D1432989

The
Law
of
Gravity

The Law of Gravity

by

Dennis Morgan Cottrell

Wyrick & Company

For Brenda

Published by
Wyrick & Company
Post Office Box 89
Charleston, S.C. 29402

Copyright © 1995 by Dennis Morgan Cottrell
All rights reserved
Printed in the United States of America

Library of Congress Cataloging-in-Publication Data
Cottrell, Dennis Morgan, 1950-
The law of gravity / by Dennis Morgan Cottrell.
p. cm.
ISBN 0-941711-25-0
I. Title.
PS3553.07682L38   1995
813'.54--dc20   95-35508
CIP

All events in this book, as well as all characters and their names, are fictitious. Any resemblance to an actual event, or to a real person, living or dead, is purely coincidental.

The
Law
of
Gravity

CHAPTER I

How I Came To Leave Home

I suspect that most everybody living below the Mason-Dixon line has heard of me, Pat Gunn, especially since all the big newspapers down here have told my story in half a dozen different ways, none of them exactly right, and now that one of my old school pictures has been flashed across every durn TV screen between Memphis and Mobile.

I'm pretty famous, but I'm not stuck on myself. Even if I was, the old folks I live with would set me straight in about two seconds flat. Now some people in this little town who knew me way back when do think I have the bighead, and a few of them go around trying to low-rate me, telling reporters and other outsiders that I never had any raising, that a few years ago I was just another dumb, white-trash kid jerked up by the hair of the head.

That's all right. The truth is the truth. I've learned a few things in my life, though, even if I did come by a good part of my education in a trailer park. One thing I know, you can change a whole lot about yourself, but you can't change where you came from or who your kinfolks are. Another thing, most of the wrong stuff that's happened in the past can't ever be made right, so just leave it lay. Going on a TV talk show and bellyaching in front of the whole world won't change a blessed thing, except to make you look like one more ignorant fool.

1

But I'm a good one to talk. Lots of times late at night my mind starts turning everything that's happened over and over like that big agitator at the Econ-O-Wash and won't stop. Before long I'm flouncing around on the bed for two or three hours, trying to wear the worry out of everything that's gone wrong. The next morning I'm all wrung out, and the sheets are twisted in a wad, but as soon as my feet hit the floor, the same old troubles get up with me.

I still study a lot about my dead kinfolks, too. I'm not ashamed of them, not all of them, anyway, but sometimes I wish I'd belonged to somebody else. Now most of my folks weren't low-down mean people, just mainly blind. I mean they all had good eyes in their heads, but look like they couldn't see what was right in front of them, and then again, they couldn't seem to see far off, either.

I think about Granny Gunn. I reckon because she was a poor woman who lived by herself way back in the diggings, she couldn't see any better than to name my daddy Tommy. Tommy Gunn. Granny had a radio, and later on a TV, so I know good and well she'd heard of Eliot Ness and *The Untouchables* or Al Capone or Bonnie and Clyde. But as far as I was ever able to tell, it never crossed her mind that she was naming her only child after a submachine gun. My daddy spent all his elementary school days being teased to death. He quit school in the eighth grade, and years later I ended up getting the daylights beat out of me because he was still rubbed raw inside.

And then there's my mama. Papa Prince tried to raise her according to the Bible after his wife died, but he was too strict and religious with her. He meant well, I'm sure, but she ran off to Iuka, Mississippi, with my daddy when she was fourteen years old. She was just wanting to get away from home and have some fun like a normal teenager, but ended up with a sorry dickens who used her for a punching bag.

My mama never had been free, so that was why she had

to run wild. When I was nine or ten years old and my daddy was off on a long haul, she'd pack me off to Granny Gunn's so she could ride around all weekend with a bunch of women from the trailer park. They'd all get drunker than Cootie Brown at the Starlite Club and then cruise up and down Broadway—Broadway in Broad Plains, Tennessee, not New York City. Broadway is the main street in town, about two miles long with four traffic lights, and teenagers drive back and forth on that strip of blacktop all weekend long. Teenagers don't have anything better to do, but what's pitiful is to see older people like my mama or divorced people out on Broadway trying to make out like teenagers again.

Anyway, when I was eleven my mama took up with this nigger, Reggie somebody, who worked with her at Tennessee Shirt Designs, and they left town together. My daddy would've shot them both if he'd ever caught them, but he didn't. Like Granny Gunn said, I reckon the Devil got them first. That old yellow Grand Ville convertible they were riding in blew out a front tire going down Monteagle Mountain, and it took the highway patrol and the rescue squad all one day to bring them back up, both dead to the living world.

My daddy didn't even go to the funeral, but Granny Gunn took me. It's still like a dream, people I didn't half know hugging on me and pressing dollar bills in my hands, my mama's eighth grade graduation picture propped on top of this white casket. And flowers. Lots of sickly sweet flowers.

Papa Prince didn't come to the funeral, either. He never spoke a word to my mama after she took up with my daddy, and he never had much to do with me, except to send me a miniature Bible once on my birthday. I didn't care anything about a Bible. When he died, I didn't go to his funeral, on account I didn't know that much about him.

I don't claim to be smart, but I have figured out a few

things. I know you can put the wrong name on a letter, or the wrong address, and it might just end up in Nashville or Timbuktu. Put the wrong label on a person, though, or try to head him in some direction he's not supposed to go, and he's liable to end up in hell, or cause somebody else to.

If I'd had sense enough to play my own cards right, I could have lived with Granny Gunn and saved myself a peck of trouble. My daddy had half a notion to let her raise me, anyway. After my mama got killed, he didn't want to stay around Broad Plains anymore because, naturally, his pride was hurt. And he sure didn't need a snot-nosed pissant tagging along in a semi with him, reminding him of things he'd just as soon forget.

But I couldn't be satisfied living out at Granny Gunn's. She lived way out in the sticks, and there was absolutely nothing to do. When I lived in the trailer park, I would ride my bike around town all day or play the game machines up at Jiffy Mart with my friends.

Now, Granny, she would've tried to do right by me. She was like most old people. Living so long had hulled everything that was hard out of her. But I just couldn't stand being so lonesome way out there, missing my mama so bad I ached and not having anybody to talk to. Granny would try to talk to me, but she couldn't carry on a real conversation because she didn't know anything. It's bad to say your granny was ignorant, but she was. She was good as gold, but she didn't know about football or any sport or even who the Vice President was. She couldn't even get the answer right on "Wheel of Fortune" when most of the letters were filled in.

I couldn't eat her food, either. She cooked mostly gross stuff like pinto beans and cornbread and turnip greens and something else that stunk up the whole house. Cabbage, I think it was.

After supper we'd go out on the porch, and she'd cut us

off a big plug of Red Man with a little yellow-handled pocket knife she kept in her apron. We'd rock real slow in the swing and spit in a Folger's coffee can. Directly, she'd say something like, "Hit looks like rain over yonder in the east, Pat," or "Them crickets is fiddling a jig, ain't they, son?"

About dark we'd get up and go back inside the house, which always had this smell that's hard to describe, not nasty or anything, but musty and old, like all the living air had been sucked out of it. We'd watch television if we could pick up a channel out of Memphis. Sometimes I'd have to go up on the hill behind the house and turn the antenna, and Granny would holler out the kitchen window when we finally got a picture.

After I left the country, the cable people strung a line out Granny's way, and she got hooked up. Just about every time I rode way out there on my bicycle, she'd be watching country music videos. Then one Saturday the home health care nurse found her dead in her easy chair with the TV going full blast.

I felt real bad about her being out there by herself when she died, and I reckon I always will. She might be alive today if somebody had been there with her when she took sick.

But I couldn't be satisfied living with Granny, not realizing what I was in for when I begged my daddy to let me come back to town. Before I knew what was happening, I was back in the trailer park and getting the dickens beat out of me when he rolled in drunk.

He started doing short hauls on account of me, so he said, and money was tight. Then he got it in his head that people were all time talking about him behind his back. Even before my mama took off with Reggie, he used to come in drunk every once in a while and work me over, nothing much, just some pushing and shoving and cursing.

He saved the rough stuff for my mama. But when I came back home from Granny's, he started the rough stuff with me.

I was just a measly little old stick of a boy, going on twelve years old, and that sorry thing would come in mad at the world and beat the stew out of me with a belt or an extension cord or anything else that was handy.

What turned me against him for good was the time he came in late and I had the door locked, like a body naturally would in a trailer park, unless you want everything you own toted off, and he started shaking the door nearly off the hinges. I'd been sound asleep and was trying my best to undo the latch while he was jerking on the door and calling me every name in the book. I reckon he thought I was trying to lock him out when I was really trying to let him in. Finally, he yanked so hard that the latch broke, he fell backwards, and I tumbled head first down the trailer steps. "You goddamn little bastard!" he hollered at me, jumping up and kicking me in the butt as hard as he could.

I tried to get up and run, but he kicked me in the ribs twice and then a time or two in the head. I don't remember exactly what happened next, but I reckon Jessie Pratt's mama, who'd been cut before with a straight razor from her right eyelid down to her chin and weighed about three hundred pounds, saved my bacon. Jessie said she heard the commotion and ran out of their trailer next door with an aluminum baseball bat. She threatened to brain my daddy if he laid another hand on me, and then he must have come to himself. He backed off, anyway, and Jessie's mama made me spend the night with them.

The next morning I was pretty stove up and my head was about to kill me, but Jessie's mama gave me two Tylenols and made me eat some grits and eggs I didn't want. I've got a weak stomach. Their trailer smelled like stale cigarettes and soured towels, so I was kind of glad to get out of there, even if I did have to go home.

My daddy had already fixed the door and was sprawled out on the couch drinking a beer when I got home. "Hair of the dog," he said, smiling friendly at me, but I didn't ever want anything else to do with him. I just went on back to my room and stayed still.

Directly he commenced snoring, and I slipped back out. Jessie got me to go with him up to the Jiffy Mart for a pack of cigarettes. He bought a pack of Marlboros (for his mama, he told the clerk,) and then he slipped two packs of generics down the front of his jeans. We went across the street to the Econ-O-Wash and smoked until we were both as dizzy as a witch.

Jessie said his mama said I could stay with them, at least for a while, but I couldn't stand the smell inside their trailer. I didn't tell Jessie that, though. He was a little red-headed runt not much bigger than I was, even though he was fourteen or maybe fifteen at the time. The following summer he was visiting his cousin in Nashville and drowned while swimming with a bunch of teenagers in the Cumberland River. I hated that. Jessie was all right.

After that last beating, I figured that the best thing for me to do was to be gone when my daddy came in drunk. He always got drunk after he finished a haul, because that was about the only time he ever had any jingle in his pockets. Sometimes he'd sleep twenty-four hours at a stretch when he first came home, but after he got rested, he'd clean up. When I saw him shining his boots and trimming his mustache, I knew he was headed for the beer joint.

By then it was summer. I started taking my fishing tackle, blankets, and some eats, and camping out down at Shoal Bluff Bridge. I'd fish all day up and down the creek. I'd eat a snack when I got hungry or take a little snooze under a shade tree when I felt like it. About dark I'd strip off and take a bath in the creek and then cook some supper.

When it was raining I slept right under the bridge. The

pigeons bothered me a little at first, cooing and flying up in front of my face sometimes before I knew what they were, but I got used to them.

In two or three days I'd pack all my stuff and head back to the trailer park. Usually, my daddy would be moping around the trailer, all washed out looking and needing a bath and a shave. He wasn't too hard to get along with when he was sober. I'd always leave him a note telling him where I'd gone, but he didn't seem to care one way or another. He might say something like, "Where the hell you been, you little mutt?"and I'd say, "Down on the creek fishing," and he'd just nod his head and rub his hand over his flattop like everything was all right. Pretty soon he'd leave me a little money for groceries and then take off again.

When I wasn't on the creek, I was hanging around the Jiffy Mart with Jessie and some other boys. The clerks ran us off once or twice a week for swiping stuff or spitting Skoal in the floor. They'd tell us not to step foot in the store again, but there were so many of us living out at the trailer park, and we all looked so scraggly, they couldn't tell us apart. We stayed outside the store most of the time, anyway, unless the cashiers got a big run on customers. Then we'd go in and lift a few things we needed, Cokes and Fig Newtons and snack crackers, stuff like that. About four o'clock the work hands from the factories started filling up the place, and that's when we made another haul. Jessie and some of the others would take things like cigarettes and playing cards and sunshades, but I never did feel right doing that. Stealing is stealing, no two ways about it, but I never took anything I couldn't eat or drink.

Jessie didn't ever camp out with me, because he had to be home at night to take care of his little sister while his mama worked second shift at the cookie plant. Before long, though, Chigger kind of took up with me.

Chigger was a year or two older than I was, but we were

in the same class at school because he'd failed kindergarten or something. He wasn't dumb or anything. He just didn't come to school, so he'd usually spend about the last three or four months of the term in juvenile detention over in Memphis. He was a little blonde-haired boy who had one whole arm and half of another. He was riding around uptown one day with his mama and had his arm hanging out the window when some old woman broadsided the car and clipped his arm off right below the elbow. Chigger claimed his arm didn't bleed or even hurt for an hour or two, but that his ghost arm itched so bad sometimes he could hardly stand it.

He had a funny thing about his name. He wouldn't tell anybody what his last name was. He went by Bitner at school, but that wasn't his real name, only his mama's maiden name. People would try to guess his real name, but he wouldn't let on one way or another. All he would say was that his first name was Doug.

I knew what his real name was, though. One time I had to take this slip of paper over to school saying that I'd had all my shots. This was right after school had turned out for the summer. Miss Jones had called my daddy and told him state law said that I couldn't come back to school unless I had a doctor's slip saying I'd been vaccinated for measles and smallpox and DPT. So I took this slip of paper from the health department over to school after my daddy had ranted and raved on me for being so much trouble, like I could help it. Anyway, Miss Jones was working on some records in her room, and just as I was handing her the piece of paper, I saw Chigger's picture stapled to the top of this folder. "Douglas Darren Dick" was printed in dark letters across the top of the folder.

I never let on to anybody, though. Chigger aggravated the dough out of me sometimes, but I couldn't help liking him. He'd give you his last cigarette if he had one.

I think that Chigger would've fit in right well with the

other boys at the trailer park if he'd had two whole arms and less lip, but I was always different. I mean everybody seemed to like me well enough, even the rough boys who'd done time in juvenile detention, but I didn't like doing the same things they did, at least not all the time. After a week or two of riding bikes and hanging around Jiffy Mart all hours of the day to see what I could pick up at a five-finger discount, I was bored to death. Hardly anybody at the trailer park fished or camped out, but I liked getting off to myself, away from my daddy, especially, but away from other people, too. Finally, though, I reckon the other boys got fed up with Chigger and his aggravating ways, so that's when he started tagging along with me.

We pretty much lived on the creek when the weather was warm. I know the year I was twelve, we camped out down there the whole summer, except for a week when we had a flood.

Now in August of that same year, I naturally got ready to go back to school, but Chigger decided he'd just stay put. The day I headed for home, I found a pasteboard box a refrigerator had been packed in behind Turnbow's Furniture and Appliances. I turned around and toted that big thing back down to the creek, thinking that Chigger could sleep in it when the weather turned cool, but he wouldn't have it. He told me he wasn't about to live like a homeless person, and then durn if he didn't throw that box into the creek!

I got so mad I wanted to knock the living daylights out of him, but I can't stay mad for long. Over the next few weeks, every time my daddy decided to pull a drunk—and he was pulling lots of them about that time—I'd slip off down to the creek and stay with Chigger for a day or two.

The trouble was, school had started on the sixteenth of August, and by Labor Day I'd already missed seven days of school. I was really getting behind in my work, especially in algebra, but I couldn't help it. I wasn't exactly surprised, either, when Mr. Hardwick, the attendance teacher, called me into the front office for a talk. I shot him this bunch of bull about being sick off and on with a stomach virus.

Old man Hardwick had already heard every excuse in the book. Before I knew what was happening, he was trying to contact my daddy by phone, by registered mail, and even by visiting our trailer. The next week, after he couldn't ever find my daddy, he flat out asked me why, just as I walked sleepy-headed into the schoolhouse on Monday morning. I was caught off guard, and without even meaning to, I blurted out that my daddy stayed on the road two or three weeks at a time. The next thing I knew, Mr. Hardwick had his head together with the people at the Department of Human Services, and by the middle of that same week, my daddy was standing with me right smack in front of the juvenile judge.

The judge was this white–haired fellow whose cheeks drooped down real low and looked like they belonged on some sad old hound dog. You could tell by the way he looked at you that he'd done heard it all, and that he wouldn't put up with a lot of foolishness.

My daddy was madder than a wet hen because I'd gone and got him into trouble. He knew the judge could fine him plenty if he took a notion to, so he'd already warned me to keep my mouth shut and let him do all the talking. He was aiming to let on like some of his trucker buddies had been watching after me while he was on the road. But first thing, the judge says, "Mr. Gunn, I'm going to ask you to leave the courtroom while I talk with Pat here in private. Have a seat out there in the lobby."

My daddy shot me a look that said, "You better watch it, mister," and strutted bowlegged out of the courtroom. He was wearing his tight Wrangler jeans and his snakeskin boots, and as that old judge watched him leave, he wiggled his nose like he'd got wind of a fart.

The judge came down off his perch and sat in a chair

beside me. He didn't have much flesh on his bones, but he was still a big man. He didn't fuss on me, but he told me right off the bat that he already knew the whole truth, no use in me lying for my daddy. The social worker had talked with some of the neighbors and the teachers at school and even the people that owned the Jiffy Mart.

Now like I said, he didn't talk mean. His voice was as soft as the cotton plug in an aspirin bottle. So when he asked me how come I missed so much school, I just up and told him. I said, "I camp out on Shoal Creek when I know my daddy's going out to get drunk. I ain't got the heart to come to school after sleeping in my clothes on the hard ground all night."

"Does your father actually abuse you when he's drinking, Pat?" the judge asked.

I said, "He hits me with anything handy, if that's what you mean, and he keeps on hitting me until he wears out or passes out, one."

The judge commenced clicking his old yellow nubby teeth, and his eyes got real bright. "How old are you, son?" he said.

"I turned thirteen the first day of September," I told him.

"So you stay by yourself a lot, do you?" he said, and I told him just like it was. I said, "Most of the time, but that's the way I like it. I don't want my daddy staying at home anymore than he does already."

He nodded, all the time looking me right straight in the eye, and then he told me to go out and get my daddy and for me to stay put until somebody came to get me.

So I walked out in the big marble lobby of the courthouse, my knees rubbery, and there was my daddy leaning up against the wall looking at me hard, like he was trying to figure out how he was going to beat me up once we got home. He was baring his teeth so that I could see the empty space where his front tooth had got knocked out somewhere, probably in some beer joint when he was drunk.

12

"That old judge wants to talk to you now," I said.

Before I could blink twice, he'd done grabbed me by the shoulders and was shaking the dickens out of me. "Damn your time, you better not've told him nothing on me!" he said, hissing like a cornered alleycat. "What the hell did you tell him?"

About that time my daddy saw that the judge was looking through the crack of the door right behind me, and then he tried to let on like he was hugging me. It might near made me sick. The judge said, "Come on back in here, Mr. Gunn. We need to talk about some things."

My daddy looked at me like he wanted to jump right through me, and I knew then that my goose was cooked.

They stayed inside talking for the longest time. I'd flop down on the bench outside the door for a while. Then I'd get up and stretch and go get a drink of water. Every five or ten minutes seem like I'd have to go pee, and then I'd come back and flop down on the bench again. I was as miserable as I could be, not knowing what was going on in there and not knowing what was going to become of me once we got back home.

After about an hour, this youngish woman with a boy's haircut stuck her head out the door and told me to come on back inside. She grabbed me by the hand once I was inside the courtroom and led me right past my daddy, who was sitting in a chair up front. He was looking down with one hand on each side of his head like the old judge had done blistered his ears. That woman led me right up to the place where a witness gets grilled inside this little pen. The judge was sitting on his throne, looking real sour like he'd been eating green persimmons. The woman opened the gate and motioned for me to sit down, and when I did, she came inside, too, and stood behind me with her hands on my shoulders.

By this time I'd done figured out that the woman was

somebody from Human Services, and that my daddy was fixing to catch the devil. All of a sudden, the judge cleared his throat and looked right at me. "Pat, do you love your father?" he said, his voice sounding like rolling thunder.

That question really took me by surprise, because I hadn't ever thought much about who loved who and what love was, anyway. But I tried to answer with the truth, because talking to this old judge was kind of like talking to God. "Nosir," I said, my words sounding like somebody else's words. "I don't think I do. Everybody I love is dead."

You could've heard a pin drop in that courtroom. My daddy looked up at me like I'd never seen him look before. He didn't look mad. He looked like he'd finally had to swallow a dose of his own medicine.

The woman made some kind of noise in her throat like a hiccup, and for a long time the judge looked at my daddy and just nodded his head. Then the judge said, "Pat, we've already decided here this afternoon that your daddy can't take care of you in a way that's fitting and proper. Until he can prove to me that he is capable of providing you with a stable home, I'm placing you in foster care. Miss Thistle here will help acquaint you with your foster parent." He reached over and shook my hand. "Good luck, son."

Miss Thistle grabbed my hand and let me out of the courtroom. When we passed by my daddy, he reached out his hand to me, but I never let on like I even saw him.

CHAPTER II

I Get Put In An Old Lady's Home

It's funny how you can go for the longest time and nothing out of the ordinary happens, every day just about the same as the next, and then all of a sudden, everything happens at once.

One minute I was in court, knowing that my daddy was fixing to beat me black and blue when he got me home, but the next thing I knew, I was in Miss Thistle's Corolla riding over in this neighborhood next to the junior college on my way to my new home.

Directly, we pulled up in the driveway of this big old red brick house. It had a porch that wrapped around two sides, tall white columns, and fancy trim work that kind of put me in mind of icing on a birthday cake. I was studying to myself all this time, not really thinking about what I was saying, and I blurted out something plumb ignorant, about like something Chigger would say. I said, "What in the world is this, a funeral home?"

I was real got away with, and I saw Miss Thistle wanted to burst out laughing, but she caught herself. One thing I had to give her credit for, she didn't make fun like most highfalutin folks. A lot of people think that because you're poor, you don't have feelings, but she didn't. She tried not to laugh in my face, and I appreciated it. "No, Pat," she said, grinning a little and patting me on the arm. "This is where you're going to stay for a while."

I could hardly believe it, but I wasn't going to make her out a liar. We got out of the car, and about the time we set foot on the stoop, out the front door walked this old lady.

She looked like a stick woman, she was so tall and skinny and straight. She had white curly hair and big eyes the color of old nickels. She was wrinkled up pretty bad, and blue veins ran down her arms like little biddy rivers. But she didn't look mean or anything. "Well, this is Pat, Miss Armistead," Miss Thistle said, kind of like she was apologizing because there wasn't much size to me or something.

Miss Armistead smiled real big at me and stuck out her long hand for me to shake. It was crinkled like crepe paper. I declare, she was as old as the hills but still had every single tooth in her head, looked like about forty-eleven, and every other one was plugged up with gold. I was might near scared to shake hands with her, because I wasn't sure my hands were clean, and she smelled like a bank of pure honeysuckles. But I shook hands with her anyway, and she said, "I'm Appolonia Armistead. Now is it Pat or Patrick, dear?"

If she'd had on a pink feathery hat, I'd have passed her off for the Queen of England. "Pat, I reckon," I said. "But I wouldn't mind atall if you called me Patrick. I kind of like the way you say it."

Miss Thistle puckered up her mouth like she was trying to keep from laughing in my face again, but Miss Armistead never cracked a smile. "Then Patrick it will be," she said, turning and motioning me on in the house with a wave of her long skinny arm.

Miss Armistead and Miss Thistle talked out on the porch for a minute, so I just stayed put right inside the door. I didn't want Miss Armistead to think I might try to steal something. I could've heard every word they said as plain as day, but I wasn't even trying to listen. I was too busy trying to take in this house.

I could see myself in the wooden floors. I was standing in a hallway that went clear on back to the kitchen. On my right were these high twisting stair steps that curved around to the second floor. I couldn't figure out what was holding them up there in the air. Over every two or three stair steps were hung pictures of old timey people in gold frames. The walls were painted yellow, the color of egg custard, and down in the hall was this couch that was yellow, too. The front legs on it looked like two giant eagle claws had snatched hold of two big wheel bearings. Over the couch was a big picture of pirate ships shooting cannons at one another.

Directly, Miss Thistle left and waved good-bye to me through the screen. Miss Armistead came on in the house then and kind of looked me over good from top to bottom. I reckon she was trying to figure out how big a mess she'd got herself into. "Oh, pardon me, Patrick," she said all of a sudden, like she was just waking up of a morning. "I must have been staring. How awful I must seem!" She grabbed hold of her throat like she'd got a fish bone hung in it. "I was just thinking about what size clothing we needed to buy you."

I had on my good high-top Nikes, my new Guns N' Roses T-shirt, and my best pair of black jeans, but durn if I didn't feel poor as Job's turkey standing there in front of that old hotsy-totsy lady. My best get-up was like rags to her, I could see that. "I won't be needing no new *clothing*," I said, sounding hateful like my daddy. "These here are plenty good enough for me."

She turned about four shades of red. "But of course, Patrick," she said. "I am so sorry. I'm afraid I've made a very bad beginning."

I could see that she had tears in her big gray eyes, and her hand was trembly when she touched me on the shoulder. Durn if I didn't feel lower than a snake.

Right then I burst out crying. I don't know why. I reckon because everything had happened so fast and all, and here I was in a big fancy house with this nice old woman that I'd

17

done insulted, and I needed to pee so bad I could hardly stand it, but I was scared to death to pee in her bathroom or even ask her where the durn bathroom was.

The next thing I knew, we were both sitting on that yellow couch, and I was crying on her shoulder to beat the band. She kept smoothing down my hair and saying, "That's all right, that's all right," and I was nearly too ashamed to stop bawling and look at her, but finally I did.

When I looked her in the eye, I saw she'd been crying, too. It beat all!

"You're a mighty nice old lady," I told her, "but I reckon I don't belong here. I've been living on the creek most of the summer, and this house is so big and shiny, I feel like I'm still inside the courthouse."

She smiled and patted me on the back. "Well, now, you just let me tell you a little story, Patrick," she said, straightening up and drying her eyes with the tips of one finger.

I hated little stories. When I was in the third grade, old Miss Gooch used to tell us little stories about good boys and girls and bad boys and girls. Good things always happened to good boys and girls, and bad things always happened to bad boys and girls. I never believed any of that stuff myself. Granny Gunn never did any harm to another living soul, and she died all by herself in front of the TV set, nobody even there to hold her hand when she went.

But Miss Armistead wanted to have her say, and I wasn't going to insult her again if I could help it. I wondered, though, how she was supposed to take care of me, her nerves not being that good and all.

"Once there was a girl who lived far away from here," she said, looking first at me and then fiddling with her ring that was jam-packed full of rhinestone sets. "She lived down in Mississippi, near a little town called Dennis. Isn't that a funny name, now?" she said, looking at me kind of sad.

"Yeah, I guess," I said. "It's right funny."

"She was a poor girl who lived in a log cabin without running water. The girl's father made whiskey for a living, and one day the revenue men caught him and sent him to prison."

"Seems like I've done seen this on HBO," I said.

"Perhaps you've seen something similar," Miss Armistead said kindly, "but this is a true story."

That was what Miss Gooch always said, too.

"The girl's mother got very sick and had no real means of supporting the child, so she pinned a note to her collar and sent her on the bus to her aunt's house in Memphis."

"I bet the girl missed her mama," I said, looking off down the hall. "Wonder if she ever got to see her again?"

Miss Armistead's eyes looked like two puddles of clear rainwater. "No," she said. "She never did. Her mother died of tuberculosis."

"My mama got killed in a car wreck with a nigger," I said. "She told me she was just going up to Jiffy Mart for a pack of cigarettes."

"Yes, dear, I know," she said, looking like she had something on her mind she started to say but didn't. I reckon she was trying to be careful of my feelings, too. Directly, she went on. "As I was saying, the girl was sent to Memphis. Her aunt worked in a hosiery mill there and was not well off herself. Her husband was dead, and she had two small children of her own to care for. So when the girl was twelve, her aunt found her a job working in the kitchen of a well-to-do family."

"I just got over being twelve, myself," I said. "I'd hate to think I had to go live with some old rich people."

I could've gnawed my tongue off at the roots for saying that, but that's me, saying the first ignorant thing that pops into my head. Miss Armistead never let on, though. She went right on talking, never missing a lick. "It was a big house, even bigger than this one. The girl was afraid of the big house and most of the people who lived there. They

talked strange and had strange ways she didn't understand."

"Talk about strange," I told her, "old Miss Tommy
Holland who lives close to me at the trailer park won't
touch pennies. She won't take pennies when they give her
back change at the Jiffy Mart. She says she was struck by
lightning when she was little and pennies shock her. Ain't
that something?"

"How interesting," Miss Armistead said, but she didn't
act like she was too interested to me. She sounded like one
of my teachers at school, Miss Ordway, who always said
one thing when she meant something the exact opposite.
Miss Ordway said she was being ironic, but I think she was
just plain ornery, myself.

I shut up, though, because I knew how grown people
were. It's all right for them to put their two cents worth in,
but they don't want young folks to. Miss Armistead went
on, "There in that house the girl met the youngest son of
that prosperous old family. He was a lonely boy her own
age, and she thought that he was the most handsome lad she
had ever seen. He had curly brown hair and eyes the color
of emeralds. Some years earlier he had developed a bone
disease that left him partially crippled, so he was often left
out of the games other children played. He loved books and
music and art."

Miss Armistead stopped talking for a minute and then
started fiddling with her ring again. I didn't know if this
was all of the story or not, but I sure didn't like the way it
went so far. "Was this boy a sissy or something?" I said.
"He sounds like James Lee Bates at the trailer park. James
Lee paints his fingernails with clear fingernail polish, but he
can draw might near anything."

"He was like no one else, to be sure," she said, sounding
like she wasn't even talking to me. Now she was looking
straight up, like she was talking to the ceiling or something.
"He taught the girl to play the piano. He lent her books to

read. He brought her little presents. He even paid for her class ring when they graduated from high school."

"Sounds like a right good-natured sort of fellow," I said. "Most folks don't care nothing about nobody else."

Miss Armistead looked down like she had just noticed me for the first time. She smiled sort of sad like and then took my right hand and held it between both of hers. She held it right in her lap, and I was kind of embarrassed in a way, but I never let on.

"Oh, Patrick," she said, craning her head sideways, "it was all so very long ago."

"I don't get this story," I said. "I guess it's just me."

Miss Armistead smiled, squeezed my hand, and then shook it a little like she was aggravated with me, only I could tell she wasn't. "Such an impatient boy," she said, turning loose of my hand and brushing my hair out of my eyes. "When his father died in 1939, the boy, who was no longer a boy but a young man in college, came into his inheritance, and on Christmas Eve of that same year, he married the girl who worked in the kitchen. Ain't that something?"

It sounded funny hearing Miss Armistead say "ain't," but I knew she was just teasing me a little about my English. Usually I talk good. "That girl was you, wasn't it, Miss Armistead?" I said. "I figured it out right off the bat. That was your husband, the crippled boy, and I bet he's dead. That's the way all good things turn out, even on TV."

There I'd gone again with my big mouth, saying stuff I didn't have any business saying about her husband and all. Miss Armistead looked at me real sad. Then she put her arm around my shoulders and gave me a little squeeze. "Yes, dear," she said, putting her hand up to her neck and clearing her throat. "That's my own story. So you see, Patrick, I do know what it feels like to be afraid of strange people and big houses. I'm here to be your friend, if you'll let me. We can talk about whatever you want to talk about, and if there's ever anything you don't understand, just ask me. Will you do that for me?"

"Yes, ma'am," I said, trying not to show how bad I had the wiggles.

Miss Armistead looked at me out of the corner of her eye. "Are you uncomfortable, Patrick?"

"Yes, ma'am, I sure am," I said, plain forgetting my manners. "Whereabouts is your bathroom? I'm about to whiz in my pants."

"Oh, dear," she said, laughing as she lifted me up by the arm. "We can't have that, now can we?"

She led me fast down the hall and showed me where to go, and by then I knew that this rich old woman was all right. That didn't mean I was aiming to live with her, though.

When I came out of the bathroom, Miss Armistead gave me a tour of all the rooms downstairs and then led the way up the long winding stairs to my bedroom.

My bedroom was as big as Granny Gunn's whole house if the partitions had been knocked out. Even standing on my tiptoes, I couldn't have touched the ceiling with a broom handle. The wallpaper wasn't paper, but blue and white cloth that showed these George Washington type men in kneepants bowing low in front of women with high hairdos. The very same cloth was used for the curtains and bedspread. It all kind of made me dizzy when I stared at it too long. The bed was so high that a body had to use these little portable steps to crawl in it. Chigger wouldn't believe me in a thousand years if I ever told him about this place. "I hope this will be satisfactory," Miss Armistead said, smoothing out the bedspread. "There's blankets in the trunk at the foot of the bed if you should get cool during the night."

"Yes, ma'am," I said. "Anything's good enough for me."

Miss Armistead frowned. I didn't know what I'd said

wrong, but I knew from watching TV that rich folks got their feelings hurt mighty easy. "Perhaps you'd like to spend some time alone before supper," she said, walking over to the door like she was fixing to leave.

I sat down on the bed steps. "I'm not much hungry," I said. "I reckon I'll just go on to bed directly."

Miss Armistead's eyes got a little rounder in her head. "So early?" she said, her voice hitting a high note. "Why, dear, the sun hasn't even set yet."

I told her the truth about not being very hungry, but mainly I was wanting to get rid of her so I could be by myself. I needed to think. I figured at first she was like Granny Gunn and would go to bed with the chickens, but look like I'd figured wrong. "Miss Armistead," I said, "it's like this. A long time ago, I lived with my granny way out in the country. She got me in the habit of going to bed early and getting up early."

"Well, of course, dear," Miss Armistead said, walking back over and putting her hand on my shoulder. "That's perfectly all right. This must have been a very tiring day for you. I'll leave you now, and you go right to bed if you like. If you should get hungry during the night, I'll leave you a nice plate of cold cuts in the refrigerator."

"I appreciate it," I said.

"Well, you're quite welcome," she said.

I sat real still on the steps and held my breath, waiting for her to leave. I saw she wanted to hug me or something, because her hands fluttered like nervous birds looking for a place to light, but finally she turned around and walked back to the door. "Good night, then," she said as she closed the door.

"Good night, Miss Armistead," I hollered, thinking to myself if this old lady didn't get out of my sight for a minute, I was going to hop right out of my skin.

CHAPTER III

I Run Away

As soon as I was by myself for a minute, I knew exactly what I had to do.

I opened the trunk, took out two thin plaid blankets, and rolled them up into one.

I hated to steal from Miss Armistead, but my own blankets were over at the trailer park, and I had no intention of going over there with my daddy still mad and probably dog drunk by now. But I had no intention of staying here in this big house, either.

I liked Miss Armistead right well, but I couldn't stay with her. This house was too different from any other place I'd ever lived. I'd shrivel up and die here. I'd been lonely lots of times in my life, but never like this. Bad as my daddy was, I'd take him any day over living in a strange house with a strange old woman.

I couldn't go back home any time soon, but I knew one place I could go.

I picked up the blankets, tiptoed outside the bedroom, and eased the door shut. At the end of the upstairs hall was a big arched window that looked out over the front yard. Lucky for me, when I peeped out one side, I spied Miss Armistead talking with one of her lady neighbors across the street. They both had their backs turned, and Miss Armistead was pointing toward some red flowers that her neighbor had growing in these square white boxes on the front porch.

I hopped down those stairs two at a time and was out the kitchen door in a flash. I didn't run, but I didn't let any grass grow under my feet, either, as I hiked across Miss Armistead's long back yard out to the street. If any of her neighbors saw me, I don't know what they thought, me toting a big roll of blankets across my shoulder. I never looked one way or another, though, just kept walking like I had important business to tend to and didn't have time to stop and talk.

Looking back now, I don't know what in the world I was thinking. I don't reckon I was.

When I got down to the creek around seven o'clock, dusk was fading fast, but a bright moon was drifting out from behind the clouds.

Even though Chigger had left all our cooking stuff out in plain sight on the bank, I didn't see hide nor hair of him. I didn't much care, to tell the truth. I hadn't seen him in about a week, so he didn't know what had happened to me, and I didn't feel like explaining everything to him.

I cleared a place on the gravel and set down the blankets. Then I decided to strip off and take a bath. I'd had a good shower earlier that morning, but it seemed like I needed to wash away something that had settled on me.

Creek water gets cold again during dog days, so I didn't linger long. I was drying my shivering chickenskin off with my T–shirt when all of a sudden I felt something splatter on top of my head. I figured that a pigeon had squatted on me, because I was standing pretty close to the bridge where they nested. So I commenced tiptoeing barefoot across the sharp gravel down to the edge of the creek. I was all bent over washing my head when all of a sudden somebody hollered in a high fake voice, "Yoo-o-o-who-o! Full moon tonight!"

I didn't recognize the voice at first, but I thought it sounded mighty familiar. I was still naked as a jaybird, so I hopped up fast, covering my particulars as best I could, and scampered back under the bridge before I was completely mortified. About that time I spied that durn Chigger leaning on the bridge railing, his shaggy blonde head bobbing over the side. "Better stay out of the water with that little worm," he said, about to die laughing. "A bluegill would nibble that off in one bite."

I was mad as a hornet, I tell you I was! He let fly another long squirt of spit at me, but this time I ducked back under the bridge. "You asshole!" I hollered.

I started once to rock him, but even then I reckon I knew he couldn't help acting a fool. When I finally tugged up my jeans over my wet hind end, I'd just about got over my mad spell, anyway. "You might as well come on down," I said, making sure my head stayed under the bridge. "I'm fixing to get you sooner or later, anyway."

"I got stuff to cook," he hollered down. "You promise not to hit me?"

"Come on down, chickenshit, and find out," I said.

Directly, he crept down the big rocks that shored up the bank beside the bridge. He carried a limp paper sack in his one good hand and kept looking back over his shoulder at me, none too sure that I wouldn't beat the devil out of him. I thought once about throwing him in the creek, but then I decided that I didn't want to work up a sweat over nothing. He walked over and dropped the sack at my feet. "Truce," he said. Then he grinned and gave me a high five.

I was prouder to see him than I let on. "I reckon," I said.

He sat down and lit a cigarette. I could tell he was intending for me to do the cooking, but that was all right, because he wasn't exactly the cleanest person in the world. Back in the early part of the summer, we'd found lots of good camping stuff in the dumpster behind Jiffy Mart, a skillet with just a little of the Teflon peeling off, a set of knives and forks that were still packed in the box, and a big round grill rack. Propped upon some rocks, the grill rack made a good cookstove.

In a few minutes I'd gathered up driftwood and had a fire going. In the sack was a pack of weenies and a sixteen ounce can of pork and beans. I got the skillet hot and fried up all the weenies, then opened the beans with my pocketknife and dumped them in on top. I wiped two spoons off on the tail of my T-shirt, and we ate right out of the skillet. Chigger had about half of a jumbo size Snickers in his shirt pocket, and we ate that, too.

I let Chigger use one of Miss Armistead's blankets, and we hunkered down like Indians around the fire and had ourselves a smoke. The big white moon rose up higher and threw our shadows on the gravel bank. Way off down the creek, a coyote barked, making the hairs on the back of my neck stand up. Lightning bugs winked at us, and over in the bottom, crickets fiddled in seesaw time with the wet rubbery croaks of frogs. I could hear the creek trickling over the slick limestone rocks of the shoals and smell the peppermint growing on the opposite bank. It was good to sit still and quiet in a place that was alive and peaceful at the same time.

Directly, Chigger said, just right out of the blue, "Wouldn't never a better car built than a '57 Chevy."

I stirred up the fire with a forked stick. "I've heard some people say a Porsche's better," I said.

"Well, I ain't never heard of no car by that name," he said, acting like if he'd never heard of a thing, it didn't count.

"It was first made by Doctor Fred Porsche over in Germany," I told him. "I reckon he was a car doctor."

"I still ain't heard of it," he said, like I had to prove something to him before it could be so.

"You have, too," I said. "I just told you. *Porsche.*"

"Porsche," he repeated and then spit. "It sure don't fit right in your mouth. Sound like something you ought to hawk up."

He laughed like he'd said something awfully funny and then flipped his cigarette over into the creek.

The gnats were beginning to bite, so I got up and threw some more brush on the fire to smoke them off. The fire crackled and blazed up in a shower of orange sparks. In the firelight Chigger's pointed face and his pointed nose poking out of his blanket put me in mind of a rat down at the city dump. I felt bad thinking about him that way, but he acted so durn ignorant it was pitiful. When I sat back down I told him, I said, "James Dean was killed in a Porsche on his way to some big car race."

Chigger snorted. "He wouldn't done it," he said. "He sells sausage on the television all the time."

"That's Jimmy Dean," I said, taking the last drag off my cigarette before dropping it into the fire. "I'm talking about James Dean the actor."

"Jimmy Dean's a singer and a actor, too," he said, spitting over to one side. "I seen him playing in something not long ago, so he ain't dead."

My ears commenced getting hot like they always do when I'm fixing to get mad. "Hell yes, he is," I said. "The one I'm talking about is. He got killed way back when, in fifty something."

"He's about fifty something, probably," Chigger said, "but he ain't dead."

"*James Dean,* durn your time," I said. "Not Jimmy Dean. They're two different people."

Chigger was so slow in the head that you couldn't reason with him like a regular person. "James is the same name as Jimmy, ain't it?" he said. "Just like Bob's the same name as Robert."

"Yeah, but..."

"So they're the same person."

"No, they're not."

"You just said they was," Chigger said, smirking at me across our campfire. "Make up your mind."

I shut up then before I really got mad and hit him in the head with a stick or something .

Directly, he said, 'You ain't mad, are you?"

He said it like he would be just tickled to death if I was. Chigger had rather aggravate somebody than eat. Most of the people at school wouldn't even fool with him. The only reason he didn't get the tar beat out of him on a regular basis was because nobody wanted the name of fighting a one-armed boy. It would be as bad as fighting with a girl. "Naw, I ain't mad," I said. "Hardly anybody ever makes me mad."

He was ready to pick at me again, but all of a sudden he jumped right straight up and hollered, "Whoa!" and commenced shaking his hand like it was on fire. He shed his blanket as he got up close to the fire and turned his hand every which way, looking real keen at it.

"What's wrong?" I said, getting up to look for myself. "Something bite you?"

"I can't tell," he said, his voice quivering as he reached across the fire for me to take a look.

Chigger's fingernails were gnawed down to the quick, and his knuckles were dirty and chapped. I didn't think about it then, but I guess it was hard for him to wash one hand without the other. He was trembling like somebody with chills and fever. I turned his hand over twice on both sides, but I didn't see a puncture or any swelling. "I don't see anything out of the way," I said, thumping him on the shoulder. "You ain't going to die."

He didn't seem too sure. He stuck his hand under his arm and scrunched up his shoulders. "Something cold and slick run right across my hand," he said, closing his eyes and shivering.

"Probably just a little old waterdog," I said, tickled under my skin now that I knew he hadn't been snakebit. It served him right, arguing with me when he knew durn well I was smarter than he was.

After shaking out his blanket, he eased over to my side of the fire and huddled down beside me. "I hope it wouldn't a scorpion," he said, still shivering. "My Uncle Daryl got bit by one when he was pulling up some boards in this old house, and his hand rotted to the bone. It was one of them blue-striped scorpions."

I knew better than to correct him, but I couldn't help myself. "There's no such thing as a blue-striped scorpion," I told him. "Most of them are kind of tan looking. You don't hardly ever see a scorpion around these parts, anyway."

He looked around, his eyes as keen as a straight razor. "I reckon Daryl ought to know!" he said, snarling out of one side of his mouth. "He had to have a transplant at Baptist Hospital in Memphis, Tennessee. He's still got a sunk–in place on the back of his hand as big as a half a dollar. You ask anybody."

He nodded at me for good measure and then took his hand out from under his armpit. He looked at it for a while in the firelight and then put it back.

"I'll tell you what I bet bit your uncle," I said directly. "It was that brown kind of spider. You know, they're all over the place, in old barns and houses, just about everywhere. It's brown with a fiddle on its back. Brown recluse spider, ain't that what they call it?"

"I don't call it nothing," he said like a big smart aleck. "I called it right the first time, a blue-striped scorpion. Uncle Daryl's silver service, so I 'spect he knows a thing or two."

Old Daryl Tate was Chigger's mama's brother who got sent off to the state pen for killing somebody in a car wreck when he was dog drunk. He was a trusty in prison, but Chigger was all the time bragging that his uncle had a state job. I guess in a way he did.

"Listen here," I said, trying to reason with him. "What you're talking about is a lizard, a blue-striped lizard. They call them skinks, or something like that."

"I call them scorpions," he said, drawing his blanket tighter around his shoulders.

"Naw, now, there's just one poison lizard in the whole United States."

"I know it," he said, "and it's got blue stripes."

"No, dammit to hell!" I hollered, throwing off my blanket. "It's not poison!"

Chigger threw off his blanket, too, just like he was aiming to fight. Our campfire flickered yellow in his eyes, and his jaw jutted way out. "You said it was," he said, poking his forefinger hard in my chest. "You said it was a poison lizard, now didn't you?"

I grabbed ahold of his hand and slung it back. "Shut up!" I said, daring him to make something out of it.

He cocked back his head and stared hard at me. I stared right back until I'd stared him down.

I decided then that I'd not talk to him atall. I figured he'd take the hint after a while and leave.

The trouble with Chigger, he couldn't get along with anybody. He knew just a little bit more than everybody else, that was his trouble. If it hadn't been for me, he wouldn't have had a friend in the world.

The old dead wood I was burning spewed and popped. Every once in a while a pigeon cooed and clucked under the bridge. Across the creek two squeaking bats fluttered around like they were crazy drunk and fixing to run into something, but they didn't. In the moonlight I could make out the white snouts of five gars circling right under the surface of the water.

This was a good place to be. As long as you watched where you put your hands and feet, and you didn't swim too soon after you'd had your eats, couldn't anything bad happen to you here. Most of the living things on the creek, even the poison snakes, didn't want to bother you unless you tried to bother them first. One night I woke up and found a coon as big as a feist dog nuzzling my big toe with his wet nose. Lots of times in my sleep I'd heard deer moving around in the thickets on the far side of the creek, or big fish surfacing, or turtles and muskrats dropping heavy off the banks.

I knew Chigger would finally have to say something or die. He couldn't keep his mouth shut. "I've always wondered about something," he said, acting like there never had been a cross word between us. "Hulen Jones down at the pool hall is all the time talking about his double first cousin up in Detroit. What is a double first cousin, anyhow?"

I shrugged like I didn't know, but I did. I'd already learned my lesson. No matter what I said, he would try to make something else out of it. You couldn't argue with a fool.

He sniffled and wiped his durn nose on Miss Armistead's blanket that he had wrapped around himself again. "Well, I think I've got it figured out. Hulen's cousin has a twin. I've studied about it and studied about it, and that's the only way it comes out right in my head. That would make him have a double first cousin."

"That's not right," I blurted out before I caught myself.

One side of Chigger's mouth curled up over his eyetooth. "I figured you'd know," he said. "You're just trying to make me out a liar. What is it then, if it ain't what I said?"

"I don't know," I said, yawning real big like I was plumb wore out. "I forget."

Chigger leaned over until he was right up in my face. "Why did you say you did, then?" he said. "Turd."

"I don't know," I said, laughing because he was batting his eyes at me like something foolish. "I told you, I don't know."

"Is that a echo I hear?" he said, laughing himself and jabbing me hard in the side with his nub. "Huh? Huh?"

He was hurting me, so I shoved him back. "Do I hear a damn fool who don't know his ass from a hole in the ground?" I said.

"Yeah, boy," he said, scooting farther away from me. "You hear yourself, don't you?"

He doubled over laughing then, slapping one knee like he'd said about the funniest thing that had ever been said in the world. He laughed so hard that Mr. Aaron's dogs commenced barking across the bottom.

"Listen here," I said, after he'd finally laughed himself out. "A double first cousin is when two men who are brothers marry two women who are sisters. Their kids are double first cousins, smartass."

Chigger wrinkled up his nose like he smelled something dead. "Anybody knows better than that," he said. "It's against the law for brothers to marry sisters. Dumbass." Then he stuck his finger down his throat like he was making himself puke.

I got up and walked over to the bridge before I had to hit him.

The moon had everything so lit up in frosty white light that I could make out every rock on the bank. Little dark speckled frogs hopped in front of my feet, and across the creek a possum hid at the edge of a canebrake. A few pigeons clucked and fluttered above me as I ducked under the bridge and hauled out two big trash bags I'd stashed behind one of the short pilings. In each bag were three foam rubber couch cushions that I'd found in the dumpster about a week earlier and hidden from Chigger. He liked to claim everything we found as his own. I carried a bag in each hand and walked back to the campfire.

"What you got there, hoss?" Chigger said real friendly.

I never let on like I heard him. I took the cushions from one bag and spread them out end to end. I folded my blanket longways, using half of it to cover the cushions and half of it to cover myself. "I'm going to sleep now," I told him, my voice as cold as spring water. "There's some more cushions in that other bag if you want them. You can stay here with me tonight, or you can go on back home. You just suit yourself. I don't care one way or the other."

"Man, you're too touchy," Chigger said, beginning to fix his bed like mine. "You ought not to get to mad all the time. Everybody says so. You're always getting hot under the collar about nothing much atall."

"I'm not mad," I said, playing like I was drifting off to sleep. "I don't ever get mad."

"And you don't ever rub your nubbin, either, to hear you tell it," he said, laughing.

I didn't want to laugh, but I couldn't help it. "At least I got one to rub," I told him.

"Not much of one," he said, flipping a piece of gravel at me.

"Shut up," I said, even though I wasn't really mad at him anymore. "Less us go to sleep."

Chigger stretched out on his bed and lit up another cigarette. "You want a smoke?" he said. "I got one if you want it."

"Naw, I've done gone to bed," I said. "You're not supposed to smoke in bed, anyway. You might catch the house afire."

"Yeah, right," he said, laughing a little.

I lay still with my eyes half closed looking at the stars in the eastern sky. I knew people at school who could tell one constellation from the other, but stars always looked like one jumbled-up mess to me, except for the Northern Star. Heaven was supposed to be way up there somewhere beyond the stars, but I couldn't believe it myself, not all the time, anyway. Seem like the stars were as hard as diamond bits, the sky cold as black ice, and nothing or nobody could be way up there.

"You know what?" Chigger said directly.

"What?"

"The shortest distance between two points ain't a straight line. It's a circle. There ain't but one man in the whole United States smart enough to understand it, and he's got a office in the White House, just in case he needs to explain it to the President all of a sudden. Do you believe that?"

"Yeah," I said.

"You ain't just saying that, are you?"

"Naw, I believe every word of it."

"Well, it's the truth," he said, sounding like he didn't much believe it himself.

Chigger went on and on with a bunch of foolishness for a long time. Way in the night his voice began to sound muffled, like he'd covered up his head with the blanket and was talking from under it. The last thing I remember before falling asleep was him explaining how hummingbirds really didn't hover, they just seemed to, because not flying like an ordinary bird went against some law of gravity.

Over in the east, a long needle of sunlight poking out from behind a big sycamore jabbed me in the eye.

I sat up so fast that my head got dizzy. All of a sudden, the cold truth sank in my belly like a lead weight. It was already daylight, I'd run away from my foster home, and I didn't have anywhere else to go. I couldn't go back to the trailer park, even if I wanted to, and if I stayed down here on the creek with Chigger, sooner or later I was going to end up in juvenile detention over in Memphis.

I let Chigger sleep, because there were some things I couldn't make him understand. I gathered up Miss Armistead's blanket, shook it out, and folded it. I'd have to leave the other blanket, because Chigger had it wrapped tight around his bony shoulders and was all drawn up in a knot. I figured that Miss Armistead had so much stuff already, she surely wouldn't miss one little blanket. Besides, she'd be so mad about me running off, she wouldn't be studying blankets.

As soon as I crawled up the far bank and got back on the highway, I took off in a run.

I knew good and well when I walked across the back yard

that I'd been locked out of the house. I was trying to get prepared for a big commotion, but when I tried the knob on the kitchen door, durn if it didn't turn!

Now, I didn't think I was home free. I tiptoed inside the house, doing my level best not to make those old floors creak, half expecting Miss Armistead to jump out any second and start hollering and fussing on me. But when I passed by her bedroom door in the downstairs hall, I heard her sawing logs.

I couldn't believe my good luck. I eased upstairs, put the blanket back in the trunk, and took a long, hot shower.

I didn't stir from my bedroom until I heard the coffee percolating downstairs in the kitchen. When I came down to the breakfast table, the first thing Miss Armistead said was, "Did you rest well last night, dear?"

I couldn't look at her, because I was afraid I'd laugh in her face. She was like most old people—easy to fool. "Yes, ma'am," I said. "Right well."

Every single day I lived at Miss Armistead's, the last thing she did at night before going to bed was to check all the doors. It's funny, now that I think back on it, how she forgot to check the kitchen door that one time.

CHAPTER IV

I Turn Into A Prep

I'll tell you what's the truth. I believe I learned more in a week at Miss Armistead's than I'd ever learned in a month at school.

She had about a zillion books in this room she called a study, only you didn't have to study in it. She didn't try to make me sit down and learn foolishness like the four main products the United States imports from Chile, like they did at school. She just let me look at whatever I wanted to, books or magazines or the stamp collection. She had stacks and stacks of *National Geographics*, and on rainy afternoons I'd plop right down there in the middle of the floor and go through a big pile of them, and old *Life* magazines, too. I liked to look at the advertisements for all these old-timey cars, only the cars weren't old-timey then, they were new. She had books with nothing in them but pictures people had taken with a camera, and some of them were scary, like a man shooting another man in the head with a pistol, and a woman jumping out of a big tall building because it was on fire. And she had this real thick book called *Gray's Anatomy* that showed what a body looked like inside and out, right down to your particulars. Chigger would've loved it, he was so nasty-minded, anyway. It made me feel sort of funny looking at some of that stuff, but Miss Armistead told me that I could look at any book in that room, so I took her at her word.

I figured that Miss Armistead would commence correcting my manners and such, but she didn't. I went out of my way not to hurt her feelings, though, because her nerves were kind of bad and all. So I tried to straighten up the best I could by listening to her and watching her moves. I knew all along how to talk right, but people at the trailer park didn't like people trying to get above their raising, so I talked like everybody else as long as I was there. I wasn't there anymore, though, so I commenced using good English.

Before long I figured out that you used the little fork for the salad and the long fork for everything else. You ate with just one hand. Eating that way really didn't make a lot of sense to me, because I'd always been taught to use one hand to rake and one hand to sop, but Miss Armistead didn't sop. I'd never used a knife before, either, except maybe for whittling off a plug of Red Man, but Miss Armistead used hers for cutting up pork chop and breast of chicken. I could've done a heap better gnawing the bone like I used to, but like I said, I didn't want to upset Miss Armistead, because she was mighty kind to me. Before long I could use a knife about as well as she could and knew where to put it on the plate when I got through with it.

And I thought maybe Miss Armistead would start on my long hair sooner or later, but she never did. My hair had grown way below my shoulders, but I kept it clean. I'd always kept it clean, even when I was at the trailer park or camping down at the creek. I never could stand to be nasty, like some of the people I knew. At Miss Armistead's I had this big blue bathroom all to myself, and I could take a shower ten times a day if I wanted to, and use as many towels as I wanted to. I didn't have to worry about taking dirty clothes to the Econ-O-Wash, either. This man came by the house every other day in a van to pick up our dirty stuff and brought it back clean when he made his next round.

But it was funny about my hair. I reckon I thought I was old Samson or something, cut off my hair and I'd be too weak to crawl to the dinner table. Or that's the way I was at the trailer park. My daddy would say things like, "I'm going to have to buy you a brassiere and some lace panties," or "Patty needs a ribbon in her hair," mean stuff like that, letting on like I wanted to be a girly boy. I couldn't say why, but the more he aggravated me, the more I knew I couldn't cut my hair. I thought if I cut my hair, something bad would happen. That may not make any sense, but that's what I thought.

At Miss Armistead's, though, I got to feeling a little out of place about my hair. I'd be going to pick up the garbage cans at the curb or just sitting out on the porch steps looking at magazines, and seem like people that passed by kind of looked at me funny. I figured it was my hair, because when I had it pulled back out of sight in a pony tail, they didn't seem to take a second look at me.

Of course, they may have been staring at my clothes. Miss Thistle had rounded up the rest of my clothes at the trailer and brought them over, but they were all thin from washing and mostly worn out. By now it was early December, the days were beginning to get nippy, and I'd lost my good blue jean jacket at school the year before. Now I wished I'd kept my big mouth shut when I told Miss Armistead I didn't want any new clothes. My drawers were so raggedy you could've pitched broomstraws through them.

One Saturday morning when there was a big frost on the ground, I told Miss Armistead at the breakfast table, "Miss Armistead, reckon you can run me by the First Assembly of God? They give out clothes on Saturday, and I'm might near naked."

She looked up from her plate and said, "I'd be happy to, Patrick." Then she looked down and pushed her scrambled eggs around some. "Of course," she added, "if you'd rather, I can buy you some new ones."

That was what I was wanting her to say in the first place, but I had my pride. "Yes, ma'am, I'd like to have some new clothes. But you've got to let me do something extra for them," I said. I didn't have anything to do at her house except study my lessons, take out the garbage, and sweep off the porch every once in a while.

All of a sudden, she clapped her hands and reared way back in her chair. She was acting right foolish if you ask me, but then rich people are different. "Patrick, I know just the thing you could do for me," she said, grinning from ear to ear.

"Okeydoke, what?" I said, knowing that she wouldn't expect me to do much of anything.

"It's rather underhanded, I'm afraid," she said, looking at me kind of sideways. "No, I couldn't ask you to do that. It wouldn't be right."

I knew good and well she really didn't want me to do anything bad, but I played along with her. In lots of ways I was a whole lot smarter than she was, but I never let on. "What?" I said, acting like I was suspicious. "What do you want me to do?"

She leaned over close to me and talked in a low voice like somebody was aiming to hear her. "Well, you see," she said, "I belong to the Readers' Circle. You've seen the members here before, if you'll recall."

I remembered, all right. I came in from school one day and about forty-eleven old ladies with their glasses hung around their skinny necks on chains looked me over like I came from Mars. "I don't want to belong to a club with old ladies, now," I said. "I'd do might near anything else for you, Miss Armistead, but I've got to draw the line there."

"Oh, no, dear, " she said, covering my hand with hers. "It's a ladies only club, you see. What I want you to do..." she eyed me for a second or two and then shook her head..."no, I couldn't possibly ask you to do that. You're my ward, and I mustn't lead you astray."

To tell you the truth, she'd done got my curiosity stirred up. "What?" I said, nearly hollering. "What do you want me to do?"

"Nothing, dear," she said with a flip of her hand. "Forget I mentioned it."

"I bet I know," I said. "You want me to go through their purses when they ain't looking."

"Oh, my goodness, no!" she screeched, grabbing hold of her throat.

That was the first time I'd ever heard her raise her voice, and it kind of scared me. Now she could hit a high note. She put her fingers up to each side of her head like she was going to come down with a sick headache or something. Directly, she said, "Patrick, you know I would never ask you to do anything like that."

"I know it," I said. "I just said that to get your goat."

She narrowed her eyes and pursed up her mouth, but then she commenced grinning a little. "I'd best tell you, I suppose, before I cause more trouble than I'm worth," she said, having to clear her throat. "What I want you to do for me is to read some books."

Boy, that hit me like a truckload of bricks! *Read!* I hated to read. I never did read the stories at school I was supposed to. I'd do book reports on books that had movies made about them. "What do you want me to read for?" I said, feeling a sickly hot feeling all over.

"Well, you see, dear," she said, talking low again, "I have to read these books and report back to the Reading Circle on whether or not they're worth reading. I'm afraid I've gotten terribly behind on my reading and need some help getting caught up." She looked at me real pitiful. "These old eyes aren't what they used to be."

"I know what you can do, Miss Armistead," I said. "Play like you've read the book and just watch the video."

Miss Armistead shook her head. "Oh, I've tried that,

she said, "but wouldn't you know it, some of those ladies ask some very picky questions about these books, and some of the things they ask are not in the movie."

"I know what you mean," I said. "Teachers do that, too."

"So I'm afraid we're just stuck with reading them, Patrick." She closed her hands together like she was praying and rested her chin on them. "I'm so happy that you've agreed to help me. You really are such a kind boy."

I didn't remember agreeing to anything, but since I didn't want her bawling at the breakfast table, I just sat still, miserable as a mangy dog. "Well," I said directly, "I didn't know grown people had to do book reports, but I reckon I can do yours. How many books do you want me to read?"

She commenced gathering up the breakfast dishes and didn't answer right off. She kept working her mouth and screwing up her eyes toward the ceiling like she was doing some deep studying. In a minute she said, "Oh, I think perhaps one a week for now."

I might near passed out! I couldn't say a thing, I was so shook up. Durn if she didn't charge a high price for some clothes. When I was finally able to say something, I said, "Reckon you couldn't throw in a haircut, too, Miss Armistead?"

"Oh, I think I could manage that," she said, looking mighty pleased with herself as she handed me the blue well-aware dishes to take to the dishwasher. "Let me get on the phone and see if Berniece down at Fantastic Sam's can't work you in today."

Up in the morning Miss Armistead backed her big white Lincoln Continental out of the garage, and we got ready to go shopping. This old Lincoln was a 1962 model, she told me, and the last thing her husband gave her before he fell dead of a heart attack in the post office. It looked brand new and was about as long as the house.

Miss Armistead didn't drive fast, now. We headed out
for Memphis, poking down the highway about thirty-five
miles an hour. The highway was crooked in places, and
before long we had a string of cars backed up behind us for
about three miles. Every so often a car would whiz around
us and just about get hit head-on by an oncoming car. I was
a nervous wreck, but Miss Armistead didn't act like anything out of the ordinary was happening. Then some smart
aleck wearing a beard and camouflage clothes flew by in a
four-wheel drive pickup and shot us one. Miss Armistead
glanced over at me. I didn't want to get her upset, because
she couldn't drive worth a flip to begin with, so I said,
"That man must know us, Miss Armistead. I saw him
throwing up his hand at you."

She smiled real sweet and reached over to pat me on
the shoulder. "No, dear," she said, "he was firing us the
bird, I believe it's called."

I shut up then. Miss Armistead wasn't as big a fool as
I'd thought.

It took us so long to get to the mall, and I had so many
scares along the way, I felt gray-headed by the time we got
there. And you might know, I had to pee bad.

I never had been to a mall before, but Chigger claimed
he had. He said it was so big that a man got lost in it once
and starved to death before he was found, but that was
Chigger for you. This one was sure enough big, and we
drove around the parking lot a half hour before Miss
Armistead found us a parking place and maneuvered that
big Lincoln between two cars. It took her two or three tries,
and she fought that steering wheel like it was a wildcat.

Once we got inside the mall, I stayed close to Miss
Armistead. Seem like I was afraid somebody might try to
bother me or something.

We walked a long time before we came to this big old
store, and then we walked a good piece inside this store

until we came to the young men's department. We moseyed around a little bit, looking at first one thing and then another, and directly this prissy man with a yellow tape measure strung around his neck walked up to us. He was dressed real spiffy in this greenish suit with double rows of buttons, but there was something funny about his hair. Up close I could see that he was wearing fake hair, and the more I looked at it, the more it looked like a bird's nest or something. It was all I could do to keep from laughing in his face. "We'd like to look at some of your suits, please," Miss Armistead said, frowning at me a little so I wouldn't mortify her.

This fellow gave us the quick once over and said, "We have some slightly irregular suits over here on the sale rack that you might be interested in."

All of a sudden, Miss Armistead looked like she'd been sprayed with starch and dried. She was wearing what she called her gardening attire, plain tan pants and a jacket with lots of pockets. This outfit didn't look like much, I have to admit, but it cost a lot of money. She had four or five outfits just like it that she wore when she worked in her flower beds or ran errands. She ordered these clothes and all kinds of gardening stuff from some place way up in Maine, and even a pair of scissors that she used to cut the heads off flowers cost about fifty dollars.

When the salesman got over to the sale rack and turned around, he soon found out that we hadn't followed him. I'd started to, but Miss Armistead slung out her arms like a turnstile and blocked me.

She never moved an inch. She looked mighty put out, standing real straight and tapping one foot like she was keeping time with music. The salesman soon saw he'd made a big mistake low-rating us, because he pranced back over to where we were in a hurry. "If you're quite ready," Miss Armistead said, her voice cold enough to freeze a car radiator, "you may begin by measuring my young friend for a suit. *Your best suit.*"

Miss Armistead never did act that way to me, but I saw she sure did know how to put on the dog.

In no time flat that feisty dickens had me measured up and down and across my shoulders and around my waist. Miss Armistead had him running around that store like a chicken with its head cut off, showing us ten brands of everything, and she acted like none of it was good enough for me. The salesman led me into this little stall and commenced throwing clothes over the door. I tried on stuff until I felt like I'd done a day's work.

Finally, Miss Armistead helped me pick out a blue suit and a striped tie and a white shirt. I didn't say anything, but I didn't have much use for a suit. I reckon she thought I needed one in case I died or ever decided to go to church, whichever happened first. She asked me every Sunday morning if I wanted to go to Sunday school with her, but I always told her that I'd rather stay home and look at magazines. Sunday school reminded me too much of funerals.

The next thing I knew, we were over a little ways looking at school clothes, and I was trying on a bunch of stuff again. Miss Armistead told me to pick out the kind of jeans I wanted, so I got the best pair I could find, figuring she'd just buy me one pair. The ones I picked out cost sixty dollars a pair. They were the kind that all the preps at school wore, but durn if Miss Armistead didn't up and tell the salesman that I needed seven pairs. He and I both must have been standing there with our mouths hanging wide open, because Miss Armistead turned to me and said, "You need a pair for each day of the week, dear. No need being without when you don't have to."

I was beginning to feel uneasy about her buying me so much stuff. It just didn't seem right, me taking things off her, and she wasn't through buying by a long shot. She bought me a bomber jacket, a dozen long sleeve shirts, and oodles of T-shirts and socks and underwear. I bet it took that old salesman twenty minutes to ring up everything and put it down on Miss Armistead's plastic card. Then, to beat all, she took me by the shoe department and bought me two new pairs of Nikes, two pairs of loafers—one black and one brown—and some lace–up shoes that the salesman there called "dirty bucks."

Miss Armistead bought me more clothes in two hours than I had ever owned in my entire life. It was all we could do to tote all the packages out to the car, and people looked at us and grinned when we walked through the mall, we being so loaded down and all.

After we got everything packed away in the trunk and back seat of the Lincoln, we went on back inside the mall to get us some dinner. We went to this cafeteria that had every kind of food you could imagine to eat. I got right nervous, there was so much of it, and people behind us seemed like they were in a big hurry, and I wanted to pick the best stuff. Miss Armistead set a good table, and I was gaining weight fast, but I'd never seen anything like this place. "Just get what you want, Patrick," Miss Armistead said, and durn if I wasn't picking up stuff left and right. When this woman rung us up at the end of the line, I had so much food on my tray that I could hardly tote it to the table Miss Armistead picked out for us.

We took our stuff off the trays, stacked our empty trays on this little doodad of a table, and commenced to eat. I took one bite of coconut pie and couldn't seem to eat anything else.

I had the biggest mess of food in front of me, but all of a sudden, I wasn't one bit hungry. Durn it, one minute I was sitting there wondering how I was going to force everything down, and the next thing I knew, I was sniffling and hiccuping and getting ready to bellow like a bull calf. I know Miss Armistead thought I was the biggest tittiebaby she'd ever seen. "Whatever's the matter, Patrick?" she said, looking real sorry for me and digging in her purse for a pocket handkerchief.

"I don't know," I said, and I was mostly telling the truth. Here I had all these new clothes and a table full of food right in front of me, and I didn't want any of it. I just wanted to slip off somewhere and bawl my eyes out.

She reached right across the table and dabbed at my eye with a Kleenex. Durn if I wasn't embarrassed. She didn't mean anything by it, but she was treating me like I was six years old or something. "There," she said, brushing my hair out of my eyes. "I think that's better. Now, can you tell me what brought that on, dear?"

I couldn't look at her. I figured all these other people sitting around us were looking at me, so I just kept my head down. "I don't know how to say it," I said, shaking my head. "Something about you buying all this stuff for me and me not being worth the trouble."

"Not being worth the trouble," she said, not mocking me or anything, but letting on like I'd said about the dumbest thing in the world. "Nonsense. You're a perfectly good boy, and I won't ever hear otherwise, not from you or anyone else." I glanced up and saw that she'd got real tight around the mouth. "Do you understand me?" she said, sounding right hateful and kind at the same time.

"Yes, ma'am," I said.

It's awful not to be able to say what you're feeling. I sat there and ate most everything in front of me and didn't taste any of it. Every so often Miss Armistead would reach across the table and pat me on the hand, but I was still so durn sad I could hardly stand it.

I thought a right smart of Miss Armistead, but I didn't know how to explain my feelings to her. Or maybe I was just too ashamed to explain them to her, I don't know. Granny Gunn didn't have but one good dress to her name, and she was buried in it, and I remembered that my mama couldn't even afford to have her teeth fixed. Now here I was with everything a body could want, and both of them were dead and buried.

There was no fair in the world, and no God, either, and anybody who thought there was didn't know a blessed thing.

Seem like I could barely put one foot in front of the other by the time we walked on down to the other end of the mall toward the barber shop. I was plumb wore out.

I hadn't ever seen so many stores and all the things they had to sell, stores jam-packed full of clothes and toys and records, so much stuff it made me dizzy just trying to see it all. "Come along, dear," Miss Armistead would say to me every so often, and I'd nearly have to run to catch up with her, she was so spry and all. Granny Gunn could hardly walk from the eating table to the back door without catching her breath, she was so heavy on her feet, and her hips were so bad, too.

When we got to the barber shop, one of the women working there told us that the lady who was supposed to cut my hair was still eating her dinner, so we sat down in these chrome chairs out front to wait. Miss Armistead picked up this women's magazine off a table and was reading it, when all of a sudden she burst out laughing. "He did have perfectly awful hair, didn't he?" she said, and then I burst out laughing, too.

"He looked like a possum had died on top of his head," I said, and Miss Armistead clapped her hands and laughed even harder.

Finally, Miss Armistead stopped laughing and grabbed her throat. "We should both be ashamed of ourselves," she said, her mouth twitching like she wanted to laugh some more.

"But we ain't, are we?" I said.

"No, we ain't," she said, winking at me.

I reckon I got to feeling better after that. In a few minutes this woman came back from eating and told us she was ready to work on me. She was a right good-sized woman, and everything about her was black. She was wearing black britches and shirt, black fingernail polish, and black lipstick, and even her hair was black as a stovepipe. She put me in mind of a good-natured witch, if there is such a thing. "Now is this your grandson or boyfriend, Miss Armistead?" she said as I crawled up into her chair.

"Neither, Berneice," said Miss Armistead. "He's a young friend of an innocent age, so we'll have none of your usual talk, if you know what I mean."

Berneice walled up her big raccoon eyes and stuck out her tongue like something stupid. Miss Armistead frowned and shook her head, acting real prim and proper, but I could tell she wasn't really aggravated with Berneice. She was just acting like an old fogey for my benefit. As far as me being innocent, I'd done seen and heard and tried things that would've shocked the daylights out of Miss Armistead, but I never let on.

"Don't you love the way she talks?" Berneice said, laughing like she didn't care one bit if Miss Armistead was mad or not. "She tickles me to death," she added, girding this plastic sheet of a thing around my neck. "How do you want it cut, hon?"

To tell the truth, I hadn't thought about the way I wanted to wear my hair. I just knew it didn't need to be long any more. "Cut it like the college boys wear it," I said.

"Hon, that could be lots of ways," said Berneice. "It's so long and pretty, I kind of hate to cut it without knowing what you want."

I got real nervous again. When my daddy used to give me a haircut when I was little, he would start whacking every which way, not caring what it looked like. I reckon Miss Armistead saw that I was getting mighty squirrely, because she picked up this big magazine off the table and handed it to me. It was a magazine of different kinds of hair styles. "Perhaps you can find something suitable in there," she said.

I started flipping the pages. Sure enough, I found something that looked right nice. "Cut it sort of like this one," I said to Berneice.

Berneice took the magazine from me and looked at it. "Yes sirree," she said, handing the magazine back to Miss Armistead. "I believe that'll look good on you."

Miss Armistead held the magazine out a ways and looked at it. "Yes, indeed," she said. "A very good choice, I'd say."

It was good to have somebody to show me things. The world wasn't nearly as scary when you knew what to do, and the more you knew, the easier everything got to be. I would never have walked inside that big old mall by myself or got in line to eat with a bunch of strange folks. I would never have hopped up in a chair and told a beauty operator how to cut my hair, not by myself, I wouldn't have.

Miss Armistead and Berneice talked about some movie they both were aiming to see, but I wasn't listening much. Pretty soon I could see my long black hair lying in little piles all around the chair, and I was partly scared and partly excited. "It's going to look real nice, hon," said Berneice, and Miss Armistead nodded so I'd know Berneice was telling the truth.

Law, that woman cut and cut and cut. I never knew a body had so much hair. I figured I wouldn't have any left once Berneice got through with me. Directly, she squirted some foamy stuff in her hand and then rubbed it on my head. I was wondering if she was going to shave me bald or something, but about that time she got the blow dryer cranked up and worked my head over good with this round brush. In about five minutes, she whirled the chair around so I could see myself in the mirror on the wall.

I had the funniest feeling. For a minute I thought I was looking at somebody else. I know you're not supposed to brag on yourself, but durn if I didn't look good!

Berneice had cut my hair short on the sides, parted it, and left it kind of long on top. "Well, how do you like it?" Berneice said. "You'd better like it."

I laughed. "I like it," I said.

"Now ain't he a doll?" Berneice said to Miss Armistead, kind of embarrassing me.

"He is quite handsome," said Miss Armistead, nodding like she was pleased with the way I looked herself.

I couldn't keep my eyes off myself. Nobody at the trailer park would even know me unless they took a second look.

But I'm like the wind, all time changing. After Miss Armistead had paid Berneice, I had a little tingly sad feeling. By the time we got back to the car, I was feeling real bad again. Seem like I'd left something in the mall, not just my hair all over the floor, but something else I needed that I'd left behind.

As we were riding home, I didn't pay much attention to Miss Armistead's driving. I kept looking up at the sky. All the clouds were purple and gray and fierce-looking. It scared me to think that there might be a God who could just wiggle His finger and stir up such a powerful mess of sky, and I figured that He didn't have much use for people who ran off and left their kinfolks, or for mamas who ran off with niggers. For a second I wondered where my mama was right that minute, but I shook her out of my head before I could think of anything bad.

CHAPTER V

I Go To Church And Take Up Reading

The next morning at the breakfast table Miss Armistead said to me, "Patrick," she says, "would you like to attend services with me today?"

"Yes, ma'am, I think I would," I said.

Miss Armistead dribbled milk she was pouring in her coffee all over the table, she was so got away with. I reckon she thought I was aiming to be a heathen the rest of my days. I didn't care a blessed thing about going to church, but I guess I felt obligated. Miss Armistead had gone and bought me everything in the world and was always real nice to me, so I figured it was my turn to do something nice for her. Going to church had never killed anybody, at least anybody I'd ever heard of.

By ten o'clock I'd taken my shower and fooled with my hair to get it just right. You might know, Miss Armistead bought me a bottle of that foamy stuff and a styling brush before we left the mall, but I had to practice a while before I got the hang of styling my hair. Used to I just washed my hair, combed it, and went on my way with it wet. I didn't care what it looked like as long as it was clean. I soon found out, though, that looking good took a lot of time and trouble.

Directly, I put on my suit and was ready for church except for tying my tie. I didn't have a clue about how to do that. My daddy never did wear a tie. I heard Miss Armistead's high heels clicking out in the hall, so I knew she was in a hurry to go. She was a big hand for being on time. I went on out there and told her, I said, "Look, Miss Armistead, you better go on to church without me. I don't know how to tie this datburn silly thing."

"Well, Patrick, that's no problem," she said, grinning like she had a secret she wasn't aiming to tell. What it was, she knew good and well I didn't want to go to church and was looking for a good excuse to stay home.

She dropped her purse and coat on the yellow couch and commenced looping that tie around every which way, putting one end through here and pulling it through there, and durn it, when she got through, my tie was tied better than any man could have done it. "How in the world did you do that?" I said, looking at myself in the mirror hung above the three-legged table.

"Nothing to it," she said, picking up her things. "That's called a double Windsor, and when we have more time, perhaps this afternoon, I'll teach you how to tie it yourself."

I started to tell her that I didn't know how I was going to have time to learn anything new, me having to read so many books and all, but I kept my mouth shut for once.

It was a pretty sunshiny day, real warm for December, so after a while I didn't mind too awful bad that we were poking along in the big Lincoln toward church. There wasn't a cloud in the sky, and all the buildings downtown looked shopworn but friendly, like old country people. The sun warmed me through the car windows. My new clothes smelled good. I knew I was as green as that stuff that covered the copper roof on the courthouse dome, but I began to feel like I'd never felt before, right grand and proper, not like somebody who used to sleep under the bridge.

When we finally wheeled into the parking lot of the church, I could tell we were already late. Almost every parking place was full. We had to circle around three or four times until Miss Armistead could find a place big enough for the Lincoln, and then it was a tight squeeze.

"Reckon we hadn't better go on back home, Miss Armistead?" I said when we walked up to these big old double doors that neither one of us looked stout enough to open. "I'll bet there's not any seats left from the looks of all these cars."

"Not to worry," she said, opening one of the big doors just as pretty as you please and looping her arm through mine.

Durn if the preacher wasn't upstairs preaching when we tiptoed in. All of a sudden, I needed to pee bad. I was nervous as a cat as we walked side by side up this wide aisle on thick red carpet, right up close to the front where there was an empty stall of a thing. Miss Armistead opened this little biddy door on the side of the stall and closed it behind us after we had sat down on a bench covered with these purple fringed cushions.

It was a sight to see, this church was. There were ten big windows made of different colored glass glued together to make a picture. There was Jesus at a fish fry, Jesus praying on a big rock, Jesus jumping down barefooted into a swimming hole, and some other stuff I didn't understand.

I saw why Miss Armistead didn't have to worry about not having a place to sit when she got to church. On the back of the bench right in front of us was a little brass plate that read, "Mr. and Mrs. John Phillip Armistead." It beat anything I'd ever heard tell of, somebody having their very own seat at church.

I never had seen a church like this one, anyway. The preacher was wearing a white dress that looked like a pregnant woman's dress over his suit. He was a plump, sawed-off fellow who talked real soft and kind. Every so often he'd open his arms wide and look straight up, like he was fixing to hug a tall, fat woman.

Sometimes everybody would stand up and read the same

thing out of a book, and then we'd sit down for a spell. Then we'd all get up again for some little shindig. It was kind of fun in a way. That preacher never did get stirred up and holler like the one at Granny Gunn's church, and the people didn't holler, either. Everybody just sat rock still most of the time, and some of the young kids and some of the old folks dropped off to sleep. Everybody asleep would wake up when a bunch of men and women in dresses like the preacher's sang a song or two while this man over in the corner played a piano with brass pipes that ran all way to the ceiling.

After church a few old people came around and shook hands with Miss Armistead and me. Miss Armistead would introduce me, and I'd say something like, "Pleased to meet you, sir," or "Nice talking to you, your highness."

As we were walking to the car, Miss Armistead complimented me on my nice manners but told me I didn't have to lay on the nice stuff too thick.

But, see, I caught on fast. There wasn't anything to being rich. Being poor was what was hard.

Of course, when I was living under Shoal Bluff Bridge, I didn't have to read no blame books, either.

I never mentioned those old books to Miss Armistead, hoping she'd be forgetful like Granny Gunn, but she wasn't. Before I knew it, she'd already brought home a stack of books from the public library so I could start paying her back for all my fancy clothes.

The first week, I read *The Red Pony*. There wasn't much to it, I told Miss Armistead, just a boy who got a pony that died. Durn if she didn't ask me a zillion questions, though, saying those old ladies in the Reading Circle liked details. Did the boy have a daddy? Yeah, he had a daddy who was kind of hateful and contrary, seem like to me. And he had a mama and a granddaddy, and once he killed a bunch of rats down at the barn. And he ate an egg that had a speck of blood in it. I figured all that would satisfy her, but then she wanted to know about the granddaddy. Well, he told the same story over and over, just like Granny Gunn, and the boy's daddy got sick and tired of hearing his old stories, and the granddaddy came in when the daddy said he was tired of hearing those old stories, and the daddy got mighty embarrassed. Was she satisfied then? Shit no! How was the boy different at the end of the story than at the beginning? Hellfire! He didn't have a durn pony!

The next book she wanted me to read was *To Kill A Mockingbird*. Man, I had my work cut out for me, it was so long. By the time I ate supper and got my lessons at school, I'd have to read until bedtime just to stay caught up. I had to forget all about television.

The funny thing about *To Kill A Mockingbird* was, the more I read, the better it got. I could picture old Jem being my best friend, but I thought Scout ought to have been a boy, too. I liked Atticus, the daddy, even if he wasn't like any daddy I'd ever heard of. Shoot, before I got through reading that book, Miss Armistead had me talking about it at the supper table. I never let on, but I think she'd already read it, but I figured she'd skipped some pages and wanted me to fill her in. That's what I thought then, anyway.

Before long I got so I didn't mind atall doing Miss Armistead's reading for her. The week before Christmas I read *Where The Red Fern Grows* and *A Day No Pigs Would Die*, both in the same week, and had started *Where the Lilies Bloom*. I'd have finished that last one in a day or two if Chigger hadn't come back to school, if everything hadn't turned out the way it did.

CHAPTER VI

I Mess Up Good

It was like this. When I was going to school over at Broad Plains Elementary, nobody paid much attention to us kids who lived in the trailer park, not even the teachers, unless we messed up the bathrooms or got into some other kind of trouble. None of us ever got picked to be in the school plays or the Christmas program. Now I don't say the teachers were mean to us. They mainly just didn't want us to cause trouble. As long as we behaved, they overlooked us.

So I learned real quick that the best way to get along in school was to lie low and keep your mouth shut. Some people never learned, though. Billy Don Holland and Gerald Haislip and Sammy Truit were always in trouble because they didn't have good sense, but they sat in the office four days out of five acting like they were big shots, when really they were dumb as a rail fence. They didn't have sense enough to do their meanness outside of school. Old Sammy was always saying I was chickenshit or a goody-goody because I wouldn't take the bolts out of desks and stuff, but I didn't see why anybody would want to go to juvenile court or to alternative school on a regular basis like he did. You couldn't tell Sammy and his bunch anything, though. They were too ignorant.

Those people who lived in regular houses didn't have

much to do with us trailer park kids, either. They were nice enough, I reckon, but we never did get invited to any of their parties. I just kept to myself at school, and most people didn't even know my name.

But then when I came to live at Miss Armistead's and started middle school, people began noticing me, especially after I got all fixed up and Miss Armistead was dropping me off every morning in front of the school in her big old Lincoln. Some kids started speaking to me in the hall, kids I didn't even know, and then some others stayed stuck up.

One morning I was walking to Tennessee history and these two preppie girls in front of me, Leslie Peale and Tracy somebody, were talking about me. They didn't know I was right behind them. This Tracy girl said, "That Gunn boy is real cute, Leslie," and then Leslie said, "Yeah, he is, but he's green as grass and kind of trashy."

Lots of people would've told them both where to go, but I never let on. I just never tried to be nice to preppie kids after that, even if they tried to be nice to me. I didn't trust them.

I didn't fit in with anybody, anyway. Now all the trailer park kids would get dead quiet and look me over from top to bottom when I walked up and tried to talk to them in the hall, and then one or two of them would always try to put me down. "Hey, prep, where'd you get them shoes?" one of them would say, or "Who's your mama now, prep?" Mean stuff like that to egg me on to fight, but I just let it go. I knew they were jealous, was all, but it didn't make me feel good.

I wasn't smart enough to hang out with the honor roll kids, and part of them were preps, anyway, so I started staying in the library after I ate lunch and reading Miss Armistead's books.

I don't reckon school was all that bad, because I had somebody to come home to who liked me. At least that's what I kept telling myself. The truth was, I missed the old days real bad sometimes, not my daddy beating on me, but living on my own down at the creek or camping out with Chigger. Sometimes I wanted a smoke or dip so bad I could hardly stand it, but Miss Armistead didn't allow any kind of tobacco in the house, nicotine fit or no nicotine fit.

Then, a few days before we were ready to get out for Christmas, Chigger came back to school.

I was leaving homeroom on my way to Algebra I when I rounded the corner and ran smack dab into him.

I hadn't seen him in about two months, and the first thing I noticed was this homemade Harley-Davidson tattoo on his nub. Right then I knew he'd been fooling around over at Dicky Simpson's. Dicky was about twenty something and sold grass to all the little kids over at the elementary school. He'd learned how to do tattoos from his uncle up in Nashville. He charged twenty dollars to do a Harley–Davidson and just five for a naked woman or HATE across the knuckles.

"Hey, watch it, dude!" Chigger said, drawing back his fist like he was fixing to hit me. At school Chigger was always letting on like he was wanting to fight, figuring nobody would take him up on it, but every so often somebody got real aggravated and beat the dough out of him, one arm or not.

I laughed in his face and pushed him back. "What's wrong with you, Chigger?" I said. "Are you blind or something? It's me. Pat."

He batted his eyes two or three times, and all of a sudden, his jaw dropped. "Good God Almighty," he said, grinning real big and looking around to see if anybody else was listening. "What happened to you? You look like a fairy." He flipped his wrist, trying to imitate a sissy.

Durn if my face didn't get hot, and I knew I was lit up like a stop light. I was halfway pissed off, but I didn't want him to know it. That would just suit him. There I was in my fancy jeans and my hair all duded up, and he still looked like something the cats had drug in, his old torn jeans about to fall off his skinny hind end and his black T-shirt so thin you could've counted every one of his ribs. His hair had grown down to his shoulders and looked like one of those round bales of hay that's beginning to rot.

"It's all my foster mama's fault," I said, running my hand through my hair so he'd know I didn't care if my 'do was perfect. "She wants me to be a prep."

He shook his head and frowned like he didn't have any respect atall for me. "I'd like to see some old pretend mama try to change me," he said, sticking his fist up close to my chin. "I'd give her a knuckle sandwich."

I didn't want to hear any more of Chigger's big talk. He couldn't whip his way out of a wet paper sack, and everybody knew it. He was all right when we were by ourselves down at the creek, at least part of the time, anyway, but school turned him into something else. I reckon he felt out of place or scared, and he had to prove to everybody what a big man he was, when really he was just a pissant.

"I've got to go, Chigger," I told him. "I don't want to be late for algebra. Miss Goodloe will give me a write-off, and I've got too much reading to do at home without doing anything extra."

He looked at me like I was a creature from outer space. "*Reading?*" he said, making a sour mouth. "Who says you got to read, anyhow? Or do a write-off?" He took a step back and tried to stand up taller. "Shitfire," he said, "do like me. Don't do no write-off or nothing else you don't want to. All they can do is send you to the office or alternative school, and who cares if they do that?"

"Yeah, well," I said, figuring I was wasting my time trying to talk sensible to him, "I'll see you later."

He was too ignorant to talk to, anyway. Besides, I was kind of ashamed to be seen with him, him with that stupid tattoo on his nub. I might not've had any friends, but I still had my pride. You'd think with a mama and daddy like mine, I wouldn't have any shame left, but I reckon shame is something that you don't ever run short of.

"Hey, wait up," he said after I'd turned and started walking down the hall.

I kept on walking like I didn't hear him. I figured if Chigger wanted to spend the rest of his school days in alternative school or juvenile detention, then that was his business, but he wasn't fixing to take me with him. "Well, be that way!" he hollered after me. "You queer."

I could've told him what a lot of people around town said about his Uncle Daryl, but I just let it go and kept going.

I barely made it through the door before the bell rang. "Some of us are cutting it mighty close," Miss Goodloe said, and I ducked my head so I wouldn't have to see everybody turning around in their seats to look at me.

I couldn't keep my mind on algebra after that run-in with Chigger.

One minute I was so mad at him I didn't know what to do, him low-rating me when I hadn't done anything to him. I was a good mind to beat the shit out of him. How come he couldn't act right at school? School was something you had to do, like taking a shower or brushing your teeth. Of course, Chigger didn't understand that, either, because half the time he stunk to high heaven and his teeth looked like they had moss or something green growing on them right up next to the gums.

Then after a while I got to feeling bad about high-hatting him. Chigger didn't have but one arm and half of another, and his own mama wouldn't have given two cents for him. There I was, living in a fancy house that smelled like the public library, it was so big, eating good food and wearing nice clothes, and Chigger and his sorry mama lived in the worst trailer in the park, an old turquoise and white rusty thing that had pasteboard stuck in about half the windows. He had never passed a single grade in his life, but most of the teachers got tired of fooling with him and passed him on. He wasn't even supposed to be in middle school, but look like in those juvenile centers they just passed him on for doing a little of nothing, too.

But he didn't have any right calling me a queer and acting so durn smart-alecky because I looked good and he was jealous. Look like he could see that he didn't have anybody fooled about being a tough guy, and he'd quit that foolishness. Look like there were just some people who didn't ever learn anything, and you couldn't tell them anything, either.

We used to have a big time down at the creek, skinny–dipping and smoking and talking to all hours of the night, but I figured that those days were gone forever.

After school I was sitting out in the front lounge waiting for Miss Armistead to come by and pick me up. She was running a little bit late because this was her beauty appointment day. Every so often I'd get up off the couch and go look out the big plate glass windows to see if I could see her coming down the street. We were supposed to go Christmas shopping. She'd already given me a hundred dollars so I could buy my school friends some presents, but since I didn't have any friends, I was planning on buying her something. Two things I was going to get her were bubble bath and some of that Passion perfume I saw on television.

Anyway, I got up one more time to look out the windows, and that's when I spied Chigger out front on his bicycle. He was talking to some rough-looking boy called Ian who'd stolen a car once and run off to Mobile. When he happened to glance up and catch me watching him, Chigger wheeled his bicycle up on the sidewalk and then laid it over in the boxwoods like we're not supposed to do.

I figured he was aiming to start something with me, and then I'd have to whip him. I'd had enough of him for one day, and I was ready to fight.

But when he strutted up through the front door he was smiling as pretty as you please. He walked right up to me and said, "Come on and go camping with me. We'll have a good time. Ian knows there we can buy some good home-made wine."

He leaned his good arm on my shoulder and looked up at me almost like he was begging. He hadn't even washed his face that morning, because he still had sleep matted in the corners of his green eyes. I didn't want anything else to do with him at school, but I still hated to hurt his feelings, so I said, "Man, it's too blame cold. We'll freeze our nubbins off down there on that creek."

"Naw, dude," he said, beginning to lay everything off with one hand. "See, after I got back from detention, I went down there and found a bunch of old tore up skids somebody had throwed away. You remember where me and you used to snag them old gars, right there on that bank below the bridge?"

I nodded, but I didn't much want to hear what he had to tell. As soon as Miss Armistead got there, I was fixing to take off and leave him.

"Well, see, here's what I done," he said, getting more and more excited as he talked. "I found me these four saplings growing close together in kind of a square, and I nailed them skid planks around them. Then over at the dump I found a big thick roll of shiny pasteboard that somebody had throwed away, probably Northwest Container, and I got that tacked to the walls."

"What did you use for the roof?" I asked, not interested or anything, just making conversation was all.

"Hell, man," he said, looking real sneaky and talking low, "you ain't going to believe this. Old man Hardiman out there on Conner Road was putting a new roof on his barn, and I kind of accidentally on purpose found two new pieces of galvanized tin." He stuck his thumb in the front belt loop and reared way back. "We're all set. Less us go before it gets dark."

"I can't go today," I said, noticing over his shoulder that Ian was taking off with a rough-looking bunch of boys. "I'm waiting on somebody to pick me up. I'll come down there one of these days and check everything out."

"Yeah, I hear you," he said, leaning up against the plate glass windows and smirking.

"Your buddy Ian's leaving," I said.

"Who gives a shit if he is?" he said, shrugging. "You can't go because that old lady you live with will be mad at you. She'll have you wearing panties, the next thing you know."

I wanted to hit that little scrawny turd so bad I could hardly stand it. "Miss Armistead don't make me do nothing I don't want to," I said. "And you don't, either."

"Tell me about it," he said, his mouth curling down in disgust. "You told me yourself she made you be a prep."

He had me there. That's what I got for lying. Miss Armistead didn't make me get a haircut or wear fancy new clothes. I'd told a boldface lie on her, and see where it got me. It didn't seem like much of a lie when I first told it, though. "I'll tell you what, Chigger," I said, thumping him in the chest. "You leave me alone, and I'll leave you alone. How's that?"

"You come on and go camping with me, and I won't think you're a big sissy with your sprayed down hair and your mama's boy shoes," he said, grinning and scratching under his nub. "How's that?"

All of a sudden I felt something grab hold of my guts and twist, something hot and mean and sour tasting. I need-ed to let it out of me, let it grab hold of Chigger's neck and wring it like Granny Gunn used to wring a hen's head off. My fingers tingled, and my eyes got blurry. I heard the books I was toting drop on the tile floor, but the sound seemed far away. I was fixing to kill Chigger, and he knew it. "Just forget it, man," he said, grabbing the bar handle on the door and backing out fast. "Don't sweat it."

I grabbed a handful of his T-shirt and had my fist drawn back ready to punch his lights out, but for some reason I pictured Miss Armistead looking at me. She never did holler and carry on if I did something she didn't like. She'd frown a little, and that was it. But seem like I could see her watching me, and she was frowning.

I turned Chigger loose. He was as pale as a dishrag, and I was so weak in the knees I felt like I'd been jolted with electricity. "Okay, durn your time," I said, my voice all trembly. "I'm going with you. But you understand." I pointed my finger at him. "You're not making me go. I'm going because I want to go."

Chigger poked out his lower lip, closed his eyes, and shimmied like he was dancing or something. "Cool," he said. "It's cool."

I don't know what in the world came over me. I left my books lying there in the floor, went outside, and doubled up with Chigger on his bike. I didn't want to go with him, because I knew good and well Miss Armistead would be worried to death about me when I came up missing. I knew I was doing wrong, but I reckon whatever had grabbed hold of my insides had creeped up inside my head, and I didn't have a lick of sense.

The funny thing was, the farther we got away from school, the less I worried about Miss Armistead. I figured she'd know I hadn't gone far, that I was probably down on the creek.

I wanted to steer, but Chigger liked to show off because he didn't have but one arm. We started off down the street, me holding on to the back of the banana seat for dear life, and once or twice we might near wrecked. When we got over to Blue Bird Drive, I hollered, "Pull over at P.J.'s One Stop!"

As we whizzed into the parking lot, this old lady about like Granny Gunn was poking along toward her car. That durn Chigger was turned halfway around, acting like he was fixing to spit on me, and just in the nick of time I screamed out, "Watch it, stupid, you're going to hit that old grandma!"

Chigger turned around right before we were about to leave tread marks across her poor old humped back, but we whistled so close to her I could smell her bath powder.

We didn't pay any more attention to her after we'd stopped and laid the bicycle down on the sidewalk in front of the store, but before we went inside, she was on us like a chicken on a June bug. "Hold on there a minute," she said, sounding mean like a school teacher or a librarian.

When we turned around, she had her skinny crinkled finger pointed at Chigger. She was so old her finger wouldn't even straighten out, and I could hardly keep from laughing. "We didn't aim to get that close to you, ma'am," I told her. "We're sorry."

She never glanced toward me or even let on like she heard me. "You little spitspurt, you nearly run over me," she said, shaking her finger at Chigger.

Chigger couldn't say a word at first, he was so got away with. He looked like he was scared of her, but she was a scrawny little old thing. Her flowery dress hung down lower in the front than it did in the back. It was all she could do to hold her sack of groceries and point, too.

"I didn't mean to," Chigger finally said, swallowing hard. He motioned with his head toward me. "This boy here was goosing me."

I ought to have hit him upside the head for lying on me, but I couldn't help sniggering. "Ma'am, he ain't right in the head," I said, trying to keep a straight face.

She made a sour mouth at Chigger. "Well, I could tell that by looking at him," she said, turning around to walk back to her car.

I poked Chigger in the side. "Got you back, didn't I?" I said.

The trouble with Chigger, he never could leave well enough alone. He had to have the last say or die. "Ma'am!" he hollered. "Yoo-hoo, Granny Clampett!"

She whirled back around. Her face looked like a hillside that the rain had washed away, she was frowning so. "I was fixing to help you across the street," Chigger said, "but I seem to have misplaced my arm."

He waved his nub at her, and she turned gray as oatmeal. I reckon she was so mad when she walked up that she hadn't even noticed his one arm. Anyway, she must have thought we were both crazy or something, because she hiked to her car extra fast and took off.

I felt like a low–down dog, but I laughed just as hard as Chigger did when she left the parking lot on two wheels.

We went on inside the store then, and I told Chigger, I said, "Don't steal nothing. I've got money."

Chigger kind of looked at me cross-eyed like he thought I was crazy or something.

I got us a basket and started piling in a bunch of stuff— vienna sausage, crackers, cheese, and such. Directly, I noticed this fat fellow in a white shirt and bow tie following along behind us, and I knew then what was up. "Somebody's watching," I whispered to Chigger, who was walking ahead of me and looking back over his shoulder every so often.

"That's a big 10–4, good buddy," he said real loud, wanting to be heard. "Say smokey's on our tail?"

He said it just to be smart, and he was making his old ragged Nikes squeak on the tile on purpose. I came a spat of marching out of that store and leaving him. I was this close to walking to the telephone booth on the corner and calling me a taxi.

I stopped right in my tracks, and the next time Chigger turned back around, he saw me staring a hole through him.

He shrugged, putting on the innocent act, but he quit squeaking his durn shoes.

By the time we got up to the cash register, he was acting pitiful, looking down at his shoes like he was too ashamed to hold up his head. Chigger was like a lot of people. He was the only one who had any feelings. He didn't like to be corrected, either. He wasn't used to it.

I wasn't about to humor him. I started getting our stuff out of the buggy and putting it on the counter.

All of a sudden, the fat man in the white shirt and bow tie walked up behind us. "Okay, empty your pockets," he said.

Without even thinking, I stood up straight like Miss Armistead and said, "I beg your pardon! What seems to be the problem?"

I mean I sounded just like her. I was right proud of myself, because then the fat man said, "Naw, not you, son, this fellow here."

He clamped his hand on Chigger's shoulder, and Chigger jerked away as mad as a wet hen. "Oh, he's with me," I said, pulling Chigger in front of me like he was a loony who needed a keeper. "We're perfectly all right. He's my country cousin from Alabama."

I tapped my temple a couple of times with my forefinger, and then the fat man grinned and nodded.

Chigger looked like he wanted to jump right through me, but he kept his trap shut for once. I pulled out my billfold and laid a hundred dollar bill on the counter. The lady cashier picked it up and looked over at the fat man like she didn't know what she was supposed to do. He winked and then patted Chigger on the back. "Sorry about that, bud," he said, more to me than to Chigger. "Y'all come back."

After the lady cashier had rung me up and counted back my change, she sacked our groceries in two plastic bags. I picked up both bags, and we headed on out of the store.

Chigger was as quiet as a graveyard when we got back outside. I knew good and well I'd hurt his feelings, letting on like he was my backward kinfolks from the sticks, but it was good enough for him. He aggravated the daylights out of everybody, and it was a thousand wonders I hadn't already stomped a mudhole in him.

I got myself balanced on the banana seat, wondering if I was going to be able to tote two bags of groceries with Chigger steering, and we took off. Chigger was too wormy to pedal fast, so we wobbled along, and every so often I'd have to stick out my legs to keep us from turning over. It took us over an hour to get down to the creek, and once I thought I saw Chigger crying, but I reckon he was having to work so hard pedaling, he was just sweating.

I have to say, he had everything fixed nice.

On the creek bank, he'd built this shack that was most-ly silver all over. It had shiny silver paper tacked up for the walls, a tin roof, and a refrigerator door for a door. He'd found some green paint somewhere, and look like he'd tried to paint part of the front with a broom or something before he'd run out of paint or got tired, one.

Inside, he'd built a real wood floor out of skid lumber, and over in one corner was a potbellied stove missing one leg that he'd shored up with a great big rock from the creek. Somehow he'd managed to punch a hole in the tin roof for the stovepipe to poke through.

It was going on four thirty and beginning to get cold and dark, so Chigger commenced building a fire out of a bunch of old dead limbs he'd stacked up against one side of the shack. "Where'd you find this stove, at the dump?" I said.

He grunted and nodded, acting like he was so busy building the fire that he didn't have time to fool with me.

"You still got our skillet?" I said.

He motioned with his head toward a big pasteboard

box over in one corner. "In that box yonder," he said.

In the box were two ragged, musty quilts, a lantern with a cracked globe, and our silverware and skillet. The handle had broken off the skillet. All the cooking things looked nasty, so I gathered them up and took them down to the creek to wash them.

After I got through, seem like I didn't want to be around Chigger for a while, so I stayed down there, skipping rocks across the water and kind of looking the place over.

Maybe it was because it was nearly dark, but the creek looked different somehow. It usually looked pretty much the same from one year to the next, but it changed its course a little bit every spring after the big rains. Some years it changed more than others. I reckoned that everything in the world was like the creek, changing a little here and there, sometimes changing a lot. People were like that, too. Even if they didn't know they were changing, they were. They couldn't help it. Something in the world kept all things in motion, even things that didn't want to move.

When I got back, Chigger had a good fire going in the stove, and the little shack was already toasty warm. "You got any kerosene for the lantern?" I asked, and he shook his head.

It was so dark in the shack that directly all I could see were Chigger's shape on the floor beside the stove and the red coals down at the grate. I knew he was pouting with me, but I didn't know how to make up with him. I figured he wanted to stew for a while longer, anyway. Sometimes nothing feels better than having your feelings hurt.

I popped open two cans of vienna sausages and set them on top of the stove to heat. I handed Chigger some individually wrapped slices of cheese, a pack of crackers, and a can of Coke. He took them without thanking me, but he wouldn't have thanked me if he hadn't been mad. He didn't know any manners.

I sat over in the opposite corner with my own eats. All I could hear was cellophane crackling and the fire popping and spewing every once in a while, but seem like every time I chewed a cracker, it sounded like a rock slide. Finally, I couldn't stand it any longer. "What's wrong with you?" I said. "You do stuff to me all the time, spitting on me and calling me names and everything else, but then the first time I crook my finger at you, you're mad. How come you can't be like me? I don't get mad at you."

"Don't worry about it," he said, and neither one of us spoke a word for the longest time.

Directly the vienna sausages started to boil over and hiss on top of the stove, so I used my shirt tail to pick up the two cans and set them down fast on the floor. We speared the sausages with our forks and blew on them and ate them without talking. "You want some of mine?" I said directly. "I got two left I don't want."

"Naw," Chigger said, so quiet I could barely hear him.

It got so still in the shack that I could hear the creek trickling over the slick green rocks in the shallows. Far away dogs barked, and an owl hooted back up in the woods behind the creek. Every once in a while I could hear something moving in the cane brake on the opposite bank, but I wasn't afraid. It was just raccoons and muskrats, probably. The shack was dark and warm. I felt like a wild thing curled up in its den. It was a good feeling, or would have been, if everything else had been right.

Finally, I got a quilt out of the box and made me a pallet over in the corner. I was about to drop off to sleep when Chigger said, "I ain't never thought I was better than you, though."

"What?" I said, raising up on my elbow. "What are you talking about?"

"What are you talking about?" he said, mocking me, and the next thing I knew, he was crying.

I never could stand to hear a body cry, not my own

71

mama or anybody else. I felt awful, like that time I was having some fun with Jimmy Dale Qualls and dunked him in the water fountain at school. All I meant was to wet Jimmy Dale's face, only he hit his front tooth and broke it half in two. "What's wrong, Chigger?" I said, might near crying myself. "I don't know what you're talking about."

"The hell you don't!" he hollered real hateful. "I seen you in the hall, the way you kept looking around to see if anybody was watching you talk to me, you in your fancy get-up. Half the time you don't even talk right no more, you sissy! Then you telling that fatass in the grocery store that I was some of your hick kinfolks, letting on like I wouldn't right in the head. I don't guess you remember any of that, neither."

Durn his time, seem like he was always snagging me up about something I'd said or done. He was too ignorant to live. He was so dense you couldn't explain things simple enough for him to understand. "Look," I said, "you don't ever know how far to go with anything. You've got to show your hind end in school or at the grocery store or anywhere else you go."

"So what's it to you?" he said in his old smart-alecky way, wiping his nose on the sleeve of his good arm. "You ain't my mama."

"I don't want any trouble," I said, ashamed because my voice was quivering, "If you want trouble, that's your business, but just leave me out. I like things nice and calm. I like living in a nice house and wearing nice clothes and not having to worry that somebody's going to come in drunk and beat me up because I ain't big enough to take up for myself yet."

"Oh, okay," he said, acting like he understood what I was saying. "You don't think you're a big shot, you just don't want people to think you're like me, ain't that it?"

"Yeah," I said. "That's it exactly."

"So why don't you want people to think you're like

me?"

"I've done told you once," I said, trying my best not to get mad at him. "Because you stay in trouble all the time, and I don't want people to think I'm like that, too. I don't want them on my case on account of you."

"So that's the way it is," he said.

"That's the way it is."

Neither one of us said anything else for a while, but finally he said, "Okay. I reckon that's okay."

I felt like a sledge hammer had been lifted out of my insides. "You got a smoke, Chigger?" I asked, scooting over and leaning against the wall beside him. "I ain't had a smoke in I don't know when ever."

"Yeah, boy," he said, reaching into his back pocket and bringing out a pack of generics. "I picked these up at the grocery store."

We both laughed, and when he flicked his butane lighter to fire me up, I saw how young he looked, like a little biddy boy, and then that Harley-Davidson tattoo on his nub. It brought a big lump in my throat to see how young he looked in the face, and then to see how folks had messed over him so.

The cigarette made me dizzy, and it didn't even taste right. I reckoned then that I'd done got weaned away from cigarettes, and maybe some other things, too.

It was cold inside the shack when I woke up early the next morning. The fire had gone out during the night, and we had scrunched up close together in our blankets. My arm had gone to sleep where Chigger's head had rolled over on it. When I wiggled my arm from under him, he moaned a little but didn't wake up.

I scooted over on the other side of the shack and tried to go back to sleep, but I couldn't, because now I was worried. I hated that I'd gone off without telling Miss Armistead where I was headed. I wouldn't have gone off in the first place if Chigger had left me alone, but I hoped Miss Armistead would understand once I had a chance to explain the situation to her. The only thing was, I could picture her walking from window to door all night, worried to death about me. Right now she probably had the law on my trail, and when I got back home, she might not even want me anymore. She didn't have to put up with me, because she wasn't my kinfolks. I knew kids at school who lived in foster homes, and sometimes the first time they messed up, they were out the door and on the way to some juvenile detention center. That's one place I didn't want to end up in, because I'd heard plenty of stories about what happened to boys there, and not only from Chigger.

I made up my mind then and there, if I ever got out of trouble this time, Chigger was never going to have a chance to get me in trouble again. I liked him, and I felt bad about his arm and all, but I had a good thing going, and I didn't aim to let him mess it up for me.

I quit trying to go to sleep and just huddled there in the corner of the shack with the quilt wrapped around me. After a while I could see pink daylight through the cracks where the roof met the walls. Chigger was snoring away on his back, his mouth wide open, his dirty, hay-colored hair standing up all over his head. In the light of day, I knew I should have told him the whole truth the night before, not just part of it. I *was* ashamed of him, and I *did* think I was better than he was. I hadn't been at Miss Armistead's hardly any time atall, but I already saw that I didn't have to live like a dog all my born days. The trouble with people like Chigger was, they couldn't picture themselves any other way except the way they were. They couldn't see themselves as older or richer or living anywhere else except where they were living then, and they couldn't picture any way of staying out of trouble or living like other folks. You couldn't call them crazy, exactly, but there was something twisted about their minds that nothing or nobody could straighten out.

I took my Cross inkpen out of the inside pocket of my jacket and wrote Chigger a note on the pasteboard box. "I've got to go," I wrote. "You eat the rest of the groceries. I'm putting thirty dollars on the inside of the lantern. Don't say I never gave you anything. Patrick A. Gunn."

Chigger was still sawing logs when I eased out the door. It was cold outside, but I was wearing my leather bomber jacket. The sun was shining bright on a great big frost, and as I made my way across the pasture to the highway, the ground looked like it was sprinkled with a zillion diamonds. I felt light all over, like I'd shucked something heavy, and kind of empty, too.

CHAPTER VII

I Go Back And Face The Music

I hadn't even walked a quarter of a mile on the highway before this old tan Volkswagen pulled over to the side of the road in front of me. When the driver rolled down the frosted window, I saw this freckled fat woman with frizzly red hair and a little keen nose. She was wearing a white uniform like she was a cafeteria worker or something. She didn't give me time to say anything before she commenced hollering, "What in the world are you doing out this early on such a cold morning? Don't you know you'll catch pneumonia? Don't your mama know where you are?"

I started not to get into the car with her, she was acting so durn bossy and all, but I figured if I didn't, she'd probably get out and run me down. "Get in here," she said, patting the ripped-up seat. "Can't you talk? Has the cat got your tongue?"

I got in and we took off, the old Volkswagen jumping and sputtering and leaving a trail of blue smoke. "You don't look like no runaway," she said, looking me up and down. "Why don't you say something, boy? Can't you talk?"

"You haven't given me half a chance yet," I said, and she looked so red in the face that I thought she might be getting ready to smack me. "I've been camping out with a friend. I forgot to tell my mama I was going off."

"Forgot?" she hollered. "You didn't forget! You slipped off, is what. I hope she dusts your jacket good! Now whereabouts do you live? I got to get to work over at Hillview Manor, and I ain't got much time to fool with you."

"I live at 411 East College, just a block away from the junior college," I said, smiling and batting my eyes at her, trying to soften the old sister up. "I'm Patrick Gunn, ma'am, and who might you be?"

"I might be a kidnapper, but I ain't," she said, making a disgusted face at me. "Don't you know you ain't supposed to crawl in the car with a stranger without even asking the first question? Do you want to end up on *Unsolved Mysteries?"*

She beat all I'd ever seen. She wouldn't even let me answer one question before she'd ask me another one. I decided that I was just going to sit there and keep my mouth shut.

"You ain't pouting, are you?" she said, reaching over and dusting off the shoulder of my jacket. "I hate a person that pouts. Some of my patients at the nursing home pouts, Mrs. Tootie Crane to name one. You got dirt on that new jacket. You're just like Daryl and Don, my twins, you don't take care of nothing, do you?"

"You don't ever stop talking, either," I said. I didn't mean to smart off to her, but I couldn't help it.

She reared back and laughed, though, slapping me hard on the leg. "That's what LeVoy says," she said. "LeVoy's my husband. LeVoy Sexton. Do you know LeVoy?"

"No, ma'am," I said, and she commenced talking ninety miles an hour about how lazy and trifling he was. He got a job in the shoe factory, but he didn't much like that, so he got a job in the foundry, but it was too hot, and now he had too much bending and lifting to do at Giant Foods. She blabbed on and on, and all of a sudden I thought about how big and fat she was, and then about her name, Sexton. She was a ton of sex all right. I'd have to tell Chigger that sometime. He'd get a big kick out of that.

Finally, we came to the forty-five mile–an–hour speed zone in Broad Plains. "You're grinning like a Cheshire cat," she said. "What are you studying about? Some meanness, I imagine."

I was still thinking about her name, but I wasn't about to let on to her. "I'm just happy to be getting back home to my precious mother," I said, which was about halfway true.

"Oh, yeah, I 'spect so," she said, narrowing her eyes and nodding like she didn't much believe me. "Now where is it you say you live?"

"Over on East College next to David Livingston Junior College," I said. "You need to hang a left at the next light."

"Oh, I know where it is," she said. "That's where I got my L.P.N. training, and let me tell you mister, they put me through the mill."

She never let up talking. She told about having to cut up pickled frogs and cats, and how on this important test she was able to name all the bones in the human body except one. I finally tuned her out, but every once in a while I'd have to nod like I was listening.

Everything looked hard and unfriendly in the bright morning sunshine. In town, the frozen windshields of cars were covered with icy white feathers of frost. The sidewalks glistened gray and gritty, and all the big old white houses on McLemore Drive were dingy and washed out with winter. We were nearly home, and now I was scared. I didn't know if Miss Armistead was fixing to run me off or not. Here it was a few days before Christmas, when people are supposed to be happy, and I'd messed up good.

"Right up there at that Hansel and Gretel looking house," I said when we turned on East College. "You can let me out on the street if you're a mind to."

"Okeydoke," she said, pulling over at the curb.

"Thank you, Miss Sexton," I said, getting out of the

car. "It's been real nice talking to you and all."

"You better go on in and get your whipping," she said, waving at me with her freckled hand. "I bet I bent your ear good, didn't I?"

"You got that right," I said and slammed the door fast.

She took off in a puff of blue smoke, the little car whining and hiccuping down the street. She was a right nice lady, but I was kind of glad to be shed of her.

I stepped upon the porch, half expecting Miss Armistead to run out and grab me, but she didn't. I tried the doorknob, but the door was locked, so I had to ring the doorbell.

Seem like I had to wait the longest time before she ever answered the door. I knew she was already up, because she got up early like all old folks. I didn't have any earthly idea what she was aiming to do, but I figured she'd either cry a little or run me off, one or the other.

"Oh, thank goodness!" she hollered after she unlatched the door and saw it was me.

She stood behind the screen for a few seconds, sighing and holding her blue nightdress together up at the neck. Her curly hair was mashed down flat on one side. All of a sudden, though, she rushed out and grabbed hold of me right there on the front porch. She kissed me a dozen times and squeezed me so hard I thought my eyeballs were fixing to pop out. Then she held me away from her, shaking her head like she was aggravated to death. Before I could catch my breath, she was hugging me hard again. "I've been so worried about you, Patrick," she said, and I could feel her old pitiful heart beating fast against mine. "I've imagined the most horrible things."

"I'm all right," I said, pulling away from her, because I didn't much like the lovey-dovey stuff. "I didn't mean to worry you."

"I'm sure you didn't," she said, shivering a little from

the cold. "Let's go on inside the house before we both catch our death."

As soon as Miss Armistead closed the front door behind us, durn if she didn't haul off and hug me again! She beat all.

I knew she wasn't going to make me leave. She was probably going to cry a little and tell me a story, and that was all. I already felt a hundred percent better. I didn't know what I'd been so worried about, anyway. "Go on into the study," she said, finally letting me go and walking over to the stairs. She held on to the banister like she wasn't too steady on her feet. "I need to go upstairs and make some phone calls. A great many people have been concerned about your whereabouts, and I need to pass along the good news."

"Do you need me to guide you up the steps?" I asked, fixing to help her.

"No," she said, waving me away. "Go on into the study like I asked you to do."

She sounded a little bit hateful, not like Miss Armistead atall. I figured she was worn out, was all. I went on in the study and flopped down in the big green wingback chair in front of the window.

The sun shining through the clean windows was warm on my face. I could smell Miss Armistead's lemony furniture polish, and the chair I was sitting in gave off a scent like an old baseball glove. Miss Armistead was a real particular housekeeper, but I could see zillions of bits of dust floating on the sunbeams like a little galaxy. I wondered to myself if all the dust motes could be planets, with people on them so tiny you couldn't even see them with a microscope. I might mention all this to Chigger sometime when we were down on the creek. I hoped I'd made it clear to him, though, that I couldn't have anything to do with him at school.

Miss Armistead had everything fixed up pretty for Christmas. There was a big plastic Santa Claus sitting in a sled being pulled by reindeer on the round reading table in the middle of the room. Pine cones sprayed gold and bunches of holly were arranged on the bookshelves and on top of the piano. The room even smelled like Christmas, because Miss Armistead had put a mess of wood chips and dried flowers and other stuff in a big glass bowl on the little table next to the leather couch. She'd told me once that this stuff she changed every so often meant "stinkpot" in some language, but it sure didn't stink. It smelled just like the Christmas tree in Kmart where Granny Gunn used to take me to see Santa Claus when I was little.

After a while, Miss Armistead came back into the study and stood with her arms folded looking down at me in the chair. She had changed into this black dress that had gold buttons in double rows up the front. She didn't look like she felt good. I figured she was about to come down with a sick headache, her being so worried about me and all.

"How dare you do me like that!" she said, screeching like an old witch right out of the blue and shaking her finger about an inch away from my nose.

I came up out of that chair I know a good foot, she scared me so! I felt like I'd been jolted with a hundred and ten volts!

"The very idea that you would leave me to worry all night long about you! How dare you!"

I didn't say a word. I didn't think that I could talk, anyway. Miss Armistead had done gone as crazy as a bessybug.

"You have no idea how I felt driving up to that school and finding nothing there but your books," she said, ranting and raving and pacing this way and that. "Now I'm going to ask you a question"—she stopped pacing then and looked me hard in the eye and spoke low—"and I want you to think very carefully before you answer." She swallowed hard. "Because if I think you're lying to me, I don't know what I might be forced to do."

She was threatening to get rid of me, sure as the world!

Her big gray eyes bored a hole right through me. "Where were you last night?" she asked.

I thought about telling her I was kidnapped by this old lady named Miss Sexton, and that her twins Daryl and Don tied me up to a tree and stole thirty dollars off me. But then I figured the police would eventually find Miss Sexton, and then she'd be in trouble, and before long, I'd be in a sure enough mess. So I said to Miss Armistead, my hands trembling, "I was camping out with Chigger, and that's the gospel truth. I didn't want to go camping, but he shamed me into going."

Miss Armistead stood there like a general with her skinny legs spraddled out and her hands behind her back.

She craned her head a little to one side and quirked up her mouth like she wasn't sure I was telling everything straight. "And just who is this Chigger person who is able to get you to do things against your will?"

I sat there in that big wingback chair, my heart fluttering like nobody's business, and tried to explain to Miss Armistead about Chigger, how his mama just more or less turned him out on the street and how he didn't have but one arm and part of another. I told her how he always had to argue about everything, and how he liked to let on like he was bad business, but everybody knew he couldn't hit any harder than a girl, he was so weasely.

Directly, Miss Armistead's face kind of unfroze and sagged. She looked old and tired. "You may tell your friend to come and stay here with us," she said, sighing real big. "Of course, some legal arrangements will have to be made, but Judge Parsons is an old friend of mine."

I had no intentions of telling Chigger anything. If he ever set foot inside this house, he'd be trying to take over, the first thing. "I'll tell him what you said," I told her, "but he'll never come here. He can't be tamed."

"I wouldn't trying to 'tame' him, as you put it," she said right hateful, "but I would certainly expect him to behave and to be responsible."

I knew she was throwing that at me, and I caught it on the first go around. "Miss Armistead," I said, getting sort of aggravated myself, "I couldn't help it because Chigger wouldn't leave me alone. You don't know him. He just keeps on and on and on. I didn't want to go off down there on the creek, but he kept pestering me until I went. Looks to me like you could understand that."

"Indeed," she said as cold as an icicle and commenced prancing again. "I suppose"—she marched to the bookcase and whirled around—"I suppose if Mr. Chigger told you to climb the steeple on the First Baptist Church and jump off, you'd do that, too."

Grown people just don't understand some things, and you can't make them understand. They get old and forget how they used to feel and how they used to think. But if Miss Armistead wanted to act like a smart aleck, I could act like one, too. "No, ma'am," I said, "I wouldn't do that. I can't look off the front porch without getting dizzy. But if Chigger was to pester me long enough to rob a bank, now I might do that."

She stopped dead in her tracks and looked hard at me for the longest time. I'd found out that she had a temper, and I knew she was fixing to fly into me again.

She commenced grinning, but it wasn't happy grinning. It was dangerous grinning. Miss Armistead didn't have much color about her to begin with, and now her face was sickly white. She walked over and rested her hand right on top of my head, and I couldn't help flinching. For all I knew, she was fixing to snatch me baldheaded.

"I suppose I'm supposed to be very angry with you now and strike you, is that it?" she said, tilting my head back so she could stare me in the eye.

She was asking me one of those grown-up questions that, if you've got good sense, you don't answer, so I didn't.

"Well, I *am* very angry with you. I'm so angry that the

thought of striking you is quite appealing, but I shall not strike you," she said, taking her hand off my head.

I let out a big puff of air. I was so scared that I didn't realize that I'd been holding my breath.

Miss Armistead folded her arms and looked down her long nose at me. "You will sit there in that chair and think about what you've done," she said, acting like the Queen of Sheba. "You may get up to use the bathroom, and I shall bring your meals to you if necessary, but you will sit there until you can admit the wrong in what you've done."

Mister, I got mad then! She was just like some of those old teachers at school, making me do some durn shitting crazy nonsense for doing wrong, instead of beating the tar out of me! Where in the world did they come up with all that stuff, I wanted to know. Miss Gooch made me put my nose in a circle she'd drawn on the board because I hadn't learned my times tables, and old Miss Edwards in second grade made me suck a fooler when I cried one time. Durn it, I wasn't going to put up with such foolishness, me thirteen years old! "No, ma'am," I said, acting like I was fixing to get up, "I'm not about to sit here in this chair any longer than I want to. You're not big enough to make me, either."

"Perhaps not," she said, leaning over and putting a hand on each arm of the chair. "But I can call someone over at the sheriff's department to help me, if need be." She took her hands off the chair arms then and raised back up. "And besides, you're going to have to walk over the top of me to get out of this house, and I just don't think you're going to do that, young master Gunn."

I eased back down in my chair. I was afraid I'd give her a heart attack or something, she was so durn old and feeble. It beat all I'd ever seen, anyway. Here was this old woman who was sweet as pie one minute and mean as a snake the next. A person ought to be one way or another, that's what I thought. "Well," I said, telling her a thing or two, "I'm not sitting here if you're fixing to send me around the bend."

She closed her eyes and put her fingertips to her temples like she always did when stuff got to her. Directly, she opened her eyes and said, "I have no intention of sending you away. You will have to decide when it is time for you to go." She stood up taller and reared back like a preacher stirred up with a sermon. "Unlike some people, I do not renege on my responsibilities to others."

"What does that *renege* word mean?" I said, aiming to make a joke so she'd get off my case for a while. "Is it something to do with niggers?"

Durn if she didn't fly into me all over again!

"I've tolerated these racial slurs of yours quite long enough," she said, shaking her finger and looking at me like I was a slug in her flower bed. "Only the most ignorant, most unfortunate people use that word, and you will never use it again in this house. Do you understand me, young man?"

"Hell yes!" I hollered, and then I burst out crying.

It just didn't seem right, her talking to me like I wasn't anything. I figured after she'd bought me so much stuff and all, she thought a right smart of me, but now I wasn't so sure.

"I think in this case, tears are very appropriate, Patrick, considering what you've done," Miss Armistead said, walking out of the study real fast. Her high heels sounded like somebody was hammering nails in the floor.

For a second I thought about just getting up and running out of that house as fast as I could and never turning around to look back. I could hit the road with Chigger. He'd go with me, too. That would be right up his alley, hoboing across the country without a care in the world.

But it was already cold weather, and I didn't have but fifty something dollars to my name. Besides, I really didn't want to take off with Chigger. I didn't like to go to school any more than the next fellow, but I be durn if I wanted to end up as ignorant as Chigger, my arms covered with home-made tattoos and moss growing on my teeth. People on the road sometimes picked up boys like us and did all kinds of bad things to them, too. I didn't want somebody to find my bones in a ditch somewhere a year or two after some psycho had slit my gullet.

Miss Armistead didn't have any right letting on like I didn't have any raising, though. At first maybe I didn't know which fork to eat with or to stand up when a woman walked into the room, but at least Granny Gunn tried to show me right from wrong, whether it took or not. One time Granny Gunn turned right around and marched back inside Piggly Wiggly because the cashier had given her back too much change.

Miss Armistead was hardheaded, that was her problem. She just wanted me to say everything was all my fault because I'd slipped off with Chigger, but if she'd been acquainted with Chigger, she'd have known I couldn't help what happened. She was wanting me to say I was wrong because she thought I was wrong, and if you didn't agree with grown people, then they were mad at you.

What was I supposed to have done? Durn it, Chigger was one of those people you might near had to whip sometimes just to make him leave you alone. I guess I could have fought him instead of taking off to the creek with him, but then old man Moneypenny the principal would have put me in detention for fighting in school, and Chigger would've been mad at me until the creek ran dry. Look to me like it was six of one or a half dozen of another. Anyway you looked at it, I was bound to get into trouble.

Grown people halfway expected you to get into some trouble with people your own age, but never with them. It was all right for grown people to talk to you like a dog, too, but you sure better not talk to them that way. Old Miss Gooch used to call me stupid, but if I'd called her that, my hind end wouldn't of held shucks when she got through with me. Miss Armistead didn't call me bad name, but she didn't care how much trouble I had with Chigger, so long as I didn't cause her to lose any sleep.

I sat there in that big green chair a long time saying to myself that I wasn't about to take all the blame for what had happened, but I knew all along I was fixing to give in to Miss Armistead. That was life. Every once in a while you had to say things you didn't believe and act ways you didn't feel and let on like you were sorry for something you weren't. It whittled away at your insides when you had to be that way, but people generally didn't really care about the truth. They just wanted to hear what they wanted to hear.

I turned everything over in my head two or three times, and the answer always came out the same. I was going to have to let on to Miss Armistead like she was right and I was wrong, or I would have to find myself another place to live.

I hadn't slept much the night before, and with all this hard studying on top of that, I was dead tired. I was sound asleep when Miss Armistead's high heels tapping on the hardwood floor woke me up.

Miss Armistead was carrying a big wooden tray piled with sandwiches and cupcakes, but I wasn't hungry. She was looking mighty hurt, but she managed to smile just a little biddy smile when I took the tray from her. "Miss Armistead," I said, having a hard time looking her square in the eye, "I reckon you were right about everything. It was all my fault I took off with Chigger and kept you up at night worrying about me. I'm sorry, and I won't try to cause you any more trouble."

She commenced blinking her eyes, and I knew she was about ready to tune up. She turned around and walked over to the bookshelves so I wouldn't see her cry. She let on like she was looking for a book, but I knew better. She could put her hand on any book in the study without thinking twice.

Directly, after she'd straightened up her she face, she said, "Thank you, Patrick. I know you're genuinely sorry for everything that happened, so let's put it all behind us and not speak of it again."

"Yes, ma'am," I said.

She looked so pitiful and all I reckon I had to forgive her on the spot. She was old and had forgotten what it was like to be young. She was rich and had forgotten what it was like to be poor. She hadn't meant any harm, though, and she couldn't help it because she wasn't as smart as I was about figuring things out. She was a grown person who was set in her ways, and you couldn't make anything else out of her.

Seem like all the next day we couldn't get used to one another, or at least Miss Armistead couldn't get used to me.

It was Saturday, but I stayed in my room and tried to be extra quiet. Miss Armistead couldn't do enough for me. She made me divinity candy and brought me hot spiced tea and wanted to know every five minutes if there was anything special old Santa could bring me. I never let on to her, but I wasn't studying about Christmas, because I had too many tumbled-up notions in my head that I needed to piece together. I was thinking about Chigger and my mama and Granny Gunn, but Miss Armistead was tapping on my door every time I turned around, acting like she was the maid in the house instead of the owner. "May I come in, dear?" she'd say, acting real nervous, and then she'd fidget in my room for a spell, then walk out again like she was in a big hurry. She got on my nerves so bad I could hardly stand her.

Up in the day she finally left me alone, and I got some reading done. Reading wasn't all that much fun, but it took my mind off things for a while.

I finished reading *Where the Lilies Bloom* late that afternoon and was telling Miss Armistead all about it at the supper table, how a bunch of kids my own age learned to take care of themselves after their daddy died. Directly, she said to me, she said, "That story reminds me of your friend Chigger. You could invite him over tomorrow if you like. You need to associate with more young people."

I didn't tell Miss Armistead that I wasn't young inside, because some things other people can't understand. "I don't think Chigger would come over here," I said, which was the truth, even if it was the handy truth. "There's no telling when I'll see him again, either. Next year, probably."

I went on and explained to her that Chigger wouldn't come back to school until he got good and ready or until the sheriff picked him up.

She looked at me a long time while she was chewing, like she had something on her mind she wanted to say but decided not to. "People are often a lot of trouble to us," she said finally, worrying her front teeth with her tongue. "Especially the ones we love."

"I don't love Chigger," I said, feeling myself turning beet red in the face. "Boys ain't supposed to love other boys."

She burped into her napkin. "Oh, I see," she said, acting like she didn't already know that, but I knew she did. "When you see him again, you must tell him what I said about coming here. You will do that, won't you, dear?"

I wasn't about to say anything to Chigger about coming over to our house to live. "Yes, ma'am, I'll sure tell him," I said.

We ate a while without saying anything else. We were having roast beef and potatoes and carrots all cooked together. I kept my eyes on my plate mostly, and she kept her eyes on hers. Every so often we'd look up to spy on the other one and lock eyes. Finally, she said, "I'm sorry I spoke so harshly to you yesterday. I was very upset because I thought I had allowed something terrible to happen to you, and I overspoke, I'm afraid." She put her hand up to her throat and leaned forward a little. "I love you very much, you see."

Durn if this old lady couldn't embarrass the living day-lights out of a body! I could feel myself turning red right up to the roots of my hair. I didn't know what to say, and Miss Armistead was looking at me like she was waiting for me to say something. I commenced stammering and stuttering and then blurted out, "I don't know whether I love you or not, Miss Armistead. I don't hate you or nothing, but I usually don't know I love somebody until they're dead."

She stood straight up from the table, and I didn't know what was up, whether she had roast beef hung in her throat and I was going to have to do the Heimlich on her, or whether she was mad at me again. But durn if she didn't walk over behind my chair and wrap both her arms around my neck and lay her head down on top of mine. "I love you enough for both of us," she whispered.

She held me like that for the longest time, but I didn't mind too much.

I gave Miss Armistead a big bottle of pink bubble bath for Christmas and a comb that looked like turtle shell, only it was plastic.

She gave me a bicycle and a watch. The watch wasn't new. It belonged to her husband, her "late" husband, as she always put it. I reckon if you're dead, you're late for every-thing, but I didn't tell her that. The watch was square and had to be wound up by hand. I couldn't wear it to school because it was solid gold and worth a ton of money. It was the second nicest thing anybody had ever given me. I liked my new bicycle, too, but I'd heap rather had an old one I didn't have to worry about scratching up. Miss Armistead made me set this one on the back porch every night. She was a big hand for taking care of your stuff.

It ought to have been a good Christmas, but it wasn't. We had oodles of good things to eat, things I'd never even heard of before, like mincemeat pie and oyster dressing and tomato something that was kind of like jello except it wasn't sweet.

Seem like I couldn't think of anything but Granny Gunn all Christmas Day.

The last Christmas she was alive, she gave me this little toy dog that ran on batteries. It could walk and bark and open its mouth, too. Granny didn't have much money, but she saw this little dog at Jiffy Mart and bought if for me when she was getting her Social Security check cashed. I was way too old for a toy like that, but Granny always thought I was six years old. My daddy said to me when he saw it, he said, "Well, mama's baby got a play pretty, didn't he?" One night he came in drunk and kicked it across the trailer, and then it never worked right again.

I never did buy Granny a present. I never even thought of buying her one, and I don't reckon my daddy did, either. I thought about her being dead on Christmas, and me sitting up eating fancy stuff and having the best of everything, and it might near broke my heart.

CHAPTER VIII

I Find A Good Hideout
And Meet A Sissy Boy

The weeks passed off fast at Miss Armistead's. I was getting my lessons and reading books and going to church on Sunday, and seem like a week was used up before I knew it.

I was doing right well in school, making nearly all B's. I hadn't seen hide nor hair of Chigger anymore. Some of the kids at school said that he'd been sent off to juvenile detention in Memphis again, and I guess he had.

As long as I told Miss Armistead where I was headed and what time I was aiming to be back, she let me go down to the creek on Saturdays when the weather got warm up in April. She'd always tell me not to get snake bit and not to drown, like I would on purpose.

I'd pack up a big bunch of stuff, boloney sandwiches and bananas and potato chips, and head off early in the morning on my bicycle. I'd hold my groceries and fishing rod in one hand and steer with the other one. I couldn't pedal too fast, I was usually so loaded down, and sometimes cars honked at me because I wouldn't get off the highway.

In a way it was a good thing that Chigger had been sent off. He would've had a fit if he'd seen what had happened to his camp. Some sorry dickens had ripped the sides off the shack and slung one of his quilts way up in a tree. I looked off the bank and saw his potbellied stove lying upside down in the creek. It looked like a swollen dead pig with three legs sticking straight up in the air.

Right down below the bridge where we used to camp, the creek ran through a big pasture that this old farmer named Bill Aaron kept bushhogged. He didn't much like people messing around in his pasture, because one time somebody shot one of his cows. Chigger told me that Mr. Aaron used to run him off all the time, but Miss Armistead had called him and fixed things up so he wouldn't bother me. Once I got off the blacktop, I could ride my bicycle a good mile through level pasture before I ever got to any real woods. I'd hide my bicycle in the woods and wade up and down the creek all day, fishing and swimming and generally having a fine time.

There was one place, though, where I'd have to get out of the creek and walk around, because back in March a tornado had blown about a dozen big oaks over in the water. I figured there was a good fishing hole in there among those trees, but I could never get inside, because all those big oaks were stacked like Lincoln Logs on all four sides. I could work my way inside only about two or three yards, and then it was like I was in a big briar patch, limbs scratching and poking me everywhere. I liked to have worried myself to death trying to figure out a way to get to all those bass I knew were swimming around those limbs and roots.

Then on up in May, there was a big flood in Broad Plains. It rained all day long for four days, and water even got inside the First National Bank and McDonald's and a whole bunch of stores around the square. We couldn't have school for two days, which was all right with me, except then we had to make up two days before we got our summer vacation.

Miss Armistead wouldn't let me go to the creek for about a week. She was afraid I'd fall in swift water and get carried off. I'd had to look after myself ever since I was a little biddy boy in the trailer park, but I couldn't make her understand that. She was always afraid that I was fixing to do something dangerous and get killed. She just didn't understand how I lived before I came to stay with her, how I sometimes had to monkey with the fusebox in our trailer before we had any electricity, or how Jessie and I used to jump off the Riverbend Overpass onto the tops of slow-moving boxcars.

Anyway, I finally persuaded her to let me go back to the creek the Friday after we got out of school.

It was one of those mornings when you feel like everything in the world is just right and nothing can go wrong. All the trees were fresh green with tender leaves, and big banks of honeysuckles tumbled over fencerows along the highway. Wrens chirped and hopped and fluttered in the thickets. The whole countryside looked like it was getting a fresh start, and I felt good riding my new bicycle down that smooth blacktop, knowing that school was out and I had the whole summer to myself. I didn't have a thing in the world to do at home except to sweep off the porch and read books. I was about finished with *Robinson Crusoe*, and I hadn't minded reading it atall. It was right up my alley.

I didn't take any groceries or fishing tackle with me this day. I figured I'd just explore to see how the creek had changed since the flood. The sun began to get hot as I rode along, and finally I turned up the collar on my knit shirt to keep my neck from blistering. Sweat was trickling down the hollow of my back when I finally got down to the creek.

All the trees on the bank were wearing grass skirts where the water had risen so high. Chigger's shack was all washed away now except for the door. I saw it wedged between two willows on the other side of the creek.

Everywhere I looked, there was trash. I saw old rusty spray cans, car tires, and all kinds of plastic junk bobbing up and down in the shallows. It made me durn mad to see how people had dumped garbage in the creek because they were too trifling to tote it off right. Big greenish blue snake doctors and little gray butterflies were flitting around in all that mess, and in places rainbow colored scum was floating on top of the water.

I'd told Miss Armistead not to expect me back before suppertime, so I took my time exploring. I had money to buy me something to eat at the store when I got hungry.

I liked being off to myself. Sometimes I pretended I was Daniel Boone or De Soto or some other famous explorer I'd read about in school. Sometimes I sang, too, but I wouldn't dare sing in front of anybody at school or at church. If I wanted to talk to myself or break wind or pee up against a tree, nobody knew any different. I thought back to things that had happened at school and fixed them up to suit myself, like that time Leslie Peale said I was trash when she didn't know I was walking right behind her. I let on to myself like I'd tapped her on the shoulder and said, "Leslie, since you've already got two earrings in each ear, why don't you poke one through your snout so it won't turn up on the end like it does now?"

After a while I came to that spot where all these big water oaks were blown over in the creek. I wasn't paying much attention at first, because everything looked about the same there, but all of a sudden, I glanced down and saw something shiny deep in the water.

Then I could see that the trunks of three big oaks had shifted around just enough to open up a space in the water about a yard across in the shape of a triangle. Somebody had dropped a fishing line down in that open space and gotten snagged on a limb. What had caught my eye was a fishing lure, and a good one, too, one of those seven or eight dollar jobs at Wal-Mart.

I dug out my pocketknife and whittled off a forked limb. I stuck the limb down in the water and tried to tangle it around the lure, but I didn't have any luck. That limb was too short, so I cut another one. I lay down flat on the bank and worked around with that limb for the better part of an hour, but I still couldn't jar the lure loose. Finally, I just threw the limb in the water and got ready to go on somewhere else.

I'd already walked off a little piece when I had an idea. It was dangerous, but I knew I was going to do it, anyway. I could feel my stomach sinking cold the way it always did when I knew I was fixing to do something that I knew I shouldn't. What I was going to do, I was going to get down between those three trunks, go under water, and pull that lure loose or else prize it loose with my pocketknife. I knew good and well I could get down there and get tangled up in a root, or else I could bump my head and get knocked out cold and drown. I knew a boy from school who drowned that way. Glenn Romer drowned under a bank one day when he was fishing for bluegill with Calvin Barnes. Glenn got his line tangled in some roots, went under a bank to pull it loose, and drowned before Calvin realized he wasn't coming back up.

What was crazy, Miss Armistead gave me five dollars every week as regular as rain, and I could've bought a lure just like the one I saw. It wouldn't have been the same, though, because this one was free for the taking. Everything in the world is naturally supposed to cost something, but I was always one who liked sliding under the fence instead of paying at the gate.

I was as nervous as a cat in a roomful of rockers, but I had to get that lure. I stripped off naked and took off my black plastic watch that Miss Armistead had given me for everyday and laid it on top of my clothes. All of a sudden, I got a picture in my mind of somebody coming upon my clothes after I'd drowned and knowing that's where I was, wedged down there under those big tree trunks, my nubbin shrunk to a peapod and my eyes rolled back in my head. I almost put my clothes back on then and walked off, but that lure kept twinkling and winking and waving in the water like it was begging me to come after it.

I slipped down off the bank, my bare hind end scrubbing through old gray clay and roots, and eased between the tree trunks. Hot as the weather was, the creek was still cold, and my hide looked like a pullet's skin after it had been scalded and plucked. My particulars drew up inside me like they were looking for a warm place to hide. I held on to one of the tree trunks for a few seconds, took three good breaths, and dunked myself under.

Here the water was clean enough for me to open my eyes. I could see the lure as clear as day, but it was farther down than it looked from the bank. I grabbed hold of the broken limb it was snagged on and followed it down about six feet. The hooks on the lure were sunk in deep, and as I was trying to get my pocketknife open and hold on to the limb so I wouldn't float back to the top, I dropped my durn knife. It was a Case and cost forty dollars, so I had to go on down to the bottom to see if I could find it.

I didn't have any trouble getting down. I'd just grab hold of a limb and pull myself along, then grab another one and go a little farther. Lucky for me, I spied my knife right away lying about ten or eleven feet down on the gravel bottom. Any other time I wouldn't have been able to see it, because the handles were deer antler, about the same color as creek gravel.

It wasn't really scary down there, no roots to get tangled around your feet or anything. I could look up and see daylight, and I knew I could pop back up to the top in five or six seconds. I could see how all three tree trunks lay on top of one another and noticed that they weren't sunk down all the way to the creek bottom.

I decided to look around a little more before my air ran out. I grabbed hold of the bottom tree trunk and eased on around some limbs to the other side of it, and I could look up and see daylight there, too, so I swam toward the top on this side to explore. I didn't really expect to find anything except maybe another place where the trees had shifted and opened up a good fishing hole, but when my head popped out of the water, what I found was the best hideout in the world.

I was at the edge of a big dome of trees. Across from where I was now holding onto a root was a good twenty-five feet of level gravel bank, plenty big enough to camp out on and build a fire. I dogpaddled over to the bank and walked around for a while just inspecting everything. All anybody could see from the outside was a giant logjam of water oaks, but inside the tree limbs looked woven together on purpose. And even though these trees had blown down back in the spring, most of them were still putting out leaves. I could squat down right where I was, and nobody would ever spot me in a thousand years if I didn't want them to. There was plenty of speckled daylight shining through all the leaves, so the whole place was warm and shady at the same time.

I wasn't ever going to tell anybody about this place, not even Chigger. Well, someday I might tell Chigger, if I ever ran into him again.

There was only one way in and one way out right now, and that was swimming down under the big tree trunk and coming out on the opposite side. The trouble was, once I was inside this hideout at night, I wouldn't be able to see under water to get out. I would be in a cage, so to speak, and that didn't make me feel too good the more I thought about it. I figured, though, if I had a good handsaw, I could cut a tunnel through the thick limbs in a couple of days. That's what I decided to do, once I found a good place to come in and out.

I stayed inside for a long time, swimming for a while and then just sitting on the bank planning how I was going to get my stuff inside my hideout. After a while I decided that I could load up groceries and matches and fishing gear in a big garbage bag, squeeze most of the air out, and then haul everything underwater with me. I could do the same thing with my clothes, and then nobody would know where I was.

I thought about Chigger again, and then I wished he was with me. He'd get a big kick out of a hideout like this one. I decided that I'd get everything fixed nice, and then I'd show it to him as soon as he came back home. I knew I was bound to run into him sooner or later.

Around the middle of the afternoon, I swam back over to about where I came in, got a good breath, and went back down. The water wasn't as clear on this side of the logs as it was on the other side, and for half a second I got scared as I was making my way through the limbs to the bottom. Then I saw five or six old gars swimming around, and ordinarily I wasn't afraid of them, but I reckon I was just a little nervous about being down under those big logs by myself. I soon got under the bottom tree trunk and paddled straight up toward the triangle of light, and to tell the truth, it felt kind of good to be out in the hot sunshine again. Funny thing was, I had my knife, but I'd forgotten all about that fishing lure. It could wait, I decided.

I stopped at PeeWee Mason's Texaco and Deli and bought a boloney sandwich and an Orange Crush. Then I went out to the picnic tables at the side of the store to eat.

Directly, PeeWee came out of the store, hitched up his old slouchy green pants, and walked over close to where I was eating. He was a big, red-faced man who wore a cap all the time so folks wouldn't know he was baldheaded. His belly hung way over the front of his pants and looked like it was about to burst out his shirt. "What you say, bud?" he said, hawking and spitting over to one side.

"Reckon where a fellow could get a saw?" I said.

He never even looked toward me. He was humming some song as he looked way over toward a field of young corn. "What's that?" he said.

"A saw. Reckon where a fellow could get a saw?"

He glanced around then, running his tongue over his teeth and studying me. "What you want a saw for, boy?" he asked, spitting again and pulling on the bill of his cap.

"I need to cut some stuff."

"Yeah," he said, looking down at his feet and kind of grinning, "that's generally what people use a saw for. What kind of saw are you wanting?"

"A saw saw," I said, making a motion with my hand to show him how a saw worked. "You know."

"A handsaw?"

"Yeah," I said, "a handsaw."

He kept grinning like he was getting a kick out of aggravating me. "Now just how big a stuff are you talking about cutting?" he said.

I made a circle with my hands to show him. "I want to cut some tree limbs about this big."

He laughed like he was making fun of me. "Hell, boy, you don't need no handsaw for that. You need a chainsaw."

I got up from the picnic table and walked over to where he was standing. "You got a chainsaw?" I said.

"Got two," he said, sticking his tongue through a space where some of his bottom teeth were missing. He hitched up his pants again and started walking back to the store.

I tagged along behind him. "Will you let me borrow one and show me how to use it?" I said to his back. "I won't need it long."

"Nope," he said, turning around and spitting might near on my feet. "You'll cut your damn leg off, and then I'll be in a big lawsuit."

"I've got money," I said, looking him square in the eye. "I'll rent it from you, but you have to show me how to turn it on and off."

"Nope," he said, shaking his head before taking off his cap to smooth down a few greasy strings of hair on top of his head. "Can't help you, mister. Won't help you."

I stayed right behind him when he walked back inside the store. "I've got ten dollars," I said, digging two fives out of my jeans pockets.

He leaned his big hind end against the counter and eyed me for a minute. "When do you want it?" he said finally, reaching out and snatching my money.

"How about the first of next week?"

"Okay," he said, jerking his head toward the back door of the store. "Come on out here and I'll show you where I keep it. You cut your damn leg off, don't blame me. I'll swear to God you stole it."

We went to a little shed out back, and PeeWee filled the saw with gas and oil mixed. Then he showed me how to crank it up. There wasn't much to it. It was about like a lawnmower except the choke was a little different. He told me what to do and what not to do when I was using it, and before I left he said again, "You better not cut your damn leg off."

I got back home around three o'clock and saw we had company sitting in the porch swing beside Miss Armistead.

I recognized Miss Marcella—Miss Marcella James— right off the bat. She lived next door in a house as big as Miss Armistead's and belonged to the Reading Circle. She was an old widow woman like Miss Armistead and didn't have much of a chin to speak of. She had gray teeth, and the two front ones looked like a squirrel's. She wore long fancy dresses that put me in mind of undergarments.

"Hidy, Miss Marcella," I said, sitting down on the front steps. "Hasn't this been a beautiful day?"

"Yes, but the humidity is a bit high," she said, lifting the front of her dress a little. Nothing was ever exactly right with Miss Marcella.

"Tory!" Miss Marcella hollered over her shoulder all of a sudden. "Oh, Tory! Oh, Tory!"

Miss Marcella sounded like she was singing that hollering kind of music that fat ladies sing. I glanced over at Miss Armistead to see if she knew what was going on here, but she just smiled and said, "Did you have a good time? You didn't see any snakes, did you?"

Before I could answer, this boy about my age kind of sidled up behind the swing from the side porch where I reckon he'd been standing. He was a plump pink boy with curly blonde hair. He put me in mind of one of those storybook angels that shoots a bow and arrow and makes people fall in love. Chubbies, I think they're called. He was wearing a blue alligator shirt and khaki shorts and white low-cut Nikes. His glasses were round and wire–rimmed. He had prep written all over him.

"Here, Gran," he said in a high voice, putting his hands on Miss Marcella's shoulders.

I knew right away he was a big sissy. I was real sure I didn't want anything to do with him.

Miss Armistead cleared her throat, which was the signal she always gave when I was supposed to stand up and introduce myself. I knew you had manners on the inside of the house, but it never crossed my mind that you had to have manners on the porch, too. But I got up and walked over to the swing. "Patrick Gunn," I said, sticking out my hand for him to shake. "Pleased to make your acquaintance."

The boy prissed out from behind the swing and shook hands with me. "Tory James," he said in his high soft voice. "Nice to meet you, too."

His hand felt like a damp frog. I started to wipe my hand off on my britches leg, but I knew Miss Armistead was watching. Sure enough, when I turned around, she nodded her head and smiled like I'd done right.

"Tory's going to be staying with his grandmother for a while," said Miss Armistead, patting Miss Marcella's hand.

Miss Marcella bit her bottom lip with her little squirrel teeth and looked like she was ready to burst out bawling. I figured then that this Tory fellow must be a real stinker if he caused his own grandma this much grief.

He didn't look like somebody who'd ever been in any meanness, though. In fact, he looked real uneasy, kind of jumpy and like he didn't know what to do with his hands. When I leaned up against the side of the house, he did the same thing, like he was trying to fit in with me or something. "I stayed with my grandma once," I told him. "I got lonesome, though, and moved back home to live with my daddy."

I saw then I'd done said the wrong thing, because durn if he didn't look like he was about ready to tune up, too. He turned his head away from me, playing like he was looking at something over on the campus of the junior college. I saw his shoulders draw up once or twice like he had the hiccups, but he didn't.

"Why don't you take Tory and show him your room and your things," said Miss Armistead. "I'm sure you're going to be famous friends."

I was sure I didn't want to be friends with this boy atall, but I motioned with my head toward the front door, and he followed me. I held the door open and let him go inside first like I was supposed to, but I felt kind of funny doing that. "This is the hall," I said, "but I guess you can see that for yourself."

This Tory fellow grinned a little, but he still had big tears in his eyes.

I guess I started acting like a big shot. "These floors we're standing on are ash. These were trees when George Washington was President, Miss Armistead says."

He bent down and rubbed his plump fingers across one of the wide planks. "That's really something," he said, sounding just like a girl. "I'm fascinated by historical houses."

"And these fellows up here on the wall are Miss Armistead's dead husband's kinfolks," I told him, imitating the way Miss Armistead always waved her arm when she was showing you something. "Now Miss Armistead's kinfolks were all poor, so none of them are up here. Miss Armistead's daddy went to the pen for making whiskey, so the only place you'll see his picture is in the post office."

I thought that was right funny, but this Tory fellow never cracked a smile. He looked at me like I'd just told him that he had to go to school on Saturday. I could tell there wasn't a bit of fun about him.

"Well, come on," I said, going over to the banister. "I'll show you the upstairs now. I reckon your feet are clean. Miss Armistead is mighty particular. This runner is from Brussels, Belgium, and it's a lot of trouble to take loose from these brass rods and send to the dry cleaners."

He held on to the banister with one hand and inspected each one of his feet before following me upstairs. I showed him the picture in a fancy gold frame that Miss Armistead kept on a tripod at the top of the landing. "This here is a watercolor of Paris, France, painted by Miss Armistead's dead husband when he was sixteen years old," I said.

Tory bent down and squinted at this picture of a big courthouse in the middle of a flooded field. "No," he said, raising his head and looking real serious. "This is Venice, Italy, not Paris." He put his finger on the water. "See, this is the canal."

I saw right off that he was a durn smart aleck. "Yeah, Venice, that's what I said. Didn't I say Venice? That's what I meant, anyway," I told him.

"You said Paris," he said, looking like he wanted to laugh in my face so bad he could hardly stand it.

"You're not supposed to touch it," I said, shaking my head. "Miss Armistead would have a fainting spell if she knew you touched that."

"It's under glass, after all," he said, looking me hard in the eye and frowning.

I didn't like people looking me in the eye. Seem like they were trying to peep inside me and see things I'd rather keep to myself. It was as bad as somebody you didn't know or somebody you didn't like seeing you naked. "Well, she won't have fingerprints all over her stuff," I said, and he cocked his head back and acted like he didn't believe me. "Now I'll show you my room, I reckon."

I walked on down to the end of the hall and opened the last door. When I showed this Tory inside my bedroom, I noticed that he took tiny quick steps like a penguin.

"Well, this is quite nice," he said, looking around every which way.

"You durn right it is," I said, grabbing hold of my bedpost. "This is what you call a rice bed, because it's got bunches of rice carved right here on the posts, see?"

"Yes, I know that," he said, and grinned. I didn't like his grin. When somebody is whispering mean stuff about you to another person, and then this person looks at you and grins, it was that kind of grin.

"I bet you don't know why the old folks built these beds so high off the ground back in pioneer days," I said, fixing to get him back for being such a smart aleck.

"I believe there was a problem involving snakes, if memory serves me," he said, yawning out loud.

He acted just like the preps at school, letting on like he knew everything and looking at me like I was dirt. Where did they learn to act that way, I wanted to know. Granny Gunn used to say my daddy didn't learn his meanness from her, he went to meanness school. I reckoned that preps must go to prep school to learn how to look down their noses at everybody.

This old Tory boy commenced running his fingers across the green top on this little table that had some tin soldiers and other doodads on it. "Malachite, I would say," he said, looking at me like I was supposed to know one kind of plastic from another.

I decided to tell him a dirty joke. Everybody liked dirty jokes. "Hey, Tory," I said, grabbing him by the shirtsleeve and kind of leading him out of my room. "If you're an American citizen and you're using the bathroom in Paris, France, do you know what you are?"

His mouth tightened, and he rolled his eyes up at the hall ceiling. "No, what?" he said, acting like he was tired to death and didn't feel like fooling with me.

"*European,*" I said, and laughed.

He batted his big blue eyes a couple of times and then looked at me like I didn't have good sense.

"It's a joke," I said. "*You are a peeing.* Get it? *European.*"

He stood real still for a minute, pinching a little piece of skin on his throat and looking sideways. "Oh, well, yes," he finally stuttered. "A joke. I get it. Yes."

He grudged me a smile, and I felt like a durn fool! I saw then that he was just too slow for me. "Less us go back downstairs," I said, and he followed behind me.

When we got back to the porch, Miss Marcella had already gone, and Miss Armistead was out in the yard pulling dandelions. She looked up when she heard us come out the door and said, "Tory, your grandmother said for you to visit for as long as you liked. We'd love to have you stay for supper, wouldn't we, Patrick?"

"Yeah, stay for supper, Tory," I said, but I didn't put much wind behind it.

"Thank you, Miss Armistead, but I think I'll go home now and take a nap," he said, sticking out his hand for me to shake again. "I'm afraid I had a rather tiring plane trip from Jackson."

"Of course, dear," said Miss Armistead, taking off her weed–pulling gloves and walking back to the porch so she could shake hands with Tory. "Don't wait for an invitation," she went on, drawing me close to her and putting her arm around my waist, "because Patrick and I both enjoy company. Don't we dear?"

"Yes, ma'am," I said, looking down at my feet.

"Well, thanks again," Tory said, and prissed across the yard and through the privet hedge to his house.

I was glad to see him go. Chigger would sure get a kick out of him.

Miss Armistead and I were at the supper table eating breast of chicken and early peas and new potatoes. "Pass me another biscuit, please ma'am," I said. "I believe I'm hollow tonight."

"You must have had an exciting day," she said, passing the wire basket where the biscuits were wrapped up in this cloth of a thing.

She was trying to pick me, was what she was trying to do. She had a way of getting me started on something, and if I wasn't real careful, I'd tell her a whole bunch of stuff before I knew it. I was getting too smart for her, though. "Well, it was okay," I said. "I explored all up and down the creek and found me another good fishing hole. I went swimming for a while, too."

"Oh, I didn't know you took your swimming things," she said, setting down her fork and dabbing her mouth with her napkin.

"I didn't," I said without thinking. "I went in my birthday suit."

All of a sudden, she put her napkin back up to her mouth, and at first I thought I'd done shocked the daylights out of her. Then I saw she was tickled. "Indeed," she said, straightening up her face. "That sounds like wonderful fun."

I couldn't imagine Miss Armistead swimming in her birthday suit, and I didn't try, either. It looked to me like old people ought to be thinking about other things, church and flower arrangements and such as that.

"I'm sorry, Patrick," she said directly. "I believe I've embarrassed you." I could tell it was all she could do to keep from laughing out loud.

"That's okay," I said to change the subject. I commenced talking about our company. "Is that Tory boy going to be here for the whole summer?"

I'm glad you brought that up, dear," she said, laying her knife and fork across her plate and leaning back in her chair like she was full. Miss Armistead didn't eat enough to keep a bird alive, but she was all time acting like she was one of those Roman gluttons I'd read about. "I'm afraid I must hold you in the strictest confidence."

"That means I can't tell anybody, right?"

"Yes," she said, looking serious. "Tory is here with his grandmother not necessarily because he wants to be, but because he has nowhere else to go."

I almost blurted out something then, but I bit my tongue just in time. It was a thousand wonders that something ignorant didn't pop out of my mouth like it usually did.

Miss Armistead looked at me funny. "Yes, dear?" she said, her eyebrows raised.

"Nothing," I said. "I was just thinking."

I don't know how one person is able to read another person's eyes, but you can sometimes, and I read Miss Armistead's. She knew what I'd been thinking, sure as the world. "Yes, I suppose you were, and I understand," she said, reaching over to pat my hand. "You see, Tory's father was sent to prison because he didn't pay his taxes for a number of years. Tory's mother has remarried, and Tory seems to be in the way at the moment." Miss Armistead's mouth tightened like she was disgusted.

Then it hit me! No wonder Tory acted so funny when I told him that Miss Armistead's daddy had gone to the pen. No wonder his granny was about to cry out on the porch, and him, too. I felt about yea high.

"I realize that the two of you probably have very little in common, Patrick," Miss Armistead went on, "but I would appreciate it if you would be nice to him. Try to be his friend."

"Yes, ma'am, I will," I said, and I meant it.

"You know, dear, I have very serious reservations about your going to the creek alone, much less your swimming alone down there. I think it would be wonderful if you invited Tory along from now on. You can look after each other."

I could have told her quick, I didn't need anybody to look after me. Me and my durn big mouth! Boy, Miss Armistead really knew how to put a quietus on somebody's plans. Now I was going to have to let this Tory boy in on the secret about my hideout.

"I can see that you're disappointed," Miss Armistead said, "but do this for me. I do worry about you when you're off all day by yourself."

I started once to pout, but I despise a pouter. "Yes, ma'am," I said, pushing back my plate because my appetite was gone.

The next afternoon I was stretched out in the porch swing with two big pillows under my head and was reading the rest of *The Once and Future King*. I'd started reading it way back in the winter on my own, but I'd just been reading a little bit at a time. This book was might near as thick as a dictionary, because it wasn't one book, it was four books in one. It was about King Arthur and Camelot and all that stuff. One chapter told how Merlyn the magician got younger as he went back in time, and I lay there in the swing studying for the longest time, trying to figure out how that could be.

I'd about nodded off to sleep when that Tory boy stepped upon the porch. He was wearing blue jeans and another alligator shirt and dirty bucks like mine. His alligator shirt was white and had a big spot of mustard down on the belly of it. "Had hotdogs for lunch today, didn't you?"

I said, not thinking of how smart alecky that sounded until after I'd said it.

He just laughed, though, and didn't seem to get mad. He had straight white teeth. Mine look like white niblet corn, but when Miss Armistead took me to Dr. Charlie, I only had one cavity. Dr. Charlie reamed it out and plugged it up with real gold.

"Yeah," he said, looking down at his shirt, "how'd you guess?"

We both laughed this time. I decided that this Tory fellow wasn't so bad after all. We had just started off on the wrong foot, was all.

He walked over toward the swing, sat down on the porch, and leaned his back against the side of the house. "Did you ever read this?" I said, holding up the book so he could see the cover.

He craned his neck to see. "No," he said. "What's it about?"

"Well, it's a long story, but here goes," I said, and then I commenced telling him a lot about it, how Merlyn showed Wart how to be king and to use Might for Right, and how King Arthur had this wife, who took up with Lancelot, who happened to be King Arthur's best friend and the greatest knight in the world.

"Sounds like my mother," Tory said.

"Who?" I said, raising up on one arm.

"King Arthur's wife. My mother took up with my father's best friend, George Henry Lee. He's my stepfather now. He's not the greatest anything, though, except a drunk. He might be the greatest drunk in the world."

"Now that sounds like *my* daddy," I said. "I ain't seen him in might near a year, and I don't care if I don't see him for another one."

"Yeah, I know," Tory said. "I've already heard about him."

I must have turned all colors, because Tory's mouth

dropped like a person's does when he knows he's really stepped in it. I didn't say anything, but I sure wanted to. I wanted to know who had been talking about me behind my back. I figured it was Miss Marcella who'd been low-rating me to Tory.

Neither one of us said a word for a long time. I let on like I was reading, figuring he'd finally get tired of sitting on his fat butt and leave. Directly, though, he said, "I didn't mean to hurt your feelings about your father. I happened to ask Gran how you were related to Miss Armistead, and she told me why you were here. I really am sorry."

"You didn't hurt my feelings," I said, turning the page and acting like I didn't have a care in the world. "Can't anybody hurt my feelings."

"Miss Armistead told you about me, too, didn't she?" he asked.

I hadn't counted on him bringing up that subject. I was stuck between a rock and a hard place. I'd promised Miss Armistead I wouldn't say anything about what she'd told me, but I knew good and well my face was giving me away. "What?" I said, my voice hitting a high note.

"You heard me," he said, grinning because he knew he had me pinned down. "She did, didn't she?"

"A heap of times it's better not to talk," I said, holding the book in front of my face. "I'm not saying she did, and I ain't saying she didn't."

"She did," he said, and laughed. "You're from the country, aren't you?"

"I'm not neither!" I said, sitting straight up in the swing. "I'm from over yonder at Meadowview Manor Trailer Park. I stayed for a month with my granny out in the sticks, but that was all!"

"Hey, now, I didn't mean to insult you," he said, putting out both hands like he was fixing to have to push me back. "Come on. I'm not making fun of the way you talk."

I tried to cool down before I knocked this Tory in the head, but my hands were all trembly, I was so mad. I didn't know how to take him. One minute he was acting like a know–it–all, and the next minute he seemed like maybe he was okay. Then he'd turn right around and start acting like a turd. Anybody ought to be one way or the other, not changing like the wind.

"I'm not from the country," I said directly. "I may not talk like a city slicker all the time, but I'm as good as the next fellow."

He scratched both his ankles and looked way off down the street. "I didn't mean anything by what I said, I promise. People make fun of the way I talk," he said, turning to look at me. "They call me a sissy and worse stuff than that because I don't have a deep voice."

I thought he talked funny, too, but at least I had enough raising not to let on. "They don't have any right to do that," I said. "People don't have a right to be making fun of anybody, anyway. People can't help where they come from or if they turn out to be a sissy."

All of a sudden, Tory got up from the porch and sat down in the swing beside me. I didn't much want him doing that, but he did it, anyway. "Are we going to be friends or what?" he said, pushing up his glasses with his thumb.

I wasn't all that thrilled about being his friend, but I'd halfway promised Miss Armistead that I'd try to be. I'd felt sorry for this Tory fellow at the supper table, and now I was having to pay up for my pity. Maybe someday I'd learn to keep my big mouth shut. "If you don't go low-rating me again, I reckon we can be," I said.

"Done deal," he said, giving me a high five.

CHAPTER IX

I Whip Tory's Butt And He Saves Mine

Early Monday morning I was ready to take off to the creek.

I gathered up my fishing tackle and a bunch of good stuff to eat—Pop Tarts and apples and crackers and a whole pack of cheese. I put all my eats in a big paper sack along with three garbage bags.

Miss Armistead hadn't stirred yet, but I'd already cleared everything with her on Sunday. I was supposed to take Tory with me and be back home before suppertime. Sunday night I'd called him on the telephone to tell him to be ready to go at five o'clock. We were fixing to camp out all day on the creek. He acted like he didn't know what camping out was, but he said he knew his granny would let him go.

I eased out the back door, being careful not to wake Miss Armistead. Tory was supposed to be waiting outside in our driveway, but I didn't see hide nor hair of him.

I can't stand for somebody to tell me they're going to do something and then not do it. People at the trailer park were like that, always promising that they were going to do some big something for you, but when time came for them to deliver, they acted like you were a durn fool for believing them in the first place. Buck Nobblit told me one time that he'd give me the handlebars off his old bicycle when he got a new one for Christmas. Well, when he got his new bicycle, he sold his old one to Pukey Hobbs, handlebars and all. I said to him, I said, "Buck, where's my handlebars?" and he goes, "Well, shit, Gunn, you know good and well I sold my bicycle to Pukey. You didn't expect me to keep the handlebars and give them to you, did you?" He acted like I was stupid, and I kind of felt that way myself.

I started thinking about Buck as I waited for Tory, and durn if I didn't get mad all over again. People were the same everywhere. You couldn't believe a thing they said.

I decided to go off and leave Tory. I wheeled my bicycle down off the porch, broke down my fishing rod, and tied it across the handlebars with a piece of fishing line. I gathered up my groceries in one arm and headed out.

I didn't get any farther than the four-way stop at the end of the street. Durn it, I knew Miss Armistead would rake my hind end over the coals if I didn't do what I said I would. I was going to have to sit around on the porch half the morning waiting on city boy. I had him figured for the kind that would sleep half the day and then complain about being tired the other half.

I pedaled back and sat down on the porch for a little spell. Over on the main highway, I could hear the cars of the work hands rushing to the factories over in Industrial Park, but here on the side streets everything was quiet. A big gray mockingbird was gurgling out a song up in the top of Miss Armistead's tulip poplar, and a few wrens fluttered around in the privet hedge. Over in the east the sky was pinkish red. My tee shirt was already sticking to my back, so it was going to rain before we ever got off, look like.

I decided to go over to Miss Marcella's house and wake up Tory. The trouble was, I didn't know which room was his bedroom. I felt like a low-down sneaky dog looking in a body's windows, but I was fixing to, anyway. I knew Miss Armistead would have a hissy fit if she caught me.

I looked through Miss Armistead's kitchen window to

see if she was making coffee yet. The percolator wasn't hiccuping, so I knew Miss Armistead was still abed. I slipped around to the far side of Miss Marcella's house, which had exactly ten windows on the bottom floor. The first window had a wasp's nest up in the corner, so I decided to go to the next window and come back to that one later if I had to. The second window was covered with thick fancy curtains, but there was a little sliver of light showing through where the curtains didn't exactly meet. I took a quick gander at the other houses, and when I didn't see anybody else stirring, I bent over and peeped in.

It was Miss Marcella's bedroom!

Boy, I hopped back fast! Miss Marcella was propped up in bed with toilet paper wrapped around her head like a mummy, and she had her mouth wide open. She was lying in a big poster bed with the sheet pulled up to her neck and both hands holding on to the top of it like somebody was fixing to slip in and jerk it off her. Lord God Almighty, what kind of person had I turned out to be, peeping in old ladies' bedrooms?

I slipped over to the window with the wasp nest in the corner. It was too early for the wasps to get stirred up if I didn't shake the window, but I was still mighty careful when I peeped in there. There were just blinds on this window, but they'd been slanted up from the inside. I squatted down low on the ground and tried to look up, but all I could see was a lamp fixture with six white globes. I figured that this was the dining room, so I was out of luck again. I didn't know what else to do but keep on looking in all the other windows, but I knew better than to go around on the other side of the house where Miss Armistead might catch me.

Just about the time I was bending over to peep in another window, I caught a glimpse of something striped in one of the upstairs windows that had an air conditioner sticking out of it. It was Tory, and he was standing there in his pajamas looking right straight down at me. I didn't know how long he'd been standing there, but something told me he'd seen me peeping in his granny's window. I felt lower than a snake's belly.

I let on like I hadn't been doing anything, though, or like I didn't think a thing in the world about it. I mouthed out the words, "Hurry up," and motioned for him to come on down. He looked stony-faced at me for a second before disappearing from the window. I went back and sat on the porch and waited on him some more.

I waited and I waited. Finally, he slow-poked out the front door wearing white overall shorts, a polo shirt, and high-top Nikes. His hair was still kinky and wet where he'd taken a shower. "Ready?" I said, trying to act friendly, because I didn't know how he was going to take what he caught me doing.

"Ready as I'm ever going to be," he said right hateful, walking back to the shed behind Miss Marcella's house and wheeling out his bicycle. It was an old beat-up looking purple ten-speed, and I could tell by the shifter and cable that he'd done messed up his gears. Mine was a jet black all–terrain, and I knew he was just as jealous as he could be, even if he didn't look like he was.

"I've got everything we need," I said when he rode up beside me. "You just follow me."

I pushed off, but I hadn't pedaled any farther than the end of the driveway when I heard him say, "Does Miss Armistead know you're a pervert?"

I braked so fast my rear end slid around, making me drop all the groceries. Tory hadn't even taken off. He was sitting on his bicycle with his legs spraddled out and his arms folded. He had his mouth all turned down like Miss Austin the librarian at school did when you talked too loud. "See what you made me do?" I said, getting off my bicycle to gather up everything. I was acting mad, but I was really scared. My stomach had that hot electric feeling it gets when I know I'm fixing to get into trouble. "I wasn't trying to be a Peeping Tom, so you just shut your face. All I was trying to do was to find your bedroom so I could wake you up. We were aiming to leave at five o 'clock."

"We were aiming to leave at five o'clock," he said, mocking me and trying to sound backward like he thought I was.

I'd already told that four-eyed turd about low-rating me! Mister, I dropped all my groceries again and went after him. I saw a big jar of Planter's Peanuts rolling right out in the street, but I didn't care.

When he saw me coming with blood in my eye, he slung one leg over the crossbar and let his bicycle drop right there on the concrete. Then he slung his glasses back over his shoulder. You could tell he was the kind who'd had everything given to him on a silver platter, because he didn't take care of his stuff.

I figured he was fixing to tuck tail and run for his granny, but he didn't. I had my fist drawn back and had done popped him a good one upside the head before he could say "Jack Robinson," but durn his time, he got lucky and hit me hard in the gut. It cramped like the dickens, but I went after him again. I laid a goose egg right above his left eye, but durn if he didn't pop me hard on the chin! If I'd had a glass chin, I would've been a goner for sure. I reeled around a couple of times, dizzy as a bat, and ended up holding on to an elm tree.

Directly, I flew into him again, and I saw he'd just about had enough, because he was wheezing like an old race horse. I didn't let up, though. I dotted that other eye for him.

Then he did a low-down sneaky thing when he knew I'd done got the best of him. I wasn't paying any attention to his feet, figuring he wouldn't be the kind to fight dirty, and he hauled off and kicked me right in the particulars!

I was bent double, hurting so bad I couldn't help crying, but I managed to crawl over behind the big oak at the end of the driveway so Miss Armistead wouldn't see me. I couldn't tell her where I was hurting if she ran out the door and asked me, anyway.

That sissy Tory was standing over me wringing his hands like an old lady and looking like he'd done seen a ghost, he was so pale. "You won, okay? Okay? You won," he said, his voice quivering like he was fixing to cry. "I didn't mean to hit you there. Honest, I didn't mean to."

I couldn't answer for a minute. I thought I was going to puke or pee in my pants, I hurt so bad. "You a durn lie," I said, drawing my knife and working open the long blade. I didn't aim to cut him, but I meant to scare him good.

Then he did commence crying. "Please don't tell Gran," he bawled, digging his fists in his eyes. "Please don't tell her! She'll make me go back!"

I didn't care if she did make him go back to live with his drunk stepdaddy and his mama who didn't want him. That would serve him right, and I told him so.

In a minute I got to feeling some better, as long as I didn't move too fast. I was still mad, but I folded up my knife on my britches leg and slipped it back inside my pocket.

We were both a sight to behold. Tory had a welt right up above each eye, his nose was running, and he was still blubbering and hiccuping like a big tittiebaby. My knees were all burned and skinned up from crawling across the driveway, my jaw was might near too sore to move, and I'd been crying a little bit, too. Of course, I had good reason for crying.

Funny thing was, all of a sudden I looked at Tory, and he looked at me, and then we both burst out laughing! It beat all! The next thing I knew, he was helping me up, and we both started hunting for his glasses. We found them tangled up in the hedge, and all they needed was straightening out some. Then I told Tory, I said, "That was a dirty common trick you pulled, but I don't reckon I'll tell on you if you don't tell on me. I ought to, but I ain't no tattletale."

"Well, I certainly have no intentions of ratting on you," he said, grinning like a jackass eating sawbriars.

He helped me gather up the groceries that were scattered every which way. I was sore as a rising all over. "You still want to go camping?" I asked him after we'd finished. "I won't be mad at you if you don't."

"Yeah, I really want to," he said, hopping on his bicycle and coasting over to where I was. "Here. Give me the sack, and you lead the way."

I handed him the groceries, and we took off. After we got over on Broadway, the main drag, the sun snuck out from behind the clouds, and it looked like it was going to be a right pretty day after all.

I left Tory waiting outside the store when I stopped to pick up the chainsaw. I didn't want PeeWee to get nervous and back out on me.

PeeWee and I were in the shed out back. "How are you going to carry this thing on a bicycle?" PeeWee said.

I hadn't thought much about that, to tell the truth. "I'll figure out something," I said, picking up the saw. It didn't weigh any more than a big sack of sugar.

"Hell, naw, you won't," PeeWee said, hitching up his pants. "We got to figure out something here. That damn blade there'll snag you before you know it. Looks like something's already snagged you. What you been in to?"

"I don't know," I said, shrugging my shoulders.

"Yeah, I bet you don't," he said, narrowing his eyes and grinning. "Looks like you've been playing with the cat. Is that what happened?" He wiggled out his tongue in a wet nasty way and winked. "Been playing with the pussy, boy?"

I thought about the difference between PeeWee and Miss Armistead, how she wouldn't think about saying something ignorant like that to me or anybody else. I kind of looked off to one side and grinned, but I didn't see anything funny.

PeeWee looked around the shed for a minute and then went over to the far corner where a bunch of tow sacks, an old turning plow, a big roll of baling twine, and a lot of other junk were piled up. "Bring me that saw here," he said, and when I handed it to him, he wrapped the blade with two tow sacks and stuck the whole saw down inside another one. Then he tied up the open end of the sack with a piece of baling twine and handed it back to me. "Reckon that will fix you up, partner?" he said, hawking and spitting. "Can you tote it like that?"

"Yessir, I believe I can," I said. I figured that I could sling the whole sack across my back and carry it that way if I wanted to, or else I could lay the sack across my fishing rod on the handlebars, hold on to it with one hand, and steer with the other.

"You bring that saw back before dark, now, or I'll have the law on you. I don't know nothing about renting you no saw," he said, nodding for good measure.

I hightailed it out of his sight before he had a chance to change his mind, and in about fifteen minutes, Tory and I were riding in the pasture alongside the creek.

We stopped every once in a while so I could show Tory some of the places I used to camp out with Chigger. I told him a lot of things about Chigger, how he only had one arm and all, and how I got in trouble that time for slipping off with him and not telling Miss Armistead. Tory said, "He seems like a lot of fun and a lot of trouble, too," and he commenced telling me about this friend of his in Jackson, this Carter Blankenship, who was fixing to make a record because he'd won the big singing contest on "Star Search." Chigger hadn't done anything that would come up with that, so I shut up about him.

We pedaled on for a good piece, but before we got to the woods, I had to stop and rest. I was still right sore from that whipping I gave Tory. Holding on to that chainsaw I'd

120

laid across the handlebars was tricky and hard work, too.

I was hot, so I decided to pull off my shirt and tie it around my waist. When Tory saw what I was doing, he unfastened his galluses and peeled off his shirt, monkey see, monkey do. Without his shirt his hide was white as a grubworm, and he had titties, too, but I never let on. I wouldn't want anybody at school seeing me hanging around with him, but I was beginning to like him right well when we were off to ourselves.

We hid our bicycles in a little thicket at the edge of the woods. I carried the chainsaw, and Tory toted the rest of our stuff. We walked inside the woods, me leading the way. All of a sudden Tory squealed out like some little old girl, "Ooo–wee!" and sputtered and picked at his clothes something fierce.

I could tell right off he'd never been in the woods. I couldn't help laughing at him. "It's just a spider web," I told him. "Don't worry about it. That spider's done long gone."

He shot me a hard look like it was my fault he'd run through a spider web. I didn't twist his arm to make him come to the creek, and I started to tell him so, but I didn't.

We walked a little piece farther before we got to the creek. The first thing I saw was a water snake curled around a tree snag out in the middle of the creek. I told him before he saw it, I said, "Now Tory, over yonder on that old gray snag is a water snake. They ain't nothing to be afraid of. The only ones you have to be afraid of in the water are some that look right black and swim on top of the water. They're cottonmouths, but there's not many of them around these parts."

"Ooo!" he squealed, shivering like he had the chills. He didn't even look toward that snake, either. He just scrunched up his shoulders, shook his head, and closed his eyes. He beat all I'd ever seen. He didn't even act much like a boy, and he fought dirty, too. One minute I kind of liked him and the next I didn't. He was too different from anybody I'd ever known.

We walked down the creek about a hundred yards and came to my hideout. I said, "Well, Tory, here's my hideout. Go on in."

He looked at that big bunch of stacked-up trees and batted his eyes three or four times like he always did when he didn't understand something. "I'm afraid I don't see it," he said finally, setting the groceries and my fishing rod on the ground.

I commenced laughing at him again, the way he said, "I'm afraid I don't see it." He sounded just like the rich fat kid in the movies who doesn't know his butt from a hole in the ground.

He poked out his lips, getting sulky, but I couldn't help it, I laughed that much harder. He knew good and well I was making fun of him about something, but he didn't know what. I guess he saw how it felt to be made fun of. "I'm afraid I don't understand all this redneck humor," he said, smirking mean at me like he aimed to make something out of it.

I came this close to smacking him upside the head, but I didn't want to hurt him again. "Don't get your panties in a wad," I said, thumping him on the shoulder. "I just thought it was funny because you couldn't see my hideout. You're not supposed to see it, see?"

"Oh, yeah, right," he said, rolling up his eyes.

He was just mad because I'd pulled one on him. I pointed to the triangle of water in the middle of the big logs. "We have to get in the water there," I said, "and swim on down to the bottom log. It's not hard to get to, but when you get down there to that bottom log, go under it, and when you come up on the other side, you'll be inside the hideout. You're not going to believe it until you see it, how good it is."

"It sounds somewhat risky to me," he said, scratching his head and looking like he didn't want to have any part of this business.

I knew he was a big chicken. He was hard as get along with, too, but look like I was going to be stuck with him, for the time being, anyway. "Listen, buddy, there's nothing to it," I said, beginning to take off my clothes. "You just follow right behind me, and I'll show you the way."

"Now how are we going to get all our things in there?" he asked, motioning toward the water with his head and rubbing circles on his white chest. He was trying to come up with a good excuse to get out of going under the logs, and I knew it.

"I've already got that covered," I said, reaching inside the grocery sack and pulling out a garbage bag. "We'll put our eats and other stuff in here, make sure all the air is squeezed out, and just tie up one end. Then we'll be all set to take it inside with us when we go."

"I guess," he said, frowning and kicking off his shoes.

"We'll go down the first time so you can learn how to get in and out," I said. "We can come back for our stuff later."

"Okay," he said, but he didn't sound too happy.

I'd already stripped off, so I hunkered down and waited on Tory. I was sore, but I still felt good. When I was in the woods or on the creek, seem like everything about me perked up. My eyes could pick up every periwinkle on every rock, my ears could hear a branch snap fifty yards away, and my nose could smell the creek, honeysuckle, clover, and bitterweed, all at once. For a minute I pretended I was an Indian scout in *The Last of the Mohicans*. If I died and went to Heaven, if there was such a place, I wanted to run naked and free through cool green woods that stretched for miles and miles, sleep at night in a big swaying tree, and fish and swim in clean, clear water.

Tory was slow as Christmas. He folded everything like he was packing for a trip. Without his glasses he looked like somebody had coldcocked him, real dazed looking. He set his glasses down on a dried cow pie. I reckon he thought it was a big mushroom or something. "Hurry up," I said.

He had his thumbs hooked in the elastic band of his underwear, and all of a sudden he got real fidgety and red in the face. I commenced rubbing my skinned-up knees like I wasn't paying him any attention. When I kind of glanced around at him again, he'd shucked his underwear. He didn't have but a few cornsilks growing around his nubbin. I didn't care one way or another, but I figured he did, so I didn't tease him like Chigger used to me. "Come on," I said, getting up.

I eased off the bank and slid down into the water. "You need to get a good breath of air," I said, "and just use the tree limbs to pull yourself along. It's as clear as a bell down there."

"Okay," he said, his legs dangling from the bank now. "I'm right behind you."

I ducked under then, opened my eyes, and pulled myself down with the limbs. I saw my fishing lure still stuck in the tree limb. I was so excited about finding my hideout the other day, I'd forgotten to prize it out.

I looked back over my shoulder and saw Tory's feet and then the rest of him sink down into the water. His cheeks were puffed out so big that his eyes were squinted like Chinese eyes. I motioned with my hand for him to come on and turned back around.

All of a sudden, I felt something slide across my foot and ankle. I just barely felt it, sort of like somebody had tickled my foot with a feather. I figured it was a minnow or maybe a water snake, but water snakes won't bite you. I gave my foot a good shake and went on about my business. I swam down maybe a yard more, and then something yanked me back hard! Whatever it was had circled around my ankle and was pulling me back every time I tried to go forward.

The most awful thoughts skittered through my head,

like maybe somebody had turned loose a little biddy Florida alligator a long time ago in this creek and it had grown up, or I had stirred up a nest of cottonmouths, like I'd heard Granny Gunn tell about people sometimes doing. It was all I could do to turn around and look, but I knew I had to, or else something was fixing to gobble me up for sure. But when I did turn around, all I saw was Tory's face coming up behind me a few feet away.

I could see both my feet and nothing had hold of me. I gave my foot a hard yank, and again I felt something bite into my ankle, and then I saw a cloud of red swirl around my foot and disappear.

Then it hit me! I knew what had hold of me!

That fishing lure stuck in the limb probably had three or four feet of ten pound test line hanging from it, and my foot had somehow gotten tangled in it.

My heart was pounding a mile a minute, and I couldn't think straight. I jerked my foot back again. This time a big cloud of red circled my foot, and the fishing line bit into my ankle so deep and hurtful that I hollered underwater.

In a second or two I was choking to death, but somehow I managed to motion toward my leg so Tory could see. He looked at me and then at my ankle and back at me. I motioned again and tried to swim back up, but Tory was in my way and kept pushing me away from him. Finally, he kicked me in the chest and started swimming toward the surface. He was aiming to leave me to drown because he was a damn chicken!

My eyes got blurry, and I didn't feel anything after a while. My ankle didn't hurt or my lungs or anything else about me. I thought about Miss Armistead and what would become of her. She would blame herself for what had happened. I thought about Jessie, too. I tried once more to swim back up, but seem like somebody's feet were pushing against my face. The last thing I remembered down in the water, I thought I saw Granny Gunn reaching out her hand to me.

The next thing I knew, I was holding on to a big log up at the surface and about to cough my insides out. And then Tory was standing on the log dragging me up by my armpits. He carried me across his back up the bank like I didn't weigh ten pounds. He laid me out flat on the ground and pushed on my back so hard that water gushed out of my mouth and nose like a hose pipe. Hot water and old slimy stuff kept coming out of my mouth, and my throat and insides felt raw.

After Tory had played me like an accordion for the longest time, he finally helped me to sit up, and that was when I saw my Case knife open on the bank in a little puddle of mud. When I thought Tory was running off scared to let me drown, he had come back up here after my knife and then gone back down in the water to cut me loose.

Tory James might have to squat to pee, but he was all right, and I'd whip anybody who tried to say otherwise.

CHAPTER X

We Get Into A Sure Enough Fix

Tory was sitting a few feet away looking down between his knees at the ground. Every once in a while he'd glance over at me, but when he'd see me turning my head toward him, he'd hang his head again. He looked embarrassed, and right then I wasn't sure why. He was a funny person.

I didn't feel exactly right. I was cold on the inside, but the sun was beating down hot on my shoulders and back. Nothing looked right. The leaves on the trees were greener, the sky was bluer, and the air smelled fresher than the first day of spring. It scared me for a few seconds, thinking that maybe I really had drowned, and this was Heaven. Maybe dead people never even realized that they were dead, or maybe being dead took a long time to dawn on you. I shook my head to clear out the crazy thoughts.

Directly, I said to Tory, "How about handing me my knife over yonder. I don't want my blade to rust. You can't walk around with a rusty blade."

He didn't get it, but he did hop up and get my knife for me. He looked away when he handed it to me and then went over and plopped back down. His white hind end had two muddy circles where he'd been wallowing on the bank, and I started once to kid him about that, but then I didn't.

I figured he was embarrassed enough already because he'd saved my life, or something like that.

I was mighty sore and little dizzy-headed when I first stood up. My hide felt like somebody had gone over it good from my neck to my knees with a sheet of number six sandpaper. My ankle wasn't cut very deep, but it was oozing blood and looked like it had been scored with a knife all the way around.

I didn't feel like I was ready to jump the fence rows any time soon, so I sat back down. I cut up my T-shirt with my knife and tried to bandage my ankle, but I wasn't too good a hand at it. Tory saw me trying to patch myself up and came back over to where I was. "Here," he said, getting down on his knees, "let me show you how to do this. I did Red Cross first aid for one of my badges."

He ripped some more strips off my T-shirt and bandaged my foot as pretty as you please. It made me feel right funny at first, him doctoring me, but I soon saw he knew what he was doing. He wasn't like anybody I'd ever known, and I couldn't stand him in my sight about half the time, but when somebody's saved your bacon, I don't reckon you ought to talk too bad about him. "What do you mean about getting a badge?" I asked him after he'd finished patching me up. "Surely you're not the police."

Then he explained how if you wanted to be an Eagle Scout, you had to do a whole bunch of things like learn sign language or study the stars or build an electric motor. When I asked him how much this paid, being an Eagle Scout, he said it wasn't a job, it was an important goal for any young man to have. Seemed to me like a lot of trouble for nothing.

After a while Tory said, "Are you about ready to go inside your hideout now?"

To tell the truth, I didn't care too much if I ever went back to my hideout again. "I'm still not feeling too good," I said, letting my shoulders droop so I'd look puny, "but you go on in if you're a mind to."

He was sitting on the ground beside me, and he sort of cut his eyes around when I said that, like he was quick to catch on to things. "No, that's all right," he said, standing up and walking over to where he'd piled his clothes. "I think I'll wait on you. I bet by tomorrow you'll feel more at ease in the water."

Durn his time, he was going to shame me into doing what I didn't want to do, so I got up and hopped over to the edge of the bank. "I guess I'll be all right," I said, easing down on one of the logs and dangling my sore foot in the water. "I don't reckon I'll pass out on you or nothing."

"I'll be right there in case you do," he said, acting like he couldn't wait to see my hideout, even if it killed me.

But seem like that one foot was all I could make myself get wet. I took three or four good breaths, but about the time I was ready to jump into the water, something grabbed hold of me and held me back, just as sure as that piece of fishing line had held me back. And that was what it was, that fishing line. It was still holding me back in my mind.

I felt Tory grab hold of my shoulders, and at first I thought he was fixing to shove me in, and I was fixing to let him, because look like that was the only way I was going to get back in the water. But he didn't offer to shove me, and when I turned halfway around, he said, "Hey, why don't you let me go first? I think I understand how to get to it."

"Suit yourself," I said, and he eased down between the big logs. Then he held on to one log and looked back up at me standing there, my knees knocking.

He reached out his hand to me. "Come on," he said. "Let me help you. I imagine you're pretty sore as scratched up as you are."

I squatted down on the log and let my legs dangle in the water for a second or two. I could hear my heart beating in my head. I didn't feel exactly right about doing it, but then I took hold of Tory's hand, because I didn't know what else to do. I couldn't get back in that water by myself.

I was trembling all over as I slipped into the water and wrenched loose my hand. "Shoo-wee," I said, letting on like the cold creek water was what was making me shake. "This water's like ice. I need to get used to it so I won't get the cramps."

I didn't look, but I could feel Tory cutting his eyes around at me again. You couldn't fool him, "Yeah, okay," he said.

In a minute or two I was fine, just like nothing had ever happened. We were both holding onto the log, and I said, "Ready when you are."

Tory nodded his head, sucked in a big breath, and we went under.

I waited until I saw his feet about a yard in front of me, and then I followed him. On land Tory walked just like a fat penguin, but in water he was a regular waterdog, slithering in between the limbs like nobody's business. When he got down to the bottom, he looked back up at me, and I pointed the way under the log. He nodded, and in a few seconds, all I could see were the soles of his feet, and then a second later, nothing. Directly, I went under the log myself, and when I looked up at the surface of the water, I saw him sprawled out in a deadman's float looking down at me. When he saw me, he grinned. Then his legs came down in the water, and I could see all of him except for his head. He was treading water as he waited for me.

Just as soon as my head shot out of the water, he said, "Gee! This is fantastic! This is too much! Man, it's just like a great big wigwam!"

If Chigger could've heard Tory carrying on like that, he would've laughed in his face. Nobody we knew said stuff like "Gee." Most people in the trailer park just cursed a blue streak. At first I wasn't real sure what a wigwam was, either, but I figured it must be some kind of hat.

We swam over to the long gravel bank and rested for a minute. Then we walked around some and tried to figure out where would be the best place to cut a path in from the outside. To me, it didn't look like it mattered much, but Tory had a different notion. "Let's cut it there," he said, pointing over to the right side of the gravel bank where there were shallows across the width of the creek. "Let's cut it out in a zigzag pattern, too, instead of straight through. That way no one can see in from the outside."

I didn't much like Tory taking over so. It was my hideout, and he was just a visitor. He had a good idea, but I didn't aim for him to be the boss. "Okay," I said, motioning with my thumb, "you go get the saw. Make sure you wrap it up good in a garbage bag before you try to bring it in here."

"Okay," he said, wading out in the water and then swimming to the spot where we first came in. He held onto a tree limb and looked back at me.

"What's the holdup?" I said, thumping a piece of gravel in his direction. "I thought you were fixing to get the saw for us."

"I am," he said, "but I thought you were coming, too."

Right then I thought I knew what his trouble was. "You wouldn't be afraid of snakes, now would you?" I said.

He looked a puzzle. "No, not after you told me that most of them are harmless," he said, frowning like he had the sun in his eyes. "I just thought you were following me so you could bring in the rest of the stuff."

"Gee," I said, shrugging and feeling my face turn as red as a rooster's comb. "I forgot all about that."

It wasn't as easy as I made it out to be, bringing in everything underwater in garbage bags.

Tory got the chainsaw inside with no trouble atall. Of course, it was easier to work with than the stuff I had. I snagged up the sack with my fishing rod inside on a limb, and as I was trying to untangle it, durn if I didn't hang up my grocery sack. I just turned loose of my fishing rod, figuring the water wouldn't hurt my reel too bad, and finally got the groceries loose and over to the other side.

"Did you get everything?" Tory asked me when I dumped the groceries on the bank.

It made me about halfway mad. He should've seen that I had my hands full, me with a fishing rod and groceries, too, and him carrying nothing but a chainsaw. "Shit, naw," I said, slinging the water out of my hair and kicking out my leg so my ears would unstop. "I snagged up my fishing rod because I had too much to carry all by myself."

"Well, poor little baby," he said, smirking and patting me on the head.

I came within an inch of smacking him in the mouth, but I knew I was too stove up to fight. He saw I was mad, too, because I didn't crack a smile, just stood there staring a hole through him. He didn't know how to get along with people. I figured he was backward, coming from Mississippi, but he thought he knew everything. I started once to say, "I'll baby your fat butt, you four-eyed sissy," but before I could bless him out, he said, "I'll go get your fishing rod. I didn't realize that you had your hands full."

I let him go get my fishing rod, too. When he came back, he'd changed his tune. He couldn't be nice enough to me. He said, "Are you feeling okay? Boy, you're scrubbed-up looking."

I told him I was perfectly fine, thank you very much. I untied the sack with the chainsaw and told him to stay out of the way. He wasn't about to be the big buck in everything.

I set the choke on the saw and yanked the cord. It grunted and rattled but didn't start. I tried it again, and it did the same thing. The third time I tried it, and it still didn't start. Then Tory said to me, he said, "You may need to push in the choke a little. Want me to try?"

I didn't say anything, but I shot him another one of my hard looks. He looked a fool standing there batting his eyes, his hair all plastered down on his forehead and his big white belly poking out. It wasn't any of my business, but he didn't have anything but an acorn for a nubbin, either. "Guess not," he said, looking away so I wouldn't see him grinning.

I don't reckon I could help it, because I grinned then, too. I knew good and well he hadn't been trying to start anything with me, and that I'd been taking out my troubles on him. "I'm so wore out I can't do the first thing right today," I said, handing the saw over to him. "See what you can do with this contrary thing."

He pushed in the choke some, and durn if that saw didn't catch on the first pull. "What do I do now?" he hollered, holding the saw way out like it was fixing to jump back and bite him.

I eased the saw out of his hands and commenced cutting where he'd decided we ought to. Directly, I showed him how to use the saw, and he'd cut some, and later I'd cut some. While one of us was sawing, the other one pulled out the cut limbs and stacked them over on the bank.

In a half hour or less we had a nice little passageway about a yard high and a yard wide cut through to the outside. The entrance came out behind a good-sized hackberry that was leaning way over toward the water. We'd cut our entrance in a zigzag pattern like Tory had suggested, and sure enough, it would take somebody with keen eyes to ever see his way into our hideout from the outside.

By now it was the middle of the morning. We were both hot and sweaty, and itchy, too. "Less us take a little swim and get cleaned up some," I told Tory, and we did.

He was a good swimmer, but I dunked him under a time or two. He started to dunk me, too, but I let out a big war whoop when he raked his hand across my sore chest so he left me alone after that. I didn't get mad at him, though.

Finally, we came back upon the gravel bank and sat down on some flat rocks to eat. We had cheese and crackers and Spam spread. We had big Winesap apples from

Kroger, cherry Pop Tarts, and peanuts. To drink we had a six pack of Orange Slice. We ate a lot, and then we lay out in the shallow water on our backs to let our dinner settle.

It was a hot day, but our hideout was shaded by the limbs of the water oaks overhead. The sunshine looked like big golden flakes on the water. I could smell mint and honeysuckles and the fishy creek. Far off down in the bottom a rain crow cooed, giving me a shivery feeling, and a bull bellowed somewhere out in the woods. I was still sore and achy, but little hot fingerprints of sunlight touched me all over, and cool water trickled through my fingers and toes. It was a good feeling to know that Tory and I had a secret place to do as we pleased, to swim or camp or fish, and to know we could always come back here when we wanted to get away from everybody and be by ourselves.

We wallowed out there in the shallow water for a good long spell, neither one of us saying much of anything. The trees overhead swayed in the breeze, and every so often leaves fluttered down and made boats in the water. Minnows pecked and nibbled at us, and tiny waves lapped us clean. I was just about asleep when Tory rolled over on his side toward me and whispered, "Hey, Patrick, listen."

At first, all I heard were cars over on the highway. Then, directly, I heard what Tory had heard, somebody poking around outside our hideout, over at the bank where we'd come in. Sometimes I couldn't hear anything, like somebody was standing still listening, and then I could hear somebody switching through the undergrowth. Then somebody hollered, "Hey! Anybody there?"

It sounded like an old man. I figured it was Mr. Aaron that Chigger had told me about. He didn't like strangers fooling around in his pasture. Miss Armistead had asked his permission for me to fish in the creek, and he'd said it was all right, but she didn't mention anything about a hideout. I thought he might not like that, so I put my finger up to my lips so Tory wouldn't give us away.

134

He hollered again, "Anybody there? Who's over there? Hey!"

We stayed still, so still that all I could hear were the tree trunks creaking together every so often and the creek trickling over the shoals. Whoever was out there had to know we were around somewhere, because we'd left our clothes up there on the bank. We hadn't even thought to bring them inside once we'd cut out our entrance.

Then out of the blue the person hollered, "Oh, my God!"

I didn't know that to think, but whoever was out there had taken off running, it sounded like. When I looked over at Tory, he made his eyes go big and round, and then he shrugged.

After we didn't hear anything for the longest time, Tory laughed and said, "Man, we fooled him, didn't we? I bet we were nearly close enough to touch him, and he couldn't even see us."

"I know it," I said, hunkering down as I waded across the shallows to the entrance to peep out. I didn't see a soul in the woods. "I bet you money that was Mr. Aaron, the man who owns this land. He's a mean old dickens when he wants to be. He used to run Chigger off with a shotgun. He told Chigger to his face that he didn't like his looks. We might ought to go."

Tory waded over and squatted down beside me. "I guess so," he said, craning his neck to see if he could see anybody. "That old fart might come back with a gun and run us off, too."

We'd eaten all our groceries so we didn't have much to tote out. Tory wrapped the chainsaw back up in the tow sacks, and I took my rod and reel. After we'd waded back across the shallows to the entrance, we looked at our hide-out for a minute. It was a good place, and we kind of grinned at one another because we both knew it was. Tory said, "Ready, friend?"

Chigger and I never called each other friends, even though we were, I reckon. It didn't seem right somehow, calling somebody your friend to his face, even if it was true. "Ready when you are," I said. "Friend."

After we slipped out behind the hackberry hiding our entrance, we had a cross a little branch that fed into the creek. Tory splashed across first, wagging the chainsaw. Soon we came to the far end of the bank there we'd come in earlier. Tory climbed up, me right behind him.

All of a sudden, he whirled around so fast that he might near hit me with the chainsaw. He had the funniest look on his face, and his eyes were big as guinea eggs. "Our clothes!" he hollered, dropping the chainsaw and covering his particulars with both hands, just like we both hadn't been buck naked all day long. "Someone has taken our clothes!"

I used to dream sometimes about being naked at school and having to squeeze inside a locker to hide, but this was no dream. This was the real thing, and it was a nightmare.

"Gran's going to kill me," Tory said, shaking his head and beginning to blubber.

"That low-down devil," I said. "That sorry thing."

Tory kicked up some dead leaves with his bare foot. "Damn, damn, double damn," he said.

Whoever took our clothes took my good knife and even Tory's glasses. "Now just how are we supposed to get back home?" Tory said, putting his hands on his hips like a prissy old maid. He said it like it was my fault that we'd ended up in such a fix.

"Same way we got here, I reckon," I said right hateful. "Unless you know how to fly or something."

He commenced batting his eyes and looking mean like he wanted to make something out of it, but he knew better. He knew I'd dotted both of his eyes for him that morning, and I could do it again if I took a notion to. "I don't know why I came down here with you today, anyway," he said, spitting over into the creek. "You have no idea of even how to be civil."

I didn't know what he meant by that last thing he said, but I wasn't aiming to let him know I didn't. I figured this Civil was one of his sissy friends down in Jackson, Civil Treetop IV or something. "I can't be Civil," I told him, unwrapping the chainsaw. "I can't be anybody but myself."

"You said it, I didn't," he said, acting like he'd got one on me.

I didn't know what I said or didn't say, so I just let it drop. The only thing wrong with him, he was worried that his old granny would get mad at him and ship him back.

I was too busy to fool with him. After I got the tow sacks off the chainsaw, I spread them out flat on the ground. I stood there a while trying to figure out some way to make me some clothes. I thought maybe I could cut some holes in one sack and make me sort of a shirt, but I didn't have a knife, and without a needle I couldn't see a way to make pants. "What are you thinking about doing?" Tory said directly, nudging one of the sacks with his big toe. "You can't cover up with these. They're too scratchy."

He was right, but I wasn't about to let him know he was. That burlap would rub me raw, and I was already raw from where Tory had pulled me over that log to get me out of the water. "I wasn't fixing to make clothes out of these," I said, acting like he was the biggest fool that ever was.

"Yes, you were," he said, pushing my shoulder. "I could see the little wheels clicking in your head."

"You don't see anything in my head," I said, laughing because I was fixing to get him good. "You can't see shit without your glasses, four eyes."

"Well, you're right," he said, reaching out with both hands and feeling the air like he was a blind man. "Where are you?"

You can't make anything on a fool, so I just let on like

I didn't see him. I kept studying to myself, but then he said, "Hey! Wait a minute. Why not try the plastic bags?"

He grabbed up the one the saw was wrapped in and tore the bottom out of it. He stepped inside it and pulled the bottom end up between his legs and tied it in a knot with the loose part that was left over from around his waist. "Well?" he said, taking a step backwards and spreading out his arms so I could see his work. "Ta–dah! What do you think?"

"I don't reckon it looks too bad," I said, lying like a dog. "Kind of like a big black diaper, but on our bicycles maybe people can't tell it's not shorts."

I took my rod and reel out of the bag and did what Tory had done. "You look like a swami snake charmer," he said when I got through.

I didn't know if that was good or bad, so I didn't say anything back. I'd already seen that he could insult a fellow without him even knowing he'd been insulted until it was too late.

We walked barefooted through the woods, taking our time so we wouldn't step on a stob or in poison oak. This time I toted the chainsaw and my rod and reel, too. I just wanted Tory to see that I didn't need him for anything. Every once in a while he'd stop and say, "Sure you don't want some help?" and I'd say, "Naw, I got it," just like I wasn't loaded down and about to die.

After a while we came to where we'd hidden our bicycles in the thicket, and by that time I was plumb worn out. "Here," I said, handing him my rod and reel. "You take this. Try not to tear it up."

"Try not to tear it up," he mumbled under his breath loud enough for me to hear.

I didn't let on like I heard him. He was a big baby, anyway.

He pulled up the handlebars on his old ten-speed so that he had two hooks to lay the rod and reel in and to guide with, too. I hated to admit it, but he was pretty smart sometimes. About some things he was even smarter than I was, but if you added up everything we were both smart about, I came out way ahead.

I had to hold the chainsaw across my handlebars with one hand so I'd have the other hand free to guide my bicycle. I started once to ask Tory if he could think of a better way to carry the saw, but then I didn't. He liked to boss too much already.

We took off riding through the pasture. The sun was blazing hot out in the open where there was no shade. In a minute we were both sticky slick from pedaling over that soft ground. We had to dodge rocks and cowpies, and I kept my eyes open for copperheads. The sweat trickled down my neck and stung my scratched chest. Up ahead I could hear Tory sucking air hard. Every once in a while he'd sling a line of sweat out of his hair. I felt like I was cooking inside that plastic bag, and I knew he had to be feeling the same way.

When we got close to the highway, we stopped, leaned our bicycles against a big oak, and sat down behind it to rest for a while. It wouldn't be as hard pedaling on the blacktop, but I was wondering what people in cars might think when they saw our get-ups. Mine didn't even want to stay on. By the time we'd got off our bicycles to rest, it was flapping in the wind like a loose sail and had to be girded back up. I guess sometimes things look all right in one place and not too good when you get to where you're going. I told Tory, I said, "Listen. You stay outside when I drop off the saw. I'm not going inside that store looking like this. I'm just going to slip out back and leave PeeWee's saw in the shed."

"And suppose something happens to it and he doesn't know you returned it? Suppose someone steals it?" he said, blowing the sweat off the tip of his nose.

"That's not my fault," I said. "I can't help that."

"I suppose not," he said, walling up his eyes and acting

like a goody-goody.

"Do you want to take it in for me?" I said, bending over so I could stare him in the face.

He looked way off in the distance and didn't answer.

"Well, do you?"

"No," he finally said, still not looking at me.

"Okay then," I said, nodding my head for good measure. "And another thing. We're not going home the usual way. When we get to McLemore Drive, turn into the alley, and that will take us all the way to the back of our houses. Maybe we can slip in before anybody sees us."

"Yeah, right," he said, quirking his mouth on one side. "Gran's not going to notice that I'm wearing a black plastic loincloth and that my glasses are missing."

"Tell her you got robbed," I said. "I'll back you up. It's not a lie, anyway. We did get robbed."

He didn't say anything, just looked at me like I was common as dirt. I wasn't too good a hand at lying, and I didn't believe it was right, but I knew every once in a while you ran upon people who were too nervous and finicky to be aggravated with the truth. Tory's granny would probably faint and fall out when she saw him in that get-up, and then she'd probably have to go to the hospital after she found out what had happened down at our hideout, about him swimming under big logs and stuff. But I figured all along he was aiming to tell her everything, come hell or high water, and that meant that I'd have to tell Miss Armistead the truth, too, because all old ladies compare stories and husbands and recipes.

I picked up the chainsaw and got back on my bicycle, but Tory didn't get up right away. I was spraddled on my bicycle waiting while he sat there breaking up little pieces of tree limbs and throwing the pieces over in the grass. I figured he was still pouting because he thought that everything was my fault, so I said, "Tory, I ain't never met anybody exactly like you, and I don't think you've ever met anybody exactly like me. So we're even there. Sometimes I'll get you into trouble, and sometimes you'll get me into trouble. That's just the way it is. I'm not perfect, and you're sure not, either. You're a good swimmer, and sometimes you have good ideas. But you're a smart aleck, and you don't fight fair. But I have to say, you're right brave. I wouldn't be here this very minute except for you, and I'm mighty grateful you were with me today. So shut up and quit acting like a big baby."

He didn't answer at first, but he'd been paying attention to me. Every time I'd said something he didn't like, I saw him clamp his teeth together, and his jawbone would stick out. In a minute he stood up and got back on his bicycle. "I guess I was blaming you in a way," he said, letting out a big breath of air. "I didn't much want to come down here today, but after I got here, I had a good time. Then when somebody took our things, I blamed you for getting us in such a mess. I'm sorry."

He stuck out his fat hand for me to shake, and I shook it, but I didn't much want to. Who ever heard of boys shaking hands, anyway? In some ways he was just like an old man. "I'm sorry, too," I said. "I forget just exactly what I'm sorry for, but I'm sure I've done some little something to you today to be sorry for, too."

He batted his weak-looking eyes a few times and then grinned. "You're so ugly you could raise a blister on a limestone rock," he said and thumped me on the head.

I thumped his ear a good one. "When you were born, the doctor slapped your mama," I said.

He punched me on the shoulder and took off all of a sudden. "Your fat butt looks like a great big raisin," I hollered and took off after him.

When we got to PeeWee's, Tory waited on the far side of the gas pumps next to the highway while I jumped off my bicycle with the chainsaw and hightailed it to the shed out back.

There were a bunch of cars at the store, probably factory hands getting ready to go on second shift. I didn't tarry. In the first place, the pavement was so hot on my bare feet that I felt like I was walking across a skillet, and in the second place, I didn't aim for anybody to see me.

I got to the shed, and durn if it didn't have a combination lock on it!

I had no intentions of stepping foot inside that store, no matter if PeeWee sicced the law on me or not. I just set the saw down by the door of the shed and ran as fast as I could back to my bicycle. Just as I straddled it, a blue Monte Carlo slowed down in front of the store, and some high school boys whistled real loud at Tory and me. Then they set down on the horn before they took off, burning rubber.

About that time PeeWee opened the door to see what all the commotion was about outside. He was wearing an old raggedy T-shirt that struck him so high I could see his bellybutton. "Your saw's out back," I hollered at him, and we took off as fast as we could pedal.

"Wait a minute here!" he hollered, but we never broke stride.

We pedaled as fast as we could going into Broad Plains, too. Somebody in another car blew when he passed us, but I think he just wanted us to know he was behind us so we wouldn't get run over. My rod and reel were bouncing up and down on Tory's handlebars, and I just knew it was fixing to hit the pavement any minute, or else fly back and switch me across the face. I hollered at Tory to slow up, and he did, and when I glided up beside him, I told him to pull over at the old Moonglow Drive-in.

We hid behind the ticket shed for a minute to see if we were being followed, but we weren't.

We rested a little and took off again, and this time Tory followed me. We turned off McLemore Drive and went up a long alley that crooked around and ran in behind College Street where we lived. All of a sudden, old Miss Feinstein's Chihuahua started barking and snipping at me, so I had to kind of nudge it hard with my foot. When we got to the privacy fence behind our houses, we parked our bicycles and peeped over.

The first thing I saw was the police cars, two pulled up in the driveway between our houses and one parked on the street. I looked at Tory, and he looked at me. He didn't have a bit of color about him except for his nose, which was blistered.

"Hotdamn!" I said, not meaning to swear. "The police are done after us. That durn PeeWee must've turned us in or else somebody saw us pedaling down the highway in our altogether and reported us."

Durn if Tory didn't tune up! "I've had it now," he whimpered.

"Now don't start that," I said, getting ready to climb over. "Maybe we can slip inside my house without them seeing us and at least get on some clothes."

Tory turned away so I wouldn't see him crying. I felt sorry for him, but I didn't have time to pet him. I wanted to get out of the open.

But as soon as my feet slapped the ground, somebody hollered, "Lord have mercy, there they are!"

Tory was still straddling the fence, so I gave him a hand down. Before we knew what was happening, a whole slew of people were running over to the fence, Miss Armistead and Miss Marcella and police and neighbors and just about everybody. They looked like a wagon train, there were so many of them circling around us, and Miss Armistead was crying and hugging and kissing me, and Miss Marcella was crying to beat the band, too, and people we didn't even know were patting Tory and me on the back and rubbing our heads.

It was the worst commotion I'd ever seen, and at first I

didn't have a clue why everybody was acting this way. I thought we were fixing to be arrested, but the police didn't offer to handcuff us. It beat all.

"Just look at you, child!" Miss Armistead said after the longest spell of boo-hooing and laughing at the same time. She had me by one arm holding me out so everybody could see my get-up, and she reached over and grabbed Tory so people could see him, too. I don't know why she did that, because we were kind of hard to miss to begin with. She was out of her head, I reckon, and didn't mean anything by it, but people commenced laughing at us like we were two fools.

I got about halfway mad, myself. "What's going on here?" I said. "Somebody let me in on the joke."

"Mercy me," Miss Armistead said, laughing and then wiping her eyes on a balled-up handkerchief. "It's certainly no joke, Patrick. We thought we'd never lay eyes on you two again. We thought you'd drowned."

"Drowned?" Tory and I hollered at the same time.

"We're not drowned!" I said, and then everybody laughed again except for Miss Marcella, who was being held up by some of the neighbors, she was still carrying on so.

Miss Armistead put her hand on my shoulder and looked down at me real serious. "Mr. Aaron found your clothes where you'd left them on the bank," she said. "He called to you several times, he said, but when no one answered, he feared the worse. He brought your clothes to the police station so they would know for sure who was missing."

When Miss Armistead said "missing," her voice got quivery, and then she commenced crying again. I wanted to cry myself, and would have, if there hadn't been so many people standing around. I knew how Miss Armistead felt. When Granny Gunn told me that my mama was dead, something went numb inside me, and the feeling never had exactly come back. "Mr. Aaron didn't call us no several times," I said. "He might have hollered once or twice, I don't know, but he sure didn't holler a bunch of times, did he, Tory?"

Tory was looking at his granny when he said, "I didn't hear anything. You might have heard him, but I don't remember hearing anything."

I didn't get mad at him for lying, the way his granny was acting, but he made me look like a liar, too. People looked down at their feet or over to one side. Directly, a few women folks came over and patted Miss Armistead on the back and whispered stuff to her.

Finally, everybody spread out and left, even the police. Some of the neighbor men half carried Miss Marcella home, and Tory followed behind like a little lost puppy. His garbage bag had come loose and made a skirt, but he didn't seem to notice. "See you," I said and waved at him, but he didn't seem to hear me or notice me, either.

After Miss Armistead had straightened up her face, I led her back to the house, and we sat down in the porch swing. We didn't say anything to one another for the longest time. The crickets were chirping shrill and loud, like they were agitated about something, and big moths were swirling around crazy-like, bumping up against the porch light and ceiling. Miss Armistead didn't mention supper. I was on nettles. I hadn't meant to do wrong, but here I'd gone and caused her some more trouble.

I wasn't a fortuneteller, though, so how did I know what Mr. Aaron would do? I didn't make him run off with our clothes and make everybody think we were drowned. I knew Miss Armistead was going to be mad once she got over being sick at heart, but somehow it didn't seem right that I was in trouble again. I sat there in the swing and studied about everything that had happened, and when I couldn't stand Miss Armistead not saying anything any longer, I said, "Miss Armistead, I'm mighty sorry for all the trouble

I've done caused you. I didn't mean to. I want you to know that."

I figured she'd say something like, "That's all right, dear," real hurt and all, or else she'd fly into me with both feet, but she didn't say a word. All I heard was the squeaking of the chain holding up the porch swing and those durn crickets complaining.

I just kept on talking because I didn't know what else to do, and I couldn't stand Miss Armistead looking straight ahead like I wasn't even there. I was used to her listening to me, even when I said something ignorant. "Listen, Miss Armistead. I've sat here and studied about everything that I did today, and I know I didn't mean any harm. All I can figure I did wrong was not to answer Mr. Aaron when he called. I thought he might be mad at me if he found us in our hideout on his place. I see now that I should've answered him, but I couldn't see it at the time."

Then Miss Armistead put her arm around my head and pulled me right down to her bosom, just like Granny Gunn used to do when I was little and cried for my mama. "So what must you do?" she said in a whisper. "Because we can't always predict the consequences of our actions."

"I reckon do the right thing in the beginning, and then whatever happens, you're not to blame," I said.

"Yes," she said, squeezing me trembly hard, and then everything was all right, except for those damn crickets.

CHAPTER XI

Tory Has A Plan

The next morning I was sweeping off the front porch when I spied Tory coming through the privet hedge. He was barefooted and wearing nothing except a pair of khaki shorts. His eyes looked tired because he wasn't wearing his glasses. I figured they were still at the police station with the rest of our stuff.

I stopped sweeping, and he walked over and sat on the edge of the porch. "What happened to you?" he asked, and then I could see he'd already been crying again, early as it was.

"Nothing much," I said. "I have to see Dr. Cohen in the morning so he can check me over, and Miss Armistead said at the breakfast table that I can't go to the creek again for a month, and then somebody will have to go with me."

"It won't be me," Tory said. "I can't go anymore."

"Never?"

He turned his head so I wouldn't see him crying. I didn't know what to make of all these crying folks. People I knew didn't cry, people at the trailer park. But I felt bad about him getting into trouble, because I knew Miss Marcella didn't make over him like Miss Armistead did over me. Miss Marcella was like me in a way. She didn't know how to make over people. She never even hugged Tory when she found out he wasn't drowned. She'd just cried and carried on so that some menfolks had to carry her to her house. Last night I'd thought about Tory being over there in that big house all by himself, and I'd asked Miss Armistead if he could come to our house to sleep, but she'd said she reckoned his granny would want him there with her. I reckoned that his granny didn't want him there in the first place, but I didn't contradict Miss Armistead.

I leaned the broom against the side of the house and sat down beside him. I didn't look him in the face, because I didn't want to shame him. I didn't like looking people in the face, anyway, because sometimes I saw things in people's faces that I didn't want to. "Ah, she'll change her tune," I said, swinging my feet back and forth together like I didn't have a care in the world. "That's old folks for you. They let on like at first they're never going to let you do something again, but then they always do."

He wiped his eyes on the back of his hand and turned toward me. His eyes were all puffy and bloodshot, and his nose looked like he had a bad cold. "You don't understand," he said. "She's going to send me back down to Jackson. I've got to leave here as soon as my mother and stepfather get back from Hawaii."

I knew better than to ask him why he hadn't gone to Hawaii with his mama. I'd just about learned to keep my mouth shut until my mind was in gear. "You can stay right here with us," I said. "I know Miss Armistead will let you, because she said Chigger could stay here if he wanted to, and she didn't even know Chigger. Now see?"

He shook his head and bit one of his fingernails. He didn't have much in the way of fingernails to begin with. "No, I've already asked her," he said. "She said it would shame our family if I lived with someone other than my own flesh and blood."

I knew Tory didn't mean to, but he stepped on my toes when he said that. "What are you going to do then?" I said. "You have to live somewhere."

"I thought about living at the hideout," he said. "I don't know where I'd get anything to eat, though." He looked at me like he was wanting to ask me something but just didn't know how to.

"I could bring you stuff to eat, as far as that," I said, "but they'd find you there first thing. Even if they didn't, the creek's too cold to camp on in the winter."

I thought about Chigger, and how he'd camped out winter and summer. Tory wasn't Chigger, though. I couldn't see anything for him to do except go on back and live with his mama and his sorry drunk stepdaddy. "When are your mama and them getting back?" I asked.

He shrugged. "A couple of weeks, a month, who knows? I'm not going back, anyway," he said. He'd quit crying, but he was breathing through his mouth, he was so stopped up.

"Well," I said, "if you can't stay here, and you're not going back to Jackson, what are you aiming to do?"

He looked at me real funny, and the worst thought hit me. A shiver ran right straight up my back like a cat had stepped on my grave. He was fixing to kill himself! "There's no need of doing that, now," I said, putting my hand on his shoulder. "You're no good to anybody when you're dead, especially yourself."

He frowned and looked at me like I smelled bad. "What are you talking about?" he asked.

I took my hand off his shoulder. "I thought you meant you were fixing to k--"

"Kill myself?" he said, grinning and frowning at the same time. "I hadn't even thought of that, but thanks so very much for the idea."

I don't reckon he could help being a smart aleck, even when he was down and out. "Well, what were you talking about then?" I asked.

"You can't tell anybody," he said, looking me square in the eye. "Not even Miss Armistead. *Especially* not Miss

Armistead.

I hopped down off the porch. I hated to say it, but I told him, I said, "Don't tell me then. I can't make a promise like that. Ain't no telling what it would lead to."

"Sometimes you sound just like somebody's hillbilly grandaddy," he said real hateful, hopping off the porch himself and prissing toward the hedge. "Why don't you learn to speak English like the rest of us?"

I don't know why, but seem like half the time I was around that boy, I couldn't talk right. He made me nervous or something, because I knew good and well if I ever said anything the least bit wrong, or if I as much as crooked my finger at him, he was fixing to low-rate me. "You listen here," I said, talking to his back, because he was already stepping through the hedge, "I know your daddy's in the durn pen, but I don't throw it up to you all the time. The trouble with you, you've had everything but raising."

He turned around fast and barged back over to where I was standing in front of the porch. I figured I was going to have to fight him again, and I didn't want to. His eyes were real keen, and he was huffing and puffing through his mouth. His head was lowered, too, like he was fixing to charge me. "My daddy's not in the damn pen, for your information," he said, pointing his stubby finger right in my face. "He's on parole and living in a halfway house. He'll be home before long, and I'm going to live with him. He doesn't beat me up like your father does you."

The funny thing was, even after Tory said what he did about my daddy, I really wasn't mad at him. Getting beat up didn't seem like anything to be ashamed of once somebody else had put words to it. "How are you planning on getting to your daddy's?" I asked. "Where does he live, anyway?"

He turned around and started walking back toward his own house. "That's for me to know and you to find out, you redneck," he said over his shoulder.

"I may be a redneck," I said, "but at least I don't have

a daddy who has to live in half of a house."

"Asshole!" he hollered from the privet hedge.

"You're another one!" I said, scooting back upon the porch and laughing because I'd got him good for once.

I reckon he thought I was just trying to tease him out of being mad, because all of a sudden he commenced laughing, too. Then he walked back over to the porch and squatted down in front of me. "You're not going to tell anybody, are you? Okay?" he said.

"Naw. Not unless I have to."

He batted his eyes, studying me good for a few seconds. Then he said, "My daddy's got a house in Starkville, Mississippi. That's where I'm headed."

"Does he know you're coming?"

He shook his head and then sat back in the grass and wrapped his arms around his knees. "He'll let me stay, though," he said. "Right before Gran gets ready to send me back, that's when I'm taking off."

"How are you going to get there, though?" I said. "It's too far to ride your bicycle."

He grinned but didn't say anything at first. Then he got up, brushed off his hind end, and craned his neck over toward his own house. I know he was looking to see if his granny was around anywhere. In a minute he motioned with his head for me to follow him.

We went out back to the shed where Miss Marcella kept her long blue Electra. This shed leaned a little to one side, but it was real big, and there was a bunch of stuff in there. I saw a push mower, rakes, a shovel, and a lot of tools held up by nails tacked into the walls. There were wasps flying around, too, so I wasn't too keen about staying in there too long.

Tory was grinning all the time like he had a big secret. He walked over to the far left hand corner where there were several old paint cans stacked up and pointed toward this heavy-looking cloth covering something that looked about the size of one of those big round bales of hay. He looked at the thing a second and then back at me so I'd get my curiosity up. Then, all of a sudden, he jerked the cloth off, and there it was.

It was the prettiest little red car I'd ever seen, a Volkswagen convertible. I could tell it was one of the older models by the bumpers, but it looked might near brand new. "Gol-ly!" I said, walking over and running my fingers over the front fender. "Where in the world did you get a car like this?"

"Gran bought it for my father when he left for college in 1964," he said. "It's supposed to be mine when I turn sixteen. I'm going to take possession of it a little earlier than that, though."

His car was white inside and had a white top. The rims on the tires were red like the body. In the center of the steering wheel was the picture of a wolf on top of a castle. I would've given my eyeteeth for a car like that. "Does it run?" I asked. "I bet it doesn't run."

"Like a sewing machine," Tory said, beginning to cover it back up again. "The owner down at Texaco comes and gets it every so often. He drives it around some and makes sure everything's working okay, changes the oil, things like that."

I helped him get the cover on straight. "You can't drive, though, can you?" I asked. I was hoping he couldn't. I couldn't, and I didn't have a car like this, either.

"How hard can it be?" he said, shrugging his shoulders. "Everybody drives."

He couldn't drive. He wasn't going to get very far in this car, but I never let on. He was fixing to have to go live with his mama, and that was all there was to it.

As we were walking out of the shed, I got to thinking. What if he took this little red car out on the road and got hit by a semi or something? Would it be my fault? I wasn't a tattletale, and anybody at school who knew me would say the same thing, but was I supposed to tell on somebody if he was fixing to do something foolish? I wasn't sure, but I was aiming to pussyfoot around a little with Miss Armistead and find out. I sure didn't want something else bad coming back on me because I hadn't done the right thing.

We hadn't much more than got out of the shed when Miss Marcella hollered from the back door, "Oh Tory, oh Tory!"

Tory made a disgusted face. "I've got to go," he said.

"Okay," I said. "See you later."

"Not if I see you first," he said, thumping my ear and making a dash for his back door.

CHAPTER XII

Two People Come For A Visit

I liked Dr. Cohen. He had a big wooly beard but not much hair on top of his head, and his clothes looked like he'd slept in them.

He acted kind of like a smart aleck, but not in a mean way, not like Tory did sometimes. "What did you do, Tarzan, slide down a pine tree?" he said when I showed him my belly and what all else I'd done to myself.

"I don't know," I said.

"I don't know," he said, mocking me and sticking out his tongue and generally acting goofy. He looked my ankle over good and felt of my insides. "Time's all that's going to cure you, partner, so get out of here and stop wasting my time," he added. "Keep Neosporin on that ankle and stay out of the creek until it heals."

Dr. Cohen even knew how to give a high five. For a grown person, he did right well.

After we got home about middle of the afternoon, Miss Armistead went to her bedroom to take a nap.

I couldn't go to the creek, so I decided to get my book and read out in the swing. My book this week was *A Member of the Wedding*. It was a pretty good book, funny in places and sad in places. It was about this girl who felt all left out of things, and she planned on going to live with her brother who was getting married, but you knew from the beginning that she'd never get that she wanted, because people don't ever get what they want. There's nothing on Earth that can come up with what you imagine in your head, and anybody ought to know that.

I'd eaten a big dinner at McDonald's, and before long I got tired sitting there in the swing reading, so I just lay down and propped up my head with a pillow. It was a hot day, and the swing rocked gently in the breeze coming across Miss Arnistead's long wooden porch. Soon, I'd read something and then have to read it over again, I was so tired and sleepy. Then I thought I'd rest my eyes for a second or two, and the next thing I knew, I was sound asleep.

I knew somebody was standing over me even before I woke up, but I guess in my sleep I figured it was Miss Armistead. Sometimes I'd go to sleep reading on the couch, and she'd take the book out of my hands and cover me up with one of those africans. I reckon after a while, though, something told me that whoever was standing over me wasn't Miss Armistead this time. I opened my eyes and looked right up at my daddy.

He was grinning, and I saw that somebody had knocked out another one of his front teeth. What teeth he had left had turned yellow from smoking so many cigarettes. He'd had a haircut, and the top of his head looked skinned and naked. "Hey, mutt," he said, cuffing me upside the head.

"Hey, watch it!" I said as I put up my hands in front of my face.

He laughed and smacked me again, this time knocking the book out of my hand. It landed next to these concrete flower pots on the edge of the porch. My daddy went over and picked up the book and flopped down hard in one of Miss Armistead's wicker chairs a few feet away from me. "Well, well," he said, turning the book over two or three times in his hands. "Now ain't this something? Mama's baby is reading books like some little old girl."

He slung the book away from him like it was something nasty. It skittered across the porch and dropped off the edge. He looked hard at me, and I looked hard right back at him.

He wasn't much to look at in the first place, but now he looked worse than ever in his stupid crewcut. His fingernails were all broken and black, and he was wearing a red muscle shirt to show off his tattoos. His tattoos were mostly homemade, and one of them even showed a woman's titties and her private place. Anybody with any sense would've covered that up, but he was proud of it.

When he hiked up his foot across his knee, I noticed that he was wearing a new pair of snakeskin boots. He always liked snakeskin. "What are you staring at, you little shit?" he said. He pointed to that old sexy tattoo and laughed mean. "Is this what you're looking at? I can fix you up with one just like it if you want me to. In fact, I can fix you up with the real thing, if that old lady hadn't already turned you into a fairy."

He made me shiver all over, just like he carried the cold with him. I was hoping somebody would hurry up and see him. He wasn't supposed to come near me unless somebody else was with us. I glanced over my shoulder to see if Tory was out in the yard, but I didn't see hide nor hair of him. Any other time Miss Armistead would've been out on the porch watering her flowers and ferns, but not now that I needed her.

My daddy sat up straight in the chair and kept eyeing me. "You done got to be a big shot, ain't you, boy?" he said, winking at me. "What do you call them shoes there you're wearing, girly shoes?"

"Bucks," I said.

"Bucks," he repeated and acted like he was studying about something for a minute. "Bucks. That's a good name for them. I bet you think you're a big buck now, don't you?"

"I don't know," I said.

His eyes looked like little dark slits. He twirled the ends of his handlebar mustache and then said, "What do you call that watch there you're wearing?"

"It's a Hamilton," I said, "but it ain't mine. It belonged to Miss Armistead's dead husband, and she just lets me wear it."

He squinted one eye and grinned his old low-down grin. "I bet she just lets you wear them shoes, too, don't she? Who do they belong to, her dead sister?"

He threw back his head and laughed like he'd said something real funny. I didn't see anything funny about him, myself. I couldn't figure out to save my life how Granny Gunn had raised somebody as ignorant as my daddy. He wasn't only ignorant, he was ignorant and proud of it.

"What's wrong, boy, cat got your tongue? Why can't you talk to your old daddy? Ain't you glad to see me?" he said, kind of hanging over the arm of the chair.

"Sure," I said. "I couldn't hardly wait."

He changed his tune then, hopping to the edge of the wicker chair like he was aiming to pounce on me. "That'll get you a assbeating in a New York second," he said, pointing his finger at me and acting like he just dared me to say something else.

I sat up in the swing. If he came after me, he was going to have to catch me first. "You lay a hand on me and I'll holler so loud they'll hear me all the way down to the courthouse."

I was expecting him to take me up on my bluff, but he didn't. He eased back in the chair and stuck his tongue in the space where he was missing his front teeth. He didn't even look at me or say anything for the longest time. I thought at first he was trying to catch me off guard so he could grab me, but he stuck both of his legs out straight and crossed his feet. Finally, he tilted back his head and looked up at the blue porch ceiling. "I'll tell you what, boy," he said. "Things have changed since I seen you last. I got me a nice brick house in another state and a new truck. I got me a leather sectional sofa and a big wide-screen TV. I think you might want to come on back home now."

"I don't think so," I said.

"You don't think so, huh?" he said, still looking up at the ceiling. "Well, it don't matter what you think." He turned his head sideways and cut his eyes around at me. "You may wear bucks now, but you ain't going to be no buck for long. Once we get home, I'm fixing to take you down a notch or two."

All of a sudden, I heard Miss Armistead coming down the stairs. So my daddy wouldn't hear her, too, I said, "You still trucking?"

His face changed, and he winked at me again. "I'm in the transportation business, so to speak."

I didn't know what he meant by that, but I kept talking, hoping that Miss Armistead would catch him out here and call the law. "What kind of truck do you have?" I asked.

He looked at the front door and then back over at me again. I didn't know whether he'd heard Miss Armistead or not, but I figured he had by the way he acted. "What difference does it make to you?" he said, snarling like some mean backalley dog. "You don't care nothing about me. You said so yourself right there in the courtroom. You're a big shot, now, reading books and wearing a dead man's gold watch. Got that hair all duded up, too, ain't you?"

He got up, and I got up, too, and went behind the swing. "I ain't going to bother you, mutt," he said. He sneered and showed his yellow dogtooth. "Not now, anyways. I'll be back, though, you can count on that."

He jumped off the porch right over Miss Armistead's boxwoods and never once looked back, just strutted across the yard in his tight Wrangler jeans and muscle shirt and disappeared down the street.

I was shaking all over, and my stomach was doing flip-flops. I found my book where my daddy had slung it and sat back down in the swing, but nothing I read made any sense.

A few minutes later, Miss Armistead came out on the porch and commenced pinching the dead blooms off her mums. I kept looking at the book, letting on like I was reading. She wouldn't interrupt me while I was reading. She stayed out on the porch a pretty good spell messing with her flowers, and finally she said, "Are you having difficulty with that book, Patrick? I don't believe you've turned a page since I've been out here."

When Miss Armistead smiled, I could always see lots of gold in her teeth. She was smiling like she thought I was possuming and trying to get out of my weekly reading. "No, ma'am," I said. "I was just thinking, was all."

She came over and sat down beside me in the swing. "Deep thoughts?" she said.

"Pretty deep," I said.

"Did Tory go home?" she said.

"No, ma'am, he ain't been here," I said. I was this close to telling her about my daddy, and I don't know why I didn't.

"Oh, I thought I heard you talking to someone," she said.

"Naw, it wasn't anybody," I said. "It wasn't anybody atall."

That night I had so much bearing on my mind I couldn't go to sleep.

Seem like when I turned off the lights and hopped into bed, I could see somebody in the room. I got up and opened the curtains so the moon could shine in, and then seem like I could see somebody standing next to a telephone pole

159

down close to the street. I locked my door before I got back into bed.

Then, I started thinking about my daddy. I could've thought a right smart of him if he hadn't been so low-down mean. Seem like he was afraid I would care something about him, but that didn't make sense. And I couldn't understand why he wouldn't leave me alone, especially since he didn't seem to care one bit about me. Look like he just wanted to aggravate me. But that wasn't exactly the whole picture. Maybe in his own way he did care a little something about me, but he couldn't stand the thought of the law telling him how to raise me. He thought the law was picking on him like people used to pick on him at school on account of his name. He used my mama and me to get back at everybody because we were handy. But how could you keep on mistreating people if you loved them? It didn't make sense.

I was dead tired and wanted to get some rest, but troubles are like babies cutting teeth. They don't just lie down and go to sleep when you bring them to bed.

Granny Gunn wasn't the blame for my daddy turning out mean. She didn't know any better than naming him something foolish. She was just ignorant. I'd already seen that if you didn't want the bad to come back on you, you had to do right from the start. But then to do right, you had to know right. You couldn't exactly do right if you were ignorant, so you owed it to yourself and everybody else to learn as much as you could. Poor old Granny Gunn, though, was so ignorant she didn't know she was ignorant. Somehow you had to let ignorant people know they were ignorant, and then that way they could learn to do better.

All of a sudden, a big moth hit the window, and I jumped might near a foot off my bed. I knew in my head that it wasn't anything but a moth, but I got out of bed anyway and peeped out the window.

Miss Marcella's house was dark, but toward the back I

could see flashes of blue light like lightning. Tory was watching TV with the lights off. I started once to slip downstairs and go over there, but I thought Miss Marcella might not like it. She was funny about things.

I climbed back into bed and tried to go to sleep, but every time I was just about ready to doze off, I'd wake up. I'd hear something squeak in the hall like soft footsteps, or something bump against the side of the house. The refrigerator would kick on and thump, and then I'd hear something walking across the front porch. I decided that I might as well stay awake all night and go to sleep when the sun came up. Miss Armistead didn't care how late I slept, anyway.

I started thinking about Tory. He low-rated me every time he got mad, but then he had saved my life. I owed him something, but I didn't know how to pay him back. I didn't know if I was supposed to tell on him or lie for him. If I told on him, I'd be wronging him, because I promised I wouldn't tell on him unless I had to. But then if I didn't tell on him, maybe later I'd find out I'd wronged him because I hadn't told. If he got hurt or killed, everything would come back on me because I hadn't told.

It made my head spin, trying to figure out the right and wrong of it all. Doing right didn't used to seem like much trouble until I started trying to do it.

Another big bug thumped against the window, but this time I just lay still. I knew it was nothing.

A few seconds later, something else hit the window, and before I could get out of bed, whatever it was hit the window again.

I crawled on all fours over to the window and peeped out the corner. This time I did see something. This time it wasn't my imagination.

I saw somebody standing down under the big oak tree at the edge of the driveway. I saw right off it wasn't my daddy. It was somebody my own age or thereabouts, and at first I thought it might be Chigger, but this person had two arms and short hair. He was gathering up something under the tree, look like, and in a minute he came over to the side of the house.

I soon saw what he was up to. He was throwing twigs against the windows on this side of the house. He'd hit one window and come on down and hit another. At first I figured he had to be a crazy person or somebody on drugs, but when he stepped out in the moonlight, I saw it was Chigger after all!

He was looking me up, durn his time!

I raised the window and then the storm window and whispered through the screen. "Chigger! Up here."

He cocked back his head like a rooster. "Is that you, Pat?" he said quietly. He probably couldn't see me because the tree was casting big blotchy shadows against the side of the house.

"Yeah, it's me," I said. "Come on around to the back door. I'll come down and let you in."

He scratched his belly and looked from one end of the house to the other. "I don't know," he said. "Maybe you ought to come on out here."

"Okay," I said. "Give me a minute and I'll be on down."

"10–4," he said and stepped back under the big oak.

I slipped on my khaki shorts and deck shoes and got my door key out of the nightstand. Then I eased down the steps. Miss Armistead slept in a bedroom behind the parlor. She snored like nobody's business. When I got down to the long hallway leading back to the kitchen, I could hear her sawing logs. She never let up when I tiptoed past her bedroom. I snuck right on out the kitchen door and locked it behind me.

When I walked up to Chigger, I almost offered to shake hands with him. I'd been around Tory too long. Instead, I thumped him on the shoulder. "Hey, turd," I said.

He put up his dukes and made like a boxer, dancing

around and punching the air close to my head. "You ain't had the shit beat out of you lately, have you?" he said.

I held out my palms, and he socked them three or four times. "Not by no pencil pecker like you, I ain't," I said.

In a minute we stopped fooling around, and Chigger said, "Less us walk over to the Jiffy Mart."

"Okay," I said, and we took off down the street.

Chigger looked like he'd shot up about three inches, and his short haircut made him look different, even in the moonlight. He didn't look wormy anymore, either. He'd done filled out. I wanted to ask him about his arm so bad I could hardly stand it, but I didn't want to hurt his feelings. Chigger was touchy about a lot of things. He didn't have a metal hook. He had a mannequin-like arm and hand.

The funny thing was, we hadn't seen each other in a long time, but neither one of us had much to say as we walked along under the shadows of the big oaks lining College Street and McLemore Drive. I couldn't get over how much he'd changed. He even sounded different, his voice sometimes squeaky and at other times deep and hoarse.

It was a hot night. By the time we'd walked two blocks, both of us were blowing sweat off the ends of our noses. As we ran across the big intersection there at Terrace Lane and Highway 24, I noticed that Chigger didn't have his tattoo anymore.

By the time we finally got over to Jiffy Mart, we were both soaked with sweat. Chigger took off his Perrier T–shirt and wiped off his back and belly with it. He laughed and offered it to me, but I shook my head, and then he stuck part of it in the back pocket of his shorts and let the rest hang out. He was wearing blue jeans shorts, not cut-offs, either, but GUESS?, the same brand Miss Armistead always bought me. I didn't know where he'd been or what he'd done, but he sure didn't look like the same old Chigger.

We went inside Jiffy Mart and sat down in one of the

orange and yellow booths close to the deli. "What do you want to drink?" he said, and I told him, "I got some money."

I told him I had money because I figured that he'd try to get a couple of drinks with the five-finger discount. "Naw, that's all right," he said, wiping sweat off the blonde fuzz on his upper lip. He was getting a mustache, but I didn't have a sign of anything growing up there in that direction yet. "I got it. Besides, I owe you."

"Naw, you don't owe me nothing, man," I said. "That thirty dollars was a Christmas present."

He frowned. "A Christmas present?" he said. "I ain't never bought you no Christmas present."

"Well," I said, "buy me a Mountain Dew. I'll pretend it's got a bow on top of it."

"Whatever, dude," he said and shrugged. He went back to the cooler and took out two drinks and went up to the register to pay. When he walked back to our booth, he was cradling the drinks next to his belly with his fake arm. If Chigger had been wearing a shirt to cover up where his new arm harnessed on, you couldn't have told it was fake unless you looked real close.

He handed me my drink, and after he'd sat down, I said, "How long have you been back? I ain't seen you around anywhere."

"Ain't been around," he said, his voice croaking like a bullfrog. "I've been over in Memphis since the first of the year."

"How'd you find me?"

"Makes you wonder, don't it?" he said, grinning. His teeth were clean and white, like he'd had the moss scraped off them. "Old lady Pratt told me she heard you were living over on the corner of College Street in a big brick mansion. When I saw your house, I knew it had to be the one."

"Are you back with your mama now?"

He leaned back in the booth and yawned. "Just for a

few weeks," he said. "I'm going to be living in Memphis from now on, though."

I had a sinking feeling when he said that. Now that he'd come back, I was hoping we were going to have the summer together, camping out and fishing up and down the creek. "How come your mama is moving to Memphis?" I said.

He glanced over to one side. "She ain't," he said, and when he looked at me again, I thought I saw something in his green eyes I didn't want to see, and something he didn't aim for me to see, either. "I've got a legal guardian now. A doctor over there in Memphis."

I couldn't stand the suspense any longer. "Tell me everything from the beginning," I said, leaning on the table-top. "Tell me how you got your arm and why you don't have a tattoo anymore. How come you look so different than you used to?"

"How come you do?" he said right hateful. He took a big swig of co-cola and eyeballed me.

"If you talked to Miss Pratt, you know why," I said. "Miss Armistead took me in. Come on, now. Tell me."

"You're as nosy as somebody's grandma," he said. He was letting on like he was aggravated, and maybe he was a little, but I knew he was aiming to tell me everything. Sure enough, directly he shrugged and said, "I don't know, dude. Things just happened."

"Things just don't happen," I said. "Miss Armistead says that all the time. People make things happen."

"Yeah, and I ain't Miss...how do you say her name?"

"Armistead."

"Yeah, right. I ain't that old lady."

I decided to prod him along some. "They sent you off again for missing so much school, didn't they?"

Chigger commenced peeling off the Styrofoam on his co-cola bottle. "Yeah, they did. To Jackson Street Detention Center. They hauled my little butt up there in

January, and the first day I was there, me and this colored dude from Germantown had a little trouble."

"You mouthed off and he beat the tar out of you, didn't he?" I said and laughed.

Chigger kind of grinned and looked down, because he knew I'd hit the nail on the head. "Something like that," he said. "Anyhow, he kept picking on me after that, and one day when we were out on the softball diamond, I cold-cocked him with an aluminum bat."

"You didn't do no such thing," I said. Chigger always talked big, but he didn't ever get the best of anybody.

"Yeah, I did, too," he said. He was stuffing the Styrofoam peelings down inside his empty bottle, and when he looked up, I saw that he was serious. "I didn't mean to, though."

I laughed real loud, and the cashier craned her neck around the corner and looked mean back at us. It was about midnight, and we weren't really supposed to be in there. If the county mounties caught us, they'd take us home in the police car.

"I can just see it," I said, playing like I was swinging a bat. "Oh, sorry, dude, I didn't mean to hit you upside the head with this aluminum bat."

"Naw, really, I didn't," he said, laughing along with me. "He come out there trying to start some stuff with me, and I started swinging so he'd stay back. He walked right into that bat. I reckon he thought I'd stop swinging or something, I don't know."

"Then what happened?" I asked.

Chigger shook his head like my question wasn't worth answering. "Ah, I don't know. Just a bunch of stuff."

"You got into a lot of trouble, didn't you?"

He began spinning his drink bottle around on the table top. "Naw, not really," he said. "They sent me to a head doctor, this dude named Dr. Biley over at Baptist, to see if I had good sense or not."

"I could've saved them the trouble," I said. "I could've told them you ain't never had good sense."

Chigger grinned, but it was forced. I was just teasing him, but I could tell he didn't like it. His face looked like somebody's who'd been told real bad news, and the tops of his ears got red. He stopped spinning the bottle and set it upright on the table. "He said I did," he said. "Dr. Biley said I had a lot more sense than people give me credit for."

"I didn't mean to low-rate you," I said, "I was..."

"It don't matter," he said, waving his real arm toward me like he was shooing away a fly. "Me and Dr. Biley figured out why I stayed bent out of shape so much. Me and him got to be pretty good buddies, and that's who I'm staying with now, and that's how I got my arm. We drove all the way to Lexington, Kentucky, to get this arm fitted at the Shriners." He stuck his arm out on the table for me to see. "Pretty neat, huh?"

"It looks like it would get hot where it fastens on with that sock of a thing," I said, "but it sure looks like a real arm."

"It is a real one, dogface," he said, chucking me under the chin with it and laughing. "It's a *real plastic one.*"

"That wasn't a real tattoo you had that time, was it?" I said. "It was just one of those stuck-on kind."

Chigger turned his shoulder toward me and pointed. "It was stuck on, all right," he said. He pointed toward this dark patch of skin that was might near covered by his suntan and all those harness wires. "It was stuck on with a big sewing needle, and right there is where I got it burned off." He sneered at me. "Stuck on, my ass."

"Did they burn if off with a blowtorch or something?" I said. The thoughts of it sent chillbumps up my back.

Chigger laughed and shook his head. "You're about dumb, Pat, do you know that?" he said. "Ain't you ever been nowhere?"

The only times Chigger had ever been out of the county were when he'd been sent off for skipping school. I might be about dumb, but he about had the bighead. I hadn't meant to low-rate him, and I didn't want him low-rating me. "I've been to Venice, Italy," I said, "and I got a picture at home to prove it. I've even waded in the canals there."

"You a lie," Chigger said and looked around behind him to see if there was anybody else in the other booths. He was wanting to shame me in front of some other people if he could, which was low-down mean, if you ask me. He hadn't changed much after all, just on the outside. He was still an aggravating pissant.

"Forget it," I said. "I don't care if you believe me or not."

He cocked his head to one side and grinned at me like he was having a fine time. "Don't get mad, now," he said. "You know good and well you ain't been to Venice or nowhere else. That old lady keeps you penned up like a little puppy dog, is what I hear. You're backward as reverse."

I capped my drink and started to get up. I wasn't messing with him anymore. He was ignorant as ever, and I wasn't aiming to tell him about my hideout, either. "Wait a minute, hoss!" he said. He clamped his real hand hard down on my arm. He was stouter than he used to be. "Still got a temper, don't you?"

I jerked my arm loose and made a fist down at my side. I couldn't say a word, I was so mad. I knew if I opened my mouth I wouldn't be able to talk. Every time I got real mad, I sounded like I was fixing to cry, and I wasn't going to give Chigger anything else to aggravate me about.

He rose halfway out of his seat and made a time-out sign. "Whoa! Come on, now, Pat," he said. "Don't be like that. You told me I didn't have good sense a minute ago, and I didn't fly off the handle about that, now did I?"

I shook my head. He was right, which made me feel even worse.

"All right, then," he said and flopped back in the seat.

I sat down again, too. "Man! Dr. Biley would say you're carrying around a lot of baggage."

I didn't know what in the devil he was talking about, but I was afraid to open my mouth to ask, because most likely he'd try to low-rate me.

He leaned over the table and talked in a low voice. "See, man, the reason I was mad all the time was on account of my arm," he said. "I didn't like to go to school because I thought people were staring at my arm, and I guess they were sometimes. Then I got so far behind in school I was ashamed to go, because I didn't know the stuff everybody else knew."

The clerk came down the aisle beside the booths and commenced mopping. Chigger shut up then, and I looked out the window toward the gas pumps. An old stray dog walked up the street and came on over to the sidewalk in front of the store. He sniffed at the rocking horse and the weight machine like he was hungry. He went on around behind the store when an old purple Javelin with splayed wheels pulled up to the air pump. Tommy Lee Trigg got out and put a quarter in the machine and aired up his front tires. Tommy Lee lived in the trailer park with his mama and wife and girlfriend, all of them in the same trailer. He got a pension because he'd been shot in the head in the war. Every once in a while he used to let Chigger and me shoot his pistol at rats down at the city dump. I started once to tap on the window and throw up my hand at him, but I didn't figure he'd know me anymore.

Directly, the clerk moved over to another aisle, and Chigger said, "You're mad about what happened to your mama, or about your daddy beating on you and stuff. That's why nobody can't get along with you."

I stared a hole through him. "I wondered what this rigmarole was all about when you brought up your doctor friend, and now I see," I said. "I got news for you, Chigger. I don't ever think about my mama anymore. I'm not hard to get along with, either, when people treat me right." I'd make him think.

"Forget it, then," he said, acting hurt like I'd done something mean to him. "What were we talking about before?"

"Your tattoo," I said. "We were talking about your tattoo, and then you got to be a smart aleck."

He narrowed his eyes like he was studying me. "Oh, yeah," he said. "One of Dr. Biley's buddies at the hospital burned it off with a laser. Smelled just like burning hair."

"Didn't it hurt?"

He looked down at the table top and grinned. He was still aiming to make light of me, and I knew it. "They deadened it, Pat. You know, with a needle."

"I know how they deaden stuff. See?" I opened my mouth and showed him my back tooth plugged with real gold.

"Yeah, right," he said. He got up and picked up his bottle, and I did the same thing. "Hey, man, I'm wore out," he said, throwing his bottle into the trash bin over by the door. "Come over to the trailer sometime. I'm going to be there about another week."

"Okay," I said. I dropped my bottle into the trash, too, and we walked on out to the sidewalk. I was mostly over my mad spell, but it didn't make me feel good, Chigger acting like such a big shot since he'd been to Memphis. "Listen," I said, giving him a play punch on the shoulder. "Maybe we can go to the creek. I've found a hideout like you wouldn't believe. Don't anybody know about it except me and this boy next door."

Chigger frowned and looked at me like he thought I was crazy. "*Hideout,*" he said. "What do you want a hideout for?"

"I don't know," I said, shrugging and feeling my face turn red. "You can go there and camp out and stuff, and nobody knows you're there. It's fun."

"If you're ten years old," he said. He shook his head like he didn't know what to make of me. "You ever heard of girls, Pat? How old are you, anyhow, thirteen or fourteen?"

"Of course I've heard of girls," I said. "What's that supposed to mean?"

"Never mind," he said, turning and walking down the sidewalk. "Catch you later, man."

"Sure," I said.

I commenced walking home. It had cooled off outside. It was late, and I didn't see many lights still on in the houses. Some houses had doorbells that lit up. They put me in mind of a dog's eyes in the dark.

I was glad to be by myself. I didn't want to see anybody or talk to anybody or answer anybody.

When I got over to McLemore, I sat down on a retaining wall to rest for a minute. The clouds overhead looked like long scarves, and directly the tail end of one raked across the moon. Even with the streetlights, everything felt dark and closed in.

I got up and walked on home, knowing what a coon knows, or a skunk knows, or a fox in the henhouse knows. The dark is nothing to be afraid of, especially when you're after something or something's after you.

CHAPTER XIII

I Get Bamboozled
By A Low-Down Dog

"My dad's supposed to be home by the fifteenth of this month," Tory said.

It was middle of the morning, and we were sitting out on the side porch playing Chinese checkers. Playing checkers was Miss Armistead's idea of fun, not mine. Tory and I had played five games, and he'd won every single one. "Are you still going to slip off?" I said. "Maybe now your granny's not going to send you back to your mama."

He pushed his glasses back up with his stubby thumb. "Not a chance," he said. "She's already spoken with my mother in Hawaii and told her everything." He jumped a whole bunch of my marbles. "You're not too good at this game, are you?"

"I don't like games," I told him, scooting back against the porch post. "I don't see no sense in them."

The sun was hot, but it felt good on my bare skin. I wasn't wearing a stitch except for shorts that were made out of this funny cloth from India. These shorts changed colors every time they were washed. My skin was turning real dark, like it always did, but Tory's skin was still about the color of flour. He wasn't wearing anything but shorts, either, and his bellybutton looked like a dark train tunnel.

"I don't like football," Tory said. "Most everybody

seems to, but I don't."

"I don't much like soccer," I said. "People are always kicking me in the shins."

About that time Miss Marcella crept around the side of the house and looked across the hedge at us. "I'd like to sock her," Tory whispered. "Right in the kisser."

We both turned our heads and sniggered. Miss Marcella didn't know we were laughing at her. She said real sweet, "Having fun, boys?"

"Yessum," I said, and then she walked down to the street to pick up a paper bag and some other junk somebody had thrown out of a passing car.

Tory scooted back against a post, too. "She gripes my butt," he said. "You'd think I'd robbed a bank or something, the way she acts. She won't let me out of her sight ten minutes."

I stretched out longways on the porch and closed my eyes. "That's just old folks for you," I told him. "Miss Armistead gets on my nerves, too, sometimes, but she don't mean anything by it. I know she sure stays on my case when I don't brush my teeth regular."

"She's not sending you packing, though, is she?" Tory said.

I was glad I had my eyes closed. I let on like I was half asleep and just sort of grunted. He was right, and I didn't know what to say to him.

"By the way, who was your company yesterday?" he asked me right out of the blue. "Who was that man?"

"Huh?" I said, opening my eyes but still acting like I was addled. Tory was grinning on one side of his face like he knew something on me.

"You heard me," he said. He stuck out his foot and jarred my legs. "I was coming out of the bathroom and heard old Mrs. Anderson's collies barking like somebody was trying to take her off, and then I saw this guy walk right across our lawn and go over to your porch."

I looked up at the blue porch ceiling like I was in a deep study. "Well, let's see now," I said. "Yesterday." I didn't want Tory to know that Tommy Gunn was my daddy. His daddy had been in the pen, but still I knew he was the kind of fellow who wore a gray striped suit and a gold pinkie ring. I hadn't ever laid eyes on him, but I could picture him clear as day.

"I don't care, anyway," Tory said and slapped his shoulder. "Damn mosquitoes!"

I don't know why in the world I told him the truth then, but I did. I said, "It was my daddy. Miss Marcella has already told you he ain't worth killing. I didn't want you to know that was him."

"Nothing to me," he said and shrugged.

I wasn't sure what he meant by that. I didn't know if he meant that he didn't care enough about me as a friend to care if I had a sorry daddy or not, or if he meant that he still liked me as a friend, even if I did have a sorry daddy. I thought about what Chigger had said the night before, accusing me of being hard to get along with and all, so I didn't fly off the handle. "I'm glad you saw him, in a way," I said, raising up and stretching. Then I scooted over to the edge of the porch and let my legs dangle off, my back to Tory. "I thought he might be fixing to beat me up again. Miss Armistead didn't know he was there, or she would've sicced the law on him."

I could feel Tory's eyes on my back. In a minute, he came over and sat down beside me. He raised his hand like he was aiming to touch me on the shoulder or back, but then he didn't. I was glad he didn't. "I had no idea he was your father," he said. "He didn't look like he belonged over here, so I stayed by the phone until he left. If he'd tried to bother you, I was ready to call the police."

Tory was saying that my daddy wasn't good enough to be seen in this neighborhood, and even though I didn't care anything about my daddy, I didn't want anybody but me low-rating him. If Tory thought that about him, then he probably thought the same thing about me. I knew Tory was trying to be my friend, though, and I realized for the first time that even a smart person like him had an ignorant side, or maybe a blind side would be a better way to say it. He didn't miss seeing much with his eyes, but he didn't have the kind of sight to see himself in my place, to understand how I felt. Once I understood this, a lot of things cleared up in my head, and some of the hard feelings I had for him went away.

I nudged him in the ribs with my elbow. "You're all right for a fat boy," I said.

"And you're all wet," he said and spit right down my bare leg!

I got him in a half nelson and was fixing to skin his head, but he wiggled away from me and ran over to the spigot. He got the hose pipe and shot a big long squirt at me. He got my left side good and was fixing to wet me all over, but I hopped upon the porch and took cover behind a post. "You can't get the porch wet!" I hollered at him, and he hollered back, "Watch me!"

About that time Miss Armistead opened the side screen door behind me. She was triggered up in one of her flowery dresses and was headed to the Reading Circle down the street at Miss Haislip's house. I turned around and looked at her with my mouth wide open, and she looked at me funny, and right then Tory drenched her from head to toe before he even realized she was standing there.

When Tory saw what he'd done, he turned the color of concrete and looked toward Miss Marcella's house like he was considering making a run for it. His eyes looked like two wild things looking for a place to hide. Then Miss Armistead said, shaking her hands down at her sides, "I do believe we've had a sudden cloudburst, Patrick. Perhaps I should take my umbrella."

Tory didn't know what to make of her at first, just

stood there real cowed down, holding the dripping hose pipe and batting his big eyes and stammering how sorry he was. When he finally caught on that Miss Armistead wasn't mad atall, he managed to grin a little, but he still looked like somebody in pain who was trying to be brave.

I got a big kick out of him, myself.

I was walking home from the public library with two good-sized stacks of books.

I'd tried to put a stack under each arm, but there were just too many to carry that way. I'd drop a book every four or five feet, so finally I stacked them in one big stack and carried them right in front of me like the girls did at school. Every so often a car would come down the street, and then I'd kind of hang my head so nobody would see me and think I was a sissy.

Miss Armistead had told me to wear shoes, because the public librarian was always fussing on people who came in without them. There was some law or something that said you couldn't go into a public building without shoes. Anyway, I didn't pay any attention to Miss Armistead, and sure enough, when I got to the public library, the librarian fussed on me, but I didn't pay any attention to her, either. Besides, she looked like she enjoyed fussing.

But as I was walking down that concrete sidewalk at two o'clock on a hot day in June, I wished I hadn't been so durn hardheaded. The soles of my feet had just about baked. Every once in a while I'd have to set down my stack and lay two books on the sidewalk to stand on for a minute. If that hateful librarian had seen me doing that, she sure would have fussed. But I didn't have a choice. People on our side of town were all old and rich, and they didn't appreciate anybody walking on their grass. They thought God made grass to look at.

Anyway, I was doing a fast tiptoe down that sidewalk when all of a sudden this old rusty Ford van pulled up

alongside me, and this man who hadn't shaved in forty fore-
vers hollered to me, "Hey, bud, can you tell me how to get
to the college?"

I thought to myself, *It's might near right in front of
you, dumbass,* but I minded my manners. I set down my
stack of books and walked over to the curb. "It's right over
yonder," I said, pointing to the Administration Building.

"I can't see it," he said as he leaned over the seat and
looked out the opposite window. Then he got out of the van
and walked around to the passenger side.

He shaded his eyes with one hand and looked in the
direction I was pointing. He was a short, fat man. He was
wearing some old gray work pants that looked like they
were fixing to fall off his hind end and drop right around
his ankles and a greasy checked shirt that was ripped down
the middle of his back. "Where'd you say now?" he said,
motioning for me to come over and show him again.

I walked over beside him and pointed. He stunk to high
heaven. "Look, mister," I said. "You mean to tell me you
can't see that big building with those gray and red squares
stuck up between the windows? See?"

He grinned a funny little grin. "Yeah, I see now," he
said. "Yeah."

I hadn't even had time to turn around when I heard the
passenger door of the van open, and before I knew what
was happening, my daddy had me cinched up by the waist
and was dragging me kicking inside.

There wasn't a seat on the passenger side, so he'd been
hiding in the back all along. In the back were rusty pipe
wrenches and a bunch of junk—jumper cables and beer
cans and such. I didn't have time to think or put up much
of a fuss, everything happened so fast. One minute I was
standing there talking to that low-down dog, and the next
thing I knew, my daddy had me slung on the floor of the
van.

I landed on my shoulder and hip and then rolled over

and banged the left side of my forehead good on an old battery that was inside a pasteboard box. The van backfired, and we took off in a wild lurch.

"Don't you say a damn word," my daddy said. He was on his knees pointing his finger in my face, and I smelled his sour beer breath and old sweat.

At first I was dizzy as a witch and couldn't have said anything if I'd wanted to. Directly, my daddy decided that I wasn't going to try to jump out, I reckon, so he scooted over and leaned back against the side of the van.

I sat up then and rubbed the hen egg on my forehead. That low-down dog who was driving kept looking back through the rearview mirror and grinning at me. He was driving as fast as that old van would go, and he was driving wild. I was used to slow driving, and all that speed and being scared, too, made me start sweating, even though both windows were rolled down and the breeze coming through them was about to blow us away in the back.

"Now wouldn't he a nice boy?" that low-down dog hollered back at my daddy. "Wouldn't he a regular Boy Scout?"

"I'll Boy Scout him," my daddy hollered back, and that low-down dog winked at me and then laughed. He had long yellow teeth that stuck way out and didn't have any gums around them.

"Where are we going?" I said when I finally got up my nerve. "Where are you taking me?"

"I'm taking you where you belong," my daddy said, aiming his finger at me again. "Now shut the hell up."

"We're going on a picnic," that low-down dog said and giggled.

All of a sudden, my daddy picked up one of the empty beer cans and slung it toward the front. It bounced off the back of the driver's seat. "Give it a rest, Dewayne," he said. "I got a headache, and you're about to get on my nerves."

Dewayne poked his tongue in his cheek to keep from

laughing. Every once in a while he'd cross his eyes in the mirror to make me laugh, but I didn't think he was one bit funny.

I sat back there on that dirty van floor and bounced around every which way. This old van had these long strips of metal about an inch apart that stuck up from the floor, so there was no way to keep my tail out of the cracks. I was wearing my brand-new blue checked shorts that Miss Armistead had bought me at Dillard's and a solid blue knit shirt. My shorts had a long smear of greasy dirt up one side, and my shirt had a pull in it. My hip felt raw, and I figured I was skinned up good on my left side.

After a while, we turned off on a dirt road. We were still going fast, too fast, because the rear end of the van kept sliding. We hadn't had any rain in a week or two, and dust was flying through the windows all over us. It was might near strangling me. It finally got to my daddy, too, because he hollered, "Dammit, Dewayne, slow down! We ain't going to no fire!"

Dewayne laughed, showing his long ugly teeth. "All right, boss man," he said, and then we slowed down some.

It made me durn mad to think how I hadn't bothered a soul, and then that sorry low-down dog had bamboozled me so my daddy could cart me off to Lord knows where. Here I'd ruined a good set of clothes, and I didn't have a blessed thing on my feet.

If I'd had a loaded gun that very minute, I would've shot my daddy deader than a doornail, and I'm not stretching it one bit.

I knew one thing. My daddy had me for now, but he was fixing to have to watch me twenty-four hours a day. As soon as he turned his back, I was going to be gone. I still had ten dollars in my pocket, and that and my thumb would take me a pretty good ways.

All of a sudden, I thought about my watch. I was wearing my good gold watch, even though I wasn't supposed to wear it for everyday. My daddy would probably take it away from me if he saw it, and maybe he already had. Old Dewayne kept looking back through the rearview mirror every minute or two, and maybe he'd seen it, too. I decided that it wouldn't hurt to try and hide it. If my daddy caught me trying to fool him, he'd smack me upside the head, but he was fixing to do plenty of that, anyway.

I had my legs stretched out longways and was leaning back on my hands so I could lift up and rest my hind end every so often. I drew up my legs toward my chest real slow and then hugged my knees. I clamped my right hand over my watch and rode that way for a pretty long spell so neither one of them would think anything.

I made the mistake of looking at my daddy. He had his legs all spraddled out, and his eyes looked closed. "What are you looking at, mutt?" he said.

"Nothing much," I said.

Before I could dodge, he let loose and kicked me in the thigh. It didn't hurt too bad, but it knocked me off balance so that my head banged against the side of the van.

"Hey, now." I heard Dewayne say, and the van slowed down to where it was just barely moving. "Ain't no need of that. He's just a kid."

My daddy hopped up fast and twisted hold of Dewayne's shirt collar. "Who the hell asked you?" my daddy said. "Huh?"

I saw that he had his knife out, a long, pearl-handled switchblade that looked sharp enough to shave with. Dewayne was grinning, but his face was oily with sweat. "Put that up, now, Tommy," he said and swallowed hard once or twice. "You know I didn't mean nothing. Ain't nothing to me."

My daddy grinned his mean grin and then turned loose of Dewayne's shirt collar. "That's what I thought," he said and looked back at me. He wanted to make sure I understood who was running the show from now on.

He closed the switchblade on his britches leg and slipped it into his back pocket. We took off again, and he crawled back over across from me and leaned against the side of the van. Then he raised his eyebrows and said, "Better learn to watch your mouth, mutt. You know what I mean?"

I nodded, but I kept my mouth shut. I was sitting up again by then. While my daddy had been threatening Dewayne, I'd managed to unstrap my watch and slip it inside my pocket.

I didn't know where we were now. There weren't many towns in the county, but there was a slew of dirt roads and pig paths going off every which way. We drove for the longest time, seem like, turning off one dirt road onto another, until finally we came to this old junky-looking brown trailer wedged upon a pine bluff out in the middle of nowhere. There were five or six old cars and trucks with the hoods up piled out in the middle of this field below the trailer. It was a hot, scrubby place, nothing growing there except pine trees and sumac and bitterweed.

Dewayne pulled up in the driveway leading to the trailer. The driveway was chert with a big gully washed out down the middle of it. The van rocked from side to side as we drove up it. Through the windshield I could see a new black Jeep Cherokee parked behind the trailer.

Dewayne parked on the far side of the Jeep. Then, my daddy motioned with his head toward the door. "Get out and stretch," he said, beginning to get up himself. "You can run off if you want to, but there ain't nowhere to go."

After all three of us were out of the van, Dewayne hitched up his pants and looked over at my daddy like he wanted to say something, but not in front of me. "Go on and get in the Jeep," my daddy said. "I'll be on in a minute."

Dewayne and my daddy walked around to the front of the trailer. I could hear them talking low, but I couldn't make out what they were saying.

I looked at the Jeep, and then I looked at the country-side. I thought about making a run for it up through the pines behind the trailer, but I didn't know these parts. It was hot weather, and I knew I could stay lost for days before I ever came to pavement or found water. Here I was bare-footed, and there was nothing a rattlesnake liked better than a cool pine thicket. I figured I'd better bide my time.

So I got in the Jeep. It still smelled brand new. Directly, my daddy and Dewayne came back around to where I was. Dewayne bent down and looked in the window at me. He winked and gave me a thumbs-up sign. "Check you later, partner," he said.

I turned my head like I hadn't heard him. He might not have been as low-down as my daddy, but I still didn't have any use for him. He'd done me wrong, and now he thought he could make up for that by being friendly. I had news for him. One of these days his meanness was fixing to come back home to him, and I would finger him in court before he could blink twice.

My daddy got in the Jeep, and we inched back down the washed-out driveway. Dewayne waved at us, but my daddy never let on like he saw him, either. Dewayne turned around and went in the back door of the trailer.

I didn't say a word to my daddy, and all he said to me was, "Roll up the window, and I'll turn on the air condi-tioner." He didn't say it hateful or anything, and one time he reached over and felt of one of the knots on my head and then kind of grinned. He didn't really know how to act like a daddy, though.

We drove for a long time on winding dirt roads. The hood of the black Cherokee was covered with reddish tan dust that put me in mind of the face powder Miss Armistead dabbed on her nose to keep it from shining.

I wondered what Miss Armistead was doing now, whether he knew I was missing or not. It might be two or three days before anybody came along and found those books stacked on the sidewalk, or somebody might just make off with them and never tell anybody. Miss Armistead might think that I'd slipped off somewhere again without telling her, or that I'd managed to get into some kind of trouble, or that I'd drowned down there in the creek. I'd already done enough to worry that woman to death. That was the only trouble about having somebody who cared about what happened to you. You had to worry about that person worrying about you, and then you couldn't do half the stuff you used to. You couldn't be free anymore once somebody cared about you, and you cared about that person, too.

Then I wondered about Tory, if he'd slipped off to Starkville in that little red convertible car. I never did have a chance to figure out what to do about him, whether to tell on him or not, but if he got killed running off down there in a car he didn't even know how to drive, it would be partly my fault. Nobody would ever accuse me, because nobody knew about Tory's plan except for the two of us, but I didn't know if I could live with myself if something happened to him. It wasn't like we were kinfolks, or that I cared about him or anything. I mean I liked him well enough as a friend, but the main thing was, he'd saved my life, so I had to do him a mighty big favor to be even. That's really what had me worried. I was afraid something might happen to him with me still owing him, that's all.

I thought about Chigger, too, and how much he'd changed. In some ways he was like the old Chigger, but in some ways he was different. He didn't argue about everything like he used to. He acted grown up, like he knew what was what. I used to boss him around and stuff, and now he acted like he knew a whole lot more than I did. He wasn't even touchy anymore. I was the one who was touchy. Seem like somehow we'd switched places, and I didn't much like it. I couldn't figure out why he'd bothered to look me up, either. He didn't seem to be all that tickled to see me.

Finally, we came to some pavement and turned right. The road sign said we were on Highway 100 going toward Henderson. I knew about Henderson, because that's where my mama and Papa Prince had lived before my mama ran off with my daddy. I wanted to ask my daddy to show me the house where my mama had been raised, but I knew I couldn't.

In ten minutes we were passing right through Henderson. It wasn't much size. We passed a service station and a few old houses stuck here and there, and I wondered what my mama thought when she was living here, and what she felt getting up of a morning, and if she'd ever seen exactly the same sights I was looking at now. I wondered if she'd been scared when she went to first grade, like I'd been, or if she'd played hopscotch, or if she ever had to stay in at recess for talking too much. It made the nape of my neck throb to think about all this, so finally I tried not to think atall. My daddy drove real fast through Henderson, and his jawbones stuck way out from his face.

Directly, we turned north on Highway 22. I didn't know where we were heading. I never had been up this far, that I could remember. I'd been to Memphis once before Miss Armistead had taken me. In the sixth grade, Miss Lumpkins took us on the bus to the museum to see all this stuff somebody had dug up in Egypt a long time ago. This stuff belonged to a king named Tut, and he had a false face made out of solid gold.

Before long we came to the interstate, Interstate 40. I'd been on this interstate before, but we headed in another direction, toward Nashville.

I figured it was going to be a long ride to wherever we were going, so I just kind of leaned my head against the window and closed my eyes to shut out everything. The Jeep tires hummed and thumped down the interstate, and before long I was sound asleep.

CHAPTER XIV

Nashville

My daddy shook me awake. "Damn if you ain't just like a baby," he said. "Put you in something moving for a few minutes, and you're dead to the world. Get up, we're in Nashville."

He laughed, his mouth looking like a dark, empty cave. He was trying to be friendly, the best he knew how. "I'm up," I said, rubbing my eyes. "How long have I been asleep?"

"About a hour and a half, if you ain't been possuming," he said, opening the door and climbing out of the Jeep. "Less us go in here and see if we can't find a room."

Out on the highway cars were whizzing by like they were all late to somewhere. We were pulled off the road under this little carport of a thing, and on the driver's side of the Jeep was an office. My daddy lit a cigarette and stretched. I got out and stretched, too. The asphalt was cool in the shade, but I knew everywhere else it would be hot enough to curl up my toes. Every time I didn't listen to Miss Armistead, seem like I got into trouble.

My daddy hopped up the steps to the office and swung open the door halfway. "You staying or coming, mutt?" he said.

"I'll look around out here if you don't care," I said, and he went on inside without answering.

185

I hadn't had any experience with motels, but this place sure didn't look like much. There was an upstairs and a downstairs part, and water was dripping from the upstairs air conditioners down off the balcony. At one time the doors to the rooms had been painted orange, but some of them had gotten torn up and been replaced by secondhand ones that nobody had ever bothered to paint. In front of the downstairs rooms were shrubs that had turned yellow in places. There was a little swimming pool surrounded by this iron fence over next to the highway, but a sign at the gate read, "Pool Close For Repair."

In a minute my daddy came back out with a key. "It's around on the other side," he said, and we got back in the Jeep. Our room turned out to be there on the end as we rounded the corner.

After my daddy fiddled with the lock for a while, he finally got the door open, and we went inside. It was too cold in the room, and the air smelled funny, kind of like an old refrigerator that somebody had plugged in after it had set out on the back porch for a long time. The carpet was red and stained in a bunch of places. I could feel something gritty like sand on the soles of my feet when I walked across it. There were two pictures on the wall, one of a skinny bullfighter leaning way back with his cape draped over his sword, and the other one of a fanning woman with a white flower on each side of her head. There was only one bed, and it looked like it had seen a right smart of use. It was covered with a red bedspread that had fringe around the bottom, only part of the fringe was torn loose.

My daddy went in the bathroom and peed. He didn't close the door, just hauled out his business and went to it. When he came out, I went in and closed the door. I was about to burst. My daddy hadn't even flushed the toilet. Miss Armistead sure didn't put up with trifling ways like that. As I was peeing, I saw we had a bunch of towels hung up on the rack. They didn't look like Miss Armistead's towels. These were supposed to be white, but you could tell people had used them for things they shouldn't have.

As soon as I came out of the bathroom, I saw my daddy sprawled out on the bed with his boots on. He had his hands behind his head and looked mighty pleased with himself. "You hungry, mutt?" he said.

"Yeah," I said. There was an orange plastic chair like the ones in the Econ-O-Wash over in the far corner, so I went over and sat down in it. I wasn't really hungry, even though it was probably around four o'clock, and I hadn't eaten anything except a bowl of cereal all day long. I was wanting him to get out of my sight for a while so I could think. It made me nervous just being in the same room with him, even though I knew he wouldn't beat on me when he was sober unless I smarted off to him.

After a while he got up and went back into the bathroom. I heard water splashing and him snorting as he washed his face. He came out a minute later jamming his shirttail down in his jeans. "You stay put," he said, walking over to the door. "I'm fixing to get us something to eat. Watch television or something until I get back."

"Okay," I said, and he went out.

I hadn't counted on him leaving me by myself. I reckon he figured I wouldn't try to run for it in a big town like Nashville, me with no shoes on or no way to find my way home. He was right, at least this time. I knew he wouldn't be gone long, and I needed a good head start.

I got up out of my chair and went over to the window. I eased down on all fours and peeped out the corner of the window where there was a little crack of light between the curtains and the window frame. My daddy's Jeep was gone, but something told me he was trying to trick me. I crawled over to the other side of the window and peeped out there.

Sure enough, he'd backed the Jeep out of the parking place but was still waiting inside it a good piece down the parking lot.

I went over to the television, flipped it on, and then fell back on the bed. I couldn't even consider running off for a while. I had to come up with a plan first, and then I had to get up my nerve. But I would get away from my daddy, sooner or later. Once you've lived like a human being, you can't go back to living like a dog.

This sorry television didn't even have a flipper. I'd have to get up and turn the station myself. There wasn't anything on but talk shows and soap operas, anyway. One thing Miss Armistead and I had in common, we didn't see any sense in soap operas. All they did on those shows was to fuss and argue, lie and cheat. We couldn't figure how come anybody would want to see something like that, because we both had already seen enough of the bad stuff in real life ever to want to see it playacted for fun.

Finally, I just cut the TV off and tried to think some things out. One day my daddy would have to leave me by myself. He had to do something for a living, drive a truck or whatever. Once he wasn't worried about me taking off, that's when I'd make a run for it. I'd have to hitchhike, no way around that. Miss Armistead had already warned me a hundred times not to get into a car with somebody I didn't know, but she thought I was still going on six years old. She didn't have to worry. I wouldn't get in the car with a sweaty fat man, or a bunch of young niggers, or a Yankee-talking man, or a man wearing sunshades. I knew a few things.

The first thing I had to do, if I was aiming to leave right away, was to get out of this town. There were too many cars and big semis in towns like Memphis and Nashville, all weaving in and out of the lanes real fast, and everything was spread out so, how could a body tell if he was coming or going? I couldn't figure out why anybody would want to live in a big town in the first place, cars whizzing along at eighty miles an hour and nobody even waving at anybody else.

I was going to have to be careful with my money when

I hit the road. No telling how long it would take me to get back home. I couldn't be eating at McDonald's with just ten dollars to my name. I'd have to eat out of the grocery store—vienna sausage and crackers and stuff like that.

The doorknob wiggled. My daddy came in toting a big bag of Krystals and another big brown paper sack. I ate Krystals that time Miss Lumpkins took us to Memphis, and they were little but good. "Have at it, mutt," my daddy said, pitching the bag of Krystals at me.

In the bag were about a dozen Krystals and a bunch of french fries and ketchup. I didn't think I was hungry at first, but as soon as I ate one hamburger, I was ready for another one. Before I knew it, I'd eaten eight Krystals and most of the fries.

I ate right on the bedspread. Miss Armistead would've had a hissy fit if I'd done that at home, but this wasn't home. The trouble was, living with my daddy would make it mighty easy for me to get weaned away from all the good habits I'd learned at Miss Armistead's.

All this time my daddy had been sitting on the edge of the bed, drinking beer and watching me eat. He'd bought a whole case of beer, look like. "Hungry, wouldn't you, mutt?" he said and grinned. "Save me a couple of them burgers, now."

"Okay," I said. "I'm full, anyway."

"Naw, now, go on and eat what you want," he said, raking his knuckles across the top of my head. "Don't say I don't feed you."

He was trying to be good to me the best way he knew how, and I didn't want to cross him, so I ate one more hamburger. This time I really was full.

He popped open another beer and laid back on the bed. "Turn on the tube," he said, pulling both pillows loose from the bedspread and stuffing them under his head.

After I turned on the TV, I went back over in the corner and sat down. The news was on, but my daddy didn't seem to be listening. I reckon he just wanted the TV for company. He lay there propped up drinking beer, and as soon as he finished one can, he'd tell me to open him another one. I did what he told me, but I didn't want to. I didn't like the smell of beer. It smelled like somebody had belched in your face.

He drank six beers before staggering off the bed to the bathroom. He peed for the longest, then staggered back to the bed. I was fixing to open him another beer, but he shook his head. Before long he was snoring.

I'd sat in that old hard plastic chair for over an hour, just getting up long enough to open my daddy a beer.

I had the wiggles bad, being cooped up in this little biddy dark room that was too cold and smelled funny. I tried to sit still and think of other things, like my hideout and all the fun Tory and I could have if he didn't run off or get sent back to his mama.

Finally, though, I had to get out of that motel room or die. I couldn't stand it any longer. I tiptoed across that old nasty carpet and unlatched the bolt and slipped out into the hot sunshine.

It felt good. I was might near chilled to the bone. The sidewalk wasn't hot, because we were in a room under the balcony.

I walked around the corner and over to the other side where we first came in. There wasn't much to see or do. I decided to go look in the pool.

That asphalt was blazing hot. I couldn't walk flatfooted on the soles of my feet but for a second or two before I'd have to walk on my heels and then switch to my tiptoes. When I got over to the pool, I saw this green stuff that looked like plastic grass all way around the edges. I hopped over the fence and cooled my feet on that plastic grass. There wasn't a drop of water in the pool, and streaks of gray-looking stuff were all up and down the sides of it. All of a sudden, somebody hollered, "Get away from there!

Can't you read?"

I turned around and saw this young fellow about twenty something sticking his head out the office door. "I ain't hurting nothing," I said, and then he walked out the door and stood there on the porch with his hands on his hips staring at me.

"I said get away from there," he said, but he didn't holler as loud this time.

I crawled back over the fence and hightailed it back under the shade of the balcony. The young fellow shook his head and laughed at me. "Where's your shoes?" he said.

I could tell right away he was a smart aleck. He was wearing green shorts and a T-shirt and a red baseball cap turned around backwards. I wasn't aiming to fool with him, but I made sure I got my lick in. "I can, too, read," I said. "I'm not as backward as you. You've even got your cap on bassackwards."

I was fixing to make a dash back to the motel room, but he just laughed and took off the baseball cap. He combed his long blonde hair with his fingers and put the baseball cap on backwards again. "You can't read," he said, but he didn't really sound mean, just kind of like he was joking. "What do you read, the back of a cereal box?"

He stepped off the porch and started walking with his hands in his back pockets down to where I was standing under the balcony. I knew he couldn't hit me, or he'd be in big trouble with his boss. "I finished reading *A Member of the Wedding* by Mr. Carson McCullers about a week ago," I said.

"Is that a fact?" he said when he came up to me. He raised his eyebrows, poked out his lower lip, and nodded his head a few times, looking me over.

"You ain't never read that, have you?" I said, daring him to say he had.

"As a matter of fact, I have," he said and grinned. He had square white teeth with spaces between them. "I have to tell you, though, that Carson McCullers was a miss, not a mister."

"What?" I said. I didn't know what in the world he was talking about.

He gave me a play punch on the chin. "Carson McCullers was a woman, old buddy, not a man," he said. "What's your name?"

"Pat. Patrick Gunn," I said. I was beginning to like this fellow all right. He wasn't too bad a smart aleck, a little maybe. He was right funny, too, letting on like Carson McCullers was a woman. Women can't be named Carson, and he knew that as well as I did.

"Geoffrey Herring," he said, and he stuck out his hand for me to shake. I shook hands with him, and then he said, "Want a Coke or something?"

I was dry as a bone after eating all those Krystals and french fries, and I won't drink water. "Yeah," I said, and he motioned with his head for me to follow him back up to the office.

Inside the office was this long desk and a few chairs scattered around and a bunch of papers framed on the wall. He went over behind the counter and got a drink in a can out of this little refrigerator setting on a table with a coffee pot and some other stuff. He came from around behind the counter and gave me the can, and then we sat across the room from each other in the chairs out front. The drink was a Sprite, and it was good and cold. "I appreciate it," I said.

This Geoffrey fellow threw his legs up over the arm of his chair. "You're welcome, bud," he said. "You on vacation?"

I choked a little on the Sprite, because I wasn't counting on him asking personal questions. This fellow seemed like somebody who might help me, but I couldn't tell him my daddy had kidnapped me. He might want to call the police, and knowing my daddy, somebody would end up getting hurt with that switchblade knife, maybe this fellow.

He looked like a nice city boy, and he didn't know how mean people like my daddy could be. But I reckon the main reason I wasn't going to tell him anything was because I didn't want him to know how sorry my daddy was. "Uh-huh," I said. "We're on vacation all right."

"Where y'all from?" he said, yawning and then taking off his cap again to comb his hair.

I knew he wasn't trying to be nosy. He was just passing the time of day, but he was making me mighty nervous. "We're from Broad. . . Memphis," I said.

He looked at me funny, kind of frowning and smiling at the same time. "Broad Memphis?" he said. "Where's that?"

"Memphis," I said, and right then my daddy walked through the door.

I could smell beer on him clear over to where I was sitting. He was weaving a little as he stood there, his eyes looking like two red razor slits. He looked at Geoffrey and then at me. He motioned with his head back over his shoulder, and I got up fast. "May I help you, sir?" Geoffrey asked and got up, too.

My daddy never answered him. He turned around and grabbed me by the nape of my neck as I passed by. My drink splashed out on my feet and on my daddy's new boots, but he never broke stride as he guided me out the door fast and down the steps and under the long balcony. As we were rounding the corner, I saw Geoffrey standing on the steps watching us, but he didn't offer to help me. I didn't much blame him, though.

My daddy held me by the neck even as he was unlocking the door, but once we were inside the room, he slung me as hard as he could. My daddy was a strong man, if you're talking about muscles. I flew across the room and turned a flip right over the bed and landed flat on my back on the other side. I wasn't really hurt, but the breath was knocked out of me for a second. "What the hell were you doing?"

my daddy hollered. He stood over me and poked my ribs with his pointed toe.

"Nothing," I said. "I wouldn't doing nothing."

I saw him draw back his foot, so I tried to roll out of his way, but his toe caught me right in the crack of my butt.

It hurt so bad I couldn't help crying. "I got damn tired in here with nothing to do!" I hollered up at him, and I braced myself for another kick, but it never came.

"Why didn't you tell me that before you slipped off, you little sneaky asshole?" he said, letting on like I was lying to him, but he didn't seem hardly as mad now.

"You were asleep, and I knew better than to wake you up," I said. I grabbed hold of the bed and pulled myself up. My backside felt like it was split plumb in two. I sat on the bed and tried not to move so it wouldn't hurt so bad. My daddy hadn't moved, and I knew he might fly into me again, but he looked like he'd done got over most of his mad spell. He rubbed his hand over his flattop and then his face like he was studying about something.

Directly, he cut his eyes in the direction of the office. "What did you tell pretty boy up yonder?" he said. "You didn't tell him anything about our little trip this morning, did you?"

He was watching me like a hawk to see if I was lying. "Naw," I said, "honest I didn't. He asked me if I was on vacation, and I told him I was, and then he asked me where I was from, and I said Memphis."

My daddy had his head cocked to one side and was running his tongue over his teeth. Finally, he nodded and said, "All right, mutt. But don't ever let me catch you trying to slip off from me."

I got up and rubbed my hind end. "I ain't trying to slip off," I said. "I don't have any money, and I don't have any shoes. How am I going to slip off anywhere?"

He grinned then and turned around and went back into the bathroom. "Ain't no need of you ever trying to slip off," he hollered to me as he was peeing. "I'll get you sooner or later. I've done showed you that."

He came back to the bed, flopped down, and popped open another beer.

I went into the bathroom and closed the door. I stripped off naked and looked myself over. My left hip looked like I'd been sliding on pavement, it was so skinned up, and my shoulder had a big purple bruise. There was a mirror over the sink, and I turned around and tried to look over my shoulder at my hind end. It was right embarrassing, but I needed to see it. It was red looking, but that was all. No harm done.

I took a hot shower and used two towels to dry on. I got the bathroom all steamed up and couldn't see to fix my hair. I didn't have a comb, anyway, so I just brushed it straight down on my forehead and let it go. I put my clothes on and went back out.

My daddy was still lying on the bed drinking beer. I sacked up the cold hamburgers and put them over on top of the television. Then I stretched out on the bed as far away as I could from my daddy and turned my back.

I lay real still like I was resting, and directly I heard him get up and turn on the TV. He went back into the bathroom, and then I turned over and played like I was asleep.

After my daddy came out of the bathroom this time, he went over to the window and peeped out behind the curtains. He stood there looking out a long time and then came back and sat on the bed with his back to me.

He picked up the phone and dialed out. When I saw he was fixing to turn around, I closed my eyes. Somebody answered on the other end, because he said, "I ain't got it yet." He listened for a minute and said, "Hell, yes, I will. Tomorrow," and slammed down the receiver.

I grunted like I was coming out of sleep and turned back over. I heard the weather announcer saying something about a cold front hitting a warm front and there was going to be rain tomorrow.

I lay still and listened to the TV. Granny Gunn used to tell me how in the old days there wasn't any TV, and people listened to radio, only you couldn't listen to it all the time like people did TV, because the radios ran on batteries. There wasn't any electricity back in those days, either, so people saved their batteries for Saturday night when the Grand Ole Opry came on. She told me a lot of stuff about the old days, even about having my daddy without a husband. Her mama and daddy ran her off when they found out she was expecting, so she had to go live with these people up the road and keep house for them. Granny Gunn said she had a secondhand piano at her mama and daddy's that she'd paid for by hoeing cotton, but when she went back home after it, they wouldn't let her have it. She sicced the law on them, though, and got her piano.

I didn't have much use for the law, myself. When Jessie and I used to hang around Jiffy Mart, they'd come in there all the time, strutting around with their .357s strapped around their big bellies and acting like they were tough stuff. One time I was wearing my Metallica T-shirt, and one of them cornered me outside and asked me if I was a devil worshipper and killed cats and stuff. That was old Bobby Joe Brown, and he was just trash himself, a big lardbutt who couldn't keep a job at the factories in town because he was so durn trifling. I told him, I said, "That's for me to know and for you to find out," and he said, "What are you fixing to do now, punk, put me on your Satanist hit list?"

And one time Chigger's mama got picked up because she was drunk at the Econ-O-Wash and broke the glass door in one of the dryers, and they hit her four or five times hard in the head with a blackjack. I was sitting on the sidewalk outside Jiffy Mart and saw every bit of it. They knew who they could beat on, and they always beat on people from the trailer park.

It made me durn mad to think about the law, but when

you let your mind wander like a stray dog, it brings home a lot of stuff.

All this time my daddy sat on the edge of the bed, drinking beer and smoking cigarettes. He'd drink one beer after another, crushing the empty cans and dropping them on the floor. After three or four, he'd get up and go pee.

I knew he was getting real drunk, because once he ran into the bathroom door and gave it a hard kick. I was so nervous I was shaking. It was cold in the room, too. I didn't try to get under the cover, though. I knew my best bet was just to lie still until he passed out, and then everything would be all right.

About seven o'clock he lay down on the bed and said something to me I couldn't understand. He reached over and shook me some, but I lay still, playing like I was sound asleep. In a minute, he was dead to the world. His snoring sounded like a woodpecker tapping on an ironwood tree.

I eased up off the bed and stretched. I was stiff as a board after lying there so long in one spot trying not to move. My daddy was all sprawled out on the bed with his mouth wide open. One of his new boots had a dark spot across the instep where my drink had splashed on it, and his Wrangler jeans looked like he'd been wallowing around under an old car all day in them. His black T-shirt had hiked up around his hairy navel, and slobber was bubbling out of one corner of his mouth. He stunk. The whole room stunk. It smelled sour and stale and nasty. A thin blue cloud of cigarette smoke hung up around the ceiling. I counted twelve beer cans he'd twisted up and slung on the floor, and there were three more in the trash can over by the TV.

I knew better than to leave the room again, so I sat down in the orange chair and watched TV. I didn't even change the channel, because I didn't want to do anything that might wake him up. I watched these two movies, *Grease* and *Hiding Out*. I'd already seen the first one forty-eleven times, but I hadn't seen the second one. It was about this boy who played like he was still in high school so these bad guys couldn't kill him. I didn't see the end of it, because I went to sleep sitting right there in the chair, and when I woke up, the TV was snowing. I didn't have to see the end of the movie to know that the bad guys didn't get the boy. It wasn't like real life.

I slipped out my watch and saw that it was after twelve-thirty. I thought about sleeping on the floor, but that old red carpet felt so nasty on my bare feet, I just didn't think I could do it. So I tiptoed over to the bed and eased down on it with my hind end first. I put one leg up and then the other one, being careful not to make the springs squeak. Then I lay back real slow. I sure didn't want to sleep beside my daddy, but I was so worn out, before long I didn't care one way or the other.

CHAPTER XV

I Make My Getaway

At first I thought it was the TV I heard, but even in my sleep I realized that all the stations were off the air, and somebody was saying, "Judy, Judy." Then I figured I was dreaming and went right on sleeping.

My mama's name was Judy. When I was a little biddy boy, we used to take a nap every day on this green plastic couch that sagged in the middle. My mama would wrap her arms around the front of me, and we'd sleep like spoons. In the summertime my face would be hot and damp when I woke up, and my mama would take a cool washrag and wash it off. I was dreaming that I was little again, and she was holding me against her. I'd had this dream lots of times since she'd got killed. The dream was so real that I could feel her heart beating against my back, and I felt safe and warm. I snuggled closer to her, but I knew somehow that this was just a dream, and I didn't want to wake up.

I did wake up, though, because my daddy's rough whiskers were rubbing against my neck, and he was about to squeeze me in two.

I tried to wiggle loose, but he just squeezed me that much harder. "No, Judy, no," he said, slobbering on my neck and back, and I knew then he was dreaming, too.

I didn't even think. I elbowed him in the ribs as hard as I could and commenced kicking. "It's me!" I hollered, shaking and wiggling and kicking. "Wake up, it's me! It ain't her!"

All of a sudden, he got dead still, and I quit struggling. He took his arm off me and turned over. In a second he was snoring, but it didn't sound like real snoring to me. I reckon he was embarrassed because I caught him dreaming about my mama, and he'd thought I was her.

I got out of bed and sat in the orange chair. I knew he didn't intend to bother me anymore, but I couldn't stand the thoughts of him being that close to me. It made chillbumps all over me, thinking about him touching me, about him rubbing his whiskers against my neck and slobbering on my skin.

Finally, he went back to sleep for real. I tiptoed over to the window and peeped out. The sky was the color of a peach that was about ripe. Some old humpbacked man wearing white shorts and socks pulled all way up to his knees was jogging real slow around the parking lot. Cars were already rushing down the streets both ways. Way off in the distance I could see a big square building that looked like it was covered with some kind of copper plates, and another tall skinny building that had a big L and C on the top of it. I was so lonesome I could hardly stand it, being stuck in a big old town and not knowing the first thing about how to get out.

When I turned around from the window, my daddy was awake looking at me. Overnight, his beard had grown out bristly and black, and his eyes were glassy. His lips were coated with pasty looking stuff, and I turned my head so I wouldn't have to face him and went into the bathroom.

After I'd peed, I got me a washrag down off the rack and washed my face and neck and back. I was a sight. My hair was sticking up on one side where I'd slept on it wet, and my eyes were bloodshot from not getting enough sleep. I wet my hair down some to try to make it lie down, but it just sprung back up. I looked like Buckwheat, and my clothes were all dirty and nasty from rolling around in that old van and being slung across the room. I wanted to cry, but I knew that wouldn't do any good.

When I came out of the bathroom, my daddy was sitting on the side of the bed looking down at the floor, but when he heard me, he looked over and said, "What's up, mutt?"

"Nothing," I said and went back to the chair.

He rubbed both hands over his face and head. "Oh, God," he moaned. "I feel like somebody's done beat hell out of me."

The first time he tried to get up from the bed, he fell back down. The second time he was able to stand, but he was weaving like a sapling in a wind storm. He lurched over toward the bathroom and held on to the door facing a minute before he went on in. "Oh, God A'mighty!" he hollered, and I heard him drop hard down on his knees. He puked his guts out, and it about made me sick, listening to him heaving and coughing and splattering in the toilet, and smelling it, too.

He grunted like a big boar hog when he finally got up off the floor and began to stumble around in there like he was still drunk. The toilet flushed, and then the lid banged down. I jumped about a foot out of my chair.

The shower cut on, and I heard him bumping heavy and wet against the stall. Directly, he came out naked, drying his hair and face in a towel. He didn't know any better than to come out naked in front of me, or maybe he thought that was smart or something. I tried not to look toward him. "Can I go get something to eat?" I said. "I'm hungry."

"Hungry?" he said, like I wasn't supposed to get hungry. "Damn, mutt, you eat enough last night to kill you."

I never answered, and he went on back into the bathroom. I heard him washing out his mouth and gargling. When he came out this time, he had his clothes on except for his boots. He went over to the side of the bed and commenced putting them on. He smelled better, but he didn't look much better. He looked like a bum with his beard all grown out, and his T-shirt was sticking to his back where he hadn't dried good.

All of a sudden, he broke wind and laughed. He got up from the bed and walked over to the door. "You-wee," he said, laughing still and showing his missing teeth. "I had to walk away from that one."

I kind of grinned so he wouldn't start on me, but I didn't think being gross and ignorant was one bit funny.

He opened the door. "I got to go see a man about a dog," he said. "I ain't going to be gone long. When I get back, we'll go get us something to eat."

I got out of the chair and stretched. "Okay," I said. "I'm fixing to take a shower while you're gone."

"Good deal, Lucille," he said, but when I started to walk into the bathroom, he motioned me over to where he was. I didn't know what he was aiming to do, but he didn't seem mad. "Hey, sport, I didn't mean to roll over on you last night," he said. He lifted up my chin with the crook of his finger, but I couldn't look him in the eye. "I didn't mean to bother you. Hear?"

"You didn't bother me," I said, and then he turned me loose.

He nodded two or three times and looked down at his boots. "All right," he said. "Go on and get your shower and I'll be back after while."

I nodded and went on into the bathroom. As I turned on the shower, I heard the door close.

I went back to the window and watched him leave. For some reason I didn't think he would try to trick me this time. He took off in a big hurry, his tires squealing in a cloud of blue smoke, and just as soon as I saw his Jeep whip around the corner, I left the shower running and took off myself.

As I eased around the corner of the motel, I was scared and excited at the same time.

My daddy's Jeep was nowhere in sight. I knew he would half kill me if he caught me trying to run away, but he was fixing to have a hard time finding me in a big place like Nashville.

I ran across the parking lot and out to the street. I didn't see which way my daddy had gone. All I knew, I was getting away from this place. Cars were whizzing by so fast I could feel the wind from them picking at my shirttail like fingers. There were lots of businesses on this stretch of highway, nightclubs and motels and places to eat. I was so scared that I didn't even think about being barefooted. I stayed over on the shoulder of the road and ran as fast as I could, and when I got winded, I stopped and rested for a little spell and then took off again. Cars kept blowing at me, but I never paid any attention to them or to my feet, either. I was running over sharp gravel and bottle caps and no telling what all, but I didn't feel a thing.

I ran a long ways, probably three miles. In the middle of this four lane I was running down was a bunch of trees. I saw a doughnut shop over on the other side of the street, and when the traffic let up for a second, I darted to the trees, and then as soon as I got a chance, I hightailed it the other side. I was fixing to get me a bite to eat. I'd already decided that I was home free now, anyway. If my daddy happened to find me in an eating place, all I had to do was kick up a big fuss and tell the people there that I'd been kidnapped. The only thing was, I didn't want to have to fool with the law if I didn't have to. I could get back to Broad Plains by myself sooner or later without having my face on the six o'clock news. Miss Armistead was worried sick by now, anyway, and I didn't want her to see me pulling up in front of her house in a police car.

I stepped upon this little concrete porch and had my hand on the door ready to open it when this man came out.

He had his head turned and was still talking to this other man sitting on a red stool in front of the counter, so he didn't see me and might near knocked me off the porch. I stumbled back a little but didn't fall because I was holding on to the door handle. "Whoa, hoss!" the man said when he saw me. He grabbed me by the arm to steady me.

He was a skinny, wrinkled man wearing white overalls and a white cap, "You all right, son?" he said, turning me loose. "I didn't mean to knock you down."

Right then I saw a good chance. This man didn't look like he would harm anybody. He wasn't much bigger than I was, anyway. I put on my best Sunday manners, trying to sound like Miss Armistead, and said, "That's quite all right, sir. No harm done. And where might you be headed this fine morning?"

I guess I laid it on too thick, because the man got rock still for a second, and then he hunkered down a little and stared at me like he was trying to look up under my eyeballs. "You on drugs, boy?" he said right hateful, sniffling and running his finger under his nose.

"Nosir," I said. "I'm just tired from running."

He took a step closer, and I couldn't move without falling off the porch. "Who are you running from?" he said. "What are you doing out this early, anyhow?"

I saw then I'd done run into trouble. I stood up straight and let on like I'd been highly insulted. "I'm not running from anybody," I said. "I was trying to catch my daddy's Jeep was all. We're visiting from Memphis, and he ran off to my grandmother's house without me while I was in the shower at the motel. He didn't know I was wanting to with him. My grandma's a Episcopalian, and she's got her own seat in church with her name on it."

I'd never had too much practice at lying, but seem like I had the gift. Take a little truth and kind of blow it up like a balloon, that's all there was to it. That lie rolled off my tongue so smooth that I halfway believed it myself, and so did the wrinkled fellow. "Well, why didn't you say you needed a ride in the first place, boy, instead of beating around the bush?" he said, pulling on his ear like he was embarrassed. Then he put his hand in the small of my back and guided me toward his truck. "Whereabouts does your grandmama live? Now I can't go way over yonder in East Nashville. I got to get to work."

The trouble with me, I can't always think on my feet. "Uh," I stuttered, "uh, I, uh…"

"You got speech troubles, son?" he said, reaching in the bib of his overalls for his keys. "You tongue-tied?"

The red plastic letters on the side of his truck read, "S & P Painters, Inc. Frankli, TN." "Frankli," I said. "I'll get it out in a minute."

He started to put the key in the door lock but stopped to study me again. His wrinkled face put me in mind of one of Granny Gunn's apples she used to dry under screen wire on the roof top. "You mean Franklin?" he said, talking real loud and cocking his head sideways. "Frank-lin? Franklin, Tennessee?"

All of a sudden, I noticed dried glue on the truck door where a letter had fallen off. My heart was thumping like the native drums in a Tarzan movie. "Yeah," I said. "Franklin. That's what I meant. Like you say, I got a speech pediment."

"Okay," he said, unlocking the door and motioning for me to hop in and scoot across the seat. "That's just where I'm headed. I had to pick up some paint this morning. I got to paint the trim on two new houses if it don't rain."

I got in the truck, and we took off.

I was hungry, but I could wait to eat. I didn't know the first thing about the streets of Nashville, but after we drove a little piece and made two or three turns, we were back on the interstate. Before long I saw we were on Interstate 65 heading south. I needed to go west, but that was all right for now. I remembered how Tory and I cut out the entrance to our hideout, kind of in a zigzag pattern, so we could fool people. If my daddy started looking for me, he'd probably think I'd be heading west. I'd fool him this time.

Directly, it started to rain, and I mean sure enough rain. The wind blew so hard that the trees looked like women with big hairdos shaking their heads back and forth, back and forth. All the cars had to slow down on the interstate. Big long sprays of water flew back from the rear wheels of the cars and trucks. "This is what you call a rain," the wrinkled man said. His windshield wipers were thumping as fast as they would go. Our tires sounded like a big skillet of bacon sizzling on the stove. "Won't be no painting today," he said. "This has done set in."

"Yessir," I said. "This reminds me of the time we had us that big flood in Broad Plains."

He leaned closer to the steering wheel and wiped off the inside of the windshield with his palm. "What?" he said. "I don't believe I understood you."

"I said it reminds me of that big flood we had…" Right then I caught myself. I didn't know if I'd given myself away or not. He hadn't seemed to be listening, and he didn't act like he'd caught on to anything. "That flood we had in Memphis," I said.

"Oh, yeah," he said, still wiping the fog off the windshield. "That was a doozy, that one was."

After a while, the rain let up some, and we both cracked our windows a little so the windshield would stop fogging up. "I don't believe I heard your name, son," he said.

"Patrick Armistead."

He grinned sideways and winked. "You sure it ain't Patty or something like that?" he said.

I didn't like hearing grown people making sex jokes. It didn't seem right. "I'm not a girl," I said. "And I'm not a boy who wants to be a girl, either." I told him that in a hurry, just in case he had some ideas.

"Ah, now, don't go acting like an old sore-tail cat, boy. I was just teasing you a little," he said, sticking his tongue under his lower lip like he had a big cud of tobacco there or something.

He acted about halfway miffed at me, but I didn't care. We rode along for four or five miles, neither one of us saying anything. Every once in a while I'd glance over to my left and see his eyes in the mirror. I wasn't sure what he meant about my name. I started thinking about *Unsolved Mysteries* on TV and got a little uneasy. People were always disappearing on that show because they got in the wrong vehicle with the wrong person. Seem like lately every time I thought I was smart about something, I found out later that I was as dumb as a rail fence.

Finally, I said, "I don't believe I heard your name, either."

"Porter," he said and switched on the radio.

"Porter Wagoner, I guess," I said. I figured he was giving me one those fake names, anyway, so I'd just show him a thing or two.

He threw back his head and laughed. He had false teeth like Granny Gunn had. "You're a real cutup, boy," he said. "A.Z. Porter, that's my name, and painting's my game."

"I've never heard of anybody named A.Z.," I said. "What does A.Z. stand for?"

He scratched the back of his neck and grinned. "It don't stand for nothing. I weighed fourteen pounds when I was born, and my mama told my daddy that I was going to be the first and last youngun she ever birthed. So my daddy named me for the first and last letter of the alphabet." He winked again. "They had nine more after me."

He didn't seem to be lying, but I figured he might be as good a liar as I was.

Country music kept fading in and out on the crackling radio. Over toward Franklin a long streak of lightning

made chicken tracks across the purple sky. It was still driz-
zling, but the sun came out hot and bright. The smell of
ozone tickled my nose. "Sun's shining, so it'll rain again this
time tomorrow," he said.

I'd heard Granny Gunn say the same thing a hundred
times, so I got to feeling that he was all right. You don't
have to worry about many country people, anyway. "We're
not far from Franklin, are we?" I said.

A.Z. cut off the radio and glanced over at me. "About
five miles," he said. "Whereabouts does your grandmama
live in Franklin?"

I began to get squirrely again. "I don't remember the
street," I said, "but her house is just a little piece off the
square."

"Uh-huh," he said, looking right keen at me. "Off of
the square in Franklin, or Broad Plains, or Memphis?
Which one is it, son?"

"Franklin," I said, my voice hitting a high note. I
sounded like somebody who was scared to death because he
knew he'd done been caught up with. "Just like I told you.
Franklin."

"Wellsir," he said, "then that's where I'm fixing to take
you, to the police station in Franklin." He looked at me and
nodded. "Now how about that?"

That made me mad, him acting like a durn smart aleck.
"How come you want to be so low-down mean?" I said. "I
ain't done one blessed thing to you, and I ain't done nothing to have to go to the police, either."

He looked straight ahead and drove with both hands
on the steering wheel. "Maybe you have, maybe you ain't,"
he said. "You're not telling the truth, nohow."

The truck was moving too fast for me to jump out, or
I'd have jumped in a second. For a while I sat there studying, trying to figure out how I was going to get out of this
fix.

After I thought about the situation some, I decided that

I might as well tell A.Z. the truth. He was aiming to take me to the police station, anyway, so there wasn't any use in lying. "Okay, Mr. A.Z., or whatever your real name is," I said. "I live in Broad Plains with my foster mother, Miss Armistead. Yesterday when I was coming home from the public library, my daddy and one of his old sorry friends kidnapped me right off the sidewalk on Cow Street. He took me to this motel, and I slipped off this morning right before I ran into you."

A.Z. didn't say anything for a long time, just sat there looking straight ahead and working his jaws. "How come you live with somebody else other than your own folks?" he said finally.

"My mama ran off with this man and got killed in a car wreck," I said, looking down at my hands. "My daddy's so mean when he's drunk can't anybody live with him."

A.Z. stuck his tongue under his lower lip again and shook his head like he could hardly believe what I'd told him. "I ain't got no respect for a man who runs over his kids," he said directly. "You want me to take you home?"

"I couldn't ask you to do that," I said. "It's too far."

He reached over and grabbed my arm above the elbow and shook it. "You ain't lying now, are you?" he said, raising one eyebrow as he cut his eyes around at me.

"Nawsir."

He turned me loose. "Okay, then," he said. "I can't work today, anyway, and I ain't got no trains to catch. If I go home, the old lady'll have a job for me before I can set down."

"I'm much obliged," I said. "Miss Armistead will make it up to you."

"Ain't no need of that," he said. "You had anything to eat today?"

"Nawsir," I said, "but I've got ten dollars if you'll stop somewhere."

"I tell you what, partner," he said, reaching over and

smacking me on the knee. "We'll hit the drive-through at Hardee's, and then we'll head over to I-40 and run you home. How about that?"

I felt like I had wings and could fly. "That's the best news I've heard in a long time," I said, and I turned my head so he wouldn't see the tears in my eyes.

I ate a sausage biscuit, a ham biscuit, a cinnamon and raisin biscuit, and an order of hash browns. I drank a large orange juice, but A.Z. just had coffee. I was full enough to burst, but I was still as light as a feather all over.

After we set out on Highway 96, the rain started again, and by the time we got to the interstate, it was coming down in long flapping sheets. Water was hitting the windshield of the truck like somebody was throwing it at us from a bucket, and finally A.Z. pulled over on the side of the road to wait for the rain to let up a little bit.

Lots of others cars and trucks were pulled over, too. The windshield got all fogged up again as we sat there on the side of the road. It was kind of nice sitting in the cab of the truck, listening to the rain thumping hard on the roof, knowing I was safe and headed home. It put me in mind of the rainy nights I spent with Granny Gunn, lying in a feather bed upstairs with old quilts pulled up to my neck, listening to the rain tapping on her tin roof.

After a while the cab got stuffy, so we cracked the windows a little bit to let in some fresh air. We talked about first one thing and then another, and somehow we got on the subject of school. A.Z. said he liked geography, but he didn't like English or arithmetic. I told him I didn't like a single thing about school except three o'clock. Then he asked me, he said, "You ever get a whipping in school, Patrick?"

I told him I'd had lots of whippings in school, but really I hadn't, and he said he had, too. Then he told me about his brother Floyd who lived in Elkhart, Indiana. He said, "I bet you ain't never heard one to top this. Floyd got a whipping at school when he was thirty-one year old."

He must have been mighty slow in his books, I told him, to still be in school when he was thirty-one. I thought maybe A.Z. was just pulling my leg, so I went right along with him. "Wellsir," he said, "Floyd wanted to go to college on the G.I. Bill, but he never had finished high school, so he went back. One day he got to cutting up with a bunch of high school boys on the school bus, and the school bus driver turned them in to the principal. The principal whipped all the high school boys, but when he got to Floyd, Floyd said, 'Ah, but naw, you can't whip me, I'm a grown man with a wife and two younguns.' The principal said, 'Okeydoke, Floyd, then I'll have to expel you.' Wellsir, if Floyd got expelled, goodbye G.I. Bill, so he had to let the principal whip him. Now what do you think about that?"

"Must have been awfully embarrassing," I said. "Is that really true, or did you just make it up?"

A.Z. laughed. "Naw, it's true," he said. "I can't make up tales like some folks. Speaking of which, mister..." he pointed his finger at me..."I'm going to be one upset man if we get to Broad Plains and there ain't no Miss Arm and Hammer."

He laughed again, but I knew he was serious. "You'll see," I said. "You better not call Miss Armistead anything but her right name, though. She'll clean your plow."

"Sounds like a right tough old bird," he said, cranking up the truck and pulling back on the interstate. It was still raining pretty hard, but now at least we could see the highway. The interstate looked like a long curving river, and looking back through the side mirror, I saw our tires splashing up water like paddle wheels.

"Miss Armistead's strict in some ways, and in some ways she's not strict atall," I told him. "I remember one time she took me to see this movie called A Room With A View, and it had naked people in it, but she didn't let on like

211

she thought a thing in the world about it. But now she makes me brush my teeth with baking soda and peroxide every morning and every night, if you can believe that."

"I don't have to worry none about that," A.Z. said, all of a sudden poking out his pink upper plate and then sucking it back in. It was funny, and for some reason I thought of Tory. He would've fainted and fallen out if he'd seen somebody's false teeth. Granny Gunn always kept hers on the arm of the couch while she was watching TV. Tory didn't know much about real folks, though. I could just picture him with Chigger.

"Miss Armistead couldn't care less how much you eat, though," I told A.Z. "I can eat the house down, and she won't say the first word. She's sure not like my daddy. Used to if I ate three slices of loafbread, he'd say, 'Better save some of that for tomorrow, mutt.' And Miss Armistead doesn't care how much money she spends, either. She's got lots of that, enough to burn a wet mule."

"Widow woman, is she?" A.Z. said and made his eyebrows raise up and down.

"She's not studying menfolks, if that's what you mean. She wouldn't have a regular man, anyway. Her husband was a big lawyer and judge, and he could paint pictures and write poems and play the piano."

"I can turn my eyelids inside out," A.Z. said and showed me.

"I wouldn't do that in front of Miss Armistead," I told him. "Besides, it might be a good idea to keep your eyes on the road in case we hydroplane or something."

"You ain't a bit of fun," A.Z. said, but he was just teasing.

Sometimes the rain poured down, and then we would come to long stretches where the interstate was dry as a bone. Sometimes we talked for a long spell, and then neither one of us would say a word for ten miles. I wondered where all the cars and trucks were headed, and what the people in them were like. They mostly looked just like people I'd seen everywhere, but I didn't know any of them and they didn't know me. They got out of bed every morning just like I did, and they probably went to the bathroom first thing and then ate breakfast and brushed their teeth. They were about like me, had to be, but they lived their whole lives somewhere else. I never would know them, and they never would know me. They would die someday, and I wouldn't even know anything about it, and I would die, and they wouldn't know anything about me, either. You were only important to people who knew you, and sometimes not even to them, because humans were about as common and ordinary as wrens. It was a shame, when you thought about it, that everybody couldn't know everybody else, that everything you'd felt and heard and thought and went through didn't matter to other folks. Seem to me like there ought to be some way to get acquainted with everybody.

We got off the interstate at Jackson and headed south on Highway 18. It was just a little past dinnertime when we finally rolled into Broad Plains, but I felt like I'd traveled a million miles.

CHAPTER XVI

I Hear Some Surprising News

"This it?" A.Z. said when we pulled into Miss Armistead's driveway.

"This is it, " I said. I rolled out of the truck and stretched. "Come on in and meet Miss Armistead."

I was halfway up the sidewalk before I realized that A.Z. wasn't behind me. He'd got out of the truck and was standing there beside it with his hand on the front fender. He was looking over Miss Armistead's house. I could've told him it didn't need painting. Miss Armistead kept people fixing stuff around the house six days a week.

I motioned with my hand for him to follow me. "Come on," I said. "She won't bite you. And she won't look down her nose at you, either, unless you act like a fool, and I know you won't do that."

A.Z. took off his white cap, smoothed down his thin red hair, and then put his cap back on. He was still eyeing the house when he said, "I better not. I need to be getting on back."

I saw that A.Z. wasn't fixing to come in. He was kind of backward, like I used to be. I walked back down to where he was standing and emptied my pockets. I had a dollar and some change. "Here," I said, rolling it all up in a wad and offering it to him. "This ain't near enough, but Miss Armistead will send you plenty more if you'll let us know where to send it."

He pooched out his lips like he smelled something bad and shook his head. "I ain't taking that, now," he said, looking off to one side. "You get on in the house and let that old lady know you're all right."

I don't know what came over me, I reckon because I'd lived with Miss Armistead for so long, but durn if I didn't haul off and hug A.Z. At first he kind of jumped back a little like he'd been burned, but then he patted me a couple of times on the back and said, "That's all right, buddy, now you go on."

I looked around to see if Miss Armistead had heard us drive up and had come out on the porch. She hadn't. When I turned back around, A.Z. had already opened the truck door and was getting in. He backed out of the driveway fast, and I waved at him, but a tree came between us, so I couldn't tell if he waved back or not. It didn't matter, anyway. He was like one of those people I saw on the interstate. I wouldn't ever see him again, and he wouldn't ever see me.

I jumped upon the porch and tried to open the door, but it was locked. I didn't have my door key on me, so I rang the doorbell. I listened for Miss Armistead's footsteps, but I didn't hear anything. I rang the doorbell again, and this time I still didn't hear her coming to the door, so I went around to the back door. I was always forgetting my door key, so Miss Armistead started leaving one on top of the meter box if she had to go somewhere when I wasn't home. I stood on my tiptoes and reached way back and then felt all around on top of the meter box, but there was no key.

I kicked the back door, forgetting that I didn't have on any shoes, and I cursed for the first time in a long time.

I went through the hedge to Tory's grandmother's house and rang the doorbell. Nobody answered there, either, so I rang again. Durn if anybody was at home there, so I came back to Miss Armistead's and sat down in the porch swing. I figured she'd be back before long, and boy would she be surprised.

I waited and waited. I still had my watch in my pocket, and I kept taking it out every few minutes to check the time. Finally, I'd already waited two hours.

I was tired and hungry and aggravated. I didn't know what in the world had happened to everybody. I'd been hauled all over kingdom come, and then when I'd finally made it back home, I couldn't even get inside my own house. It beat all.

I got up out of the swing and went around back again. I felt like a fool doing it, but I felt on top of the meter box again to see if I'd somehow overlooked the key, but I hadn't.

I knew it wasn't any use, but then I tried the windows. Most windows in old houses are painted so many times that you can't raise one to save your life, but not the ones at Miss Armistead's. Her windows were scraped to bare wood before they were painted, and you could lift one up with your little finger if it wasn't locked. Her windows were hooked up to pulleys and weights inside the walls. Anyway, I tried first one and then another, but I didn't have any luck. Miss Armistead didn't ever forget to lock a door or latch a window. She ought to have worked at the jail.

I was about ready to go back and sit in the swing again when I remembered the window out back that let light in this narrow hall that led into the kitchen. It wasn't a regular window. It had eight sides and was about the size of a number two tub. I didn't think it let up or down, but it was the only one I hadn't tried. It was pretty high up off the ground, so I drug a garbage can over and stood on top of that. I tried to push this window up, but it wouldn't go, so then I figured it was either locked or not meant to be raised in the first place. All of a sudden, though, my legs got kind of shaky, and somehow I happened to push in on the window. It shot back and caught on a little brass latch kind of like the ones that hold up the lid of a cedar chest.

I wiggled through the window as far as my waist, and then I saw that I was going to have to drop about four feet down to the floor. There wasn't a chair or table under the window I could grab hold of, so I just shoved off and fell head first. I slapped the floor with the palms of my hands, banged both my elbows hard against the wooden floor, and flopped over on my side. The fall knocked the breath out of me, but I wasn't really hurt. One of my elbows was bruised and ached down next to the bone, but that was about all.

I hollered for Miss Armistead, but I knew she wasn't home. I went into the kitchen and looked inside the refrigerator for something to eat. I was might near starved to death. I found a lot of leftover meat loaf and scalloped potatoes and lima beans. I scraped all of it into a big plate and stuck it in the microwave. While that was heating up, I got out a half gallon of milk and swigged right from the carton. Miss Armistead wouldn't care, because she didn't drink milk, anyway, except in coffee. It gave her discomfort, she said. On the kitchen counter was a glass plate covered with tinfoil. When I peeped under the foil, I saw that Miss Armistead had made me chocolate oatmeal cookies. Miss Armistead didn't like chocolate, either. The beeper went off on the microwave, and I got my plate out and ate right there on the counter. I ate cookies and meat loaf and everything all together.

I ate so much I felt like I was fixing to pop. I put my plate in the sink and went upstairs to my bathroom. I was nasty as a dog, so I stripped off and got into the shower. I lathered up good and rinsed off, and then I lathered up again and rinsed off again. I stayed in the shower about thirty minutes, just letting the water beat down on me.

I got out and dried off and brushed my teeth good. I was so tickled to be back home again I didn't know what to do. I felt like I'd been gone for a year instead of overnight.

I slung my wet towel and washrag and dirty clothes down the laundry chute. Then I put on some clean underwear and shorts and went downstairs. The house smelled kind of musty, like the public library when they first open it of a morning, and there was dust on the long dining room table. Usually Miss Armistead wouldn't leave the house unless everything was so-so, and I wondered where in the world she'd taken off to in such a big hurry. She'd never forgotten to leave me the key before. I opened the front door and got the mail. Miss Armistead hadn't even picked up last night's *Banner* or this morning's *Tennessean*. She always read the *Banner* before supper and the *Tennessean* before breakfast.

I was too tired to try and figure it all out. Miss Armistead would surely be home before dark, because she couldn't see to drive at night. I laid the newspapers and other mail on top of the mail table in the hall and went back upstairs. I was on the landing before I remembered that I had opened the front door and the window in the kitchen. I came back downstairs and closed both of them. I figured that my daddy wouldn't dare come back to Broad Plains soon, because he knew the law would be after him. I wasn't taking chances, though, because he didn't always have good sense when he was drinking.

I went back upstairs and pulled off the covers and flopped in bed. I hadn't slept much last night, and I was worn out from running away and then riding back home on the interstate. My room was cool and my sheets were clean and fresh. I had that heavy sleepy feeling you get when you know you can't stay awake any longer, and sleep feels as good as sitting down hungry in front of a table that's loaded with a bunch of good things to eat. I remember hearing a mockingbird gurgling in the top of the big oak tree outside my window, and then I was dead to the world.

I just meant to take a little nap. I didn't want to be sound asleep when Miss Armistead came in, because then I'd have to come downstairs and shock the living daylights out of her. I meant to be awake so I could meet her at the front door, or maybe I'd be sitting in the swing when she drove up in the driveway. But that wasn't the way things turned out.

I'd wake up and still be dog tired, so I'd decide to rest for maybe five more minutes. The next thing I knew, I'd slept two or three hours. One time I woke up and noticed that it was getting dark outside. I started to get up then, but I didn't hear anybody moving around downstairs, so I closed my eyes for a minute. The last time I woke up, it was pitch dark outside.

I sat up on the side of the bed and switched on the lamp. It was eleven-thirty! Now I was going to have to go downstairs and wake up Miss Armistead so she'd know I'd got back home. I figured she probably wasn't sleeping much, anyway, me being gone and all.

I turned on the upstairs hall light and the light over the landing so I could see to get downstairs. When I got to the newel post, I peeped down the hall straight through the dining room into the kitchen. Miss Armistead always left the light over the sink on at night. Sometimes she got up at night and made a cup of coffee and read when she couldn't sleep.

The light wasn't on. I knew then that something was wrong. Everything began to add up in my head. Miss Armistead hadn't picked up her mail. She wasn't in the house. Then I thought, *Maybe she is, too.* I thought of Granny Gunn and the home health care nurse finding her in front of the TV.

My heart commenced thumping in my chest like it was trying to get out. I walked down to her bedroom and knocked on the door, but nobody answered. I knocked again hard and hollered, "Miss Armistead, it's me, Patrick! Can I come in? It's me, Patrick!"

I got real still and listened. All I could hear was the ice maker in the refrigerator dropping a row of ice cubes into the pan.

I took a deep breath and eased open the door. I couldn't make out anything in the room but her big tall cannonball bed. Then I reached around the door facing and flipped on the light.

Her bed was still made up neat as a pin with her green and gold brocade bedspread that she said came from Italy. As far as I could tell, nothing had been touched in her bedroom.

I went from room to room looking for her, but she wasn't anywhere in the house. I didn't know what in the dickens was going on.

I got the flashlight out of the kitchen cabinet and went outside to the garage. The door was down and locked, and when I flashed the light through the window, I saw her old Lincoln was still where she'd left it.

When I turned around to go back inside the house, I noticed a blue light flashing on and off in the back of Miss Marcella's house. Tory was still in the den watching TV. Maybe he'd know what was going on.

I stepped through the hedge and tapped on the window. "Who's there?" I heard Tory say like he was afraid. It really wasn't funny, scaring somebody, but I couldn't help laughing.

"It's me, dumbass," I said, hunkering down and peeping in the window. I couldn't see hide nor hair of him.

All of a sudden, he stuck his white face in the window, and I jumped back, and he jumped back, too. I reckon he'd been standing over to one side of the window trying to see who I was.

I laughed again when I came to myself, but Tory wasn't cracking a smile. He looked like he'd just seen a ghost. I motioned for him to come to the door, and then I went back there.

Tory opened the door and unlatched the storm door, but he didn't offer to step aside to let me in. He was batting his eyes and looking paler than usual. I held the storm door open as I talked to him. At first I figured maybe Miss Marcella had told him not to be inviting me over because I was a bad influence on him.

"So you're back," he said, acting like he was still afraid of something. He wasn't wearing anything but his underwear, and his fingers were orange from eating Cheese Curls.

"Yeah," I said. "My daddy took me off, him and this other old dude, but I snuck away from him in Nashville and hitched a ride home. I'll tell you all about it later. Right now I've got to find Miss Armistead. Where is she, anyway?"

"You don't know, do you?" he said in his high voice. "I don't believe you really know."

"Of course I don't know," I said, getting right aggravated with him. "I told you my daddy took me off yesterday."

"Yeah, I know," he whispered, taking a step back.

"How do you know?" I said. "How come you're acting so durn weird?"

I took a step inside the house, and Tory took another step back. He was acting like I had head lice or something. "What's wrong?" I said. "Where's Miss Armistead?"

"Sick," he said, his voice sounding like it had got stuck down in his throat. "She's sick. She's in the hospital."

Every time I took a step toward Tory, he moved a step back. "What's wrong with you?" I said. "What's happened to Miss Armistead? How'd she get sick?"

Tory eased around this short flowery couch and stood behind it. "They think she's had a stroke, Gran says," he said. He looked back over his shoulder at the door leading into the den. "They think she got too upset when you turned up missing."

I began to get light-headed and felt like I was fixing to throw up. I put my hand down on top of this TV tray to steady myself, but it folded up and banged down on the tile. I swallowed hard two or three times, tasting bile, and sweat popped out on my forehead. "Don't make so much noise,"

Tory said. His fingers tapped on the back of the couch like he was typing. "Don't wake up Gran. You wouldn't do anything to hurt her, would you?"

Nothing was making any sense here. People died of strokes lots of times, and Miss Armistead might die on account of me. I hadn't brought her anything but bad luck from day one. Tory was acting plumb crazy when I needed him to explain things to me. "What in the hell are you talking about?" I said. "What's wrong with you?"

I backed back and grabbed hold of the door, because the room was beginning to spin. Tory was looking at me like something you pay a dollar to see at the county fair. "Now nothing personal, understand," he said. He came around from behind the couch a little ways. "But after what happened to your father, I just thought..."

"You thought what?" I said. I could feel something dark and shivery creeping up my back. "What about my daddy? What's happened?"

"You really don't know, do you?" he said, walking over to me then and grabbing me by the arm. He started pulling me away from the door and toward the couch. I jerked away from him, but he reached toward me again. "You don't look so hot," he said. "Come on. Sit down."

"What's happened?" I said, beginning to cry. "Tell me what's happened."

Tory put his arm around my shoulder. I didn't want him touching me, but I knew he meant well. "The motel clerk found your father late yesterday in his room," he said, and I felt his whole body tense up. "Somebody had cut his throat, and the police think it was you."

"Hold on!" I heard Tory say, and the black thing on my back covered my eyes and took the breath right out of me.

When I came to on that hard tile floor, Tory was squatting down beside me and bathing my face with a cold washrag. "You passed out," he said, sort of grinning.

"Good thing I had hold of you."

I shook my head a little to clear my blurry eyes and sat up slowly. "I didn't faint," I said. "I ain't never fainted. Tell me I didn't faint."

"You didn't faint," Tory said, grinning and showing his straight white teeth. "But you did."

"I can't believe my daddy's dead," I said. "It's not true. It can't be true. I just left him this morning."

Tory stopped grinning then and handed me the washrag. I held it over my face for a minute and then put it on the back of my neck. I didn't love my daddy, but seem like somebody had knocked my insides out, I was so empty feeling. I looked down at my feet, and they were still my feet, but they looked different. My hands looked different. Tory looked different. Everything was still the same, but everything had changed, somehow. It was funny how somebody died and the world changed into a whole different place but still stayed the same. It was a crazy thought, so I tried not to think about it anymore.

Tory helped me up, and we went over and sat on the couch. I could walk all right, but I felt kind of like I'd just got over the flu. "Just go ahead and tell me everything," I told Tory. "I'm okay now. I need to know."

Tory rubbed his hand over his face and let out a big breath of air. "It's been a madhouse around here, let me tell you," he said. "Gran took to her bed late this afternoon when we finally got home from the hospital. What happened was, Gran, Miss Armistead, and I were all sitting on the front porch yesterday afternoon when the sheriff's deputies came and told Miss Armistead that Miss Elsie Shaw over on Cow Street saw two men put you into a van. They asked us all a bunch of questions. After they left, Miss Armistead started to get up out of the swing and just keeled over. I called 911 and the ambulance was here in no time."

"I'm glad you were here," I said, and I meant it. Tory had his faults, but he was a good hand at saving folks.

"Gran and I stayed all night at the hospital with her," Tory said. "She got worse around lunch time, and now they won't let anyone in the room with her except for a few minutes every four hours. She's in I.C.U."

I didn't care how ignorant Tory thought I was. I said to him, "What's I.C.U? That don't make any sense."

"Intensive Care Unit," he said, but he didn't snigger or try to low-rate me. "That's where they put people who are very sick."

"Does that mean she's fixing to die?" I asked. I put my hand on his shoulder and shook him a little. "Tell me the truth now."

Tory looked down at his hands and shrugged. "I don't know, Patrick," he said. "Doctor Cohen says he doesn't know himself yet. If she lives another twenty-four hours, her chances will be better."

It didn't seem possible that I could come home after being away one night and so much had happened. "How come the police think I killed my daddy?" I asked. "I didn't kill anybody."

Tory squirmed on the couch. "Well, see, Miss Shaw got a tag number, and the county picked up the man who was with your father. He spilled the beans, and then the county put out a state-wide bulletin on you and your father."

"The police didn't pick us up," I said. "We never saw a sign of police."

Tory shrugged. "Guess they didn't see you, either," he said. "Anyway, the county notified the police up in Nashville, because that's where the man driving the van said you two were headed. Then when your father came up dead, everybody wondered what had happened to you. When the police started asking, somebody at the motel said they saw you running across the parking lot early this morning."

"That was this boy named Geoffrey, probably," I said. "He worked at the motel. But my daddy wasn't dead then.

He'd just left in the Jeep, and I was running away."

Tory shrugged and said, "I believe you. I'm just telling you what the sheriff told Gran when he came over today. He and the deputies were poking around the house late this afternoon."

Nothing was really funny, but I laughed, anyway. "What a bunch of durn fools," I told Tory. "I was sound asleep in the house then they were trying to find some sign of me."

Tory scratched under his arm and looked away. "Maybe you just ought to turn yourself in and tell them what you've told me. It all makes sense to me, the way you explained it."

I told him right quick, I said, "I'm not having anything to do with the police. I know how they are. They have ways of making people say things that aren't true. All they care about is getting everything wrapped up all nice and neat. They don't care about the truth."

"Well, what are you going to do, then? You can't hide out forever."

"That's what I'll do!" I said. "I can go to the hideout for a few days until everything blows over."

"No, you can't go there," Tory said, shaking his head. "That's one of the first places they'll look, probably. Remember? You told me the same thing yourself just the other day."

He was right. I wasn't thinking straight. They'd go up and down the creek with dogs until they flushed me out. "I don't know what I'm going to do." I said. "I need to get off by myself and think."

"You can go with me," Tory said almost in a whisper. "I'm leaving here, just like I told you I was. I'm not about to go back to Jackson."

"Your daddy's not going to want me in Starkville, me on the run from the law, and even if the law wasn't after me, he wouldn't want somebody else to take care of," I told him. "I can't go with you, and you know it. So don't talk it."

Tory sat up on the edge of the couch and began laying everything off with his hands. "No, see, what we can do, we can go to Starkville together, and then you can go on your way to wherever. Nobody will ever think to look for you in Mississippi. Nobody ever goes there on purpose."

He laughed, but I couldn't see anything funny myself. "How am I going to live out on the road?" I said. "You tell me that."

Tory was breathing hard, he was getting so excited. "I've got money, nearly two hundred dollars," he said. "You go with me, and I'll give you half." He reached over and grabbed me by the shoulder. "Hey, I'll tell you what! Why don't you get your friend Chigger to go with us? Can he drive?"

"I don't know," I said. "I'll see. When do you plan on leaving?"

"How about in the next five minutes?" he said, his blue eyes getting bigger and bigger. "Now's as good a time as any. My mother and the sot are driving up from Jackson this weekend, so I have to be gone between now and then, anyway."

I couldn't think. So many things had happened so fast, my mind wouldn't stay on track. I'd try to think about whether I should do this, or do that, and what would happen if I did this, or did that, like Miss Armistead had tried to drill in me, but too many things were coming at me at once. Here I was trying to figure out the smart thing to do, Tory was aggravating me, Miss Armistead was might near dead, the law was after me, and I kept seeing my daddy lying dead in the motel room with his throat cut. So I gave up and struck out in the dark. I told Tory, I said, "Okay, less us go. Give me a minute or two to gather me up some stuff."

"All right!" Tory said and gave me a high five.

I didn't know how in the world Miss Marcella had slept through all the commotion we'd made. She must have been like a lot of old folks, couldn't hear it thunder.

Tory followed behind me when I got up and went out. "Hey, listen," he said, grabbing me by the belt loop for a second. "When you get ready, I think we need to roll the car out to the street. I don't think we should try to start it in the garage."

I knew why he wanted to roll the car out. He was afraid he'd run into something if he tried to back out. I almost told him right then that I didn't want to take off with him, but I didn't. I didn't know where else to go or what else to do. "All right, " I said, "but maybe you better let me drive until we get out of town."

He scratched his head and looked down at his feet. "Now I don't know about that," he said. "Can you drive?"

"I know how to hold it in the road, if that is what you mean," I told him. "I've never driven a straight shift before, but I know it's kind of like a ten-speed bicycle. You use the lower gears to pull with, but you have to push in this clutch thing before you can change gears."

"I knew that," Tory said, cocking his head to one side. "Yeah. Okay. I know all that." He rubbed his chin. "Which one of those two pedals in the floor is the clutch?"

I shook my head. "I don't know," I said and started cutting across the yard. "We'll figure it out in a minute. I've got to get my stuff together."

"Okay," he said, "but hurry up."

I've noticed this. People hardly ever get in a hurry to do things they need to be doing, but they can't wait to rush into something that's likely to cause them a world of trouble.

CHAPTER XVII

I Say Goodbye To Old Friends

I grabbed a garbage bag from the pantry and headed upstairs. I started gathering up what I thought I might need. I took enough underwear for a week, three pairs of jeans, an armload of T-shirts, and four pairs of shorts. I folded my clothes so they fit better in the bag. Then I went into the bathroom and got my toothbrush and deodorant. I put them in the bag with my clothes, slung the bag over my shoulder, and went downstairs, turning out the lights on my way.

My next stop was the pantry. I loaded another bag with cans of soup, tuna, and pork and beans. I threw in crackers and bread and cookies. I emptied all the fruit out of the fruit bowl on the kitchen counter. I found three two-liter bottles of Coke in one of the bottom cabinets, so I bagged them up, too.

I turned out all the lights downstairs and went out the kitchen door, my three bags bouncing off the door facing. I was so loaded down I could hardly walk.

Tory was already waiting over at the garage with a flashlight. All he was carrying was a Nike tennis bag. "You must have brought the kitchen sink," he said, shining the light on me. "Why did you bring so much stuff?"

I knew why he didn't need much. He had a home to go to. "I wish you'd get that durn light out of my eyes," I said, and he did. "I brought food, just in case one of us decides he'd like to have a bite to eat along the way. And clean clothes. I like to change clothes every once in a while so I don't stink."

He crinkled his lips like he was put out, but he didn't smart off to me. He knew better. "I don't care one way or the other," he said. "We won't be on the road long, though. I figure we'll be in Starkville before breakfast."

"You won't be on the road long," I said, dropping my bags on the ground in front of him. "That's you, not me. Do you have the keys?"

"To the car?"

"Naw, to that airplane we're fixing to fly away in."

"Of course I've got the keys," he said, pulling them out of his pocket. He'd put on some denim shorts but still wasn't wearing a sign of a shirt. "You don't have to be so hateful. I feel bad about all that's happened, but it's not my fault. Don't take it out on me."

"Nobody's taking anything out on you," I said. I stepped inside the big shed Miss Marcella used for a garage, and Tory followed me. "Sometimes you can be so dense."

Tory bristled like an old cat that's had its fur rubbed the wrong way, but he didn't say anything. If he'd smarted off to me again, I'd have told him where to go, and I'm not talking about Starkville, either.

I took the flashlight from him and shined the light over in the corner of the shed while he took the cover off the little car. Then he unlocked it and got in. He rolled down the window and said, "All right, Patrick. Get up front and start pushing."

I didn't know why I had to do the pushing. This trip wasn't my idea, but I handed him the flashlight and did what he said, anyway. I braced my feet against the side of the shed and pushed as hard as I could. That car never moved an inch. I really put my back into it the second time, but all I could do was rock the car back and forth a little. I knew something that small with wheels shouldn't be that hard to move. I walked around to the passenger side of the car. "Have you got the brake on?" I asked.

"I don't know," Tory said. He flashed the light around every which way like he'd lost the brake and was looking for it. "You were supposed to tell me what was what."

"Unlock this door," I said, and when he did, I got in beside him. "This is the hand brake," I said, taking the flashlight from him and shining the light on everything as I explained it. "I think you have to push in this little button on the end to let it down. Yeah, there it goes. The car won't go anywhere with it up. Now. Look down yonder at your feet." He was wearing high-top Nikes with no socks. "One of those two square pedals is the clutch. I believe you have to hold it in before the car will roll."

"It won't go down but a little ways," Tory said, mashing the pedal on the right. "See. That's as far as it will go."

"Try the other one," I said. He did and mashed it all the way to the floor.

"So this left one is the clutch," he said. "Now what?"

"Just hold it in while I'm pushing. I'm pretty sure you have to hold it down when you start the car, too, and I know you have to push it in when you change gears. See. Look on the knob here. It shows you where all the gears are."

"Okay," he said. "I guess you can start pushing again."

It was his car, but I could've done a lot better if he'd been the one pushing. He always had to be the big buck in everything, though.

I handed him the flashlight, got out of the car, and started pushing again. This time the little car rolled back easy as pie, but I soon saw that Tory didn't know much about steering. The tires were making tracks like two spreading adders across the gravel inside the shed. "Watch where you're going," I said, and about that time he scraped the right front fender on the side of the shed door.

He threw on the brakes, and I tumbled over on the hood of the Volkswagen. He jumped out of the car and flashed the light on the fender. "Well, I hope you're satisfied!" he said. "Look what you made me do."

I limped around to the side of the car to look. I'd scraped my heel good on the bumper after I'd peeled myself off the hood. The fender didn't have much of a scratch atall. "I didn't make you do anything," I said. "I'll make you think. It was your own durn fault, and you know it."

"But if you hadn't been pushing me so fast," he said, and his voice kind of trailed off into thin air.

"I'm not going to argue about it," I said, and I meant it. "I'm driving. You get behind and push so I can straighten this thing up."

Tory poked out his lips and narrowed his eyes like he was aiming to sull on me, but then he did what I said. I took the flashlight and made him push me all the way back to the back of the big shed, and then I had him get in front and push me straight back out the door and halfway down the driveway. I stopped the car then and got out to get my stuff.

Tory started to get in the driver's seat when I got out, but I said, "Ah but naw, not if I'm going with you, you're not," so he scooted across the gear shift and over to the passenger seat. I wedged my garbage bags in the back seat and got in. "Ready?" I said, and he turned his head the other way, pouting. A second later, though, he grinned and gave me the thumbs-up sign.

Before I ever turned the key, I said, "I've got to make a stop."

He got tight in the mouth again and looked like he'd had it up to here with me. "You should've thought of that before we got in the car," he said, sounding like Miss Marcella. "Just go in the shed. I do myself sometimes."

"I'm not talking about that," I said.

"Oh, you mean you want to stop to see if your friend wants to go with us. Chigger. No problem. Let's go."

"I'd forgot about him. We have to make two stops then."

"What *two?*" he said, the corners of his mouth turning down. "You said one. Make up your mind, will you?"

"I'm aiming to see Miss Armistead before we leave," I said.

Some of the icy hardness melted in Tory's face, but after he pushed up his glasses, he shook his head. "You can't see her, Patrick," he said. "They won't let you see her since you're not family. I've already told you she is in I.C.U. Besides, the police are looking for you. They may be there at the hospital."

I didn't tell him, but I halfway hoped the police did catch me. I wouldn't have to worry about what to do next. "I don't care," I said. "I can't leave her in the hospital without saying goodbye. I might never see her again."

Tory got real still and didn't say anything, just bit his fingernails and looked out the window. The moonlight shining through the window made him look sickly white. Even his hair looked white. There wasn't any color about him atall, like the very life had been drained out of him. Right then I was pretty sure he was fixing to back out of going, but directly he said, "Okay. But you've got to make it snappy. We need to get on the road before Gran wakes up and finds out I'm missing. And I'm not stepping foot inside that hospital. You're on your own there."

I never had asked him to stand by me before, so I don't know why he thought I would now. I didn't need him to depend on. I didn't need anybody. "You don't have to," I said. "I never asked you to."

Tory mumbled something under his breath and looked out the window. I didn't even want to know what he'd said.

I pushed in the clutch and cranked up the car. It started the first time, but seem like it made a right smart of noise, kind of high and whiny. I guess I was afraid Miss Marcella was going to wake up and catch us, because I knew old folks didn't sleep clear through the night. I put the car in reverse and let out the clutch.

The little car hopped about ten feet forward and stopped right in front of the shed. Tory's head bumped the windshield.

"Durn it to hell!" he said, rubbing his forehead and staring a hole through me. "You can't drive any better than I can!"

My heart was pounding, and my guts were cold and crawly. "Get out and push me back again," I said, sounding mean, but the truth was, my nerves were giving up on me. "I must've not had it in reverse."

"Oh really?" Tory said like a big smart aleck as he got out of the car and slammed the door.

This time I let him roll me all the way out in the street. I cut sharp and backed up close to the curb. He got back in, and I started the car.

I monkeyed with the gearshift until I figured I'd hit first for sure. I let the clutch out real slow this time.

The Volkswagen whined and all of a sudden lurched forward.

"Turn on the lights, fool!" Tory hollered. "We're going down the street with no lights!"

I don't know how he thought I could do everything at once. I pushed in the clutch and shifted to second. I reckon I didn't hold in the clutch long enough, because the gears grated hard, and the car had a hopping fit before it took off smooth again. Tory reached across me looking for the light switch. I couldn't see to drive with him right up in my face. He didn't smell too clean, either, kind of like a puppy that's been out in the rain. He turned on the windshield wipers by accident and honked the horn with his elbow. Finally, he found the lights and got the wipers cut off. I couldn't think and drive, too, and by this time the transmission was whining like it was fixing to pop wide open. I clutched and shifted again, and this time I about jerked our heads off. Tory looked at me hateful, but he knew good and well he couldn't do any better.

I really was getting the hang of driving, though. I figured out that I needed to let up off the gas when I was shifting. I didn't do too bad atall when I hit fourth, and I looked over at Tory and smirked for meanness. I'd make him think, calling me a fool.

We came to the first stop light over on Arrowhead Drive. I clutched and braked like I was supposed to, but when we got ready to take off, the car didn't seem to want to go. It shivered and shuddered and stopped cold.

Brakes squalled. A truck behind us just about ran up my tailpipe. "Damn fool!" some old man driving a GMC pickup hollered. He honked his horn as he whipped around us.

Tory's hands were shaking. "Do something!" he said, squealing like some little old girl. "You're going to get us both killed!"

Right then I was ready to hop out of that car in the middle of the street and walk home. Nobody had any feelings or patience with anybody, didn't look like to me. Everybody was always thinking of themselves, and nobody cared how you felt or what you'd been through. "Shut the hell up!" I said. I aimed my finger at his nose, and he slung my hand hard against the dashboard.

"You fatassed prep!" I said, and I scooted up in the seat some so I could draw back and knock the shit out of him.

"Look!" he said, hissing like a snake and pointing across my shoulder. "There is a cop standing over there at Delightful Market. Let's get out of here."

I'd already figured out what I'd done wrong at the stop light before Tory started acting like a turd. I hadn't started off in first gear. I'd been trying to take off in fourth.

I looked over at the Delightful Market. Sure enough, a cop was standing close to the pumps and staring over the roof of his car at us. I broke out in a sweat, and my leg was so trembly I could hardly hold in the clutch. I was breathing hard, and I could hear Tory breathing hard, too. "Hurry," he was whispering. "Hurry up. He's going to get us. I know he's going to get us."

I put the Volkswagen in first and took off. The little car moaned a right smart, but I hit second fine, then third. Tory was looking in the mirror to see if the cop was coming after us. I shifted to fourth just as pretty as you please. "Is he coming?" I asked.

"No," Tory said, letting out his breath.

"Can you still see him?" I said.

When Tory looked in the mirror again, his mouth flew open. "Oh, God!" he said. "He's pulling out, sure as the world!"

I sped up. "I'll turn here on Cherokee and lose him," I said.

"No!" Tory said, grabbing the steering wheel so I couldn't turn. "He'll think something's up for sure then. Drive on like you don't think a thing in the world about him being behind you."

That was easy for him to say. Through the side mirror I could see the big gray and blue Caprice easing upon us like a shark coming in for the kill. My heart sounded like somebody thumping on a balloon, and sweat was trickling down my back like I'd sprung a leak. The Caprice looked like it was aiming to gobble up my back bumper any second.

The hospital was on Creek, so I flipped on my signal like I was supposed to before we stopped for the light. My clutch leg was so weak and trembly that I had to hold it down with both hands. "Be cool," Tory said, still staring at the cop through the rearview mirror. "Be cool. He's lighting a cigarette now. I don't think he's going to pull us over."

"He is if you don't stop staring at him," I said, and then the light changed.

I don't know how I ever did it, but I took off as smooth

as warm butter. Tory was right. The cop went straight through the intersection.

I felt as empty as shucks, and I needed to pee. "Way to go," Tory said, giving me a punch on the arm.

Tory was all right sometimes. His trouble was, when he got scared, he started getting hateful and smart alecky and blaming other people. He wasn't grown up like I was, and I was just going to have to try and overlook him as best I could. "You can't make a silk purse out of a sow's ear," Granny Gunn was all time saying, and she was right.

In a minute we got to the hospital, and I parked under a big floodlight in the visiting section. When I cut off the motor, Tory said, "They're not going to let you in. Visiting hours are over at nine o'clock, and I'll bet you there's a security guard in the lobby there." He nodded toward the front of the hospital. "It's all over town by now about you killing your daddy, and you're going to wind up in jail, just wait and see."

Maybe he was trying to help me, I don't know, but he sounded like somebody who didn't want to get mixed up in something that would get him into trouble. I handed him the car keys and got out of the car. "I'll be back when you see me," I told him.

"I'm going with you," he said and got out, too.

"Back there at the house, I thought you said you weren't coming," I said. "I don't want to put you out any, now."

"I've changed my mind," he said. He looked at me funny, like he knew something I didn't, or maybe like he was up to something sneaky. Right then I didn't know whether I could trust him or not, but it didn't look like I had much choice.

We walked up the sidewalk toward the hospital. It was a one-story building, but it had arms that went out every which way like an octopus or something. It was a gray brick building with a flat roof. I always wondered how water ran off a flat roof, but I didn't want to ask Tory. He was like Chigger; he had a notion about most everything as it was.

When we got to the entrance, the doors didn't have any handles. They shot back by themselves and let us right in.

"Can I help you?" this old guy wearing a gray uniform said as we walked through the doors. He was sitting behind a desk with two clipboards in front of him. He didn't look like he could run too fast, so I was about ready to hightail it out the door, but Tory spoke up big and said, "Nosir. My aunt's in I.C.U., and I'm afraid she's taken a turn for the worse. Dr. Cohen has called the family in."

"Well, son, I'm real sorry to hear that," the old guy said, shaking his head in a hopeless kind of way. "Is your mama and them already here?"

Tory hung his head and sniffled. "Yessir, they are," he said. "It was just my cousin and I here by ourselves at home when we got the call."

The old guy got up then and came from around behind the desk. He patted Tory on the bare back and said, "You want me to take you back there, Bubba? I'll take you back there if you want me to."

"Nosir," Tory said, pinching the bridge of his nose. "I appreciate it, but we know the way. We stayed there most of the night last night."

The old guy shook his head again. "Well, I'll say," he said.

Tory grabbed me by the arm and pulled me along. "Come on, Henry," he said. "Let's hope we're not too late."

We rounded the corner and went through these two big wooden double doors, and then I flew into Tory. "You're the biggest durn liar in the state of Tennessee," I said and gave him a big shove so that he banged into the wall. "I wouldn't be surprised to find Miss Armistead dead, you lying like that."

He rubbed his shoulder and grinned. "I got you in, though, didn't I?" he said. "I could tell you didn't know whether to shit or go blind back there."

"Shut up," I said. "You're not supposed to curse in a hospital. The trouble with you, you're never had any raising."

"Raisin bran, is that what you mean? No, I never touch the stuff."

We were walking down a long hall where there were a bunch of nurses and other people going about their jobs, or else I'd have hit Tory upside the head.

The hall had blue carpet and smelled funny. The walls were a lighter shade of blue and had these signs with arrows showing the way to different rooms. We came upon this nigger man pushing a square-looking machine that was cleaning the carpet. He was wearing a tan uniform and a plastic shower cap on his head. I didn't know why he had the shower cap on. "Pardon me, sir," Tory said. "Could you tell us how to get to I.C.U.?"

The nigger grinned and shook his head. He had big white teeth, but one was missing on the side. "Nawsir," he said. "I don't work here. You need to ax one of the nurses."

"Well, thanks anyway, sir," Tory said, and we walked on down the hall.

"Ain't that just like a nigger?" I whispered to Tory. "Saying he didn't work here. What is he doing here, if he don't work here?"

Tory rolled his eyes up at the ceiling and said, "He meant that he wasn't a regular hospital employee, Patrick. He probably works for a cleaning service. Honestly, you can be such a redneck sometimes."

"Miss Armistead has done preached me that sermon about saying *nigger,* so you shut up. I forget sometimes, and I'll bet you do, too," I told him.

A few seconds later, we passed this room with the door wide open. This big fat man was lying in bed asleep with a tube of a thing taped to his lip and running up his nose. He was naked as a jaybird. I turned my head.

"That was Joe," Tory said, grabbing me by the arm and whispering in my ear.

"Joe who?" I said, whispering right back.

"Joe daddy!" Tory said. "Got you!"

"My daddy's dead," I heard myself say, and my voice sounded far away, like part of me was way off and trying to reach the other part of me that was here.

Tory put his hand on my shoulder and said, "Yeah, I know. I forgot. Bad joke."

"It's okay," I said, walking fast to wrench his hand loose from my shoulder. "You didn't think."

We came to the end of that hall and rounded the corner into another hall. All of a sudden, Tory pointed and said, "Hey, look."

There was a sign on the wall that read, "I.C.U. Waiting Room." Underneath the sign was an arrow that crooked around. That meant we were supposed to turn there before we got to the end of the hall.

We followed the arrow and came upon this little room with two couches and a TV. Right beside this room were two big double wooden doors, and over the top of these doors was a sign that read, "I.C.U. Visiting Hrs. 5:00 A.M., 9:00 A.M., 1:00 P.M., 5:00 P.M., 9:00 P.M., 1:00 A.M. Knock at the appropriate time, and nurse on duty will allow you to enter. One visitor at a time, please. No more than five minutes per visit. Thank you."

I checked my watch by the clock on the wall in the waiting room. They both said 12:48.

There was nobody in the waiting room, so I sat on one couch and Tory sat on the other one. He squirmed around for a minute or two like he had ants in his pants, and directly he got up and stretched. "Listen," he said. "I'm going to get a Coke. You want one?"

"Naw, I don't think so," I said.

Tory scratched his big white belly. "You can go with me if you want to," he said. "We've got plenty of time

239

before they'll let you in."

"Naw, I think I'll stay here," I said. "Thanks anyway."

"Suit yourself," he said and took off. His Nikes were untied, and I could hear his feet shuffling up and down inside them as he walked down the hall.

I was glad to be rid of Tory for a while. Seem like I couldn't think straight when he was around. I wondered how Miss Armistead was doing. It made me feel funny knowing that she was in the next room, but I might as well have been in Africa as far as helping her was concerned. But then I figured that distance didn't really make a difference, anyway. Being right next to somebody couldn't make you any closer, and being far away didn't make you any farther apart.

I wondered, too, if my daddy was going to have a funeral, and if anybody would come if he did. It was good in a way that Granny Gunn was dead. She'd already seen enough trouble in her life without having to contend with some more. If Miss Armistead had been on her feet, she would have wanted me to go. I didn't want to see him laid out, though. I wouldn't have been in the mess I was in if it hadn't been for him. Besides, I could cover him up in my mind without having to see him covered up in the grave-yard.

I still didn't much want to leave town with Tory, but I didn't know what else to do. I knew Miss Armistead would-n't want me to go. It was just the kind of thing that would get her all up in the air. But I needed to get away from Broad Plains for a while. Things would probably clear up by themselves sooner or later. A.Z. would back me up. He knew I didn't cut anybody's throat.

But then I thought about how I'd lied to A.Z. He knew I'd run away from my daddy. How would he know that I didn't kill him? He wouldn't, not really. He might think I'd lied about that, like I'd lied about having a grandmother in Franklin. Not only that, but somebody at the motel had seen me running across the parking lot. When the police put two and two together, they weren't going to come up with five. It sure looked like I'd killed my daddy, and that was probably the way the cops were going to see it.

I got hot and sweaty thinking about all this, and I tried to put it out of my mind.

I watched the clock in the waiting room, and I watched my own watch, too. Directly, it was time to go in. When I walked out into the hall, I didn't see hide nor hair of Tory. I figured he 'd done got lost in this big old hospital and couldn't find his way back. It was a good thing I hadn't gone with him.

I knocked on the big double doors that led into the I.C.U., and in a minute this young nurse with her blonde hair done up on top stuck her head outside. She smiled at me and said, "Family of Miss Armistead?"

"Yes, ma'am," I said, and she opened the door for me to come inside.

The room wasn't much size, but it had all kinds of machines in it. Beside Miss Armistead's bed was this TV screen that had a dot going up and down.

Miss Armistead looked awful. Her hair was mashed way down on one side and standing way up on the other. She was gray looking, and her mouth was all drawn up on one side like she was talking out of one side of it, only she wasn't. Her hands and arms were the color of a bruise, and she had big black spots on the insides of her arms and on the backs of her hands. I decided then and there that I never wanted to live to be old. I didn't want to end up pitiful like Miss Armistead and Granny Gunn, other people having to take care of me after life had beat the fire out of me.

"You can talk to her," the nurse said, touching me on the back. "She can't respond much yet, but she knows what you're saying."

The young nurse went over to her desk and wrote something down on a clipboard. There were two more little rooms like this one. The walls came up halfway, and the rest was glass. In one of the back rooms, another nurse was sitting in front of some kind of machine and fiddling with it.

Miss Armistead had a clear plastic tube stuck in her arm that ran up to this box on a stand with wheels. There were red numbers in the box that kept changing. Above the box hung a plastic bag full of watery stuff that was bubbling down through the tube right into Miss Armistead's arm. I didn't say anything, but it looked to me like these nurses were doing Miss Armistead a lot of hurt to get her well.

I got close to Miss Armistead so the nurses couldn't hear me and whispered, "Hi, Miss Armistead. I'm all right now. You just get well. I'm fixing to read a bunch of books for you."

I noticed her left hand opening and closing. I put two fingers in the palm of her hand, and she squeezed them. I knew then she knew who I was, and I felt a whole lot better. Then I got to thinking: *Here I am feeling good because I've still got somebody I can count on, but the person I'm counting on is old and sick and may die. She needs me to count on, not the other way around.* I got tears in my eyes thinking about how she needed me, and I needed her, and neither one of us could do the other one any good right now.

The nurse came back over and stood on the other side of the bed. "Miss Armistead," she said real loud. "Miss Armistead."

Miss Armistead batted her eyes once and moved them a little bit toward the nurse. "She's starting to focus," the nurse said, looking across the bed at me. "That's a good sign."

"That means she ain't going to die for sure," I said. "She ain't going to die now, is she?"

The nurse smiled at me, but it wasn't a happy smile. It was a smile like the teachers at school smiled when they wouldn't let you do something you wanted to do, like get a drink of water or go to the bathroom. "She's beginning to respond, and that's always a good sign," she said, patting Miss Armistead's shoulder.

I wiggled my fingers out of Miss Armistead's hand. "I've got to go now, Miss Armistead," I said. "Don't worry about nothing but getting well."

The nurse looked at me funny as I was starting to leave. "Aren't you her grandson?" she said. "I thought you were her grandson."

"Naw, I ain't her grandson," I said, walking over and opening the door. "This here's a lady. I ain't nothing but a trailer tramp."

Before I knew what was happening, the nurse had two fingers tugging on my shirt tail. "Now how are you connected to Miss Armistead?" she said. She turned me loose, but she cocked her head back like a chicken and looked me over good.

"I don't know," I said. "We ain't kin by blood, if that's what you mean. All I know is, if she dies on me, ain't nothing ever going to be right again."

All of the air kind of went out of the nurse then. Her shoulders drooped, and she looked tired. She didn't exactly know what was up, but she knew I was telling the truth. About the time she opened her mouth to say something, I walked out the door.

I thought maybe she might come out after me, but she didn't. I peeped in the waiting room, and there was Tory all sprawled out on one of the couches watching some old black and white cowboy movie. "Come on," I said. "We got to get out of here."

Tory got up in a hurry and followed me. "Did you see her?" he said as we beat it down the hall.

"Yeah, I saw her," I said.

"What did she look like?" he said, getting close to me and whispering like I was fixing to tell him something nasty.

I walked faster. "Shut the hell up," I said. "Why didn't you wear a shirt? You look like a big naked baby."

Tory rubbed his hands over his white belly like he was trying to cover himself and then turned red in the face. He started to say something, but he couldn't seem to get it out.

We came to the end of the hall, rounded the corner, and were back to the first hall we came in. We went through the big wooden double doors that led back to the lounge. The old man in the gray uniform was at his desk reading a newspaper. About the time we got ready to go out the door, he laid down the newspaper and looked at us real sad. "I'm so sorry, boys," he said.

"I am, too, sir," I said, and we hightailed it to the car.

When we got out there, Tory handed me the keys. "You drive," he said.

He really couldn't say anything else, but I didn't throw it up to him about not being able to drive. We got in, and this time I remembered to switch on the lights. I backed up the Volkswagen with no problem, except maybe we went back a little fast, and when I threw on the brakes, we were jerked some. I got the car in first on the first try, and we took off on Creek Street headed for the trailer park.

We turned on Shawnee and crossed the intersection of Highway 100 and 18. The trailer park was about two miles out on 18 headed toward Bolivar. We were almost there when Tory said out of the blue, "Do you have a T-shirt I could borrow? I'm a little bit cold."

He wasn't cold. He was ashamed. I didn't mean to hurt his feelings, I was just upset about Miss Armistead and everything else, but he ought to have thought about the way he looked going out in public without a shirt. Miss Armistead would've sure set him straight if he'd been her grandson. "Get one out of that middle bag there," I told him, and he did.

I couldn't keep from laughing. The Volkswagen didn't have a lot of room inside to maneuver in the first place, and in the second place, Tory was a good-sized boy. He did a lot of grunting and tugging getting that shirt on. Granny Gunn used to sew up these cloth sacks about as big around as my arm to pack her sausage in at hog-killing time, and Tory put me in mind of those sack sausage. He looked mighty squeezed in and lumpy and little bug-eyed.

Things were still hopping over at Meadowview Manor. As we pulled in, I could hear a good many stereos going full blast and all playing different music. A bunch of little kids were out playing there at the entrance. They were throwing rocks in a big mud puddle, trying to splash one another. Some old woman with jet black hair was sitting in the door of her trailer and smoking a cigarette. She didn't have any teeth, and every time she took a drag, her chin nearly met her nose.

Tory was really taking everything in. He didn't know what to think about a place like this. I noticed him frowning as he looked at all the junk. People at the trailer park never kept junk off their yards. They'd make a big pile in one place, and when that one got full, they'd start another pile.

Over at the Pratt trailer, four or five boys were standing around a '76 Impala and drinking beer. Seem like everybody at the trailer park liked '76 Impalas with mag wheels. All my old neighbors were always wanting to buy one and fix it up. The funny thing was, nobody ever got them fixed up. They'd sand off one door or patch a rear fender with Bond-O, and that was about as far as the fixing up ever got. I'll bet there were ten '76 Impalas in that one trailer park, but there wasn't a single one that wasn't all spotted with primer and parked on bald radials. That was the way of trailer park folks. They had plans like everybody else, but they never got around to finishing anything.

The lights were still on in Chigger's trailer. That didn't matter one way or the other, though, because I was aiming to wake him up even if he was asleep. I wouldn't have bothered him if his mama had been there, but she wasn't. She closed down the Hilltop Lounge, and it usually didn't close until daylight. That was when the law made their rounds and made them close.

I parked the car and got out. "What do you want me to do?" Tory said out the window. He was still looking around every which way like he'd just landed on the moon.

"Suit yourself," I said. "Come on in if you want to." I stepped upon Chigger's lopsided porch that was built on stilts. "I shouldn't be too long if you want to stay out here, though."

He looked like somebody with an upset stomach who's going to have to hop out of his seat any second and be sick. "I believe I'll stay out here, then," he said.

"Fine with me," I said, "but if Chigger decides to go with us, it'll probably take him a few minutes to gather up some stuff to take along. Don't be calling him no hillbilly, either, when he gets out here. He's not as easy to get along with as I am."

Tory didn't answer, I guess because he thought he was fixing to be outnumbered. I knocked on the door, but I didn't hear anybody stirring inside. I knocked harder and waited. I knocked again, and just about when I was ready to leave, I heard somebody walking.

When Chigger opened the door, he was rubbing his hand over his face and hair. He wasn't wearing his fake arm. "Hey, dude," he said, sounding kind of like he had a cold, and unlatched the screen. "What's going on?"

After he stood aside to let me in, I saw where he'd been lying on their old sagging plaid couch with two ratty-looking pillows propped on the arm. The TV was snowing. "Woke you up, didn't I?" I said, poking him in the ribs.

"Hey, watch it, man," he said, laughing and cuffing me on the side of the head. "I might have to hurt you."

"I need to pee bad," I said. "Where's the john?"

Chigger pointed to the back of the trailer. "Down at

the end of the hall on your left," he said. "Don't fall in or nothing."

I went inside his bathroom and closed the door. Chigger hadn't flushed the toilet, and his aim wasn't too good, either, didn't look like. His shower and bathtub were covered with old white soap scum, and there was mildew growing in the cracks between the tiles. I didn't used to notice stuff like that until I went to live with Miss Armistead. I'd a heap rather peed outside if there hadn't been so many people still up. Trailer park folks went in and out all night long. I flushed the toilet after I peed and washed my hands, but there wasn't anything to dry on. I used the sides of my shorts.

When I got back to the living room, Chigger was sitting on the couch. "Who's the albino?" he said, yawning and jerking his thumb in the direction of the car.

I plopped down in the lounge chair across from him. "That's Tory," I said. "He's all right. He pulled me out of the creek here a while back when I was fixing to drown."

Chigger leaned over on his elbow and peeped out the door. "Looks like a girl," he said. "Got titties like one, anyhow."

Chigger hadn't been home but a few days, but he was already beginning to sound like the old Chigger. I didn't know why I thought he'd changed. Like I told Miss Armistead one time, Chigger couldn't be tamed. "He's the biggest durn smart aleck I've ever run into," I said. I felt kind of sneaky saying that.

Chigger sniffled. "Why are you hanging out with him then?" he said, using his nub to scratch his bare chest. He wasn't wearing a shirt, just these long Hawaiian shorts that came down below his knees. "You used to be mighty particular about who you fooled with."

He was throwing that at me, and I got it the first go around. I could feel my face turning red. "He's not perfect by a long shot," I said, "but he's still my friend. Right now he's helping me get out of town. I'm in a little trouble."

Chigger yawned again and rubbed his eyes. "Naw, Pat, you ain't in trouble," he said directly. "You're in deep shit."

"What do you know about it?" I said real hateful.

"*Know about it?*" he said and smirked. "Hell, dude, *everybody knows about it*. They think you killed your old man." He peeped out the door again. "I wouldn't hang around here too long if I was you. The county mounties have already been over here nosing around. Course, everybody over here hates them bastards. They wouldn't tell them nothing if they knew."

My insides began crawling like a nest of snakes. "I didn't kill my daddy," I said. "You know me, and you know I didn't kill my daddy."

Chigger shrugged and looked pleased with himself. "I don't know nothing, man," he said. "I don't much think you did, but I don't know."

"Well, I didn't!" I said, my voice sounding like somebody's who's in trouble and trying to lie his way out of it. "I snuck out of the motel early in the morning right after he left and hitched a ride back home with Mr. A. Z. Porter. Anybody that won't believe me can ask him. He paints houses in Franklin, Tennessee."

"Okay, it's cool," Chigger said and shrugged again. His eyebrows were arched like he was saying to himself, *Yeah, and I've got some oceanfront property in Arizona.*

I noticed him glancing at the clock on the end table beside the couch. "I got to go," I said. "I wanted to see you before you went back to Memphis."

Chigger spread his good arm and his nub real wide. "Well," he said, "here I am. You've seen me."

I got up out of the lounge chair. I didn't know what I was fixing to do. My fingernails were biting into my palms, my hands were clenched so tight. "How come you're acting like this?" I said, ashamed that my voice was quivering. "You looked me up a'purpose just so you could show me how cool you'd got to be in Memphis. Why didn't you leave me alone if you didn't want to be friends anymore?"

Chigger looked me square in the eye and spoke so low I could barely hear him. "Maybe I wanted to show you how it felt."

"What are you talking about?" I said, taking a step closer to the couch.

Chigger never offered to move. He didn't act like he thought a thing in the world about me being so mad. He acted like we were talking about football or cars or drag racing. "You remember the last time I saw you at school? You remember the last time we camped out together?" he said, leaning back and spreading out his arm and his nub on the back of the couch like a big shot.

"Yeah. What about it?" I said.

"You remember what you told me then, don't you? About why you couldn't hang out with me at school?"

"Because you were always getting into trouble and acting like a fool, that's why," I said. "You know it's the truth, too."

"That was just part of it," he said, still talking low. "You said you had a good thing going with that old lady and didn't want me to mess it up for you."

"I didn't say that. I don't remember saying that."

"You said it. Maybe not in them exact words, but you said it."

"Maybe I did say it, I don't know." I tasted hot bile in my throat and swallowed hard. I didn't know whether I wanted to throw up or hit Chigger or cry. "If you were in my place, you'd have done the exact same thing."

Chigger took his arms off the back of the couch and leaned forward. His squinty green eyes were hard and bright. "I am in your place now," he said. "I got a good thing going in Memphis, and I ain't aiming to let you mess it up for me. I don't want you hanging around here long. You're the one in trouble now, see. You come here to get me to help you, didn't you?"

Chigger acted like he was glad I was in trouble. Seem like people weren't much different from that roving band of dogs at the trailer park. If one of those old dogs came up lame or sick, the others would gnaw on it until it died.

He wasn't going to have to tell me twice to leave. I turned around and walked over to the door. "You tell me one thing," I said, pushing open the door latch but not looking back. "What was I supposed to do for you? You just tell me that."

"I don't know, man," he said. "Just like I don't know what to do for you. We're in the same boat, see."

"Yeah, I see. I see right through you with my back turned," I said and walked into the night.

Tory had rolled up the windows on the Volkswagen, and now they were all fogged up. I was glad in a way, because he couldn't see what shape I was in. I dried my eyes on my shirt tail.

From the porch I could see where our old trailer used to be. Somebody had already hauled it away, and now there was an empty space in the two rows of old rusty trailers, like a gap in a mouthful of bad teeth. I didn't have a home here anymore, or any friends.

It was time to move on.

CHAPTER XVIII

On The Road

I hadn't been gone five minutes, but when I opened the car door, Tory was sound asleep with his mouth wide open.

He woke up when I started the car. He dug his fists in his eyes and licked his lips. "He coming with us?" he said, still half asleep.

"Naw," I said, "he's got other fish to fry."

I stuck my head out the window and backed up slow. As we headed back to the entrance of the trailer park, I glanced over at Tory. He'd scooted way down in the seat, his head lolling on the armrest. He looked like he'd settled in for the night. I shook his shoulder a little. "Hey," I said, "what's the best way to go to Starkville from here?"

"Take 18 South," he mumbled. "It runs into 7."

I wasn't exactly sure what he meant, but I didn't want him to think I was any more backward than he already thought I was, so I didn't ask him anything else about the directions.

We came in on 18 South, so I at least knew where to start. As I pulled out on the highway, I glanced down at my watch and saw that it was one-thirty in the morning. It was past Tory's bedtime, but I wasn't a bit tired. Seem like I had so much energy I was might near ready to jump out of my skin.

By now I pretty well had the hang of shifting. After I got into fourth gear, the little car puttered along a good piece before it ever got up to fifty-five. I saw I didn't have to worry about speeding in this car, but it felt the right size for me. I liked driving.

Tory commenced snoring. Every once in a while I'd hit a rough place in the pavement, and his head would roll back and forth across the armrest like it was fixing to snap off at the stem, but he never woke up. Now and then he'd grunt and shift around in the seat some, but that was all I heard out of him. I could see the moon in his glasses.

For some reason I thought about a book I'd read a while back, *The Pearl*. Kino and Juana, this poor Indian man and his wife, found a big pearl and thought it was the answer to all their prayers. They would look into the pearl and imagine owning all the things they had ever wanted. As the story turned out, though, the pearl brought them nothing but bad luck. They had to leave their village because bad people kept trying to steal the pearl from them. Their little baby Coyotito ended up getting killed. When they came back to their village, everybody was afraid of them. They had lost what was most important to them, not the pearl, but their baby, and when you've lost everything that's important to you, you're not afraid of anything anymore, and you'd just as soon kill people as look at them, and they know it. I wondered if I was heading in that direction myself, people dying on me right and left, one friend helpless and the other turning his back on me.

Directly, I crossed the Hatchie and headed into Bolivar. Bolivar looked kind of like Broad Plains, only a little smaller. The only person I saw there was a boy checking the rear tire on his yellow Roadrunner under a flood light. I threw up my hand at him when we passed, and he threw up his hand at me. In the rearview mirror, I saw him look back over his shoulder at me for a long time.

If so many bad things hadn't happened to bear on my

mind, I'd have enjoyed driving that little red car out on the highway late at night. There were hardly any other cars on the highway. A cool breeze slipped under my shirtsleeve and flapped around inside my T-shirt. The big bright moon was bleached as white as a bone you find in a pasture. The air was sweet with the scent of hay and honeysuckle. Bugs tapped and spattered against the windshield. I turned on the radio for company and picked up this station way down in Mexico. It was funny to listen to those people talk, especially when they did commercials.

I was safe for now. The cops wouldn't think about me driving this little red convertible to Mississippi. By morning Tory said we'd be in Starkville.

I began to think about what I was going to do once Tory got to his daddy's house. Tory had promised me half of his money, so I could always take the bus somewhere if the Greyhound passed through Starkville. It didn't even stop in Broad Plains anymore. I'd just have to wait and see.

Then I got to thinking about that I was going to do once I got to where I was going. I couldn't get a regular job, because I was too young. You couldn't even get a job at McDonald's until you were sixteen.

I got hot all over and commenced sweating again. What was I thinking, running off down here? I wasn't thinking, that was the problem. The law was fixing to catch me sooner or later, and running off just made me look that much more guilty. There really wasn't anything for me to do but to go on back and take whatever was coming to me. Like I told Miss Armistead that time she thought I'd drowned, if you do right in the beginning, then you're not to blame for what happens later on. Except I'd done wrong by running off. I saw that now, so no matter what happened to me later on, I was partly to blame.

I started once to turn that Volkswagen right around in the middle of the road and head on back to Broad Plains, but I couldn't do that, either. I'd already got Tory all mixed up in my trouble. I'd agreed to go with him to Starkville, and that was what I had to do. I couldn't just leave him with the car, either, because he couldn't drive and would probably end up getting himself splattered all over some Mississippi highway. I'd go with him as far as Starkville, I decided, and then I'd either hitch a ride back home or ride the bus. That was all I could do.

I tried not to think about Miss Armistead and my daddy. I put them upstairs in my mind along with a lot of other old stuff that was always trying to tumble back down the steps. I couldn't contend with my troubles right now. Miss Armistead told me once that when life got the best of you, you had to pack away your troubles and put one foot in front of the other until things got better. That was what I was doing now.

Tory groaned and coiled up in the seat and rested his head against the window. The moon shone over his left shoulder and reflected off the wolf on the steering wheel.

The blacktop snaked south through broad fields of tasseling corn, and once an owl rose up heavy from the side of the road carrying something that was still wiggling, a ground squirrel, probably. Way off on the horizon, a tall grove of trees looked like the towers of a spooky castle.

I drove on through the night, not really knowing where I was going or how I was supposed to get there.

All at once the Volkswagen began to jerk and then take off again, jerk and take off. Tory raised his head a little and looked frowning over his shoulder at me. "What are you doing?" he said, fixing his glasses back on his ears.

"I'm not doing anything," I said. The Volkswagen was bucking and snorting like it wanted to go but couldn't. "It's the car. Something's wrong with the car."

Tory sat all way up in the seat and held on to the dashboard. "Nothing's wrong with this car," he said, looking at me hateful like I was doing something a'purpose. "Gran keeps it in tiptop shape. It's the driver, I think."

I was fixing to turn the wheel over to him after he said that, but then the motor stopped. Lucky for us, the road had a wide shoulder, and I pulled all the way off the highway so nothing would rear-end us.

I felt like a complete fool, because I saw right off what was wrong. The needle on the gas gauge was way over past E. "Durn it," I said, hitting the steering wheel with my fist, "we're out of gas! Out in the middle of nowhere without any gas!"

Tory craned his neck so he could see for himself. "It's a fine time to be telling me now," he said. "Why didn't you tell me before we left that we were low on gas?"

"I didn't pay any attention to it," I said. "Why didn't you tell me?"

Tory's eyes got big and his mouth flew open. "Me tell you?" he hollered. "You're the driver. You're the one who's supposed to watch all the gauges."

"You're a lot of durn help!" I hollered back. "Asleep over there with your fat butt stuck up in the air!"

He stared hard at me, and I stared him down.

Directly, I got out of the car and sat down on the front fender. Under the full moon, the night was light as daybreak. The stars in the sky looked out of place, and everything stood still and quiet, the crosses of telephone poles, the long empty blacktop that sharpened into a point far away, the fields where nothing stirred. It was almost like the night had hushed when I stepped foot out of the car. All the trees and bushes alongside the road looked tensed up, like they were ready to jump out and grab something.

I wondered what in the world would happen to me next. The preacher at Miss Armistead's church was always saying that God didn't put any more on a person than he could handle. I thought to myself if that preacher could trade places with me for the last couple of days, or the last couple of years, for that matter, he might change his tune.

After a while Tory got out of the car, too, and came

over and stood beside me. "What are we going to do?" he said. He wasn't acting so high and mighty now. In fact, he sounded kind of scared. "Any ideas? I'm all ears."

I started to tell him to go to hell, he was all mouth, but I didn't. "All I know to do," I told him, "is to sit here until somebody stops and helps us. I don't think we ought to take off walking yet."

He nodded. "That's more or less what I was thinking, too," he said. "I think you're supposed to raise the hood so people will know you need help."

I got off the fender and raised the front end, and he went back and opened the rear end. "I tell you what," I said. "I think we need to get back in the car, roll down the windows a little bit, and then lock the doors. We might as well get some sleep if we can."

"Okay," he said, and we both got back in the car.

We sat there a long time without either one of us saying a word. We were both depressed and give out, I reckon. All I could hear were the crickets and tree frogs and Tory breathing heavy through his mouth. He told me one time that he had to take a shot once a week because he was allergic to everything in the country, even grass. Good thing he wasn't a cow.

I scooted the seat back as far as it would go and tried to stretch out my legs. The back of the seat wouldn't let down, so there was no good way to rest. Every time my eyes got the least bit heavy, my leg would go to sleep or my back would start aching from my sitting so far down in the seat on my backbone.

Finally, I reached back in the back seat and found a bag of cookies. I ate a handful of them, and then my mouth was dry, so I opened us a two-liter Coke and drank it hot right out of the bottle. Tory let on like he was asleep, but I had a feeling he was possuming. He was wanting something to eat so bad he could hardly stand it, knowing him, but he had his pride. After a while, though, I said to him, I said, "Tory, you wouldn't want a cookie, would you?" and sure enough, he opened his eyes right up and said, "I might have a couple." He ate about a dozen and swigged out of the Coke bottle after me without even wiping off the top. The boy didn't have any raising.

I had an idea. I scooted my seat up as far as it would go and crawled over into the back. I wedged two of the garbage bags behind the seats and put the one with my clothes inside on the driver's seat. "Stretch out across the front seats and use that bag for a pillow," I told Tory.

"Good idea," he said, and after a lot of shaking and shifting around, we both settled down for the night.

I didn't feel sleepy atall, I was still so keyed up, but directly I must have drifted off, because the next thing I knew, it was already daylight and somebody was outside the car tapping on the windshield.

CHAPTER XIX

Two Men Offer To Help Us

He was a great big fellow with a head shaped like a hen egg. He didn't have but a few frizzly strands of red hair growing on top. He hadn't shaved in several days, and his face was bristly as a boar hog's belly. When I raised up on my elbow to get a good gander at him, he grinned from ear to ear and waved at me through the windshield. His teeth had rotted into black points, and his gums were red and swollen looking.

I could hardly move, we were so cramped in the car, but I finally managed to sit up in the seat. Tory was still snoring with his mouth wide open again. It was hot inside the car, and his hair was damp and kinked up like a baby's. I saw his glasses lying over behind the gear shift. When I shook his shoulder, he came awake with a start.

"What?" he said real hateful.

"We've got company," I said. "Get up."

While I was waking up Tory, the big man had walked over to the driver's side and was standing in front of the window. His big, hairy white belly was hanging out from under a gray knit shirt that was about four sizes too small for him. "Don't roll the window down far," I whispered to Tory, who was looking around for his glasses. "Behind the gear shift," I said, pointing.

Tory got his glasses on and scooted over to the passenger seat. Then he leaned across the garbage bag in the driver's seat and rolled down the window about another inch.

The big man squatted down and held on inside the window. His fingernails were long and dirty. He was grinning again, and I could smell him clear through the window. He hadn't had a bath in a long time. "You little boys had car trouble?" he said in a voice that was might near as high as Tory's. "You need some help?"

I didn't know what Tory might blurt out, because he didn't know about people like this stinking dickens, so I beat him to the draw. "Nawsir," I said. "We're all right. We're out of gas, is all. Our daddy's gone after some. We look for him back directly."

Tory frowned and looked at me funny, but he didn't say anything. I didn't know whether he'd caught on or not.

The man turned his head and said, "They say they're out of gas, Jubal."

I turned around myself then and looked out the back window. A short, skinny man wearing a yellow suit was leaning against the grill of an old '70s model Bonneville. This man didn't look old, and he didn't look young. His hair was long and roached up on top like a country music singer's. His hair was yellow like his suit, but it wasn't blonde. He was smoking a cigarette, and when he took a long drag, I saw that his lower teeth were sharp and white like a dog's. He said something I couldn't hear to the big man squatting down beside the car. Then the big man turned back around and said, "Jubal says which way did your daddy go for gas?"

I pointed south. "Down the road yonder, I think," I said. "I'm not real sure, though. It was dark when he left, and I was still kind of sleepy, too. He ought to be back any minute."

The big man got up, leaving a dirty smear on the window, and walked back to the Bonneville where the skinny one was. "Why did you tell him that?" Tory whispered to me. "What's wrong?"

My heart was thumping so fast it sounded like it was fixing to run off and leave the rest of me. "I don't know exactly," I said. "Just don't let them in the car."

Tory rolled up his eyes at me. "We're in a convertible, Patrick," he said. "All they have to do if they want in is to cut the top."

He didn't have enough smarts to be afraid. "Durn it, I've got sense enough to know that," I said. "Don't open the door for them, is what I'm saying. If they start cutting the top, holler and scream and kick like the dickens." I looked through the back window again. "Here they come."

The man in the yellow suit walked around the Volkswagen and looked it over good. He didn't seem too interested in us. The big man was squatting down at the window again grinning. "Jubal says we going to siphon you some gas so you can get on your way," he said and giggled real silly. "Maybe you can meet your daddy down the road and he won't have so far to walk."

"Thank you, sir," I said, but he didn't seem to hear me as he raised up and went on back to the Bonneville.

Directly, the big man cranked up their car and pulled off the road in front of us. That old Bonneville had rusted out, and the paint had turned kind of pinkish purple. The tail pipe might near touched the ground and vibrated so bad that it looked like it was fixing to drop off.

I couldn't keep track of the man in the yellow suit. One minute he'd be standing back at the motor of the Volkswagen, and before I knew it, he'd be somewhere else. It was almost like he could disappear into thin air.

The big man rolled out of the Bonneville and opened up the trunk. It was full of junk. He moved stuff around for a minute or two and then set this wide pasteboard box on the ground. It was full of telephone books, the kind with hard plastic covers you find in the booths connected to the shelf with a little chain.

Before long the big man found a siphoning hose. It wasn't a makeshift job, either. It was one of those store-bought kinds with a hand pump. He unscrewed his gas cap and then unscrewed ours under the hood and commenced siphoning.

Tory turned around to look at me. "They're all right," he said. "They're helping us, aren't they?"

"Yeah, I reckon," I said. I reached between the front seats and drug the garbage bag to the back seat. Then I climbed back into the driver's seat. Now the man in the yellow suit was standing beside the big man as he siphoned gas. "He sure is giving us a lot of gas," I said.

"They're nice men, I think," Tory said, looking at me to see if I was going to agree with him.

My heart had slowed down some, but I still felt uneasy. "I hope so," I said. "That old big one ain't got good sense or something. I know he's weird. He talks funny, like...well, he's weird."

"You know," Tory said, putting his forefinger under his lower lip like some people do when they're studying somebody, "you're very judgmental. You don't like black people, or people from more fortunate backgrounds than your own, or people like those men out there. You don't like anyone who's different. I'd say you're a Republican."

"I don't know if I am or not. All I know, I like people who do to suit me, and I'm not going to say any different."

"You never have liked me, have you?" he said, like he was daring me to say different.

"This is not the time to start a fuss with me," I told him. "I like you right well when you're not being a smart aleck, which is almost never."

Tory started to say something, but he didn't. I figured he finally had sense enough to know that we might be in trouble and needed to stick together. He bit his fingernails as he watched the two men.

After the longest time, the fat man pulled the end of the

siphoning hose out of their car and drained it into the Volkswagen. I heard him screwing the gas cap back on our car, and then he let down the hood. The funny thing was, he left the siphoning hose under our hood. He came back over to the window and said, "Pump it a couple of times and then see if she'll start."

I did exactly what he said, but the car didn't offer to start. "Try her again," he said.

The car still wouldn't start. Then the man in the yellow suit came over to the window. He bent down and stared in at us. He was wearing a white shirt buttoned up at the neck. His eyes were so dark they looked like two black holes. His skin didn't look like any other skin I'd ever seen before. His face looked like it was covered with soft purse leather. He wasn't wrinkled like old folks exactly, but he had a thousand little cracks in his face. Miss Armistead owned some Japanese vases that had all these little cracks in the finish. I remembered asking her if they'd been broken and glued back together again, but she said no, they were supposed to look that way. She said those vases had been crazed. This fellow's face had been crazed, too, look like. "Let me try it," he said in a soft voice that sounded like a preacher's.

He had his hand on the door handle. "I don't know," I said.

All of a sudden, Tory reached all the way across me and flipped up the door latch. "For goodness sakes!" he said, shooting me a hard look. "Let the man try it. Can't you see they're just trying to help us. Honestly!"

I saw then that I was outnumbered by a fool and two men who were probably up to no good. "Okay, whatever you say," I said, opening the door and getting out. "It's your car."

As soon as I was out, the man in the yellow suit slid into the driver's seat. I stood next to the pavement, and the big man eased over to where I was and put his arm around me. "It's going to be all right, honey," he said and hugged me.

I got chickenskin all over. The fat man stunk worse than a dead dog. "Roy," the man in the yellow suit said real quiet, sticking his head a little ways out the window. The fat man turned me loose and took a step or two off to one side.

The man in the yellow suit tried to crank the car, but it didn't want to start for him, either. He got out of the car and went back to the motor and fiddled with it for a while. Then he got back in the car, and this time the motor cranked up on the first try.

"Thank you, sir," I said, walking up to the door and opening it. "How much do I owe you?"

The man in the yellow suit didn't have much lips, just kind of a straight line where his mouth was supposed to be. The straight line widened a little bit, and he stuck out his hand for me to shake. When I came from behind the car door and held out my hand, he wrapped his long fingers around my knuckles and squeezed. He wasn't hurting me, but I felt foolish having him shake my hand that way. "Jubal is the name," he said, his voice gentle and quiet. "Lee is the surname. Jubal Lee."

CHAPTER XX

Tory Smarts Off Once Too Often

He was like a lot of the old men at church. After they shook your hand, they forgot to turn it loose. "Nice to meet you, Mr. Lee," I said, all of a sudden hearing the big man behind me and smelling him, too. "How much do we owe you?"

"Roy's behind you," Jubal Lee said, blinking his dark eyes once. "He used to have a last name, too, but he forgot it."

Behind me Roy giggled. Right then I knew we were in big trouble. I don't know how I knew exactly, because neither one of them had really done anything bad to us, but I knew we were in for it.

"Roy's not what you call a mental giant," Jubal Lee said, and then turned toward Tory like he'd just noticed him for the first time. That was funny, because I'd seen Tory saying something to him in the car. "Now where did you tell me you were headed?"

"To our grandmother's in Starkville," Tory said. "I know she's worried sick that we haven't already arrived. She probably has the highway patrol out looking for us now." He glanced up at me like he was trying to tell me something without saying it. It was a fine time for him to be catching on that these two were up to no telling what.

"I'm from around in those parts myself," Jubal Lee

said. He was talking to Tory, but he kept watching me. I eased my hand back and felt his grip tighten. "What did you say her name was?"

I saw Tory's Adam's apple bobbing in his neck. "Miss Marcella James," he said, choking out the words.

Jubal Lee looked up at the sun visor like he was studying about something. "Miss Marcella James," he repeated, looking at me. "Roy, bring us the box."

Jubal Lee turned sideways toward me and put his feet on the ground. His shoes and socks were yellow, too. He kept pulling me closer toward him, but without hurting me or anything. When Roy set the pasteboard box down at his feet, he turned me loose, but I was still blocked between Roy and him. "Now let's see here," he said, opening a phone book, looking through it a minute, and then throwing it back in the box and picking up another one.

He did the same thing three or four times until he found the phone book he was looking for. Behind Jubal Lee's back, Tory made big eyes at me and shrugged. Jubal Lee had the phone book on his knees and was running his finger down a list of names. Directly, he looked up at me and said softly, "Does your brother know it's wicked to lie? Does he know how absolutely vile a lie is the sight of the Lord?"

"I don't know," I said, my voice beginning to quiver. "You'd have to ask him."

"I'm asking you," he said, never raising his voice. He spread out the fingers on his right hand and looked down at them like a woman will do sometimes when she thinks she has pretty hands.

"I guess he does," I said, scooting along the door panel away from him and glancing back over my shoulder. Roy had one hand on the edge of the door and was still grinning that stupid grin.

Jubal Lee kept looking at his hand. His fingernails were too long for a man, but they were clean and filed into points. "You guess he does," he said.

I looked down the highway to see if I could see a car coming, but there wasn't one anywhere in sight. The black-top curved off toward the left into a sharp knife point and disappeared into pine trees.

"People don't get out much in these parts," Jubal Lee said, his black eyes locked on mine all of a sudden. He made a motion backward with his head. "What's your brother's name?"

Tory threw his arm over the back of his seat, trying to act casual. "It's Tory," he said. "Tory James."

"I'm not talking to you," Jubal Lee said almost in a whisper.

"Okay," Tory said, pushing up his glasses with his thumb. "Be that way. But my name is still Tory James."

Jubal Lee moved so fast that I wasn't sure at first he'd moved atall. He lifted both feet off the ground, swung around in the seat, and caught Tory smack in the temple with his elbow. It sounded like somebody had thrown a baseball into mud. Tory's glasses flew across the seat, and he flopped over on his back with his mouth wide open and started sliding down in the seat.

Right then I aimed to kill Jubal Lee. I heard a sound in my throat I hadn't ever made before, and I took a flying leap toward him, fixing to break his neck if I could.

I had my hands reached out so I could grab him by his roached-up yellow hair, but something jerked me back like a sucker on a snatch hook.

That durn stinking Roy had me by the nape of the neck, holding me an inch or two off the ground. I would have kicked the living daylights out of him, but I couldn't. Something like electricity was shooting through my arms and legs, and I couldn't make them do anything I wanted them to. Then I couldn't get my breath, either.

"Roy," I heard Jubal Lee say, and the next thing I knew, I was feeling sharp gravel on my arms and knees.

Directly, I got up on all fours, and then I saw Roy's feet in front of me. He was wearing these old brown loafers that were busted out on the sides. "Help him up," Jubal Lee said.

Roy reached down and picked me up under my arms like I didn't weigh ten pounds. I kept jerking first one shoulder and then the other, trying to get away from him, but his fingers dug hard into my ribs. "Leave me alone, you bastard!" I hollered. "I've got to see about Tory!"

For some reason he turned me loose, and I ran over to the other side of the car. The door was still locked, but I saw Tory down in the floorboard with his knees touching his chin. At first I thought he was dead, but then I saw his head raise up a little and his right hand wiggle down at his ankle.

I looked at the broad scrubby fields on both sides of the highway. I could take off running now, and neither one of them would be able to catch me. Roy was too big and fat, and Jubal Lee was a smoker. I could get away and maybe find somebody to help me. There was no telling what was fixing to happen to us if we both stayed. There was no need for both of us to get hurt. Everybody looked out for themselves first, anyway, when you got right down to brass tacks. That was a law of nature.

"You want to run, don't you?" Jubal Lee said. He was still sitting down, so I don't know how he knew that.

I never answered. Roy came over and propped his big rusty elbows on top of the car, crossed his hands, and rested his chin on top of his hands. He acted like he was posing for a picture, grinning at me with his pointy black teeth.

Jubal Lee got out of the car and looked across the top of the car at me, too. He reached inside his jacket and brought out a cigarette. "You won't run," he said.

He put the cigarette between his lips and lit it but never took his eyes off me. Seem like his eyes drew me toward him like an undertow, and seem like he knew things about me I didn't want him to, all the secret and dirty and underhand-

ed things I'd ever done. He took a deep drag off the cigarette and blew a perfect smoke ring that rose up over his
yellow head like a halo. "I admire loyalty above else in a
boy or a man," he said his voice as kind as a praying dea-
con's. "I hate lies."

He lowered his eyes for a second and then looked back
at me. "There's no grandmother in Starkville," he said.
"She's not listed in the phone book."

"Well, maybe..."

"No."

He crooked his finger, motioning for me to come closer. I moved a little closer, but still not close enough for
either one of them to grab me. "Let's try this again," he
said, his voice soft and patient. "Be careful, son. Don't
make me change my opinion of you."

I didn't offer to answer him. I glanced down for a second and saw Tory rubbing the side of his head. If he had
any sense left after that lick he took, he might think to
unlock the door and jump out. Right now he didn't look
like he was able to do much of anything, though.

"He'll be all right in time," Jubal Lee said, taking
another long slow drag off the cigarette. This time he blew
out two smoke rings and made one go through the other
one. Roy clapped his hands, and the rings lost their shapes
and disappeared. "There's no grandmother in Starkville,"
Jubal Lee repeated. "There's no grandmother in Starkville
with an unlisted phone number, either. Old ladies seldom
have unlisted numbers." He raised his eyebrows to show me
he was asking a question and aiming for me to answer.

"Nawsir," I said. "There's no grandmother in
Starkville."

Roy looked from me to him and giggled. Jubal Lee
glanced down the highway and then back at me. "The nearest gas station is probably twenty miles from here. Your
daddy had a long walk." He locked his eyes on mine.
"Except there's no daddy."

I didn't say anything until he cocked his head one-sided and raised his eyebrows again. "Nawsir," I said. "My daddy's dead."

He ran his tongue over his front teeth and spit out a little piece of tobacco. He never took his eyes off me, and they kept reeling me in, seem like. "Yes, I think he is," he said. He took another long drag off the cigarette. "You two are too young to be driving, so that means you've run off. You're not out for a joyride. You've got the car loaded with your things."

"Yessir," I said.

Jubal Lee took the cigarette out of his mouth and flipped it right at my eyes.

I swatted at it, but it stung me like a wasp above my left eyebrow. One of my feet slid out from under me in the gravel, and I grabbed hold of the antenna, bending it down to the ground with me.

Before I had time to run or do anything, Roy had me by the nape of the neck again and was holding me spraddled across the hood of the car. I twisted my neck to see where Jubal Lee was. He was still in the same place and was looking back in the direction they had come.

A second later his eyes were boring a hole through me. "You're a polite boy at least," he said. "I like that. Too bad you're a liar, too." He lit another cigarette. "Bring him here, Roy."

Roy yanked me up off the hood and walked me around to the side of the car. Jubal Lee kept one elbow resting on the roof of the car as he turned sideways to look at me. He took a deep drag off the cigarette, and thick coils of blue smoke snaked out his nose.

He placed his thumb on my left cheekbone and his forefinger on my right one, and then he ran his long fingers down the sides of my face real slow until they met on the sides of my chin. He raised up my chin until I was looking into his eyes that were dark as a moonless night. "I like you," he said, holding my chin tight between his thumb and forefinger. He took a deep drag off the cigarette and flipped the ashes from the end.

It was a dream. None of this could be happening, not after everything else that had happened to me. None of this was real. It was happening to somebody else.

Jubal Lee held the cigarette like a piece of chalk about a foot away from my face and moved it back and forth, back and forth. My eyes began to ache from following it. Roy was holding me hard by the nape of the neck and giggling. "Don't ever try to lie to me or fool me again," he said, his gentle voice suddenly crackling like dry leaves. "I'll burn both your eyes out if you do." He held my chin up higher until my neck was stretched like a man hanged. "Do you believe me?"

"Yessir," I said, barely able to speak.

The cigarette kept moving closer to my face. I could feel the heat from it as it passed from one side of my face to the other. "I can't keep an eye on you all the time," he said, once again talking as kind as a Sunday school teacher. "You must never, never, forget what I've told you."

"Nawsir," I heard myself whisper.

"I'm going to keep you around as long as you're useful to me. Do you know what happens if you're no longer useful?"

"Yessir."

His thin lips widened a little bit. I could feel Roy's hot breath on my neck. "Yes, I think you do," he said. Hs held the cigarette an inch from the tip of my nose. "Your brother's no longer useful."

Something in my mind shut down. I was so scared I didn't know what I was saying. "He's not my brother," I said. "He's just a friend."

Jubal Lee's mouth widened even more, and this time I saw the white tips of his dog teeth.

All of a sudden, he flipped the cigarette over the top of

my head. Roy turned me loose, but Jubal Lee still held me by the chin. "That's better," he said. "I didn't want to hurt you, son." He jerked his thumb toward the inside of the car. "He's not your friend, though. He's not even like you, is he?"

"Nawsir, not much," I said, breathing a lot easier.

He turned my chin loose and put his hand on my shoulder. "He just fills up what's missing in you," he said. "He's empty stuffing." He hawked and spit on the pavement. "He's had a soft life, not like you and me. He's never had to be afraid, either."

"You're right about that," I said. "He ain't afraid of nothing. He looks like he would be, but he ain't."

"You were born afraid," he said, taking his hand off my shoulder and reaching for another cigarette in his coat pocket. "Sometimes it pays to be."

I had a funny, crazy feeling about this Jubal Lee. Seem like I'd been knowing him all my life. Seem like he'd always been in the shadows behind me, and if I'd turned around fast enough, I could have met him before now. He was mean as a snake, and he'd put my eyes out in a second, just like he said he would, but there was still something about him that I liked. He looked inside me and saw things that nobody had ever seen before, and he still liked me. He understood me in ways I couldn't exactly put into words. It didn't make any kind of sense, me feeling that way about him, especially after what he'd done to Tory, but I reckon there's more kinds of sense than what comes from your head.

"We'd best be on our way, Roy," Jubal Lee said. He looked at me and nodded toward the car. "What all do you have in there? Clothes?"

"Stuff to eat and drink is in two of the bags," I told him. "That one there in the back seat is the only bag with clothes in it."

"Take your clothes and throw them in the trunk of the

Pontiac," he said. "Put that pasteboard box in the back seat of your car."

When I opened the car door to get out my clothes, Tory stirred. He glanced up at me, but he acted like he couldn't see, or his eyes wouldn't focus, or something. His glasses were lying over in the back seat. I bent the frames back in shape and tried to hand them to him, but he didn't offer to take them. "What's wrong with you?" I said, shaking him by the shoulder. "Are you all right?"

He mumbled a few words, but I didn't catch what he said. His eyes were funny looking, like he was inside a fishbowl trying to see out. "Don't worry about him," Jubal Lee said behind me. "Hurry up."

I laid Tory's glasses behind the back seat and toted the garbage bag out to the trunk of the Bonneville. I knew I'd never see my clothes again, but that was the least of my problems.

Jubal Lee and Roy were talking low as they watched me pick up the pasteboard box and slide it on the back seat. Roy was scratching behind his neck like people do when they don't understand something, or don't like something, and Jubal Lee just looked at him and didn't say anything else.

It was fixing to be a tight fit with all of us riding in this little car. My mind was trying to tell me something, but I wouldn't listen.

"Let's go," Jubal Lee said.

CHAPTER XXI

Riding With Death

I scooted across the back seat to the far corner and unlocked the passenger door for Roy. He opened the door but didn't get in. Jubal Lee had his hand on the corner of the other door. "He can ride in my lap," Roy said across the roof of the car. "I don't care none."

"No," Jubal Lee said. His voice sounded like somebody's nice old granddaddy.

"Jubal, he won't be in the way," Roy said, whining like a little kid who's sleepy. "Let him set in my lap."

"Throw him in the trunk like I told you," Jubal Lee said.

I felt just like I did when Granny Gunn met me at the door of our trailer and told me about my mama being dead. I got real hot, and my head commenced to spin, like I was the one who'd been hit in the gourd. I opened my mouth to speak, but nothing came out. It was like one of those dreams where you need to explain something to get out of trouble, only you can't talk, or you need to run away from danger, but your feet won't move. This wasn't a dream, though. This was a nightmare even worse than a dream nightmare.

Tory was fixing to die, and probably me, too. A warm wet spot spread down the legs of my shorts. I didn't care.

273

My mind shut down again so I wouldn't care about anything.

Roy shifted his weight over on one leg. "You're kidding, ain't you, Jubal? You're trying to scare these little boys so they'll behave," he said.

Jubal Lee didn't answer.

"You do it, then," Roy said. "I ain't going to do it."

"Now Roy," Jubal Lee said barely above a whisper.

"Hell, naw, I ain't about to do it!"

I saw Jubal Lee reach in his back pocket for something. He brought it out and held it down against his skinny leg. It wasn't big, whatever it was, because his long fingers covered it up. Then his fingers wiggled up like spider legs, and I saw then that it was a nickel-plated pistol.

"At least kill him first," Roy said. I could see the points of his elbows in the convertible top.

Jubal Lee's thumb flicked off the safety.

Roy shifted his weight again. "How would you like it if somebody closed you up alive in the trunk of a car on a hot day, you sorry bastard!" he said, his voice whining like a bad starter on a car.

As Jubal Lee's hand made a wide arc and came up over the roof of the car, I saw that the pistol had pearl handles and a little gold button.

He shot. Tory jerked his head back. It sounded like somebody had thrown a firecracker in the car with us. I heard something land over in the grass by the side of the road, and gunpowder stung my nose. "How do you like not having a face, Roy?" Jubal Lee said.

Roy didn't move for the longest time, so I thought Jubal Lee had just shot close to his head to scare him. Then I saw the print of his fingers making furrows across the convertible top. Then his knees banged the side of the door, and he fell over and landed in the gravel on his back. His legs were drawn up, but his knees flopped out wide. He peed in his pants, just like me.

I tried not to look at him, but I couldn't help it. He had a red hole about the size of a dime in his left eyebrow, and his head was lying in the biggest puddle of blood I ever saw. I never knew there was that much blood in a body.

"Get out of the car," Jubal Lee said, not looking inside but motioning me out with the pistol.

He stepped back from the car as I got out. My legs were rubbery, and I could hardly get my breath. I held on to the roof of the car for a second so I wouldn't fall down.

Several beads of blood, bright as a cardinal's feather, were dotted across the white vinyl. I closed my eyes, because I didn't want to see Jubal Lee pull the trigger when he shot me. "Straighten up," he said, so I tried to stand taller.

I heard his footsteps in the gravel and felt his hand on my shoulder again. "Get hold of yourself, is what I meant," he said.

When I opened my eyes, he was smiling. He was smoking another cigarette, and the pistol was nowhere in sight. He leaned close to me, his forehead almost touching mine. He smelled like motel soap and tobacco. "I'm sorry I had to do that," he said low and gentle. "He was going to hurt your friend. Do you understand?"

I didn't like people touching me, but I didn't mind Jubal Lee putting his hand on my shoulder. I don't know why. Maybe because he was talking to me nice, like a daddy should talk to his son. "Nawsir, I don't really understand," I told him. "I thought you were talking about killing Tory."

"No," he said, his eyes hard and shiny as a beetle's shell. "I had to say those things to fool Roy. He was fixing to hurt you both." His long fingers kneaded my shoulder. "You believe me, don't you?"

I felt light as shucks all over, like my spirit was about to leave me or something. I knew I was fixing to say the wrong thing, but I had to say it, even if he shot me dead, too. A powerful thing stirred inside of me, and it rose up like a coiled rattler and struck. "Nawsir," I said, "I don't believe a goddamn word you say."

Jubal Lee took his hand off my shoulder and spit his cigarette out. His face already had a thousand tiny cracks, and now it had that many more. The muscles in his cheekbones wiggled like snakes trying to break out of their shells. He reached behind his coat. "What did I tell you?" he whispered, his hand resting on his hip.

I looked at the blue sky. It didn't look any different than it ever did. The pine trees looked like pine trees, and the blacktop smelled like warm tar. Except for Roy lying dead a few feet away, everything looked as ordinary as could be. I guess I halfway expected a movie of my life to appear before my eyes, or the sky to split open and swallow me up. I was about to die, and nothing happened. "You told me I'd better not never lie to you or try to fool you," I said. "So I told you the truth when you asked me if I believed you."

When his hand came back around, my heart hit my breastbone like a fist.

There was no pistol in his hand. He clapped his hands once and threw back his head and laughed. His laugh was high and wild, like a peacock's call. Shivers went all over me like somebody had dropped ice cubes down my back.

When he finally stopped laughing, he lit another cigarette. Seem like he never was without a cigarette. It was like he was made of bones and hide and smoke.

He took me by the arm and led me over to where Roy was lying sprawled out on the shoulder of the road. He nudged Roy's foot with his yellow shoe. "Drag him down there in the field a ways," he said. "No need of anybody finding him."

I tried not to look at Roy's face again. Two or three green flies were already humming and buzzing around him. His head was lying a foot away from an embankment that dropped about a yard. I started once just to roll him off it, but that didn't seem fitting. So I backed up between his spread-out knees, picked up his feet, and turned him around as much I could. He was real heavy.

Jubal Lee didn't offer to help. He smoked and watched me.

I got Roy's feet over to the edge of the embankment, and then I jumped down. About the time I grabbed him by the feet, I saw something that looked like a piece of broken white saucer lying over in the tall grass. It was the back of Roy's head.

I turned my head and heaved up water and green stuff. Jubal Lee stood up on the embankment smoking and never let on like anything out of the way was even happening.

I was weak and trembly all over, but I finally slid Roy down off the embankment. His shirt rolled up under his arms. He stunk, but something fresh and raw smelled even worse than he did. I wouldn't look at his head.

Foot by foot I commenced dragging him through a field of bitterweed. "Pull him behind the trees over yonder," Jubal Lee said, pointing to a small grove of sycamores about a dozen yards away.

Both of Roy's shoes came off, and so I ended up dragging him by his bare heels. I couldn't move him but a foot or two at a time without stopping to rest. My arms felt like they were fixing to fall off, and I hurt down in the lower part of my back.

Finally, though, I got him pulled behind the trees. The ground was mushy there, and I heard a little branch trickling nearby. "That's good," Jubal Lee said. "On your way back, pick up his shoes and throw them over there with him."

I was so tired I could hardly walk, but I did what he said. When I started climbing up the embankment, he reached down and gave me a hand up. His hand was as smooth and cool as a granite tombrock.

I sat down on the ground for a minute and got my

breath. Jubal Lee walked over to the trunk of the Bonneville and took out a metal toolbox. He opened the hood of the Volkswagen and put it inside. "Let's go," he said, so I had to get up then. My legs ached down to the bone.

He was holding his arm curved out as I walked up to him, and he put it around my shoulder. He led me around to the driver's side of the Bonneville. "I want you to get in this car, little friend," he said, "and drive down the road until it runs out of gas. Then pull over on the shoulder and pop the hood. I'll come along behind you."

As I climbed into his raggedy old car, I asked him, I said, "You won't hurt Tory anymore, will you, Mr. Lee? He won't cause you any more trouble. I'll see to that."

He shut the long, heavy door for me. "No," he said as kind as anybody's old grandma. "I won't hurt him. We've got plenty of room in the car now."

As he turned and walked back to the Volkswagen, his yellow coattails rose up around him like wings.

I cranked up the old Pontiac and took off. Back through the rearview mirror I could see him opening the passenger door. I didn't know what he would do to Tory, but I didn't have any choice but to drive on.

I drove pretty slow, trying to see what was going on behind me, but part of the headliner was loose and flapping in my way. The old Bonneville roared and hissed and smoked.

I rounded a curve in the road and lost sight of the Volkswagen. Another quarter mile down the road and I was out of gas.

I pulled over on the shoulder of the road and found the hood release. I got out and let up the hood like Jubal Lee had told me to. Then I went back and sat on the trunk, sat there as pretty as you please, waiting for Jubal Lee to pick me up or kill me or whatever he was aiming to do.

Something had happened to me since last night, something bad in my head. Seem like the power had gone off in my brain, just like the electricity sometimes went off in a house, and nothing worked right. When I'd try to think of a way to get out of this mess, my ideas would fuzz and tangle like a piece of baling twine, and I couldn't straighten them out. I couldn't even remember ordinary stuff. I didn't know what day of the week it was. I couldn't remember Tory's last name or what street we lived on. I did finally remember my birthday, but I didn't know my age anymore.

In a minute Jubal Lee pulled up beside the Bonneville. Before I even opened the door, I spotted Tory lying on his side in the back seat with his knees drawn up. I hopped in, and we took off.

I turned around in the seat to look at Tory. He was pale and sweaty and had lines of dirt in the creases of his neck. "Get my bike?" he said, batting his eyes at me. Without his glasses, his eyes looked watery and weak.

"What?" I said. "What bike?"

"Braves," he said. "I think this year the Braves."

"What's wrong with him?" I said, touching Jubal Lee on the arm. "Something's not right about him. He's not making sense."

Jubal Lee looked down at my hand on his coat sleeve. "Don't touch me," he said.

I drew my hand back like I'd touched a stove eye. "I didn't mean to," I said, watching his knuckles turn white as they gripped the gearshift. "I wasn't thinking. I'm like you. I don't like anybody touching me, either."

I sat still and didn't say anything else. "He'll be all right," he said after a while. He didn't sound mad, but then he hardly ever did. "Keep talking to him. If he tries to go to sleep, wake him up."

I turned back around again. "We've just crossed the Mississippi state line," I said. "Mississippi is the Magnolia State."

"And the armpit of the world," Jubal Lee said, cutting his crow's eyes over at me. I thought he was joking at first,

279

but he didn't offer to smile.

I talked to Tory about how I wanted a motorcycle and how I hated algebra and what was the best way to cast with a spinning reel. I told him about my second grade teacher, Miss Clara Hopper, and how everybody called her Miss Clodhopper behind her back. We rode along for several miles, me talking about the first thing that popped into my head, and every so often Tory would say something else that didn't make sense.

Jubal Lee didn't talk atall. He gripped the steering wheel with one hand and drove as fast as the little Volkswagen would go.

The winding highway was narrow and cut through miles of kudzu and pines and old scrubby stuff like sumac and mimosa. The sides of the road were all time closing in on us, seem like. For a long spell, we wouldn't see a single house or hardly any people on the road, either. What houses we saw were mostly poor. They set upon raw, red bluffs and in gouged-out places in the pine woods. We passed one car, an old silver '81 Cutlass with rust showing through the paint. It was so jam-packed full of poor white folks that the rear bumper might near dragged the ground.

As we passed through this little town called Holly Springs, Tory raised up on his elbow a little and batted his eyes. "Patrick," he said.

"That's right!" I said. I held up my hand to give him a high five, but he wouldn't raise his. "I'm Patrick. Do you know everything now? Are you all right?"

He laid back down and closed his eyes, so I reached back and shook him. "You can't go to sleep," I told him. "What's my name?"

"Ted Turner," he said.

Out of the corner of my eye I saw Jubal Lee's mouth widen a little. "Come on now," I said. "Be serious. What's my name?"

His big blue eyes were walled-up and glassy. "Where's

the fire?" he said.

I saw then that it was no use trying to get him to talk sense. I didn't answer him, but every time he tried to close his eyes, I shook him hard. Directly, Jubal Lee said, "Get you something to eat if you want to, but don't feed him."

I didn't know for sure why he didn't want me to give Tory something to eat, and I didn't ask. I could always slip him something later. If Jubal Lee caught me, he'd probably kill me, but he was going to kill us both, anyway. It might be today or tomorrow or a month down the road, but he was fixing to kill us all the same.

I reached behind the seat and dug out a two-liter Coke, a banana, and a bag of chocolate chip cookies. "Would you have something to eat with me, Mr. Lee?" I said, sounding like Miss Armistead.

He touched my bare knee with the tips of his cold fingers. "I don't eat in front of anybody," he said. "Don't worry about anybody else. Take care of yourself."

He didn't say it like he was trying to be mean or smart-alecky. He sounded like he was trying to teach me something that I needed to know. I knew good and well it didn't make any sense, but seem like he did kind of like me, just like he said he did.

I didn't know I was hungry until I commenced eating. I ate the banana and at least a dozen cookies. I swigged down about half of the Coke. It was warm and foamy, but it still tasted good to me.

Tory lay there watching me eat, but I don't think he really saw me. If he did, he didn't know what I was doing. I don't think he did, anyway.

Jubal Lee kept smoking one cigarette after another. The fingers where he held his cigarette were yellow all the way up to his knuckles, and even the fingernails on those fingers were brown and yellow. "Stop looking at me," he said, and I did.

I put my chin on the back on the seat and kept an eye

on Tory. Directly, though, my left leg went to sleep, so I had to turn around to rub some feeling back in it. Right then I saw a road sign that said we weren't far from this place called Oxford. I remembered Miss Armistead saying her husband went to school there, but didn't seem like it was in Mississippi. Then I remembered that this place was across the ocean. All we'd crossed was a creek called the Tallahatchie a while back. I'd heard that name somewhere before, but I couldn't remember where.

All of a sudden, Jubal Lee slowed down fast and turned right on this dirt road, only it wasn't a road, exactly. It was more like a pig path with two ruts to drive in and tall grass growing down the middle. We drove about a hundred yards, the little car rocking from side to side and grass switching underneath, and came to this bobwire gate. I wondered where in the world we were headed. "Get out and undo the gate," Jubal Lee said. "Pull it over to one side and leave it lay."

I capped the Coke and hopped out of the car. The gate post was held up by a loop of baling wire at the bottom and another one at the top. After I unhitched the gate and got it stretched out of the way, I climbed back in the Volkswagen, and we drove on.

The path bore around to the left. Another hundred yards, and the field we were passing through was grown up higher than the car. Up ahead, though, I saw the tops of three oak trees, and I figured then that we were coming to a house or maybe a barn.

Sure enough, the path led to this little shack, somebody's old homeplace. All the windows were broken out, and a wild rose bush was growing through the front window. Over on the right was a well house with the roof caved in. In the back I noticed a bunch of old peach trees that were twisted and black.

Jubal Lee pulled right up to the front porch and stopped. Most of the porch planks were rotted out, but somebody had nailed down two new two-by-fours from the step to the front door, making a kind of footlog. "Put your stuff inside and then come back and get him," Jubal Lee said.

I got out and toted the two garbage bags across the footlog. Broken glass was scattered all over the floor inside. Dry strips of old wallpaper hung down off the walls, and dirt daubers had made nests in every corner. Something or somebody had messed on the fireplace hearth, but it was mostly dried up. Two other rooms went straight back, but I could see big rusty holes in the tin roof above, and the floors had completely rotted out. There were beer cans and food cans and old newspapers scattered everywhere. The front door was off the hinges and propped against the wall where I came in. Somebody had written ugly stuff on it about this girl named Tammy.

The horn beeped. Jubal Lee was wanting me to hurry, and I knew better than to keep him waiting.

When I got outside again, he'd let the top down on the Volkswagen and was leaning on the front fender smoking a cigarette. Tory was sitting up in the back seat with his chin resting on his chest. "Get the lead out," Jubal Lee said.

I opened the passenger door and let the seat forward. "Come on, Tory," I said. "Give me your hand."

Tory didn't try to get out, but he did raise his head. He sat there looking at me but still acted like he wasn't exactly seeing me. I grabbed him by the wrist and tugged a little, and then he grabbed hold of my arm right below the elbow and raised up. He held on to me like a blind man and stumbled out of the car. I backed up to the step and led him that way across the footlog and into the house. I cleared a place on the floor with my foot and pulled him down. He flopped down hard and rolled over on me. "Sit up, Tory," I said, helping him. "Don't try to go to sleep, now."

I didn't hear Jubal Lee walking up the footlog, but when I looked up, he was standing in the door blocking out the light. His shadow looked like a man wearing a cape. "I'll be back after a while," he said. He stared at me, and I looked away, but I could feel his eyes crawling over me like big night bugs that are drawn to the light.

"Okay," I said. "You go right ahead, Mr. Lee."

He drew back his coattails and slipped his hands inside his pockets. "I don't need to tell you anything, do I, child?" he said.

I knew exactly what he meant. "Nawsir," I said.

His straight line of a mouth widened, and he nodded at Tory. "He's beginning to come around," he said.

Before I could answer, he disappeared. The shack was dim inside, like he'd taken all the light with him when he left. I heard him crank up the Volkswagen, and a second later I saw the top of his yellow head pass across the window sill.

CHAPTER XXII

Tory Comes Around

After a while I couldn't hear the car anymore, but I stayed put for a good long spell, figuring that Jubal Lee was stopped somewhere watching to see if I'd try to run off. He didn't have to worry about that—not yet, anyway.

Tory didn't look like he was doing much good to me. He was dripping with sweat, and seem like he was having a hard time getting his breath. My T-shirt he was wearing was wet across his back and looked like it was about to cut him in two.

I picked up a long piece of glass off the floor and snagged a hole in the back of the T-shirt and ripped it off him. He moaned a little like I was hurting him. His flesh kind of sagged down in a puddle around his waist, but he looked relieved. I managed to tear all the T-shirt off except for the band around his neck, and I finally cut that off with the glass, too. All this time he didn't move, just sat there with his fat white legs all spraddled out looking like Miss Armistead's statue of this Japanese god named Bubba.

With Jubal Lee out of sight for the time being, seem like my own head was clearing up some. I started thinking about what to do. This morning I was ready to give up and die, but that was this morning. I reckoned will power ran out of gas sometimes like a car.

If I stayed on my toes, I figured I could save myself for sure. Sooner or later, the time would come when I could make my getaway.

Then something hit me, something that Miss Armistead was always saying. *There's no time like the present.* Jubal Lee wouldn't ever find me in all these piney woods unless he got awfully lucky. Why didn't I go now, while the coast was clear?

Tory. He was still too addled to run away with me. I hated myself for thinking it, but just for a minute I thought about leaving him behind. Nobody could blame me. It was the natural thing to do. *Save yourself,* a voice inside my head told me. *It's the natural thing to do.* I shook my head, but the voice kept nagging me.

I knew all the time I was thinking about leaving Tory behind, I wouldn't do it. Or would I? It didn't make sense for both of us to die. I might never get another chance to get away again.

I got a hollow, sinking feeling thinking about what Jubal Lee would eventually do to us, but I decided that I couldn't leave Tory. He'd saved my life, and I owed him.

But that still wasn't the reason I couldn't leave him. He'd be dead the second Jubal Lee came back and found him there without me. Suppose I did get away and got back home and every single bit of that mess I left behind in Broad Plains was cleared up with the law? I still had to get up of a morning and look myself in the mirror when I brushed my teeth. I couldn't eat my supper or wash my face or even walk around like a human being for the next fifty or sixty years with that monkey on my back. I had to do right, not because I was good, but because I had to live with a conscience that was as overbearing as a schoolteacher.

Or was all that a lie? Was I just too scared to run off and leave Tory? I didn't really know for sure. Since I'd run into Jubal Lee, nothing was clear in my head anymore.

I stood up and looked out the window. I didn't see a

sign of Jubal Lee, but that didn't mean anything. I halfway expected him to appear in a puff of smoke. "I'll be back in a second," I told Tory. "I ain't peed in a year."

Tory moved his head a little to one side like he was trying to hear me better, but I don't think he understood me.

I walked across the footlog and then around back to the peach orchard. The weeds were high and snaky out there. Blackberry vines were tangled everywhere. Birds were chirping overhead in the trees and in the thickets. I peed a mile.

As I was zipping up my fly, I listened to see if I could hear the car anywhere. What I heard was water, a little trickling branch. Then I spied a small clump of willows and sycamores. I had a pretty good idea where the branch was.

I looked around and found a twisted piece of peach tree limb about a yard long. I beat back the high weeds and blackberry vines. This was just the place for a big copperhead to be hiding, and I probably would be covered from head to toe with chiggers, but I wanted to find that branch.

About fifteen yards away I did find it, except it wasn't a branch. Where the flat land began to gently slope back toward a long line of trees, a clean, cold spring bubbled out of a little shelf of limestone and splattered down on some slick green rock. Somebody had driven an iron pipe into the limestone, making a spigot, and a rusty dipper hung over the pipe.

I rinsed out the dipper and got me a drink. The water was so cold that it made my filling ache. I felt like taking off my clothes and standing under the spout, but the water was way too cold. What I did was take off my shorts and underwear and wash them out. I rinsed off with my hands as best I could. Then I put my clothes back on wet and went to check on Tory.

He was still sitting there where I'd left him, but he lifted his head when I came in. "Hot," he said real hoarse. "I'm hot."

I saw then that Jubal Lee had known what he was talking about. Tory was coming around. Things were looking up.

I decided to try and take him to the spring. I got behind him and grabbed him up under his arms. "Help me, now," I said. "Come on, stand up."

He weighed a ton, seem like, but directly he started bending his legs back, trying to stand up, and finally he did. He was still mighty wobbly, so I kept my hands up under his arms and guided him out the door. "Just go straight," I said. "I'm right behind you. I won't turn you loose."

We shuffled across the footlog. "We're at the step, now," I told him. "There's two of them. I've got you. Just take it easy."

After we got down the steps, I turned him at the side of the house. We walked down the path I'd beaten back. Once we got to the spring, I sat him in the shade of a little sycamore.

I took off my T-shirt and soaked it under the spout. I wrung it out some and put it on Tory's face and the nape of his neck. "Feels good," he mumbled. "Water. Give me some water."

It was pitiful to see him reaching out toward the spigot and trying to lick the drops off his face. Jubal Lee said not to give him anything to eat or drink, but I didn't care.

I got a dipper full of water and brought it over to him. He grabbed it out of my hands and spilled most of it on him. He was snorting and gurgling like he was starved to death for water, and then he held out the dipper for more. I got him some more, but after he'd drunk all that and held out the dipper again, I told him, I said, "Tory, you've been hit hard in the head. You're not supposed to drink anything. Don't you tell anybody I gave you water. I could get in big trouble. You understand?"

He nodded three or four times and blinked his eyes. "Hit," he said. "Hit hard."

"Yeah, for real," I said. "So you remember that, do you?"

All of a sudden, he grabbed one side of his head and rolled over on his side. He kicked back with one leg, not like he was trying to, but like he couldn't help it. "My head," he moaned.

I soaked and wrung out the T-shirt again and rolled him over on his back. He was lying in itchy grass and leaves and sticks on his bare back, so I sat down behind him and put his head in my lap. I felt funny doing that, but nobody was ever going to know about it except us. I kept bathing his face and forehead with the damp T-shirt, and directly he closed his eyes again. I hated to do it, but I shook his head. "You can't go to sleep," I said. "I've already told you that. Wake up!"

As soon as he opened his eyes, I knew for sure he was going to be all right. His eyes were clear, like somebody had skimmed the scum off them. "I'm awake," he said right hateful. "Where in the world are we, anyway?"

"I don't know," I said, beginning to ease his head up out of my lap. "Somewhere in Mississippi."

He commenced wiggling and then sat up by himself. He rubbed his hand through his hair and looked like he'd just come awake from a hard night's sleep. "Somebody helped us, didn't they?" he said.

"They helped themselves to your car," I said, "and might near killed you. That's the kind of help we had." I reckon I had to get my dig in. "But it wasn't my doings."

I hated to throw it up to him, about him unlatching the door for them in the first place, but I couldn't help it. I was worn out with everything and everybody.

Tory rubbed his eyes and groaned. "The last thing I remember, one of them hit me with something," he said.

"With his durn elbow, upside your head."

Tory touched the side of his head and then looked at his fingers. "He told me something in the car," he said.

"That one with the funny eyes. I knew we were in trouble when he said something, but I can't remember. I think I tried to let you know. I can't think."

I saw that Tory's mind was still scattered, so I told him everything from start to finish, except the part about him trusting them in the first place. There was no need in beating a dead horse to death. And I didn't fill in all the details about Roy getting shot, because I wished I hadn't seen that myself, and there was no need of him picturing something awful in his mind when he didn't have to. What I wound up trying to get through his thick skull was that he'd better keep his mouth shut when Jubal Lee was talking and not be smarting off.

"He hit me in the head just because I told him my name?" he said, touching the side of his head again like it was still tender. "And he was going to let me suffocate in the trunk of the car? Honestly."

I stood up and brushed my wet hind end off. "You'd better remember what I said," I told him. "He'd just soon kill you as look at you."

Tory put both hands over his ears and frowned. "Don't talk so loud," he said. "He made a believer out of me without you going on about it. I get the message." I don't reckon Tory could help being a smart aleck. I wrung out my T-shirt as best I could and tugged it back on.

I knew I looked a sight. "Come on," I said, offering Tory a hand up. "We need to go on back to the house. If Jubal Lee catches us down here, he might think we're trying to slip off. I've done seen how he acts when somebody crosses him."

Tory waved my hand away. He got up on all fours and then stood by himself. He was still weaving a little on his feet, but I didn't have any doubts now that he was fixing to be all right. "You go on," he said, kind of turning red in the face. "I'll catch up with you in a minute."

I understood why he wanted me to go on, so I turned

around and walked up to the end of the path. Directly, I heard him moving toward me. He sounded as heavy as one of Mr. Aaron's old steers as he made his way through the tall grass. When he got up to where I was, he was pale as cornmeal and out of breath. It was going to take him a while to get over that lick, look like.

We walked back to the shack and sat down on the steps. Tory was sweating and still breathing hard. His eyes looked weak and tired without his glasses. "So what are we going to do?" he said. "Maybe the car was all he wanted, and he won't be coming back."

Something moved out in the tall grass in front of the shack, and in a heartbeat four fat quail rose up in a flapping flutter and flew far away. "He'll be back," I said. "He needs us for something, and we'll have to go along with him for the time being. I don't know anything else to do."

"So why don't we just take off now?" Tory said, waving his arm out toward the rank fields on both sides of us. "He couldn't find us out there in a million years."

Everything had gotten still. The birds were no longer chirping out back in the peach orchard. Not even a breeze stirred. Way off in a distance, buzzards circled under the blazing sun. "What's wrong?" Tory said.

"I'm not sure," I said. "It's just a feeling I have. I think he may be watching us right now."

Tory shivered, even though he was sweating still. "Then let's go," he said, bracing himself on my shoulder as he tried to stand up.

I pulled him down. "You see? You're not yourself yet. What if you were to pass out on me while he was running after us?" I made a motion with my finger like I was cutting my own throat. "He's already told me what he'd do if I ever tried to trick him. Besides, we don't know anything about this country, but he does."

Tory let out a big breath like he was about halfway put out with me. "Well, I don't know," he said. "Right now running away seems like a pretty good idea to me."

My heart began to race. "Running ain't done me any good so far, has it?" I said, knowing all the time that I was a hair away from doing what he wanted. "I ran away from my daddy, and now the law and everybody else thinks I killed him. I ran away from Broad Plains, and now look what a fine mess we're in."

"Yeah, but what if you'd stayed up there in Nashville with your father?" Tory said. "If you didn't kill him, then somebody else had to, and whoever killed him would probably have killed you, too."

I hadn't even thought about that. "I guess that's right," I said, swallowing hard. I pictured myself lying dead in that motel room with my throat cut from ear to ear like my neck was smiling.

Tory rubbed the nape of his neck and leaned his head back for a second. "Of course I'm right," he said. "And we're going to be in big trouble if we don't hurry up and get away from here. That is, if that Jubal Lee person comes back. I'm not convinced he's coming back."

Right then both of us heard a car slow down and pull off the road. "We'd better get in the house," I told Tory.

"We should've run," he said.

CHAPTER XXIII

Jubal Lee Uses Us

I got up and started walking across the footlog, but Tory was still standing on the step. He had his head cocked toward the pig path. "That's not my car," he said. "That's not a Volkswagen I hear."

I went back and grabbed him by the arm. "Come on, durn it!" I said, pulling him along. "He's switched cars. He knows by now the police are probably looking for us."

We got inside the house just in time. We squatted behind the rosebush growing through the front window and watched as Jubal Lee drove up to the porch and parked the car. The car was a blue Plymouth Reliant, one of the older '80s models.

I knew what he'd done. We weren't far from Oxford, and he'd gone there and traded off Tory's car. No telling what Tory's car was worth, but he'd never see it again. Somebody would snatch that little car up in a minute.

We were both sitting on the floor when Jubal Lee appeared at the door. He could step lighter than any man I had ever seen. He never raised his voice, either, even when he was mad. The only thing loud about him was his clothes. "You're wet," was the first thing he said, his eyes crawling over Tory and me like two beetles over a carcass.

I didn't answer. I figured the less said, the better, with Jubal Lee.

"You're wet," he said again, this time raising one of his eyebrows.

Tory sat rock still and stared down between his feet like this had nothing to do with him. "I wasn't trying to be nosy, Mr. Lee, but I found the spring," I said.

"Did you?" he said. He looked at me but pinched the middle of his lower lip between his thumb and forefinger like he was studying about something.

"I washed out my clothes and got me a cold drink of water," I said. "I didn't have anything here to drink but some old hot co-cola."

He reached into his coat pocket and brought out a cigarette. After he lit it, he pointed at Tory. "What about you?"

Tory was still looking down at the floor and didn't know that Jubal Lee was talking to him, so I nudged his knee with my elbow, "Mr. Lee wants to know how you're feeling."

Tory looked up and shrugged. "I'm okay," he said. "I feel better."

"I'm sure you do," Jubal Lee said, thick twisted coils of smoke curling out of his nose. "Patrick here took care of you. Kept you awake and bathed your face in cool spring water."

He *had* been watching us! I didn't know where he'd switched cars, but now I knew he hadn't had time to go to Oxford to trade.

He took another step closer. He didn't look mad, but you never could tell about him. "Did you think about running away?" he asked.

Tory was drawing X's and O's in the dust between his legs. "Yessir," I said, barely able to get my breath.

He was standing over us now. The sun was jabbing through the broken windows in wide bright blades, but he didn't cast a shadow. Granny Gunn had a big white Bible she had bought from a traveling salesman when she was a girl. Over the years the leather backs had turned brownish yellow. Jubal Lee's face looked like the covers of that Bible. "Time to go," he said, jerking his thumb toward the door.

I didn't know who he was talking to, Tory or me, or if he was fixing to take me outside to shoot me. "Come on, Tory," I said.

Tory got up without any help from me. Jubal Lee stood aside and let us pass. We stepped off the porch and waited in front of the car. "Go on and get in," Jubal Lee said from the doorway. "Both of you get in the front."

I calmed down then. I knew he wasn't going to kill us, not here and now, anyway. I scooted across the vinyl seat and straddled the hump. Tory was a good-sized boy, and after he climbed in, we were sitting elbow to elbow. Tory didn't smell too sweet, but I don't guess I did, either.

The car was old but real clean. I saw that it didn't have but 22,000 miles on it. It was an old lady's car. Knowing Jubal Lee, he'd probably shot some poor old lady and taken it. But then I figured he wouldn't do that, not here, anyway. I had a notion that this was his homeplace. He knew how to get rid of one car and get another one in a few minutes, so he had to be acquainted with some people in these parts. Everything added up. He probably did his meanness away from here and came back when things got too hot for him elsewhere.

In a minute or two Jubal Lee got in the car, and we headed back up the pig path. Then I remembered something. "Mr. Lee," I said, "we forgot to get our stuff. Our eats."

"We'll be back, country boy," he said.

We passed through the gate and stopped. "Get out and close it," he said. I started to crawl over Tory, but Jubal Lee grabbed me by the arm and pulled me back down on the seat. "Not you. Fat boy there."

My heart skipped a beat. I figured that Tory couldn't help saying something smart back, and then he'd end up killing us both. But Tory didn't open his mouth. He hopped out of the car and commenced putting up the gate.

I said to Jubal Lee, trying to act like I was just making conversation, I said, "This is your old homeplace, ain't it? I'll bet it used to be pretty when it was fixed up."

At first he didn't answer or even act like he heard me. He was watching Tory through the side mirror. Tory finally got the gate hitched up and crawled back in the car. When we pulled out on the highway headed south, Jubal Lee said, "Sometimes it doesn't pay to know too much. It pays to forget."

"Yessir," I said.

I knew we weren't safe, but I felt better being out on the highway. We were meeting cars every now and then. If this Oxford had any traffic lights, maybe we could jump out when the car stopped and run for help. The only thing was, I didn't know how to let Tory in on what I was thinking.

Jubal Lee put his hand on my knee again. "You know," he said, "there's two ways to forget something you don't want to remember. Do you know what those two ways are, Patrick?"

I knew then I'd made him mad when I'd tried to pick him. His fingers pressed spots around my knee. "Nosir," I said. "I'm sorry if I spoke out of turn. I wasn't trying to be nosy."

"One way is to get so old that you forget everything," he said, his voice barely above a whisper. "Do you know what the other way is?"

"Nosir," I said.

Tory said, "He means to die. When you're dead, you don't remember anything." Tory leaned across me and said to Jubal Lee, "You don't have to worry about us, sir. Neither one of us remembers a thing. I sure don't."

"Shut up, fat boy," Jubal Lee said, cutting his eyes around at Tory. "Nobody pulled your string."

Tory stared out the window and didn't answer. He'd

learned his lesson. I was about to learn mine.

All of a sudden, something like a big jolt of electricity shot up my leg. Jubal Lee was squeezing hard on both sides of my knee, making me squirm around every which way on the seat. I was in Tory's lap, but he didn't turn loose. He kept squeezing harder and harder. My knee hurt like the worst toothache in the world. "Please, stop!" I hollered. "Please, please!"

About the time I thought I was going to pee on myself again, he stopped. I had tears in my eyes, and my nose was running like a wet weather spring. I was hurting all over, from my leg to my insides to my fingertips.

Tory eased me back down in the seat. He was looking all puffed up like he was aiming to spout off something, but I shook my head to keep him quiet. Jubal Lee yawned like a cat and showed his sharp white teeth.

We drove on a little piece, none of us talking. My knee ached right up into my arm, but I sat as still as I could. I found out that I was really going to have to watch myself. Everything I said to Jubal Lee was weighed and counted, and he was smart enough to know when somebody was trying to fool him.

We were a few miles from Oxford when he turned left and headed out Highway 30. Seem like every single thing I'd thought of, he'd already thought of it first. In my head I knew that wasn't possible, but I had a feeling that he'd already figured out that I was fixing to jump out of the car in Oxford. The straight line of his mouth widened as he watched me out of the corner of his eye.

It wasn't pretty country we were passing through. I could tell it hadn't rained here in a good long spell. The fields and the grass alongside the road looked dry and dusty. The trees were far off and lonesome looking. Seem like everybody who lived here was lying low somewhere until times got better. Maybe it was just my own misery I was feeling, but I felt misery in the baked, flat fields and the narrow bridges and the patched-up blacktop.

We must have been close to this place called New Albany when Jubal Lee pulled off the shoulder of the road and switched on the radio. He punched buttons and tuned the radio until he got this station where a man was first telling some news about what was happening in the United States and overseas at this big conference in Stockholm. Directly, there were commercials about State Farm Insurance in Tupelo and some funeral home that would fix everything to suit you when you died. I got nervous, and then real hot, even though Jubal Lee had the air condition-er going. Then the newsman said that the time was twelve-fifteen and started telling the local news.

Jubal Lee reached inside his coat and brought out a long skinny notepad like the one Miss Armistead wrote her grocery list on and a little stubby green pencil. The news-man talked about something the county commissioners had voted on and how short the county was on rain and how some men were going around trying to cheat old folks out of their Social Security checks. There were some more com-mercials about a furniture store selling a bunch of tents and a grocery store having the lowest prices anywhere.

Jubal Lee had the notepad resting on the bottom part of the steering wheel, but he didn't write anything until the newsman came on again and started talking about people in the county who had died. Then he commenced writing as fast as he could. He didn't bear down hard on his pencil. From where I was sitting, his writing looked like spider webs. All the time he was writing, I played like I was look-ing straight ahead, but I saw that he was writing down names. There were just two people who had died, but he wrote a page full of names. When the newsman said that sports and the farm report were next, he switched off the radio.

He cut off the motor and took the keys. "Don't run off," he said, getting out of the car and walking back to the trunk.

Tory mumbled something dirty under his breath when he thought Jubal Lee couldn't hear him.

Jubal Lee opened the trunk. We could hear him moving stuff around back there. "What's he doing?" Tory whispered.

I could look through the rearview mirror and see Jubal Lee's waist and hands through the crack where the trunk was let up. "The phone books," I said. "He's getting out a phone book. He did that once before, when he looked up your granny's name in Starkville and couldn't find it. That's why he got so mad at you, because he found out you had lied to him, and then you smarted off."

"I know what he's doing," Tory said as Jubal Lee slammed the trunk lid.

We both shut up. Jubal Lee got in the car carrying a phone book in a blue plastic cover and his notepad. He cranked up the car again and started leafing through the phone book. He stopped every so often and wrote stuff beside some names and crossed one or two names off his list.

Before long I figured out that he was writing down the addresses of people who had outlived the dead people on the radio. He stopped writing for a second and without looking at me said, "Do you know what I'm doing, Patrick?"

"Nosir," I said. "I don't see anything, and I don't know anything."

He reached over smiling and ran the eraser end of the pencil gently down my cheek. "Good boy," he said and then started turning through the phone book again. "I'll bet the filthy-mouthed fat boy over there knows. Tell the filthy-mouthed fat boy about people who know too much."

I didn't look at Tory. "They need to forget," I said.

Jubal Lee kept writing and turning pages. "You're an intelligent boy, too, Patrick," he said, his voice as soft as warm butter. "What's the fat boy's name? I don't believe I've ever heard it."

I could hear my heart knocking like an old car with bad pistons. I still didn't look at Tory's face, but I saw he'd made two fists between his legs. "Tory James," I said, my voice cracking like dry kindling.

"Tory James," Jubal Lee repeated. "Yes, I believe I have heard that name somewhere before, now that you mention it." He closed the phone book then and reached over behind me to drop it in the back floorboard. He kept his arm around me. His cold fingers brushed the short hairs on the back of my neck. "Is he any kin to Jesse James, do you suppose?"

"I don't know," I said. I had chickenskin all over, and the fuzz on my arms and legs was standing straight up.

All of a sudden, Tory squalled out in my right ear.

Jubal Lee had his ear lobe pinched between his yellow thumb and forefinger. Every time Tory would start to put his hand on Jubal Lee's hand, Jubal Lee would stretch his ear lobe out farther. Before long Tory's head was pulled over on my shoulder. "Are you kin to Jesse James, Tory James?" Jubal Lee said. He sounded like somebody's sweet old uncle asking about kinfolks at a family reunion.

Tory squirmed and bucked and breathed in quick little breaths. "Yessir," he said, his voice even higher than usual. "Yessir, I am."

Jubal Lee looked at me like we were buddies sharing a secret. "Tell us all about it, Tory James," he said, his cigarette breath in my face. "Tell Patrick and me about it."

Tory's hand was raking up and down my leg, but he didn't even know it. "He was kin to my great-grandfather somehow," Tory said, squeezing his eyes shut and breathing like he couldn't get a good breath of air. "His brother Frank James is buried in this graveyard in Lawrence County, Tennessee. My dad and I went to see his grave one summer when we were visiting my grandmother in Broad Plains."

Jubal Lee smiled at me. His eyes didn't look like any eyes I had ever seen. You couldn't tell where the black dot began and where it ended. "She moved to Starkville, did she?" Jubal Lee said. "Your grandmother."

Tory was trying to keep from crying, but tears were running down his face and dripping off his chin. "Nosir," he said. "It was a lie I told you."

Jubal Lee turned him loose then. When Tory raised up his head, his ear was red and stretched looking, and blood was oozing down his neck where Jubal Lee had torn the bottom corner of his ear lobe away from his head. Tory kept rubbing his neck and looking at the blood on his hand like he couldn't believe it was his own. "It's not bad," I told him. "I know it hurts, but it's not bad. Maybe an eighth of an inch cut."

"Tell Patrick what happened to Jesse James, Tory James," Jubal Lee said, licking his fingers and wiping his hand on the seat.

I knew what had happened to Jesse James, because I'd read a story about him, but I never let on. "He got shot," Tory said. He covered his ear with his hand and kept it there.

"Yes indeed," Jubal Lee said, putting the car in gear and pulling out on the highway. "Somebody shot him in the back of the head. He didn't get the picture straight."

Tory turned away from me, sniffling and hiccuping. I felt so sorry for him I didn't know what to do. He might be the biggest smart aleck in the world, but that didn't give Jubal Lee the right to do what all he'd done to him. Tory didn't know anything about people like Jubal Lee, how low-down mean white trash was. He didn't know how to deal with people that hated everybody and everything.

I wanted to kill Jubal Lee so bad I could feel something like a snake crawling up my throat, and my fingers ached to the bone. He wasn't going to hurt Tory anymore. He might shoot me or cut me or smother the life out of me, but he was fixing to leave this world at least knowing that I'd been there.

We were coming into New Albany. Jubal Lee drove with just his wrist resting on top of the steering wheel. The notepad was lying in the seat between us. The top name on his list read, "Harvel Lewis, Ripley Rd.," and the phone number was written under it.

Jubal Lee cut his eyes over at us. "We're coming into town," he said. "Let's not be like old Jesse, now. Let's make sure we've got the picture straight." The line of his mouth widened and then shrank. "I've got cancer, boys. It feels like a big hand trying to claw out my backbone. Do you know how it feels knowing you're about to die?"

I didn't know which one of us he was talking to, because he was looking straight ahead, but I said, "Yessir. I might near drowned here a while back, and I thought you were fixing to kill me two or three times today."

He changed hands on the steering wheel and rubbed my face with his bent forefinger. "Yes, I was, Patrick," he said. "I think you must remind me of someone I used to know. That may not keep me from killing you later on, but it has so far."

I wondered then if he'd killed who he was talking about, but I knew better than to ask him. I saw Tory's reflection in the window, and when he saw me looking at him, he closed his eyes.

Jubal Lee reached in his coat pocket for a cigarette and pushed in the cigarette lighter on the dash. "I'm telling you about my cancer because I want you both to know that I have nothing to lose by killing you," he said. "I'm already a dead man." He pointed the cigarette first at Tory and then at me. "Either one of you tries anything with me, I'll kill you deader than a doornail. I don't care if we're in McDonald's or on the courthouse steps, you'd better do what I say, when I say."

"Yessir," I said.

"Yessir," Tory echoed.

We were inside the city limits now. New Albany wasn't much size, but it looked like a nice little town, the kind where you could sit outside in your porch swing at night without anybody bothering you. The truth was, it wasn't that kind of town atall, and no other town is, either, because there's always people like Jubal Lee roaming in and out like mad dogs.

When we stopped at the first traffic light, Jubal Lee said, "Hey, fat boy, if you're so smart, tell Patrick here why I wrote down these names and addresses and phone numbers." He picked up the notepad and waved it in my face.

Tory looked down at his feet and spoke like a child who's just had a whipping. "They're survivors of the people who've died around here. While they're at the funerals, we're going to their houses." He looked at me then. "To steal their things."

It didn't seem possible that anybody could be so low-down mean, but then I knew Jubal Lee could do anything. He could blow a man's head halfway off without even blinking an eye or tear a boy's ear loose from his head like it wasn't anything but playing. I felt a fool thinking that there was anything likable about him. He didn't like me or anybody else. He was dying, and he didn't care how many people he took with him to the graveyard.

He was watching me again. "Why the long face?" he said, lighting his cigarette off the lighter that had popped out. "You've never stolen anything before, Patrick? Now don't tell me that. You have that needy look, and the needy take."

I felt myself turning red because Tory was sitting there beside me. "Yeah, I've stole," I said. "I've stole stuff to eat before at the Jiffy Mart back home. I've stole stuff for Miss Pollard at the trailer park, too, when her money got low at the end of the month. She spent most of her check on medicine, but she had to eat like everybody else."

Tory looked at me with his big blue eyes. He didn't look mad, but his face was as stony as the statue of the Confederate soldier on our town square.

"Well, you're a regular Robin Hood," Jubal Lee said as we took off from the light. We headed out north on Highway 15. "I'll tell you what. We'll play like you're Robin Hood and fat boy over there can be Jesse James." He leaned close to the steering wheel and looked over at Tory. "How about that, Jesse?"

"Yessir," Tory said, staring straight ahead.

There were no other cars behind us. Jubal Lee slowed down and pulled over on the shoulder of the road when we came to a mailbox. "What's the name on that box, Jesse?" he said.

The name was plain as day, but Jubal Lee couldn't see it. He couldn't see good! And I'd thought he could see everything.

Tory was leaning forward and squinting. "I can't read it," he said.

"Can't read it?" Jubal Lee said. "What do you mean you can't read it? You go to school, don't you?"

"He's lost his glasses," I said. I knew where they were, but I sure wasn't going to tell Jubal Lee.

"I'm not talking to you, Patrick," Jubal Lee said. His hand crept down my leg toward my knee like a tarantula. I froze stiff as a board.

Tory turned to face him. "Sir, I've lost my glasses. I've been wearing glasses since I was six years old. I can't see much without them."

"With them, either," Jubal Lee said, taking his hand off my knee. "Switch places with him, Patrick, and read me the name.

I crawled over Tory, and he scooted toward Jubal Lee a little ways. "It's Todd," I said. "R. L. Todd."

Jubal Lee pulled back out on the highway and drove slow. He pulled over again at the next mailbox. "Arthur

James," I called out.

Jubal Lee had his arm around Tory, pulling him closer. "Some more of your kinfolks, Jesse?" he said, just barely touching Tory's other ear lobe.

Tory jumped like somebody had stuck him with a needle. "Nosir," he said, his eyes closed.

At the fifth or sixth mailbox I called out, "Harvel L. Lewis, Beefmaster Farms," and Jubal Lee smiled.

We drove up the highway a little piece, turned around in somebody's driveway, and headed back real slow.

At first I couldn't see the house too well because it set back off a long paved driveway in a grove of maple trees. Little by little I made it out to be a long, one-story white brick with black wrought iron around the porch. It put me in mind of Miss Gooch's house back in Broad Plains. Miss Gooch was my third grade teacher who always told those stories I didn't like. I could tell her a few of my own, now, if I lived long enough.

Jubal Lee sped up after we passed the house and drove back to New Albany. This time we headed out east and did the same thing all over again. Jubal Lee would slow down and pull over on the shoulder of the road, and then I'd read the name off the mailbox. This time, the second name I read was Marvel W. Lewis. I knew that was the name Jubal Lee was looking for, because the other house we looked at belonged to a Lewis, too.

This house was a big white two-story perched upon a bluff. Down in front of it was a big weeping willow shading a fish pond. There was a concrete bench under the willow, and a little dock stuck out into the pond.

Jubal Lee kept looking at it and worked his jaw from side to side like he was studying about something. then he nodded his head, and we headed back to New Albany again.

CHAPTER XXIV

Somebody Gets Too Nosy

We drove around town for about five minutes. Jubal Lee kept working his jaw and looking on both sides of the road like he was trying to find something. "One-horse towns," he said under his breath like he was aggravated. He didn't usually let on one way or another about how he felt.

Finally, we drove a little piece outside the city limits and wheeled up to this tiny grocery store with two gas pumps out front. Jubal Lee put the car in park but didn't cut off the motor. He picked up the notepad off the seat and looked at it. Then he turned over a leaf and got the stub of a pencil out of his coat pocket and wrote something. He tore out the page and handed it to me. There were two phone numbers written on it.

When I looked up at him, his dark eyes seemed to latch on to me. He reached from behind Tory and touched the back of my neck. "Now listen, Patrick, and listen good," he said, his voice as soft as a featherbed. "Go inside the store and ask to use the phone. Call both numbers. If anybody answers, hang up. If nobody answers, let the phone ring at least twenty times before you hang up. Do you understand?"

"Yessir," I said. "You want me to check to see if anybody's at home before we go break into these houses."

The corners of Jubal Lee's mouth twitched. "I do believe the country mouse is about to catch on, Jesse," he said, rubbing Tory's neck. "Okay. Do what I told you. Don't act scared. Get in and out of there as fast as you can." He still had his arm around Tory, and he tapped my shoulder with his fingers. "Now, Patrick."

I got out of the car and opened the screen door to the store and stepped inside. The store was dim and cool. It smelled like feed sacks and tobacco and the upstairs at Granny Gunn's homeplace. An old ceiling fan was whispering overhead.

Behind a long counter stood a short, skinny woman with her gray hair rolled up in a ball on top of her head. There was a pencil sticking out of her ball. She wore glasses that looked like the top half of them had been cut off. "Can I use your phone, ma'am?" I said as I walked up to the counter.

"You can if you may," she said, smiling at me. She had lots of gold in her teeth like Miss Armistead.

I didn't really understand what she was talking about, but she was pointing down to where the counter crooked around toward the wall. There on that end of the counter was the phone. "Local call?" she said, watching me.

"Yes, ma'am," I said.

I picked up the phone and dialed the first number on the list. As the phone began to ring, I tried to think about what I needed to do. I was pretty sure that Jubal Lee wasn't going to break into any houses himself. He just liked to be the big buck and give orders. I figured that Tory or I would have to do all the housebreaking. He'd keep one of us with him in the car at all times so the other one couldn't run off. He knew we wouldn't leave one another.

Nobody answered the phone, so I hung up and dialed the second number.

It crossed my mind then that if somebody on the other end did answer, I wouldn't have to let on to Jubal Lee.

Whichever one of us broke into the house would get caught and be safe. But then Jubal Lee would likely kill the other one. I might have been willing to take a chance with my own life, but I knew I didn't have a right to gamble with Tory's.

The lady at the end of the counter seemed nice. I could tell her what was going on and have her call the law, but just as soon as Jubal Lee saw that the law was after us, he'd kill Tory and me both. He'd know for sure I'd tricked him. Seem like he could almost read what was going on in your mind by studying your eyes. Except he couldn't see worth a flip. That was weird, how he could see without his eyes.

It looked like we'd have to go along with whatever he wanted us to do for the time being. I knew if I could get off to myself for a while and study things, I might could come up with a plan. All the time I was riding in the car with that low-down devil, I was too nervous to think. My mind stayed tangled up like cheap fishing line.

Nobody answered the phone at the second number, either, so I hung up and started out. "Thank you, ma'am," I said.

She looked at me over the tops of her glasses. "No luck?" she said. "What party were you trying to reach?"

I had my hand on the screen door already, and I thought about going on out without answering her, but then I thought she might get suspicious. "I wasn't trying to reach a party, ma'am," I said. "I was trying to ring up this person."

She grinned real big and then put her hand over her mouth like Miss Armistead did sometimes when she had to belch and didn't want anybody to hear. When she took her hand down, she still looked tickled about something, and she said, "Hon, what person were you trying to call?"

My heart commenced beating fast, and I could feel myself getting hot all over like I always did when I got nervous. I thought about Jubal Lee waiting on me out there in the car. "Harvel Lewis," I said.

The woman pushed her glasses up higher on her nose and leaned across the counter. "You a local boy?" she said, eyeing me keen.

I wasn't counting on anybody being so durn nosy. "No, ma'am," I said.

She took off her glasses and stuck one handle in the center of her chin like she was thinking. "Now whereabouts are you from, young man?"

"Tennessee."

She walked from behind the counter and came over to where I was beside the door. "Whereabouts in Tennessee, hon?" she said, putting her glasses back on and getting right up in my face to look me over from one side to the other.

"West Tennessee. You've never heard of the place I'm from, though."

She looked out the screen door. "Is that your brother out there in the car? Is that y'all's daddy?"

"Yes, ma'am," I said. "Nice talking to you, but I've got to go now."

She didn't offer to move out of my way. "What were you wanting with Mr. Lewis?"

I eased around her and scooted out the door. "We wanted to see him about some cows," I said.

She followed right behind me, but I couldn't help it. I didn't know what to do to get rid of her. Sweat was trickling down the gully in my back. I got in the car quick. "Let's go," I said. "They're not home, either one of them."

Jubal Lee didn't answer or even look at me. The woman was tapping on his window so he would roll it down. He rolled it down a couple of inches, and she said, "Mr. Lewis's daddy passed away the night before last. They're all at the funeral home. He won't be able to do any cattle business with you today."

"Is that right?" Jubal Lee said, nodding his head. "I'm sorry to hear that." He cut off the motor and took out the keys. "I think I'm out of cigarettes," he said to the woman.

She laughed. "Well, we have some for sale," she said and started walking back toward the store.

Jubal Lee caught up with her. He held the screen door open for her, and they went inside.

"Tory," I said, my insides turning to clabber, "he's fixing to kill her, and I can't do a thing in the world about it."

"I know it," he said, covering his ears. "Let's don't listen."

We both jumped at the same time when the pistol went off.

Jubal Lee was smoking as he walked out of the store. He looked up and down the highway before he got in the car.

"Snap out of it, Patrick," he said as he cranked up the car. "You couldn't help it. Curiosity killed that cat."

We left in a hurry, squalling tires. We rode a little piece and swung back north again. I knew right away where we were heading.

Jubal Lee drove fast. "There's a crowbar under your seat, Patrick," he said. His eyes darted toward me for a second and then back to the road. "Reach under there and find it."

I did what he told me. Something sharp snagged the end of my thumb as I was pulling out the crowbar. It wasn't cut bad, but it bled some. I held my forefinger over it until the blood got sticky and stopped oozing.

Tory kept glancing at the crowbar and then at me. I knew what he was thinking, but I didn't have the guts to hit Jubal Lee with it. I didn't even dare look at Jubal Lee, afraid that he might read something in my eyes. I was like Chigger. I talked a good act, was about all.

"A penny for your thoughts, Patrick," Jubal Lee said, and I jumped like I'd been shot. Tory jumped, too.

"I wasn't thinking," I said. I was holding the crowbar

between my legs. I lifted it to my lap and held on to it with both hands.

"Stop fidgeting," Jubal Lee said. For a second his eyes seemed to take flight, lighting and flicking across the crowbar like a snake doctor. "There's nothing to be nervous about. I'm going to pull up to the back of the house and let you out. Prize open the back door. Knock out the glass if it's a French door, and then reach inside and unlock it. If you hear a buzzer or anything go off, get out of there and start running down the road."

"Where are you going to be?" I said.

A butterfly smacked the windshield in front of my face, leaving one black wing and a long yellow smear. "Old Jesse and I are riding up the road a little piece. We'll cruise back down and pick you up. You've got five minutes to get in and out of there. I want you standing at the back door ready to jump in when I pull up. Any questions?"

"I don't exactly know what to do once I'm in there," I said. "What am I supposed to do?"

"Don't be so damn stupid!" he said, raising his voice for the first time and reaching across Tory to point his long yellow finger at me. "You go to the biggest bedroom," he said, jabbing the air with his finger, "and look through every drawer and everything that's on top of the dresser. Pull everything out and just dump it on the floor. Look through the closets. Any jewelry you find, any coins, any watches, put them in a pillowcase." He jabbed his finger hard at me once more. I was drawn up in a knot as close to the door as I could get. "Now is that too hard for you to understand, country boy? Do I need to draw you a goddamn picture?"

"Nosir," I said, wanting to cry but too afraid to even sniffle.

Tory was sucking in his big belly like he was trying to disappear in the seat. Jubal Lee had really made a believer out of him.

311

CHAPTER XXV

I Get Lucky

We came to the driveway of the Lewis house and swerved in on two wheels. Jubal Lee fought the steering wheel to straighten up the car. Tory grabbed hold of me, and I held onto the door handle.

The driveway bore around to the back of the house where there was a big square of asphalt laid out so cars could pull in and then back out without any trouble. There was a new red Ford pickup parked on one side of the square. Jubal Lee pulled up beside it, slammed on the brakes, and backed out in a wild arc. "Get out!" he hollered, and I had no more turned loose of the door handle before he took off, burning rubber and fishtailing down the driveway. I saw Tory's arm reaching out to close the door as they rounded the corner.

I didn't have to use the crowbar. Somebody hadn't pulled the back door all the way shut. When I put my hand on the knob, I saw that the people hadn't even locked the door in the first place.

The back door led into a room where there were two green couches, a wide-screen TV, and a pool table. The far wall had a fireplace, and over the mantle was a mounted deer head. On the wall opposite the fireplace were pictures of old farm houses and one picture of this sad-looking mule.

I felt awful being in there. I could smell the people who

lived in this house. I felt dirty, like I was one of those people who peeped in windows at people taking baths and such.

The first room led out into a wide hall. There were two bedrooms on one side of the hall, and a bathroom and another bedroom on the other side. At the end of the hall was the biggest bedroom. It had a brass bed with something that looked like big marbles mounted in different places on it. A jewelry box lay wide open on the chest of drawers. On the dresser were earrings and perfume bottles and a round box of bath powder.

I yanked out all the drawers and dumped them in the floor. There wasn't anything in them but people's personal stuff, underwear and socks and nightclothes. There was a wedding band on the nightstand, but I didn't take that. Jubal Lee didn't have to know everything.

I opened the drawer of the nightstand and found a little square, black flashlight. I saw some more stuff in the back, so I pulled the drawer all the way out, and a shiny, short pistol hit the tan carpet and bounced under the bed.

I scrambled under the bed and got it. It wasn't much size atall, but it felt heavy and solid in my hand.

Tommy Lee Trigg at the trailer park had one just like it that he'd won in a pool game. He was all time flashing it around and bragging because it was a Beretta. He used to let Chigger and me shoot it some at rats down at the city dump. I knew how to use it.

Everything in my head was as clear as a bell then. I knew just like that what I was fixing to do. I picked up the phone on the nightstand and dialed 911. This woman answered right off the bat, and I told her, I said, "This is Patrick Gunn. I'm in a lot of trouble and need help."

"Calm down," she said. "Tell me what kind of trouble you're in."

"I took off with Tory James from Broad Plains, Tennessee, because we were both having trouble back there.

We didn't know what trouble was, though, until we ran off."

"What kind of trouble were you in in Tennessee, Patrick?" the woman asked.

I didn't have time to go into all that, so I said, "No offense, lady, but never mind about that now. There's this man named Jubal Lee who's kidnapped Tory and me. He's making us rob houses."

"Where are you now, Tory?" the woman said. I could tell she was doing something else while she was talking to me, either writing things down or calling the law, one.

"I'm not Tory," I said. "I'm Pat. Patrick Gunn."

"Sorry, Patrick," she said. "Where are you now?"

"I'm in Mr. Harvel Lewis's house out on Highway 15. I'm robbing the place."

"Is this Mr. Jubal Lee in the house with you? Where is Mr. Jubal Lee?"

This woman acted like I didn't have good sense. I wasn't sure she did, either. "He's up the road a piece with my friend Tory," I told her, my heart beating like a car with the choke stuck. "He's fixing to come back and pick me up. If he finds out I've pulled a fast one on him, he'll kill Tory or me or anybody else who gets in his way. He's already killed two people today."

I heard the woman suck in her breath. "Who has he killed, Patrick?" she said.

"This man named Roy who was his sidekick. He made me pull him off in some trees on the road to Oxford."

"You said he killed two people. Who else did he kill?"

"I don't know her name. It was this woman who ran a little grocery store outside New Albany. He killed her because she got too nosy."

"Is Mr. Jubal Lee anywhere near the house now, Patrick?" she said.

I pulled back the curtain and looked out. "I don't see him anywhere," I said. "But that doesn't mean he's not out there. He may be in the house with me right now for all I know. He's tricky."

"What's behind the house, Patrick? Are there any houses nearby?"

"I see a big fenced-in pasture," I said. "I don't see any houses."

"Okay," the woman said. "Listen to me now. Are you listening?"

Out in the hall the floor creaked. "Yes, ma'am," I said. "I'm trying to. Hold on a second."

She was still talking when I set the phone down. I tiptoed to the corner of the door and peeped around.

I didn't see anything. He could still be in the bathroom or one of the other bedrooms.

I went back to the phone but kept facing the door. I didn't want him to slip up on me from behind. "I'm back," I said.

The woman sounded like she needed to calm down some herself. "Get out of that house, Patrick. Run as fast as you can down through the pasture. If this man happens to see you, don't stop or try to go back. Just keep running as fast as you can. Someone is on their way to help you."

"I can't run off," I told her.

"Listen, Patrick, get out of that house! Go now."

"No, ma'am," I said. "I can't do that. Jubal Lee will kill Tory if I run off."

The woman was breathing almost as hard as I was. A second or two later she said, "You are not responsible for what Mr. Jubal Lee does. You have to leave the house. Leave now."

"I've not told you everything," I said. "I found a gun. It's loaded, and I know how to use it. I'm not going to use it unless I have to, but I'm not aiming for him to hurt Tory again."

"Leave the gun in the house, Patrick," the woman said real loud. "Do you hear me? Hide it somewhere and go. Go now!"

Right then I heard tires squalling as the car rounded the corner of the driveway. "He's back!" I whispered, jamming the pistol in my back pocket and pulling the tail of my T-shirt over it. "I've got to go!"

The car had pulled up outside. I could hear Jubal Lee gunning the motor so I'd hurry.

"Tell me what kind of car he's driving," the woman said.

"I've got to go, I told you! I can't think, ma'am," I said. "We're headed east, I think. It's a blue car."

The woman was still talking a mile a minute when I slammed down the phone. I yanked a pillow from under the bedspread and stripped off the pillowcase. I got the jewelry box off the chest of drawers and emptied everything into the pillowcase. Then I picked up the crowbar off the floor where I'd dropped it and ran through the house and out the door.

Jubal Lee had already pulled up and turned the car around, ready to head out of there. His jaws were clenched, but he didn't say anything when I hopped into the car.

As soon as my hind end hit the seat, he took off, burning rubber and might near snapping my head off at the stem. He was driving so fast and wild, he didn't even look when he pulled out of the driveway onto the highway.

Tory was sitting close to Jubal Lee. He was pale, and he wouldn't look at me.

Jubal Lee didn't slow down until we got back inside the city limits. In a flash he reached across Tory and snatched the pillowcase out of my hand.

He held it between his legs and reached down and grabbed a handful of stuff. He looked at it for a second. Then he slung it under the seat and reached for another handful. His mouth curled down like a tipped over parenthesis. He rammed the second handful back inside the pillowcase and handed the pillowcase to Tory. Then he looked at me, his nostrils black and flaring. "Bunch of shit," he said. "A damn bunch of shit. You knew that was a bunch of shit."

I didn't answer, just looked at my feet like I was ashamed. I could feel the pistol easing up out of my hip pocket. All I had to do was to reach back and flip the safety off. That's all I had to do, but still that pistol seemed a million miles away. I needed to pee so bad I could hardly stand it. "Give Jesse the crowbar," Jubal Lee hissed. "You little son of a bitch."

I didn't want to give Tory the crowbar, because I didn't know what he might do, but I didn't have any choice. Tory took it, his hand trembling. He held it down between his legs and rested the end of it on the hump. He still wouldn't look at me.

We turned off, just like I'd figured, and headed out east on Highway 30. I looked straight ahead, but I could feel Jubal Lee's eyes lighting on me like flies. He knew something wasn't right about me, and he was trying to figure it out. I knew something was funny about Tory. I felt my heart beating in my head, and sweat crawled inside my T-shirt like ticks.

Five minutes later, we were spinning up the gravel driveway that led to the big white house on the bluff.

When we whirled around to the back of the house, I saw that the driveway made a loop around this above-ground swimming pool before it went back down. There was a two-car garage with a picnic table stuck right in front of the doors. Somebody had been working on a lawn mower on top of the picnic table. There were two doors on the far side of the garage, and the first one was standing wide open. You could see the bottom of some steps that led upstairs.

"All right, Jesse," Jubal Lee said to Tory, "your turn. You won't be needing the crowbar. Shove it under the seat and head out. Let's see what you can do."

Tory couldn't get the crowbar under the seat at the

hump, so he handed it to me. I shoved it back under the seat for him. When I straightened up, I could feel about an inch of barrel still sticking in my hip pocket.

Tory crawled over me. Blood had crusted down his neck in the shape of a Y. "Hurry up, Jesse," Jubal Lee said. "We're on our way to Tupelo if you can find me something worth a damn."

As soon as Tory set foot out the door, Jubal Lee took off, the wheels slinging gravel every which way. Through the side mirror I could see Tory with one shoulder hunched up and his arm over his eyes. Gravel was pelting him all over his bare belly and side.

Once we were out on the highway, Jubal Lee drove fast in the direction of the Natchez Trace Parkway. Directly, he looked over at me and said in a soft voice, "What's wrong, Patrick? Tell me what's wrong."

He sounded almost like Miss Armistead, but I knew he didn't care anything about me. I shrugged my shoulders and looked out the window. "Nothing's wrong with me," I said. "I'm fine as froghair."

"I didn't mean to raise my voice to you," he said, sliding his skinny arm across the top of the seat. His long yellow fingers hung down like spider legs. "Don't worry, you'll do better next time. It just takes a little practice."

"You did something to Tory," I said, hearing myself talking but not wanting to say what I was saying. My voice didn't even sound like my voice anymore.

Jubal Lee didn't show a sign that he'd even heard me. Telephone poles zipped by. He steered with the crook of his wrist and the heel of his hand.

Finally, he did turn and look at me for the longest time, his dull dark eyes searching over my face like they were looking for a place to get in. I halfway expected the car to run off the road, but it hugged the yellow line like it had a mind of its own and knew exactly where to go. "You're shaking," he said, the tips of his yellow fingers on my shoulder. "Tell me why you're shaking."

I looked down at my hands. "I'm afraid of you." I said. "Anybody with good sense would be afraid of you."

As he began to trace the inside of my ear with his finger, the short hairs on the back of my neck stood up. "Fear is the beginning of wisdom," he said, his voice barely above a whisper. The car was moving faster and faster down the highway, sucking up the yellow line. Only when the steering wheel began to vibrate did Jubal Lee slow down some and start to watch the road again. "It's wise to be afraid. You need to be afraid of me."

The pistol slid out of my back pocket and dropped down in the crack of the seat. I pressed my tailbone against the handle. Everything was all right for now, but Tory would have to get back in the car. I'd have to be careful.

"Don't squirm and draw away from me, Patrick," he said, his two fingers walking like midget legs across my shoulder. "Fearing me is loving me. You do love me, don't you, Patrick? Just a little?"

"Yessir," I said, not knowing if what I was saying was true, because I didn't know if fear was supposed to be connected to love or not.

Now the palm of his hand was over my heart. "Do you know how to release this fear so it won't take control of you? Do you, Patrick?"

"Nosir," I said, knowing that if something didn't happen soon, I was fixing to die. Jubal Lee might not kill me, but I was going to be dead all the same. Just by touching me and talking to me, getting me all mixed up, he was doing something awful. I didn't know the name of the thing he was doing, but it was worse than anything my daddy had ever done to me.

He was looking at me so kind, and speaking so kind, that I had a hard time remembering that he was the same man who had killed two people today. "Give your fear to someone else," he said, taking his hand off me and grabbing a handful of the seat and twisting it. "It's so simple, but then the truth is always simple. Make everybody afraid of you. Scare them. Hurt them. Kill them if you want to. Nobody cares anymore."

He began to slow down. Up ahead on the right was a dirt road. On the near side of the road was a tin shelter somebody had built for their kids so they wouldn't get wet meeting the school bus. The tin said "Purina" all over it.

Everything looked so ordinary, the road, the houses here and there, that stupid shelter with Purina written all over it. No matter what happened, the world never let on. Birds were still perched on the light wires, and the sky was still blue. If Tory and I got killed, kids would still meet the bus under that shelter when it was raining. The county men wouldn't come and grade up this highway because a low-down murderer had driven up and down it. Tory and I would get a write-up in the newspaper, but people would soon forget about us. Fall and winter would come, and then spring. The creek at home wouldn't change directions on account of us being dead. The world didn't need you, and it didn't care when you were gone.

We pulled in on the dirt road, turned around, and headed back. Jubal Lee lit a cigarette and smoked it fast. One of his yellow fingers tapped on the top of the steering wheel as he drove. "I'll tell you what I've decided to do," he said, all of a sudden leaning over in my direction so that he was sitting on his right hip. "I'm going to let you kill old Jesse. We don't need him. He's not your friend and never has been."

I wiggled a little in the seat like my hind end had gone to sleep. The short cold barrel of the pistol touched my bare skin above the hip.

I wanted to shut my mind against Jubal Lee. I was afraid I'd go crazy if I listened to him anymore. He talked crazy, but I knew his crazy talk might begin to make sense if I listened to him long enough. "You'll be amazed how fear drains out of you once you kill," he said. "Especially when you kill someone you love."

"I don't love Tory," I said.

"Yes, you do," Jubal Lee said. "You love everybody, and that's the reason everybody hurts you."

I couldn't help thinking then how much better off I'd have been if I'd never cared anything about all the people who'd ever done me wrong, from my dead mama and daddy to Chigger and Tory and even Miss Armistead. Granny Gunn never wronged me, though, so I held on to her in my mind.

We came to the driveway of the big white house and slid in on two wheels. I jerked over toward Jubal Lee, acting like the swerving car had made me lose my balance, and slipped the cold pistol inside the right pocket of my shorts.

He didn't see me.

So he couldn't read my mind or see through my eyes to the inside of my head after all. He wasn't anything but an ordinary man with something left out of him and something oozy black in the empty place.

The car was fishtailing like crazy, but Jubal Lee never let up off the gas. We looped sideways around the swimming pool and finally slid to a stop just as we were ready to head back down the hill toward the highway. My head was swimming, and I had to grab hold of the dash to steady myself.

Jubal Lee looked through the dust toward the house and beat a rhythm on top of the steering wheel with his thumbs.

All of a sudden, something caught my eye in the side mirror. A white speck moved way up in the woods behind the house. I looked away quick. I didn't need to look again.

Tory wasn't in the house. He was making his way through the woods, hiding behind the trees as he went.

I didn't blame him in a way, and in a way I did. He was the kind of person who was brave until he got scared, and then he wasn't brave anymore. If a body didn't have sense enough to be scared, or had never had a good reason to be scared in the first place, then being brave wasn't too hard. Not being scared wasn't brave atall. That was ignorance.

Tory had really left me in a fix. If Jubal Lee happened to spot him, I was dead, because I didn't have the heart to shoot a man in cold blood. Jubal Lee would have to make the first move to kill me, but after he'd made his move, I'd be dead.

I felt closer to dying than I ever had before, even more than when I was drowning. I kept looking for that picture show of my life to appear before my eyes, but all I saw was gray dust boiling up like smoke, and the only light I saw at the end of the tunnel was the truth.

I was no different from Tory, and Chigger was no different from me. I'd turned my back on Chigger, just like Tory had turned his back on me. We were three peas in a pod.

I thought about Miss Armistead. I got real worried about her, just like I wasn't sitting there in a car with a crazy man who'd kill me if I looked at him cross-eyed. I got worried about her then because I knew at that very moment that I loved her, and always before I never knew I loved somebody until the person was dead. Maybe she was dead now.

Jubal Lee was looking at me with eyes so keen that they might have been the black cracks under rocks. He jerked his thumb toward the house. "Go get him," he said.

"Yessir," I said, opening the door.

His hand clamped hard around my wrist. "You're not going to tell him, are you?" he said. He had no more light in his eyes than the inside of a well. "I'm going to kill him, anyway, whether you tell him or not."

"Nosir," I said. "I'll not tell him. It's best he don't know." His cold hand slid away. "I'll get him."

I ran back up the driveway and entered the door with

the steps showing. I wondered if Jubal Lee had seen the gun flopping in my pocket.

The steps went right up to a door that led into the kitchen. Directly across the room from that door was another door that opened onto a side deck. Beside the second door was a wall phone. I picked it up as soon as I spotted it and dialed 911 again.

The very same woman answered. "It's me, Patrick," I said. "I'm out on Highway 30 at the Lewis house. There's a weeping willow out front and a fish pond. Jubal Lee's out in the car. Tory's got away. The car is a blue Plymouth Reliant."

"Slow down a minute," she said. "Is this Patrick?"

"I just told you I was Patrick, lady," I said, watching the stairs. "You've got to get somebody out here quick. He'll try to kill me when he finds out Tory is gone. He thinks he's in the house, but I saw him running through the woods behind the house."

"Who's in the woods?" the woman said. "Mr. Jubal Lee or Tory?"

"Tory is, durn it!" I hollered, slamming up the receiver.

A kitchen counter divided the kitchen from the dining room and living room. The dining room and living room were one long room together. At the far end of the living room was the front door.

The best I could remember, if I went out the front, there was a bobwire fence and a grove of pines over on the left. If I could make it to the pine grove without being seen, chances are I could circle behind the house and find Tory in the woods.

I ran to the end of the living room and yanked open the front door.

Jubal Lee was standing behind the storm door, his arms stretched out and holding onto each side of the door like a man crucified. He was smiling. "Going somewhere,

Patrick?" he said.

I jerked the pistol out of my pocket and aimed it right at his head. "Keep your hands where you've got them," I said, my hand trembling like a feeble old man's. "You move, and I'll kill you deader than a hammer."

He stopped smiling. "Now, Patrick, you're not going to shoot anybody," he said, his voice soft and his eyes moving all over me like invisible fingers. "Throw the gun down on the floor, and let's get out of here. We'll forget about old Jesse."

He eased his hands away from the door facing.

I pulled the trigger.

Nothing happened.

Jubal Lee must have seen my trigger finger moving, though, because he slapped his hands back on either side of the door.

I saw then what was wrong. The safety was on. I flicked it off with my thumb.

Jubal Lee began to sweat. I had never seen him sweat before. Sweat was trickling down both sides of his face and running out from under his yellow hair. His breath made a foggy circle on the storm door. "There's no need of this, son," he said, shifting his weight on one foot.

He was scared! I knew then that he didn't have cancer, either. He just told Tory and me a big lie so we'd go along with anything he told us to do. "I've already told the police all about you on the phone," I said. I wasn't scared anymore. Something bigger than fear had taken hold of me. My stomach tingled like I was riding down from the top of the Ferris Wheel. "I told them about you killing Roy and that woman in the grocery store. I told them everything."

"Listen, you stupid little hick!" he hissed, leaning closer to the door, his bottom teeth showing white and sharp. "You're mixed up in this to your eyeballs. I'll tell the cops you killed Roy and that bitch."

Jubal Lee's eyes moved in all directions. They looked

like two tumblebugs trying to find a place to hide back in his head. "I'm sure they'll believe you, too," I said, smiling at him for spite. "They're going to be here any minute, so you can tell them your side of things then."

I saw him squat down a little and lean over to one side, and I knew what he was aiming to do. I was ready for him.

In the blink of an eye, he tried to throw himself out from in front of the door. I pulled the trigger. The little pistol bucked up in front of me like something alive. I pulled the trigger again.

Jubal Lee had disappeared. My ears ached inside. I flopped down on my belly and rolled away from the door.

I listened. At first I couldn't hear anything.

Then I heard him scooting along the outside wall. A second later he was back at the door and holding onto the door facing again. He was looking inside.

From where I was lying I could see a spot of blood no bigger than a rose right where his white shirt buttoned up at the top.

I got up, keeping the pistol aimed right at his head, and went back to the door. He was gurgling deep inside his throat and trying to say something. Where my bullets had gone through the storm door looked like a big spider web, and Jubal Lee stayed there squirming like he was hung in it.

Directly, his eyes walled back up in his head, and he fell backwards on the brick porch. His head rolled over to one side, and his pistol that I hadn't even seen fell out of his hand and clacked down the steps.

I stayed there aiming my pistol at him through the storm door until two white police cars drove up. Then I laid the pistol on the coffee table in the living room and sat down on the couch. The weight of the world had lifted off me. I knew no matter what else happened, I would be all right.

I was free.

CHAPTER XXVI

How Things Stand Now

All that was six months ago, but it doesn't seem like it. Sometimes it seems like everything happened yesterday, and at other times it seems like it happened a million years ago.

Lot of nights I lie here in bed at Miss Armistead's and think about how much trouble I went to for nothing, and how many people wouldn't have been hurt if I'd used my head. Miss Armistead keeps telling me that that's just the way life is. You don't get through it without hurting people and messing up a whole bunch of times. Still, lots of things bear on my mind.

I thought it was weird that the police didn't even handcuff me when they took me off to the police station in Tupelo, but once I got there, I found out that I wasn't even being charged with anything. The medical examiner up in Nashville had already figured out that I hadn't killed my daddy. He had died because somebody had shot him full of enough cocaine to kill a team of mules. Whoever cut his throat did that for good measure, but he was already dead. The police seem to think he was messing around with drugs. I don't doubt it.

Tory and I made the news in several states. I spent two days in the hospital getting tests and X-rays, and the doctors and nurses had to run the newspaper and TV reporters off about a dozen times both days.

As soon as Dr. Malone, my doctor, decided that I was okay, he let me pick out one reporter to talk to. I chose this young girl from some big Memphis newspaper. She had red hair and was named Chloe, but I never could learn how to say her name exactly right. She was nice, though, and I told her everything from start to finish. She sent me a copy of the newspaper. The headline read, "TEENAGER RECOUNTS ODYSSEY OF TERROR." I liked the fact that she used the word *odyssey*. I read a book once called *The Odyssey*. It was about a great Greek warrior who helped fight a war against the Trojans and had to go through all kinds of troubles before he got back home.

I've not seen hide nor hair of Tory to this day. The police didn't find him in the woods until late the next day, and when they did, he'd gone out of his head again. We stayed in the same hospital in Tupelo, only he had to stay for two weeks, and the doctors wouldn't let anybody in to see him except his family. His mama and stepdaddy flew him out on a plane to Jackson as soon as he was able. Miss Marcella won't speak to Miss Armistead and me anymore. I don't care myself, but I feel bad for Miss Armistead. She couldn't help what I did.

I had to stay in the Christian Home for two months until Miss Armistead was able to come home from the nursing home where they sent her to get better. The people at Human Services didn't think she was ever going to be able to wait on me anymore, but she and the old judge pulled some strings, and here I am. We have a cook and a housekeeper now. And since September the seventeenth, I'm Patrick Gunn Armistead, legal. That's right. I'm Miss Armistead's son now.

It's funny how things sometimes connect and disconnect and then connect again. Miss Sexton, the fat freckled lady who gave me a ride home that time I'd slipped off to the creek with Chigger, comes to our house two or three times a week to help Miss Armistead do things she can't do by herself. Miss Sexton works for Home Health Care now. She's still right bossy and still a big talker.

Chigger's back in Broad Plains, I reckon for good. I don't know what happened to him over in Memphis, why he didn't stay with the doctor, because I don't talk to him. He turns his head every time I see him. I see him every once in a while when Miss Armistead and I are out on errands. I've got my permit and do all the driving now.

Mr. A.Z. Porter drives over to see me about once a month when he's not too busy. One weekend he took me up to Percy Priest Lake to go fishing. I had a pretty good time. He knows lots of stories. Some of them aren't very funny, but I laugh when I think I'm supposed to.

Jubal Lee didn't die. He's not dead. He's sitting in jail with a store-bought voice box and still waiting for trial. When they get through with him down in Mississippi, Tennessee and Arkansas are going to put him on trial, or try to. They say he's got some young public defender who's trying to get him off because he doesn't have good sense. I'm going to have to testify at the trial in Mississippi, Tory and I both, if he ever goes to trial. If Tennessee ever gets him, we'll have to testify again.

I still read a lot. Miss Armistead doesn't have to trick me into reading now. I read because books have some sense to them. Since so much happened to me, I can't watch TV. None of those shows have anything atall to do with me.

The big white moon is hanging from the lowest limb on the tall oak tree outside my window. It doesn't look like much, the moon, but it's a powerful thing. I recollect one of my elementary schoolteachers, Miss Annabel Longshore, telling us kids how the moon had such a strong gravitational pull that it tugged back all the big oceans and then turned them loose again, and this was what caused tides. Back then when I was little, it didn't seem possible that there could be such a thing as gravity, but I know now there is. Sometimes, like tonight, a big wave of blue rolls right over me, dragging me down, pulling me back to the old days when I was barely keeping my head above water, so to speak. I don't believe in God and such, just in what I know, and I know somehow, so far, I always come bobbing back to a good place, held up by something more powerful than all the things I can see, more real than all the things I can touch.

I believe in gravity.

TRIPLE HOMICIDE

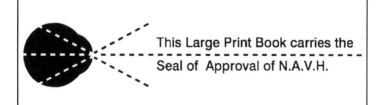
This Large Print Book carries the
Seal of Approval of N.A.V.H.

TRIPLE HOMICIDE

CHARLES J. HYNES

THORNDIKE PRESS

An imprint of Thomson Gale, a part of The Thomson Corporation

Monroe County Public Library
Key Largo Branch

THOMSON
™
GALE

Detroit • New York • San Francisco • New Haven, Conn. • Waterville, Maine • London

MONROE COUNTY
PUBLIC LIBRARY

THOMSON

™

GALE

Copyright © 2007 by Charles Hynes.

Thorndike Press, an imprint of The Gale Group.

Thomson and Star Logo and Thorndike are trademarks and Gale is a registered trademark used herein under license.

ALL RIGHTS RESERVED

This is a work of fiction. All the characters, organizations, and events portrayed in this novel are either products of the author's imagination or are used fictitiously.

Thorndike Press® Large Print Crime Scene.

The text of this Large Print edition is unabridged.

Other aspects of the book may vary from the original edition.

Set in 16 pt. Plantin.

LIBRARY OF CONGRESS CATALOGING-IN-PUBLICATION DATA

Hynes, Charles J.
   Triple homicide / by Charles Hynes.
     p. cm. — (Thorndike Press large print crime scene)
   ISBN-13: 978-1-4104-0298-1 (alk. paper)
   ISBN-10: 1-4104-0298-3 (alk. paper)
   1. Police — New York (State) — New York — Fiction. 2. New York (N.Y.)
— Fiction. I. Title.
   PS3608.Y58T75 2007b
   813'.6—dc22
                                2007034920

Published in 2007 by arrangement with St. Martin's Press, LLC.

Printed in the United States of America on permanent paper
10 9 8 7 6 5 4 3 2 1

12/07
LP

MONROE COUNTY
PUBLIC LIBRARY

For my wife and best friend, Patricia, for your constant encouragement and support.

To the men and women of the New York City Police Department whose courage, integrity, and strength have made New York City safe for the people they selflessly protect.

ACKNOWLEDGMENTS

I want to especially acknowledge those who helped me make this book possible:

Sean Desmond, formerly of Thomas Dunne Books, St. Martin's Press, and my original editor, who provided great editing skill and creative ideas, turning this book from what I hoped was an interesting story to what we both believe is an exciting mystery novel.

To Howard Kaminsky for your encouragement and help in finding a publisher.

To New York State Supreme Court Justice, Honorable Edwin Torres.

Peter Israel for your ideas.

To Thomas Dunne for believing in the worth of this project.

Special thanks to Catherine Schauf and Maureen Kravitz.

Thank you to Anne Swern and Mortimer Matz.

To Honorable Robert G. M. Keating,

dean of the New York Judicial Institute, Harvey L. Greenberg, and Joanna Zmijewski with gratitude.

Finally, to James E. Kohler, Esq., deceased, a great trial lawyer whose ideas contributed so much to this book.

PROLOGUE

The story that I am about to tell is mostly true. I have changed the names of the characters out of my concern for their privacy. Much of this tale was told to me by an extraordinary journalist who was perhaps the last of those insightful observers and courtroom commentators working in New York City up until the 1970s. Those in that elite club included Jimmy Cannon, from the *New York Post,* Scotty Reston and Russell Baker, both of the *New York Times,* and, of course, the great Murray Kempton, who for years wrote for the *New York Post* and who ended his distinguished career as a columnist for the New York City and Long Island newspaper *Newsday.*

I'll call my guy Morty, not his real name, because that's what he wanted. "If," he once said to me, "you ever get around to writing about this, leave me out." Then he added, "Ya see, if I wrote it, it would sound so far-fetched that no one would believe it, and I got a reputation to keep. You, on the other hand — you're a fuckin' lawyer, so it doesn't matter if anyone believes you!"

For years, Morty covered the New York City Criminal Court in Brooklyn for a great parochial newspaper, the *Brooklyn Eagle.* It was during the late 1950s and early '60s, and it was a glorious time to be a reporter. In those days there were ten major daily newspapers; the *News* and *Mirror* (many people thought that they were one newspaper, as in "da *News 'n' Mirror*"), the *Post,* the *Times,* the *New York World Telegram and Sun,* the *Herald Tribune,* the *Journal American,* the *Staten Island Advance,* the *Long Island Press,* and, of course, the small but mighty *Brooklyn Eagle.* Just as so many great trial lawyers learned their basic skills and honed them early in their careers in the local criminal courtrooms, working for the Legal Aid Society or the district attorney's office, these same venues provided exceptional training for young journalists. And just as the lawyers cut their teeth on this invaluable experience and began to develop their technique through the sheer volume of cases available to them, so, too, did Morty and his peers learn their trade. They learned the critical need to make a deadline in order to get a story printed, how to cultivate sources, and how to find ways to get tips and scoop the competition. For these police reporters, particularly the young ones, the criminal court was unvarnished high drama, with its share of heroes and villains, joy and tragedy, chaos and pathos. Morty never permitted himself to lose his enthusiasm for covering the courtroom scene. He called the court at 120 Schermerhorn Street in Brooklyn "the Hall of Hell." The hall, actually called the Criminal Court for the City of New York, is a huge ten-story building whose facade was constructed of gray sandstone blocks. It houses a dozen courtrooms, judges' chambers, clerks' offices, a large complaint room, where criminal charges are first docketed, and offices for the assistant district attorneys and for the lawyers from the Legal Aid Society, an organization known elsewhere in the country as the office of the public defender. The building, which occupies nearly three-quarters of a full city block, is filled each day with hundreds of police officers, hundreds more victims and defendants, and an equivalent number of tragic stories.

I first met Morty in 1963 when I worked as a criminal defense attorney for the Legal Aid Society at the Criminal Court. Our

11

meeting was one of instant and mutual dislike. I was representing a federal agent, charged in a series of brutal sodomy attacks on seven children in separate incidents. None of the children was older than nine. While each act was particularly vicious, performed at gunpoint, there was a serious question whether any of the children had correctly identified the assailant. The children separately described the assailant as much heavier and considerably taller than the defendant. The only accuracy of the identification was that both the assailant and the defendant had facial hair, although even that similarity created difficulty for the prosecution because the hair color described by each victim ranged from bright red to jet black. The agent, a childhood friend of mine whom I had not seen in years, was in the lockup — the holding cells located in the basement of the courthouse. He spotted me while I was interviewing one of my clients. This subterranean cellblock could have been designed by Dante. It was poorly lit and permeated with the ubiquitous stench of urine and body odor, which clung to the walls and the clothing of everyone who passed through the holding area. In sum, it was a dungeon, which echoed with the ceaseless ramblings of the detainees packed together in several adjoining cells, creating a loud, frightening din. It most certainly was a terrorizing experience for a federal cop from the other side of the criminal justice system.

Special Agent Frank O'Sullivan of the Federal Bureau of Investigation was dressed in a blue golf shirt and tan slacks with worn brown penny loafers. His smoker's face was prematurely aged with deep lines, and his hair was an odd mix of white and gray with clumps of each in no particular pattern. His slumping shoulders made him appear even shorter than his five feet six inches. He was leaning against the bars of his cell when he first spotted me. He was sadly self-conscious of the dried tears that streaked his cheeks, and through a voice breaking with fear, he begged me to represent him at his arraignment on the criminal charges. An arraignment is part of the initial court proceeding where a person charged with a crime is formally told the specifics of the charges. He told me that his lawyer was delayed and he had been told by the correction officer in charge of the detention area that his case would not be called until his lawyer appeared. I telephoned my boss and got permission to represent O'Sullivan for the arraignment. I was directed to make it clear to the judge that the Legal Aid Society was appearing on O'Sullivan's behalf only for the arraignment.

When the case was called, the courtroom was filled with the anxious and angry parents of the seven little victims, several dozen police officers and court officers, and seemingly every reporter in New York City. This only served to piss off the local police reporters, Morty in particular, making them all the more ravenous for inside news in order to show up "those people from the City," as the regulars referred to their invading colleagues. Of course, the children were kept in another room, protected by a detail of police officers and watched over by several social workers from the citywide trauma unit of the Victims Services Agency.

The court officer motioned to O'Sullivan, who was seated in a holding area in the courtroom, and directed him to come forward as he called the docket number and the name of the case, which included the name of the defendant. This particular announcement has a daunting effect on the defendant because it proclaims the awesome power of the state, "The People of the State of New York against. . . ." Then, turning to me, he directed, "Please give your notice of appearance." A notice of appearance is one of the court system's numerous anachronisms. It means simply that the attorney must give his or her name, address, and affiliation for the stenographic record of the proceeding, which is preserved for future review — for example, to show that a defendant was properly advised of the charges brought by the prosecutor. I replied, "Charles J. Hynes, associate attorney, the Legal Aid Society, representing the defendant."

"Does he have a name?" was Judge Cromwell's curt inquiry.

"Yes, of course he does, Your Honor, and it was just announced by the court officer, when the case was called." Judge Cromwell, a huge man whose distended belly and florid face were the marks of the final stages of a diseased liver, the result of decades of gluttonous boozing, immediately took offense. In a booming voice for all to hear, particularly the families of the victims, but especially the assembled media, he demanded, "Why is the Legal Aid Society representing this federal agent, who surely has the resources to retain private counsel?" Nothing I could say by way of explanation would keep the judge, one of the worst political hacks we had to deal with, from getting his moment in the sun. Judge Cromwell closed his tirade against the Legal Aid Society in general and me in particular with "Bail is set in each of the seven cases at one million dollars. Each," he added, not sure that he was fully understood. Then he ended with this:

"If this defendant, a federal agent" — and here, in a loud and melodramatic voice, he pronounced and spelled O'Sullivan's full name — "Francis Emmett O'Sullivan can put up seven million dollars to secure his return to court when necessary, then perhaps you, Mr. Hynes, and your organization, which exists to represent indigent criminals —"

"Defendants," I shouted, interrupting the judge.

"Don't you dare interrupt me or I shall set bail on you!" he screamed, with such intensity that it was accompanied with a noisy belch and the unmistakable odor of rye whiskey, part of his breakfast routine, assaulting everyone within five feet of the judge's bench. He kept his menacing stare fixed on me for almost a full minute. Then he continued.

"Very well, if he makes bail I assume he will pay for his own lawyer." My poor friend Agent O'Sullivan was too shaken to attempt to reply to any of this as he was led away in handcuffs. He looked plaintively in my direction and shrugged his shoulders. As he was being led away, handcuffed behind his back, to the detention cell, I mouthed, "Don't worry," and then I raced from the courtroom. It took less than an hour for me to prepare and serve a writ of habeas corpus on the New York City Department of Corrections, which was holding O'Sullivan.

A writ of habeas corpus is an ancient legal remedy that is a birthright of every American citizen and is one of the foundations of our protection against the vast power of government. The writ is an order issued by a judge directed to the custodian of a person held in confinement. The opening words of the document demand, "Habeas corpus ad subjiciendum" — or, in substance, "You shall have the body brought before me immediately!" Like so many other rights available to American citizens, it has its roots in English law. It is perhaps the most celebrated writ in English law and is revered universally as the "great writ of liberty."

New York State Supreme Court Justice Peter King, who heard my application for the writ and who promptly granted it, at first laughed. Then, when he realized that Judge Cromwell was involved, he shook his head and said, "That asshole!"

I rushed back to the courtroom with the writ. It was there that I first encountered Morty. In fact, I ran smack into him, just as he stepped in front of me and in one breath snarled, "I'm Morty — of the *Brooklyn Daily Eagle.* How do you get off representing this bum, anyway?" Morty was not much more than five feet tall with a rasping voice, the result of too many years of inhaling Camel cigarettes. He reeked of nicotine. His face was framed by an odd-looking porkpie hat, and he had a huge yellow pencil resting on his right ear. He was wearing a cheap cardigan sweater, dark gray trousers, and a loud red-and-white-striped shirt; it appeared to me that he chose his outfit for what he believed was the appropriate dress of his trade. I recalled that most of the other reporters in the press section of the courtroom wore similar attire. Morty repeated as if I hadn't heard him the first time, "What the fuck gives you the right to use taxpayer money to represent a bum like this?" After my ugly encounter with Judge Cromwell and his absurd brand of justice, I was in no mood for Morty or anyone else, so I pushed him aside and tried to ignore his shouts and complaints that I should be arrested for assault as I made my way to my office. Morty's persistent telephone calls to my office, eleven of them, I left unreturned.

Later, after the writ was granted and Agent O'Sullivan was released without any bail set, Morty accosted me again. I ignored him and resisted a powerful temptation to take his head off.

As the years passed I went on to different jobs, mostly in government, but with some time spent in the private practice of law as a criminal defense attorney. I began to notice Morty's byline on a number of significant crime stories. While I didn't forget our first unpleasant encounter, I admired his writing style. It was clear, thoughtful, and comprehensive, and it contained no personal judgments. Soon he had a column in a major New York City tabloid three times a week, and I became an avid reader and very soon an admiring fan.

In 1985, our paths crossed again. In June that year, New York Governor Mario M. Cuomo appointed me the corruption special prosecutor for New York City. One of the first calls I received was from Morty, who asked to meet with me. He made a luncheon reservation at Forlini's Italian restaurant on Baxter Street in lower Manhattan, not far from the federal and state courthouses and a favorite hangout of prosecutors, defense attorneys, and judges.

The restaurant is divided into two rooms. The main room, entered from Baxter Street, and its attached rear room have an identical placement of booths along the wall on the right side as you go in. Both in the middle and on the left side of each room, there are neatly arranged tables properly spaced for privacy. The booths in both rooms each have a small plaque affixed to the wall, identifying a famous customer, usually a judge, such as New York Supreme Court Justice Edwin Torres, the author of *Carlito's Way.* Justice Torres is famous for a line in a sentencing speech he gave to some incorrigible drug seller: "Listen to me, pal. With the sentence I'm about to give you, your parole officer hasn't been born yet!"

One of the booths bears a plaque dedicated to the current district attorney of New York County, Robert M. Morgenthau, the well-respected dean of the state's district attorneys. Another honors John Fontaine Keenan, a federal judge, formerly the brilliant chief of the Homicide Bureau in the office of the legendary Frank S. Hogan, a feared and respected predecessor of Morgenthau in the DA's office.

The lighting in Forlini's rear room is subdued, so it appears to be a more confidential setting than the brightly lighted entry room. In truth there is really no difference. It just seems more private, although the occupants of the booths, seating four, are often seen leaning over, in secret huddles. Naturally the front room is usually occupied by people who want to be seen. It is generally filled with lively conversation and a great deal of laughter, interrupted by new important arrivals.

The bar at Forlini's could easily be a setting for one of Damon Runyon's stories. It is the venue where the various levels of the court system meet with little thought to class distinction. Court officers, defense attorneys, police officers, prosecutors, and judges freely mix in a convivial setting, gathered around a very long bar. The open kitchen sends waves of tantalizing garlicky smells throughout the bar. The bar is dark, and when you enter through its separate Baxter Street door, the patrons look more like shadows until your eyes adjust.

The bar area is filled at lunch hour, and some of its regulars remain late into the evening. It is mostly dominated by loud conversation, and the din it creates ironically offers more protection for confidential conversation than the rear room.

Appropriately Morty and I met in the rear chamber to discuss our mutual fascination with public corruption and, in particular, police corruption. Before we got to that subject Morty opened with, "So kid, what ever happened to that fed child molester you represented, watshisname O'Reilly or . . . ?"

"O'Sullivan," I corrected him. "It was a tragedy seemingly without an end in sight. You may not remember the details but Frank O'Sullivan was accused by seven little girls, none older than nine years, of separate or unconnected sodomy assaults in different neighborhoods throughout Brooklyn. He was arrested despite the fact that the only evidence was the eyewitness identification by the children, each of whom offered a contradictory recollection of his facial hair. The hair color given to the police by the kids immediately after each assault ranged from bright red to jet black, nevertheless the nature of the brutal attacks, which were identical, was so horrific that the district attorney refused to dismiss even though O'Sullivan's facial hair was distinctly blond. He concluded that the discrepancies could be explained away by the age of the children and the traumatic circumstances of the assaults.

" 'Besides,' the DA said to one of O'Sullivan's lawyers, 'there hasn't been a similar attack since your guy was arrested.'

"O'Sullivan went to trial six times and as I said the facts were identical, so much so that the police department's sex crimes unit characterized the attacks as 'pattern sodomies.' In every case the victim was accosted inside an elevator of a residential building by an assailant with prominent facial hair, sideburns, and a goatee, wearing a bright bandanna which partially covered his face as well as the facial hair. Each victim said the attacker was armed with a small silver plated handgun held against their head. The assailant spoke only once and then briefly. He was somehow able to bypass floors as he took each little girl to the top floor of the building, usually the sixth floor. He then took her roughly by the arm and dragged the terrified child to a metal staircase resembling a fire escape that led up to a room containing the machinery which operated the elevator system. He then forced the victim to kneel."

At this point in my story I decided to give Morty a glimpse inside the trial where I defended O'Sullivan. I wanted him to know what we were up against.

"The assistant district attorney carefully brought the tiny seven-year-old victim through her first contact with her assailant, making it quite clear that her identification was solid.

" 'As you waited for the elevator were there lights on in the lobby?'

" 'Yes.'

" 'Were they very bright?' The prosecutor knew it was an improper leading question but he also knew that the judge would not rule in my favor had I objected because of the child's age and the stress she was under. It didn't really matter because I had no intention of objecting, which I believed would have upset the child and had an adverse effect on the jury.

"The child answered, 'They were very bright.'

" 'Were you alone?'

" 'Yes,' she replied softly and then she added almost in a whisper, 'for just a few minutes.' Here the judge leaned over and said solicitously,

" 'Sweetheart, you will have to speak up so the jurors can hear you.' The little victim then pointed to Frank and blurted out in reply, 'Yes, until he came.'

"At this point tears streamed down her cheeks and she began to shake as she seemed to recall the ugliness of it all. I glanced in the the direction of the jury box and I could see the reactions of some of the jurors, from sadness to anger to disgust.

"After the assistant DA had established that the lighting conditions were bright aboard the elevator and repeatedly asked the child where she was looking as she was abducted and throughout the ordeal leading toward her testimony about the assault in the machinery room he had clearly demonstrated to the jury that she had had ample opportunity to identify her assailant." It was at this point as I recalled her testimony that I carefully watched Morty's reaction.

" 'What happened after you were forced to kneel down?' the prosecutor continued.'

"Now the child sobbed out of control as she described how her attacker zipped down his pants and . . ."

When I finshed describing the wantonness and brutality of the assault I looked at Morty and saw his face had blanched and that he was angry.

"How could you have defended that pig?"

"But Morty," I said, "the guy was innocent."

I completed the account of her testimony where she recalled that the assailant told her, "Count to fifty or else." Then to emphasize what he'd do if she did not, he cocked the gun and pushed it against her head.

Then he disappeared out the door and quickly down the metal staircase.

"Frank went to trial six times represented in each case by an experienced and competent trial lawyer. He was convicted in each case on all counts, which included kidnapping, attempted assault, and sodomy. By the time I took him to trial the appellate division had reversed the two prior convictions and dismissed the charges citing the unreliability of eyewitness identification in general and in particular these two cases. In my trial, not only was the facial hair significantly different in color and in length, the attacker was described as having jet black sideburns and a fully developed jet black goatee. Frank's sideburns were blond like the rest of his hair and his arrest photograph showed a goatee with blond fuzz. There was also a serious problem with the height and weight description given to the police. The victim described her attacker as forty pounds heavier than Frank and at least six inches taller." None of that mattered any more than it mattered to Morty, and Frank O'Sullivan was once again convicted.

"By this time O'Sullivan had been fired from his job following his first conviction although he was appealing the ruling by the FBI. That administrative review by the bureau was rendered moot after his next conviction. Of course, his administrative appeal was put back on track after the second reversal which once again was halted upon his third conviction. Finally his marriage of ten years ended in divorce and he lost custody of his nine-year-old daughter. His wife, Rosemary, had stayed with him through the third trial but then said that she could no longer be sure of his innocence and that she was afraid for their daughter. At this point Frank, whose physical condition had deteriorated and who was fighting depression, said that he was pretty much resigned to what had happened to him and that he fully understood Rosemary's decision.

"Several months later Frank's third conviction was reversed and the case dismissed but the DA refused to change his decision to continue the prosecution. Frank was tried and convicted three more times and in each case there was a reversal and dismissal based on what the appellate court concluded was a flawed eyewitness identification. But it was the language of the court's sixth consecutive reversal and dismissal of *People v. O'Sullivan* that sent a clear message to the district attorney. In what would be the appellate division's last unanimous decision in the O'Sullivan matter, the presiding justice of the court, Honorable R. Herbert Dayon, wrote with eloquent yet direct language, 'No piece of evidence has so disturbed the courts of this state as that of the testimony of an eyewitness without any other support. While this Court does not reject such testimony entirely, every prosecutor who wishes to do a fair job must carefully weigh this evidence with a full appreciation of its potential for a perverse and unjust result.' Dayon then added these words: 'How many times must this Court reverse based on the facts in the O'Sullivan case before the district attorney of Kings County more fully understands that his job is not just to convict but to do justice?' O'Sullivan would not stand trial a seventh time."

Morty, who had recovered from his emotional reaction as he began to understand Frank's predicament, asked, "So what happened to him?"

"He was restored to duty with back pay," I replied, "but the last time I saw him a few years ago he was still in pretty bad shape and doing everything he could to restore his marriage. A few months later I called him at his office in St. Louis where he was reassigned and he told me he was still not having much luck convincing Rosemary to take him back."

We both realized that the O'Sullivan travesty had consumed most of our lunch, not leaving much time to discuss corruption, and at this point Morty, now in his late sixties, said, "By the way kid, you ain't ever gonna end police corruption. They've tried everything and nothin' works." I smiled and shrugged my shoulders.

Following a delicious meal of veal francese and a side of spaghetti drenched with garlic and oil, we skipped dessert and opted instead for some espresso and a touch of anisette. Suddenly Morty stood and said, "There's some guys at the bar who would like to meet you." "Like who?" I said warily. These were alright guys, he said, a few reporters from the courthouse, a prosecutor, and a defense lawyer. "You know most of them, and," he assured me, "it'll be off the record."

It was Friday afternoon, getaway day, when court calendars were adjourned, and as we entered the bar area, I recognized, at the far end of the room near the door, Bobby Kaminsky, a homicide prosecutor with twenty years in the New York County DA's office, talking to Carlos Rivera, a kick-ass defense lawyer for the last fifteen years.

Rivera earlier in his career had ten years in the office of the New York County district attorney. He had just been nominated to the State Supreme Court and with the support of the Democratic organization was assured of a fourteen-year term after the November election. He and Kaminsky were celebrating.

Rivera and Kaminsky were very close, some said like brothers. Carlos Rivera was a solid five feet eight inches tall, with a barrel chest, carefully hidden by tailored Baroni suits. He favored broad-brimmed fedoras and dark gray tweed overcoats with velvet Chesterfield collars. His black Italian leather shoes were always spit-shined, a habit he'd kept from the Marine Corps. His speech was street tough, with salty language picked up and retained from his years of growing up in El Barrio — Spanish Harlem. His jet black hair glistened and was always combed straight back. His friendship with Bobby Kaminsky developed when, as a veteran homicide prosecutor, he was directed by a supervisor to break in Kaminsky. Bobby Kaminsky was six foot five, with a trim two-hundred-pound frame kept solid with a daily exercise regimen that began each morning at five. He had a full head of sandy-colored wavy hair, and as a forty-five-year-old bachelor, he was very much in demand. Kaminsky and Rivera always seemed to be together at Forlini's, either in the restaurant or at the bar. Neither drank much, preferring the give-and-take of the bar scene, mostly sipping Diet Coke or an occasional beer. Their respective statures reminded older patrons of the comic strip characters Mutt and Jeff.

Standing between them were three reporters: Sid Lyons of the *New York Daily News,* with an ever-present series of chain-smoked cigars; Jimmy Fess of *Newsday,* short, fat, and loud; and Barney Golden of the *New York Post* with his checkered sports coat. The three were heavy-duty drinkers. I recognized the reporters from the court scene, but I don't think I ever spoke with any one of them. I knew both Kaminsky and Rivera as superb trial lawyers. It was difficult to get a seat at one of their trials. When they competed, all the brotherly love was left outside the courtroom, and a furious struggle ensued until a jury announced its verdict.

Morty quickly introduced me, more by title than by name. Fess of *Newsday,* barely bothering to acknowledge me, spoke first and offered the following unsolicited observation: "If the state doesn't go broke, the only thing you can be sure of from your fuckin' job is a paycheck every two weeks, because there's no fuckin' way you'll ever do anything about cop corruption, or for that matter judge corruption! It's an institution!" When I asked Fess why he was so certain, Sid Lyons gruffly interrupted and said, "If you don't know why, what the hell makes you qualified to be our special state corruption prosecutor?" To underscore his sarcasm, Lyons slowly and carefully pronounced each syllable of my job title. Kaminsky jumped in and said, "Hey, give him a break, he hasn't even started." Now both Rivera and Golden of the *Post* chimed in, shouting over one another. "Bobby, tell the kid about Mulvey," Golden said. "Tell him," said Carlos Rivera, "how that fucking blue wall destroyed a good cop." Golden continued, "Ya see, every cop knows what happened to Mulvey, and while most of them are honest, hardworking Boy Scouts, because of Mulvey and what the police department did to other cops, no honest cop will ever help you end police corruption." "And," added Morty, "that's why you'll be just another flop in a job that should have been abolished years ago. But in the meantime, take Jimmy Fess's advice. Relax and enjoy your paycheck." I wasn't particularly surprised by the cynicism; it was nothing new. But I wanted to hear about this cop Mulvey.

What they told me that afternoon was shocking enough, but what happened to Mulvey's nephew years later was outrageous. The story of that young cop, Steven Robert Holt, and his uncle, Sergeant Robert Mulvey, is a profoundly tragic example of the culture that created the NYPD's Blue Wall of Silence and why it had to be destroyed in order to end the cyclical evil of police corruption in New York. This story of police corruption begins in an unusual way. It begins with murder.

1

Suffolk County, Long Island, New York, December 20, 1990, 7:30 a.m.

"Oh my God, David." Alyson Keeler sobbed uncontrollably at her gruesome discovery. "Come here, quickly," she pleaded, her body trembling.

Alyson had soft blond hair with streaks of chestnut, worn slightly above her shoulders. Her large hazel eyes were deeply set above high cheekbones in an oval-shaped face. Her aquiline nose was neatly sculpted, and her lips were drawn up in what seemed to be a perpetual smile. She was very pretty, perhaps even beautiful, but this morning her lovely face was twisted by fear, contorted with revulsion at the sight of what lay on the ground only a few feet away from where she stood. She looked at the bodies lying there and then looked away, only to look back again. She repeated this sequence a few times until her fiancé, twenty-three-

35

year-old David Rapp, joined her and held her closely, protectively. The bodies of two young men, who appeared to be in their early thirties, lay there on the snow-covered beach looking peaceful enough, staring skyward. A brief glance might have suggested that they were lost in contemplation of their majestic surroundings. But on close examination, each man had a bullet hole on the left side of his temple, haloed with a small pool of coagulated, frozen blood.

Alyson Keeler, twenty-one years old, was a sophomore at the Stony Brook campus of SUNY, or the State University of New York, located in Long Island's Suffolk County. She was enrolled in the school's premed honors program. David was in his third year of premed at the same school. They had driven earlier that morning to Robert Moses State Park, named for New York's notorious master builder. They arrived early enough to see daybreak. It was their favorite time of day at their favorite place.

Alyson's shocking discovery was two dead men dressed in denim shirts and trousers. They wore canvas jackets with cheap imitation black fur collars and sleeves. Their footwear was worn black work boots.

When she had somewhat recovered, Alyson used a nearby phone booth to summon

36

police. As soon as Alyson's call to the Suffolk County 911 Police Emergency Operation Center was transmitted to a police car patrolling the perimeter of the park, every emergency unit with a police monitoring scanner would, with flashing red lights and blasting sirens, begin to roar toward Robert Moses State Park. Police cruisers from both the Suffolk County Police Department and the New York State Police, fire engines, emergency medical vans, and investigators from the Suffolk County district attorney's office would soon be joined by a full armada of news media.

Two murdered men found five days before Christmas in a crime-free suburban state park was a twenty-four-hour news story. Who these murdered men were would only increase the interest.

The first responding police officers notified their patrol sergeant. "We got two male Hispanics, apparently shot to death with one bullet each to the head. It looks like they were carried here from the main road after they were shot. We found pay stubs — probably their own — from a factory in Brooklyn on each of the bodies."

Ned Leon, the on-duty reporter for Long Island's cable television Channel 21, was the first reporter to hear the call over his police scanner, which was mounted on the dashboard of his mobile van, along with his unauthorized red police emergency light. Leon had been a police reporter for more than a dozen years, having spent much of his early days with the now-defunct *Long Island Press.* His heavy drinking and chain-smoking were habits he intentionally acquired trying to fit the image of a hard-bitten, leather-tough street crime reporter. These abuses were having predictable results on Ned Leon, who was afflicted with chronic coughing and bleeding ulcers and the sad and drawn look of an old man. Leon and, for that matter, all so-called police reporters loved the trappings or the instruments of police authority. Some carried phony police badges, and some even carried licensed guns. They flaunted these symbols, without having to deal with the awesome responsibilities and the dangers faced by real cops. Still, Ned was respected by the cops and the other police reporters because he had the uncanny investigative skills of a street detective. His ability to analyze raw data often led to the solution of a case before an arrest was made.

Two Hispanics killed execution style in 1990 meant one of only two things to Ned

Leon: These two victims were taken out in a bad drug deal in Brooklyn, or the murders were racially motivated. A veteran reporter like Leon, whose workday went from idle speculation to the ugly reality of homicide, abused wives, and abandoned kids, could not conceive of any other reason. Since the factory where the two murdered brothers, Hiram and Ramon Rodriguez, were employed was in a notorious Brooklyn neighborhood where drug-related murder was commonplace, and since race relations in New York City, and even its eastern neighbor counties of Nassau and Suffolk, could not have been worse, Ned Leon's guesses were not merely cynical. But his conclusion wasn't even close.

"Jimmy," said Suffolk County Police Chief of Detectives Phil Pitelli, "my homicide detectives think that those two guys we found in Moses State Park yesterday morning were killed by a city cop."

"What proof do they have?" DA James Crowley demanded.

"Frankly," Pitelli responded slowly, "they don't have much other than a few facts and a cop's instincts. The ME places the time of death, based on the degree of rigor mortis, sometime between six and eight hours before the bodies were discovered. Since the victims were from Brooklyn, my guys figure that they were killed there and brought to Moses to be dumped." Pitelli waited for DA Crowley to respond. When he didn't, the chief continued.

"The doc retrieved two rounds, one from the head of each victim. Our ballistics lab identified the rounds as those used in a .38-caliber Police Special, which, as you know, is a revolver issued to the NYPD. And then there's this: A gas station attendant on the Northern State Parkway gave a fill-up to a guy in a van about two in the morning of the twentieth, the day the bodies were found. He said that the driver looked like a cop and that the two passengers in the van also looked like cops. Finally, the attendant said that when the driver took out his wallet to pay for the gas he had a gun butt protruding from his waistband."

"Well," Crowley observed, "now if we only had a confession."

"Now, Jimmy," Pitelli scolded, "just be patient. My guys are working with the NYPD's Internal Affairs. Who knows, if we get the right photo maybe we'll have your confession."

"Why not?" replied Crowley. "With thirty thousand city cops, maybe you'll get lucky and give me that confession before my term ends in '93."

2

Kenny Rattigan,
1990 and 1991

In 1989, W. Carlton Richardson won a stunning victory to become New York City's first African American mayor. The Brooklyn district attorney, Sherman "Buddy" Cooper, an old friend and ally of Richardson, recommended Kenneth J. Rattigan, his Rackets Bureau chief, as Richardson's first corporation counsel. The corporation counsel is the city's lawyer, whose staff represents all New York City agencies in claims brought against them. Traditionally, the corporation counsel is not only the mayor's chief lawyer but also his closest confidant. District Attorney Cooper thought Kenny Rattigan was a perfect choice. Rattigan's judgment was near flawless, and he was fiercely loyal.

As Rattigan was completing his first year, he was loving every minute of the job. Despite no experience on the civil side of the practice of law, Rattigan adjusted by recruiting first-rate lawyers with extensive experience in a number of specialties, including corporate, financial, and real estate law, as well as hard-fisted trial lawyers he deployed to the combat zone of negligence law. Rattigan particularly enjoyed being part of the mayor's inner circle with its direct access to Richardson, giving him a say in virtually all major policy decisions.

Following the appointment of the corporation counsel, the next critical appointment is the police commissioner. Since Kenny Rattigan was the only member of Richardson's cabinet to have experience in law enforcement, the mayor accepted his recommendation and appointed a little-known captain, Sean J. Nevins. It was a startling development that sent shock waves throughout the hierarchy of the police department. It would also set in motion a major offensive on one of the department's most enduring problems, police corruption. The appointment did much to establish Rattigan's influence with Mayor Richardson.

Mayor Richardson's power base was Brooklyn's Bedford-Stuyvesant section and South Jamaica in Queens County, both black enclaves, every bit as rich in African American tradition as Manhattan's world-famous Harlem. The rivalry among these communities was mostly friendly except when it came to politics. Richardson filled his inner circle with his political supporters, who were in the main African Americans, leaving Corporation Counsel Rattigan very much in the minority. But he looked forward to each new day and each new challenge, and he enjoyed fending off the good-natured comments from the other members of the mayor's kitchen cabinet, especially one deputy mayor who would wonder aloud, "Does our white guy have any colorful thoughts this morning?"

The daily meetings at Gracie Mansion began promptly at seven o'clock and quickly became free-for-alls — loud debates presided over by Richardson, a workaholic who seemed driven by the need to prove himself all over again every day. The exhilaration of each morning's often fierce debates was for Kenny a natural high, and it filled the vacuum created by the separation from his first love, the battleground of the trial court.

But Rattigan's time at the mayor's elbow soon ended. In November 1990, Sean Patrick, who had served as the Queens County district attorney for more than a dozen years, suddenly resigned. At Mayor Richardson's urging, New York State's governor and fellow Democrat David Laurel appointed Kenneth Rattigan the interim Queens County DA. The appointment would last until the next general election, in November 1991. The mayor convinced Rattigan to take a shot at elective office. He promised and delivered the support of the powerful African American community in South Jamaica, and in November Kenny Rattigan was easily elected to fill the remainder of Patrick's term.

"Kenny, it's Rose. The boss wants you." Rose Chauf was Brooklyn DA Cooper's longtime secretary and confidant. To Kenny Rattigan, despite the fact that he and District Attorney Cooper were colleagues, Cooper would always be the boss.

"Kenny, I have some terrible news." Cooper knew that Rattigan would be shocked, so he chose his words carefully and uttered them very slowly. "The Suffolk cops have been investigating the murder of two young Hispanics found shot to death in Robert Moses State Park."

"Yeah, Boss," Rattigan interrupted, "I remember the case."

"Well, they were tipped by telephone, anonymously," Cooper continued, "that if they searched a certain factory in Brooklyn they would find the body of Scott Ruben, a cop who disappeared some time ago. The caller added that the guy who murdered all three was a New York City police officer and that if they recovered his gun, they would have all the evidence that they needed."

"Who's the cop, Boss?" Rattigan asked anxiously.

Cooper replied, "The caller said that it was a Sergeant Steven Holt."

"Ah, that's just bullshit, Boss." Rattigan was angry.

"Wait a minute, Kenny. The medical examiner's office checked the dental records of the corpse found in the warehouse, and it was identified as the body of Scott Ruben. The word is that Steven was furious when Ruben somehow managed to avoid being arrested in that roundup of all those corrupt cops last year."

"Yeah, but that's quite a leap to conclude that he killed him."

"But Kenny, what if the tip is right about Steven's gun?"

"I still wouldn't believe it, Boss. Hey, I'm sorry, I gotta make a call." With that, Rattigan abruptly ended the conversation.

Rattigan's first call was to Robert Mulvey, retired and living with his family in upstate

New York.

"Robert." Rattigan tried to sound casual. "How do I find your nephew?"

"He's still at the Seven-five in East New York over in Brooklyn. Is there a problem?"

"Nah," replied Rattigan, "a question came up about a case we worked on."

"Seven-five Precinct, PAA Sloan, how can I help you?

"May I please speak with Sergeant Holt? This is a personal call."

"May I tell him who is calling?" responded the police administrative assistant, a civilian working for the department.

"Sure, this is the Queens County district attorney, Ken Rattigan, but this call is unofficial."

Moments later, the PAA was back on the phone. "I'm sorry, Mr. District Attorney, but Sergeant Holt is in conference, and he can't be interrupted. I'll tell him you called."

East New York, Brooklyn, the 75th Precinct, April 23, 1991

Inspector Thomas Newell and Sergeant Reggie Jobloviski, both of Internal Affairs, greeted Sergeant Steven Holt. Holt had met both men some months before when he was interviewed by them for a position in the Internal Affairs Bureau of the New York City Police Department. Shortly after the arrests in a major police corruption case in Brooklyn during 1990, Holt had responded to a departmental order issued by Police Commissioner Sean Nevins inviting officers of all ranks to apply for a transfer to a "new" Internal Affairs Bureau.

While both Newell and Jobloviski were impressed with Holt's intelligence, enthusiasm, and knowledge of corruption, particularly what he said about its causes and various strategies he thought should be used to contain it, they were not inclined to recommend him for transfer to the revamped corruption unit for two reasons. First, his age. He was, after all, the youngest sergeant in the police department. Second, his answers to some of their questions suggested that he needed more maturity. They were particularly concerned that he considered the elimination of police corruption not only a priority mission for the department but a personal passion.

Sergeant Jobloviski concluded in his report that Holt's application for a transfer to IAB should be put on hold for a year or two to allow him more patrol experience and time to gain the necessary maturity. "The applicant is very bright and will surely hit a fast promotional track, but at this stage of his career, his concerns about corruption allegations within the department cloud his objectivity and judgment," he wrote.

Today, though, Inspector Newell and Sergeant Jobloviski were not in the captain's office at the 75th Precinct to discuss Holt's transfer application. Steven was puzzled to see others in the room, particularly a few uniformed officers with shoulder patches identifying them as members of the Suffolk County Police Department.

Inspector Newell made the introductions. "Sergeant Holt, this is Assistant Chief Phil

Pitelli, chief of detectives for Suffolk County. Detective Sergeant Brenda Murphy, who is in charge of the Homicide Division for the Suffolk County Police Department, and Assistant District Attorney Wallace Goss, chief of the Suffolk County district attorney's Homicide Bureau."

The scene would have been comical with all of these people jammed into the captain's modest-sized office except everyone's face was so solemn.

"These folks would like to ask you a few questions, Steven. Any problem with that?" Newell continued.

"None that I can think of, sir," Holt replied.

Chief Pitelli motioned to Sergeant Murphy and said, "Brenda, why don't you begin."

"Sergeant, how well did you know Police Officer Scott Ruben?"

Holt was immediately curious, because Sergeant Murphy referred to Ruben in the past tense.

"Not well at all. We both work here at the 75th Precinct, but he works a steady tour supervised by another sergeant."

"And who is that?" she asked.

"There are several. I don't recall their names."

"Did you know two brothers, Hiram and Ramon Rodriguez" — Holt thought, *She's using the past tense again* — "who were employed by Leib Electrical Supplies, located in the Bush Terminal in Brooklyn?"

Holt looked at each of the three people in civilian clothing who had been identified as officials from Suffolk County. He glanced toward each of the uniformed officers, also from Suffolk but not introduced. He then directed a question to Inspector Newell. "Has anything happened to these guys?"

"Yes," Sergeant Murphy replied, not waiting for Newell's response. "They are all dead. Ruben, too. They were murdered."

Holt shot out of his seat and, raising his voice, said, "I think maybe I should speak to my SBA delegate before we go much further." A police officer's union — in Steven's case, the Sergeants' Benevolent Association — would be the first line of defense in such a situation.

Inspector Newell stood and walked to where Holt was standing and said, "Sergeant Holt, that of course is your right, but I must ask you officially if you are willing to proceed with this interview."

"No, sir, I am not, at least not until I speak to my union representative and decide whether I should be advised by a lawyer. By

51

the way, am I in custody?"

Chief Pitelli, assuming his best folksy manner, put his arm on Steven's shoulder and said softly, "Of course not, son, and if you want to wait until you consult a lawyer or a union rep, you can and you should."

Inspector Newell said, "Sergeant Holt, as a result of a preliminary inquiry, I am authorized by the police commissioner of the City of New York to suspend you for a minimum of thirty days, and I am directing you to immediately hand over any weapons you have in your possession and to surrender your shield. And finally, I order you to report to the office of the chief of detectives tomorrow morning at One Police Plaza at 0800 hours. Am I clear?"

Holt could feel the anger building. His cheeks were red hot, and he felt frustrated and humiliated. "Yes, sir," he finally blurted.

But the ordeal was just beginning for the young police officer, because it was Assistant District Attorney Wallace Goss's turn to speak. Clearing his throat for his moment, Goss clumsily removed from his inside coat pocket a piece of paper, orange in color and perhaps three-quarters the size of business stationery. He handed the paper to Holt, who did not offer to accept it until he noticed that Goss's hand was quivering.

Goss solemnly intoned, "Steven Robert Holt, the grand jury of Suffolk County hearby summons you to appear before it to give testimony in the matter entitled *The People of the State of New York Against John Doe.*" The name John Doe or Richard Roe is used in the identifying title of grand jury investigations when that body has not received sufficient evidence to name or charge a particular individual.

Holt took the paper, folded it up, and began to leave. He stopped, however, at the door and addressed Newell and Jobloviski. "What you two have done today is just disgraceful."

Newell tried to interrupt, but Holt cut him off. "No, Inspector, be decent enough to listen to me. I assure you that I will not be as disrespectful to you as you have been to me. I have put my life on the line for the people of this city. I fought the corruption that this department permitted to fester and grow unchecked for decades. And now, in the presence of strangers, you didn't grant me the common courtesy or fundamental rights you would give as a matter of routine to some street mutt who injured or killed a police officer."

The room had become eerily silent. Pitelli was genuinely embarrassed by what had occurred. Even Goss looked uneasy.

Holt finished, "What you have done today is a huge mistake. You should all be ashamed to call yourselves law enforcement professionals."

Suddenly Holt was gone, out the door, not waiting for any complaints or comments.

The following morning, Steven Holt reported to One Police Plaza. There Chief Pitelli was waiting, accompanied by two Suffolk County detectives and a lieutenant from the NYPD IAB. They approached Holt, and Pitelli said quietly but firmly, "Sergeant Holt, please turn around and place your hands behind your back."

Steven complied immediately, allowing Pitelli to rear-cuff him, but when the chief began to give him the Miranda warnings — "You have the right to remain silent . . . anything you say" — Holt interrupted.

"No, don't you dare treat me like a perp!" he shouted. "I am a sergeant with the New York City Police Department, and I damned well know my rights. Don't you disrespect me in front of the other cops."

Pitelli raised his voice and said, "Son, I have no choice. It's the law."

What wasn't either the law or a procedural

requirement was to march Steven, hand-cuffed from the rear, through the hallway of the headquarters of the New York City Police Department, past cops and civilian employees, to an elevator and then to the garage for his ride in a gated police van to the Suffolk County jail. It was something Holt would never forget nor forgive, and years later he certainly would recall that it was April 24, 1991, his birthday. He was twenty-seven years old.

4

Steven Holt, Brooklyn,
1964–1969

Steven Robert Holt was born on April 24, 1964. At his baptism into the Roman Catholic faith he was given the middle name Robert to honor his mother's brother, Robert Mulvey. Robert Mulvey, then twenty-one, was a brand-new member of the New York City Police Department, assigned to the 67th Police precinct in the Flatbush section of Brooklyn. Mulvey's strong young body was neatly packed into a six-foot frame that easily supported 180 pounds of carefully conditioned muscle. His sharp facial features, in particular his pointed chin, his broad, large nose, his jet black hair, and his dark searching eyes made him look like a descendant of Native Americans rather than one whose ancestral roots were in County Derry, Northern Ireland.

Police Officer Robert Mulvey, who wore

shield number 1050, was so very proud to be a member of the department that he dressed for the baptism in his crisp blue uniform and specially shined his gleaming black shoes. He was particularly proud that his sister Mary had asked him to be Steven's godfather. During the baptism ceremony, Steven's father, Harold, perpetually drunk and out of work, could not contain himself from mocking this serious young police officer. Harold became so loud and abusive that Father Dwyer ordered him to leave the baptistry. Harold happily obliged and headed for the nearest gin mill.

As Steven grew up, he became more and more attached to his uncle. And Robert Mulvey soon became much more than an uncle, especially after he kicked Steven's father out of the family's apartment in 1968.

Typically Harold's episodes with alcohol made him increasingly violent. He began to direct his violence against Steven's mother, first with humiliating sarcasm and then with an occasional slap across her face. The physical assaults escalated, and he beat her so severely early one morning that she had to be rushed to the hospital, where she needed sutures to close a deep gash over her left eye. For Mary, the worst part of this ordeal was that it was inflicted on her in front of their son, Steven, who was at the time only four years old. Soon the frail little boy began to have terrifying nightmares about these beatings, and Mary decided that they would have to leave.

Not long after she reached this decision, her brother Robert dropped by unexpectedly. As he approached the front door, he heard Mary's screams and his nephew Steven's convulsive sobs. Mulvey burst through the door and found Mary lying on the floor of the kitchen with Harold's foot drawn back about to kick her in the head. Mulvey grabbed the drunk's raised foot and threw him backward into the kitchen stove. Harold hit his head and lost consciousness. Steven, his little heart beating so rapidly he thought it might explode, watched all this while cowering under the kitchen table. When Harold came to, he was on the sidewalk in front of the home he would no longer share with his family. Robert had piled all of his clothing and two suitcases neatly next to where he had thrown Harold. "If you ever go near my sister again, I will break every bone in your body." Mulvey said this as he was holding Harold's hair, pulling his head back so he was staring directly at him and so there could be no mistake about the seriousness of his threat. Harold never saw his wife or son again, although he did try to contact her and Steven a few years later while he was serving time in a federal prison for tax fraud.

Uncle Robert Mulvey was not only a surrogate father to Steven, he was his idol and best friend. During the summer of 1969, Mulvey taught the little boy how to play baseball. He took him to the movies and to Mets games at Shea Stadium. It was the Mets' magical summer, the year they won the World Series. When Robert's sister chided him that someone nearly twenty-seven years old should marry and settle down, Robert would say that between the job he loved so much and the time he spent with his "best buddy" Steven, he had little time for anything else. He managed to say this in front of the boy, and the five-year-old beamed.

Not long after, a tragedy struck the City of New York that would have lasting repercussions for Robert Mulvey, and for his little nephew Steven.

5

Flatbush Avenue and Avenue U, Brooklyn, August 23, 1969, 2:25 p.m.

By early afternoon Brooklyn was experiencing one of its annual August dog days when the sun seems, in that turn of the calendar, to stand still. The temperature had reached 96 degrees by 1:30 p.m. and with humidity above 90 percent, Brooklyn was baking.

Overheated automobiles on both Flatbush Avenue and Avenue U, where the two major arteries intersect, were proof of the futility of attempting to use the relatively new automobile air-conditioning. The result left many of these vehicles, not much more than helpless metal hulks, clogging the streets.

No one paid much attention to the battered dark blue Ford sedan pulling over to the curb on Flatbush Avenue, a few feet west of the intersection. The unmarked but unmistakable detective squad car contained Detective Harry Lewis behind the wheel and his partner of more than a dozen years, Detective David Cordo, in the passenger seat. They had gone a short distance outside of their assigned area, so that Lewis could buy some cigars at his favorite tobacco store.

In 1969, cigars and wide-brimmed porkpie hats were the trademarks of a New York City detective, and Harry Lewis was every inch, and with every move, a New York City detective. A thin little Dapper Dan of a guy, with elevated lifts in his shoes, he was just a hair below five feet seven inches tall. His eyes betrayed more smiles than he'd allow his lips, but they communicated more cynicism than humor, the result of years interrogating suspects. His high forehead would draw attention to his receding hairline, but it was always concealed by the way he wore his porkpie hat, down but jaunty on the left side of his head. He thought this made him look like Humphrey Bogart. To complete the picture, Detective Lewis always wore loud striped and oversized sports jackets. The large jacket was used to conceal his cannon, as he called his huge Colt revolver. He could very well have just stepped out of Central Casting.

As Lewis walked slowly toward the store, Detective Cordo stepped outside the police cruiser to escape the heat trapped inside.

Cordo was originally from Puerto Rico. He preferred neatly pressed dark suits, blue shirts, conservative ties, and highly polished shoes. His look was more FBI than NYPD, the polar opposite of his partner, Lewis. He smiled broadly and constantly with his gleaming white teeth, at nothing in particular. His high cheekbones and a perfectly sculpted nose and jet black wavy hair blessed him with the swarthy good looks of a Latin matinee idol complemented by a firm, lean body. He could have easily passed himself off as a recently retired professional athlete, perhaps a major league baseball player. As Cordo rested against a nearby telephone pole, he began to think how good the ice-cold beer would be at McNulty's, the favorite haunt of the cops and detectives of the 67th Police Precinct.

The sight of a tall, thin young woman, with bleached blond hair neatly shaped in pageboy style, walking slowly down Flatbush Avenue in his direction distracted Cordo. Her yellow tank top barely hid her supple breasts; her overall look was very inviting. She smiled sweetly, acknowledging his attention. She slowed, seemingly interested in stopping, at least for a moment. Detective Cordo started to speak when suddenly, from the cigar store, he heard the popping sounds of a handgun. He instantly drew his .38 and started racing toward the store. His adrenaline shot up and his heart was pounding against his chest, but his training took over as he quickly assessed his first tactical problem.

The store's entrance was guarded on the side nearest Cordo by a large green bench, which held an assortment of daily newspapers. The back of the bench was about four feet wide and nearly six feet high, completely blocking Cordo's view of the store's interior from that side. Cordo passed this partition cautiously. Detective Lewis's body was sprawled across the entranceway. Harry was on his back, motionless, with his empty hands outstretched against the wall. At the rear of the small store behind a six-foot-long counter, some fifteen feet from the entrance, Detective Cordo spotted an elderly man, arms raised in the air, with a terrified look on his face; he seemed to be motioning with his eyes to someone off to the side.

Cordo shouted, "Police, freeze!" and assumed the shooter's crouch. Two blurred forms suddenly appeared from each side of the counter, firing their guns repeatedly in response. *Pop, pop, pop, pop.* Detective Cordo took two bullets in the chest and two in the stomach. He was dead before he fell to the sidewalk.

Detective First Grade Harry Lewis, age fifty-one, was married and the father of five children, and Detective Second Grade David Cordo, forty-six, was the widowed father of two girls and two boys. They became the fourth and fifth members of the New York City Police Department murdered in the line of duty in 1969.

Steven Holt would always remember the morning of August 24, 1969. His mother had just finished preparing Steven's breakfast when they heard the two familiar knocks followed by the opening of the door to their apartment. Robert looked at Mary and Steven, then stopped abruptly at the doorway. Robert's ever-present smile was gone. His eyes were moist and red. It was clear that he'd been crying. He was clutching in his right hand a copy of the *New York Daily News.* As he unfolded the newspaper they saw the terrible headline: "Two Detectives Executed in Brooklyn."

Every uniformed cop in the 67th Precinct knew Lewis and Cordo. Mulvey especially looked up to these two charismatic detectives. One of his dreams was to one day get the gold shield of detective in the NYPD.

6

Church of the Holy Innocents, Brooklyn,
August 27, 1969

Perhaps the most cherished tradition of the New York City Police Department is the tribute it gives to those of its members who fall in the line of duty. It is called an inspector's funeral, probably because it was thought that the ceremony would be fitting for someone of that rank, although no one recalls a funeral for a police inspector who died in bed ever equaling the one given to police officers below that rank who are killed on the job. The tradition dates back many decades. With its pomp, pageantry, and ornamental trappings, the ceremony is not unlike a majestic church service.

As the time for the funeral Mass grows near and the street becomes filled with people, tension builds with mournful anticipation. No one who has attended such a funeral will ever forget it.

When Detectives Lewis and Cordo were murdered, tradition at the time gave to the commanding officer of the precinct the privilege of selecting the honor guard from among the police officers who worked under his command. That unit, usually a contingent of ten, took turns, two at a time, standing guard at attention on each side of the casket during the viewing hours chosen by the family. The honor guard also remained with the body during all public displays until the burial, vaulting, or cremation.

Captain Sean J. Nevins, the commanding officer of the 67th, chose Robert Mulvey as the first member of this elite unit. He did so for reasons other than Mulvey's flawless appearance and exceptional personnel evaluations. Mulvey's evaluations were indeed outstanding, and with his looks, his physique, and the way he cared for his uniform, he could well have been the ideal model for a police department recruitment poster. But Nevins chose him for his character and in order to send the message to the rest of the officers assigned to the 67th Precinct that in the eyes of their commanding officer, integrity counted above misguided loyalty.

Mulvey's appointment to the honor guard at the joint funeral of Detectives Lewis and

Cordo would affect his nephew Steven in a way that was impossible to predict at the time. And it set in motion circumstances that would change Robert Mulvey's life forever.

The inspector's funeral and Mass was held at the Church of the Holy Innocents, in the Flatbush section of Brooklyn. The church is a huge Gothic structure built in the late nineteenth century, a third of a city block wide and a full block deep. It is constructed mostly of sand-colored blocks of stone of various sizes and shapes, with some dark-colored pieces creating a unique design. The main entrance is located on East 17th Street and has three twelve-foot-high arched doorways made from darkened oak. The lower two-thirds of these doors, which lead to the church's vestibule, are inlaid with morocco leather imported especially for the church by one of its parishioners, an enormously wealthy investment banker. The upper portions of the doors, composed of stained glass, depict various scenes from the life of Christ. Each of the doors has huge brass rings, polished regularly so that they glisten in the sunlight.

In 1969, the Church of the Holy Innocents was the crown jewel of the Diocese of Brooklyn, which includes all Roman

Catholic parishes in Kings and Queens counties. Holy Innocents Parish included worshippers such as the Trumps, who built thousands of affordable housing units in high-rise apartment houses in Brooklyn and in neighboring Queens County. The McAllisters, whose tugboats dominated the harbor, were also prominent members of the parish. Both families were extremely active in every aspect of church life, particularly fund-raising. Successful lawyers, bankers, and physicians poured contributions into the maintenance of this magnificent structure. No expense was considered too much by these important lay leaders. Of course, not all of the parishioners were wealthy. Most of the other church members were from comfortable middle-class families, including teachers, small business owners, firefighters, and police officers.

The Church of the Holy Innocents was chosen for the joint funeral for the two detectives mostly because Harry and Monica Lewis and their children were members of the parish and devout Catholics. The Cordos were not practicing Catholics and claimed no parish for their own. Muriel, David Cordo's wife, had died of cancer when she was only thirty and left behind four little children to be raised by their father. Her death left David angry and bitter. Although initially David followed Muriel's wishes and raised the children as Catholics, he and they soon fell away from all association with the Church. So when the oldest Cordo child, twenty-three-year-old Billy, a probationary New York City firefighter, was asked if he had a preference for his dad's funeral, he replied that his father and "Uncle Harry," as he called Detective Lewis, "should remain partners, even at the funeral."

The day of the funeral was another August scorcher. By nine o'clock, the temperature readings were nearing 80 degrees with 75 percent humidity. Sanitation workers scurried along East 17th between Cortelyou Road and Beverly Road, cleaning every inch of the asphalt roadway, the curbs, and even the sidewalks on either side of the street. The sun rose rapidly, quickly burning off the small veil of fog. The sweat poured through the sanitation workers' shirts, but no one complained. Their job, willingly and proudly done, was to make this city street spotless, a fitting place of honor for two heroes who would soon be delivered in their coffins to begin their funeral Mass.

Mary Holt and her son stood on top of the

rectory's stoop to observe the funeral procession. Mary's face was ordinarily a sad one. Her hair was gray and rapidly turning white, and the skin below her left eye was permanently discolored, the scar left over from the last beating by the fists of her husband, Harold. During that vicious attack, the bones above and below her eye were shattered and she suffered a concussion. Her brother Robert would later recall that after that brutal assault Mary rarely ever smiled again. She always maintained her erect posture, holding her head up in a dignified way. Her clothing was mostly hand-me-downs from close friends or family members, but today she wore a tasteful dark blue linen suit with soft makeup including pink lipstick. Sheer stockings complemented her shapely legs, and with her dark blue pumps, she appeared taller than her five feet five inches. Her outfit was completed by an elegant white straw hat with a dark blue band around the crown, which she angled sharply and wore on the left side of her head. It was worn in a way to conceal her substantial hair loss, the result of the aggressive chemotherapy administered by her doctors to destroy the cancer cells surging through her body. Nevertheless, for one rare time, Mary Holt looked stunning.

Little Steven, with long, tousled blond hair, possessed a sweet and yet devilish smile. He had been smartly dressed by his mom in a starched white oxford shirt, a blue-and-green-striped tie, and navy blue shorts with matching knee socks. His black loafers that he'd shined earlier that morning sparkled in the sunlight.

By ten minutes before eleven, thousands of uniformed police officers from New York City were joined by hundreds more from cities throughout the country, including Boston, Chicago, and Washington, D.C. The massive contingent created a wall of blue filling both sides of East 17th, five deep, for its entire length. The mayor and the governor had arrived, together with other politicians and union officials. All the officials took places in front of those police officers who were lined up directly across from the church.

From about three blocks in the distance, the vast crowd began to hear the unmistakable strains of several bagpipes with no identifiable tune, just sad noises as the pipers rehearsed with their instruments. Suddenly there was an eerie silence. It lasted a full ten minutes. Many of the mourners had begun to look in the direction of the last sounds when all at once the slight beat of muffled drums was heard in the distance. The beating of the drums grew louder as the contingent of pipers and drummers came within view of the church. Soon the twelve drummers were just a few yards from the line of dignitaries, and the powerful beat of their drums and the click of their leather heels against the asphalt caused goose bumps to rise on more than a few of those in attendance. The drummers led fifty silent bagpipers, each carrying his instrument on his right side parallel to the ground.

This part of the ceremony meant that the heroes had arrived, led in historic tradition by a protective band of warriors with drumbeats marking the pace — the proud members of the Pipe and Drum Corps of the Emerald Society of the New York City Police Department. Dressed in dark blue jackets with bright-colored tartan kilts, each carried on his right hip an automatic pistol in a leather holster. Completing the uniform was a broad green, white, and orange sash, the colors of the Republic of Ireland, fastened at the top of the left shoulder and worn diagonally across the chest and down past the waist. Their black shoes were spit-shined for the occasion, and they wore dark blue knee socks with bright green trim. A long, sheathed knife with a huge black handle hung on the outside of the stocking on each man's right leg. The pipers marched solemnly, parading ever so slowly toward the Church of the Holy Innocents. Their leader, the drum major, Ryan O'Farrell, was in full command at six feet four inches, with flaming red hair laced with puffs of white. O'Farrell's high, ruddy cheekbones stood guard over his ample and sharpened nose, with its reddening tip. His broad, powerful-looking shoulders bulged from his tunic, as did his swollen belly, the result of years of beer drinking. He used his graveled smoker's voice effectively, shouting out commands. The regal way he wielded the six-foot-long silver baton slowly from side to side as he marched, almost with a prance in his step, completed the picture of decorous authority not tolerating any challenges.

Suddenly the drums grew louder when a robust roar of engines was heard — the sound of forty motorcycles as they made their way slowly toward the church. They came two abreast, each one ridden by a young policeman. The riders wore dark blue tunics with highly polished copper buttons — from which the slang word for police officer, "copper," or "cop," is derived — and soft uniform caps trimmed in black leather, different from the blocked and steam-pressed caps worn by other police officers. Each had a black leather strap worn diagonally left to right across his chest, attached to a belt of the same material. On the right side of each belt was a black leather holster carrying a .38-caliber police revolver. The motorcycle cops completed their uniforms with dark blue trousers, more like the jodhpurs worn by horseback riders. They also wore jet black, well-polished boots, coming to just below the knee. The NYPD cyclists were followed by at least twenty more motorcyclists from police departments in Suffolk and Nassau counties as well as several cities in New Jersey and Connecticut. The final motorized contingent included twenty green-and-white police patrol cars, ten on each side of the street. The NYPD patrol cars were followed by another twenty patrol cars from police departments across the tri-state area.

Now came the funeral cars bearing the bodies. They moved deliberately down East 17th Street, hulks of polished steel, one jet black, the other a deep dark gray, glistening in the late morning sun, first the one carrying the body of Detective Harry Lewis, followed by the hearse carrying Detective David Cordo. At the front and rear of each hearse, the members of the police honor guard, with their shoulders back and their heads erect, strode with military precision, in a determined silence broken only by the cadence of their heels beating on the pavement.

Steven, his little heart pounding, immediately spotted his Uncle Robert marching at the right front fender of the car carrying Detective Lewis. Little Steven Holt later would remember that Uncle Robert was everything he wanted to be. The honor guard carefully began removing the caskets of the two detectives, and at that exact moment a voice loudly commanded, "Detail, attention." The order was dutifully responded to by the thousands present. Once the caskets were removed and placed on the shoulders of the officers assigned to the honor guard, and the various members of the families lined up in sight of the caskets, the voice commanded, "Detail, hand salute." Immediately the uniformed thousands brought their hands to the brims of their uniform caps while the civilians brought their right hands across their chests.

As the bodies were carried toward the church entrance, a lone piper played the strains of "Amazing Grace." When the sound of the instrument stopped, the voice boomed, "Ready, two," and all the mourners brought their right hands to their sides. The families and as many of the officers as the church could accommodate, together with the politicians, filed in and took places in the pews for the solemn Mass of the Resurrection. For those who could not cram into the church, the entire ceremony, including a particularly moving homily by the senior Roman Catholic police chaplain, Monsignor Patrick Kellchan, was heard through large loudspeakers placed in various spots near the front of the church and down the complete length of East 17th Street.

When the service concluded, those police officers in the church poured out to join their comrades once again, setting up a blue wall of tribute. Soon they were joined by the mayor, the governor, and the other politicians and union officials to await the families and then the caskets of the two heroes. When the families exited the church, they stood off to the side. As the caskets left the church, the American flags covering them were carefully folded and offered with an attentive salute by two lieutenants to Monica Lewis and Billy Cordo.

As soon as the flags were presented, an NYPD detail of helicopters flying in a missing-man formation appeared from the eastern sky and passed over the funeral scene below. During the flyover, the piper played taps, followed by "America." The final scene began as the Pipe and Drum Corps led the cortege from the church for several blocks. The tune they played was "Going Home." The maudlin cry of the bagpipes, at first hitting high notes and then low notes, wailing the lyrics, "Going home, going home," was accompanied by the deliberate beat of muffled drums. As Robert Mulvey passed by Steven and his mother perched on the rectory's stoop, admiration and pride overtook the youngster, and he threw up a smart hand salute as tears ran down his cheeks.

Someone else at the funeral noticed Police Officer Mulvey. That someone, Captain James Patrick Connolly, would have a profound influence on Robert Mulvey's career, and his life.

7

Larry Green,
April 25, 1991

"Kenny," the voice of Robert Mulvey quivered, "they're going to railroad my nephew. We need help."

Mulvey explained to Queens County District Attorney Ken Rattigan that Steven Holt had been arrested for a triple murder and was being held without bail in the Suffolk County jail. Of course, news of the arrest of a New York police sergeant for a triple murder was headlining radio and television programming all morning, so Mulvey's call was no surprise to Rattigan. What was a revelation was that Steven had been given a subpoena by the chief of the Homicide Bureau of the district attorney's office allowing him the "opportunity" to appear before the county's grand jury investigating the deaths of Scott Ruben and Hiram and Ramon Rodriguez.

"Stay calm, Robert," Rattigan answered. "I know the Suffolk County district attorney, and there is not a fairer prosecutor in this state."

Mulvey paused, holding back a sob, and said, "But Kenny, what if the evidence makes it look like Steven is connected to all of this? I mean, they took his gun." He now sobbed out of control. "This is my sister's only child. Please, you gotta help us."

"Larry, do me a favor, take a look at this for me, will you?" Rattigan detailed for Larry Green as much as he knew, which wasn't a whole lot, and finished by saying, "This is very important to me."

His plea was answered, first with a grunt and then with Green's trademark growl, "Hey, Kenny, you're a fucking prosecutor, but you sound like a goddamned social worker."

Lawrence Lewis Green was fifty-eight years of age and still at the top of his game. He was almost bald and kept whatever hair was left at crew-cut length. He had a portly appearance maintained by a gourmet diet with generous amounts of special vintage French red wine consumed over long lunches. His perpetual scowl, like his acerbic and confrontational style, was part act and part gout, caused by his affection for his favorite red wines. When asked by his doctor, who was bold enough to suggest a change in his diet, whether he drank a lot, his answer was "As compared to whom, W. C. Fields?"

Throughout the years that Buddy Cooper served as the Brooklyn district attorney, Larry Green was always his first choice for an appointment as special DA in those cases where the district attorney was faced with a conflict of interest. For example, if one of Cooper's assistants was a crime victim, it would not be appropriate for him to remain as chief prosecutor. And for all those years, it was not uncommon to hear District Attorney Cooper's raspy voice bellow to his secretary, Rose Chauf, "Get me Green."

Larry Green was a natural in the courtroom and a Brooklyn legend. His trial skills, while marked by his unique brand of bellicosity, were rounded out by meticulous preparation of the facts and knowledge of the law. He refused to let anyone conduct any investigation unless he supervised each step. One prosecutor, who had dismissed him as a one-man band after what turned out to be a regrettable miscalculation of Green's ability, soon changed her mind. Following an acquittal in a case she thought was a slam dunk, she said, "He's no one-man band, he's more like the damn New York Philharmonic. He served me with thirty-seven fucking motions. I had to assign three people from my Appeals Bureau to work full-time just to stay even."

For the next several days, Green met with Sergeant Holt, Inspector Bernard Pressler, a longtime friend and mentor to Steven, and a number of Holt's friends and associates so he could get a full picture of just who this young man was and determine whether anything about him suggested that he was capable of murder. He also met with Suffolk County District Attorney Jim Crowley and Crowley's Homicide Bureau chief, Wally Goss.

Green had known Crowley for several years, and they had teamed up and lectured many times to meetings of the New York State District Attorneys Association and at law enforcement conferences held in various parts of the country by the National District Attorneys Association. Before Crowley's election as Suffolk County's district attorney, he had been Long Island's most celebrated criminal defense attorney, and since Green was the Brooklyn DA's top pinch-hitter as special district attorney, the two would take turns acting out the parts of prosecutor and defense attorney. Their styles contrasted dramatically: Crowley the blustering Irishman who tried to dominate the courtroom, and Green his cantankerous adversary, the quintessential Brooklyn Jew whose speech inflections suggested to most people the way the notorious mobster of Murder Incorporated, Meyer Lansky, must have sounded. Between these two characters, a dynamic was created that regularly filled lecture halls to standing-room-only capacity. Green and Crowley both enjoyed a drink or two . . . or three, so their professional respect for one another developed into a social relationship.

So Green's meeting with Crowley was friendly enough, with a half hour or so devoted to war stories, which had a different hero depending on who was the narrator. Crowley, large and gregarious, sat in front of his long mahogany desk, wearing a huge white Irish-knit sweater. His gray hair, streaked with black strands, was more like a mane that fell long over his ears and flowed over and covered most of his neck. His thick black eyebrows loomed over his deeply set dark eyes, which twinkled regularly in concert with a disarming smile.

When the good-natured ribbing had run

its course and the meeting turned to the charges against Steven Holt, it did not look good, and Larry Green was very troubled.

Green's last interview before reporting his findings to Kenny Rattigan was with Robert Mulvey and his wife, Shannon, a retired special agent with the Federal Bureau of Investigation.

Green got right to the point with Mulvey. "So you had trouble in your career until someone at One PP saved your ass. Why did they do that?"

Shannon attempted to speak, trying to protect her husband, but Green raised his voice and continued, "How much of this did your nephew know, and when did he find out?" Then Green faced Shannon and shouted to her, "Listen, lady, get this straight. I don't like feds, and it doesn't matter to me in the least that you're retired, because you never lose your inflated sense that you're better than everyone else."

Now it was Shannon's turn to shout. "Dammit, don't you dare put me in one of your FBI mental cubicles, and don't you treat my husband like this. Robert Mulvey was and is a hero, and he was screwed by the NYPD. You know nothing of the circumstances that nearly destroyed both of us, so don't you be so fucking callous."

Mulvey stood and said slowly and firmly, in a way that was clearly intimidating, "You can ask anything you want about me, but stay away from my wife, you hear me?"

Green replied, "I hear you, and I'm sorry, Mrs. Mulvey, that was out of bounds." Green was very calm, and he spoke in a deliberately measured tone. It was the soft side of Green he usually tried to hide. He felt guilty about the way he was treating them, but he didn't offer more than that flat apology because he had to make it clear what they were up against.

However painful it was for both Robert and Shannon Mulvey, Robert told Green the entire story of his fall into the gutter and how Kenny Rattigan and Inspector Bernie Pressler saved him and finally how Police Commissioner Virgil Sampson permitted him to remain a police officer. He also told the lawyer, who was taking copious notes on a yellow legal pad, that he had told Steven none of the details but only that he had some difficulty and was then assigned to Internal Affairs.

Green looked up at this point and said, "And you spoke to him sometime in 1990, right?"

Mulvey looked puzzled and said, "Is it a

problem that I didn't tell Steven what I just told you?"

Shannon asked, "Is someone suggesting that there's a motive?"

Green permitted himself a rare smile. "I thought you were an FBI agent, Mrs. Mulvey. You sound more like a major case squad detective."

"It's Shannon, Mr. Green, and I was a brick agent."

Special agents of the Federal Bureau of Investigation who were assigned to field or street investigations, in contrast to those who reviewed books and records to build fraud cases, were known as brick agents, and they were every bit as effective as any New York City detective. Larry Green certainly knew as much.

Green did not respond directly to this but simply said, "That's about it, and as you both probably know, a prosecutor in state court doesn't have to prove motive, but it sure helps them when they have one."

Because of their backgrounds in law enforcement he told the Mulveys a little more than he would usually be inclined to reveal. "Your nephew was furious that Police Officer Scott Ruben and his partner, Police Officer Gabe Perone, were crooked cops and were permitted to remain on the police force. You both know how quiet and reserved he is, but he has repeatedly displayed anger and frustration and has told anyone who will listen how wrong it was for them to have escaped and remained on the job. He feels outraged by the way you were treated by the department, transferring you to a unit that was held in contempt by most members of the service."

"Are you suggesting," Shannon asked, "that Steven felt that Robert's transfer was disrespectful and that, coupled with the department's lax attitude toward police corruption, led him to execute three people?"

Green paused to let everything he'd said sink in and then said, "Shannon, he has worshipped Robert all his life."

Shannon walked over to where Green was sitting and asked, very softly, "And do you think that kid could kill three people . . . out of love for his uncle?"

Green looked up, and Shannon thought she saw a flash of anger as he said, "A lawyer's nightmare is to be forced to defend an innocent person, but right now my biggest problem is that I don't know whether he's innocent."

"Kenny," said Green, "let's get a beer."

When they had finished their first drink,

Green stared directly into Rattigan's eyes and said, "The only real hope is that asshole Wally Goss. Why Crowley would assign someone like him to try the case is beyond me. It's as if he's going into the tank, throwing the case. But that's not like Crowley."

"Well, Goss is the chief of the Homicide Bureau," Rattigan responded.

"Yeah, he's supposed to be a good investigative lawyer, but I can't find anyone who can remember the last time he's been on trial. Besides, during our meeting with Crowley, it was clear that he didn't know dick about trial strategy. He kept repeating that his case was a lock, as if that was supposed to scare me."

Rattigan observed, "Well, maybe Crowley thinks it's such a tight case that he doesn't need a heavy-duty trial lawyer, and he's rewarding Goss for making the case."

Suffolk County Jail,
May 28, 1991

Steven Holt was held in isolation for two reasons: one, he was a police officer, and two, given the brutal nature of the charges, and that he faced upon conviction three consecutive prison terms of twenty-five years to life, there was a serious concern that he was a suicide risk. He was guarded around the clock in three shifts, with two deputy sheriffs assigned to each shift. He was kept in a comfortably sized bedroom, with a double bed and a writing table with a small chair and tabletop lamp. During evening hours, the lamp remained lit. The door to the room was made of bulletproof glass, permitting the deputies to view Steven at all times. He was given access to any newspaper he chose, and he was permitted to read any of the books that were kept at the jail library. He was fed in the room three times a day, and when he needed to relieve himself, he was marched to a secure bathroom on the same floor that was available only to him.

"Hey, Sarge," one of the deputies shouted, after knocking on the translucent jail door, "you've got a visitor." Standing in the doorway was Sergeant Joseph Kurland. Though he was wearing civilian clothing, a blue windbreaker and khaki pants, Steven recognized the heavyset but powerfully built Kurland from the 75th Precinct in East New York, where Steven had been assigned after graduating from the Police Academy. Kurland occasionally had the duty of the turnout sergeant, the supervisor who presided over roll call at the beginning of each shift. Since Steven had virtually no contact with Kurland during the few years he served at the Seven-five, he was curious about the visit.

Kurland spoke first. "I just wanted you to know, son, that the entire SBA is solidly behind you. Last night, I was at one of the beer rackets." Kurland watched Steven's reaction. There was none. He continued, "And I told the membership that I knew you at the Seven-five, ya know, not personally, or close, but I knew you was a great cop and a decent guy who could never have done what they're claiming. They told us that a ballistics test matched the bullets from your service gun to the bullets taken from those three dead guys. Do you have any idea how that happened?"

Steven finally spoke. "Sarge, I have no idea. All I know is that I never killed anyone."

Kurland followed up quickly. "But they say you knew Scott Ruben, and you didn't like him because he was a crooked cop —"

Steven interrupted, raising his voice. "Listen, Sarge, my lawyer said I was not to speak to anyone about this case, so let's end it here. Ruben was a crook, and worse than that, but I am not going to discuss it with you or anyone else. But the fact is that I had nothing to do with his murder. Is that clear?"

"Sure, son, and don't get angry with me. I'm here to help."

"I think you'd better go," Steven said firmly. As Kurland turned to leave, he stopped and, grabbing Steven by the shoulders with his powerful hands, said, "The membership is running a fund-raiser to help you pay for your lawyer. Larry Green is very good and very expensive, so we're gonna come up with as much as it takes so that you're not in a hole."

Now Steven smiled. "Thanks," he said. He waved as Kurland was leaving.

As Steven sat back down his thoughts were about Chief Connolly and how it might have been different for his Uncle Robert if he and Connolly had never met. He began to reflect on the ironic parallel path his life was taking, rapidly descending toward chaos very much the way Uncle Robert's life hit some rough times. Oh, to be sure, their paths toward descent were quite different. Robert, after all, nearly succumbed to job-related stress. Steven, on the other hand, was plainly and simply the victim of a diabolical frame-up. Yet Steven could see the dark connection between Robert Mulvey's hero worship of James Patrick Connolly and his own worship of an uncle who was his guardian angel for most of his life. He was the reason Steven was a cop. And becoming a cop was why Steven sat in this makeshift jail cell in Suffolk County facing life in state prison for three murders he did not commit.

*Captain Connolly and the Christmas List,
September 1969*

James Patrick Connolly at age thirty-seven
was one of perhaps a half dozen bright
young executives in the New York City
Police Department who were known to be
all job. "All job" was a description given to
very few officers, particularly bosses, and it
meant a total commitment to police work,
together with fierce loyalty to the department.

At the time of his baptism into the Roman Catholic faith, Connolly was named
for James Connolly and Patrick Henry
Pearse, both martyred heroes of the Irish
Revolution.

By 1969, James Connolly was one of those
young captains in the New York City Police
Department considered to be the future
leaders of the department. In fact, some
senior chiefs saw in Connolly a potential

police commissioner. He had rugged good looks with a broad face and a high forehead. His broad, powerfully constructed jaw and his large, prominent nose were softened by wavy light brown hair and pale blue eyes. He was solidly built with 185 pounds on a frame slightly under six feet. His otherwise handsome face carried a jagged five-inch maroon-colored scar that started just under his left eye and traveled down his face, ending just above his lips. He had been attacked while he was attempting to arrest a knife-wielding maniac who was threatening one of his cops.

In lightning fashion, Connolly passed the promotional tests for sergeant, then lieutenant, and finally captain, the highest rank available for civil service testing. All higher ranks are attained solely by the appointment of the police commissioner upon the recommendation of a police promotional review board. The ranks of deputy inspector, inspector, deputy chief, and assistant chief are so political that one bitter senior captain observed that in order to be promoted you had to kiss ass and undergo a frontal lobotomy. This frequently passed-over captain added, "And don't make waves . . . ever!"

None of that, though, seemed to apply to the hard-charging James Connolly. He consistently took maverick positions during policy discussions with his bosses, but he never contradicted his superiors once they had made a decision. He carried out each command assignment with skill and exuberance. For example, when he was put in charge of the 60th Police Precinct in Brooklyn's Coney Island section, drug houses had virtually overwhelmed the neighborhood. Connolly, armed with search warrants and battering rams, led wave after wave of raids against these drug dens until every last dealer had fled. During one of the raids, a drug dealer armed with a shotgun blew off part of Connolly's right shoulder, but he was able to return fire, and the cops assigned to the Six-oh had one less drug dealer to bother with.

Connolly soon acquired the reputation of being a cop's cop. Anyone familiar with the politburo mentality at police headquarters at that time knew that it was not a recommended part of the formula for promotional advancement. But James Connolly was different. The bosses liked him, and while at times he would disagree with policy, it was always done respectfully. When he was overruled, it was always answered with a "Yes, sir," and Connolly made certain that the policy was carried out in meticulous detail.

What the super-chiefs saw in young Captain Connolly was a superb police executive and a future leader.

Just past Labor Day in 1969, Police Officer Robert Mulvey was summoned to Captain Connolly's office at the site of the 1964 World's Fair in Queens County. The Special Operations Division, or SOD, of the New York City Police Department could mobilize to meet any contingency. New York City, the borough of Manhattan in particular, is a mecca for huge indoor and outdoor events drawing crowds at times into the tens of thousands. Special Ops will, depending on the size of a gathering, typically assign hundreds of foot patrol officers reinforced by a dozen "scooter cops" and mounted police officers. This kind of crowd control is fairly routine, but Special Ops is particularly effective in responding to spontaneous demonstrations that have the potential of escalating into a riot. In this division, Connolly had command override, the power to supersede command authority for any police unit. If, for instance, there was a concert in Prospect Park in Brooklyn and the fans became rowdy, the local police precinct commander could notify Special Ops and a directive would be sent by Connolly ordering all police commands in a predefined area near Prospect Park to respond and take up positions and implement crowd control. Every detail of this procedure is part of a preset plan regularly practiced by police units throughout New York City. Connolly's selection as the commanding officer of the SOD was a clear indication of how well his career was developing.

Mulvey knocked at the captain's door and was told to enter. "Sit down, son, and just relax."

Mulvey could not relax, so he sat at attention.

Connolly pretended not to notice. "Do you like the job, son?"

"Yes, sir," Mulvey replied, trying to avoid Connolly's searching eyes, which peered out from either side of his massive yet perfectly shaped nose, set in contrast with soft rounded cheeks, marred by the massive scar on the left side of his face. Connolly's deep tan was maintained by a daily run along the beach near his home at Breezy Point in Queens, a peninsula nestled between the Atlantic Ocean and Jamaica Bay. Connolly's imposing figure and his very direct way of speaking intimidated the young officer.

"How long have you been assigned to the

Six-seven, Officer?"

"Ever since I graduated from the academy, sir."

"Do you know why you were picked for Detectives Lewis and Cordo's funeral honor guard?"

Mulvey reddened slightly as he softly said, "No, sir."

"Because your captain didn't want any fucking crooks guarding two heroes!" Connolly replied. Although he rarely used that kind of language, it seemed to him appropriate for the circumstances.

"Now, tell me about the Christmas list," he demanded.

Mulvey's face was now fully crimson, and he could not immediately reply.

Connolly rose abruptly from his seat and continued, "Listen to me good, Mulvey, there is a line drawn on the floor of this office and you better goddamned well see it. You can step over it and be with me, or you can stay there, take off your shield, spit on it, and throw yourself in with those fucking dirtbags on Snyder Avenue."

The fury of Captain Connolly's ultimatum so unnerved Mulvey that he was having difficulty speaking.

Connolly shouted again, "Tell me about the fucking Christmas list or get the fuck outta here."

Suddenly Mulvey recovered and stood. As he stepped back from Connolly, he tripped and all but fell into a nearby chair. He put his face in his hands, and as anger, guilt, and fear of the consequences nearly overwhelmed him, he froze with concern and uncertainty. Connolly put a reassuring hand on his shoulder and waited. After a few minutes, Mulvey began to talk of last year's Christmas season.

Before the NYPD began to replace police officers with civilians in certain clerical jobs, virtually all tasks were performed by uniformed police officers. It was neither efficient nor cost-effective, and it took police officers away from fighting crime. One of these positions was the job of station house administration. Each precinct had an officer who was known as the "124 man," taken from Section 124 of the Police Patrol Guide, the NYPD's detailed bible of protocol for just about everything. As the name suggested, the 124 man was the precinct's paper shuffler, who recorded everything involving the police personnel assigned to the station house. These tasks included the essential duty of recording each police officer's days off, sick leave, and vacation time.

The information was vital to the decisions made by the precinct commander, who had to know available patrol strength to make appropriate deployments of his officers.

The importance of the 124 man was never taken for granted by anyone in the station house, and to the extent he had virtual control over the roster, he was respected if not feared by the officers assigned to the station house who might need his grant of a favor.

By the mid-1960s, a 124 man received a nominal tip from a police officer who wanted a day off, usually a ten-dollar bill. He also designated which police officers on patrol would be assigned the Christmas pickup list from local merchants who would be asked to give an annual contribution to the officers who regularly patrolled in the vicinity of their stores. It amounted to only a few dollars each year, but no store owner was ever known to refuse.

In some police precincts the 124 man was also the CO's bagman, who would regularly collect bribes from the more substantial store owners in the precinct for a variety of favors. The bagman would turn over most of the bribe money to the boss and would receive a 10 percent share. Of course, there is no honor among thieves, and many of the bagmen would pocket some of the money before turning over the rest of it. In the 1960s these 124 men, particularly those who operated as the precinct's bagman, became all-powerful, and their requests for tips became demands; they might get as much as a hundred dollars from a police officer, depending on the kind of favor allowed. A police officer who paid this tribute typically would recover that cost by taking tips from motorists stopped for violations, who in return for ten or twenty dollars would be let off with a warning.

Police corruption of this kind had become pervasive in New York City by 1968. Honest cops looked the other way. One anticorruption police chief described the crooked cops as falling into two very different categories: the grass eaters and the meat eaters. Grass eaters would take money only when it was plainly opportune — say, from the stopped motorist who with a toothy smile would offer a driver's license and an automobile registration folded around a twenty-dollar bill.

On the other hand, meat eaters would start every tour of duty with the resoluteness of a perpetrator, or a perp, singling out targets for prey. They would enter a bar tightly regulated by the SLA — the State

Liquor Authority — go into the bathroom, and steal the soap required by the SLA and the city's health department to be available to customers. Then the officer would boldly approach the bartender and say, "Hey, pal, what kind of a pigpen do you run? You know the SLA rules about soap!" In 1968, most bartenders, familiar with the routine, would silently turn to the cash register, hit the No Sale key, and remove a ten- or twenty-dollar bill and pass it across the bar discreetly to this guardian of the public's hygiene, who swiftly left to be on his way to the next score. The practice was briefly interrupted with the arrival of soap dispensers, a momentary inconvenience for the meat eaters, until they found a way to remove the liquid soap from its container.

The 124 men of the late sixties were so organized they appeared to have their own membership association — a cadre of crooks from which precinct commanders could draw for replacements. Commanders of the various police precincts who were getting kickbacks from their 124 men would exchange these officers when the need arose, but without giving much information or direction to the reassigned officer. This practice led to sloppiness and the assignment of clerical police personnel who did not have the ability to identify those officers in the precinct who could be trusted.

So it was that Officer Hartwell, the 124 man of the 75th Precinct in the East New York section of Brooklyn, got himself in serious trouble and inadvertently caused an eruption and near chaos at the 67th Precinct in the Flatbush section of the borough, where he was temporarily assigned during the holiday season of 1968.

Meyer Hartwell was as unlikely looking a cop as you could imagine. Short, overweight, and mostly bald, Meyer had grown his black hair as long as he could from the left side of his head and then folded it over to cover the rest of his bald pate. The effect was an unintended burlesque look. Meyer had a perpetual crown of perspiration hanging on his forehead. His distinctive and certainly in no way attractive face brought attention to itself with a large, bushy black mustache flecked with gray and strange-looking pieces of debris that remained from a recent meal. His tiny dark and deep-set eyes were obscured by a long, thin nose discolored by popping blue and red veins. Protruding aimlessly from his nostrils were several strands of nose hair. Police Officer Hartwell appeared to have selected his uniform each day from the bottom of his closet. Frayed and always wrinkled, his uniform shirt with the lower two buttons missing hung over a belt forced out by his bulging stomach. His black shoes were almost gray with scuff marks. None of this mattered, though, because he had graduated third in his class from the Police Academy, and because of his grades his first commanding officer at a police precinct in the Bronx tapped him to be the 124 man. It was soon clear that Hartwell and his CO were a perfect match. They were both crooks. It was this first assignment that Meyer Hartwell used to hone his skills as a 124 man, providing for the needs of every officer at the precinct willing to meet his price. That experience, and even more his reputation, helped to land him a spot at the 75th Precinct, a particularly fertile place for a 124 man to make extra money.

Police Officer Meyer Hartwell's reputation in the Seven-five, as an aggressive meat eater quickly earned him the nickname of "Meyer the Buyer." Meyer had a price list, which included a fee for every favor offered to the police officers assigned to the Seven-five, from thirty dollars for an unscheduled day off to seventy-five dollars for a choice seat in a police patrol car on the midnight to 8:00 a.m. shift. This late tour was infamous as most conducive to police scores, because there were fewer sergeants around, so there was little or no supervision. It was known throughout the job as the theft shift, where two aggressive cops could make up to three hundred dollars a tour by raiding bars that failed to stop serving booze after 4:00 a.m. and pulling over drunk drivers who would be forced to pay the officers twenty, fifty, or a hundred dollars to avoid an arrest.

Some of the Yiddish-speaking merchants on Pitkin Avenue in East New York, whose businesses were patrolled by the police officers assigned to the 75th Precinct, when observing Officer Hartwell strolling down their street would exclaim, "Oy vey, here comes Meyer the Buyer!"

On one occasion, Mendick the kosher butcher said to Hartwell, "Meyer, why don't you go bother the goyim? I have no more gelt for you."

Hartwell smiled and replied, "That'll cost ya!"

Hartwell had a friend at the New York State agency that supervised the dietary laws required to be observed by kosher butchers in the preparation and sale of meat to observant Jews. His inspector friend would regularly drop by Mendick's market, look around, and, as he left, exclaim, "Meyer says you run a good store. You know, he's right!" Every six weeks or so Meyer would receive seventy-five to one hundred dollars from Mendick for his stamp of approval, which he would split with the kosher meat inspector.

Shortly before Christmas 1968, when Meyer learned that the 67th Precinct's 124 man was going on a short leave, he asked his uncle, a captain assigned to police headquarters, if he could arrange for a transfer.

So, early in the third week of December, Meyer Hartwell arrived at the Six-seven to begin his 8:00 a.m. to 4:00 p.m. shift as the temporary 124 man.

Meyer fingered his way distractedly through the paperwork on the desk until he found a sealed white business-sized police department envelope. It was addressed simply "Hartwell." Opening it quickly, Meyer found a note from the previous 124 man listing the names and locations of businesses for each assigned police patrol sector of the precinct.

Meyer marveled at the number of businesses listed in each sector. His eyes danced with delight as he read over the parentheses by each business. The numbers varied between $50 and $250. The high figure of $250 was assigned to Bloomstein's department store at the corner of Flatbush Avenue and Snyder Avenue, only half a block from the station house. The hundreds of stores stretching side by side for miles down Flatbush Avenue would produce quite a bundle of money. Each list was headed by the name of the police officer assigned to the 8:00 a.m. to 4:00 p.m. patrol that day — except for Sector Charlie, which had no assigned officer.

A note attached to the list stated simply and directly, "Meyer, thanks for filling in for me, but don't get sticky fingers. Billy!"

As Meyer happily reviewed the Christmas list, which he expected would yield for him a generous share, the morning routine of the precinct was carried out. The turnout sergeant conducted the morning's roll call. Police Officer Robert Mulvey got excited before each tour. For this young and dedicated police officer, it was another adventure about to start, with no way of predicting how it would end. Also, roll call always reminded him of Sergeant Bernard Pressler, the tough, powerfully built instructor at the Police Academy whose military bearing and manner Mulvey so admired.

Standing at attention, his firmly proportioned five-ten frame erect, Pressler had once said something Mulvey never forgot: "What makes us so different from the people we are sworn to protect is the uncertainty. We never know whether we will be injured or killed before our tour ends." The words shocked Robert, but he always seemed to remember them just before he took any action. He began to regard those words as his safety net.

As the turnout sergeant concluded his roll call instructions, he said quite matter-of-factly, "Those officers on Flatbush Avenue patrol, see the 124 man." Each police officer so assigned stepped over to Hartwell's desk and received his typed Christmas list — everyone except the police officer assigned to Sector Charlie.

"Who's got Charlie?" Hartwell shouted.

"I'm sorry," replied Police Officer Robert Mulvey nervously. "I've got it. I was just assigned this morning."

"Okay, kid," said Hartwell, handing Mulvey the list. With a chuckle, he added, "Don't drop any singles."

Curious, Mulvey took the list. As he walked across the precinct floor, glancing at it, he became more and more perplexed. "Brockman's grocery store, 740 Flatbush

Avenue (50); Mickey Brennan's Bar and Grill, 836 Flatbush Avenue (100); Sid's Stationery, 850 Flatbush Avenue (50) . . ."

As Mulvey got to the front door, suddenly the turnout sergeant ran up to him and, grabbing the piece of paper out of Mulvey's hand, shouted, "That's not yours, kid. It's a mistake."

"But what is it?" stammered the young police officer.

"It's nothin'," snarled the sergeant. "Now get out there on patrol, like you're supposed to!"

Still confused, Mulvey stumbled down the concrete front steps of the station house and began walking toward Flatbush Avenue.

He couldn't hear the turnout sergeant's screams as he slammed Meyer the Buyer against the wall of the precinct's locker room. "You fuckin' asshole, are you outta your head? Who the fuck told you to give that list to that fuckin' Boy Scout?"

Robert's mind raced as he walked back and forth patrolling Sector Charlie. Everything had happened so quickly. As he recalled looking at the typed sheets, recognizing the names of businesses located on the patrol route next to the parenthetically enclosed numbers, then thinking about the sergeant's bizarre behavior, all of it seemed surreal. He decided, with nothing more than instinct, that something was wrong, very wrong.

"Let me speak to the captain. It's Police Officer Mulvey."

It was 1315 hours, or 1:15 p.m. Mulvey was on meal break, although he couldn't eat.

"Boss, this is Mulvey, Officer Mulvey," he sputtered when the captain picked up.

"I know, you called me" was Captain Nevins's gruff but typical reply. "What do you want?"

"Boss, I've got to see you after my tour."

10

Lookout Point, Nassau County,
Late Summer 1992

For New York Police officers and firefighters, particularly retirees, Lookout Point was a kind of Shangri-la. It was home to people who enjoyed the summer tranquility of a bungalow colony and who at season's end would join other snowbirds in various settlements on both coasts of southern Florida. There they would remain until Memorial Day weekend would summon them back to what they lovingly called "Nassau-by-the-Sea." Yet some of the regulars who stayed behind in the off-season knew that Lookout Point was an incredibly peaceful oasis.

One of these was retired New York City First Deputy Police Commissioner Brendan Moore. While most of his neighbors headed toward warmer climates, Commissioner Moore and Peggy, his wife of forty years, enjoyed the turn of autumn by the seashore.

"Brendan." The voice was unmistakably Robert Mulvey's, although many years had passed since they last spoke. "I promise not to take more than an hour of your time."

"Sure," Brendan replied, "come on down."

"Thanks, and do you mind if I bring Shannon with me?"

"Of course not. Peggy and I would love to see both of you. Why not come in the afternoon and plan to have dinner with us and stay over? We've got plenty of room."

11

Suffolk County Jail,
January 1992

During the months that followed the Suffolk grand jury's finding, charging Steven with three counts of murder in the second degree, his physical condition steadily declined. His once firm and wiry body had lost considerable weight. In deference to the fact that he was still a police officer, and one holding the rank of sergeant, he was not required to wear the coveralls and T-shirt issued to other inmates. The collared sports shirts he favored seemed draped onto his body, and his khaki trousers were so loose at his waist that he had trouble finding a belt to hold them up. Steven's dark brown eyes were set back in shrunken sockets made more prominent by his bony cheeks. His light brown wavy hair was showing spots of gray, and his hairline was receding. The deputy sheriffs who watched him constantly were beginning to become alarmed because he would sit for hours in his desk chair with an expressionless stare. At times, when they tried to make conversation, Steven appeared to be listening politely, but they knew he understood little of what they were saying. The only time he came alive was during the daily visits from his fiancée, Lee Moran.

Lee was in her midtwenties and was also a New York City police officer with the rank of sergeant. She shared the anguish of Steven's nightmare from the very beginning. She had long, soft, blond hair with a touch of red, frequently swept back in a ponytail. Her emerald green eyes set in an oval face were disarmingly gentle and yet quite sexy. Lee Moran literally turned heads each day as she glided up the steps of the county jail on her visits to Steven. Her body had near perfect proportions, with full rounded breasts enticingly concealed in a woolen sweater, or sometimes in a soft blouse or tailored jacket. Her narrow waist, her firm, attractive, and softly curved calves, and elegantly turned ankles completed the picture of a very attractive and photogenic young woman.

Since Steven's arrest and detention in the Suffolk County jail, where he was held without bail, awaiting trial, he had managed to keep his sanity through the comfort this lovely creature brought him each day. On leave from the police department without pay, Lee Moran was a constant source of reassurance and hope. Waiting for Lee was no different this morning, although the hour was approaching noon and Steven was becoming anxious. He was suddenly roused from his thoughts by a sharp tap on his translucent door.

"There's a certain sergeant here, Sergeant," Deputy Sheriff Foley announced with his usual broad smile. Of all of the deputies, Foley was Steven's favorite. When Foley had the duty he would regale the young officer with endless war stories and lots of unsolicited legal advice. "It's really too bad that my nephew Liam is a government attorney. There's the lad who could spring you from this hoosegow!" he once burst out.

"You okay?" Lee asked hopefully.

"With you here, it's always okay." Breaking into a laugh, he motioned toward the cell door. Deputy Sheriff Foley insisted on covering the glass door with a blanket to give Steven and Lee privacy. It didn't matter at all to Foley that this serious infraction could cost him a heavy sanction, or even the loss of his job. It didn't matter to Foley because he was convinced that Steven had been framed.

"Any word from Green about a trial date?" Lee asked.

"Unfortunately, if we don't get started within the next month or two, Larry is committed to a trial in federal court in Manhattan. It's scheduled to go the beginning of April. It's a racketeering case, and he expects that it will go for at least four months."

"I just don't know how you're able to get through this, Steven. What are you going to do if Green gets stuck in federal court? Are we sure he's the right lawyer for us?"

"It's bad enough to be innocent, but the one break I got, apart from you, was getting my lawyer. Usually when someone is jammed up for the first time and doesn't know anything about the system, finding a lawyer is a stab in the dark. That's the way I felt when they threw the handcuffs on me and put me in a holding cell. But thank God for Uncle Robert and his friend District Attorney Rattigan. Their recommendation was really all I needed. And now that I've watched Larry Green in action at the pretrial skirmishes with that asshole of an assistant DA Wally Goss, I know I have the best." Steven stood up, leaving Lee Moran sitting on his bed alone. He walked a few steps and then turned around. She could see the hint of tears in his eyes as he said, "You know that next to you, I loved nothing more than being a member of the service. It's something I've wanted to do since I was a kid. Be a cop and do good. And regardless of what they did to my uncle or do to me, I will never stop being a cop."

Steven returned to his bed, sat down beside Lee, and gently kissed her on the forehead.

Lee stared silently at Steven for a minute or two and then began to speak. "I don't think you ever told me why you decided to become a cop."

Steven smiled and sighed. "It's a long story, but we have plenty of time."

Steven Holt's Road to the Job

Steven's mother had over several years been in remission from cancer, which had attacked different parts of her body, but finally in 1984 she lost her last fight to lung cancer diagnosed the year before. His father drank himself to death nearly ten years before that. So Uncle Robert was his only living relative to attend the ceremony at historic Madison Square Garden in Manhattan when he graduated from the Police Academy in 1985. Afterward, Robert took Steven to dinner at a venerable downtown Brooklyn restaurant, Gage and Tollners.

"Be safe, Steven," Robert began, "and most of all be true to the memory of your mother. Don't do anything that would not make her proud. And if you ever have the slightest concern about anything, just call me, at any time, day or night."

While there was never any doubt in

Steven's mind that he would become a police officer, as he grew up he seemed to go out of his way to make that dream impossible. In the fifth grade at Our Lady of Angels elementary school in Brooklyn, he was expelled for being disrespectful.

Immediately after Steven's expulsion, Mary Holt used some savings she had accumulated from a few odd jobs and placed him in St. Peter Julian Eymard Preparatory, a private Catholic school in Manhattan, which was staffed by a religious order of brothers known for their strictness and propensity for corporal punishment. Mary thought that the brothers would be an effective substitute for the boy's father, who was rarely around and very rarely sober.

Steven's first few years at St. Peter's Prep were uneventful. His behavior was carefully controlled by strict discipline administered most often at the end of a stick. The brothers were otherwise friendly, and many were athletic young men who taught Steven and his classmates the fundamentals of basketball and baseball. Nevertheless, they would not tolerate any disruption in class or laziness in academics. They demanded that their students reach above-average levels in reading, mathematics, and grammar. These requirements were serious problems for

Steven. While he didn't dare disrespect the brothers, because they hit much too hard, he had a quick temper with his fellow students, and he frequently used boxing techniques taught to him by his Uncle Robert to terrorize his classmates. He was very quick and extremely effective with his fists. On several occasions when an instructor had to leave the classroom to attend to something, Steven would use the time to settle a grudge against another student. Of course, when the brother returned to the classroom, Steven was severely beaten and denied his weekend pass. As his bullying and other erratic behavior increased, he was denied more and more weekends at home.

As these separations from his mother and Uncle Robert increased, Steven suffered from depression and began to withdraw from most school activities and contact with his classmates. He began to have recurring nightmares, vivid replays of the vicious beatings his father frequently gave to his mother. He would not or could not study, and soon he placed dead last in all his classes except gym. It was the only place that provided an outlet for Steven's aggression. His speed on the basketball court and his solid fielding as a first baseman were noticed by the school's athletic director, who coached both sports, but Steven's chance to join either of the school's teams was abruptly cut short when he was informed one day by the dean of academics that his grades disqualified him from all extracurricular sports. That evening while the seniors were having dinner in the school's cafeteria, Steven went to their dormitory and stole a draft card from a night-table drawer. His plan was simple. Early the next morning he would slip out of the school, find a recruiting office, and join the United States Army. He would become a paratrooper, and when he returned home after training, dressed in his freshly pressed uniform with gleaming paratroop boots and the silver jump wings worn proudly on his chest, everyone would look up to him the way they looked up to Uncle Robert. He would even go back and visit St. Peter's and see the envy on the faces of the brothers and those little creeps who made fun of him behind his back. He would never again have to put up with that "Mickey Mouse bullshit discipline from the brudders."

Steven's grand plan had a number of problems. When he forged the name of the eighteen-year-old senior whose card he stole, it was a botched job. He used a whitener to remove the inked signature and then clumsily wrote his name over it. In his panic over what seemed to him to be the crime of the century, when he noticed that the date of birth on the card didn't match his, he changed it in the same clumsy way. What the hapless forger didn't realize was that the alteration proclaimed his true age, sixteen! The Army recruiting sergeant took one look at the draft card, then at Steven, who immediately confessed and was in short order on the way back to face "the brudders."

Everyone in the family seemed to remember this incident as a turning point for Steven. The brothers treated the incident as a silly prank by a kid, but they also recognized the danger signs in this behavior, so one of the brothers was assigned virtually full-time to tutor Steven and bring him to an acceptable academic level. His classmates also looked a bit differently at him. "Geez," said one, "this guy's got some balls." Some of them even became his friends, really the first Steven ever had. While all of this did have a definite positive effect on Steven and allowed him to graduate closer to the middle of his class, his real change, a kind of an epiphany, didn't occur until several years later when he was accepted by the New York City Police Department to begin training at the Police Academy.

Steven threw himself into his studies. He drove himself to exhaustion during the physical training periods. He studied and analyzed every theory and application of police strategies and techniques, spending many hours after class in the academy's library. And he spent hours peppering his Uncle Robert with every question he could think of. At the conclusion of all this, Probationary Police Officer Steven Robert Holt had two achievements. He was given the Leadership Award by a majority vote of his class, and he graduated from the academy fourth in his class.

Holt's first assignment was to the 75th Police Precinct in the East New York section of Brooklyn.

"Of course," Steven continued, "what gave me the confidence and the desire to become a police officer was my Uncle Robert. He was and is my hero." Suddenly a pained expression overtook Steven's face.

Alarmed, Lee asked, "What is it?"

Steven was thinking again of his uncle and the infamous Christmas list. He began telling Lee the rest of his uncle's story.

13

*Captain Nevins and the Christmas List,
December 1968*

Captain Sean J. Nevins always seemed to be
at attention, even when seated. His prematurely white hair was at crew-cut length; his
jaw was perpetually clenched, and his
mouth seemed always clamped around a
very long, never lighted cigar. He had soft
blue eyes, perpetually darting with activity.
A recovering alcoholic and former chain-
smoker, the captain rose early in the morning, giving himself enough time for ninety
minutes of physical conditioning. When he
spoke, his arms and hands moved in the
animated fashion of a marionette manipu-
lated by a master puppeteer. In those rare
moments when he released his cigar, you
could see his tight, thin-set lips, which appeared to form a constant scowl or sneer.
They were just below a huge, flattened nose,
the result of years of unsuccessful amateur

boxing in his youth. He had a bulging chest made larger by the contrasting narrowness of his waist. At forty-four, he had been a police officer for nineteen years. His reputation among the police brass and among the union officials of the Patrolmen's Benevolent Association, or the PBA, was one of uncompromising inflexibility. They all hated Nevins. His troops, on the other hand, loved him, and that was all that mattered to him.

Once when a rare job action bordering on a strike threatened police patrols in the South Bronx, Nevins was assigned to turn the police officers out on patrol after roll call. He stood in front of the assembled cops and said, "There is no job action on my command," and as he said the words a kind of force field of electricity seemed to develop. "Does everyone understand that?" he bellowed.

One veteran police officer, a guy named Winter, raised his hand. "I'm the delegate in this precinct, and I want a chance to speak to the borough trustee."

Every police precinct has two union delegates, and every borough command has a PBA trustee, who sits as a member of the central board of trustees, the operating body for the twenty-thousand-member organization. Police Officer Winter was the fullback on the police department football team, called the Finest. At six-three and 240 solid pounds he seemed more than intimidating. Captain Nevins walked directly up to Winter, peered up at his face, and slapped it so hard that it made a pop like a firecracker. Winter screamed with pain.

"You get the fuck out on patrol or I'm going to kick the shit out of you in front of your constituents so they can all see what a piece of garbage you are. Now move," Nevins commanded, "all of you!"

The police officers moved quickly toward the door and on to their patrols.

Nevins shouted, "Hey, Winter, after you finish your tour you have that turd your trustee see me." He paused for effect, threw his head back, and howled, "That's if he has the balls to see me!"

The morning following Police Officer Mulvey's report to Nevins, there was a directive from the captain posted prominently throughout the 67th Precinct station house ordering all officers to meet in the assembly room fifteen minutes before turnout, with no exceptions.

"When I took over this scurvy house," Nevins began forcefully, "I warned you fucking people that if I caught you stealing

I would personally put the handcuffs on you." Nevins's face was a frightful red hue as he spit out his anger and frustration. He had until this moment believed that the sheer force of his personality together with his unique command style developed as a Marine officer in Vietnam was enough to elicit total obedience to his orders. And for most of the police officers of the Six-seven Precinct, particularly the young ones, it was. They adored Nevins, who time after time would lead raids against the hijackers who preyed on the truckers who made deliveries to the commercial strip along Flatbush Avenue. He led them with all the lust of the military operations he conducted in Vietnam.

"Whoever started a goddamned Christmas list," he continued, just below a shout, "committed a goddamned crime. Cops don't take fuckin' gratuities, at least real cops don't. You got twenty-four hours to return whatever you took from those humps on Flatbush Avenue. Those of you who don't, I'm gonna fuckin' lock you up." Glaring at all the police officers standing at rigid attention in the muster room, he shouted, "You got that?"

"Yes, sir!" came the screamed response.

"Now get the fuck out of here!" ordered

the captain.

The following afternoon, Nevins marched along Flatbush Avenue, a solitary figure of impressive stature. At each stop along the way, he received repeated denials from the store owners. Some replies were delivered so sheepishly it confirmed for Nevins that he was visiting a member of the now-defunct Christmas list.

To each store owner he gave a direct promise delivered with an unmistakable threat. "You give money to my people again and I will lock you up!" One of them was so frightened that he complained to a local Democratic district leader who forwarded his concern to Sherman Cooper, the Brooklyn district attorney. So it was that Sean Nevins and Kenny Rattigan, Cooper's Rackets Bureau chief, first met. Years later, they would recall the incident and laugh about how much both of them had changed.

Nevins, incidentally, was fined two weeks' pay for slapping Winter, the PBA delegate from the South Bronx, during the attempted "job action." It was the proverbial straw that broke the camel's back. In the years that followed, Nevins would never receive a promotion above his civil service rank of captain, a fact that didn't seem to bother him.

■ ■ ■ ■

Nevins did one more thing. He assigned Officer Mulvey to be the full-time 124 man of the 67th Precinct. The corrupt payoffs to the 124 desk stopped, of course, and few police officers at the Six-seven would have anything to do with Mulvey. After all, he couldn't be trusted.

"But how did the Six-seven, or the rest of the job, for that matter, get so screwed up in the first place?" Lee asked.

"What my uncle always said was that it was a deadly combination of bosses who cared only about covering their asses and their careers after they left the department and a PBA leadership more interested in their political power and perks than in the well-being of their membership," Steven replied.

"Hey, Sergeants," interrupted Deputy Sheriff Foley, "do you have any idea what time it is?"

Both Lee and Steven blurted out an apology for talking away the afternoon, including a full hour past the authorized visiting time. Lee planted a quick kiss on Steven's lips and was out the door.

14

The Annual PBA Convention,
August 1990

The Concord Hotel and Resort was one of the few remaining jewels of the once great summer vacation resorts located in Sullivan County in upstate New York.

In the 1940s and '50s, the Borscht Belt hotels of the Catskill Mountains were the summer places to be, but by the late 1960s and '70s, interest in the Catskills had waned. Concord and just a few other resorts survived by offering especially attractive deals for organizations like the Patrolmen's Benevolent Association, which held annual conventions at the spacious resort.

The PBA's annual convention was the highlight of the union's year. The officers and the board of trustees of the PBA used the event as a way of saying thank-you to their delegates from the various units of the

129

NYPD. In fact, all of the delegates and their spouses and children were treated to a week at the convention "on the arm" — police parlance for free.

By 1990, there were several hundred delegates from the more than seventy police precinct houses and other units of the police department. The delegates comprise the ruling assembly, whose particular power ordinarily is limited to the approval or rejection of the contract covering the wages and other benefits for the union's members. This negotiated settlement between the PBA's executive board and New York City's Office of Labor Relations is then proposed to the delegate assembly of the PBA for an up or down vote. The assembly historically approves these contracts with limited controversy. Nevertheless, this membership body remains a sleeping giant, and when aroused it can be the catalyst for throwing out the officers and the board of trustees. Hence the delegates of the assembly are treated very, very well by the union's hierarchy.

Although by 1990 more than a third of New York City's police officers were women, African Americans, Latinos, Asians, and other minorities, the seven members of the board of trustees were all white males, and the organization stubbornly maintained its official name as the Patrol*men's* Benevolent Association. Although from the beginning of the twentieth century the problems of police corruption apparently had a cyclical recurrence every two decades, no one could ever recall any initiatives proposed by the PBA to prevent this blight. Instead, the union's leadership either steadfastly denied the existence of corruption and condemned any investigation into police corruption as a witchhunt or simply ignored it.

The president of the PBA was the all but invincible Pasquale Russell Russo. By 1990, "Rusty" Russo had held the office for almost twenty years. His administration was popular with the rank and file and was regularly reelected. Russo gave the PBA much-needed stability, which forced the city fathers to bargain seriously with the union on relevant issues, in particular the all-important subject of wages.

President Russo presided over a membership of more than twenty thousand, giving him substantial political clout. No one ran for any elective office in New York City without seeking a PBA endorsement, and, since a growing majority of New York City's police officers then resided outside the city, no one ever contemplated a run for state-wide elective office without courting the support of the PBA. These endorsements were sought not so much for the votes they might produce as for the money they generated, as well as the status and recognition. An endorsement by the PBA carried with it the imprimatur of "pro law enforcement," hence tough on crime.

At fifty-four Rusty Russo maintained a trim and muscular frame with daily visits to the gym. He stood exactly six feet and never weighed more than 170 pounds. He had a small, thin face that was offset by a large, powerfully constructed square jaw. All of his hand-tailored Armani suits were dark, and his Oleg Cassini shirts were all blue. Of course, no outfit of his was complete without designer shoes and ties by Ferragamo. Rusty was very much in demand and accessible to the news media. His face had the manufactured tan of a sunlamp, part of a daily routine, and his blow-dried straight black hair was seeing its first signs of gray. His eyes were large, and their color appeared dark, almost black, because of his bushy black eyebrows. His eyes seemed to peer out from his face, emphasizing the man's intensity. He had high, puffy cheekbones and a pug nose. To some the image was that of a boxer who had taken too many head shots, but the fact is that Rusty always avoided physical contact. The total image Russo projected was success, a powerful leader of the largest police union in the United States.

Rusty Russo's speech pattern was distinctive. His predecessor was a tough street cop whose "deese, dose, and dems" and a nasty habit of repeatedly attacking public officials and the media became an embarrassment to his members. By contrast, Russo's flair for language gave him, at least to his membership, the sound of a college professor. He brought class to his position. Rusty chose his vocabulary for its sound, its length, and most of the time for its content. Slipping an occasional malapropism into his speech led Murray Kempton, one of New York City's top political columnists, to observe that "the ubiquitous Pasquale Russell Russo has never met a polysyllable or a metaphor he didn't like."

Shortly after the last plate of dessert was served, Pasquale Russell Russo mounted the rostrum of the Concord Hotel and Resort's grand hall.

"My brothers and sisters, elected officials and guests, welcome once again to the magnificence and splendor of the Concord."

The grand hall's luncheon arrangement featured a three-tiered dais filled with other PBA union officials, as well as representatives from other unions and an appropriate mix of police executives and elected officials. Attendance was a must for the police commissioner, the New York City mayor, the state's governor, several dozen members of Congress, and more than a few state and city legislators. Finally, as a show of unified support from the law enforcement community, the five elected district attorneys of New York City, representing Brooklyn (aka Kings County), Queens, Manhattan (aka New York County), Staten Island, and the Bronx, made the annual trip to the Concord, a mandatory entry on their appointment schedule.

"Regard this day and the remainder of your brief sojourn here as our way" — Russo majestically gestured toward the beaming trustees seated on either side of the lectern — "of expressing our profound gratitude to you for your unstinting and unselfish devotion to those magnificent modern warriors who daily stand between the criminals and the decent people of our city. And let us now give tribute to those heroes."

At these words, a roar of approval filled

the hall and everyone jumped to his feet. The dais snapped to attention so abruptly that one candidate for mayor nearly lost his toupee. Russo would have his twenty-minute address interrupted eight more times by standing ovations.

Eventually he continued. "Because of an inextricable confluence of calamity, the loss of family virtues, today those verities have been inexplicably replaced by violence, a growing welfare-dominated society, and the all too meddlesome influence of the American Civil Liberties Union — and if you are a police officer, that means ACLU lose!"

This line caused a cascade of laughter, which filled the dining hall. Russo now raised his hand and brought instant silence. He looked sternly first at Mayor Richardson, then for dramatic effect at each of the city's five elected district attorneys. His voice began to rise as he continued.

"We are now seeing the ravages brought upon our society by the 'street mutts.' " The term was one of only a few diversions Rusty permitted himself from his affected patrician speech, as a way of saying, *I'm still one of you guys.* "That milieu has created such an utter lack of respect for law and order that in far too many police precincts of New

York City, cops are cuffed and criminals walk!"

This last piece of rhetoric brought Rusty's desired level of snarls and shouts from every police officer in the hall.

"So tormented are our lonely guardians of public safety that the words of Sir William Schwenck Gilbert of the renowned team of operatic composers Gilbert and Sullivan sadly but clearly apply: 'A policeman's lot is not a happy one.' But, my friends, the era of criminal coddling is about to end. From this day forward this union of brothers and sisters will issue its manifesto — a message to all prosecutors of New York City: We have had enough! This morning, your board and I have unanimously agreed that your eminent counsel, William Moreland, Esquire, and his capable staff of lawyers will draw up a protocol for all of our members that will include the demand that no police officer in any criminal case will speak to a superior officer or to an assistant district attorney without benefit of counsel."

Everyone except the five district attorneys, the governor, the mayor, and his police commissioner was on his feet, cheering wildly.

Russo shouted over the din, "If those who would elevate their evil ways to the detriment of society are by law decreed to be protected by lawyers, then those who daily lay down their lives to preserve society shall also be protected by lawyers, our lawyers. It is what they deserve. It is what they shall have." At the end of his speech, Russo thrust both his hands straight up in a victory sign and for a brief moment looked very much like Richard Nixon, as the rafters of the old hall shook with the thunderous applause of the police officers and their families, who leaped to their feet.

As Rusty began to descend the stairs from the dais, suddenly one of the district attorneys, the longest-serving of the five, stepped in front of him. The district attorney of New York County, Justin Rothchild, was furious as he contemplated the chaos that would result if every police officer who made an arrest demanded the presence of a PBA attorney before speaking to an assistant district attorney. At seventy-one years of age, a former United States attorney, appointed by President Kennedy, with a national reputation, Rothchild wielded enormous power. At a trim six foot two and still ramrod straight, he was a man no one wanted as an enemy. Staring eye-level straight at Russo, and with his index finger jabbing the union leader's chest,

Rothchild said quietly but in a firm voice, "Rusty, are you fucking crazy? How do you expect to get away with this?"

Russo glared back and said, "Watch me." Then he walked away, immediately mobbed by his adoring delegates.

Police Officers Scott Ruben and Gabe Perone talked excitedly at their table about Russo's proposal. Ruben was short and squat; some said he looked like a fire hydrant. He had a seventeen-inch neck and a broad, powerful chest, and his muscular arms, made prominent by his form-fitting short-sleeved shirt, were thick with black hair. Not much more than five feet six inches in height, he had short, stocky legs, which made him quite formidable on the department's soccer team. Ruben's oval face had a large, crooked nose between bulbous eyes. His bald pate, above tiny ears, was compensated by a large black walrus mustache. His physical appearance, together with a perpetual scowl, made him a very intimidating man. It was probably one of the reasons he was elected a delegate at the 75th Precinct. Ruben's friend Gabe Perone was his alternate, and both were members of a special new breed of crooks. These two, like other delegates and alternates in every police precinct, knew about the increase of corruption in the NYPD, but they chose to look the other way. Unfortunately, most other cops during that awful period also chose that course of conduct. Ruben's reaction to Rusty Russo's challenge was "What a terrific idea — an instant lawyer, even if it's that scumbag Moreland."

Perone, a gaunt little man with a long, sallow face with slits for eyes and a long pointed nose, was puffing hard on a cigarette. His nasal voice whined, "Scott, whaddaya think, can Rusty carry this thing off?"

Before Ruben could answer, Perone's beeper went off. He quickly read the number on the display and said, "It's Frankie." Ruben nodded as Perone left the table for the pay telephone.

"Frankie," Perone shouted into the phone, "tell that fuckin' weasel if we don't get that package by Friday morning, he won't ever see his kids again." He slammed the phone down and excitedly lit up a cigarette.

15

NYPD Safe House, Prospect Park, Brooklyn, Early March 1974

Captain Nevins's decision in January 1969 to reassign Robert Mulvey as the 124 man at the 67th Precinct following the Christmas list revelation a month earlier was a sound one for the commanding officer. There would not be the slightest chance of corruption with Mulvey in charge of that sensitive position. For the young officer, though, the assignment was an immediate nightmare. Not a single cop would have anything to do with him. In every way he was shunned as the precinct's pariah. The Blue Wall of Silence not only protected corrupt cops, it blacklisted any officer who would violate the code. Observers outside the NYPD could not comprehend why honest police officers, who were a clear majority, fiercely supported this code. The reason for this will be more fully understood before our story ends.

At no time during the more than nine months Mulvey remained at the Six-seven as its outcast did he complain or ask for a transfer. He had recurring second thoughts and even some guilt as the betrayer of fellow officers. His ordeal ended with his meeting with Captain Connolly at SOD in September 1969. At the conclusion of their meeting that day, Connolly arranged to have Mulvey transferred to the Emergency Service Unit of the NYPD. It would be the highlight of Mulvey's career.

The ESU is an elite unit within the New York City Police Department. Members of ESU respond to every kind of emergency in their geographic zone of operation. They pluck babies from the arms of suicidal parents precariously perched on a building ledge and then, using whatever distraction they can create, they save the life of the despondent man or woman seconds before an attempt to jump to certain death. They race across the city to assist their sister or brother police officers confronting an EDP — emotionally disturbed person — armed with an axe. They regularly visit elementary and high schools, where they demonstrate rescue techniques and teach lessons in crime prevention. They are, according to one columnist from the *New York Post,* "firefighters with guns," a description they reject because it suggests heroic parity with their rivals. One of Mulvey's buddies, upon hearing of this comparison, said, "No, we're firefighters with brains." This was said over a beer at a local bar, the hangout of cops and firefighters, and said loud enough to invite the usual and expected four-letter-word responses.

Mulvey imagined he could do this assignment forever, or at least until he got too old for the physical demands of the job. Forty or forty-five, perhaps. By that time he'd be ready to pack it in anyway and look for civilian work.

"Mulvey," shouted his ESU commanding officer, a deputy inspector.

"Yes, sir!" replied Mulvey.

"Report to Inspector Connolly at the 13th Division, forthwith."

As Robert left his command, an unmarked but clearly recognizable police cruiser blocked his path as he turned to cross the street. Two gold shields were thrust at him and withdrawn so quickly that Robert could not identify the rank.

"Officer Mulvey," the older man said, "please get in the backseat. Inspector Connolly told us to give you a lift." Mulvey quickly got in the rear of the car, not really thinking that he had an option.

It had been more than four years since the meeting with Connolly at the Special Operations Division. While Mulvey saw Connolly at police rackets, as beer parties were called, they rarely spoke more than a greeting. Two of those rackets were to celebrate Connolly's promotions only a year apart, first to the rank of deputy inspector and then, six months ago, to full inspector.

Soon the car was in Prospect Park, Brooklyn's huge main recreational green space. The cruiser stopped at what appeared to be a bandshell with a stage. The rear of the stage contained a door leading to a dimly lighted staircase. At the bottom of the second landing of what looked like a subcellar was a rust-colored metal door. Mulvey, left alone as he descended, was told to knock and walk in. The room contained a desk and two straight wooden chairs. At each end of the desk stood a flag: the American flag at one end and the flag of the NYPD at the other. Suddenly a door to the rear of the desk opened and there stood Inspector James Patrick Connolly, commanding officer of the Thirteenth Division police plainclothes unit.

Connolly was dressed casually in fitted

gray slacks, a white collared shirt, a blue cardigan sweater partially buttoned, white gym socks, and highly polished brown loafers. He could have been a professor of literature at nearby Brooklyn College. The pipe he clutched in his left hand completed the academic look. The inspector pointed to a chair for Robert to sit. As he sat down, his eyes wandered for a split second to a corkboard, three feet by two, partially blocked by Connolly's body as he seated himself behind the desk. The board appeared to have pictures of young men and two or three young women in uniform.

"How is the job, Robert?" Inspector Connolly inquired.

"I love it, sir, and I'm about to be made a sergeant."

Connolly interrupted, "In October, yes, and you're getting pretty serious with a very attractive young woman, a special agent of the FBI, Shannon Kelly. And oh, I see you just bought a share of a place on Fire Island for next summer."

Mulvey was puzzled and a bit flustered as he saw that Connolly was reading from the pages of a blue three-ring binder.

"And you still attend daily Mass, usually at St. Rita's in Corona, Queens." Then, with a smile, "Or any other place you can find, depending on the demands of the job. Some mornings you've led us on quite a chase."

"Excuse me, sir," he said, summoning up some courage with a simple question, "but why are you following me?"

"Because, Robert" — Connolly got very serious — "I need you."

Connolly's earnestness was unsettling to Mulvey. Connolly seemed worried — not the usual supremely confident police commander — and the setting for their meeting made all of it seem ominous.

"I need your help as I have never needed anyone else before!"

For the moment, Mulvey was stunned. Connolly was someone whom he admired and would gladly help, but how? And would he have to leave ESU? His career dream was to stay in the unit, and if he was lucky enough to catch the promotional examination cycle, he could be a captain before he reached his midthirties, just like Connolly. It was unreal. James Connolly, at once the most respected, most feared, and most dynamic young police boss in the department, needed Mulvey's help so much he seemed to be pleading for it.

"Robert," Connolly began in a soft, almost inaudible voice, "what I have to tell you must remain here. You must swear an oath to God."

Mulvey's heart began to race. Fear took hold of him at the solemnity of the situation.

"Even if you decide not to help, or should I say especially if you refuse, you must under pain of sin never reveal my words." Connolly allowed the young cop a minute to reflect on the seriousness of all this and then said, "Am I clear?"

"Yes, Inspector," came the muffled reply.

"Do I have your oath?"

"Yes, Inspector."

"Do you want me to continue?"

"Yes, sir."

"Besides that business a few years ago with the Christmas list at the 67th Precinct, have you ever heard of or actually seen any other cops taking money?"

Connolly, of course, suspected the answer would be no, because Mulvey's ESU assignment placed him among a group of police officers whose integrity had never been in question.

"No, sir. Although I have heard the normal rumors you pick up at beer rackets. Nothing other than that."

"Well, Robert, here at the 13th Plainclothes Division, we have much more than a rumor."

16

NYPD Safe House, Prospect Park, Brooklyn, Early March 1974

Inspector Connolly began by giving Mulvey an overview of the work of plainclothes units like the 13th Division and a history of their corrupt activities.

The 13th Plainclothes Division was one of a dozen similar units created by the department to deal with prostitution and gambling. Plainclothes units soon became known as places where cops could make a few extra bucks off of the bookies they were charged with arresting, or from the prostitutes who worked the streets and were regarded as neighborhood eyesores. These women would approach an undercover plainclothesman, offer to turn a trick, and routinely be arrested, but that didn't necessarily mean that the officer would take the prostitute to the station house for processing on the way to criminal court. Often he had other plans for her.

Since it was the duty of these units to contain, if not eliminate, these two evils, or vices, the men and the few women assigned to this unit were soon branded with the ignoble nickname of "vice cops." It became almost immediately obvious to those cops assigned to these squads that the attempt to contain, let alone eliminate, these two immoral public activities was an exercise in futility.

If no society in all of human history had successfully eradicated prostitution, the so-called world's oldest profession, how could any New York City cop do better? So why not make some money from the pros, as they called them, by releasing them in return for free sex or a tip, or letting them ply their trade in a particular area in exchange for a percentage of the action?

As for bookmaking, since to the general public it was of little concern or interest, the vice cops received no outcry from citizens. Quite the contrary; the prevailing attitude was: Who is really hurt by Joe the Bookie? There was little evidence that wives and children anywhere were being deprived of food or clothing because of a husband's excessive bets with a bookie. There seemed to be far more evidence of deprivation for the wives and children of drunks. The difference was that the politicians made booze legal and kept gambling illegal. This reality soon led to a type of containment not envisioned by the Police Department or the penal laws of New York State — containment by the creation of the pad.

The "pad" was the euphemism invented by vice cops and bookies for payment to the cops. The bookie every once in a while would take a collar. (The word "collar" came from the turn of the twentieth century, when most men, even criminals, wore high starched collars. When a police officer made an arrest, he would typically grab the person by the collar.) The arresting officer permitted him to keep his book, or his work. The work was the detailed record of the bets made with the bookie; without it every bettor would claim that he or she was a winner. The work therefore was the bookmaker's lifeline. Since the arrest was made without the evidence of bookmaking, which is a felony, the only charge that could be brought was the misdemeanor of loitering for the purpose of bookmaking. Of course, neither the district attorney nor the judges were particularly excited about cases charging bookmakers with that low-level offense. So the vice cops and the bookies created an arrangement that worked to everyone's satisfaction.

The main reason why bookmakers paid off cops in the first place and never seriously complained when an increase in the pad was demanded was that their business was very, very lucrative. Bookies make money from their customer's losses, through the "vigorish," or the "vig," paid to them. The first bookmakers in New York City were Jewish, so they used the Yiddish word *vyigrysh,* a charge placed on bets. The vig is usually 10 percent of the face amount of the losing bet.

Bookmaking is a major criminal industry in the United States except in those few states, such as Nevada, where gambling is legal. By the 1970s in New York City, the annual gross take from bookmaking was eight billion dollars — and, no surprise, it was, as it is today, totally controlled by organized crime. The five organized crime families of New York franchise bookmaking locations and receive a weekly percentage of the bookmaker's profits. These franchises are controlled by fear. Every bookmaker knows that any violation, such as skimming or hiding profits, would be met swiftly with a severe beating or even death.

The next act of this charade would occur

at the courthouse, where the assistant district attorney, busy with more serious crime, would say perfunctorily, "Whaddaya got, officer?"

"I got a KG for loitering." KG is cop and prosecution slang for "known gambler."

The prosecutor would then ask the bookie's lawyer, usually a local courthouse hustler retained by the bookie for a sum of twenty-five dollars for each case, "Counselor, how about a plea to an attempt and a fifty-dollar fine?"

Quickly they agreed to the deal, which was presented to a judge who also didn't regard the criminal charge to be particularly serious and who would pronounce a sentence with the usual warning not to repeat this egregious behavior. So the accommodation arrest benefited not just the partnership between the cop and the bookie but also the criminal justice system, a speedy and efficient revenue-producing disposition of minor matters that could clog up the system.

Some judges, such as Judge Murray Shoenstein, who was preparing to run for the office of Kings County district attorney, always sought to curry favor — with the cops and the PBA. Shoenstein, a comically fat man whose facial features were disappearing into his jowls, had curly strawberry hair that he dyed because he thought it made him look younger. When he tried to stand, it was always a great effort; his short arms gave him no balance to support himself on his stubby legs. Ordinarily, and for obvious reasons, Judge Shoenstein avoided standing once he ascended to the bench and took his seat, but he loved to castigate bookmakers from a threatening, standing position. He would preface pronouncing the sentence he imposed on the bookie with a special warning.

"You may not think your crime particularly vile, and I suppose that even to the more sophisticated, your activity is at worst socially unacceptable, but let me tell you, sir, and make it clear, when you become the subject of this police officer's investigation, requiring him to engage in activity that puts him at risk" — at this point Shoenstein would raise his voice, demanding the rapt attention of all present, mostly other vice cops and other bookies with the same kind of accommodation arrest — "when you by your criminal conduct, require a police officer to use his training, his cunning, his intellect" — now Shoenstein was shouting — "you are placing him in harm's way with a high risk of injury or even death." The last part of his oration was uttered solemnly with a deep voice: "I can never get used to appearing at a police officer's funeral. So if you come before me again, I shall sentence you to a maximum period of jail time. Do you understand?"

The bookie would look wisely shaken — and chastened. The vice cop would usually beam and, depending on how effective the judge's presentation sounded, the court-room cops and bookies alike would erupt with cheers and applause. Whereupon Shoenstein would announce, with a broad, satisfied smile, "This court stands adjourned!"

Of course, most of the bookies that found themselves as defendants in Judge Shoenstein's courtroom had been treated to this same ranting many times over — and of course he never jailed a single one of them. In Part 3 of Brooklyn Criminal Court, where pleas of guilty or not guilty were entered, all was well that ended well. The judge made a speech; the assistant district attorney got a guilty plea; the bookie got to keep his freedom, but more important, he kept his book going. The hustling courtroom lawyer got his twenty-five bucks, and the vice cop reensured the monthly receipt of his payment from the pad.

When Inspector Connolly came to the

13th Division, he became determined to find out the extent of the corruption affecting the police officers he was about to command. It did not take long before he discovered conditions within the 13th that were so shocking he decided to recruit Mulvey for a highly confidential undercover assignment. Although Connolly knew that this young officer was intensely loyal to him, he suspected that Mulvey would find this level of corruption repulsive and probably refuse the assignment. Nonetheless, Connolly would try.

"Just settle back, son," Connolly said gently. "How I learned about the 13th is a pretty long, sorry story, and before I can ask for your help you have to know all of it." Mulvey didn't respond, but he did relax and listen attentively.

17

People v. Holt,
October 12, 1992
Too many lawyers who put themselves
forward as trial attorneys or litigators regard
the process of jury selection to be not much
more than a delaying distraction from the
main event, the trial. But to premier trial
lawyers like Larry Green, the voir dire —
French for "to speak the truth" — is the essential prelude to the case. Indeed, Green
was fond of calling the process of finding
the right jurors the very *sine qua non* of any
case. The Latin phrase means "absolutely
indispensable."

"It is during jury selection," Green lectured his trial advocacy class at Fordham
Law School, "that prospective jurors take
the measure of the lawyers. If they like you,
you have established a beachhead. If they
don't like you, then you might as well be
speaking Swahili! How," he would ask

crankily, "can you possibly pick a jury if you don't know anything about them? And you will learn about them only by asking questions that elicit complete, comprehensive answers. Only then can you assess a juror for intelligence, knowledge of current events, and the ability to keep an open mind."

Now, that did not necessarily imply Green was looking for an impartial jury. His mission, as he saw it, was to pick the brightest people he could find, those he could persuade to embrace his theory of the case.

For Larry Green, just as it was for the great pro football coach Vince Lombardi, winning wasn't everything, it was the only thing, so he had little patience and much contempt for lawyers who regarded jury selection as incidental to the trial. Such a lawyer, fortunately for Steven Holt, was Suffolk County Assistant District Attorney Wallace Goss.

Goss gave a perfunctory thank-you to the panel of citizens waiting to be chosen for jury service, followed by a series of questions that invited a one-word answer, often grunted inaudibly. "Can you be fair?" "Will you accept the law from the judge?" "Will you demand more of the prosecutor than proof beyond a reasonable doubt?" These were answered always "yes," "yes," and "no." In some cases, the judge would admonish Goss not to ask that last question because matters of law were strictly for the judge, but no matter how many times Goss was warned, he didn't get it. He remained clueless.

Larry Green's approach to jury selection had two basic goals: find out something about a prospective juror by getting him or her to talk as much as was necessary for an appropriate assessment, and develop questions to aid his strategy to win the case. Of course, his approach turned on the weight and the quality of the evidence. One technique to achieve the first goal was to ask questions that probed a juror's previous experience with a trial.

"Mr. Sullivan, you indicated before that you had previously served on a jury?"

"Yes, sir."

"Did you and the other jurors deliberate?"

"We did."

"If you did reach a verdict, without telling us what that verdict was, can you tell me the facts of the case?"

The way the potential juror framed the answer — whether it was articulate, concise, and clear; whether it showed a good recollection of the case — said a lot about the person. Even an attitude toward the system could be elicited by these responses. When Mr. Sullivan, the prospective juror, replied to Green's question about prior service, he recalled, "It was about this robber." That description of the defendant, though brief, meant to Larry Green that Mr. Sullivan had a predisposition in favor of the prosecution. Of course, Green would add that his conclusion was at best a good guess, based on experience.

Green's second goal had very much to do with his analysis of the case, and in Steven Holt's, Green found little optimism for an outcome favorable to the young sergeant. Holt's gun had been surrendered to the Suffolk County detectives and showed a clean set of his fingerprints and palm prints. The ballistics test appeared to be conclusive; the test bullets from Steven's weapon matched the bullets recovered from the bodies of the three dead victims. Moreover, Steven had some hell of a motive for killing Police Officer Scott Ruben. He hated him, and it was not just because Ruben was a crook. There was something more, something Holt was not ready to reveal.

"Criminal defense lawyers in New York State have a powerful ace in the hole, assuming," Green lectured his Fordham trial advocacy class, "they understand how to use it. It only takes one juror to screw up a prosecutor's case and create a hung jury. In some states a verdict can be reached upon the agreement of four-fifths of the jurors, but New York requires a unanimous verdict. And," he added, with a rare smile, really a smirk, "sometimes you get lucky, when an argument meant to convince just one juror gets adopted by all twelve." Here he quoted, very roughly, the writer-critic H. L Mencken, who said, "When a person is arrested and charged with a crime, a presumption of guilt immediately attaches to the case, but should that person be convicted after trial, the public can be easily convinced that the person was railroaded by the authorities!" Green decided that he would employ a strategy to frustrate if not defeat the prosecution of Steven Holt, based on the cynically held belief of many that often defendants are charged with a crime as a result of fabricated evidence.

Green began his voir dire "Ladies and gentlemen, perhaps the greatest observation one can make of the jury system is that truth is found by the collaborative effort of sincere and honorable citizens with disparate experiences. So let me begin with this question: Is there any example in your

lifetime experience of someone unjustly accused of a crime, and do you recall the facts
of that case?"

A young African American stockbroker,
perhaps in his early thirties, dressed in a
blue blazer with a white polo shirt, open at
the neck, leaned forward and said, "Lynch-
ings in the South were all too common, even
in the 1960s, and were frequently based on
trumped-up evidence."

Although Larry spent some time discussing this blight on American history with
Norton Marshal, the young prospective
juror from Wall Street, he knew very well
that Goss would use one of his peremptory
challenges to send the sincere young man
back to the stock exchange. In a criminal
case, the lawyers have two types of challenges to remove a prospective juror. One is
for cause, where it is clear that the juror
should not be seated because of bias, and
the other is a peremptory challenge, which
does not require explanation but may not
be used prejudicially — for reasons of race
or religion, for example.

Several of the other prospective jurors had
varying opinions about Green's inquiry.
After each lawyer finished a round of ques-
tioning, the panelists were seated or rejected. Not very long into the process,

Green caught a huge break. Esther Steinberg raised her hand.

"Yes, madam." Green nodded to her. "Do you have a question or perhaps an observation?"

"I do," she replied. With a broad smile she said quietly yet firmly, *"J'accuse."*

"What?" exclaimed Goss.

"Oh, be patient," counseled Green. "I'm certain Mrs. Steinberg will explain."

For the next few minutes, Esther Steinberg, a matronly seventy-year-old who was impeccably dressed and stylishly made up, spoke of what is known as the Dreyfus case.

Captain Alfred Dreyfus, a Jewish artillery officer in the French army, was falsely charged with treason and then convicted at a court-martial in 1894. He was sentenced to prison on the infamous Devil's Island off the coast of South America. In 1896, the French military had indisputable evidence that Dreyfus was not guilty, but instead of freeing him, they withheld the information, and he remained imprisoned until 1899. In 1898, the great French novelist Emile Zola penned a four-thousand-word essay in the form of an open letter to the president of the French Republic; he entitled the piece *J'accuse* — "I Accuse." Zola made a strong and compelling case that condemned the injustice suffered by Captain Dreyfus at the hands of the French military court. Zola's words ignited a firestorm of outrage from officials within the French government. The essay also led to a vile wave of anti-Semitism that swept across France. Zola was tried and convicted of criminal libel and was sentenced to serve a year in prison. He fled to England, where he remained for more than a year. By then, Dreyfus's conviction had been reversed. The captain was retried and once again convicted. Nonetheless, the French government immediately pardoned him, and he was reinstated by the army. Thereafter he was promoted and awarded the Legion of Honor. In 1906, France's highest court formally found the captain innocent. The libel charge against Zola had been dismissed years earlier, but his support for Captain Dreyfus left him financially ruined. Twelve years after this monumental injustice began, Captain Alfred Dreyfus was honored with a dress parade military ceremony.

Green was determined not to lose Mrs. Steinberg, but he made sure that it didn't appear obvious to Goss.

"Mrs. Steinberg," he began gently, "may I ask you if are you Jewish?"

She reddened slightly and replied, "Yes, I

am, but —"

Green quickly interrupted. "May I assume that your religious affiliation and your knowledge about the Dreyfus case would not interfere with your ability to listen to the evidence in this case, take the judge's charge on the law, deliberate with your fellow jurors, and render a fair verdict?"

"That is correct," she quickly answered.

Green continued, "Is there any reason why you cited the Dreyfus case when I asked you about examples of injustice? And by the way, do you think that the circumstances that led to the injustices in the Dreyfus case are the norm for the criminal justice system — say, for this country?"

"I regard the Dreyfus case to be a particularly egregious example of injustice," she replied, "but I also think that, given all of the safeguards contained in our criminal justice system, an abuse like the Dreyfus case would be rare in this country."

Her answer completely satisfied Assistant District Attorney Goss, and he accepted Mrs. Steinberg as a juror. Green was ecstatic!

Chief Louis Guido,
1973–1974

By 1973, police corruption had reached epidemic proportions, yet the leadership at One PP was unable or unwilling to mount any strategy to contain it. It would take a new mayoral administration and an innovative commissioner to turn the tide, but given the political demographics of a city controlled by Democrats and an extremely popular mayor, that was unlikely to happen. Then along came Winthrope Hargrove. No one could think of a more unlikely candidate.

For the political machine bosses of the Democratic Party, Hargrove was the ideal candidate of the Republican Party as its quadrennial sacrifice. Winthrope Hargrove seemed to be just a goofy WASP with a prep school education, topped off with a Harvard undergrad degree and a law school diploma from Yale. In a city whose Republican registration was dwarfed by the Democrats by a margin of six to one, Hargrove did not loom as much of a threat, and his slogan, "Win with Winnie," was laughable if not ludicrous. It didn't seem to matter that the Democratic leadership's once reform-minded incumbent, Phil Kersey, had become a vacuous, self-pitying shadow of the man once so much admired by New Yorkers as "Mayor Eternal" — his words. Or that Kersey's repeated and ill-advised attempts at higher office — first a disastrous run for the United States Senate, followed several years later by a half-hearted attempt at a run for governor — had worn thin his appeal with the voters and left his reputation shattered. Nor did it seem much of a problem that of the five Democratic bosses controlling each of the city's boroughs, two were serving time in federal prison and another had himself committed to a psychiatric hospital suffering severe depression. Nearly a century of repeated election victories at every level in New York City had left the Democratic Party as detached from reality as the city's mayor, who insisted on running for an unprecedented fourth term.

A confluence of circumstances fueled by Kersey's contempt for just about everyone made the unthinkable the inevitable.

The Associated Press wire story flashed around the country. "Phillip Kersey, once the enormously popular mayor of New York City's middle class, courted by three candidates for the Democratic nomination for president to be their vice presidential running mate in 1968, only minutes ago became part of the bitter history of lost elections, and with him the Democratic Party's machine has been unmasked as a paper tiger. 'Winnie' Hargrove, repeatedly vilified by the worst negative campaign in New York City's history, has overwhelmed Mayor Kersey 57 percent to 41 percent."

The first priority of any mayor is public safety, so his appointment of a police commissioner is closely watched by the press. The way Hargrove met the man he chose was purely coincidental. The place was a United Auto Workers lodge in the Brighton section of Richmond County, in the borough of Staten Island, on a summer weekend of that particularly nasty campaign for mayor. Louis Guido was a one-star chief serving as the deputy to the borough commander. Guido's career, which had peaked when he led the prestigious Public Morals Administrative Division, rapidly descended after he ordered the arrest of "Bippo" Readon, a major sports bookie who happened to be the brother of a New York City councilman who chaired the powerful Finance Committee.

Hargrove was introduced by the UAW lodge steward and took the stage to say a few words. Suddenly a drunken Democratic Party worker appeared out of the crowd and began screaming, "You fuckin' Republican phony," and threw a filled quart bottle of beer at the candidate. Hargrove quickly batted the bottle away, deflecting it from his head. Guido, who had wandered into the lodge a few minutes before to check on Hargrove's security, leaped to the stage and, smashing the drunk to the ground, knocked him unconscious. In seconds, Chief Guido had the man's arms cuffed behind his back and handed him over to an astonished young sergeant to complete the arrest procedure. When the crowd recovered, they sent up a loud cheer for Guido as he bounded onto the stage and asked the smiling candidate, "Are you okay, sir?"

The police department acceded immediately to Hargrove's request that Chief Guido head up his security unit.

Chief Louis Guido's appointment as the new commissioner bypassed eleven senior chiefs, all of whom promptly resigned. Guido in turn chose another one-star chief, Keith "Cookie" Nolan, to be his chief of department. Nolan became the only police executive to wear four stars and was the day-to-day chief executive officer of a department with thirty-six thousand officers of all ranks and twelve thousand civilians.

Some years before his current assignment, Chief Nolan had been banished by the then-serving chief of department to an obscure part of the bureaucracy hidden in the bowels of One Police Plaza. His transgression, which he could not recall, was apparently some slight that his immediate predecessor imagined him guilty of during one of the chief's endless administrative conferences. His best guess was that during one such conference with a redundant agenda about the personal hygiene habits expected of senior officers, an exasperated Nolan uttered a slight groan. The next morning he was banished from the executive floor to the basement of the building and put in charge of the motor pool.

While the traditional interaction between the police commissioner and the top uniformed commander was policy setter to policy executioner, Guido's and Nolan's history with each other would make things quite different. They had been friends since their days as police officers in the South Bronx, after they both graduated near the top of their class at the academy. This new administration would be a true partnership. In public, Nolan would refer respectfully to Guido as "Boss" — the traditional term for a superior officer in the department — and Guido would call Nolan "Chief." In private, all formality was dropped, and they set about reforming the department they loved so very much. They were determined to eradicate systemic corruption, particularly in the plainclothes division, and so it was that they decided to call upon Inspector James Patrick Connolly to begin that reform. Connolly agreed after one request was granted: assign Sergeant Bernie Pressler to help him.

Bernie Pressler from Brownsville

Ever since their first assignment from the Police Academy to the 75th Precinct in Brooklyn's East New York, James Connolly and Bernie Pressler had been each other's shadow. They were very different in many ways. Connolly, an Irish Catholic, was all spit and polish while in uniform and a meticulous dresser when he wore civilian clothing. Pressler was Jewish. He was opinionated and super street-smart. His clothes always looked as if he had worn them to bed. He was also an extraordinarily effective investigator who hated corrupt cops.

Bernard Aser Pressler was a Brownsville Jew, and if you were one, or knew what the Brownsville section of Brooklyn was like in the 1920s through the end of the '50s, those words had instant meaning. Brownsville was a lower-income village made up typically of wood-frame, one- and two-family, fully detached or semidetached homes and a large number of brownstone row houses, popularly known as railroad flats. This enclave was wholly populated by Jewish emigrants from Eastern Europe. These Polish, Russian, and Romanian settlers produced large families fiercely committed to a tradition that included a deep faith in God and a clear understanding that education was the ultimate liberator from their economic ghetto here in their adopted land. But just as other groups, similarly situated, drifted into crime as a more effective way out of poverty, some in Brownsville chose that path and were enormously successful. These hoodlums created Murder Incorporated, the Jewish mob that controlled all the rackets in Brooklyn until the emigration and the ascendancy of the Sicilian Mafia.

Brownsville Jews also dominated college basketball at Long Island University and City College of New York, which was the last college basketball team to win both the NCAA and the NIT in the same year. They even played for some of the Catholic schools: The St. John's University basketball team of the late twenties was called "the Wonder Five," and in 1929 four of the five starting players were Jewish. Brownsville also produced some of the most successful bookmakers in New York City, and some say they were behind the biggest college basketball point-shaving scandal in history.

Fighting under pseudonyms such as Battlin' Buddy McGirt and Looie the Assassin Mangano, Jews from Brownsville became highly rated professional boxers. They were the trailblazers for Jews years later who could fight under their own names. Champions like Max Baer and Gus Lesnevich would in their time pack all the major fighting arenas in New York City with a huge following of fight fans.

Brownsville also produced a haberdasher who was a man so devoted to turning kids from that neighborhood away from a life of crime to medicine, teaching, social work, and the law that he soon became a living legend. This man, Abraham Stark, was so successful that he was elected borough president of Brooklyn. For anyone today over the age of fifty, Abe Stark is remembered best for his haberdashery sign in right center field at historic Ebbets Field, then the home of the Brooklyn Dodgers. The clothing sign read, "Abe Stark — 1514 Pitkin Avenue," and invited the ballplayers to "Hit Sign, Win Suit!"

While Brownsville produced its share of criminals, many more of its residents became educators, judges, great trial attorneys, physicians, and cops like Bernie Pressler. Bernie Pressler, who had a keen intellect with high-school grades good enough to get him into any of the colleges of New York City, came from a family of seven children. It was a family, like so many others in Brownsville, that was dirt poor and simply could not afford sending a child to college. The combined incomes of all the kids and the parents were essential for survival.

At five feet ten inches and weighing 180 pounds, Bernie had developed a daily regimen of weight training and jogging at a gym not far from his home. He became so accomplished on the speed bag that the gym's boxing coach tried to convince him to take up the sport professionally. That career option lasted as long as it took for Momma Pressler to issue a firm order. "No!" So Bernie took the examination to become a New York City police officer and finished fourth out of the thousands of youngsters who applied. He was soon sworn in and was on the way to the academy.

Bernie wore his jet black hair with a sharp part directly down the middle, the favored style of bartenders in the 1940s. His wide face contained bead-sized dark eyes, prominent high cheekbones, and a huge flattened nose, a trophy from his boxing days. His short, muscular neck seemed to disappear between his head and shoulders. His lips were thin and perpetually turned down like a Ringling Brothers clown's, and it seemed to require an immense effort for him to smile.

Bernie Pressler was on the job when the Irish Mafia still ruled the NYPD; the stereotype for Jews was that they were either doctors, lawyers, teachers, or highly successful businessmen, and that they never took tough jobs like cop or firefighter. The police department he joined was parochial and distant from most new immigrants, particularly European Jews, and so at times Jewish citizens and the few Jewish police officers would fall victim to anti-Semitism. Whenever Pressler was confronted, he acted swiftly. Soon after his assignment to the 75th Precinct, in one of Brooklyn's toughest neighborhoods, Bernie overheard a big-mouthed bigot refer to him as "that Jew scumbag." He invited the officer to come to the locker room, alone, where he left him in a pile of bruises and blood.

20

People v. Holt,
October 19, 1992
On June 4, 1991, Steven Holt had been indicted by a Suffolk County grand jury. He was charged with three counts of murder in the second degree in connection with the murders of Scott Ruben, Ramon Rodriguez, and Ramon's brother, Hiram. A combination of extensive and complicated pretrial motions and Larry Green's commitment to other trials had delayed the start of Steven's trial for over a year. Now, as the court convened, he finally felt some relief.

Judge Michael J. McGowan was speaking to the jurors.

"Furthermore, if you conclude beyond a reasonable doubt that Sergeant Steven Robert Holt intentionally caused the death of Ramon Rodriguez and his brother, Hiram Rodriguez, and that he caused the death of Police Officer Scott Ruben, then you must find him guilty of the crime of murder in the second degree as charged in the first, second, and third counts of this indictment." Here the judge paused for a moment, and then he continued, "And, of course, if you don't so find, beyond a reasonable doubt, then you must acquit Sergeant Holt."

Judge McGowan was merely going through his ritual of giving the jury preliminary instructions, but Steven Holt, after months of anxiety, was beginning to show signs of paranoia and at this point cringed, believing that the judge had emphasized the standard for a criminal conviction and understated the grounds for acquittal. McGowan, on the other hand, thought he was actually benefiting the defendant through clarity and repetition. He would repeat these instructions in greater detail during his final charge, or definition and explanation of the law, to the jury, after they had heard all of the evidence and before submitting the case to them for their deliberation. Finally, McGowan added, "Verdict, ladies and gentlemen of the jury, comes from the Latin word *veredictum,* which means truth saying or telling the truth. And that, after all, is what you must try to achieve."

Judge McGowan's voice was firm and strong. It resonated clearly through the huge courtroom, acoustically almost perfect, chosen by him because he anticipated correctly that a large crowd of spectators and reporters would attend the trial of a New York City police officer charged with a triple homicide.

The walls of the courtroom were of rich, dark reddish-brown mahogany. Its floors were inlaid with expensive oak, maintained at a high polish with daily care at the conclusion of the court session. Completing the majestic image of this palace of justice was the judge's bench. The front wall of the bench was a foot thick and measured seven feet high and twelve feet wide. It was made mostly of black-and-white marble with a tastefully designed ebony base, three feet by four feet, that featured a sculpture of Justice carefully chiseled into the glistening stone. The judge's lofty perch created a formidable barrier between him and everyone else in his courtroom. High above and behind the judge's oversized green leather upholstered chair, an ancient command from the Book of Deuteronomy was written in large gold script on the mahogany wall: "Justice, justice, thou shalt pursue." All of this created a most appropriate venue for the tall, trim, austere-looking Michael J. McGowan, chief administrative judge of all the courts in Suffolk County. At nearly six feet six inches tall, with snow-white hair and a deep bass voice, he commanded the complete attention of the jurors. They sat comfortably in their jury box nearby, in large chairs made from the same mahogany as the courtroom walls and luxuriously padded with the same dark green leather as Judge McGowan's chair. McGowan, of course, had full control over the lawyers and the courtroom spectators, because he simply would not have it any other way. When he spoke, the sound of his voice was the only thing heard in the courtroom.

At the beginning of the judge's introductory charge, delivered just prior to the prosecutor's opening statement to the jury, Steven was having difficulty reading him. McGowan's reputation was that of a no-nonsense, tough, pro-cop jurist who had little patience with defense attorneys. Most police officers thought he was great. Steven was watching very carefully to see how the judge felt about this case, his case. Since Holt had no guidelines or experience in such matters, it was really an exercise in futility.

"Now, a doubt can't be flimsy. It must be

reasonable and not used as an excuse to avoid an unpleasant task," McGowan continued. Steven thought for sure that things were not going in his favor. As McGowan's words pounded against his ears like so many sledgehammer blows, he could feel the hot flashes erupting on his pale cheeks.

How . . . how? Steven thought as the fear those words caused surged throughout his body. *How the fuck did I get here?*

It was a question he frequently asked himself and rhetorically put to Lee Moran and his uncle. He had no answer. He certainly had no reason to kill two factory workers from Brooklyn he'd never met, and while he knew Police Officer Scott Ruben and didn't have much use for him, he had no motive to kill him — or anyone else, for that matter. And he didn't have a clue about how his police service weapon was used to kill all three.

It was at these times of reflection, either during moments of distraction at the trial or alone in his cell, that he would compare his plight to the circumstances that led to the poor treatment given his uncle. What united them, aside from their love for each other and the job, was their hatred for every vestige of police corruption, and while their service was separated by nearly twenty years, each was given the opportunity by bosses fed up with police corruption to eliminate it. What Steven couldn't know was that while the factors that almost crushed Mulvey and the forces that were threatening to put him in prison for the rest of his life grew out of their anticorruption efforts, the destructive paths taken by each of them were very different.

Connolly, Pressler, and the Plan,
January–February 1974

Inspector Connolly and Sergeant Pressler agreed that their initial strategy should be to set up a surveillance of a few selected locations within the operational area of the 13th Division. Pressler borrowed a van from Internal Affairs that was made to look like a utility vehicle operated by the Brooklyn Union Gas Company.

They began their observations early the following morning. At approximately 10:30, not more than an hour after they set up, they noticed some unusual activity at a liquor store and a grocery store located on the opposite sides of Nostrand Avenue about a hundred feet from the intersection of Nostrand and a major artery called Eastern Parkway. Through the smoked windows of the undercover van, they watched a steady stream of people enter the stores and leave empty-handed. Over the next two and a half hours, thirty-six people entered the grocery store, and forty-seven entered the liquor store; most of them left a short time later without a package.

While the conduct of these "customers" might appear suspicious, the law requires that a police officer have probable cause to believe that a crime is being committed before taking any action against a suspect. Connolly and Pressler decided to get some advice from Deputy Chief Virgil Sampson, commanding officer of the elite Public Morals Administrative Division.

While PMAD's main mission was to work with prosecutors to put major bookmakers out of business and into prison, occasionally it would catch some crooked cops and thieving lawyers who were in partnership with the major bookies. PMAD operated at an undisclosed location and kept its personnel strength a closely held secret. It had an unblemished reputation for integrity as well as effectiveness. Unlike Internal Affairs, which at the time was regarded as a joke by most cops, PMAD was the real deal. If PMAD detectives caught you, you'd stay caught!

Virgil Sampson stood about six feet four inches tall, with skin the color of brilliantly polished ebony. He was one of the few African Americans at that time who had reached the rank of chief in the New York City Police Department. His trim, firm body was held perpetually erect, disciplined by regular exercise and by Chief Sampson's will. His large, muscular hands, which appeared to be out of proportion to the rest of his body, were strengthened by a routine of chopping wood several days a week in the backyard of his home in a neat residential neighborhood in Brooklyn known as Crown Heights. The chief had a habit of staring through people, which intimidated most and belied the fact that he had a great sense of humor. From the first day in the Police Academy, through every promotional examination, Virgil Sampson was known as a student. While he was never at the top of the class in school or on a promotional exam, he strictly followed the advice of his late father: "Virgil, just make sure that you're competitive." Indeed, that was what all the long hours of study produced for this dedicated young man. Virgil was always in the game, always competitive.

Chief Sampson was very familiar with the area of Crown Heights where Connolly and Pressler made their observations. He had grown up in the vicinity, not far from his present home. He also knew quite a lot about the two stores Connolly and Pressler had under observation.

"The liquor store," he said, "has been in the Creighton family since they moved here from Georgia in the late 1940s. Luis Arroyo bought the grocery store from the Steward family, who started their business in late 1951 shortly after they moved to Brooklyn from the Cayman Islands. Both stores are known to handle a little sports betting action and some numbers on the side." Numbers is essentially a ghetto gambling game and the winning numbers are selected from the last three digits of the mutual handle, or the gross amount of money bet for the day at the local horseracing track. So for example if the total amount of money bet at Aqueduct racetrack in New York City in one day is $3,542,923, the winning number for the day would be the last three digits, or 923. The payoff for the right guess can run into the hundreds and sometimes into the thousands of dollars.

Pressler asked, "Chief, don't you think that so many people over a few hours indicates more than a little action?" Chief Sampson, with many more years of experience in the surveillance business than the sergeant, resisted the temptation to put Bernie down. Instead he put a question to both officers. "Well, what do think we've got?"

Connolly replied, "My guess is that either the CO of the Seven-one doesn't regard the two businesses as anything more than a nuisance, or that some cops from either the precinct or from the 13th Division are being paid off."

Mulvey cleared his throat, and although he was intimidated he got up the courage to ask, "Why was it so obvious to you, Chief, that some police officers were on the take?"

Connolly smiled, still trying without much success to relax his protégé. "The short answer is, son, that corruption in the plain-clothes division has been an open secret in this department forever. The thing is, no one has been able to prove it, but that's what the commissioner wants us to try to do."

Mulvey froze when the Inspector said "us." He shifted uncomfortably in his chair. Connolly continued his story.

When Connolly had finished his analysis, Chief Sampson looked a bit puzzled, but for only a minute. Then he said, "Fine, let's see if we can find out." He pushed the intercom button and said to his aide, "Billie, get me Lieutenant Moore. If he's in the building, send him in. If not, reach him and tell him I want him forthwith."

Not ten minutes later, there was a sharp knock on Chief Sampson's door which was answered, "Lou" — Lieutenant — "if that's you, come on in."

Lieutenant Brendan Moore quickly stepped into the room. Moore's face could have been on a travel poster for Aer Lingus. His hair, which he kept short, was jet black. He had deep blue eyes, and his cheeks had two prominent dimples. He wore a bubbly smile, and you could sense the enthusiasm as he entered the room. His gray tweed jacket and his freshly pressed chinos, accompanied by black loafers with tasseled straps, was the wardrobe he chose because he thought it made him look older. Although he was in his late forties, he was always concerned that his youthful appearance would be mistaken for inexperience. This street uniform made him look like the investigative analyst he had worked so hard to become — at least he thought so. There was no one in the department quite like him.

After the introductions, Chief Sampson gave Lieutenant Moore the details and asked, "Brendan, do we have any informants we can send to either or both of those locations to see what's going on?"

"Sure, Boss," the lieutenant replied. "I've got a guy working off a Bronx case who lives on Eastern Parkway, a few blocks from those stores." By "working off a case," the lieutenant meant that a confidential informant, or CI, had a pending criminal case in one of the five counties in New York City, and if the CI provided evidence or useful intelligence for Lieutenant Moore, Moore would agree to ask the district attorney in that county to offer a guilty plea to a lesser charge, reduce a jail sentence, or even dismiss the case. If confidential information is the currency for law enforcement undercover in drug and gambling operations, Lieutenant Brendan A. Moore was the national bank for CIs. This twenty-six-year police veteran, with two decades of experience in undercover operations, was quite simply the most highly respected police officer in the clandestine art known as surreptitious investigation. The demand for Moore's expertise from federal and local investigative agencies had become so time-consuming that Police Commissioner Guido's predecessors had to severely limit the lieutenant's activities outside the police department.

Several days later and with the assistance of Lieutenant Moore's CI, the answer was crystal clear: Both Crown Heights locations had become major sports betting operations. Moreover, those businesses were part of a network of illegal betting franchises wholly controlled by the Gambino crime family.

Moore's information did not just startle Chief Sampson, it made him furious. How could something like this happen, under his nose, in his neighborhood?

Certainly Sampson was well aware that organized crime controls and, indeed, regulates illegal gambling, not just in New York City but across the country. He was, after all, the premier expert in this area of criminal activity. Until this very moment, though, he had believed the conventional wisdom that organized crime bosses generally ignored local, small-time bookmakers, particularly those whose business largely dealt with the numbers racket.

Neither the chief nor anyone else in the illegal gambling wing of law enforcement knew of a meeting of Gambino capos held eighteen months before, when the family made a decision to get out of the narcotics business because it created too much risk, and to expand control over every aspect of illegal gambling, particularly sports betting, wherever it operated. In a remarkably short time, the revenue stream from this source would amply fill the vacuum created when the mob got out of drug trafficking.

Both the liquor store and the grocery store followed roughly the same routine. Bobby Arroyo, Luis's son, and Lance Creighton, the son of Bernice Creighton, the Creighton matriarch and owner of the liquor store, would deliver the betting slips to what appeared to be an abandoned warehouse on Staten Island located near the ferry slip. Part of the warehouse was used as a highly sophisticated wire room — acting as the nerve center of the Gambino sports betting operation in New York City.

A wire room is the depository for all the betting action, the place where all the betting slips are centrally recorded to determine who is entitled to be paid after winning a bet. It also operates to lay off bets with another bookmaking operation somewhere else in the country if the action is too much to handle. For example, if the Giants were a heavy favorite against the Cowboys, the wire room in Staten Island would lay off part of the action. So that if there was an upset and Dallas won, the Gambino wire room wouldn't be wiped out.

This particular wire room in Staten Island was heavily guarded, secured by surveillance equipment and a central alarm system connected to a security company controlled by the family. Since the annual gross at the room was six hundred million dollars, it was closely watched twenty-four hours a day.

On a bright, frigid February afternoon, Connolly and Pressler decided to put their plan into action. The design of the plan was really quite simple: Grab the Arroyo kid with all the betting slips, charging him with maximum felonies that could guarantee him serious prison time, summon his father to the arrest scene, and use the leverage to get the old man to identify the crooked cops. If they got lucky they could be well on the way to dismantling corruption in the 13th. Not bad for a new police commissioner who only took office a month before, in January 1974. Of course, it was not going to be that easy.

As Bobby Arroyo's late-model blue Mercedes neared the entrance ramp on the Brooklyn side of the Verrazano Bridge, an unmarked car cut in front of it, forcing him to the curb. Connolly and Pressler leapt from their car with their guns drawn.

"Show me your hands and freeze," commanded Sergeant Pressler, which upon later reflection he thought sounded a bit too melodramatic. Not so for poor Bobby Arroyo, who wet his pants, immediately before leaving his car with his hands over his head. Arroyo's five-foot-four, 120-pound muscular body shook violently with fear, and his small pockmarked face with its perpetually sad look had turned ashen. He cried convulsively.

"Well, looka here, Inspector," said Pressler, showing Connolly two full shopping bags of betting slips.

"Officer," pleaded Arroyo, "can I call my dad?"

"Who the fuck do you think you're messin' with?" roared Luis Arroyo, his face scarlet with rage. As soon as he received the urgent call from his son, Arroyo raced to the secluded tree-lined service road under the Verrazano bridge on the Brooklyn side. Bobby had been allowed a minute to speak to his father alone. In appearance Luis Arroyo was an older version of his son; Bobby tried to match his father in dress and mannerisms, so much so that his friends and family called him Luisito, or little Luis.

"How much more money do I have to pay

you motherfuckers?" Luis shouted, but he was stopped before completing the sentence by the pain from Pressler's fist crashing against his jaw, sending him hard to the pavement.

Pointing to Connolly, Pressler snarled, "This is a New York City police inspector, you little mutt. Don't you dare use that language with him."

Stunned, Luis Arroyo, with a voice and look showing disgust, said softly, "How much money do I have to pay to how many cops to avoid this bullshit?"

The command center of the police department's Public Morals Administrative Division was located in a closed bus depot in Staten Island. It happened to be no more than two blocks away from the Gambino wire room.

As Luis Arroyo laid out how the operation worked to Connolly, Pressler, Chief Sampson, and Detective Paul Garcia at PMAD headquarters, Connolly could feel the early signs of nausea. He was about to assume command of a police unit that, if you did the math quickly as he did, was substantially corrupt.

On the last day of each month, at a different location, Luis would meet with two police officers assigned to the 13th and give them one hundred one-hundred-dollar bills, or ten thousand dollars.

As soon as Mulvey did the math and realized that crooked cops were receiving annually one hundred and twenty thousand dollars in dirty money, he jumped up and exclaimed, "Please, Inspector, I've heard enough. Whatever you have in mind for me is not something I want to be involved with." Connolly stood and tried to interrupt the young cop, but he persisted. "If you're looking to catch crooked cops, I'm not your guy. They would see through me in a minute —"

"Robert," Connolly went on, "just listen to the rest of this and then to what I have in mind for you. If you still don't think you can help me, that will be the end of it. Fair enough?" Mulvey hesitated, and Connolly continued, "Please sit back down and let me finish."

Mulvey nodded warily and sat back down.

When Inspector Connolly reviewed the personnel roster for the 13th Division, he found that there were currently twenty-four police officers, three sergeants, a lieutenant, a captain, and an unfilled spot for an inspector, which Connolly would assume. In all there were twenty-nine officers. Connolly wondered how many cops were splitting the annual payoff of one hundred and twenty thousand dollars — from Arroyo alone.

Luis Arroyo explained that the money was given in return for all the usual benefits, including accommodation arrests for the misdemeanor of loitering for the purpose of gambling, and, of course, the gambling slips were returned to Arroyo's workers, commonly called runners. Arroyo explained that after the Gambinos took control of his operation and granted him the right to continue bookmaking, his business increased as they steered new customers to his store. The payoff demanded by the cops also increased, from six thousand to ten thousand a month. That this coincided with the Gambinos' decision to assert total control over all gambling operations in their territory was an even greater concern to Chief Sampson. Corrupt cops taking money from local bookmakers was evil enough, but the adjusted amount in the payoffs indicated a direct connection between crooked cops and the mob.

Arroyo explained that the passing of the money was accomplished in a brief meeting where no words were exchanged. Three days before the last day of every month, one of his runners would be told randomly by one of the cops, *"Muchacho, Feliz Navidad."* That "Merry Christmas" meant that Arroyo was to telephone a special number to get the location for the monthly payment. Changing these locations was thought by the crooked cops to ensure against detection.

Luis Arroyo agreed to cooperate with the police investigation in return for the release of his son Bobby, although the betting slips seized from Bobby Arroyo's shopping bags were not returned. The only assurance that Luis Arroyo got was that an effort would be made to keep him from becoming a witness against the crooks if a case developed.

22

People v. Holt,
October 19, 1992

As Larry Green rose from his seat at the defense table to begin his opening statement, he smiled briefly at Steven and then walked toward the jury box. He sensed the futility of his case, but there was nothing in his demeanor that would disclose it. Out of the corner of his right eye he caught a glimpse of some of his law students from Fordham seated in the row reserved for lawyers. He turned to look at them, and with a wink he continued approaching the jury until he was about a foot away from the forewoman, a sixty-something retired banker, neatly attired in a charcoal gray business suit. From the start of the voir dire, Green had been impressed with Ms. Drew's answers to both his and Judge McGowan's questions.

At this point, Green thought about his law

school lecture on the dynamics of an opening statement and how a defense lawyer should deal with a weak case: "One thing you never do is to waive your opening, unless," he would add cynically, "you're prepared to give your client a jailbreak plan. And that's particularly true if the prosecutor has made an effective opening." That certainly wasn't the case with Goss's opening, which was sterile, boring, and distracting. Nonetheless, as Green would caution in class, "even a lousy opening requires a response, but it has to be tailored according to the facts of the case, its strengths and weaknesses, together with any available pragmatic factors."

And so he began.

"May it please the Court, Justice McGowan, Mr. Goss, Madam Forelady, and ladies and gentlemen of the jury." Green's voice was soft and soothing. "The prosecution has brought to this courtroom a case which asks you to convict a much decorated police officer, a man whose record as a corruption fighter earned him the personal and heartfelt gratitude of the mayor of the city of New York and that of the city's police commissioner, and who was awarded the highest medal the New York City police department has to offer. And,

Madam Forelady, given the clear direction you and your colleagues will receive from this learned justice, Judge McGowan, about the burden of proof required of the prosecutor, and Sergeant Holt's right to be presumed innocent, and added to that the paucity of the evidence promised thus far in these proceedings by young Mr. Goss in his address to you, I must tell you that these charges" — Green's voice was now rising steadily — "are among the most outrageous I have confronted in my four decades as a lawyer. Let me add that while for most of my career I have defended people charged with various crimes, I have often acted as a special prosecutor by the appointment of the state's chief administrative judge in a number of counties throughout New York State. And I say to you" — now Larry Green had reached his desired level of staged indignation — "that never before in any county of this state where I have had the honor of appearing, either as a defense attorney or as the prosecutor, have I encountered a case so reckless that it relies wholly on evidence, which will soon be offered to you, that is both gossamer thin and irrevocably flawed."

Suddenly Green whirled around to look at the gallery and those members of his trial advocacy class. He smiled knowingly at his young charges because he understood they would be surprised. After all, for most of the semester at Fordham he'd taught them that rhetoric and argument have no place in an opening statement. "An opening statement is," he would say, "a promise to prove. Save your arguments for summation." He would tell them later today that he taught this division of presentations purposefully throughout his course until the end so as not to confuse them, and that during the last class session, when he would treat them to a few beers or some wine at a local bar, he'd explain that an experienced trial lawyer could, where appropriate, blend in with the promise to prove compelling arguments designed to capture the jury's attention early in the trial. Defending Steven Holt against multiple murder charges demanded, Green would tell them, "that I take the prosecutor's case apart piece by piece and shake it from its baseless foundation!"

Green returned his gaze to the jurors. "What is it that young Mr. Goss has promised you, once you have cleared away his fog of obfuscation? He has Sergeant Holt's gun" — now he shouted in mock surprise — "and lo and behold, the weapon has both the sergeant's fingerprints and palm prints."

Pausing for effect, slowly shrugging his shoulders, and with palms upturned, he threw back his head and cried, "Mr. Goss would have you believe that these conclusions are from forensic technicians who are the successors of the great Sherlock Holmes."

Green walked directly toward Ms. Drew and, leaning over to about a foot away from the forewoman, said in a soft and quiet tone, "Let me be clear, the gun that Sergeant Holt turned over to the Suffolk County detectives is his gun, and it is covered with his fingerprints and palm prints."

"Objection," shouted Assistant District Attorney Goss, "I can't hear what Mr. Green is saying."

"Overruled," Justice McGowan shot back. "Sit down and pay attention!"

"Then," Green continued, "added to this underwhelming offering, Mr. Goss assures you that the bullets from Sergeant Holt's gun and the bullets recovered from the body of each of the victims in this case are a match." Green paced up and down before the jury box, searching the eyes of each juror. He stopped suddenly and then said matter-of-factly, "I assure you that after this so-called forensic proof disintegrates before your very eyes, and is swept away by the cold wind of truth, your course will be clear."

Green turned and appeared to be returning to his seat at counsel's table, but he stopped just before reaching his chair. "Madam Forelady, and ladies and gentlemen of the jury, when you have heard all of this" — his face was now an angry mask, although he kept his voice calm — "you will ask how this flimsy case has taken away this young police officer's liberty for nearly sixteen months, and placed him under the looming fear of a state prison sentence for the rest of his life. You will wonder, sadly —"

Goss exploded from his seat, shouting, "Objection, objection, Your Honor. Counsel knows very well that sentencing and pretrial release conditions are not part of the jury's responsibility."

Green, wearing a Cheshire Cat smile, remained standing, awaiting the court's ruling.

Judge McGowan rose slowly and, assisted by his high bench, seemed to grow to an awesome size. "You had better understand one thing very clearly, young Mr. Goss. Don't you ever again lecture anyone in my courtroom about the law of this state."

McGowan ripped off his reading glasses angrily and peered down at the youthful prosecutor, who looked terrified. "The law is my domain!" The judge waited to allow his admonition to achieve its full effect. "Moreover," he continued, "for whatever period of time that Mr. Green has remaining in his opening address to this jury, you are to stay in your seat and you are not to utter so much as a sound. Am I clear?"

At first Goss, stunned, didn't reply. McGowan, whose voice until now had been measured and level, raised it and asked, "Do you understand me?"

The young assistant DA rose, unsteady on shaking legs, and spoke softly, "Yes, Your Honor."

Judge McGowan took his seat and, turning to the jury, said, "Now, members of the jury, Mr. Green very well knows, and I suspect even young Mr. Goss knows, that punishment is my obligation, not yours, and so you must not consider it, any more than you can consider the manner in which Sergeant Holt is being detained. Neither issue may be considered by you in arriving at your verdict."

Judge McGowan then addressed Larry Green. "Now, Mr. Green, please try to resist the urge to demonstrate your vast experience as a trial attorney by engaging in this kind of tactic."

Green rose immediately and, with a polite bow, said, "Of course, Your Honor. I will respect your wishes. And now, if I may, I am about done."

McGowan nodded, and Green continued. "When you think about this case, with all of its ramifications to the victims, whose lives were snuffed out, to their families, and their indescribable suffering, and how this young sergeant has been punished, you will wonder about the meaning of those words which sit high over Judge McGowan's bench; the true meaning of the ancient command of Deuteronomy, 'Justice, justice, thou shalt pursue.' But no matter how you conclude those words apply to the prosecutor in this case, I am entirely confident that you will heed their profound direction, and that you will follow the learned charge on the law by Judge McGowan to reach a just verdict. And when you do, I know that you will find Steven Robert Holt not guilty. Thank you."

As Green walked to his seat, he knew that his opening statement was good theater but lacking in substance, because there was none. He also knew that it was the only thing he had to offer. He would put his hopes on Ms. Drew or Mrs. Steinberg or just one of the others to hang the jury!

23

The Plan,
February, 1974

"You want to take a break, Robert?"

"No, sir, Inspector, I'd like to hear more," Mulvey replied.

"Good," said Connolly, "because now it becomes fascinating."

The Friday following Arroyo's agreement to cooperate, he was informed by one of his runners that some cops had called with their familiar greeting, *"Feliz Navidad,"* followed by the instruction that the meeting would be at the main public library in Brooklyn, located in Grand Army Plaza. That plaza, designed as a replica of the Arc de Triomphe in Paris, was built as a monument to the soldiers who fought for the North in the Civil War.

The instructions directed that the meeting take place at the last table in the law research section and that Arroyo bring a Nike box in a brown paper bag. This last instruction seemed to Inspector Connolly and the others to be right from the plot of a cheap spy movie. Luis explained that whatever was used to transport the ten thousand dollars would be exchanged for an empty duplicate container brought to the meeting by the cops.

Chief Sampson, Inspector Connolly, and Sergeant Pressler agreed that it was time to meet with representatives of the Brooklyn district attorney.

The evidence developed so far in the investigation was brought to ADA Kenneth J. Rattigan, chief of the Rackets Bureau in the Brooklyn DA's office, by the district attorney's new detective squad commander, Captain Sean J. Nevins. Chief Sampson told Nevins some of the facts and asked him to set up a meeting with Rattigan.

By tradition, each of the five district attorneys was assigned a squad of New York City detectives who worked from the DA's office. Since these detectives typically investigated organized crime and allegations of police corruption, they were supervised by each DA's rackets chief. Throughout the years these squads and their commanders were often recommended by the political bosses in each county, but shortly after his appointment as police commissioner, Guido decided to appoint squad commanders of unquestioned integrity, replacing some of the hacks who owed their assignment to Democratic political bosses. The commissioner wanted these commanders to be jointly chosen by him and the district attorney to cement the relationship between the city's five prosecutors and the NYPD so that there could be a coordinated strategy to eliminate police corruption. It was an inspired idea, which did not take long to yield positive results.

Kenny Rattigan was not only the chief of Brooklyn's Rackets Bureau. He was Brooklyn DA Buddy Cooper's confidant. When Commissioner Guido suggested his idea of a partnership of appointment between the DAs and him, he did it over a drink with Rattigan. Kenny thought it was a great innovation.

Guido then asked, "Any ideas who your boss would want?"

"Absolutely," Rattigan responded. "We'd want Nevins."

Guido, in his comic Brooklynese — most people didn't know whether it was feigned or real — replied, "Hey, Kenny, are you fuckin' nuts? Nevins is a straight guy, but he's a fuckin' loose cannon."

So Chief Sampson, Connolly, Pressler, and Squad Commander Nevins filled the musty, tiny corner room occupied by Brooklyn Rackets Chief Kenneth Rattigan. At thirty-five, with a thin, pallid face and soft brown hair, Rattigan was an even six feet with a body so underweight that his business suit appeared two sizes too big and his white dress shirt and striped tie hung so loosely that people would focus on his huge Adam's apple. Rattigan looked so young that he was often mistaken for one of the baby-faced detectives assigned to the DA's squad. His annoying chain-smoking filled his little office with a constant cloud and a stench that gagged most nonsmokers. His attitude in dealing with investigators who brought cases to his bureau was "No bullshit!" Kenny had a knack of evaluating cases and making a decision to move quickly or shut them down. From what he'd been told so far about this new case, Rattigan was salivating.

The plan of action they discussed demanded surprise. They concluded that the most effective way to get a true picture of the extent of corruption in the 13th Division was to get one of the two

13th Division pickup cops who met Luis Arroyo at the Grand Army Plaza library to flip. But what could the police department offer a cop who decided to turn against his co-conspirators?

Chief Sampson, who raised the question, answered it himself. "Get the DA to agree not to ask the judge for a prison sentence?"

Rattigan thought for a moment and then replied, "That's worth shit, Virgil. All these humps really care about is their pension. They know damn well that judges don't send them to jail, so there's no reason to come with us."

Rattigan now paused for effect and counterproposed something he knew very well ran against the grain of every procedure held so dearly by the police department. Before this meeting, he had cleared it with District Attorney Cooper, whose parting words were "Well, Kenny, we will soon find out if the cops are serious."

Rattigan leaned forward and said, "What if we don't prosecute one of these corrupt cops who agrees to cooperate and you keep him on the job?"

Chief Sampson shot up to a standing position as if struck by lightning but in a measured reply said, "Kenny, this department flushes its garbage. It's no go!"

"Okay, Chief, then we got nothing else to talk about."

Connolly jumped from his chair, shouting, "But Kenny, what about all those crooked scumbags at the 13th Division?"

The confident young prosecutor stood up to play his trump card and, smiling as he stepped over some of the participants crowded in the tiny room, answered, "Hey, guys, go see your friends at the FBI. They do corruption, too!" Looking directly at Chief Sampson, he continued, "The district attorney and I are frankly fed up with this bullshit. You and the rest of your department are in fucking denial. You have the chance of a lifetime to dismantle, destroy, and send to prison an entire vipers' nest of corrupt cops, and instead you want to just pick off one or two. Oh, I am fully familiar with your policy. After the arrest of these two crooks who were dealing with Arroyo, you'll announce to the press that in order to avoid the appearance of impropriety the police commissioner will reassign all of the members of the 13th Division. And you will do this with the full knowledge that the majority of those cops are crooks and that it will not take very long for them to regroup and to steal again. You know damned well, Chief, that this policy is the major reason your department can never be taken seriously when it comes to rooting out corruption. So go play with the feds, because they don't have any problem playing your game. But just remember this, Chief, District Attorney Cooper and I know what you are doing. You are trying to cover up the most extensive corruption scandal in the recent history of your department, so don't think we are going to sit back and say nothing." He closed the door behind him and left for another meeting.

"Kenny," said an obviously concerned District Attorney Cooper, "I hope you know what you're doing, letting a case like this get away."

"Buddy, aren't you fed up with these one-case-at-a-time corruption prosecutions? Every time we lock up a corrupt cop, the union and the department say it's an isolated case, a bad apple in a barrel of good apples. You piss off honest cops and their families, who feel embarrassed that their neighbors will look at them differently. Soon they and all their relatives and friends start to believe the PBA's bullshit, which is embraced by an anachronistic department which has never found a way to clean out its sewer. We have a chance that nobody may ever have again. We've got to show everyone that what we've got here is a fucking outrage; that the cops in one police unit are collecting a share of thousands of dollars. That's something that all the working stiffs in this city including you and me can understand and will not tolerate. And, Boss, if the department doesn't understand that, fuck 'em!"

At 2:30 the following morning, they were all back in Rattigan's cubbyhole of an office. On one side of the desk, sitting next to the rackets chief, were Inspector Connolly, Sergeant Pressler, Detective Garcia, and a scowling Chief Virgil Sampson. On the other side, jammed against the wall, sat Police Officer William Bosco. Bosco didn't really fit the image of a cop, certainly not at this moment. He was a short young man with not much left of his hair. His balding pate ran with nervous sweat. He was wearing a faded green jogging suit that seemed sizes too big for him as he slumped over to one side. His face was chalk white. His fingers were in constant motion, either tapping the sides of the straight-backed wooden chair he sat in or brushing away the perspiration flushing down his narrow face. His body occasionally twitched with fear and then heaved deep sighs as his eyes darted from face to face of the accusers who did not seem to take their eyes off him. Sitting inches away, glaring with his omnipresent unlighted cigar, was Captain Sean Nevins.

Many hours earlier, Bosco and his partner, Officer Benny Perez, met with Luis Arroyo at the library. Bosco placed an empty Nike box in a brown paper bag next to the similar package under the table in the legal reference section. Then, smiling, Detective Perez picked up Arroyo's package and said, *"Muchas gracias, muchacho,"* and both police officers quickly left and headed for their car.

A thorough background analysis of both officers included the facts that Bosco was twenty-eight years old, that he had two children, ages four and two, that his wife, Marie, was three months pregnant, and that they had recently purchased and moved into a one-family house in a suburb in Nassau County. All those personal and financial obligations made Bosco a prime target. By contrast, Perez was a twenty-six-year-old bachelor with a relatively carefree lifestyle who spent his off-hours driving a used MG, usually with a different girlfriend each week.

They decided to flip Bosco.

At about 12:45 Saturday morning, Bosco's

four-year-old Ford station wagon had just crossed over the New York City line into the town of Valley Stream, in Nassau County. Bosco swerved sharply to the right, leaving the Southern State Parkway, onto the cement shoulder, halting at the grass. The reason for his sudden move was two unmarked black vans — one that rammed the rear of his station wagon without warning, and one that pulled next to him and turned a hard right into his vehicle, forcing it from the road.

It seemed to Bosco that more than a dozen people leaped from the two vans with guns drawn, screaming, "Freeze, police!"

Bosco shouted, "I'm a cop," while trying to show his police shield and identification.

"You're shit, dirtbag," came the reply from someone who added, "and show me your fucking hands before I blow your balls off."

Connolly stepped out of the shadows and asked the shaken young officer, "What were you trying to get out of your pocket, son? You nearly got yourself shot."

Bosco answered quickly, "I'm a New York City police officer, sir. I was just trying to identify myself."

"Well, son, I'm Inspector Connolly of the NYPD, and we've been looking for a guy driving a station wagon who robbed a convenience store in Maspeth, Queens, a few hours ago."

"Sir, that couldn't have been me. I'm assigned to the 13th Plainclothes Division in East New York, Brooklyn, and I didn't end my tour until midnight. My partner and at least two bosses can vouch for that."

"Put the guns away," ordered Connolly, to Bosco's instant relief. After Bosco showed his ID, Connolly said, "I'm sorry for the hassle, son, but the creep who held up the store fired three shots over the head of the owner's twelve-year-old daughter, and it would help us if you could come meet the guy so he can see that it wasn't you. You won't mind, now will you?"

"I got no problem, sir, but my wife is pregnant and she expects me home."

"No problem. Sergeant Pressler here will take you to a pay phone on the way to our office," answered Connolly. "We'll have you home in two hours flat."

None of this was anything more than a ruse to take Bosco off his guard for the shock that would follow.

Once they arrived at the Brooklyn district attorney's offices, Nevins suddenly reached into Bosco's waistband and ripped his .38-caliber police special from its holster. He said matter-of-factly, "You're now an ex-cop, you piece of shit!"

Before Bosco could react, Rattigan spoke. "Mr. Bosco." He emphasized the word "Mister" to underscore Bosco's sudden change of status. "I'm Ken Rattigan, and I'm an assistant district attorney and chief of the Rackets Bureau."

It helped that Kenny had been involved in a number of high-profile police corruption cases, which were widely reported by the media. His name was known well enough by the police officers who worked in Brooklyn. He had a reputation for demanding prison sentences for cops convicted of bribery.

"Now, Mr. Bosco, I want you to sit back and close your eyes and imagine for the next half hour or so that you're sitting in the felony part of the State Supreme Court here in Brooklyn, listening to me outline my case against you, which will send you to state prison for about seven years. Do you understand?"

Bosco, who was now drenched in sweat, couldn't answer. Instead he nodded slightly.

Rattigan continued, "Mr. Foreman, and ladies and gentlemen of the jury, last year, inside Brooklyn's main public library at Grand Army Plaza, at the legal research reference section, this defendant, William Bosco, then a New York City police officer, received the sum of ten thousand dollars from a major bookmaker, an associate of the Gambino organized crime family. The money was passed to this defendant in a Nike sneaker box, which was carried in a brown paper bag. The purpose of this extortionate bribe was to pay for police protection which was provided by this defendant and other corrupt police officers assigned to the 13th Plainclothes Division, a unit of the New York Police Department located here in Kings County, in the Crown Heights section of our borough." Rattigan paused for a moment and then said, "As a result of this corrupt activity, a Kings County grand jury has returned an indictment charging this defendant with numerous felony crimes."

As the rackets chief continued laying out a powerful recitation of the evidence, particularly the testimony of witnesses, each section of the facts he promised to prove at trial came as a hammer blow to William Bosco. His hands trembled and he began to feel faint. Interrupting Rattigan, he asked for a glass of water.

Rattigan returned his request with a stern glare and said firmly, "No, you'll wait until

I'm finished!" Rattigan was too experienced a trial lawyer to tolerate a loss of momentum. He would make Bosco keenly aware of the consequences of violating his oath and selling his sacred trust.

As he concluded, Kenneth Rattigan rose dramatically, turned away from Bosco for a moment, paused, and then abruptly faced the distraught young cop and said, "I'm entirely confident, Mr. Foreman and members of the jury, that after you have heard all of this evidence and you have been given the judge's explanation of the law, and after your careful deliberation of the facts and the law of this case, you will return to this courtroom and you will deliver your verdict. When you publish your verdict in this courtroom, you will say clearly and eloquently that William Bosco has brought shame on himself, his wife, and his children and that he has dishonored the police department of the City of New York, because your verdict will be to find him guilty of every count of this indictment."

When Rattigan had finished, he went to the watercooler just outside his office and returned with a cold glass of water, which he offered to Bosco and which was accepted in his shaking hands. Rattigan then sat down and allowed the silence to focus the young cop's attention.

After a few minutes, the rackets chief spoke. "You know, you don't have to go to prison, and you don't even have to give up your job or your pension." At this, Bosco seemed to recover from the shock, and he leaned forward and listened very carefully to Rattigan.

"What you did was disgraceful. You spit on your badge and you brought shame on other police officers, and for what?" Rattigan asked. Now standing, the veins in his neck bulging, he shouted, "A few hundred dollars a month of dirty money!" Bringing his face not more than an inch from Bosco's, he continued, "Have you any dignity left? Do you want to drag yourself out of the gutter?"

Kenneth Rattigan had made his final pitch, one he had used several times before, although he thought this was one of his better ones.

After a pause that completely stilled the tiny room, Bosco said simply, "I've got to talk to my wife, but you gotta tell me what you want me to do."

Rattigan did not respond immediately. Instead, to keep Bosco off balance, which was critical to turning the shaken young cop, he looked up at the ceiling as if deep in thought.

In order to build a prosecutable case, the tried and true maxim is "To catch a thief, you must turn a thief." To turn the thief, everything had to be planned and in place.

So when Rattigan and the others chose Bosco rather than Perez to flip, part of the plan was to dispatch a female detective who was known as PMAD's diplomat. She and her partner were ordered by Chief Sampson to convince Mrs. Bosco that it was in her husband's interest to accompany them to the office of the Brooklyn district attorney. She was told only that William had been arrested for bribery and that she could help him.

"Your wife is in the next room," Rattigan said finally.

Bosco seemed momentarily stunned by the news, but before he could react, Rattigan laid out the deal.

"First you're going to tell us who else is being paid off in the 13th Division, and then you're going to wear a wire and help me send every crooked scumbag to jail." Rattigan's anger unnerved Bosco as the prosecutor carefully laid out each demand. "If you do this, my boss won't prosecute you, and the police commissioner will let you stay on the job until he figures out a way to get you retired. If you don't, then I'm still going to send a scumbag to prison — you! Now go speak to your wife."

Wearing a wire was necessary because even if Bosco agreed to testify against the other thieves, under the law of New York State he was a co-conspirator. His testimony had to be corroborated, meaning that independent evidence had to be produced to support it.

It did not take Marie Bosco very long. When she emerged from the room she said simply but very firmly, "Mr. Rattigan, William will do what you want, and if he does not, he will never again see me or our children."

According to Bosco, twenty-nine members of the 13th Division, over 70 percent, were on the pad. Twenty-nine police officers, including a lieutenant and two sergeants, were receiving monthly payments from the two gambling operations in Crown Heights, Brooklyn.

Mulvey was out of his chair again. "Inspector," he shouted, "good Lord, twenty-nine crooks!"

"Hold it right there, Robert," Connolly hastily replied. "Just wait a few more minutes. I'm certain that when you hear the extent of this corruption, the depth of their evil acts and how they disgraced the reputation of every police officer who was ever privileged to carry the badge of the NYPD, including heroes like Detectives Lewis and Cordo, you will agree that you have no choice but to join me in a historic mission." Connolly thought he was being a bit too theatrical, but from the look on Mulvey's face he knew he'd been persuasive. He watched with disguised satisfaction as Robert once again took his seat.

"And Robert, once you have heard my plan you will understand that when we bring down these vipers, the effect of it will be an avalanche of publicity, which will change the culture in this department that permitted corruption to flourish. We have an opportunity that no one has ever had before, the chance to free this department from institutionalized thievery and to put in place a mechanism which will prevent forevermore a return to the cyclical corruption that has reappeared approximately every twenty years throughout the history of the NYPD."

Connolly certainly believed what he said,

although he knew that seemingly nothing, not even something so dramatic as the arrest, conviction, and imprisonment of so many corrupt cops, could reverse decades of entrenched police corruption. Connolly, of course, couldn't know that his plan would nearly destroy this young sergeant. And he certainly couldn't know that the person who would be given the honor of eliminating the culture of police corruption in the NYPD would not be Mulvey but rather his nephew, Steven Holt.

As Bosco related each detail, the account was both astonishing and shocking. The payments were prorated according to the rank of each officer — for example, a monthly share for each plainclothes cop, a share and a half for each sergeant, and a double share for the lieutenant. In all there were twenty-nine corrupt cops. So the grocery store monthly payment of $12,000 and the liquor store monthly bribe of $7,000 was a combined annual pot of almost $230,000. The pad yielded about $600 a month for each of the twenty-six corrupt police officers, plus $900 for each sergeant, or $1,800 for the two of them, and a double share, or $1,200, for the lieutenant. The monthly total was astounding: a bit less than $19,000. In order to make the shares manageable, they rounded off the money and designated a treasurer to retain the excess, which was divided and distributed on a prorated basis to each cop at the end of each quarter of the year.

They rotated treasurers monthly to protect themselves against temptations that might be too much for any one cop. This arrangement was a result of a problem that developed when one of them who had been the permanent treasurer claimed that his automobile, which had a bag of cash in the trunk containing about $6,000, blew up in a gasoline explosion. The Corporation, which was the name they gave themselves, did not believe their treasurer for a minute, but without any proof, they could only create a procedure to guard against any further calamity. The former permanent treasurer was excluded from the rotation. Of course, their suspicions were confirmed when they learned much later that the wife of their former money handler had treated herself to a new kitchen.

The Corporation met regularly, usually the last Friday night of each month, to discuss a variety of ways to expand their financial interests.

Similar groups were formed in other

plainclothes units around the city, and in time an organizational structure was put in place. An officer wishing to join had to tender corruption credentials that would be checked out during a period of two months. No share would be distributed to the applicant until this process was complete. This procedure was concocted to protect the group against infiltration by Internal Affairs officers or, worse, by the hated and feared cops from the elite group assigned to PMAD.

When department transfers were inevitably made, something over which these thieving groups had no control, a two-months' share would be distributed from the treasury to the departing crook, usually at his or her farewell beer racket. This way a crooked cop lost nothing.

When Inspector Connolly had finished recounting this shocking story of the extent of this pervasive corruption in just one police unit, he let a period of silence settle in. He watched Mulvey carefully until the young police officer dropped his head to his chest and stared at the floor beneath his chair. Mulvey, uncertain of what Connolly wanted, began to sweat as panic overtook him.

"Robert." Connolly finally broke the tension. "This assignment is the turning point of my career. It will either make or break me, and that's why I need your help so much. I also understand that what I am about to propose to you may well be too much to ask, so if you refuse, it will not diminish in the least my respect or affection for you."

Connolly explained that Bosco had agreed to do whatever was necessary to collect incriminating conversations against every crooked cop in the division, but the inspector did not trust, as he put it, "this corrupt little weasel for an instant."

He had a plan to guarantee a successful prosecution. First, he would have Bosco wear a wire for a period of six months, gathering evidence against as many of the crooks as he could. Next he would, with Kenny Rattigan's help, get a court-ordered listening device planted at each meeting place chosen by the Corporation. Recorded conversations from four monthly meetings, together with all the other conversations gathered by Bosco, should ensure that future meetings of the Corporation would be in Attica State Prison.

Just to be sure, Connolly's trump card would be Robert Mulvey. Robert would spend six months at an assignment chosen by PMAD, getting his corruption credentials, and he would then be transferred to the 13th Division. Following his two months of initiation, during which his corruption credentials would be cleared, he would take his place at the table at a regular meeting of the Corporation. Just two meetings recorded in Mulvey's presence would finish off the Corporation. The plan would lock Bosco in because if he reneged, Rattigan could send him to prison until he was a very old man. If any of the defense lawyers tried to discredit Bosco, they would have to face the undercover officer Robert Mulvey, whose unblemished record would make it very unlikely that the corrupt police officers would be found not guilty. If the cops' lawyers forced Mulvey to testify, and if any of these crooks were convicted, Rattigan would demand and probably get maximum state prison sentences.

Mulvey stood, and Connolly watched him guardedly for a very long period of silence. Finally Mulvey said, "Boss, you have been an inspiration to me, someone I admire and respect. I have serious doubts about this, but I'll do whatever you say."

"Thank you, son," Connolly replied. "In just a minute I'm going to introduce you to the man who'll be your direct contact throughout the operation." Connolly pushed a buzzer near his telephone, and a moment later Pressler entered the room. Mulvey stood up immediately, coming to attention.

Pressler smiled and said gruffly, "You don't need to stand up for me, young man. I'm just a sergeant." Now it was Mulvey's turn to smile, and at the same time to be relieved because he recognized Pressler as the academy instructor he so much admired. He thought to himself that if Pressler was going to be his contact it would turn out alright.

"You take this number." Pressler handed him a folded piece of paper. "If I don't pick up right away, I'll be automatically paged, and I'll be back to you almost immediately."

Mulvey looked at the number and then said, "Thank you, sir."

Connolly put his hand out and shook Mulvey's and said, "Sergeant Pressler will be in touch with you shortly. Now you can return to your command." Pressler shook Mulvey's hand, and the youngster quickly left the room.

"Well, what do you think, Bernie?"

"He's perfect, Boss."

Things often don't work out as well as they are planned, but neither Connolly nor

Pressler could have predicted that at this point. The plan seemed like a sure winner.

24

People v. Holt,
October 21, 1992

Goss's prosecution proceeded much as expected. David Rapp, now twenty-five years old, and his former fiancée, Alyson Keeler, who had just turned twenty-four, testified about their gruesome discovery of the bodies of Hiram and Ramon Rodriguez on the snow-covered beach of Robert Moses State Park. Goss led each through every detail, emphasizing in particular the large holes rimmed by dried blood observed by them on the left temple of each victim. It was a predictable attempt by a prosecutor to highlight the violence.

At this point an incident occurred that began to reveal Goss's strategy and produced the first serious round of combat. As David Rapp described the wounds, a piercing scream erupted from the second row on the jury side of Judge McGowan's courtroom. Rosa Rodriguez, the mother of the two victims, who had flown from Puerto Rico to be present at the trial, began to wail convulsively. The best efforts of the female court officers could not console her, and Judge McGowan ordered a brief recess.

The jury left the courtroom. Larry Green waited for their departure, then stood and said, "Your Honor, may we meet in your chambers?"

McGowan, motioning to Assistant District Attorney Goss, replied, "Of course, Mr. Green. Come along, Mr. Goss."

The parties had barely entered Judge McGowan's inner office before he exploded, "Just what are you trying to pull in my courtroom, young man?"

Goss's face turned ashen. "I deeply resent that, Judge. What are you implying?"

"You know damned well what you are doing. By the way, who paid Mrs. Rodriguez's airfare from Puerto Rico, and who is financing her expenses while she's here?" McGowan demanded.

"We paid for her airfare and we are paying her expenses, Your Honor, and what's wrong with that?"

"Nothing," McGowan shouted, "except that it means that you have control of her in this county and you should control her emotions so that this jury is not unduly influenced. If you cannot, then don't bring her to this court again. Is that clear? Because if it isn't and there is another outburst, I'm going to hold you in contempt and you can try this case by day and spend your evenings in the county jail until this case has concluded. Is that clear?"

All Goss could say, in a voice barely heard, was "Yes, Your Honor."

David Rapp concluded his direct testimony without incident and without the presence of Mrs. Rodriguez. When Goss was finished, he turned and said to Larry Green, "You may examine."

Green rose and, looking first at the jury and then to the judge, announced what trial lawyers agree is perhaps the most difficult thing for a lawyer to say. "Your Honor, I have no questions of this young man." It was the same tactic Green used after Alyson Keeler finished her testimony. No purpose could be served by keeping Rapp or Keeler on the stand other than to confirm the accuracy of their horrifying discovery.

After the two youngsters had concluded, Judge McGowan noted that it was now past four o'clock. "Time," he said, "to give the jury a well-earned respite."

The jurors began leaving the room.

Now Judge McGowan asked, "Mr. Goss, what are your plans for tomorrow?"

"I plan to have the coroner, some police witnesses, and a ballistics expert, and that should be all," Goss replied.

Green, instinctively smelling a rat, asked, "May I inquire whether the prosecutor has plans to call anyone not currently on the witness list he has supplied?"

Goss, whose unpleasant exchanges with Green had reached a level of animosity where he would respond only to the judge, answered, "I have no plans at this time to expand the witness list, Your Honor."

McGowan glowered. "Very well, young Mr. Goss, but I warn you, don't play games in my courtroom."

"But, Your Honor —" Before Goss could say another word, Judge McGowan had left the bench.

Green turned to Goss and said, "Hey, have you ever tried a case before this judge? As a matter of fact, when was the last time you tried a felony case?"

Goss had no intention of giving him an answer, but it did not matter, because Green did not plan to stay to hear one.

25

Washington Heights, Manhattan, the 34th Precinct,
1974

Connolly had decided before speaking with Mulvey that if he agreed to help he would be placed in a police precinct known for its corruption.

His assignment to the 34th Precinct in Washington Heights, in the northern part of the borough of Manhattan, was done easily enough. No one paid much attention to ordinary transfers, and the fact that Police Officer Mulvey was leaving the prestigious Emergency Service Unit for a patrol assignment could be explained away as nothing more than his position high up on the sergeant's list, and his obvious interest in getting some time in the field before his promotion.

Mulvey replaced another police officer, who was transferred to the 60th Precinct in

Coney Island, Brooklyn, a place notorious for the high incidence of driving-while-intoxicated arrests and so a place where considerable money could be collected by a two-officer team cruising in a patrol car. The reassigned police officer, like Mulvey, had been placed in Washington Heights as part of Lieutenant Moore's network of anticorruption moles, held in reserve for the right assignment.

Mulvey's assignment immediately gave him the opportunity to make some cash protecting a local Dominican entrepreneur who ran a cockfight for the neighborhood. The cockfight he would protect in exchange for a monthly payment would later secure his passport to the 13th Division.

Washington Heights for years had been the landing point for émigrés from the Dominican Republic. They brought their tradition of Christianity, family values, and hard work with them, along with the poverty caused by displacement and few employment opportunities. For the majority of the Dominicans, their dream, like most other immigrants', was to get work, any kind of work, put in long hours supporting themselves and any family that came with them from the Dominican Republic, and send money regularly back home to those members of the family unable to join them. Their language presented the usual barrier until they could learn some English to get along. During their off-hours, particularly on weekends, they looked for some diversion, and cockfighting was their favorite. It was their spectator sport of choice, and when it was combined with their favorite *cerveza fría,* it made for a pleasurable evening out with friends. However, there was one significant problem, and that was that cockfighting was against the law in New York State.

The combatants, gamecocks, were bred for physical strength, for speed, and for their killer instinct. Usually their feathers were of various bright colors. They had long spurs on their legs, and their breeders trimmed down these spurs and attached sharpened artificial spurs made of steel or brass over them. These weapons were used to tear at the flesh of the opponent until death ended the pain and misery caused by the violence.

The fight took place in an enclosed pit. Before the fight began, the handlers held the birds close to each other and permitted them to peck at each other with their beaks until they were angry enough to fight. Spectators who surrounded the pit bet money with the bookmaker, who was the proprietor of what was often a factory-sized floor of an abandoned warehouse.

To ensure against any interruption by the local police, an appropriate bribe was agreed to by the police officer assigned to the sector where the arena was located. The payoff ranged from a flat fee of $250 to, for the more creative cops, a percentage of the house receipts, which could yield up to $700 or $800 on a good night. While the $250 was not a particularly good score, it did provide the credentials that would be used to gain other corrupt opportunities for assignments such as antihijacking squads, where dishonest police officers were paid to look the other way when a truckload of liquor was seized, or as a springboard to a choice assignment in the plainclothes divisions.

The cockfight pit was run by D'Ario Santiago and Petie Perez, who had become Santiago's main man. Perez was the front man who, among other things, handled the payoff arrangements with the cops assigned to the 34th Precinct. Petie was also working off a drug sale, which could have sent him to state prison for a term up to life, so he was cooperating fully with Lieutenant Moore. Among the dozen or so crooks with badges who were part of the approximately

175 police officers assigned to the precinct, none would question why Mulvey was allowed to catch the cockfight. In their business, you didn't ask questions if you wanted to survive. So Mulvey was quietly assigned to the sector covering the cockfight, and Petie Perez arranged the appropriate payment for him. While Perez worked out the details of the payment, Santiago, who trusted no one, designated himself to make the actual payment of the bribe. He liked, as he would say openly, the feeling of owning a cop.

Mulvey detested taking the dirty money. Although it was limited to one fifteen-minute period several times a month and it was a charade, he loathed the thought of meeting D'Ario Santiago, who always reeked of cheap wine and garlic and would toss a filthy brown paper bag at Mulvey with a big smile and a "Here, *amigo.*"

It did not matter to Mulvey that immediately after the transfer of the money he would go to the lot in the rear of the warehouse, where one of Lieutenant Moore's officers would count the money in front of him and have him sign a receipt. It did not help Robert Mulvey to know that the corrupt money would be vouchered for the day when that slob Santiago and his creeps would have their operation raided and shut down and that they would be locked up for many, many years. What filled Mulvey's recurring and restless thoughts while he tried to sleep the night before each money transfer was that this piece of shit thought he was just another crooked cop who could be bought for a few hundred bucks.

He got out of bed, found the piece of paper he got from Pressler, and dialed the number. After several unanswered rings he hung up and waited for the promised return call. When it hadn't come fifteen minutes later, he repeated the call. When that went unreturned, he found a bottle of vodka under the sink in the kitchen, poured a long drink, and sat on his bed wondering what was going on. He drained the glass and tried to fall asleep.

The monthly meeting of the Corporation was set for the basement of Officer Sharon Mickens's brownstone located in an upscale part of Bedford-Stuyvesant. Sharon's years on the pad enabled her to socialize with this moneyed class that included physicians, stockbrokers, lawyers, and entrepreneurs. Officer Mickens deflected questions about her apparent wealth with a story of a huge inheritance from an uncle in Panama.

For six months, Detective Bosco tape-recorded dozens of conversations involving corrupt payoffs to the police officers assigned to the 13th Division. These bribes were paid to the cops by the bookmakers they protected. The payments were always made to a pair of cops, partners working a particular investigative shift. By prearrangement, Bosco was carefully moved to fill in when one of the regular partners had a day off, was ill, or was on vacation. Soon, without attracting any particular notice, Bosco became the division's "relief partner." The subtlety with which this was accomplished was lost on the crooks, who were more interested in their payments than concerned about being detected. It was, of course, a fatal mistake. The plan that moved Bosco from cop to cop was enormously successful. Over the six-month period not only did he capture on tape virtually every corrupt cop assigned to the division, recording each one receiving a payoff from a bookie, but he recorded six monthly meetings of the Corporation. All this evidence provided sufficient probable cause for Rackets Chief Kenneth Rattigan to seek a court order for eavesdropping devices to be installed at Mulvey's debut at a future meeting of the

Corporation. The next meeting's location, the basement of Police Officer Mickens's brownstone, was turned into a sound stage, with listening microphones backed up by recording equipment everywhere. Seven different listening devices had been planted by a special unit of Lieutenant Moore's undercover squad. Not a syllable would be lost, not a whisper unheard.

Mulvey rose before dawn the morning of his first meeting as a full-fledged member of the Corporation. He had patiently waited out his two-month period at the 13th Division before his acceptance was granted. Some of the Corporation members had quietly checked out his credentials with their buddies at the 34th Precinct in Washington Heights. Richie Goodwin, one of the plainclothes cops at the 13th Division, made it clear to Mulvey that not only was he satisfied to have him as a colleague but he was very impressed with reports about how he handled his "cockfighting protection racket," as Goodwin called it. Still, as Mulvey dragged himself from bed that morning dreading his first formal sit-down with the crooked cops he despised, he had a knot in his stomach.

Richie Goodwin had a nose like Cyrano de Bergerac's and large, grossly deformed ears, and a scrawny body barely five feet eight inches tall. He was known by everyone as "the Weasel." His hair was thick with pomade and combed into a comical pompadour. If that wasn't enough, his body gave off a stench that could fill a room. Goodwin had not always been a slob. Prior to his assignment to the 13th Division he had worked for eighteen months in the Narcotics Bureau as an undercover cop. He played up his part as a mostly stoned junkie as if it were a movie role. He grew a beard, lost thirty pounds, and got used to sleeping in the street on some cardboard he kept hidden during the day. Without benefit of any regular bathing, his acquired filth became part of his act. He even occasionally peed in his pants so the smell of dried urine filled the air around him.

He was also a thief. His operation was really quite simple. He teamed up with his partner, Police Officer Billy McGinn. Goodwin would buy some drugs from a local drug dealer. Afterward he'd radio McGinn, who together with his team would swoop down on the dealer and arrest him. They would confiscate all the dealer's drugs and money. They kept all the money and most of the drugs, which were divided equally at the end of their tour among Goodwin,

McGinn, and two other members of the team. For example, if they seized fifty bags of heroin or crack, they'd voucher ten as evidence and divide up the forty. Thereafter they would resell the drugs to some of the street junkies they worked with regularly for cash and information about other drug dealers they'd set up for a score on another day. When the defendant was taken to court, McGinn or one of the other two police officers would tell the assistant district attorney that they realized they had made a lousy search, that they got too anxious and really didn't have probable cause. The case would then be dismissed. On other occasions they would tell the prosecutor that the defendant was a cooperator or was a stoned-out junkie who needed drug treatment. They employed a variety of schemes resulting in the defendant being cut loose. All of this had the effect of producing a happy junkie who would never tell anyone that he or she was ripped off. To avoid creating a pattern that could be discovered, they were always careful never to use the same assistant prosecutor more than once. During his eighteen months as a narc, Richie Goodwin pulled in thousands of dollars, which gave him sufficient credentials to earn him membership in the 13th Division's Corporation.

The Weasel probably would have remained longer in the Narcotics Bureau except for an incident that began as an affair of the heart and ended in the arrest of a team of narcotics detectives operating very much like Goodwin's crew. Unfortunately for the NYPD, Goodwin's corruption cell was not unique in the Narcotics Bureau. There were small, very controlled nests of corruption in every part of the Narcotics Bureau in every county of New York City. The demise of one of these began in the bar at Forlini's, the fabled gathering place of the power brokers of the criminal justice system in Manhattan. Twenty-six-year-old Blossom Zim, an associate attorney for the Legal Aid Society, was on her first date with Aaron Stevens, a thirty-year-old assistant in the office of the New York County DA. They were having a few break-the-ice drinks before adjourning to Forlini's dining room, and they were talking shop.

"You know, Aaron," Blossom began, "your office is too much a bunch of hardasses when it comes to dealing with junkies. Lucky for us that some of the narcs have the guts to admit making a mistake."

"Like what?" Stevens responded cautiously.

"Well, just in the last few months," Zim

explained, "there's a team of narcs operating around Times Square who have admitted to me twice that they were involved in bad searches and told me that they jumped the gun without having probable cause."

"What did you do with that information?" Stevens inquired. "And what do these cops look like?"

After describing the team of narcs in some detail, Blossom continued, "Well, of course, I told one of the assistant DAs what happened, and after it was confirmed by the cops the case was dismissed. But why do you ask about the police officers?"

"Because those guys told me the very same thing last month. So I wonder why they would have made three tainted searches in just a few months. It sounds fishy to me."

"Now, that's the problem with prosecutors," Blossom huffed. "You are just too goddamned suspicious."

"Or maybe you guys are too naïve," Stevens quickly rejoined. "But what the hell," he added, "let's have some dinner." He said this not wishing to blow the first date, but he would surely look into these coincidences the next day.

It did not take much effort to uncover the scheme that Narcotics Detective Brian O'Hurley and his two buddies had cooked up, and once Internal Affairs got the co-operation of a dozen or so junkies it was over for at least that collection of crooks. Less than six months later each police officer pled guilty and received several years in the upstate prison system. Of course, long before that Richie Goodwin used his contacts and was on the way to the 13th Division to steal again. But there was no real need for haste, because Internal Affairs concluded its investigation with O'Hurley and his friends, refusing to believe that there was a pattern of corruption.

"Hey, Mulvey, whaddaya think?" the Weasel asked in his whiny nasal voice, leaning close to Mulvey. "D'ya have any way of getting a buddy of mine that cockfight deal?"

Mulvey held his breath, fearing serious danger to his health if he inhaled his environment. "No, Richie," he quickly responded as he began to walk away. Then he said vaguely, "They already have lined someone up."

"Okay, I understand," replied the Weasel. "I just thought I could pick up some quick bucks as a finder's fee!" Somehow Mulvey was not shocked, but he quickly became depressed as the Weasel shouted after him, "I'll see you tomorrow night at the meetin'.

I'll sit next to you and sorta let you know what's goin' on."

That wasn't what was troubling Mulvey this morning, though. It had more to do with the apprehension he felt having to sit among a bunch of crooks who thought that he was just like them. He knew how dirty he'd feel, the same way he felt when D'Ario Santiago would throw him the dirty brown bag filled with money after a cockfight in Washington Heights. He decided to call Shannon Kelly. She'd know what to do. She always did.

"Robert," Shannon said, trying to wake up, "do you know it's not even six o'clock?"

"I know, sweetheart, and I'm sorry," he replied timidly, "but I need your advice. I just can't sleep."

"Alright," she said sympathetically. "I'll put on some coffee. Come on over, you big baby!" Shannon was the youngest of six children and the only girl, but as she reached young adulthood and trained to be a special agent with the Federal Bureau of Investigation, she soon became the commanding presence in her home, particularly after her mother died. Her father and all the boys constantly sought out Shannon for advice, sometimes for the simplest problem. Handling Robert Mulvey as she did so well came with years of training and experience.

He sat on her overstuffed brown leather sofa. At first he just studied his shoes, and after a few minutes he crossed his long legs and folded his arms. Then he held his right elbow in his left hand and cupped his right hand under his chin. He said nothing for nearly ten minutes.

Finally Shannon broke the silence. "Hey, friend, what do you say you drink that coffee I just put in front of you and let's you and I talk about this problem." She waited for that to sink in. "Otherwise," she added defiantly, "I'm going back to bed. It is after all Saturday." Now Shannon stood as if to threaten, and Mulvey began to speak.

"I can't go through with this. I don't want to sit in that room for five minutes with that group of lowlifes and let them think that I'm a piece of shit like them."

"Sure, honey," she replied. Then, carefully selecting her words, she proceeded. "It's your call, completely your decision, but you ought to think about a few things before you make up your mind. Like how you have already invested eight months of your life to infiltrate these dirtbags and that you just have two meetings to attend. And that you've already been through the roughest part: dealing with lice like that Santiago.

And that you are so very close to breaking the back of one of the most shameful corruption conspiracies in the history of the NYPD." He listened very attentively, as he always did when she gave advice. "Besides," she continued, "didn't you promise Inspector Connolly that you'd see this thing through?"

"But he's got Bosco, and that crooked bum's gonna walk away from all of this with his badge and his pension because he has everyone on tape."

"Sure," she rebutted quickly, "and any defense lawyer worth his salt will destroy Bosco and show him up to the jury for the rat he is. No, Robert, you are Connolly's ace in the hole. You can't take that chance and allow these crooks to be acquitted." Shannon paused for a moment and then used her strongest argument. "What does it matter what those worthless bastards think of you? You know who you are, and I certainly know who you are, and soon every cop in your department and every citizen of this city will know who you are. You put your life on the line in Washington Heights for half a year. Robert, you are a hero, and what's more you have been chosen, given an opportunity that is so rare in life. There is a reason why you go to Mass every day. It has led to a calling that you cannot ignore."

A full ten minutes passed before he finally responded. "Alright," Robert said quietly, and then got up to leave. "But can I come back here later tonight after the meeting?"

Shannon winked and threw him a devilish smile. "Sure, but don't forget the champagne. I've got a feeling we will have lots to celebrate about!"

The meeting in Police Officer Sharon Mickens's basement started typically late for a police affair. The beer immediately flowed, and Sharon had chosen a special bottle of Sancerre, which she planned to share with the only other female police officer on the Corporation, Tina Trumboli. Sharon and Tina reminded most people who met them for the first time of Stevie Wonder's near-legendary ballad "Ebony and Ivory." Both young women were in their late twenties and had magnificently proportioned figures, with beautiful, almost angelic faces, high cheekbones, lovely almond-shaped eyes, and small but sculptured noses. Their sensuous mouths were drawn up into a perpetual grin, and when they smiled their teeth were gleaming white. They looked very much alike. Even their skin color wasn't all that different. Sharon's was a light milky brown, and Tina had perfectly blended olive-colored skin derived from her Mediterranean roots. Needless to say, they were the object of numerous failed attempts at conquests by their brother police officers. They shared the dream of the perfect score, a husband with unlimited wealth, but in the meantime they shared another passion: They would make as much money as they could by protecting the bookmakers operating within the confines of the 13th Division.

Tonight's meeting of the Corporation would have its full board present, all twenty-two members. Mulvey marveled at them, so many cops with a collective dedication to greed. He glanced quickly at each, one by one, trying to determine if there was anything about them that would suggest that they were out of the ordinary. But there was nothing. Only twenty white males and two females, one black and one white, whose dress, looks, or mannerisms gave no clue about them. It was only when they spoke, as they did frequently, about their obsession with money that the enormity of their conspiracy was so startling — particularly to Robert Mulvey, whose belief in the honor of the badge was as deep as was his faith in God.

They sat around a huge oak table, comfortably lounging in burgundy-colored upholstered leather chairs. Long ago Sharon Mickens decided that if her basement was to be the Corporation's monthly meeting room, its décor and appointments should appropriately reflect the style of a corporate boardroom. Accordingly she assessed an amount of money from the pad before its distribution to the cops, enough to buy a proper conference table, the matching chairs, the floor-to-ceiling thick velvet drapes, and the massive wet bar and full kitchen. Across the room at the opposite end from the kitchen was a comfortable seating area with two large corduroy-covered couches and four large matching club chairs facing a forty-inch television screen. It had what Sharon thought must be the look of an executive lounge. While the consumption of alcohol in all forms was encouraged, smoking was strictly prohibited.

The reason for the full house this evening was that there was a particularly significant agenda. The Corporation would formally consider Robert Mulvey for membership, which was perhaps the real reason he was so apprehensive. They were also going to discuss whether the time had come to demand that the pad payments by the bookies be increased, something that had not occurred in nearly eighteen months. Finally, Sharon had suggested she had her own item, which she refused to disclose in advance. She did say that it was so important that it required the attention of all twenty-two members.

The Corporation's meeting was chaired by Police Officer Tom Huss, an eighteen-year-veteran of the job. Although he was outranked by Lieutenant Franks and Sergeants Bowers and White, he had been elected chair because he held an MBA from John Jay College of Criminal Justice. A consensus had been reached long ago by the membership that they needed a good numbers person as chairman. Besides, Huss had all the attributes of a leader.

Huss, an imposing, trim, and athletic six-footer, was, despite his age — he was nearing forty — the mainstay wide receiver for the Finest, the NYPD's football team. He was also the team's captain. With sun-bleached, curly blond hair and deepset blue eyes, he had the perpetual tan of a Southern California surfer. He had a preference for casual clothes — jeans and polo shirts — which made him look considerably younger than his age. When he walked into a room, the way he carried himself exuded charisma, and whenever he directed a Corporation meeting to come to order, there was immediate silence. From the moment he stepped into Sharon's basement with his long, determined strides, wearing his custom-made boots of alligator leather, no one would question who was in charge.

Robert was fortunate enough to squeeze into a seat between Sergeant White and Officer Tina Trumboli, leaving a somewhat miffed Weasel Goodwin on the opposite side of the conference table looking particularly glum.

The first item, the proposed increase in the pad, was introduced by Sergeant Bowers. His case was built on the recent across-the-board police raise negotiated by the city with the police unions. "It's an outrage," he fumed. "We got fuckin' sold out. Nothin' in the first year with 2 percent in year two and 3 percent in the last year for a total of a measly 5 percent over the three years. If we don't increase the pad, that kind of raise won't even cover the cost of living."

A bemused Mulvey watched a spirited debate ensue that considered the pros and cons of increasing the percentage of a shakedown. It continued for more than an hour before Chairman Huss raised his hand and said calmly, "I think it's time for a vote, but just remember this fact. It wasn't that long ago that we had twenty-nine members on the pad splitting nearly nineteen grand a month. Today, because of transfers and retirements, we're down to just twenty-two unless we add Mulvey. The bottom line is our net take, which I remind you is tax free. It's a hell of a lot more than it was before, and none of the bookies are complaining. Why risk making one of these bums an enemy? Right now if they get banged by PMAD there's no incentive for them to cooperate against us. But if we get too hungry, who knows what they will do?"

It was the winning argument, and a vote wasn't needed.

Next Sharon's hand shot up. Huss eyed her sharply and asked, "You want to speak about this some more?"

"No, Tommy," she purred, leaning forward from across the table, revealing a tantalizing cleavage from her tight dark brown cashmere sweater. "But since we're talking about the pad, I'd like to go to my item before we consider Mulvey. It relates to both the pad and the need to discuss new members."

At this point, Tina Trumboli put her left hand over Mulvey's right, which she found resting on his knee, squeezed it, and whispered in his ear, "Just watch this, sweetie."

Mulvey stirred uncomfortably and quickly put his hand on the table. He thought that Tina was taking too much time removing hers from his knee. She finally took her hand away but then placed it on the table near Robert's, which was quivering slightly. She giggled softly and whispered, "Don't worry, babe, I'm not trying to seduce you." She then added, "At least not for now." Mulvey could feel his cheeks redden and kept looking straight ahead without even thinking of answering Tina.

"Very well, Sharon, lay it out."

"Well, for openers," she began forcefully, "look around this room and what do you see?" The question was rhetorical, and she answered herself immediately. "Everyone here is a white male except for me and Tina, and I'm the only black cop. There is something wrong about this."

Mulvey watched in utter disbelief for another hour during a heated discussion, which at times came very close to acrimony. At its start, most of the boys, as they referred to themselves, thought Sharon's complaints were not made seriously, so there were heckles and catcalls. Those stopped abruptly when Sharon stood up and shouted, "No, dammit, you listen to me. There are three other black cops in the

13th who are just as anxious to make a few bucks on the side. Why can't these guys get in? And please don't tell me it's their skin color that keeps them out. Even if you think it, you better not say it."

This she uttered with a level of defiance that made Huss uneasy. He jumped in. "No, Sharon, this discussion will not be about color but about economics. It's about, Why should we shrink our take?"

"Okay," she shot back, "then why are we thinking about Mulvey, because he's white?"

"Not at all, Sharon. Mulvey has credentials." At this Robert cringed as he thought, *There, it's said; I'm a crook just like them.* Then all he could think of was how incredible this all would sound when it was played at the trial of these criminals.

Finally Huss ended the discussion by agreeing to an interview process that included Mickens, Trumboli, and the two sergeants. Huss would act as the chairman. The panel was given the task of checking out each of the three black male officers currently assigned to the 13th Division to determine if they were ever involved in corrupt acts that would qualify them for membership in the Corporation. In an offer that pleased Sharon, Huss said he would go out to other parts of the police department to see if there were other corrupt black cops they could trust. He committed to adding a total of three African American police officers to their membership.

Later, at Shannon Kelly's apartment, Mulvey's stories about his first Corporation meeting became more and more hysterical, particularly with each glass of champagne.

"One thing is for sure, honey," Shannon beamed, "whatever else the jury thinks about Ms. Mickens, after they hear these tapes, they sure won't compare her to Rosa Parks!"

The headline in the *New York Post* screamed, 22 CROOKED COPS NABBED. Even the conspicuously reserved *New York Times* devoted the full right-hand side of its front page, above the fold — generally where particularly important stories are placed — to the headline POLICE LIEUTENANT, 2 SERGEANTS, 19 POLICE OFFICERS ARRESTED IN MASSIVE CORRUPTION SCANDAL; MOB TIES ALLEGED. The accompanying story about the indictment not only detailed the almost unbelievable allegation that more than 70 percent of one police unit was corrupt, it included unnamed sources who said that similar levels of corruption existed elsewhere in the police department.

At one of the many press conferences held in the days that followed these unsettling revelations, the mayor, the police commissioner, and Brooklyn District Attorney Cooper faced the media in the mayor's ceremonial blue room. The three officials were joined by an impeccably dressed, distinguished-looking man who appeared to be in his late sixties.

Judge George M. Scarpo, senior associate judge of New York State's highest court, the Court of Appeals, had agreed to resign from the court and undertake, as the mayor promised, "the most comprehensive review of police corruption in the history of this department." Judge Scarpo would head up an investigative panel appointed by the mayor to end police corruption forever.

"Judge Scarpo and other panelists, whom I shall appoint, will be supported by all necessary staff and other resources in order to institutionalize anticorruption efforts within the police department," said the mayor.

At the rear of the huge room, Captain Sean J. Nevins, with his ever-present un-lighted cigar bouncing from one side of his mouth to the other, turned to Sergeant Bernie Pressler and said simply, "It's all bullshit, Bernie. This ain't ever gonna end until cops act like cops."

Overhearing this, the local police reporter from *New York Newsday* asked, "What's that supposed to mean?"

Nevins replied over his shoulder as he and Pressler left the room, "Was I talkin' to you, dickhead?"

"Well, what *does* that mean, Sean?" asked Pressler earnestly.

"It means, Bernie, just what it says." And the captain dismissed any further conversation about the subject.

The fact was that Nevins was correct. No commission, no new initiatives, no commitment of resources could address the recurring reality of police corruption. For those who studied the issue it seemed that in a workforce of twenty-five or thirty thousand people, just as in the general population, there would be some percentage of law-breakers; there would always be some rotten apples. The difficulty in accepting this as fact was that these violators were police officers, sworn to protect the public and dedicated to upholding the law. Worse than that, police corruption had become by the mid-1970s so pervasive as to threaten the very purpose for which young men and women became police officers in the first place. After all, they had become police officers to do good, and it was a pity that Nevins's cynicism about how any attempted reform would be doomed to failure had history to support it.

Soon after the mayor introduced his corruption commissioner and issued his executive order declaring the end to institutional corruption in the department, he summoned Police Officer Robert Mulvey to join him at the podium. The mayor then nodded to the police commissioner, who took a place next to the mayor. Mulvey moved to the side and stood next to his family.

The mayor now spoke. "This department has been served nobly by the undercover efforts of Sergeant Robert Mulvey, whose dedication to the people of this city that he and the women and men of the New York City Police Department so proudly protect is exemplary. We are deeply indebted to him. In recognition of his unstinting courage in undertaking a profoundly dangerous mission, the commissioner will make a presentation." The police commissioner opened a blue felt box and lifted out a gold medal shaped in the form of a cross attached to a dark blue ribbon.

"Sergeant Mulvey," the commissioner

commanded, "approach." The young officer snapped to attention and walked smartly in the commissioner's direction. As he passed the mayor, he paused and saluted. The mayor awkwardly raised his hand, attempting to return the salute. When Mulvey reached the commissioner, he stood directly in front him and came to attention. He brought his right hand smartly to the brim of his uniform cap. He waited until the commissioner returned his salute and then brought his hand to his side. Next Mulvey removed his cap and bent his head slightly as the commissioner spoke.

"Sergeant Robert Mulvey, I now present to you, on behalf of a proud department and a grateful city, our second highest honor, the Combat Cross." After placing the medal around the young sergeant's neck, the commissioner raised his hand in a salute, which was quickly returned by the somewhat embarrassed young officer.

The Commissioner continued, "The citation which accompanies this medal recounts the eight long months of undercover work carried on by this heroic police officer who daily risked his life knowing that his cover would be broken and that he might be seriously injured or killed. His actions led to the breakup of what was the most pervasive example of police corruption in the history of our department and will stand out for all time as a clear warning to those who would think to defile their badges. Sergeant Robert Mulvey now joins the ranks of those special few who have contributed to the well-being of this city and made their sister and brother police officers proud to wear the uniform of the NYPD."

As Mulvey, in his immaculately pressed uniform with a chest full of ribbons, smiled for the horde of cameras, his girlfriend, FBI Special Agent Shannon Kelly, and his little nephew Steven stood next to him beaming with pride. Only a few feet away, Mary couldn't take her eyes off her brother. At one point he returned her smile, sadly knowing that she would soon die from the cancer attacking her body. All eyes were on Robert Mulvey, but none at this triumphant ceremony could have suspected what was in store for him.

People v. Holt,
October 26, 1992

Assistant District Attorney Wally Goss was thorough and methodical to the point of mind-numbing boredom. Goss's preliminary witness list included chemists from the forensic unit of the NYPD who droned on endlessly about the condition of the bodies of the Rodriguez brothers and Police Officer Ruben when they were discovered. The testimony of the experts included evidence of the trajectory of the bullet to the head of each Rodriguez brother and gunpowder residue found at the temple of each victim to establish that the gun had been fired at very close range. This highlighted the fact that the murders had been done execution style. The testimony about the decomposed body of Officer Ruben brought outcries of sobbing and gagging. After it was stipulated by Green that the murder weapon was owned by Holt and that it contained his fingerprints and palm prints, it remained only for the ballistics expert to testify that each of the bullets came from Steven's weapon.

Finally, there was the question of motive. While motive is not necessary to support a conviction for murder in New York State, there was evidence that Steven was angry at the way his uncle was treated by the department following his heroic role as an undercover cop in the 13th Division scandal. He was particularly infuriated that Ruben, a notoriously corrupt cop, was allowed to remain a police officer while Robert Mulvey was set adrift from that very same department and permitted to descend into drug abuse, despair, and disgrace.

When Steven wasn't trying to listen carefully, he found himself repeatedly distracted by thoughts of his uncle and the department. It somehow made him forget for a time how shabbily he was being treated by that very same organization.

27

Lookout Point, Nassau County,
Late Summer 1992

Peggy Moore answered the door. She greeted Robert and Shannon each with a kiss and then ushered them into the Moores' comfortable and tastefully decorated study. Brendan Moore had made a fire a few minutes before the Mulveys arrived. To the right of the ornate fireplace of marble and cobblestone were floor-to-ceiling windows. They took up the rest of that side of the study, providing a breathtaking water view. Presently Brendan Moore entered and hugged both of his old friends.

Peggy brought in a tray of coffee, and the four settled around the center of the room facing the water.

"Brendan, we don't know where to turn," Robert Mulvey began. "Since Steven's arrest, we've had an opportunity to review the evidence. Quite frankly, it looks overwhelming."

Shannon added, "They've got forensic evidence and motive." Although Shannon appeared to interrupt her husband, they had agreed before the meeting with Brendan Moore that she would lead the plea for help, because Robert was too emotional about all that was happening to his nephew. Despite Shannon's strongest arguments, Robert believed that he was at least partially responsible for Steven's indictment, but his more serious concern, which he did not dare mention to Shannon, was a nightmare that haunted his sleep: that somehow the charges against Steven were true.

After laying out the case against Steven, Shannon paused to assess Moore's reaction. There was none. He had learned after two decades of investigative experience that no benefit is gained by showing a reaction, unless it is a planned reaction. Shannon continued, "The prosecution is prepared to offer witnesses who will establish that no one had a better motive than Steven, and —"

Now it was Brendan Moore's turn to interrupt. "Look, Larry Green is probably the best criminal lawyer in New York today. By the time he gets finished with the DA's forensic experts, they will be performing magic tricks for the circus. I've seen this guy in action."

Shannon's response was almost distraught. She was growing desperate that she was not convincing Brendan how much he was needed. "But Brendan, Larry thinks that Goss, the assistant district attorney, has a witness he hasn't told us about." Shannon saw that Moore was beginning to understand her anguish. "Steven believes that the Blue Wall of Silence exists not just among honest police officers who protect the crooked ones out of some misguided fraternal obligation, but that this damned wall, as he calls it, has been permitted to exist for the benefit of brass at One PP to cover their backsides against any media exposure, until they can move on to some cushy job as security director for some department store chain." As Shannon concluded, she could feel she was losing it, but she managed to say, "And Brendan, you know very well that for too many years, that's the way it's been. Steven is obsessed by his firm conviction that this policy nearly ruined Robert and probably destroyed or nearly destroyed many other decent young men and women who signed on to serve the public in this city and instead were corrupted by that fucking wall."

Moore blanched at Shannon's profanity, and she immediately apologized through a torrent of tears. Moore waited until Shannon seemed to regain her composure, responding to Robert's hugs and gentle kisses as he tenderly wiped her cheeks dry. Then he said, "Shannon, Green will tear that theory to shreds!"

Now Robert spoke. "Brendan, we are at our wits' end. Larry, as usual, poured himself into the law books looking for anything that might be used to dismiss the indictment. He found no way out. And as you know, the reason he works alone is, there is simply nobody his equal when it comes to legal research or creative strategies to end a prosecution pretrial. He used a team of his best investigators to conduct a complete canvass throughout the Bush Terminal complex, where Ruben's body was found. Nothing. No one has been found who can tell us anything about Ruben's murder. We told Larry about your network of informers, and he said that we have to find someone soon who might have been at the terminal that evening, or someone who might have seen something, anything."

Moore protested, "You both know just how quickly sources dry up. Informers get busted and go to jail, they overdose on drugs and die, or they become someone else's stoolie. That can happen in just a few months. I'm out of the job for almost a year. You know I'd like to help, but I'm out of this stuff and I don't want to get back in. Look at the life Peggy and I have now. I'm very sorry."

Robert and Shannon got up to say good-bye and to thank Brendan for listening, until Peggy Moore, who had been listening carefully to every word, took Brendan by the hand and said, "Sweetheart, won't you at least try?"

28

From Lookout Point to Suffolk County Jail, Late Summer 1992

During the long automobile ride from Lookout Point to their home in upstate New York, Shannon and Robert at first barely spoke. While Shannon drove, Robert settled back and pretended to sleep.

He began to review his discussion with Brendan Moore and to tick off the points that the prosecutors had assembled. The more he recalled all of this, the more troubled he became. However much he wanted to believe in Steven's innocence, the facts simply didn't support that conclusion.

For a time, Mulvey wasn't sure whether he had fallen asleep or was deep in reverie, but in any event he was transported back in time to when Steven was very young, back to a dusty sandlot with patches of rich dark green grass. The sun was blistering hot, and Mulvey, sitting in the grandstands, wrapped a water-soaked towel around his neck seeking relief. His sole distraction was watching Steven, then about eighteen years of age, gracefully maneuvering around first base. He was a natural, and each time he executed a play it was done flawlessly, after which Steven would glance over to his uncle for approval. When Robert nodded or gave the youngster a thumbs-up, Steven smiled broadly. What Mulvey remembered most was Steven's sheer adulation, a love that transcended the normal relation of older brother or best friend. Steven made no decision without first asking for Uncle Robert's advice. Although he possessed the skill necessary to give serious consideration to playing baseball professionally or at least applying for a college scholarship, his admiration for his uncle was sending him off on another path.

As they walked toward Mulvey's car, sipping Cokes, suddenly Steven stopped and said, "Uncle Robert, I want to be a police officer. I've wanted that for a very long time."

Suddenly a wave of sadness and guilt engulfed Mulvey. Now fully conscious, he nearly shouted to Shannon, "Honey, pull over."

"What's wrong with you?

"Please, Shannon, pull over. Don't you see? Steven is guilty!"

Shannon exclaimed, "What are you talking about?" She guided the car from the right side of the Long Island Expressway to the wide shoulder within sight of the next exit, where she brought it to a stop. It was now quite dark, so Shannon turned on the hazard lights.

"You don't understand," he insisted. "Had he known the truth about me, he wouldn't be facing life imprisonment. I've got to go see him before it's too late." Robert leaned over and tenderly kissed Shannon on the forehead. "After Steven came to see us, I didn't tell you everything because I knew it would upset you. I told Steven about my assignment to Washington Heights and how my undercover role led to the takedown of the Corporation and the arrest of all those corrupt cops in the 13th Division. But when I began to tell him what happened to me, he cut me off. He just wouldn't listen. He said he didn't care to listen to any of it because his inspector said I was screwed by the job."

Now it was Shannon's turn to speak. "Look, Robert, I don't know where you're going with all this, but I won't let you demean yourself by telling Steven the rest of the story. The fact is, what you did was nothing short of heroic, and the department had an obligation to give you every last bit of support you desperately needed. Instead they walked away from you. But nothing that happened to you can ever take away your dedication to the people of this city and the risks you took for police officers everywhere." Shannon's face turned crimson with anger, and she shouted, "I will not let you disillusion that kid. You were a hero and you remain a hero and even the department finally came to that recognition. No, you are Steven's idol, and whatever else may be taken from him, let him at least keep that."

"But, Shannon," Mulvey said firmly, "had he known the truth about me, he wouldn't be facing life imprisonment. I've got to see him before it's too late. Maybe if he knows what I did he'll let Green cut him a deal. Let's find a motel, and tomorrow you can drive me over to the Suffolk County jail."

Nothing Shannon could say could convince her husband that he was making a mistake, but then her heart wasn't in it. The fact was that she was beginning to believe that Steven was a murderer. In any event, Shannon agreed that Robert had to go and speak to his nephew, if only to save him from spending the rest of his life in prison.

"Steven, there is something you must know." As Mulvey began his tale, Steven sat on the chair in front of his desk, crossed his legs, and listened intently.

29

Suffolk County Jail,
Late Summer 1992: Mulvey's Story
Mulvey knew that Steven Holt had worshipped him for most of the younger man's
life, so he knew that the story of his self-
destruction had to be clearly understood. It
was critical, Mulvey believed, that he wasn't
excusing his conduct but rather placing the
blame solely at his own door. He explained
first that his six-month assignment at the
34th Precinct played havoc with his personal
life. He began to drink heavily, first after
work, particularly after a payoff from D'Ario
Santiago, the cockfight thug. The alcohol
made him nasty to anyone around him,
although he did manage to conceal his
growing problem from Shannon Kelly.

All through the period of Mulvey's assignment to the 34th Precinct, he had no
contact with Inspector Connolly, who was
receiving brief but positive reports from

Lieutenant Moore. Moore's information, of course, was limited to the report he got from his undercover cop, which was limited to the quick transfer of the vouchered money given to him by Officer Mulvey.

During the first two months of his assignment to the 13th Division, there was no sign that the young police officer was experiencing any problems. Through it all he kept his drinking a secret, right up through the arrest of the Corporation members.

When Inspector Connolly met with Mulvey after the massive arrests of the corrupt cops of the 13th Division, they had a brief exchange. Connolly congratulated Robert for a superb job. "Now that you have been promoted to sergeant, where would you like to be assigned, Robert?" Perhaps the inspector should have noticed that Mulvey's eyes had a strange gaze and that he stared straight ahead at all times, or that his answer, "Your choice, Boss," was particularly flat, but Connolly didn't notice anything out of the ordinary. Mulvey was, after all, always overly deferential in the inspector's presence. Inspector Connolly decided to recommend that Robert be assigned to a prestigious police precinct located near Chinatown in lower Manhattan. When he said this to Mulvey, the young sergeant nodded obediently. Perhaps, given time, Connolly would have detected symptoms of the demons that were slowly consuming a dedicated young police officer and would soon bring him to the brink of despair — but Connolly would not get that chance.

Much of Mulvey's problem stemmed from the fact that for all of the glory he was given by the mayor and the police commissioner and the media, he was shunned by other cops. The grand predictions that Mulvey would be regarded a hero by other cops didn't come true. Soon after his reassignment, his new comrades treated him as nothing more than an informer. Not that it was ever said. He noticed that they often whispered when they were near him, or he was simply ignored, or when he entered the locker room other police officers, sometimes engaged in animated conversation, would leave immediately. This rejection and the images haunting him from his dealings with the scum of Washington Heights who thought they had a cop on the payroll caused him to become more and more isolated and at times reclusive.

The one relationship he clung to was with Shannon Kelly. Unfortunately, a particularly important and sensitive political corruption investigation involving a powerful and influential assemblyman led to her working late hours at the bureau and left little time for anything other than a few hours' sleep. As the investigation intensified, except for a few brief telephone conversations with Robert, the separation ran into several weeks. Alone in his tiny apartment, Mulvey soon began to increase his drinking, which led to weekend binge drinking. Shannon noticed a few times in their telephone conversations that his speech was slurred, but she thought little of it. These calls were late in the evening and brief. So what if Robert had a little too much at some beer racket. She had no way of knowing that the drink was vodka and not beer, or that it had begun to possess him.

Early in 1975, Inspector Connolly was promoted to one-star deputy chief and assigned to head up training at the Police Academy. Soon after, he was approaching a bank on East 21st Street in Manhattan, not far from the academy, when he spotted someone attempting to rob an elderly woman who was using an ATM in the lobby of the bank. Chief Connolly immediately ordered his driver to bring the car to the curb. Leaping from the vehicle with his gun drawn, he shouted at the gunman, "Police, freeze." The man immediately turned and emptied his MAC-9 automatic into Chief Connolly's chest. Minutes later the chief died on the sidewalk where he fell.

It was a devastating blow to Robert Mulvey, tearing him apart.

For weeks after Connolly's funeral, Mulvey spoke with no one. He took a few weeks of vacation and remained in seclusion. He repeatedly rejected his nephew Steven's attempts to visit him. He sat mostly in his darkened bedroom, drinking from a bottle of vodka until he passed out.

Late one evening the phone in Mulvey's apartment began to ring. At first he didn't move but rather sat rocking in his chair with an empty vodka bottle at his feet. Finally, as the phone rang incessantly, he stumbled out of his chair and, taking the telephone from its cradle, barely mumbled, "Hello."

"I'm so sorry, honey, did I wake you?" Shannon said hurriedly. Before he could answer, she added, "I have some great news." Mulvey didn't answer, because he couldn't. He fell to the floor in a stupor, sending the telephone crashing down next to him. Shannon looked at her watch, which said ten past seven. She'd speak to Robert about it tomorrow.

Yet the following day when Mulvey called Shannon, she decided not to mention her strange experience with him the night before but instead launched into her good news.

"Yesterday afternoon we arrested Harry Manion, the deputy speaker of the New York State Assembly. We got him accepting eighteen thousand dollars in marked money, the down payment for assuring that our undercover agent would get a judgeship on the New York State Supreme Court."

"Wow, that's fantastic."

"What's really great is that the bum makes it clear on tape that the balance of thirty-two thousand was due in two weeks."

"Unbelievable" was all Mulvey could say at first, but then he went on, "and most people believe that only cops go wrong. What can they expect a corrupt lawyer who pays fifty grand for a judgeship will do to get the money back?" Then he added, "Sounds like we should celebrate. How about dinner at Forlini's?" He suggested this because his current assignment in a downtown Manhattan police precinct was just a few blocks away from the restaurant and it was convenient to Shannon's FBI office at 26 Federal Plaza. Mulvey ended the conversation cheerfully, saying, "And I've got a little surprise for you. I'll pick you up at eight."

"Eight it is," Shannon happily responded. As she hung up, the incident of the night before was forgotten and she looked forward to her surprise.

After Mulvey hung up, he hurriedly walked to his night table, opened the top drawer and looked admiringly at a gleaming half-carat diamond engagement ring. He began to smile with anticipation, but almost immediately he wondered if she'd accept. Suddenly he noticed a slight tremor in the hand holding the ring. In recent weeks it had recurred often. He dealt with it the way he had learned to do in the past. He went to the kitchen and retrieved a bottle of vodka from the cabinet above the sink. He grabbed a glass, filled it halfway, and gulped it down. It was warm, almost hot, at first and then instantly brought a calming effect. The tremor passed and he felt good. Of course she'd say yes!

Mulvey suggested to Shannon that they get engaged immediately after he entered her apartment. She noticed right away that there was a problem — his proposal came after he'd consumed nearly half a quart of vodka only an hour before. His speech was slurred, and his bloodshot eyes frightened

Shannon.

"Robert, what's happening to you?" she said, rather than responding to his offer.

Pathetically, Mulvey could hardly stand. Outraged that Shannon had ducked his proposal, he shouted, "You just made a big mistake, sweetie." Then, slamming the door to her apartment, he disappeared up the street, heading for the nearest bar.

Heartbroken, Shannon watched out her window as Mulvey stumbled from side to side out of the walkway of her apartment house. Then she closed her drapes and wondered sadly if she'd ever want to see him again.

The next day Mulvey woke up with a horrible hangover. He made an appointment at the Medical Division, and when he confessed his problem he was granted a leave. The department psychiatrist suggested that Mulvey should apply for an inpatient thirty-day program. Unfortunately, no beds were available, and in the weeks that followed, his drinking was worse than ever before.

No one knows for sure what happened. Maybe it was the miracle from his daily attendance at Mass, which he stubbornly refused to give up, but suddenly he snapped out of his depression and stopped drinking. After several weeks he requested that he be returned to duty. Following a complete physical and psychological examination, Robert was restored to duty. His superiors decided that he should be given a low-stress assignment. He was ordered to become the supervisor of the automobile pound on Fountain Avenue in a desolate section of East New York in Brooklyn.

At first Steven sat transfixed, but when his uncle had finished describing the uncontrollable binge drinking and then his redemption, he seemed puzzled. He stood and walked toward his bed, stretching his legs. As he sat down on the bed he said, "How did it all unravel again?"

"It didn't take too long, and then it became really ugly," Mulvey replied. Holt sat down on his bed and listened intently as his uncle discussed his next assignment.

The NYPD automobile pound is a vast storage lot for vehicles from Brooklyn and the adjoining county of Queens that are recovered and held for evidence in connection with pending criminal cases or during the investigation of the theft of these cars. The police officers assigned to the auto pound were, with few exceptions, miscreants who had been disciplined repeatedly for their alcoholism, cops awaiting the disposition of charges brought against them at the police department's administrative trial room, and any number of troublemakers who had connections with the PBA and had been placed in limbo to save their pension. One of these, Officer Michael O'Leary, was in particular a problem cop.

The brass at headquarters thought that this was an ideal assignment for Sergeant Mulvey. The job required his leadership skills and his ability to motivate. They actually thought he would inspire some of these misfits and restore them to full duty. But no one understood the devastating effects on Mulvey of his separation from his beloved Shannon or the desperation and profound sadness he felt following the murder of his mentor and idol, James Patrick Connolly. While he had stopped drinking, he was still moody and at times sullen. But the real problem for Mulvey lay ahead, and no one could gauge the powerful hold Mike O'Leary would soon have on him.

Forty-six-year-old Michael O'Leary spent two tours of duty in Vietnam as a sergeant assigned to a Marine Corps rifle company. In order to get a second tour in Nam one had to volunteer. O'Leary asked to return, although he didn't disclose that his reason was that he liked combat. By his count he took out sixteen Viet Cong soldiers. Even more than killing Viet Cong, O'Leary loved cocaine. In Nam, he became a serious abuser, snorting the drug as often as he could.

During his second tour and while on a cocaine binge, O'Leary rescued a trapped Marine rifle squad, and for his heroism he was awarded the Silver Star, the country's third highest military award. That award added luster to an imposing figure of a man, an even six feet tall, with a broad, powerfully constructed face, which was topped by golden blond hair. His hazel eyes bulged, in part because of his addiction, and his large nose had been flattened during several years of street brawls as a child. He had wide shoulders that were attached to muscular arms and massively large hands, weapons he used frequently with little or no provocation.

O'Leary constantly displayed the Silver Star, wearing the ribbon on all of his civilian dress and later on his police uniform. He used it frequently as a conversation ice breaker. The award also led to his election as a delegate of the PBA for the 5th Precinct in lower Manhattan when he refused an order by a young lieutenant to remove his combat ribbon. It did not help the lieutenant's case when it was discovered that he had avoided the draft through a college deferment. No charges were ever brought against O'Leary, who in short order became the hero of those police officers assigned to the 5th Precinct.

"Good morning, Sarge," said O'Leary, snapping sharply to attention with a crisp hand salute. It caught Mulvey off guard. He was not used to that kind of military courtesy from a veteran cop, a formality that often disappeared a few years after a police officer graduated from the Police Academy.

The headquarters for the Fountain Avenue automobile pound was a dingy trailer with a desk, partially illuminated by a single table lamp. Two police officers, O'Leary and a not very successful recovering drunk from a precinct in Queens, were supervised by one sergeant. Their shift was 4:00 p.m. to midnight. The tiny unit maintained contact with the outside world with two telephones, although most of the time only one of the phones was operable. While the command was small, the responsibilities for vouchering and safeguarding hundreds of recovered stolen vehicles was no easy task. Added to the mountain of backbreaking paperwork was the reality that no citizen arriving or leaving the pound was ever happy. O'Leary's charm and streetwise diplomacy made an otherwise unpleasant assignment for a boss like Mulvey bearable. Sergeant Mulvey was grateful for the way O'Leary shielded him from the often irate public, demanding to know why their automobile couldn't be promptly released or why it had been damaged while in police custody. Of course, Mulvey didn't know that O'Leary's method of calming the angry automobile owners included a price! For a hundred dollars he could arrange a swift release from the clerk's office — so long as cash came with the request. The property clerk thief was told by O'Leary that the bribe was only fifty dollars, so his twenty-five-dollar portion seemed generous.

"Don't you understand, I desperately need this car," the woman pleaded as she pointed toward her very used Plymouth station wagon. "It's the only way I can get my three kids to school in time for me to go to work. Please do something!"

"I know, miss, but those damned bureaucrats at the police property clerk's office really don't care," O'Leary replied, "unless I'm able to show that this is a special case."

"Well, how do you do that?"

Now O'Leary played the hand he used so often. "The fact is that the guy I deal with down there is a greedy SOB who won't do nothin' for nothin'." It wasn't long before the poor woman forked over a hundred dollars.

O'Leary was trouble from the day he graduated from the Police Academy, and if Mulvey's supervisors had bothered to tell him anything about O'Leary's history, the young sergeant would have demanded an immediate transfer.

O'Leary was first assigned to the 114th Precinct in Queens County. There he had an argument with an assistant district attorney and a sergeant over the way he seized drugs from a local pusher. O'Leary didn't care much about their concern that the junk was illegally seized and that the case had to be dismissed. The argument took place on the steps of the courthouse in front of a crowd of people on their lunch hour and escalated to the point where O'Leary punched both men, knocking the prosecutor out cold. That time, his war record and his Silver Star got him off with an apology.

Now, O'Leary had an Uncle Frank, a retired narcotics detective, who while on the job supplemented his income by selling illegally seized narcotics. "I just recycle the junk for the mutts and make a few dollars on the side," he would boast to a very impressed young Officer O'Leary, who was not only his nephew but his godson.

When the story of his nephew's behavior in front of the courthouse in Queens got around to the beer rackets, Uncle Frank felt some counseling was necessary. "Now, why do you care whether two assholes second-guess you? The important thing is you know what you're doing and they don't. You better lay low for a while because unless you're careful, even those losers from IAD will nail you." Frank explained how two black narco detectives were set up by Internal Affairs and detectives from the office of the Manhattan district attorney. They were sent to state prison for five years. Frank told O'Leary that if he played his cards right, by the time the police department's Internal Affairs Division got around to taking a look at him, he could be promoted from precinct delegate to PBA trustee, granting him virtual if not complete immunity from arrest or administrative discipline.

But O'Leary would not be careful. During one of his frequent visits to the Dublin Celtic Cross pub in the Woodside section of

Queens County, which had become a gathering place for the stream of Irish illegals who landed in New York, he discovered that many of them had as strong a taste for cocaine as they did for Guinness stout. Most had come from the depressed areas of northeast Ireland, where unemployment for Catholics in the Protestant-dominated province was as much as 80 percent. Booze and, increasingly, drugs were the common way to escape, but here in the States, in Woodside, Queens, they had trouble making a drug connection.

O'Leary saw immediately an opportunity to supplement his income. The recklessness that saved the lives of his buddies in Nam and got him his Silver Star would soon threaten his freedom. Overheard on a court-authorized wiretap on the pay phone at the Celtic Cross was some reference to an Irish cop and cocaine. The wiretap, placed on the telephone by detectives from the office of the Queens County district attorney, was gathering evidence about an illegal sports betting group operating out of the bar.

When the overheard information about an Irish cop was reported to the chief assistant district attorney, she did what the law required and prepared an amendment to the original wiretap order for the district attorney's signature, to permit his detectives to collect evidence of an additional crime, the possession and/or sale of cocaine. However carefully these investigations are conducted, the more people involved, the greater the possibility of breached confidentiality.

So, once again, along came Uncle Frank to the rescue. O'Leary, whose on-duty alcohol abuse was becoming a serious problem, was sent to an alcohol treatment center in upstate New York. While there remained casual references to the Irish cop and cocaine on the wiretap, the investigation, at least of that particular crime, was over.

Nonetheless, it was clear to Internal Affairs that O'Leary's fingerprints were all over trouble brewing at the Dublin Celtic Cross. An outraged Queens County district attorney demanded a department investigation of the leak that ruined the potential drug case. While the strong suspicion pointed to the rogue cop, there was no evidence.

After O'Leary finished his rehab, a decision was made to assign him to the Fountain Avenue pound until the bosses could figure out what next to do with him.

■ ■ ■ ■

After several weeks, the combination of Mulvey's painful loneliness and O'Leary's feigned solicitude was having its planned effect.

"Hey, Boss, how about a beer after our tour?"

Mulvey, shy to begin with and becoming more and more reclusive, at first hesitated, but before he could answer, O'Leary pressed on. "Come on, Boss, it'll do you good."

A few shots of vodka followed by beer chasers and Mulvey began to loosen up, perhaps for the first time he could remember in nearly a year. Through the gathering haze produced by the booze, O'Leary's questions didn't seem so pointed or presumptuous.

"Boy, that stuff at the 13th Division must have been somethin', Boss. I guess you got there just before the shit hit the fan!" Before Mulvey could answer, O'Leary continued, "What a bunch of two-bit cowboys, riskin' everything for a few grand a year."

Mulvey's speech began to slur, and he started to see an O'Leary and a half, but he still understood and could reply. "Well, it was actually a lot more money for each thieving cop."

"But Boss, that's chicken feed. It just wasn't worth the risk."

"Well, maybe so," said Mulvey, draining the tumbler of vodka, which he quickly washed down with a glass of beer. Getting up to leave, he said, "Nothing's worth the risk, Michael."

"Maybe so, Boss, maybe so," replied O'Leary with a strange look in his eye, which Mulvey ignored.

As time passed, it didn't take O'Leary very long to introduce his increasingly vulnerable supervisor to wider substance abuse. First it was a high grade of marijuana, which when combined with the vodka and beer gave Mulvey a delectable rush and then a feeling of quiet ease and self-confidence he had rarely experienced. The problem for him was he lapsed too quickly into a stupor, which he could not control. It was followed by violent headaches when he woke up. O'Leary next introduced Mulvey to cocaine. It provided Mulvey all the relaxing joy, without the horrible side effects, but it, too, soon took hold of the young sergeant. His desire for it grew stronger by the week.

O'Leary also introduced Mulvey to a group of other cops, most of them his contemporaries in age, two of the same rank. First they drank together in the Irish bars on Second Avenue in Manhattan, then went to an after-hours topless joint where crack cocaine smoked in a pipe gave Mulvey and the others a succession of high rushes. The group began to meet regularly to discuss how they could make some money to support their habit and to put some money on the side, as one said, for retirement. Mulvey by this time was a hooked follower — hooked on drugs — but since he was often in a haze, he didn't catch on when the group discussed corruption. Nevertheless, his descent into hell was nearly complete. That phase of Mulvey's tragedy would occur shortly after O'Leary was asked by Junior Garofolo for some desperately needed help.

By the early 1970s, the neighborhood in Brooklyn known as East New York resembled Berlin in the days following World War II. Many of the single-family and two-family homes that remained standing were burned out or were otherwise empty shells. The rental income from these homes often didn't produce enough to cover the costs of ordinary maintenance care, and that led to their deteriorating conditions. Some unscrupulous landlords deliberately allowed the properties to fall into a disrepair that ultimately made them uninhabitable. Those forced out by these conditions were replaced by others who were forced to pay even higher rents. Many of these new arrivals could not afford the rent, and then they were evicted. After the cycle was repeated several times, what was left of East New York was mostly a huge slum.

With so many vacant houses and the debris-strewn lots, no one could have guessed that East New York was once a vibrant and flourishing section of Brooklyn. Nevertheless, there did remain perhaps a hundred homes and a few churches, including an African Methodist Episcopal church and a Baptist church, to provide spiritual support for those who refused to leave.

The neighborhood also included one block with beautiful brick and oak-frame homes fronted by manicured lawns and protected by wrought-iron fencing. The block included a tiny bar, a social club, and an Italian grocery store. This block on New Lots Avenue was headquarters for the Garofolo crew of the Lucchese organized crime family, led by Carmine "the Nose" Garofolo.

Carmine "the Nose" got his nickname not

only for his amply sized proboscis but because he used it so often to snort cocaine that he destroyed all its membranes. The result was that his nose was constantly red and dripping, and Carmine aggravated the condition by repeatedly blowing it, producing a honking noise, which could be heard half a block away. Carmine, who was in his midsixties, was a short, fat man, perhaps five foot three, with no neck visible to the naked eye and a melon-shaped face with bulging dark eyes. He had no hair other than a wisp of black growth just above each of his tiny ears. He wore tailored Italian suits, all of them dark. He never removed his jacket, which covered expensive and gaudy silk white-on-white shirts, because he needed to conceal a huge .357 Magnum automatic handgun. His massive hands were more like ham hocks, and their knuckles carried large, ugly scars from the days when he was an enforcer before he became a boss. When he walked, he waddled on short stumps for legs, and his feet were jammed into imported Ferragamo loafers. When he spoke, mostly in a guttural, barely audible voice, he had an annoying habit of using the phrase "Who da fuck knows?" This was accompanied by a strange gesture, his hands outstretched, palms up, all the while staring at the sky. "How are you, Carmine?" was answered with his signature gesture and "Who da fuck knows?" Or "I gotta go, Boss, okay?" left the supplicant confused by the response, "Who da fuck knows?" When people got to know Carmine a little better, they got used to the fact that the phrase meant nothing, and they ignored it.

The Garofolo crew was the Lucchese crew most feared by the other four organized crime families of New York City, which controlled everything from bookmaking to hijacking to drugs. They earned and needed this reputation because they controlled and franchised the cocaine importation and distribution network in the metropolitan New York area. They dealt with the Colombian drug cartels that were known internationally for their brutal attacks on family members to exact complete submission from rivals, and even from their customers. Children would disappear and their body parts would be returned to their families wrapped in plastic bags and packed in corrugated boxes. The Garofolos also worked effectively with similarly violent Jamaican and Latino drug gangs.

Carmine the Nose and his thugs took complete control over the drug trade in New York City through a series of vicious strikes. A beheaded Jamaican and a castrated Colombian who had his hands chopped off at his wrists and then stuffed into his jacket pockets gave reason enough for these members of the drug-dealing food chain to understand who was in charge.

The cartels were permitted to export their cocaine only if it was sold to the Garofolos, who in turn would sell the drugs to the various gangs, after inflating the price to include a handsome profit. The Nose also set up geographic franchise areas guaranteeing exclusivity. The franchisees paid for the uncut cocaine, which was either sold in pure form to snorting yuppies or cut up and mixed to make crack cocaine for street junkies. To sweeten the Garofolos' profit, the franchised areas of operation for the drug dealers were leased weekly from the crew for an average of a thousand dollars.

O'Leary and Junior Garofolo, the oldest of Carmine's three sons, began their friendship some ten years before O'Leary was banished to Fountain Avenue. They met one evening, quite fortuitously for both, when O'Leary and his partner were working the late shift in a patrol car assigned to the 71st Police Precinct, which covered parts of East New York and Crown Heights. While on patrol making the streets safe for the people of Brooklyn, as they would joke, they were also looking for a score, perhaps a drunk driver to arrest. For an agreed-upon fee, they would either let the driver go or, if he or she was so drunk as to be unsuitable for release, the arrest would be processed and then later the officers would testify falsely in court, which would lead to a finding of not guilty.

It had been a relatively quiet night for O'Leary and his partner, when suddenly O'Leary spotted a car roar at high speed out from Nostrand Avenue through a red signal light and onto Eastern Parkway. The dark green, brand-new convertible Jaguar sped east on the parkway, reaching at times seventy and eighty miles per hour. O'Leary, behind the wheel of the patrol car, remained in full pursuit and was finally able to bring the sports car to a stop by pulling in front of it some thirty blocks into the chase.

Junior Garofalo stumbled out of the car and fell into the street, his left hand clutching a wad of hundred-dollar bills. His speech was slurred, and he said, "Please, Officer, bring me to my father," as he offered the money to O'Leary. Junior was of average height and build, maybe five feet eight and 160 pounds. He had a long, thin, mousy kind of face with a high forehead, a long, pointed nose, and very large ears, a gift from his mother. His tightly drawn mouth made him look perpetually sad, and when he tried to smile, which was not very often, he revealed an incomplete set of rotting teeth. He wore jeans and a dark sports shirt and black sneakers. He had just bought some coke from a Jamaican connection on Nostrand Avenue.

When O'Leary learned Junior's last name, his heart jumped with delight. *Here's my score of scores,* he thought. Junior reeked of scotch, and his nose cavities were still filled with white powder — and there on the passenger seat and on the floor of the vehicle, in open view, were more than a dozen clear plastic packets with more white powder.

O'Leary took Junior to his father, but it wasn't a happy reunion. "You fuckin' asshole," shouted Carmine as he landed the meat of a baseball bat across Junior's nose, breaking the long beak. "Disgrace yourself, you disgrace me and the family, you piece of shit!"

O'Leary took Junior to a local hospital to have his nose repaired, but not before receiving a handsome reward from Carmine for himself and his partner; enough money for his partner to make a down payment on a dream house in the village of Lawrence out in Nassau County. Of course, there was no police action taken about the incident, not even a report.

Junior became one of O'Leary's closest friends and his main supplier of cocaine, at no charge. In the years that followed, Carmine increasingly turned his business over to Junior, who never forgot his friend O'Leary.

"Mikey," Junior shouted into the telephone, "I gotta see you right away." O'Leary told Sergeant Mulvey that he was feeling a stomach flu coming on and got permission to leave the auto pound immediately. As soon as he arrived at the social club on New Lots Avenue, he went straight to the guarded office in the rear.

Junior Garofolo, his face ashen and his hands shaking uncontrollably, said, "Mikey, they killed my father. They ambushed him up on Pitkin Avenue." Junior began to sob and shake his head pathetically from side to side. "Then I get a call and a guy says tomorrow I'm out of business, that he and his people will come over tomorrow morning to arrange my retirement."

O'Leary asked, "Do you know who the guy is?"

"Nah, but he had a pretty thick Jamaican accent."

"I'm so very, very sorry about your guinea father, mon," said the huge black man with the ample reddish brown dreadlocks spilling over his shoulders.

Junior could feel his face muscles tighten as he stared at Winston Jordan, whose half smile through his neatly combed handlebar mustache revealed three prominent gold teeth. Jordan's image of himself was completed with a massive diamond-inlaid gold circular earring swinging back and forth from his left earlobe with every one of his animated head movements. Jordan was the undisputed boss of the most vicious of all the Jamaican drug gangs terrorizing many sections of Brooklyn. He'd named his gang "the Jamaican Sled Team."

"Your fucking guinea father ruled my people too long, and then he had the audacity" — here he slowly pronounced each of the four syllables for emphasis — "to try and turn everything over to you. He went too far, tryin' to pass all of this off to you, little guinea, as if it was his inheritance to give!"

At this Junior leaped out of his chair so abruptly that each of the four Jordan henchmen, clad in matching black leather motorcycle jackets, instantly produced a MAC-9 automatic. Jordan slammed Junior back in his chair so violently that the chair toppled over, sending him to the ground.

From the floor, Junior screamed, "Listen, motherfucker, you best stop calling my father a guinea. He was very good to your people."

"No, you listen, you little guinea scumbag, your guinea father was nothing but a bloodsucker who drained the very life out of my people. Now it's over, so clear out of here before I blow your balls off and stuff them in your guinea mouth!"

"On the floor and freeze, cocksuckers, and I better see empty hands right away," O'Leary commanded, as he and six other off-duty cops, with Glocks and shields waving, burst into the room. One of Jordan's top lieutenants screeched with pain as two bullets slammed into his shoulder. He had not moved fast enough for O'Leary, who shouted, "Who's next?" Everyone quickly complied. O'Leary leaned over the rigidly prone Jordan and said quietly, "You got a big fuckin' mouth for a rum-headed junkie." Jordan wailed in horror as O'Leary reached down and in one motion ripped away his earring, tearing his lobe off, splattering blood everywhere. He then began to bludgeon Jordan with repeated blows from his Glock until the Jamaican passed out.

The six other cops began systematically pistol-whipping Jordan's men until their screams were silenced by unconsciousness. Now O'Leary filled a wastebasket with water and poured it over Jordan's head until he twitched back to reality. When the other cops saw this, each got a similar container. The cold water quickly revived the Jamaicans, and now Jordan and his men listened very carefully as O'Leary lowered his voice to a measured level and said, "Listen up, the next time you mutts are seen anywhere in New York you die — and you die slowly. You understand, dickhead?"

O'Leary had his boot against Jordan's neck, limiting his breathing so much that all Jordan could do was grunt his answer, showing he understood very clearly. The cops confiscated the Jamaicans' guns and then released the men through the back door of the social club at ten-minute intervals.

What neither the cops nor the Jamaicans knew was that as each one exited, he was blown away by one of Junior's people, waiting in the backyard and using an automatic pistol equipped with a silencer. The bodies were then stacked inside a stolen van and dumped on the sidewalk in front of the Carib-reggae club on Clarkson Avenue in Brooklyn that served as the meeting place for the feared Jamaican Sled Team.

"Mikey," pleaded a still shaken Junior, who never got used to the violence and instead concentrated his efforts on expanding the drug business, leaving the enforcement part to his people, "what happens to me if their friends come back?"

O'Leary stared hard and with disgust at this pampered wimp, who had none of the strength, leadership, or balls of Carmine the Nose, and said matter-of-factly, "Then we will kill them. And in the meantime, we'll give you all the protection you need."

At this point in his uncle's story Holt felt a wave of disgust come over him. He wondered what possessed Mulvey to remain involved with this murderous crew of rogue cops led by a sociopath. Yet Steven said nothing and continued to listen, confused but quite fascinated.

30

People v. Holt,
November 1992

Brendan Moore's prediction that Green would easily destroy the credibility of the forensic experts was not off the mark.

The ballistics expert, Detective Edmund Thatcher, had testified confidently enough about the peculiar markings the barrel of a gun makes on a bullet as it passes through on the way to a target. These markings, or grooves, were, he said, as reliable as fingerprints.

"Now, based on your experience with the science of ballistics identification," inquired Goss, "do you have an expert opinion about the origin of the bullets that were found in the skull section of Hiram Rodriguez, Ramon Rodriguez, and Scott Ruben, and the bullets you recovered after you test-fired Sergeant Holt's weapon at the police crime laboratory here in Suffolk County?"

"Yes, I do," replied Thatcher. "They were fired from an NYPD service revolver registered to Sergeant Steven Robert Holt."

Goss turned to Green with comic disdain and said, "You may inquire."

Just before Green began his cross-examination, Holt took a deep breath and turned to Lee Moran. She smiled reassuringly. He then looked over to where Sergeant Kurland sat each day. Kurland quickly gave the young officer a thumbs-up.

In minutes, Green established that Thatcher was not familiar with the works of several leading authorities on forensic science, in particular those who specialized in the science of ballistics identification. He conceded that he had not had a refresher course on the subject in at least three years, and he did not know that during that time these authorities, as well as FBI ballistics experts and experts from the New York State crime laboratory, all agreed that factors such as grit and rust can alter the markings Thatcher had compared in accuracy to fingerprints. Nor did he consider expert findings that corrosion of a bullet's shell or a weapon's barrel might lead to an inconclusive finding by a ballistics examiner.

Green pressed on. "Detective, isn't it true that in part your conclusions are based on the assumption that the gun surrendered by Sergeant Holt was used sometime in December of 1990, the same time that the bodies of the Rodriguez brothers were found?"

"Yes, sir."

"And isn't it also true that this weapon was surrendered to detectives from the Suffolk County Police Department in April of 1991?"

"Yes, sir."

"And you testified before a Suffolk County grand jury in late May of the same year? And you conducted your ballistic tests sometime between April of 1991 and May of 1991, correct?"

"Yes, sir, and if you give me a moment, I'll find the exact date."

Green quickly brushed aside the offer with a surly "It's a little late for precision, don't you think, Detective Thatcher?"

"I don't understand."

"Well, let me help you. Where was that weapon kept before your ballistics test?"

"In the office of the Suffolk County police property clerk, where I retrieved it just before conducting my test."

"And did you consider whether Sergeant Holt had properly maintained his weapon before its surrender?" Thatcher hesitated, and Green continued. "Did you check that weapon for rust or grit? Oh, that's right, you are not familiar with the technology that suggests that those factors can alter your findings, correct?"

"I did not check the weapon in any detail, but it looked clean."

Now Green shouted, "It looked clean, and that's it! It didn't occur to you to make a thorough inspection, Detective, because you have not kept up to date with these new findings, correct? In fact, since you did nothing more than a cursory inspection of a weapon which is offered for the sole purpose of sending this man to prison for the rest of his life, you have no way of knowing whether the barrel of that weapon was affected in any way by corrosion, correct?"

Goss rose and said, "Your Honor, we could check the weapon now for rust, grit, or corrosion."

"Oh, sit down, Mr. Goss," replied Judge McGowan in disgust.

Green turned to the jury. "Madam Forewoman and ladies and gentlemen, it may be lost on young Mr. Goss, but I assume not on you, that it might be rather a bit late to trust whether the authorities did anything to this weapon, such as cleaning it, after Detective Thatcher conducted his less than satisfactory ballistics test!" Green then said, "Your Honor, I have nothing more to say to this . . . expert." He carefully pronounced the two syllables.

When Green had finished, Thatcher left the witness stand. The color had drained from his face, and he looked sadly befuddled. Goss said, "Thank you, Detective, you did fine."

Flashing instant anger, Thatcher said in a loud voice, for all to hear, especially the jury, "It would have been helpful if you had spent some fucking time preparing me to testify."

Green, rarely gracious to his adversaries, except when he had a design in mind, rose to Goss's defense. Speaking directly to the disgruntled police officer, he said, "Now, now, Detective Thatcher, why must you blame young Mr. Goss here for your short-comings? Perhaps the time has come for you to return to your previous assignment for the Suffolk County Police Department, writing tickets for parking violations!"

The detective, his face beet red with fury, wheeled around and shouted, "Fuck you, you Jew cocksucker!"

Green could not have dreamed for more, especially in the presence of the jury. By the look on the face of juror number seven,

Mrs. Steinberg, he knew she was not at all happy about the remark.

Judge McGowan was infuriated. He stood and pointed a sharp finger at Detective Thatcher, who quickly understood the impact of his stupidity and tried to apologize. The judge cut him off immediately and commanded, "Show cause by nine o'clock tomorrow morning why this court should not hold you in contempt. Now get out of my courtroom."

As Goss rose, presumably to complain or perhaps to explain Thatcher's conduct, Judge McGowan roared, "You sit down." Now he spoke to the jury, "Madam Forewoman, ladies and gentlemen, I deeply regret that ugly outburst, that filthy display. I shall deal with this police officer tomorrow morning, but I must charge you that you may not be influenced by any of this in reaching a verdict, because none of it, however repulsive, has any bearing on the evidence in this case. Now, I believe we could all use the rest of the afternoon off." Motioning to the court officers to escort the jury out of the courtroom, he said, "Please enjoy the rest of the day. We will resume at eleven o'clock tomorrow morning."

When the door had closed behind the last

juror, Judge McGowan, still standing, spoke directly to Green. "Counselor, I admire your ability as a trial lawyer in every respect, but you and I both know that you goaded that police officer and intended the result to influence the jury. I warn you, if you try similar tactics during the remainder of this trial, you will do so at your own peril. The trial is adjourned until eleven o'clock tomorrow morning."

Judge McGowan did not wait for a response from Larry Green, nor was Green intending to give one. His ploy had worked, and of course he would not use any more like it in front of this judge. Instead, he had other plans to unnerve young Mr. Goss.

When Judge McGowan left the courtroom, Kurland walked up to the rail separating the spectators from the well, where Steven remained seated. Kurland leaned over and whispered, "Hey, kid, we had a great day." Holt beamed and then stood to be led back to his cell. Before he left he looked at Lee Moran, smiled, and winked.

At nine o'clock the following morning, Thatcher apologized to the judge in a way that confirmed for Green that the officer was just a run-of-the-mill anti-Semite. McGowan ordered Thatcher to apologize to

Green, imposed a thousand-dollar fine, and directed an inquiry by the Suffolk County Police Department to determine whether Thatcher was fit for continued service as a police officer.

Judge McGowan had one remaining piece of business. "Mr. Goss, I will not warn you again about your refusal or inability to control your witnesses. Do you understand?"

"Yes, Your Honor." Goss slumped to his chair as Judge McGowan left the courtroom to wait for the jury to be brought in.

Moments later, things got better for Goss. He was summoned from the courtroom by a call from the Suffolk County chief of detectives, Phil Pitelli.

"Wally, I think we have the witness we have all been waiting for. I'll see you tonight." Despite Goss's pleas for more information, Pitelli wouldn't budge. "Just be patient " was all he would say before he hung up.

Later the same day, the trial of Steven Robert Holt reached that stage of every murder case where the jury is given the testimony as to the cause of death. It is generally a pedestrian exercise conducted by a deputy medical examiner of the county where a dead body is found. The prosecutor in grand style leads the ME through a series of detailed questions eliciting information beginning with the doctor's professional experience, including the number of autopsies performed since the doctor became an ME. Next, the testimony turns to the condition of the body and a description, mostly a gory one, of the wounds. In cases such as this one, involving multiple victims, the jury is given a description of the kind of wounds inflicted on each victim. Finally, with great drama, the prosecutor, in this case Assistant District Attorney Wally Goss, steps back a bit and looks at the jury for effect and then to the physician. "Now, Doctor, based on your professional experience and your examination of the body of Officer Scott Ruben, do you have an opinion within a reasonable medical certainty about his cause of death?"

Throughout this last question, quiet sobs could be heard from the section where Scott Ruben's relatives were sitting, including those of his mother and of his young wife.

After the answer — "a gunshot wound to the head" — Goss would repeat the exercise concerning the autopsy and the cause of death of Ramon and then Hiram Rodriguez. Larry Green had nothing but contempt for this part of a murder trial, but then, he had nothing but contempt for those in his profession who proudly proclaimed that they were homicide lawyers. For Green, whose trial skills went beyond pigeonholing specialties, a homicide case was a case with one less lousy witness. Green always believed that the testimony of the ME, particularly the cause of death, should be stipulated, or agreed to by the parties, because the testimony in his opinion was a sham and a ploy to wrench sympathy from the jurors. As a result, Green developed a style of cross-examination that was unsettling for homicide prosecutors.

When Goss had completed his direct examination of Suffolk County Deputy Medical Examiner Ronald Farnsworth, MD, he turned to Larry Green and said, "You may inquire."

Larry Green rose slowly and, with a sort of amble, walked toward the witness and asked just three questions.

"Dr. Farnsworth, does your autopsy tell you who caused the death of a victim?"

Farnsworth, who had been warned about Green's penchant for confrontation, shot back, "Of course not."

"It doesn't?" mocked Green, shaking his head from side to side in feigned disbelief.

"And you are employed by Suffolk County, correct?"

Farnsworth cautiously responded, "Yes."

Now Green asked, in a booming voice, "So you get your paycheck from the same people who pay the salary of young Mr. Goss, correct?"

Goss rose to object, and Judge McGowan ordered, "Sit down."

When Farnsworth hesitated, Green said in a measured voice, "Do you have an answer?"

Farnsworth angrily responded, "My answer, sir, is yes."

"Good," said Green. "Then I have no more questions."

Larry Green had learned over the years, speaking to jurors about his approach, that they agreed with him that the testimony of the ME was indeed nothing more than a prosecutor's charade.

Holt was impressed with the job his lawyer was doing, yet he could not stop being distracted. He would from time to time glance over to where his Uncle Robert was sitting and think of all the awful things that his hero had been made to endure. Now he was in the same boat.

Goss rose and confidently announced, "That, Your Honor, subject to my application to reopen, is the case on behalf of the People of —"

Green didn't allow Goss to continue, jumping to his feet, but before he could speak, McGowan said sternly, "What are you pulling, Mr. Goss? Either rest your case or call your next witness, now!"

"But, Your Honor," Goss whined, "may we approach the bench?"

"No," bellowed the red-faced jurist. "Inside!" He waved angrily toward his chambers.

"First, of all, Goss," Judge McGowan thundered, "don't you ever again appear in my courtroom. Do you understand?"

"Your Honor, I don't know what I did to make you so angry."

"Well, for openers, you are rarely prepared, you have no sense of decorum, and you are a slick practitioner full of yourself with nothing of substance to support that conclusion. And finally you are not owed, nor do you deserve, any further explanation. So make a decision, without further delay. Rest your case or tell me and Mr. Green whom you will call." McGowan remained standing throughout and did not lower his voice. "Announce your decision tomorrow morning at nine thirty."

McGowan walked briskly from chambers, entered the courtroom, and recessed the trial, without either lawyer present.

31

Suffolk County Jail,
Late Summer 1992: Mulvey's Story

"By this time, Steven," Mulvey continued, "I was lost in alcohol and cocaine. I was in and out of reality, and in any event O'Leary made no effort to tell me about his grand scam."

Steven said nothing but shook his head in disgust.

Police Officer Michael O'Leary was already formulating a plan for a lucrative retirement package for himself and the others, who would include Robert Mulvey. O'Leary in his own perverse way had grown to admire and respect Mulvey and withheld his plan from him. Nevertheless, O'Leary could not help being pleased with himself. This would be his last and greatest score.

O'Leary and his group, including Robert Mulvey, began guarding Garofolo's interests immediately. Mulvey was told as little as possible. While he had crossed the line and done things that in the past he would have rejected out of hand, his need for cocaine had grown so great that he had to supplement his income. So he did not object to receiving his end of a payment from a desperate automobile owner willing to pay for the quick return of his car. Of course, he refused to deal directly with the citizen, but he did sign the release outside the presence of the motorist.

This relieved O'Leary from the task of forging Mulvey's name on the document as he had with Mulvey's predecessor. O'Leary always thought this was dangerous for him and made him more vulnerable to discovery and perhaps prosecution.

Having taken the small steps of corruption at the pound, it did not bother Sergeant Mulvey to perform guard duty for Junior Garofolo for a price. O'Leary told Mulvey that a mob hit had been ordered on Junior by the successors to the Jamaican Sled Team. Mulvey had followed the explosive media coverage about the executed Jamaican drug dealers and assumed that the Garofolo crew was involved. Through a haze of booze and drugs Mulvey justified guarding someone marked for execution as an appropriate part of police work.

The arrangement fully benefited O'Leary because it got both Mulvey and Junior Garofolo out of his hair to allow him to implement his grand score. It also gave O'Leary the chance to work closely with Joey Banfanti, known everywhere as Joey the Snake.

Joey was Carmine Garofolo's true second in command even though the bloodline went directly to Junior. Had Banfanti been asked by the drug-dealing Winston Jordan if it was fair that Junior should inherit the business from his father, Joey would have answered unequivocally no. Of course, Joey believed that he was the natural heir. He shared O'Leary's contempt for Junior and the new boss's revulsion toward violence. It was Joey the Snake who ordered the methodical execution of Jordan and his men. O'Leary and he would work well together. Of course, Banfanti had planned to use "that Mick cop," as he called him, to retire Junior permanently. For O'Leary's part, he knew exactly what he was doing with Joey the Snake. O'Leary told a few of his guys over several pints at Kilday's Shamrock Castle in Woodside, "That murderous little guinea Banfanti is gonna make us rich. Once he lets us know where the money is, we go, we take it, and we leave the planet."

■ ■ ■ ■

The drug trade was not all that complicated to understand, nor was it difficult to uncover. It was nevertheless very difficult to stop because most of the law enforcement resources were spent on detection, interdiction, arrest, and prosecution, and very little of what was left on reducing the bottomless pit caused by the demand for drugs.

O'Leary learned about the way the Garofolos operated their drug business from Joey Banfanti. He told Banfanti that he needed the information in order to protect the business. Joey was too concerned about keeping the business profitable until he could figure out a way to get rid of Junior to be cautious about some of the questions asked by O'Leary. What O'Leary discovered was literally beyond his wildest expectations. If things worked out, he and his small band of thieves would never worry about money again.

Mulvey had paused for a moment to get a glass of water before continuing. He looked carefully at Steven, but he couldn't figure out whether he was getting through.

■ ■ ■ ■

It took O'Leary virtually no time to figure out the chain of distribution once the drugs came under the control of the Garofolos. Their crew was importing hundreds of kilos on a regular basis, selling these kilos to the various drug dealers throughout New York City, and receiving the income from each franchise they controlled. As a result of this tightly supervised business, the Garofolo crew was accumulating an astounding profit of between ten and twelve million dollars a month. The crew set up a series of stash houses where the money was taken on a weekly basis until it was distributed to the various members of the crew at the end of each month. Junior Garofolo's monthly draw was a minimum of one million dollars.

From time to time law enforcement from federal, state, and local agencies would disrupt these operations and seize substantial sums of money and a large quantity of drugs. The drugs would be destroyed by burning the product in a huge furnace. The money would be divided up and distributed to cooperating state, local, and federal agencies. But the amount of money generated by the drug trade throughout the United States amounts to billions of dollars a year, and so the seizure of even a few million dollars by law enforcement agents is considered, at worst, an annoyance and a minor cost of doing business.

At first O'Leary and his gang guarded the transfer of the cash from pickup locations to the various stash houses, which were protected by Garofolo's soldiers. The dangerous part of the operation was the street transfer of the cash, so O'Leary's couriers traveled in well-armed threesomes. The maximum found in any one stash house was limited by order of Junior Garofolo to two million dollars. The details of the operation that began in Colombia and led to the exportation of the cocaine, and of the last step, the money laundering back through Colombia, did not interest Michael O'Leary in the least. His all-consuming interest was the money placed in the stash houses.

O'Leary's plan included pitting Joey "the Snake" Banfanti's greed and ambition against Junior Garofolo's cowardice and paranoia. He soon decided to create a fictitious story that DEA friends of his had overheard on a federal wiretap: a threat made by one of the Gambino crime family's crews to hijack the cash from one or more of the stash houses. O'Leary would convince Garofolo and Banfanti that all the cash accumulated in four separate stash houses had to be moved to a different location, a place that O'Leary would find, and held for two weeks until the threat had passed.

To make the threat seem real, O'Leary showed the two hoodlums, separately, copies of what he said were transcripts of a conversation in a social club in the Bensonhurst section of Brooklyn, headquarters for the Maroni crew from the Gambinos, which had in the past threatened to compete with the Garofolos. The transcript included a reference to Billy D'Agusta, the youngest member of the Garofolo crew, who revealed the stash house locations for an undisclosed amount of money.

Of course, before the purported transcripts were given to Banfanti and Garofolo, the body of Billy D'Agusta was found in the trunk of his late-model Cadillac not far from New Lots Avenue in Bensonhurst. D'Agusta had two bullet holes in the back of his head, an organized crime signature for execution. No one knew or suspected that the executioner was Police Officer Michael O'Leary.

The preliminaries of his plan now completed, all that was necessary was to find a house in a suitable location, have all the cash from the four Garofolo stash houses delivered there, and then complete his score by stealing every dollar. O'Leary estimated that the total amount would be at least eight million dollars, which had been converted from smaller denominations to hundred-dollar bills and larger by two bank officers currently on the Garofolo payroll. The last step for O'Leary was to figure out how he and his gang would leave the country with that huge amount of money and where to go.

One of Scotland's greatest poets, Robert Burns, once wrote something about how the "best-laid schemes of mice and men gang aft a-gley" — they go awry! He could not, of course, have been thinking of an Irish American police officer, born many years later, whose Scottish-born mother, whose married name was Burns, christened her son Robert.

Officer Robert Burns, a member of O'Leary's mob, had no trouble deciding where he would go after the big score. He would go to Ireland and help the Irish Republican Army liberate his sacred ancestral homeland. Unfortunately for O'Leary and the grand scheme for his last great score, Burns couldn't keep his mouth shut — particularly when drinking shots of Irish whiskey, chased by Guinness stout, all the while holding court in Fitzgerald's Pub in Woodside. Fitzgerald's was closely monitored by agents of the FBI.

It wasn't very long before Special Agent Shannon Kelly and her partner began to hear clear conversations about the unthinkable — a scheme devised by several New York City police officers to rip off millions of dollars of drug money and leave the country. One cop in particular, Police Officer Robert Burns, was planning to go to Northern Ireland and use his newfound wealth to fund terrorism and make Ireland united and free.

Neither Agent Kelly nor anyone else listening could know from the preliminary conversations the number of cops involved. Certainly Shannon Kelly could not have known that her former boyfriend Robert Mulvey was one of them.

The stash house to be selected by O'Leary would be carefully chosen not only to be secure but to be isolated from both residential neighborhoods and business districts. It would require access to a parkway system to permit each member of the gang a different route to exit New York City quickly. The scheme was designed to provide a separate escape plan for O'Leary, each of his six gangster cops, and Sergeant Mulvey, although O'Leary eventually decided that Mulvey was too vulnerable to be left alone and that he and the sergeant should travel together.

As to the distribution of the money, the six agreed that since O'Leary was the brains behind this great score, he was entitled to a larger share of the loot. If, as they suspected, there were at least eight million dollars, O'Leary would take two million and the six would get one million each. Anything above eight million would be evenly divided. O'Leary decided to give Mulvey a hundred thousand dollars of the first batch and a small percentage of the excess above the eight million. Initially Mulvey was told none of this because his drug addiction had completely taken hold of him and made him at times erratic. O'Leary decided that he would wait until the last minute before he and his men executed their plan. Then he would inform Mulvey, and they would leave New York together.

While poor Mulvey knew nothing and was left in the dark, Agent Kelly and the rest of the FBI squad knew everything about the plan down to the very last detail.

Even though he had not objected to it, Police Officer Burns did not think that the split that O'Leary suggested was at all fair, nor did he believe that Mulvey should receive any money. He complained bitterly to the "boyos," as the Irish illegals called themselves, as he addressed them in the rear room of Fitzgerald's. "Why," he rhetorically demanded, "should we share any of our money with that cokehead Mulvey? Why the fuck should he get a nickel? Half the time, he has no idea where he is." Burns's words were like daggers, inflicting excruciating pain on Shannon Kelly as she listened to the wiretapped conversation with a heavy heart. Burns continued, reasoning that while the money for Mulvey, at least in the first instance, came from O'Leary's share, it had the effect of reducing everyone else's.

Mulvey was now very near the end of his story.

"What you will see, Steven, is that I fell into the gutter." He said this earnestly. "And I did it by myself, making lame excuses for suffocating myself in booze and hard drugs. It was the police department that saved me."

32

Mulvey woke suddenly. It was 4:15 in the morning. The date was June 11, 1976. The place was an office inside the federal courthouse at Foley Square in Manhattan. He rose from his chair and looked around, trying to remember how he got here. The gray walls of the room seemed to close in on him. He thought that he must have dozed off after he was placed in the tiny room. He sat back down, bewildered. Slumped in the worn leather chair in the windowless room, he became aware of stacks of files on the floor. Mulvey brought himself to his feet once more and walked over to the files to read the words stenciled across one of them. The words sent a chill throughout his body.

UNITED STATES ATTORNEY, SOUTHERN DISTRICT OF NEW YORK, CRIMINAL DIVISION.

He felt a cold sweat; he was having trouble breathing. He sat back in the chair heavily, trying to understand it all. Slowly the words began to form on his lips.

"I'm a crook."

He repeated the words. Then he shouted them as he began to cry convulsively. The door opened quickly. Sergeant Bernie Pressler walked over to Mulvey and put his arms around the distraught young police officer.

"Take it easy, Robert," he said gently. "It's all over. It's goin' to get better now."

Mulvey's face looked too old for his years. The tears still streamed down his cheeks as he looked helplessly at Pressler.

"Robert, relax here for another fifteen minutes or so," said the sergeant. "Then we'll be ready to talk to you."

Robert stood up, although his knees were so wobbly that he nearly fell back into the chair. He braced himself and managed to say softly, "Thank you, sir."

Pressler headed out the door, leaving this pathetic young man standing there with his shoulders drooping pitiably. Once outside, with the door shut behind him, the sturdily built Pressler, with his military-style crew-cut hair, swept past several police officers of the elite Public Morals Administrative Division standing outside the room and muttered, "Another fucking tragedy for this goddamned job." None of the officers of this special anticorruption unit dared to say a word.

Mulvey's fifteen minutes in the holding room seemed an eternity. When Pressler returned to the room, he was joined by an assistant United States attorney, Bill McKecknie, who was the chief of the Criminal Division, FBI Supervising Agent Fred Goldman, and Chief Virgil Sampson, formerly of PMAD. As a result of the success of the 13th Division investigation, Sampson had been promoted by the commissioner to chief of a reconstituted and beefed-up Internal Affairs Division, with the three-star rank of supervising assistant chief.

Chief Sampson spoke first. "How are you doing, Robert?" Mulvey had jumped up to attention as the chief entered the room, so Sampson quickly said, "Stand easy, son."

After several hours of debriefing, it was clear to everyone that Mulvey's cocaine problem, combined with O'Leary's manipulation, had left the young sergeant not much more than an empty shell, a dupe who really had no firsthand knowledge of what O'Leary and the other corrupt cops in his crew had done.

The question remained: What could or should be done for Robert Mulvey? Later that day, after an evaluation by the substance abuse unit of the police department's Medical Division and a consultation with a drug rehabilitation center's executive director, Mulvey was admitted to Northern Hope, an internationally known drug and alcohol counseling agency located in Clinton County, New York, just a few miles south of the Canadian border.

At this point Mulvey interrupted his narrative. "I didn't want to let you know how screwed up I was, so that's why I told you I was going into a deep cover assignment for the commissioner. Of course, I didn't realize how long the rehab would take, and that was the reason I called you a few times. I knew you'd be worried."

Steven didn't react. He wanted to know the rest of the story.

The farm where Robert was sent was part of the Northern Hope complex and was called Blue Valley. It provided a multidisciplinary approach to recovery, which addressed physical and mental needs. Robert's weight had dropped to a dangerous level, under 140 pounds, as he took in less and less solid food and more and more vodka. It would take Blue Valley nearly eleven months to restore his health to an acceptable level for him to be considered at the stage in life that therapists call "in recovery": Drug addicts or alcoholics are never cured; rather, according to the treatment community, they are recovering for the rest of their lives. Shortly after his discharge from Blue Valley, Robert received department orders directing him to meet with the newly appointed police commissioner, Virgil Sampson.

Chief Sampson was just about everyone's first choice to be commissioner, and so it was that he would become the first African American to hold that job. The announcement drew rave reviews from every quarter, with the exception of at least one police officer and a local prosecutor. Brooklyn's rackets chief, Kenny Rattigan, and Sergeant Bernard Pressler had great respect for Commissioner Sampson's ability, his intellect, and his sound judgment, but they were worried about his inflexibility. They remembered his opposition to the plan that led to the dismantling of the corrupt 13th Division. While he begrudgingly gave in, he could not wait until he made it so unpleasant for Detective Bosco that this "thief," as Sampson called him, filed for retirement. And neither Rattigan nor Pressler ever forgot Sampson's fury that Bosco was granted a line-of-duty disability pension, for psychiatric reasons that a panel of physicians determined were job related, giving him three-quarters of his salary tax free for the rest of his life. Bosco and his family moved on to an undisclosed warmer climate together with his fat pension. In a rare display of foul language, the courtly chief was heard to rail, "That corrupt son of a bitch beat the system after he disgraced this department. I will make sure that this injustice is never repeated!"

As Rattigan and Pressler considered what should be done for Mulvey, both the attitude of the new commissioner and the police department's policy on drug abuse were of great concern. The department's policy was, without any exception, a mandated dismissal. Zero tolerance had to be observed so order could be maintained. That was held as the standard even as society became more and more permissive about the use of so-called recreational drugs.

Rattigan and Pressler believed that there

had to be an exception for Sergeant Robert Mulvey. When they learned that Mulvey had been ordered to report to the police commissioner's office, Rattigan called Commissioner Sampson and asked for a meeting in advance of Mulvey's appointment. He asked the commissioner for permission to bring Sergeant Pressler. His telephone call to Sampson ended on an ominous note with the words, "Kenneth, don't let us waste one another's time. Is that clear?" Rattigan answered, somewhat lamely, "Yes, sir." He warned Pressler that their mission would not be pleasant.

"No, goddammit, I will not permit this department to be stuck with a fucking cokehead junkie, and a corrupt one to boot." Commissioner Sampson's booming voice could be heard in nearly every corridor of the fourteenth floor of One Police Plaza, where his suite was located.

"Now, Virgil, calm down, because I don't plan to raise my voice," replied Kenny Rattigan, acting unusually conciliatory.

"Well, I'm not gonna keep my voice down, because what you are suggesting is just plain wrong, dammit," shouted Pressler, standing near the commissioner's desk, his face beet red.

"Now wait a minute, Sergeant —"

Before Sampson could get in another word, Pressler leaned across the desk, slammed his sergeant's shield to the floor, and with a menacing look, lowering his voice to a guttural growl, shouted, "Don't you fucking pull rank on me. You've no right to do that, so take this tin and stick it up your ass!"

The room fell to a deadly silence. Commissioner Sampson had leaped to his feet, staring at Pressler in disbelief.

"Hey, guys, we've been through too much together," pleaded Rattigan, "so can't we discuss this in a rational way?" Turning to Pressler, he commanded firmly, "Bernie, shut the fuck up and pick up your badge." Then he said very quietly to Commissioner Sampson, "Virgil, you're the boss, and whatever you decide, it's your department, we both know that, so hear us out, or at least hear me out."

Now a chastened Sergeant Pressler said quietly, "Commissioner, I am very sorry, I got a big fuckin' mouth, I didn't intend to disrespect you, so please, let me pick up my badge."

"It's alright, Bernie." With a half smile, Sampson continued. "What would we do without your big fucking mouth?"

The storm subsided, and Commissioner Sampson stated his case. "This department has had for decades, if not forever, two invariable policies: Corrupt cops could not retain their jobs and secure their pensions, and the department would not retain substance abusers, particularly drug addicts. And look what happened, we kept that mutt Bosco on the job, and not only does he take his salary for doing shit —"

The commissioner's rage level was beginning to rise, so Rattigan interrupted, gently saying, "You're right, Commissioner, completely right, but please remember that Mulvey is very different from Bosco."

"But Kenneth," Commissioner Sampson said earnestly, "it begins with the erosion of policy, and look what that piece of garbage Bosco was able to get, the fucking heart bill!"

This was a reference to a bill passed by the New York State legislature years before that granted disability pension payments, generally to police officers injured in the line of duty or those who had suffered ailments such as heart disease. It became known as the "heart bill." Since the disability payment was tax free, it created a windfall for those officers who received it. It appeared to many police officers that this retirement benefit was often abused, being granted to a disproportionate number of chiefs. One chief was denied the benefits of the heart bill but was nevertheless given a disability-related retirement pension for a hearing loss he claimed he sustained at a rock concert two years before he filed for retirement. Rattigan wondered why the commissioner was so exercised about Bosco's pension when so many of Sampson's former colleagues received such benefits routinely.

"He waltzed out of here with three-quarters tax free for life, all the while sticking his middle finger at every one of us. And just look what happened when we allowed a juicebag like O'Leary to go to rehab for his booze problem," Sampson continued, "who I should remind you has recently been convicted of murder for the killing of that young hood D'Agusta and for dozens of related felonies. How long will it take this department to live down that disgrace?"

Pressler, who had remained uncharacteristically silent, said, "But Boss, this department nearly destroyed Sergeant Mulvey. Don't you think we have a responsibility to help him?"

Pressler and Rattigan argued on into the late afternoon, taking turns trying to con-

vince the commissioner that by placing a
"Boy Scout" — Pressler's description for
Mulvey — first in Washington Heights, then
at the corruption meeting of the Corporation at the 13th Division, the department
put him in such a stressful and dangerous
assignment that he was emotionally unable
to cope. Pressler argued forcefully that the
police department should have known that
someone as straight as Mulvey could not
handle that kind of assignment.

Rattigan appealed to the commissioner on
emotional grounds: The murder of Chief
Connolly and Mulvey's breakup with Shannon Kelly had left him devastated and
vunerable. Sampson would not be moved.

Brendan Moore, recently promoted first
to deputy inspector, then to full inspector
after passing the captain's test, and now in
charge of the police commissioner's headquarters staff, joined the meeting in mid-
afternoon and, typically, just listened.

When the meeting concluded, there appeared to be no hope for Mulvey, who was
scheduled to meet with the police commissioner the following morning. Both Rattigan and Pressler thanked the commissioner
for his time and left police headquarters,
angry and dejected. They could understand
that Sampson was committed to restoring

principle to a department in desperate need of values, but Kenny Rattigan kept thinking of the words of William Shakespeare from *The Merchant of Venice:* "The quality of mercy is not strained. It droppeth as the gentle rain from heaven upon the place beneath: It is twice blessed; it blesseth him that gives and him that takes." Rattigan was lost in these thoughts as he and Pressler parted company, and they were repeated in his head over and over until he arrived home.

Alone now with Inspector Moore, Commissioner Sampson felt utterly drained by the meeting. He was very fond of Kenny Rattigan and had grown to have deep affection for Pressler, the kind of love men can have for each other because they share a job filled with danger that could only be understood by those willing to risk their lives.

"Well, Brendan, you didn't say anything, but I know you've got an opinion. What is it?"

"Boss," Moore said slowly but firmly, "you have no choice. You must respect and pay proper honor to a brave cop, a dead chief, Jim Connolly, who cannot be at peace knowing that he died before he had a chance to help this poor, fucked-up kid."

Moore's foul language shocked the commissioner because not only did he refrain from its use, he would angrily confront anyone, regardless of rank, who dared to use it in his presence. During all the years that Sampson had known Moore, his protégé had never used that language. Moore himself was shocked and shaken as he left the room, not waiting for the commissioner's reaction. He was disgusted with himself. He took the elevator down the fourteen floors to the building's lobby and then walked a half block away to St. Andrew's Roman Catholic Church, in the plaza named for it. He spent a few moments in the last pew of the church, looking at the statue of the Blessed Virgin Mary, and wondering to himself, "Is this job finally getting to me?" It was the first time in Brendan Moore's career that he thought seriously about getting out. And he made a personal decision that if Mulvey was not reinstated he would submit his application for retirement.

On May 27, 1977, New York City Police Sergeant Robert Mulvey nervously tore open the envelope addressed to him from the office of the police commissioner of the City of New York and anxiously read the order: "Effective 0800 hours, 28 May 1977, report to the Internal Affairs Division for immediate assignment."

It was signed Brendan A. Moore, Inspector and Commanding Officer, Office of the Police Commissioner.

Scrawled across the bottom of the order were these words: "I know that you will make Chief Connolly and me very proud. Good luck, Robert. Sincerely, Virgil Sampson."

When Mulvey had finished telling the story, he waited for Steven to react. His nephew remained silent.

Mulvey continued, "So you see, what I did was no one's fault, certainly not the fault of the police department. I did it to myself. But I will never forgive myself for what I did to you. Steven, let's talk to Larry Green and see if there is any way to end this."

Steven stood slowly and advanced toward his uncle, who was sitting on Steven's bed at the opposite end of the cell. Mulvey's head was in his hands, and he was trembling.

"Uncle Robert," he said tenderly, "I love you, but nothing you have just told me changes my opinion of what that damned job did to you." Steven hugged Mulvey and said, "Uncle Robert, you must believe me. I did not kill those men. I am innocent."

After meeting with his nephew, Mulvey had arranged a meeting at Larry Green's office. Mulvey was hopeful.

"Larry, Steven insists that he is innocent, even after I told him what I did to myself."

"When he told you that, did he appear agitated?"

"No," Robert anwered guardedly.

"Well, that's just great," Green said curtly. "That little pipsqueak Goss has all the evidence, and all you can give me is a denial with nothing to support it. Robert, let me make it plain to you. Given the level of violence in this case, coupled with the abuse Steven confronted at home watching his mother repeatedly beaten, there may be another answer."

"And just what is that?"

"Your nephew may very well be a murderer."

"And if he is, what can be done about it?"

"Barring some miracle from Moore, we may have to introduce quickly, and I mean now, the defense of extreme emotional disturbance. But I can only use that defense if Steven admits to the murders and if his mental condition — and its preexistence to the murders — is confirmed by a psychiatrist. If the jury accepts that defense, Steven will avoid state prison and instead will be confined to a psychiatric hospital where he can be treated. And it is entirely possible that one day he could be released. Our alternative is to continue to roll the dice!"

Green abruptly stood, indicating that the meeting was over.

33

*East New York, Brooklyn, the 75th Precinct,
June 1985*

"Stevie, my boy, this job used to be fun. Now it's all bullshit, run by Mickey Mouse and his band of Mouseketeers," observed Police Officer William Kerner. "Used to be, you'd hit the ground runnin' every day, every tour." He was smiling as he thought back. "Make some collars, get some overtime, and put the bad guys away."

Kerner, a veteran of almost twenty years with the NYPD, was performing the senior police officer's ritual of breaking in a new cop. At five feet nine inches, he had a slight build, which seemed to be shrinking because of severe health problems. His sustained anger directed toward the department, plus a disastrous divorce followed by a separation from his children, had left him with almost no appetite for solid food. The condition, of course, had no effect on his alcohol consumption, which consisted of shots of Irish whiskey washed down by pints of draft beer at Kennedy's Bar not far from the 75th Precinct. When he would finally arrive home, he would continue to drink beer until he fell into a stuporous sleep. His complexion had an unhealthy sallow look, and his facial skin was beginning to hang. All his police uniforms were ill-fitting, much too big for his body. His dark brown eyes were beginning to sink deep into their sockets, and his sharply pointed nose appeared larger than it really was. When he took a breath he made a wheezing sound caused by years of smoking. Kerner's fingers had a rusty color and his teeth were turning from white to brown from years of the habit. The smell of tobacco hung around him like an invisible cloud of pollution at a chemical waste disposal dump. But he would soon forget his physical and mental discomforts anytime he was training a young police officer like Steven Holt. Steven, with less than four months of experience following his graduation from the Police Academy, was behind the wheel of a cruiser and hanging on to Kerner's every word. Their cruiser was assigned to the night tour in Brooklyn's 75th Precinct, located in East New York. Their tour was from 8:00 p.m. to 4:00 a.m.

of the following day, known as the eight-by-four.

"Why did it change?" Steven asked in a tentative way, not sure he was supposed to speak at all.

"It's the fuckin' junkies, drugs everywhere. Junkies muggin', burglarizin', stealin' cars, stickin' up grocery stores and liquor stores. Doin' it all for a few bucks to get a fix, gettin' high and doin' it all over again."

Kerner paused for a moment, assessing the rookie's reaction. The kid was obviously impressed, which pleased the cynical veteran police officer.

"So much fuckin' drugs and crime that the system is jammed up. So, even with hundreds more cops on the streets, thousands of more jail cells, and many more fuckin' lawyers, the thing just doesn't work anymore."

Kerner was just warming up. "Then there's the ADAs. Used to be that a guy would get out of law school, join a political club, usually the Democrats, get a job as an assistant district attorney, and have a law practice on the side. He'd hustle to make a buck, didn't get nothin' without workin' for it. The guy knew how much the public wanted law and order, so he'd never break our balls. He never questioned a cop. He didn't care that we'd fuck around a little bit — nothin' serious, just enough to get the bad guys off the street. Then after a few years the ADA would graduate to a job as a judge's law secretary, sort of half an ass-kisser and half a gofer. And finally, after a while, with a few bucks placed here and there, you know . . ."

Holt didn't know, but he pretended that he did.

"He'd become a judge, and that concluded a fine career. I used to think that one of my jobs in life was helpin' a young ADA become a judge."

Now Kerner stopped, remembering wistfully the good times. "They weren't the brightest guys in the world. But shit, we were on the same side. Then that fuckin' Supreme Court in Washington started givin' the mutts all those rights which were for honest people in the first place."

Kerner appeared to be getting angry, and indeed, although he had given this speech countless times before, he got furious every time he thought of the Supreme Court and its decisions about confessions and seized evidence, shaped largely under the leadership of Chief Justice Earl Warren. Every cop knew that the Warren Court did nothing but tie their hands. Kerner told Steven about an incident in court soon after the Warren Court's historic decision on seized evidence in a case entitled *Mapp v. Ohio.*

In 1957, a woman named Dollree Mapp was arrested by police officers for possession of obscene material. The materials were seized and the arrest was made inside her apartment, despite the officers' failure to seek a court-authorized search warrant. Dollree Mapp could not have realized it at the time, but she was about to become part of judicial history. *Mapp v. Ohio* would become perhaps the most important case involving search and seizure in the history of American criminal law.

The case gave a defendant in cases involving seized evidence the right to have a hearing, known forever after as a Mapp hearing, to test whether a police officer acted reasonably under the Constitution when he or she seized evidence and arrested the defendant. If the judge presiding over such a hearing ruled that the police officer did not act reasonably, the evidence would be suppressed and the case against the defendant would be dismissed.

Kerner recalled for Steven how he was in Judge Patrick Horan's courtroom not long after the decision in *Mapp* when a lawyer named Norman J. Feldman entered. Horan was a little guy, not quite five feet tall, who had a habit of pacing back and forth behind his bench. He didn't fully realize that the snickering and suppressed laughter in his courtroom, which came from the court officers, lawyers, complainants, victims, and spectators, was caused by the fact that each time he passed behind his large leather-upholstered chair, he would momentarily disappear! Judge Horan's little body required custom-made judicial vestments, which nevertheless could not address the reality that his tiny head always seemed to have just popped out of the top of his robe. For all of that, though, or maybe because of it, Horan did maintain a good sense of humor. When he finally realized that he was the cause for the courtroom mirth, he installed an apple crate behind his chair so he was never again out of sight. Judge Horan was a former Brooklyn assistant district attorney, and he was very popular with cops.

When Horan spotted Feldman as the lawyer entered the courtroom, he yelled out, "Whaddaya got, Feldman?"

"I got a gun case, Your Honor," replied the lawyer.

"Ya want a plea?" shouted Horan.

"I'd first like a Mapp hearing, Judge."

"Did he have the gun?" demanded Judge Horan.

"Yeah, Judge, but the cop took it illegally."

Horan, turning red-faced, shouted, "Hey, Normie, that bullshit is for those old guys in Washington. I tell you what, you take a plea and your guy walks. But if you have a Mapp hearing and I don't see any so-called illegal seizure, your guy's goin' in the can for a year." Horan stopped and looked sternly at Feldman. "You got that?"

Feldman had his client plead guilty and that was the end of it.

Kerner continued, "So at first we and the ADAs worked together. We'd fudge a little bit about where the evidence was found. The prick had the gun in his jacket pocket but, you know, a cop has instincts. So we'd say the gun was on the seat next to him in the car in open view, as the ADAs would say. What was the big fuckin' deal? He had the gun, right?" Kerner watched Holt carefully to see if he was getting the message.

Holt, sensing that a response was expected, replied nervously, "Yeah, but isn't that perjury?"

The young police officer barely finished the sentence before Kerner exploded, "Stevie, what the fuck is wrong with you anyway? Those gun-carrying motherfuckers kill little kids. They fuckin' kill cops. Don't you get it? Pull over," he commanded.

When the patrol car had been guided to the curb, Kerner made sure he had the full attention of his young charge. "Stevie," he shouted, "it's us against the mutts. Cops are the last line of defense between citizens and chaos. Look what's happened to our streets. Don't you see what's happening in the DA's office? Now we got two types of enemies — the mutts and all of those young smart-assed ADAs, the white guys from the Ivy League schools lookin' down their noses at us."

Kerner was now seriously angry, trying to save his newest recruit from himself. "Even those fuckin' white guys from St. John's and Fordham, their fathers cops and firemen. Even they try and treat cops like fuckin' clerks. All of them lookin' for a chance to make their reputation on us. Get a promotion — lock up a cop for lyin' or for givin' some mutt a beatin' that he deserved."

Kerner's frustration was billowing over. "Then there's the fuckin' girl ADAs with their see-through blouses, showin' off their tits, wearin' skirts that look like they've been painted on them, all of them lookin' to trap you with a sexual harassment complaint. It's all bullshit, Stevie. None of them care about lockin' up mutts as much as lockin' up us! And if that's not enough, we gotta deal with those black ADAs. Oh, excuse me, the African American ADAs or whatever they fuckin' call themselves today. And the Latinos." Kerner spit out the last two syllables to emphasize his contempt. "All those fuckin' minorities hate all whites, and don't forget that, Stevie."

Kerner slammed his fist on the dashboard so hard that it scared Holt. "It's all bullshit. I got five months to go and then the mutts can have the city for all I care. For me, it'll be sayonara. But let me tell you somethin', pal, you'd better learn fast that your only friend is your brother cop — and I mean brother. Don't you ever fuckin' trust a broad with a badge. Don't get close to no cop unless he's white. And that's tellin' you straight."

Kerner was interrupted by the police radio. "Central to Sector George, there is a 10-31 at 445 Dumont Avenue, K." Central is the citywide police dispatcher, 10-31 is the code for burglary in progress, and the letter K indicates that a portion of the transmission has ended. Kerner snapped into action, notifying the dispatcher that their unit would respond.

The burglary location was a bodega on

Dumont Avenue, not far from Pennsylvania Avenue, the main roadway through the East New York section of Brooklyn. As the police car neared the store, Holt was surprised to see that three other patrol cars had already arrived — which was the total number of cars on duty for the eight-by-four tour in the 75th Precinct. All the police officers from those cars were already in the store as Holt and Kerner approached. The sight that greeted Police Officer Holt as he reached the doorway stunned him. He was left nauseous. Several of the uniformed officers were stacking cartons of cigarettes in a large brown cardboard box. Others were gathered around a cash register taking turns dipping their hands into the machine and extracting fistfuls of cash that they stuffed into the pockets of their police-issued windbreakers. He watched as two other officers carried an empty cardboard box into the store from the street and began filling it with more cigarettes.

After some twenty minutes of silence, as Kerner drove the patrol car back to the 75th Precinct, Holt turned to Kerner and said, "Bill, how could those cops do that, takin' those cartons of cigarettes, stealin' all that cash from the register? How could they fuckin' do that?" The perspiration ran down Holt's face. He felt like crying. "And what about you?" he demanded. "Even you took a carton. But when the cops left, you threw it on the floor — and that fat fuckin' sergeant sayin' to me, 'Take some cash, kid,' like I'm a thief, too."

Kerner spoke quietly and carefully. "Stevie, take it easy. Let's go back to the house, wash up and change. You come to my apartment. It's only a half hour from the station house. We'll talk."

It was just about 5:30 later that morning when they entered Kerner's apartment, three rooms on the third floor of a four-story walk-up. The inside was dreary and badly in need of a paint job. The smell was musty, punctuated by a strong odor of stale cigarette smoke that made Steven gag. The foyer remained darkened because of a burnt-out lightbulb. A small dining room was crowded with a large table and six chairs, relics of Kerner's former home in Merrick, Long Island. On it was the faded picture of a beautiful young woman — Kerner's wife, Florence, dead of breast cancer six years before, following their divorce. On the wall was a Cop of the Month plaque awarded to Kerner by the

Daily News, which would monthly cite the heroism of police officers and firefighters. The living room was also small and reeked of stale beer.

Holt flopped on the couch. The pillows were ripped, with little remaining padding. Kerner appeared from the kitchenette with two cans of beer.

"I don't want any, Bill," Holt protested, but he allowed the older man to shove it into his hand. He idly placed it on his right knee, holding it, staring at it as Kerner began to speak.

"Stevie, what you saw is not what cops are about. There are about 183 cops assigned to the Seven-five, and only a few dozen are like those bums."

"A few dozen!" Holt interrupted, incredulous.

"Stevie," Kerner yelled, "where the fuck did you grow up? In a goddamned cocoon? If you had two hundred lawyers or two hundred doctors, or two hundred anything, don't you think at least a few dozen of them would lie about their income taxes, be paddin' expense accounts, or takin' kickbacks? Why should cops be any different? Fact is that most of the cops come to work, bust their asses for people who don't give a shit about them, take abuse, get punched and shot at, and then go home. They never even think of takin' a fuckin' free cup of coffee. Then there's people like who we saw earlier this morning. Around the precinct they're known as Ali Baba and his Forty Thieves."

Now Holt's shock began to pass. He had heard about crooked cops before he became a police officer, and he was determined never to be in their company. Seeing so many of them at once was overwhelming, but he was beginning to recover.

Kerner continued, "For as long as I've been on the job, there's always been a few cops in every command who would steal when they would have the chance and shake down people, taking a few bucks in return for not issuing a moving violation like speeding or not arresting them for drunk driving. When I first saw it I was shocked, but I learned to ignore it and look the other way. I also did everything I could to stay away from dirty cops."

"But why did you take the carton and then leave it after the sergeant ordered us to secure the place?"

"Because I want those guys to trust me."

"Trust you — trust you! Why would you want those crooks to trust you?"

"Because, you dummy," Kerner said firmly, "one of these days you're goin' to be at a job, and you'll be surrounded by some mutts lookin' to take you out. They'll have tire irons and chains, maybe a knife or a gun. You and your partner will be in deep shit. You will radio a 10-13 for backup, and let's suppose that the guys closest to your location are those bandits you saw in the bodega, who also happen to be cops trained to fight and trained to shoot. Only they know that you're a fink. They may even think that you'd rat them out. So they'll come — only very slowly. They'll be passed by all the heroes. Only the heroes will arrive too late, too late to save you from a beatin', or maybe too late to save your life."

Now Holt's eyes were bulging, his mouth opened in disbelief.

"You think what I'm sayin' is bullshit? Well, you ever hear of Frank Serpico? Serpico got sick of seein' so many cops stealin' back in the late sixties, so he went to a newspaper reporter and bingo — there was a big scandal. The police brass and their friends at the PBA and the SBA said the scandal was all bullshit. But the mayor got scared — he's got an election to worry about, so he appoints a commission to investigate cops. And guess what? There was a scandal. Cops were taking money from gamblers and drug dealers for protection.

Cops were stealin' from store owners and drunk drivers. Cops were stealin' hot stoves. The PBA and SBA union guys got very quiet. Then great reforms were announced. The mayor and the police commissioner said they wouldn't tolerate crooked cops. The five district attorneys of New York City began to wake up and indict cops. But that wasn't enough for the mayor. He convinced the governor to appoint a special prosecutor. Of course, since cops vote, the mayor and the governor assured everyone that the special prosecutor was not just for cops — he'd investigate everyone, DAs, ADAs, judges. Sure, everyone. And the special prosecutor did arrest some judges, but their cases got tossed out — by other judges."

Kerner stopped to catch his breath. "Then, Stevie, Serpico, he got a gold detective shield for bein' such a great hero. He got assigned to the Narcotics Bureau. And you know what, Stevie? The first job that brand-new Detective Serpico goes on, he and his team bust into an apartment with a search warrant and Serpico gets shot in the face. One of the mutts shot Serpico as he tried to get in the door. His team leader said later that the shooting was a terrible accident that should have never happened. Only Serpico didn't think it was an accident. Now he's livin' in Switzerland. Stevie, I took that carton of cigarettes for my own protection, and I told that lowlife of a sergeant that you were a little nervous, so we'd grab some money out of the register when they left."

"You did what?" Holt demanded.

"Stevie, I did it for you. Stevie, get used to this shit or go somewhere else. Join the fire department."

"But aren't these guys afraid of Internal Affairs?"

Kerner started to laugh. "Who do you think they get to go in that rat-fink squad at IAD? Those guys can't find their ass with two hands. The bosses make sure that the good ones don't last."

"But why?" asked Holt, doubting his partner.

"Because, Stevie, the brass are terrified of scandal. So what they want IAD to do is Mickey Mouse shit, breakin' the balls of honest cops to keep them in line. Sure, if they get a crook cold, they'll serve charges and bust him out. And maybe if a DA is alert, he'll get the cop indicted. But one or two or three ain't a scandal. You got it?"

It was 6:30, and Holt was tired and disgusted. Besides, he wanted to go to the 8:00 a.m. Mass. He shook Kerner's hand.

The older man hugged him, thinking of the two sons he hadn't seen since their mother died. "Stevie, I'll be your steady partner till I get out. By that time you'll know who you can trust."

At the beginning of the next eight-by-four, after the turnout sergeant finished advising the police officers of the precinct conditions, he dismissed them from roll call. "Kerner and Holt, stand by," he ordered. "There's some fuckin' IAD captain who wants to see you. Did you guys call him?"

"Yeah," said Kerner, "we want to surrender." Kerner's stomach churned as the sergeant smiled, but as Holt began to shake, Kerner whispered, "Stevie, be cool. If it's serious we'll ask for our union delegate."

The two officers went to the locker room, where the captain was waiting. He appeared to be unthreatening as he smiled. "Did you guys take a job at Dumont Avenue yesterday?"

"Yes, Captain, why?" Kerner responded.

"Were you not told to secure the place?"

"Yes, sir."

"Were you told to remain until the owner came, or to make sure the front door was locked?"

"To lock up, sir," replied Kerner.

"Well, you didn't, dammit, and Kerner, you should certainly know better."

Kerner could hardly contain himself. Mickey Mouse was alive and well at IAD.

"It's a hell of a way to break in this rookie officer," the captain continued.

Holt spoke. "Beggin' your pardon, Captain, Officer Kerner has really taught me a lot so far. I forgot to lock up."

"Not your fault, son. This department demands accountability from our senior officers." Turning to Kerner, the captain said sternly, "Officer, we've reviewed your record to prepare for this interview. You've done pretty well. So we'll let this go with a reprimand, okay?"

Kerner snapped to attention and gave the captain a smart hand salute. "Yes, sir," he shouted.

In late December 1985, William Kerner, like many other officers who live the dream of "twenty and out," retired to Fort Lauderdale. In January 1986, he received his first police pension check. The following week, while playing tennis, Kerner suffered a massive and fatal heart attack. At the time of his death, former New York City police officer William Kerner was forty-three years of age.

34

East New York, Brooklyn, the 75th Precinct,
New York
Fall 1987

A newly assigned young officer was driving. Holt was in the passenger seat as the recorder, the police officer who records all official activity. The youngster had graduated from the academy three months earlier and had been assigned to the 75th Precinct for the last six weeks.

"Pull over," Holt abruptly ordered. The officer quickly responded, more than a bit puzzled because it was the first time Holt had spoken since the beginning of the tour.

"Let's get one thing clear," said Holt. "I don't fuckin' steal. If you do, I'm goin' to fuckin' lock you up. If you try to stop me, I'm goin' to fuckin' shoot you."

The bewildered young cop, turning crimson, shouted, "Yes, sir."

■ ■ ■ ■

Holt began his first tour with every new partner this way until he was promoted to the rank of sergeant on January 10, 1988.

35

Police Academy,
1988

After he was promoted, Sergeant Steven Holt was transferred to the academy as an instructor because his conduct had earned the notation on his official file "not suited for regular field command duty." Since the high command at the police department had little interest in controlling police corruption, something they believed was an aberration, they marked Steven as nothing more than a gadfly, and the way the brass dealt with people like Steven was to assign them to lecture probationary police officers about the dangers of corruption. Of course, over the six months of training given to these young police officers, only one hour was devoted to anticorruption awareness. In their world of doublespeak, the brass would explain that someone had to address the possibility of corruption, however remote, and that police officers like Steven Holt who worried so much about the hazards of corruption were appropriate to give that lecture.

Steven's other duties included attendance taking and the job of chauffeuring the commanding officer of the academy. During the five months Steven was assigned to this duty, the commanding officer never spoke to him beyond a perfunctory greeting at the beginning of his tour and an equally brusque good-bye at the end.

Then the 75th Precinct got a new commanding officer. Captain Jackie Desmond had built a solid reputation among police officers for carrying out the Mickey Mouse traditions of the high command at One Police Plaza. He was looking for sergeants he could trust. When someone told him of Holt's habit of breaking in a new partner, he decided that he had his man.

Soon Steven Holt was back at the 75th Precinct, this time as one of its patrol sergeants.

36

The Blue Wall, NYPD,
Late 1980s

The problem of corruption within the ranks of the NYPD continued into the late 1980s and seemed intractable. The recommendations made by the special commission back in the 1970s, just as Captain Nevins had predicted, had accomplished very little. Despite the mayor's upbeat press announcement immediately after the arrests of the crooked cops of the 13th Division, and his sincere promise to make positive changes, nothing was done institutionally to address the cyclical nature of police corruption. The Internal Affairs Division remained a place that no police officer wanted to be assigned, so it continued to be populated by gadflies or subpar cops and others who couldn't seem to fit in regular police assignments.

The special state prosecutor's office, set up as a result of one of the recommendations of the corruption commission, was abandoned after some spotty successes. It was resented throughout all the years it existed because the governor gave it the power that had until then been rested in the five elected district attorneys of New York City to investigate and prosecute police and other forms of corruption within the criminal justice system. None of the district attorneys ever forgave or forgot what the governor did, and as a result, none of them was particularly helpful.

Then in 1990, shortly after the newly elected mayor, W. Carlton Richardson, took office, he appointed Kenny Rattigan his corporation counsel.

Rattigan in turn recommended the appointment of Sean J. Nevins as the city's new police commissioner. The recommendation, adopted by Mayor Richardson, stunned most of the police brass. While the New York City Fire Department once had a lieutenant — and at another time in its history even a firefighter, who was the president of the firefighters union — vault over its chiefs, to serve as fire commissioner, nothing like that had occurred in the police department. And while it was true that a number of police commissioners came from outside the department, these were generally prominent lawyers with close contacts to whoever was serving as mayor. Never had someone with the rank of captain become chief executive officer of this tradition-bound police department.

Commissioner Virgil Sampson was a superb police officer and administrator, but he lacked the cunning and political instinct to deal with the intransigent high command of his department, nor would he suffer the bureaucratic minutiae that were the daily staples of One PP. Accordingly he increasingly ceded his authority and control to his deputies, who gleefully accepted it. Commissioner Sampson's successors over the following twelve years were more traditionalist, and it didn't take long for the department to settle back to its goal of making no waves. If there were no scandals, there would be no shake-ups. If everyone understood that crime has cyclical stages of highs and lows, not affected by any changes outside or inside the department, no problems would be presented for the chiefs to solve. Take credit for increased public safety during the good years, and blame drugs, public apathy, politicians, and district attorneys during the bad years.

Without muckraking by the media, police

corruption was largely unmentioned, and with the investigation of corruption left to the dolts assigned to IAD, the chiefs of One PP had a fine life. Keep the commissioner happy, keep him in the news visiting basketball centers with local kids, provide a few photo ops with senior citizens, get as many promotions to senior chief positions as you can, and then go off to head up the security department of a major business organization. Not a bad life, at least for the chiefs.

For the public, however, it was quite a different story. New York City in 1990 was fast becoming one of the most dangerous big cities in America, and one of its boroughs, Brooklyn, had become the fifth most violent municipality in the country per capita.

Police corruption had taken hold again. Soon there were intelligence reports from federal sources and from within the police department warning of a growing cancer of corruption. These reports, unfortunately, were generally ignored.

At least one police commissioner, Michael G. Keating, a seasoned cop and a superb chief, who rose steadily through merit to the top of the police department and who was in addition a well-respected retired colonel in the United States Marine Corps, tried to do something. Unfortunately, he served briefly and was not retained after Mayor Richardson's election. Were it not for the availability of Sean J. Nevins, replacing Keating would have been a major mistake.

Over the years, Pressler and Nevins tried to stay in touch. Pressler set his sights on passing as many promotional examinations as he could, hoping that higher rank would bring him the opportunity to make changes to prevent a return to systemic corruption. In just a few short years Pressler was promoted to lieutenant, then captain. By the time Nevins was appointed police commissioner, Pressler held the rank of deputy inspector.

With each promotion, Pressler was given challenging and exciting assignments, in commands such as the Emergency Service Unit and Intel, the Police Intelligence Bureau, where he had the responsibility of designing security programs to protect foreign dignitaries. Perhaps Pressler's most challenging job was his appointment to oversee a team responsible for the creation of a long-term approach to crime reduction by mandating accountability in each police precinct's command through the use of a computer-driven statistical analysis.

Pressler's innovative program, called Crime Crash, would over the next several years receive substantial credit for massive reductions in crime in New York City and would become the prototype used by police departments throughout the world.

In contrast to Pressler's command assignments, Nevins was given jobs created to break his spirit and force him to retire. But no attempt, however humiliating, could knock Sean Nevins down. He headed a unit that reviewed applications by civilians seeking pistol permits and one within the Missing Persons Bureau checking on case files closed for ten years or more; at another time he was made director of the bureau responsible for placing and removing police barriers at demonstrations and parades.

"Sean, how the fuck do you take this shit?" asked an exasperated Bernie Pressler.

Nevins, faking his favorite imitation of an Irish brogue, replied, "Inspector, dahlin', every day when those humps at One PP review the orders and see the name of Sean J. Nevins, captain, NYPD, they die a little . . . ever so slowly. So at the end of the day we shall see who remains standing."

Pressler at this broke into a smile and gave Nevins a bear hug.

■ ■ ■ ■

Corrupt cops who were still on the job in the early 1990s had learned well from those who preceded them. In order to survive and make an adequate amount of money on the side while laying low, waiting for the big score, it was important to operate in small, well-disciplined cells, modeled after urban terrorists, Communists, and yes, as one corrupt cop said, "freedom fighters." For this cop, he and his fellow freedom fighters were liberating assets from criminal activities for their own benefit and for the benefit of their families. They had also learned never to use a telephone to talk about their business, or to speak anywhere until they had checked for listening devices in advance. Finally, no new members were permitted to join a corrupt cell unless they were family. If any police officer was transferred out of the precinct, the size of the group or cell would be reduced until a personal friend or family member could be assigned.

The night tour, as always, was fertile ground for the operation of these corrupt units, because the numbers of police personnel provided to neighborhood patrols were reduced, and supervision by patrol sergeants was virtually eliminated.

"Commissioner," Assistant Chief Moore, soon to be Nevins's first deputy police commissioner, said with a broad smile, "I do believe you know Deputy Inspector Pressler." Here were these three old friends together in the office of the commissioner at One Police Plaza, which none of them would have believed possible — particularly with one of them holding the title of PC. It was Police Commissioner Sean J. Nevins's first full day of command. Following Moore's introduction the three men laughed with wild roars.

"Well, Bernie, how does it feel to be one of the Last of the Mohicans now that all those cellar-door dancers have jumped ship?" This was Nevins's signature line and favorite metaphor for all phonies. When Nevins was growing up, his Brooklyn neighborhood had trim little one-family frame homes. On the side near the front entrance, there was a door leading to the basement portion of the home. It was known as the cellar door and was angled at forty-five degrees. So for Nevins, the phrase described people who could dance over their principles the way his boyhood friends could balance themselves while dancing on a cellar door.

Nevins's appointment led to a flurry of resignations. Virtually every police boss above the rank of captain resigned in protest. It did not faze Mayor Richardson in the least, not just because he was a maverick, but because he remembered that when another mayor chose the fire department's first African American commissioner, there was a similar reaction from the FDNY brass. When asked what he thought of the mass of resignations, Mayor Richardson's uncharacteristic response was "Fuck 'em!"

Nor did it faze Nevins, who saw it to be a real opportunity to revolutionize this moribund autocracy. "Bernie, we just got the chance of a lifetime," Nevins began, "but all we have is two, maybe three years. Yet it's still plenty of time before we move on. And I want to start the change with you."

"Com—"

Pressler did not get beyond the first syllable before Nevins, ever volatile, leaped from his chair, red-faced and shouting. "Goddammit, Bernie, don't you ever fucking call me that again!" Nevins's cigar was bouncing in his mouth.

"Well, can I call you Boss?"

Nevins thought for a moment and said, smiling, "Okay, Bernie, but only in public, not here."

37

The Blue Wall Smashed,
February 27, 1990

"Sean, do you remember what you said after that judge was sworn in by Mayor Hargrove to investigate police corruption?" The commissioner didn't answer, so Pressler persisted. "You said, 'None of this will stop until cops act like cops.' What the hell did you mean by that?"

Nevins replied by reminding Pressler of the extraordinary work of the Public Morals Administrative Division, which, in contrast to IAD, was so successful in locking up corrupt cops and crooked lawyers.

"They were real detectives, whose primary mission was to disrupt and jail organized crime guys. While their investigation and arrest of corrupt cops and crooked lawyers grew out of this primary mission, it never occurred to them that they should make a distinction between these criminals. So they acted like cops."

Moore had heard this analysis several times before from Nevins, but he never gave much thought to it. It certainly made sense to him, but he had not considered how it could be applied beyond a special unit like PMAD, which had been disbanded a few years before. As successive commissioners worried more about rising levels of street crime and considered the investigation of sports betting an unaffordable luxury, fewer and fewer resources were allotted, until the effort was formally abandoned.

Unfortunately, few people in the department understood that the mob used the enormous profits gained from sports betting to fund most of its other activities, from loan sharking to hijacking to the control of drug traffic. And drug traffic was, beyond any other factor, most responsible for the seemingly out-of-control street crime. Drug-craving addicts and the greed of violent drug gangs were turning the streets of New York City into a zone of terror.

The problem in law enforcement was that so few administrators understood that sports betting was the cash cow of organized crime. The last commanding officer of PMAD surely understood the clear connection, and he often said with considerable frustration, before this elite unit was abolished, "The public has got to be convinced that every time they give a hundred bucks to Joe the Bookie it will come back to their neighborhood in the form of drugs or guns that will be used to murder children and cops." He also understood that a bookie was only a franchise operator, who had to pay a regular tribute to the mob. The network of bookies, numbering in the thousands, nationally produced billions of dollars each year that provided a steady stream of funding for the crime families.

Nevertheless, the chiefs at One PP considered this opinion to be completely out of touch, because it failed to understand that all the resources available had to be allocated to attacking street crime. The prime strategy for this attack, the so-called War on Drugs, was doomed to failure because it never made an effort to reduce the demand for drugs. Drug treatment and education programs were considered social work, not law enforcement.

These same chiefs also dismissed as a nut Chief Phil Blanton of the Transit Police Department, who said that the way to reduce crime in the subways was to come down hard on the fare beaters, aka the turnstile jumpers. What that chief recognized, and the One PP chiefs could not see, was that this kind of conduct might reveal sociopathic behavior, and if you arrested these people, a good number might have prior serious criminal records and might be out of prison on parole. When they were arrested, the transit police discovered that many had failed to keep contact with their parole officer, and many others were wanted in connection with the commission of another crime. So, the chief concluded — correctly, as it turned out — if he could take them off the streets and out of the subways, the result was a sharp reduction in subway crime.

The theory of attacking quality-of-life crime as a major tool against serious crime was not something traditionalists would embrace. It ran counter to everything they ever learned, and it was also dangerous. The police brass believed that if they announced that this approach would reduce crime and it failed, they couldn't withstand the angry criticism that they had wasted valuable resources on minor crime.

"And so, Bernie, that's what I wanted to talk to you about," the commissioner continued. "We have identified one cesspool in

Brooklyn, the 75th Precinct, where the majority of the police officers are young, dedicated, and honest. We've got to get to them before the half dozen or so crooks there infect them with the virus. Tell Bernie what you have, Brendan."

Even while Brendan Moore was moving up in rank, he maintained his extraordinary network of informants. There was no piece of information, no news or news source, that was not important to him. His information gathering was not just his job, it was his hobby, the goal of which was to expand his database. It also made him very much needed in the police department, and it became his power base.

"There's a sergeant, a nighttime supervisor who has been stealing since he got on the job," Moore began, "and he has very cleverly limited his corruption activities to protect himself against discovery. Over the last few years, he led a gang of perhaps four or six other cops, including one of the precinct's PBA delegates, Scott Ruben, and an alternate, Gabe Perone. They pick up extra money the usual ways with the drunk drivers, shaking them down, and the other one-shot opportunities, but their principal source of income is stealing drugs and money from a few gangs operating in East

New York. Of course, there is little new to this technique, except that this crew are very disciplined. They don't ever talk anyplace where they can be overheard, and they never use telephones.

"But" — here Moore allowed himself a broad, toothy smile — "they do make mistakes. They've gotten greedy, and instead of making arrests and confiscating the money and the drugs, dividing them up at a secure location, they set up franchises and allow the drug gangs to operate for a monthly share. While this has produced much more money, it's made them vulnerable."

Moore explained that the crew would arrest gang members, take the money and the drugs, resell the drugs that same night to another gang, and then split the proceeds at the end of the tour. This recycling of the drugs was safe, but it did not produce the kind of money they wanted, so they identified a leader of each of the eight gangs operating in East New York and demanded a percentage of the gross sales for the month. To ensure an honest count they conducted random raids, counted up the money and drugs, and then extrapolated to figure the monthly take. If they concluded that they were being shortchanged, that gang would have its operation suspended for three months. Once the period of suspension had been served, the cops told the gang members that if they were found cheating again, they would lose their police protection permanently, and if gang members were caught selling drugs, they would be arrested and would face a life sentence. The sanction never had to be imposed because the gangs understood very clearly the consequences of cheating. The "Bandits of Bush Terminal," as they were known, had created a very profitable enterprise.

This crew of rogue cops got their name because the meeting place for all of their collections was an abandoned warehouse in the commercial complex of several large buildings known as Bush Terminal, located on the Brooklyn waterfront adjacent to the Gowanus Parkway. The location was chosen because it was several miles from East New York, a factor the crew believed would lower their risk of detection.

Chief Moore's people knew just about everything the Bandits were doing but could not get anyone on the inside — no one, at least, until recently, when one of the Bandits made a major mistake. Police Officer Frank Patrice had arranged to meet Domingo Sanchez, the boss of one of the smaller drug gangs, for the monthly payoff of about a thousand dollars. Sanchez pleaded with Patrice for more time, saying he could not have the money until after the weekend. Patrice located Gabe Perone, who was attending the summer conference of the PBA at the Concord Hotel in the Catskill Mountains upstate. Perone's angry reaction to the possibility of a late payment so unnerved Patrice that he found Sanchez and, holding him by the feet from the sixth floor of the warehouse scaffold, screamed at him, "You motherfucker, you have that package in twelve hours or you will fly."

Up until then, the Bandits kept the drug dealers in check by threatening them with the law, never with rough stuff, which gets people worried and makes them do crazy things like ratting you out. Patrice, who was just plain dumb, panicked, and of course he didn't dare tell the boss. Sanchez also panicked, and he reported the threat to one of Chief Brendan Moore's operatives, who promised to help — but only if the frightened drug dealer would reveal the meeting place for the next payoff.

By the time Patrice had his next meeting with Sanchez, the sixth floor of the Bush Terminal warehouse had been turned into a sound stage by Moore's people, who placed multiple listening devices and videotaping equipment throughout the warehouse. The sights and sounds of the transaction between Sanchez and Patrice were later reviewed by Commissioner Nevins, Chief Moore, and Inspector Pressler. And, of course, this regular meeting place for the Bandits remained under constant surveillance by Chief Moore's unit until a plan could be found to catch the thieves.

For Nevins, at long last the time had come to test his theory that cops could act like cops and take police action against corrupt police officers, not as part of any specialized unit but as regular patrol officers assigned to precinct duty.

"Bernie, you're the guy with the reputation and respect to make this happen. Honest cops will follow you. And if you can make it work, the way cops look at corruption will change. We will be able to assign real cops to Internal Affairs on a rotating basis, make it a career path to detective, to other better assignments, in short, to make it a respectable place to work. "We" — the police commissioner stood up for dramatic emphasis — "can smash the blue wall . . . forever!"

Pressler didn't respond, waiting to see what Nevins had in store for him.

"Bernie, some day this is going to happen, but if you can't do it, I don't know anyone else who can."

Now it was Pressler's turn to talk. "But what do we do about the PBA and the SBA? As long as they protect their members regardless of the charges, doesn't that encourage police officers to look the other way?"

Nevins smiled and said, "Bernie, you're absolutely right." Turning to Chief Moore, he said, "Ask Billy Lally to come in, and see if Sean Tobin is available."

Police Officer William Lally entered the room, cautiously but with his usual broad smile. Five foot nine and about 140 compact pounds, he had golden blond hair and clear blue eyes that seemed to sparkle when he smiled. Lally was just thirty-four years of age and single, and some thought he was the typical young ladies' man of a cop. That mistake was made by an older opponent in the race for PBA president, whom Lally crushed in the election. The race to succeed the long-serving and seemingly invincible Rusty Russo created particular interest in the rank-and-file police officers because of his sudden resignation. It angered the veteran officeholders in the PBA because it left them to scurry around for a successor.

In contrast, a coalition of African Americans, Asians, Latinos, and women joined forces with young white officers to support Billy Lally. It was the right time for someone like him.

Commissioner Nevins was particularly pleased about the election results because of Lally's credentials as a progressive. Someone who could lead an increasingly diverse department of women and people of color was exactly what Nevins needed for the changes he had in mind. Since Lally's election slate included an African American, it was the first time in the history of the union that one of its trustees was other than white. Moreover, Lally immediately began grooming a twelve-year veteran police-woman, Lisa Keller, to become the first female trustee in the history of the PBA. The commissioner believed that if ever there was a union chief who would understand that the police department had reached a critical crossroad, Lally was the guy. Similarly, Sergeant Sean Tobin, the newly elected president of the SBA, was a young progressive supported by a broad coalition of young female sergeants and a growing number of blacks, Latinos, and Asians who passed the promotional exam.

"Sit down, Billy," Nevins said cordially.

"We're happy you had some time to come over."

Lally's face broke out in a broad smile as he replied, "Hey, Boss, I didn't think there was an option!"

The commissioner's secretary announced that Sergeant Tobin had arrived. Lally greeted the young sergeant. "Late as usual, Sarge."

Tobin ignored Lally. "I thought this was a private meeting, Boss," he said with a smile. "I didn't expect to see this lug, but I guess an order is an order." Tobin, the longtime fullback on the football team known as the Finest, was beginning to sag around the middle and pick up some jowls, but otherwise his stocky frame of six feet and some two hundred pounds was still rock solid. With a full mane of red hair worn too long for some of the bosses, deep dimples, and a perpetual smile, he looked like an oversized leprechaun.

It was Nevins's turn to tease, with his favorite Irish brogue imitation. "Now boys, you two dahlin' young men know my reputation as an old union fighter, and you bein' the big shots and all that, I'm much obliged you could find the time to visit a sentimental old man!" After the briefest of pauses, Nevins became very serious. He stood for a moment and then sat on the front edge of the desk once used by the most famous police commissioner of New York City, Teddy Roosevelt. The commissioner spoke softly. "Boys, I'm going to ask you to do what no other union official in law enforcement has ever done."

"And just what is that, Commissioner?" The response from Lally was flat and very direct. Tobin didn't speak.

"Before I ask you to do anything, I want you to listen to what Brendan has to say, fair enough?"

When Brendan Moore had completed his presentation, which included audio and video tapes of the Bandits of Bush Terminal, Lally shook his head and said simply, "Those mutts make it bad for all of us."

"That's right, Billy, and it's why I want you and Sean to agree that the PBA and the SBA will refuse to furnish lawyers for these criminals."

"But, Commissioner, as you know, our organization gives, as a benefit of membership, legal help to any cop in trouble. And the fact is that since legal fees are funded by membership dues, it is considered an entitlement," Lally said. Tobin didn't respond but just nodded his head vigorously in support.

Nevins walked over to where the young union leaders sat, placed a fatherly hand on their shoulders, and said earnestly, "Boys, how many cops and their families need to be destroyed before this department and your unions decide to finally tear down this fucking Blue Wall of Silence, and with it the blue wall of mindless support?" Without waiting for a reply, Nevins continued, "I promise you both that if we can pull this off Internal Affairs will no longer be a place for jackasses and flakes who waste time harassing cops with Mickey Mouse rules. It will be an honorable place to work and a positive career path because it will lock up all sorts of crooks, whether or not they're cops. The fact is, and I know you both believe this, any cop who protects a drug dealer is no longer a cop!"

Nevins now shook both union officials' hands, a signal that the meeting was over, and said, "All I ask is that you think it over. Whatever your decision is, I will understand."

Chief Moore filled out the rest of his intelligence report to the commissioner, which included patrol strength and an assessment of those who were likely to buy into Nevins's plan.

"There are 180 police officers at the 75th Precinct, including twenty-three sergeants, six lieutenants, a captain, and a deputy inspector. The nighttime supervising sergeant and six uniformed cops, five males and one female, are our Bush Terminal crowd. There are nineteen officers, including one sergeant, who are prime candidates for our team. We recommend from that list eight officers, including that young sergeant, Steven Robert Holt. His middle name is from his uncle, whom you will no doubt remember, retired sergeant Robert Mulvey." The commissioner smiled as he recalled the sincere young police officer from Nevins's days as the commanding officer at the 67th Precinct in Brooklyn. So much had happened over the years to both of them.

"Didn't Mulvey retire out of Internal Affairs and move with his wife upstate?"

"Yes, sir," Moore responded with a great deal of pride as he recalled the role he had in convincing then–Police Commissioner Sampson to restore Mulvey to duty.

"It's a small world," said Pressler, as he, too, remembered how he and Kenny Rattigan argued with Sampson to do the right thing, "but do you think Holt would be interested after what happened to his uncle?"

"We don't think he knows about that," responded Chief Moore.

"In any event," Moore continued, "the eight officers on our list are among the most active police officers since their assignment to the Seven-five and at every previous assignment. Not only has there been no hint of scandal among them, they are known in the precinct as super straight. While Holt is well respected by those police officers who have worked for him on various tours, he is despised by the Bandits of Bush Terminal."

The seven uniformed officers on Moore's list were Holt's protégés. He often chose them to team up with him on the more dangerous assignments. Pressler decided to approach Holt directly. If he could convince the young sergeant, the rest would be easy.

"With respect, Inspector, I don't want to be a damned guinea pig. I like this job too much. But as much as I despise those mutts, they are the reason Internal Affairs exists."

"But Steven," Pressler reasoned, "your arrest activity makes you one of the most productive sergeants in this job. Isn't a crime a crime?"

"Sure it is, Boss, but what do you do about other cops, the honest ones, who would treat me like a fink? What has this department ever done to change that attitude?" Of course, Steven knew, as did Pressler, that he had made a telling argument.

Pressler argued that attitudes could change if this initiative was successful and that the commissioner was committed to making sweeping changes, particularly at Internal Affairs. At the end of nearly two hours, Pressler could see that he was not getting anywhere and that Steven was becoming uncomfortable, so he decided to use what he had planned only as a last resort. He stood, as did Holt, who was relieved that this seemed to signal an end to the meeting.

"Look, son, you have every right to be skeptical about this approach and what it can mean for this job for decades to come. We've asked you to be a trailblazer in a department that does not look for new ideas. We built the Blue Wall of Silence, permitting cops to hide behind it, and we nurtured it by our inertia, and now, suddenly, with no guarantees, other than our word that we are committed to change, we place a demand on you that you have a right to reject."

Now Pressler seemed to be pleading,

something very much out of character for this gruff street cop. "Steven, don't think of the potential future benefits to the department. Think of this in human terms. How many honest and dedicated police officers have been hurt because none of us did a damned thing about corruption?" Pressler sat down and continued. "Why not speak to your Uncle Robert and see what he says about this."

"Sure, but why do you think he can change my decision?" Holt was puzzled.

"Steven, just ask him. Let him tell you why."

That evening Steven flew to Albany, where he rented a car and began the journey to Delaware County and the beautiful rural village of Delhi, where Robert Mulvey and his wife and three children had moved when he retired.

The following morning, Steven left the local motel in Delhi and, using the directions supplied by a perplexed Robert Mulvey, began the last leg of his trip. Although it was late in the summer, Delaware County was beginning to feel the first hint of fall. The slight chill was offset by the majestic though blinding sun rising over the magnificent Catskill Mountains. Soon the paved road turned to a rich, dark dirt road winding up to the top of a hill overlooking a lushly green and broad valley, which disappeared only as it reached the horizon. At the crest of the hill was a raised two-level ranch-style house, looking quite new.

In the driveway was a used brown Ford station wagon. A tall, comely woman, whose jeans and sweater showed a body still firm at fifty, answered the door. Her hair, a darker shade of blond with a touch of strawberry, was worn up and back in a ponytail. With a rich tan and a sprightly smile, delicately sculpted cheekbones, and almond-shaped eyes, softly tinted green, she could have easily passed for a woman not yet past her midthirties, but that was of no consequence to her; when age was mentioned, she almost always said, "It's only a number!" Steven greeted her with a smile and a quick kiss.

"Hi, Aunt Shannon. How does it feel to look like the farmer's daughter?"

"Now, Steven, save those lines for a future conquest. You look great. Your uncle can't wait to see you."

All those years ago, while he was in rehab, Robert wrote two unanswered letters to Shannon asking her to understand that their last horrific meeting was the product of his addiction. He pledged to her that he would remain sober for the rest of his life even if she could not forgive him.

When he was released, he received one of life's few second chances. As he walked along the crushed stone pathway away from the facility that had liberated him from his drug-induced nightmare, he was lost in his thoughts. Suddenly he heard a soft, familiar voice. "Hey, Sarge, care for a lift?" Mulvey dropped his bags and ran into the waiting arms of Shannon Kelly.

Robert had gone into town to get the newspapers and something for breakfast. So Shannon Kelly Mulvey, still possessing her FBI-agent interrogation skills, though she had retired several years ago to raise their two boys and a girl, used the little time available in Robert's absence to probe the purpose of Steven's trip with a few questions.

"Now, now, Aunt Shannon," Steven teased, "you know very well that we don't cooperate with the feds."

Not deterred, Shannon persisted, "Seriously, Steven, is there something wrong?"

Steven fixed his eyes directly on his aunt and asked, "What happened to Uncle Robert? How did he get assigned to Internal Affairs?"

Shannon's eyes welled up immediately and her nose reddened. She blurted out, "Steven, for God's sake, who put you up to this? Have you come all the way up here to break his heart?"

Confused, Holt responded, "I don't know what you're talking about."

Before another word passed, the doorway was filled with Robert Mulvey, whose broad smile evaporated at the sight of Shannon. He demanded, "Steven, what the hell is going on?"

Steven walked over to his uncle and, giving him a loving hug and a kiss on his cheek, said, "Uncle Robert, I really don't understand why Aunt Shannon is upset."

Shannon recovered quickly and said simply, as if dismissing the whole thing as a mistake, "I thought Steven was angry about your transfer to that fink squad at IAD."

"No, of course not," Steven protested. "Inspector Pressler suggested I come here to get some advice. He suggested that it was important that I see you, but when I asked him why he acted all mysterious. He said that I should ask you why. When I tell you what the inspector and the department have in mind for me, and why I've decided not to be involved, I think you'll agree with me, so I don't know what the big deal is that I should come all the way up here. Is there something I should know about you and the job?"

Mulvey answered guardedly, "Well, let's see what you have going on."

As Holt laid out the extent of the corruption that ravaged the 75th Precinct, it of course reminded Mulvey immediately of the corruption that overwhelmed the 13th Division and how he had been persuaded by Inspector Connolly to go undercover. Mulvey recalled the great success of the operation and then all of the bitterness and his destructive behavior that followed. He decided not to give Steven any of the details other than to tell him that most cops disapproved of his undercover activity because it led to the arrest and imprisonment of so many other cops. He explained that it didn't matter to most police officers that those cops from the 13th were corrupt. The culture of the police department and the mentality of most police officers was that cops don't treat other cops like perps, using undercover activity, including electronic listening devices, to gather evidence against them. Most police officers believed that was the job of the feds or IAD, and it really didn't matter that the feds were at best uninterested in police corruption or that IAD was a joke.

What truly excited Mulvey was the plan that Steven described for honest cops to conduct an investigation of rogue cops and then move in and make arrests. Finally it would be legitimate for police officers outside IAD to arrest crooks who happened to be police officers. It seemed to him to be a historic opportunity for trained and dedicated police officers to clean up their own mess.

"Steven," he said passionately, "you can't let this get away. Pressler and the other bosses see in you a true leader who can convince other honest cops to follow. Our department has suffered for too long under a false sense that snitching is wrong, and I'd be the last to attempt to convince cops that it is the only way to root out corruption. But this is very different. You've got to go for it."

Mulvey saw no point to telling Steven the complete story of his fall to the very brink of oblivion and how he ended up at IAD. He would soon decide that withholding all of that was a mistake he would deeply regret.

■ ■ ■ ■

"Alright, Inspector," Holt said, "let's get on with it."

For the next several days Steven met individually with the seven young police officers suggested by Moore; they were his first choices as well. Most of them raised the same question Holt put to Pressler: How would honest cops feel about this operation? The answer was even more difficult because none of these officers had Holt's motivation — the anger and pain he felt about what had happened to his hero, Uncle Robert. He reported back to Inspector Pressler that five of the officers were in and ready to go.

On most Friday evenings, exactly at 2300 hours, or 11:00 p.m., the Bandits of Bush Terminal would gather to divide up the purse, as they called it. The routine included each of the Bandits meeting earlier with a member of each of the drug gangs and picking up a package, which contained as much as twenty-five hundred dollars and as little as a thousand. Their leader, a sergeant, would arrange to meet with one member from each of two gangs, and the six other bandits would each meet with one member from the remaining six gangs. The assignments for the pickups were rotated and chosen by lot. This would ensure a larger share for the boss, who was, after all, the senior thief. On Thursday afternoon, the sergeant drew Domingo Sanchez, head of one of the Latino gangs, and Huey Davis, head of one of the black gangs.

Building 7 was the last building in Bush Terminal. The sixth floor of Building 7 had been the meeting place for the Bandits for more than six months, a concern for some of the crew members because they believed that habit and routine could lead to discovery.

Shortly before 11:00 p.m. Police Officer Frank Patrice arrived, followed soon by three other members of the corrupt gang of cops. Each had a package from his drug pickup. By 11:45, Patrice became concerned that the sergeant, Ruben, and Perone had not shown. He and the others did not know that this was a trap, nor did they know that their boss had been tipped off earlier in the day and had ordered Ruben and Perone to stay clear of the meeting.

Instead, the three met in the backroom of Kelsey's bar, not far from the 75th Precinct, to divide up a smaller but safer share of the money.

"What the fuck is goin' down here, Boss?" asked Perone.

"Whatever it is, you can be sure that scumbag Moore is involved. He's got his finks everywhere," the sergeant replied.

When the sergeant picked up the money from Sanchez earlier at his social club, the drug dealer told him how "that asshole" Patrice threatened to kill him and how he complained to a friend of his in the Police Intelligence Bureau. Sanchez said he was approached by some captain who worked for Moore who told Sanchez that if he didn't bring him to Bush Terminal and show him where the payoffs were made, he would put Sanchez out of business. Since the payoff locations were moved regularly, the captain's information about Bush Terminal was stale. Sanchez thought he was tricking the captain by bringing him to the sixth floor of Building 7, where he had occasionally made his payoff. What Sanchez didn't know was that while the payoff spots changed regularly, the sixth-floor location remained where the Bandits split up the proceeds.

"Freeze," commanded Sergeant Holt, as Pressler and the rest of the detail surrounded Patrice and the other crooked cops. "You're under arrest."

Holt then began a familiar recitation: "You have the right to remain silent. Anything you say will . . ." — the arrest warnings. All too familiar to cops, now converted in an instant to criminals.

One of the Bandits complained that it was no treatment for a cop. Pressler shut him up immediately, shouting, "You're not a cop, you're a fucking thief." The stark realization of his new condition caused the disgraced police officer to cry, sobbing out of control.

The news of the multiple arrest of corrupt cops by honest cops from the same police precinct didn't get the attention Mayor Richardson thought it should. The more the spin doctors from his press office tried to sell the story of cops, "real cops," arresting bad cops, the more crime-beat reporters, then columnists, and finally the editorial writers turned away from the story. They just didn't get it. During a time when police corruption wasn't very unusual, the attitude of most reporters was, "More crooked cops, where's the fucking story?"

The cynicism did not affect the pride felt by Police Commissioner Nevins. He had done it! With one strategic strike he had legitimized for street cops — perhaps forevermore, he hoped — the arrest of police officers who violated the law and who had done violence to the system of justice.

The commissioner immediately issued orders directing that no police officer could advance to the Detective Bureau and be given the coveted gold police shield without a minimum of eighteen months of assignment to Internal Affairs. Internal Affairs was no longer a division but had been raised to the more prestigious level of bureau, the equal of Intelligence, Homicide, Major Frauds, and the other high-level units of the NYPD.

Moreover, in order to be eligible for promotion through the three grades of detective, from third to second to first, an additional tour of one year at IAB would be mandated. Nor would any police officer be eligible to take any promotional test offered for sergeant, lieutenant, or captain without volunteering to serve at least six months in Internal Affairs. Finally, no captain could attain the rank of inspector or the various levels of chief without at least eighteen months of duty at IAB.

Commissioner Nevins not only had succeeded in smashing the blue wall, he had removed the stigma of serving in IAB, by making service there not only tied to promotion but honorable. Within a week, the waiting list for assignment to the new bureau required the creation of a lottery.

The day after the roundup, the PBA and SBA issued this press statement: "We have reviewed the evidence against the defendants known as the Bandits of Bush Terminal. We have decided that these charges are so substantial that the defendants are not entitled to be represented by lawyers hired by the PBA or the SBA." The statement was signed by William P. Lally, President, PBA, and Sean Tobin, President, SBA.

To the surprise of no one, certainly not Commissioner Nevins or Inspector Pressler, Steven Robert Holt was the first police officer with the rank of sergeant to apply for assignment to IAB.

38

Junior's Restaurant, Flatbush Avenue, Brooklyn,
Early November 1992

Famous worldwide for its cheesecake, Junior's of Brooklyn was the place to be seen if you were a lawyer with political ambition. Each morning at breakfast, beginning at 6:30, every table became a power center. The Kings County political leaders, Republican and Democrat, met at separate tables, with supplicants — lawyers looking for jobs as law secretaries to the various judges, whose staffs were, for the most part, controlled by these political leaders. Of course, no one would ever admit that such blatant patronage still existed. It was also an opportunity to meet with fund-raisers, who provided the lifeblood of politics: money.

These meetings also offered opportunities for constituents to ask for favors, or, as they were referred to in the political world, "contracts." A job given to a constituent, or the relative or friend of a constituent, was a contract that was filled. Of course, just as in the commercial use of the term "contract," something was always expected in return. The payback had become far more sophisticated since so many political leaders had landed in jail for bribery. They developed what one political columnist observed was legit graft — a payback, to be sure, but accomplished in such a way as to avoid criminal prosecution: a long, fun-filled weekend in the Bahamas for the political leader and his wife or his girlfriend, paid for by the wealthy uncle of the recipient of a political appointment; a generous contribution to the election campaign of one of the political leader's chosen candidates for the state legislature, months after the contract was filled, to make the connection between the job and the political contribution impossible to prove. Politics was still lucrative for those who controlled the jobs.

There was also a section in the rear of Junior's that, by an unwritten code, would remain off-limits to any other guest if it was occupied by people conducting serious and confidential business. That was where, early one Saturday morning, a meeting about

Steven Holt's case was held. It was at Brendan Moore's request, assembled in order for him to give a report about his investigation. Settled around the table were Larry Green, Shannon and Robert Mulvey, Deputy Chief Bernie Pressler, and Queens County DA Kenneth Rattigan and his longtime mentor, Brooklyn DA Buddy Cooper. Moore trusted the ability and judgment of each — with the exception of Robert Mulvey, but obviously, he couldn't be excluded.

"No one is around who can tell us anything about the murders," Moore began, "but my guys were told by the young drunks who hang out around Bush Terminal that there was a junkie who used to cop drugs, mostly crack cocaine, from them, who disappeared sometime in late December of 1990. He didn't have a name, but since he always wore battle fatigues, they called him Soldier."

Moore paused. He was actually enjoying his brief return to the intriguing world of informers. "One thing was of particular interest: Soldier only copped drugs at the beginning of the month. They remember that because they would try to sell him crack later on in the month and he would tell them that he only had a few bucks to buy Thunderbird wine."

Pressler was the first to speak, but what he said was something that the others had already guessed. "He is either dead or he still gets a pension, sent to wherever he's moved."

"Correct," said Moore, "but let's understand something. None of those mutts we spoke with said that this guy saw anything, so his disappearance may be unrelated to the murders."

"While that may be true, I sure would like to find the guy," Rattigan volunteered.

Shannon was particularly enthused about Moore's information. "I've got some friends in the postal service, and if this guy used a post office box, and he's still alive, they should be able to find out his new address."

The excitement began to get to Rattigan. "I've got a friend, a contributor to my campaign, who is the president of the check cashers association. He should be able to find out where Soldier cashed his check. He could have cashed it at a local bar not far from Bush Terminal."

Pressler followed up. "They said he had a bad limp, so I assume he didn't go very far. Hey, Kenny," he said, turning to Rattigan, "any problem with me checking that out?"

Before Rattigan could answer, Green

stood and, displaying his nastiest scowl, said, "You know, you fucking law enforcement types never fail to be predictable. Does it occur to you that Holt may be guilty and that Soldier may be the missing link in Goss's case?"

Mulvey broke the long silence with a shout. "No, Larry, no, he's innocent."

"Listen to me, Robert, and all of you, the heart is never a substitute for brains." Green hoped that this band of dedicated friends and loved ones would realize the consequences of what they were saying. "What if this fucking alcoholic junkie gives Steven up? Or let's say he can provide information to exonerate him — how do you know if he is credible? And don't answer, because not one of you, other than Brendan and I, can make an objective assessment. So here's the deal, if Soldier is found, only Brendan and I will interview him."

Green waited for the reaction. Not sensing any, he continued, "So that's settled, okay?"

One of the detectives assigned to the Kings County district attorney's office detective squad entered the rear sanctuary of Junior's and quietly approached District Attorney Cooper. He whispered in the DA's ear.

Cooper excused himself. "I've got an urgent call." He said to Green, "I'll only be a minute. Wait till I get back."

The car's horn was incessant. Its crimson-faced driver was screaming racial epithets at the car in the lane directly in front of his, waiting for the traffic light to change. Gabe Perone took his shield out of its case and began to wave it wildly, shouting, "I'm a fuckin' cop, move it!" Perone hours before had been at a beer racket in another section of Brooklyn. He was quite drunk. "For chrissake, you fuckin' monkey, get outta the way!"

The light on Lincoln Road, a boulevard-sized thoroughfare with two lanes on either side, changed to green, but the automobile carrying the Reverend Cedric Lyons, pastor emeritus of Salvation AME Church in the Bedford-Stuyvesant section of Brooklyn, did not move. Reverend Lyons, revered by the African American community of Brooklyn, had ordered his driver to hold on "while I give this young man a piece of my mind." When Reverend Lyons got out, Perone leaped from his car to confront the elderly pastor. Reverend Lyon raised his right hand and said softly, with a smile, "Now, son, what has got you acting like this?" On the sidewalk, a crowd of African American neighbors began to gather.

"Get back in your car now, or I'll fuckin' drop you," Perone ranted.

The pastor's chauffeur, a huge black man who was a former heavyweight boxer, began to walk toward Perone. He warned, "Watch your language." Perone fired twice, hitting the man in the shoulder and the right leg. He fell to the pavement.

Horrified, Pastor Lyons pleaded, "For the Lord's sake, put that gun down." Perone wheeled in the direction of the minister and put two bullets into his abdomen. He also fell to the ground.

The crowd on the sidewalk began to shout angrily, but Perone waved his gun, keeping them at a distance. In minutes the police were all over the street. Several of them ordered Perone to drop his gun. One cop smashed Perone over the head, sending him crashing to the pavement. He was manacled from behind and thrown into the rear of a police cruiser. The police commander for the local precinct, a well-respected African American inspector, was able to calm the crowd. He took immediate action, ordering officers to place the injured pastor and his driver in two separate patrol cars and rush them to Kings County Hospital. He decided that waiting for ambulances to respond would be too risky. He was told by one of his police officers, an emergency medical technician, that both victims had been stabilized and would survive. Before leaving the scene, the inspector addressed the crowd, which had grown to more than a hundred: "Most of you know me and know that when I talk, I tell the truth. First of all, Reverend Lyons and his driver are okay. Secondly, this guy we arrested is a cop, and I want you to know that I'm going to make sure he never gets out of prison."

Cooper returned shortly and informed the anxious group at Junior's, "Police Officer Gabe Perone has been arrested in Brooklyn. Perone claims that he is an eyewitness to all three murders charged to Sergeant Holt and that they were committed at Bush Terminal. He wants to make a deal."

39

People v. Holt,
November 10, 1992
"May it please the Court." Goss bowed and began cautiously, with a clumsily obsequious attempt to curry favor with Judge McGowan.

It didn't work. McGowan glowered down from his lofty perch and sternly interrupted. "Now what?"

Goss quickly responded, "Your Honor, the people found a witness late last night, and I wish to call him."

"Very well," McGowan said curtly, "call him now."

"Well, Your Honor, I can't do that right away. I —"

Before Goss could proceed, McGowan shouted, "Inside."

Sergeant Kurland walked briskly from the courtroom, as bewildered as the rest of the spectators. He spotted Lieutenant Artie Morelli of the Suffolk County Homicide Division, whom he had met at a police fraternal organization function several years before.

"So, Lou, what's goin' on?" Kurland asked anxiously.

"A police officer named Gabe Perone got busted, somethin' about a shooting in Brooklyn. He's agreed to testify against Holt," replied Morelli. Then, pointing in Holt's direction, he added quickly, "I think we've got him!"

"Steven," Kurland began quietly, "what can Gabe Perone testify about?"

The blood had drained from Holt's face, but his answer was firm and measured. "I haven't the slightest idea except that Perone is a goddamned crook, one of several of the Bandits of Bush Terminal who didn't show up the night we arrested the others. I was always certain that he and the rest of them were tipped off to our raid. But he'd probably say anything."

When Kurland told Holt that Perone had been involved in a shooting and was offering to testify in return for a deal, Steven shrugged his shoulders and said, "Hey, Sarge, what can you expect from that mutt?

But it doesn't matter, Green will tear him to pieces."

Kurland smiled and said, "So you're feelin' pretty good?" Without waiting for an answer, he continued. "But what do you think he'll say?"

Quite suddenly Holt seemed concerned as he replied in a whisper, "He shoulda been dead."

"What did you say?"

"Never mind, Sarge. Thanks for the visit. And oh, keep your ears open."

40

VA Hospital, Bridgeport, Connecticut, November 12, 1992

"The good news, Larry, is I have him," Brendan Moore began, trying hard not to raise expectations.

"Yeah, so what's the bad news?" interrupted Larry Green impatiently.

"He's been in the psychiatric ward of a veterans' hospital up here in Connecticut for almost two years suffering from a post-traumatic stress disorder."

Moore explained that sometime late in December of 1990 Soldier, whose real name was Bradley Coles, was found by police officers, wandering on a pier at the Brooklyn waterfront, several blocks from Bush Terminal. He was incoherent and appeared to be in shock. When they searched him looking for identification, they found among the papers in his wallet a discharge certificate from the Marine Corps that listed his rank as major.

The officers took Coles to the United States Veterans Administration Hospital in Brooklyn, where he was admitted for observation and diagnosis. Before his transfer to the VA hospital located in a suburb of Bridgeport, Connecticut, which specialized in the treatment of this mental disorder, Coles received his regular disability check. Using the information supplied to Shannon Mulvey by her contacts in the United States Postal Inspection Service, Moore was able to trace him there.

"I'm coming up," shouted Green.

"Okay, Larry, but it won't be very helpful," Moore replied. "The major, according to his psychiatrist, is withdrawn and frequently catatonic. When he responds at all, it's limited for the most part to guttural sounds."

Earlier in the day, one of the jurors had informed Judge McGowan that her brother had died suddenly and that his funeral was set for Monday. The judge recessed the trial without objection by either side to Tuesday morning at ten.

"That gives me four days to be up there," said Green in a call later to Brendan Moore, "and get firsthand from this guy's doctor if he can be of any help."

Assistant District Attorney Wally Goss welcomed the time off from trial to permit him a chance to negotiate with Police Officer Gabe Perone's lawyer. Because of the extended conflicts created by this new development, Brooklyn District Attorney Cooper and Suffolk County District Attorney Crowley filed a joint request with the chief administrative judge of Kings County, appointing Crowley special district attorney to prosecute the case against Perone.

At first, lawyers and community activists representing Pastor Cedric Lyons were angry and concerned that Perone would not be punished for his racist violence. In order to allay those fears, Mayor Richardson invited Reverend Lyons, his family, and all his representatives and followers to Gracie Mansion for a meeting with Cooper, together with the Queens County district attorney, Kenny Rattigan, who had a particularly good rapport with Brooklyn's African American community when he was Cooper's rackets chief. They were joined by Crowley.

Crowley did not mince words. "However important it is for us to bring justice to the memory of three people who were brutally assassinated during the Christmas season of 1990, I solemnly pledge to you that no agreement will be made with that murderous, bigoted thug Perone in return for his testimony unless he accepts a substantial prison sentence. Moreover, the terms of that prison sentence will be discussed with Pastor Lyons and his attorneys and will be subject to their approval."

Later that day, Perone's attorney, Carey Bremen, and District Attorney Crowley met at Crowley's office in Suffolk County. Bremen began slowly, "According to the press reports, you didn't give us much room to negotiate."

Crowley put on his best poker face and replied, "Carey, my boy, your client didn't give himself any room! And if he didn't have something to sell, we would be here discussing one of your scholarly treatises on the rules of evidence, and not wasting any words about that dirtbag you represent."

Carey Bremen, a former senior bureau chief in Brooklyn under District Attorney Cooper, had previously served as president of the Brooklyn Bar Association and recently been voted president of the prestigious New York State Bar Association by his peers. At age fifty-four, as an associate professor at

Fordham University School of Law, the author of half a dozen critically acclaimed legal textbooks, and the senior partner in one of the better-known white-collar criminal defense firms in New York City, Bremen would not ordinarily defend the likes of Perone. His practice mostly dealt with crooked financiers, an occasional corrupt union leader, or a lawyer facing prison and the loss of his license to practice law. He had only agreed to represent Perone as a favor to the PBA president, Billy Lally, who would from time to time retain Bremen's law firm when a conflict of interest precluded the PBA lawyers from representing one of the members.

Bremen was always nattily dressed in three-piece suits with hand-tied bow ties, the appropriate sartorial-splendor uniform of a Hollywood version of a trial lawyer. His jet black hair was receding on both sides of his head, leaving a sort of peak in the middle of his high forehead. Although he was blessed with a perpetual wistful smile, Professor Bremen felt quite uncomfortable representing the likes of Gabe Perone. Nevertheless, he was an advocate, so he would do his duty.

"But Jim," protested Bremen to the Suffolk County district attorney, "Gabe Perone is your case! Larry Green has destroyed all your forensic people, and your only hope is an eyewitness. Perone is the only other person present at Bush Terminal who can give you the details of what was quite simply an execution." Crowley never changed his expression as Bremen continued, "With Perone, you then set a solid foundation for motive. Holt is the only one with a motive to kill Scott Ruben. He hated Ruben because he escaped the Bush Terminal roundup. Your detectives have informed you that he planned to kill Perone if he hadn't been arrested."

"Okay." Crowley had heard enough. "Perone faces a sentence of between five years and twenty-five for each charge of attempted murder. You know Judge McGowan's reputation — he will have no problem giving Perone consecutive prison terms. So what's he looking at? If he cooperates, I'll ask the judge for twenty-five years, which, as you know, means that he will do seventeen and change. Of course, that is if the pastor and his driver agree. If he doesn't testify, I'll ask for fifty, which doesn't let him see the parole board for thirty-four years — if he's still alive."

Bremen appeared stunned, although in truth he did not expect much better. "How much time do we have?"

"I've ordered a special grand jury in Brooklyn to meet through the weekend. They will be ready to file at 5:00 p.m. on Monday, two counts of attempted murder." Crowley's office would delay the filing of the indictment until a few minutes before the clerk's office closed to minimize the possibility of a leak to the press.

Now Crowley stood and took hold of Bremen's right shoulder. "Carey, after the grand jury files on Monday, there will be no more deal."

41

Hospital, Bridgeport, Connecticut,
November 13, 1992

"I am afraid, Mr. Green, Major Coles can be of very little use to you or to himself," Dr. Jeanne de Lourdes, chief of psychiatric services for the Bridgeport VA hospital, began to explain.

In the eighteen months since his transfer from the hospital in Brooklyn, the diagnosis for Coles's mental health condition had remained largely speculative. Of course, his symptoms were consistent with posttraumatic stress disorder, which the psychiatrists concluded was related to his combat service in Vietnam. The thing that troubled the doctors who reviewed Coles's chart and made observations of him when he appeared to be awake was that he did not seem to respond to traditional treatment plans designed to disassociate his memories of Vietnam from present reality. His condition was worsened initially by the violent withdrawal he suffered when he was forced to abstain from drugs he regularly used on the street.

"For most patients," explained Dr. de Lourdes, "the symptoms disappear after approximately six months. But for others the symptoms are chronic, lasting for years."

She told Green and Brendan Moore that there was something perplexing about Major Coles. From time to time he would appear to be in recovery during the day, and just before he retired to bed, quite suddenly, he would revert and be subjected to violent nightmares.

"Can you be certain that the major's disorder is limited to his experience in Vietnam?" Green asked finally, after a long pause he used to reflect on Dr. de Lourdes's analysis.

"Mr. Green, our science has not reached a stage which goes beyond speculation, and without the benefit of observation during the time closest to Major Coles's discharge from the military, it's impossible to say. But hypothetically, if the major were confronted with another violent experience, it is quite possible that the symptoms of posttraumatic stress disorder could return."

Green pressed on. "What if the major was

shown something which re-created the environment where that violence occurred — for example, a picture of a jungle battlefield in Vietnam, or a similar environment, where the patient witnessed something that was particularly violent. Would that cause any reaction?"

"It's entirely possible, but what are you getting at?"

Larry Green turned to Moore and said, "Brendan, show Dr. de Lourdes the photographs."

Moore's people had shot a dozen or so angles on the floor in Bush Terminal. Moore also had pictures of Holt, Ruben, Perone, and the other indicted Bush Terminal Bandits, as well as other suspects who along with Perone got away by not showing up at the time of Holt's raid at the terminal.

Major Coles was led into Dr. de Lourdes's office. Coles was just under six feet with a trim figure, kept that way through vigorous exercise during his lucid periods. His hair was a silver gray, and the deep lines in his face made him appear much older than his fifty-one years. His greeting was a silent shy smile, which together with his hospital clothing and slippers made him look very vulnerable.

The pictures were placed on two sides of

the walls of Dr. de Lourdes's office and were covered at Green's request. The psychiatrist insisted that she be the only one to speak. She would ask the major first if he recognized the floor pictures of the warehouse at Bush Terminal, and then if he recognized the men in the photographs. Larry Green selected the order in which the pictures of these men would be displayed.

The first four pictures shot inside the warehouse produced no reaction from Major Coles, but the next two, shot from what Moore's investigators surmised was Coles's makeshift loft, brought a nod and a broad smile of apparent recognition. When the floor shots were completed, Green could feel his palms become moist. The pictures of Holt and the other three were set facedown, held by Scotch tape on a piece of drafting paper: Suddenly the doctor turned the paper over to reveal the photographs. Major Coles looked down at the display, then jumped up and, pointing with a series of jabs, began screaming, "Him, him, him!"

The attendants could not restrain the distraught former Marine officer. Coles smashed one attendant across the face, opening up a nasty gash above his right eye, causing a torrent of blood. The other received a judo kick to his groin and immediately doubled over in pain. Dr. de Lourdes had pressed the panic alarm in response to Coles's first outcry, which produced six burly attendants who with great difficulty, and aided by an injection administered by Dr. de Lourdes, brought him under control.

"Oh my God, now what do we do?" asked Green a bit later.

Moore asked the psychiatrist whether there was any way the use of drugs or hypnosis would permit a limited debriefing of Major Coles.

Her answer was too quick, in Green's opinion, and too abstractly clinical for both Moore and Green.

Green shouted, "Look, Doctor, I've got a young kid on trial for three murders he did not commit, and this guy holds the key, so don't be so goddamned quick to reject a plea for help."

Dr. de Lourdes, not prepared for Green's outburst, countered, "Don't you dare raise your voice to me or I'll throw you out of my hospital. I'm a doctor, not a magician, and you should know very well, since you witnessed my patient's reaction, that there is little I can do."

Moore raised his hand, signaling Green, whose face had turned scarlet with fury, to be quiet. "Doctor, there must be something. Isn't there anything you can do to get through to him?"

Dr. de Lourdes was immediately sorry; the grandmotherly seventy-something psychiatrist did not often openly display her emotions, and certainly not anger. She looked at these two men sympathetically. Green's face was filled with anxiety, and Moore's wore a look of frustration that she couldn't recall in anyone else. "Gentlemen, I will try to help you, but you should understand that while hypnosis can remove some symptoms, a substitute symptom often arises, and we have no way of knowing how it will manifest itself. To the extent that hypnosis has been effective in treating repressed feelings, of course I'll try it, but obviously, I'll have to wait several days."

"Doctor," replied Green quietly and dejectedly, "the trial resumes on Tuesday, the day after tomorrow. We are running out of time, and this is a long shot. In any event, we've got to tape your session with him. It's our only hope."

"You're some fuckin' lawyer, Bremen. Why don't you just get me the gas chamber?" Perone screeched in the isolated waiting room in the special security wing of Rikers Island.

The Rock, as it's called, houses inmates sentenced to up to a year in jail, people who are awaiting trial and are unable to post bail, and high-profile inmates like Perone who are being held without bail and in isolation, whose lives would be at risk if they were permitted to mix with the general population. A white cop charged with attempting to kill an elderly African American minister would not last long in a jail that has a high percentage of inmates who are African American.

Bremen at first ignored the sarcasm and allowed the explosion to subside. He then said, "Look, there is no alternative for you, nor is there certainty that you'll be held for the entire term of your sentence. If you put this psychopathic killer cop away for three consecutive life prison sentences, anything is possible. There is no guarantee, but I can move to have you resentenced, after a few years."

At this Perone shouted, "After a few years? For what?"

"For what?" Now it was Bremen's turn to raise his voice. "For trying to kill one of the most respected clergymen in New York City and for trying to kill his driver, all because you didn't like the color of their skin!"

"Oh, bullshit, it was self-defense," replied Perone.

"Okay, that's it," said Bremen. He shouted, "Officer, get me out of here."

"Hey, wait a minute," Perone suddenly pleaded.

Assistant District Attorney Wallace Goss rose confidently from his chair and with just a trace of a smile announced, "Your Honor, the People call New York City Police Officer Gabriel Francis Perone."

Goss took Perone through a series of questions, setting the stage for the grand finale, the in-court identification. It is the drama-filled moment when the witness, in front of the jury, actually identifies the so-called perpetrator of a crime.

"The Boss, Ruben, and I met at the Bush Terminal to split up money we got from the local drug dealers we protected. Suddenly two Spanish guys wandered onto the floor. I guess it must have made quite a spectacle for them to see all that cash lying near our feet. One of them claimed that he had lost his wallet at a party the previous night. As we were trying to figure out what to do, someone shouted across the huge floor of the building, 'Police, freeze.' The Boss and I didn't hesitate for a moment as we ran for the fire exit. When the Boss got out the door he scampered down the stairs. I stayed at the doorway with my gun drawn and took a shooter's position. The guy who shouted came across the floor from the opposite part of the building, and although the lights were pretty dim I recognized him right away. He stooped to where Ruben had dropped his gun and raised his hands, surrendering. The guy shouted, 'You crooked piece of shit,' and then he fired two shots, taking Ruben down. The two Spanish guys dropped on their knees and began to plead. I watched as he slowly and methodically put a round in the temple of one guy, and then he kicked the other guy to the ground and picked him up by his hair and put a round in his temple as he screamed for mercy."

"And then what did you do, Officer Perone?"

"I ran away," Perone replied sheepishly.

"Now, Officer Perone, please stand and look around the courtroom. Can you identify the person you have described as the killer of Hiram and Ramon Rodriguez and Police Officer Scott Ruben?"

"I can."

"Very well, point him out and indicate for the jury a piece of clothing he is wearing."

Pointing to Steven, Perone announced, "That's the man, and he's sitting at the defense table, wearing a blue blazer."

Assistant District Attorney Goss solemnly intoned, "May it please the Court, may the record show that Police Officer Perone has identified the defendant, Steven Robert Holt, as the one who killed all three victims?"

"Yes," McGowan replied.

"That's a shock," grunted Steven to his lawyer.

Now it was Larry Green's turn to shock Justice McGowan, Goss, and the assembled press and spectators. He rose and said confidently, "Your Honor, I have no questions for this person." Green pronounced "person" carefully, separating the two syllables to show his contempt for Perone. He knew that Perone had just committed perjury.

42

People v. Holt,
November 17, 1992

Goss stood and with a fumbled attempt at flair announced, "And that, Your Honor, is the case on behalf of the People of the State of New York."

"Very well," replied McGowan. Turning to Green, expecting him to make a motion to dismiss, which is always made in the absence of the jury, he inquired, "Do you want the jury excused, Mr. Green?"

Green stood and replied, "Oh, no, Your Honor, we are prepared to proceed."

"Very well. Do you intend to call witnesses, and how long do you expect to take?"

"Not very long, Your Honor, since I will only present one witness."

"Alright, please proceed."

"I call Bradley Coles."

On cue, the rear doors of the courtroom

flew open and Bradley Coles, accompanied by Brendan Moore, began to walk up the aisle slowly, with a slight limp. He was dressed immaculately in a three-piece blue business suit with a light blue button-down shirt and a red-and-dark-blue-striped tie. Moore escorted Coles to the entrance of the well and then took his seat in the front row. Coles continued past Holt and Green, to whom he gave a respectful nod, which he repeated for the jury and Justice McGowan. He mounted the stairs to the witness box and remained standing as he had been instructed previously by Larry Green.

"Do you swear to tell the truth, the whole truth, and nothing but the truth, so help you God?" intoned the clerk of the court.

"I do," the witness replied.

"Please state your name, state of residence, and occupation."

"Bradley Coles, the state of Connecticut, major, United States Marine Corps, retired."

Green's decision minutes earlier not to cross-examine Perone had intrigued everyone in the courtroom, especially the jury. They sat transfixed, watching Coles's every gesture.

The press, which at this stage of the trial included some of the most seasoned commentators from the national scene just couldn't figure out what the hell Green was up to. There was an air of building excitement greeting the arrival of his mystery witness. Kurland had a perplexed look on his face. Across the courtroom directly opposite where Kurland was seated, Mulvey, Shannon, and Lee Moran were huddled together. They knew what to expect from Major Coles, but they also knew that his testimony was fraught with danger. They stared in anticipation as Coles sat down, and they prayed silently.

Green knew full well that what he was doing could bring his career to an abrupt end. He strode confidently to within a few feet of the witness box, and with an uncharacteristic broad smile, he began.

Earlier, Dr. de Lourdes had told Larry Green that the hypnosis therapy seemed to be holding, and while she could assign no scientific reason for its success, she was quite certain that it had a limited duration. Green decided to withhold from Judge McGowan that Coles's testimony would be the result of hypnotic inducement. The lawyer certainly knew that such testimony was inadmissible in New York State and that if his deception was discovered, McGowan could hold him in contempt and refer his actions to the lawyers' grievance panel, which would undoubtedly recommend a sanction that might very well result in the loss of his license to practice law. Despite all of this, Green decided that he had no other choice.

Dr. de Lourdes was clear about the risk. "He could break down at any time, and since you witnessed it, I need not describe the volcanic nature of his flashbacks. Just ask your questions gently, and pray!"

"I wish I had that in my arsenal, Doctor," sniffed Green. "I mean prayer and all that stuff!"

Dr. de Lourdes had never quite gotten used to people who volunteer their agnosticism or atheism, so she answered with a smile, "Very well, then I'll pray."

Green began in a soft but firm voice. "Do you recall where you went after your discharge? By the way, what was the nature of that military discharge?"

"I was honorably discharged for medical reasons. I headed back to Brooklyn, where I lived as a kid."

"And did you arrive at your destination?"

"No, I did not," the major answered.

Coles described how he blacked out

repeatedly and found himself in a warehouse complex he came to know to be Bush Terminal. He testified about his journey into drug addiction and alcoholism, how he built himself a kind of loft high above the floor of one of the warehouses, and how he lived on his disability checks. Next Green brought him to the time of the murders, the evening of December 19 into the early morning of December 20, 1990.

"Now, Major," Green continued gently, "please describe what you observed." As Coles spoke, Green never lost control of the inquiry. It was important, he would lecture his students, that on direct examination the examiner not permit the witness to give long narrative answers, which frequently could cause jurors to lose interest. In this case that would not be a concern, but control over Major Coles's direct testimony was particularly important because of his fragile mental condition. So Green would interrupt Coles gingerly with well-rehearsed phrases such as "Please hold it there for a minute" or "Let me briefly interrupt you."

Green carefully guided Major Coles through each of the brutal executions. As Coles described the first murder, Green literally held his breath, but the Major's responses, as he recalled in vivid detail how each murder was carefully carried out, were both clear and measured.

When Major Coles had finished this portion of his testimony, Green stepped back to the rear of the jury box, which was directly across from the defense table, on the opposite side of the courtroom, and addressed Judge McGowan. "May it please the Court, may I have the defendant stand up?"

"Of course, Mr. Green," the judge replied. Green motioned to Steven, and he stood up on wobbly legs.

"Major Coles," said Green firmly and confidently, "can you point to the man whom you observed murder Hiram and Ramon Rodriguez, and later kill Police Officer Scott Ruben?"

"I can."

"Please point him out and identify him by a piece of his clothing."

As Coles stood and pointed his right hand and extended his index finger, he began to shake. For a moment, Green actually caught himself thinking of a little prayer in Hebrew he learned at yeshiva school in the Flatbush section of Brooklyn. As Green was finishing his prayer, Coles said in a strong voice, "That's him in the row reserved for police officers, the fat guy in the gray windbreaker."

Judge McGowan stood and commanded, "You, sir, identify yourself, now."

"I'm Sergeant Joseph Kurland of the NYPD."

Goss leaped to his feet and shouted, "Wait a minute. I want to cross-examine this witness."

McGowan responded, "Be quiet."

Now pandemonium broke out across the huge courtroom. The press corps had jumped to its feet like a well-drilled military squad and headed in Kurland's direction. Some of the spectators, police officer friends of Holt, stood and began to shout at Kurland. Kurland for his part began to look for an escape route.

McGowan stood, pounding his gavel, immediately demanding order and directing the court officers to control the courtroom. Next he ordered the jury removed. When the last juror left the room, McGowan pointed to Kurland and ordered Morelli, "Lieutenant, arrest that man." Morelli quickly handcuffed Kurland from the rear and began to escort him toward a holding pen behind the courtroom.

43

Forlini's,
November 25, 1992

It was a Wednesday, late in the afternoon, and the Forlini brothers made a rare exception and shut off their rear room to the public to allow for Steven Holt's celebration. In addition to Steven and his fiancée, Lee Moran, the crowd included Robert and Shannon Mulvey, Larry Green, and the three district attorneys, Cooper of Brooklyn, Rattigan of Queens County, and Crowley of Suffolk County. Brendan and Peggy Moore took their seats at the midpoint of the large table that took up most of the space in Forlini's rear room. Apart from the celebration, everyone wanted to hear Brendan describe how he and his operatives found Soldier, or Major Coles, and the circumstances that led to the dramatic dismissal of the case against Steven and the arrest of Kurland.

Moore, now savoring the spotlight following his brief return from retirement, began to spin his tale. The story he told the group was pieced together from interviews conducted by Moore and his investigators with the drug gang leaders Kurland and his crew protected and with Gabe Perone. Even Kurland, in an effort to shave some time off his prison sentence, eagerly agreed to cooperate. It did not work!

"After the crackdown on the Bandits of Bush Terminal, as you will recall, Steven, your unit began systematically taking out every drug gang which had operated under the protection of Sergeant Kurland and his crew. But Kurland had a plan for the two surviving drug gang bosses."

"Hey, Domingo, look at it this way, with the other gangs out of business, you and Davis here control all of East New York. Here's what we do . . ."

As Kurland outlined his plan on the top floor of Building 1 of Bush Terminal to the two drug gang honchos, they, together with Scott Ruben and Gabe Perone, were shocked by his recklessness. Only a week after several cops in his crew were led away in handcuffs from this very same commercial complex — although on the op-

posite side of the terminal in Building 7 —
and despite the fact that Domingo Sanchez
fingered those cops for the arrest, Kurland
was acting as if nothing had happened. He
was determined to resume full operations.
He would later explain his plan to Ruben
and Parone.

"Look, these two mutts are not planning
anytime soon to open up a Burger King or
a McDonald's. Without competition, their
business is going to explode, and they will
need our protection more than ever. In just
the last week, Holt and his fucking Girl
Scouts have been raiding every one of the
spots controlled by Sanchez and Davis."
Kurland allowed himself a rare smile, as he
continued. "And that fucking rookie sergeant is driving up our price."

Ruben protested, "But Boss, we're all hot.
They have to know we were working with
the others and —"

"Scottie, me boy," Kurland interrupted,
"they got shit on us, and even if the other
losers try and give us up, they still got shit
because we are all co-conspirators." Kurland
continued with a scholarly recitation of the
law: Without corroboration, or independent
evidence, one co-conspirator could not be
found guilty solely on the testimony of
another co-conspirator. "Besides," he rea-

soned, "the three of us are less than two years from getting out of this job, and with the kind of increased take we'll get from our boys Sanchez and Davis, we ain't never gonna worry about money again."

Both Davis and Sanchez understood the risks involved, but they also knew that when the heat was off and they were no longer being watched so closely, they would need protection as their drug-dealing enterprise boomed. Not only did Holt's crackdown increase the cost of protection, the street price for the now scarce crack cocaine tripled.

"That fuckin' guy had balls like a brass monkey, but what other choice did we have but to deal with him?" Sanchez told one of Moore's investigators.

So the payoff meetings continued at Bush Terminal Building 1, although the days were rotated — a Thursday here, a Monday there, not because Kurland thought it a safer strategy, but rather because it made everyone else feel more secure. He would even shift the meeting to different floors of the empty warehouse, suggesting to the others that this would avoid detection by sophisticated surveillance devices.

While the decision to continue operations as usual might have allayed the fears of

Ruben and Perone, it was plain stupid and was bound to blow up in Kurland's face. One reason it would fail was circumstances that Kurland could not control. Each time they gathered on the fourth floor of Building 1, they could not know of or see the pair of eyes belonging to a haunted and tired man with a constantly tear-stained face, who watched their every movement from a makeshift loft, high above the factory floor.

Those eyes of Bradley Coles would bulge on those various evenings when, among the debris, three white men would meet and count stacks and stacks of cash, more money than he had ever seen. The purse had grown with the huge increases in the drug business in East New York, now the sole monopoly of Domingo Sanchez and Huey Davis, until it averaged between fifteen and twenty thousand dollars every seven days.

The more he observed of all this, the more Coles became confused. He was too high up near the ceiling to hear anything, so all he could do was watch the routine of counting out the money and then the distribution. He could see that the fattest and oldest of the three men appeared to be the

447

leader and got the largest share.

And one night, not long after these strange clandestine meetings began, his eyes would be transfixed with fear as he watched a gruesome and horrifying sight. It so unnerved Major Coles that he fled his sanctuary and was never seen in the neighborhood again.

Hiram Rodriguez, twenty-six, migrated to Brooklyn in the summer of 1989 from a suburb of San Juan, Puerto Rico. Hiram had a slight but muscular build and the dark good looks of the Hollywood stereotype of a Latin lover. Possessed of an infectious charm and a perpetual broad smile, Hiram was the darling of the campus at the University of Ponce, from which he graduated third in his class with a degree in electrical engineering. But his class standing, his impeccable dress, and his wit and other social skills simply didn't matter, because there were no jobs for electrical engineers anywhere in the Commonwealth of Puerto Rico.

The job market was no better in New York, so he was forced to take an apprenticeship in an electrical supply company, located in Building 3 of Bush Terminal. The pay was decent, and the prospect of getting a union card with the powerful Local 3 of the International Brotherhood of Electrical Workers was fairly certain. After several months, Hiram was able to get the promise of a laborer's job for his baby brother, Ramon, who had just turned eighteen and who appeared to be drifting with no plans for his future. This, together with Hiram's concern about increased drug use by the teenagers in his hometown, led him to convince Ramon to join him in Brooklyn. When Ramon arrived just before Thanksgiving of 1989, Hiram had already secured a job for his little brother.

Each year, Sid Leibowitz, the owner of Leib Electrical Supplies, who cooperated with Moore by giving background information about the Rodriguez brothers, would throw a party to celebrate Christmas and Hanukkah for his employees, who numbered about twenty. The party grew to several hundred celebrants with all of Leib Electrical's customers, their spouses, and friends. The crowd also included police officers from the 72nd Precinct, who made it a habit to respond quickly to calls from any of the businesses housed at the terminal. The management and maintenance personnel of Bush Terminal were also invited, to show Sid Leibowitz's gratitude for the discount rental for the party space and for allowing the party to spread to several floors of the otherwise vacant Building 1.

The 1990 celebration was set for December 18. The invitation promised much food and drink and a six-piece band for the enjoyment of all, "from eight in the evening until two o'clock the following morning."

"Good Mother of my Lord," groaned Ramon, cradling his head with both hands.

"Well, Ramy," replied Hiram, using his affectionate nickname for his brother, "how many times did I tell you to lay off the booze?"

"Okay, okay, stop the big-brother bullshit and give me some aspirin," Ramon cried out.

"Oh, damn it," Hiram shouted, searching for the painkiller, "I can't find my wallet."

After a fruitless search in the apartment, the brothers decided to go to work. Hiram did take the time to cancel his two credit cards and call the Bush Terminal security desk to see if anyone had returned the wallet. The answer was no, but with a promise that a security officer would take a look through Building 1 later that day. Hiram recalled that he had about sixty dollars in cash, and since he was able to cancel his cards, it wasn't a big deal.

The brothers decided to go back to Bush Terminal after work to search for Hiram's wallet.

"Holy shit, will you look at that." Sergeant Joe Kurland was overwhelmed by the mound of money that poured from the sack carried by Scott Ruben. Gabe Perone, for one rare moment speechless, gasped and then produced a long, loud whistle.

"And it's not just tens and twenties. It looks like a lot of fifties and hundreds," Kurland continued. "I wonder just how much we got?"

Ruben beamed with pride and said, "Boss, I know we're not supposed to count, but I couldn't help —" Ruben was stopped in midsentence as Kurland slammed the butt of his off-duty automatic against the side of his head. He followed through with a fierce kick to Ruben's groin that sent him, wailing with pain, crumbling to the factory floor.

"Next time, show some self-discipline, you little fuckin' weasel."

Ruben, who had nearly lost consciousness, looked up at Kurland, terrified.

"Well, how much fucking money is there, or should I say was there?" asked Kurland with an angry scream.

"Boss, I swear on my dead father, I counted the cash and I left every bill. There's nineteen thousand, three hundred and fifty dollars."

"Wow," shouted Perone.

"Empty your pockets, motherfucker," commanded Kurland.

"Boss, please, don't you believe me?" Ruben pleaded. "I swear to you, I didn't keep anything. Please, don't do this to me."

Kurland put a full clip into his weapon, pulled back the slide, loading the chamber, and took the safety off as he screeched, "Turn your fuckin' pockets inside out, now."

Suddenly Perone bellowed, "What the fuck are you guys lookin' at?" Hiram and Ramon Rodriguez had appeared from a nearby stairwell. Perone ripped his gun from his ankle holster and ordered the two brothers to put their hands in the air.

The brothers couldn't prevent themselves from staring, first at all the cash on the floor, and then at Ruben's quivering body and the shock on Kurland's face. Kurland quickly recovered and demanded, "What the fuck are you doing here?"

Hiram spoke, trying to mask his terror by responding slowly. "This is my little brother. We both work at Leib Electrical Supply here in the terminal. We had a Christmas party in this building last night, and I lost my wallet."

"There was no party on this floor," Kurland interrupted, "so what the fuck are you doin' here?"

Hiram felt himself reacting to Kurland's anger. His fear for Ramon and himself made his body shake involuntarily. He replied, "No, sir, the party wasn't on this floor, but I thought maybe someone found my wallet, took the money out, and threw it somewhere in this building, so we have been searching each floor." It was, of course, the truth, but in Hiram's state of panic, he thought it sounded contrived.

Kurland shouted, "Get on the floor, face-down." Hiram's protest ended quickly when Kurland pointed his gun and said, "If you are resisting arrest, I'll fuckin' blow your head off."

Above the factory floor in the sleeping loft he'd built several years before, Bradley Coles could not understand or even quite believe what was going on. Coles watched in horror, certain that Kurland was about to murder Scott Ruben. When that drama was interrupted by the intrusion of the Rodriguez brothers, his fear subsided and he took a deep swig of wine, exhaling a burp and a long sigh. The respite was, however, short-lived, ending when Kurland ordered the brothers to hit the ground. It instantly reminded Major Coles of a deadly moment he witnessed in Saigon, when soldiers from the regular army of South Vietnam surrounded two teenagers they claimed were members of the hated VC. No sooner had the youngsters hit the ground than the regulars opened fire with their United States Army–issued M16s, sending their automatic fire ripping through the bodies of their hapless victims. Soon the ground around the youngsters had turned crimson with blood pouring from countless wounds. Coles could feel his sweat flowing from every pore as he recalled that nightmare.

The brothers quickly obeyed and dropped to the ground. Kurland said to Ruben and Perone, "Don't let these guys move. I'll be right back."

Coles knew it was over — at least for now. He took another gulp from his wine bottle.

Perone yelled after Kurland, "Boss, where're you off to?"

"Never mind. Just keep those two mutts quiet, and I'll be right back," Kurland shouted over his shoulder.

Kurland knew that Holt, "that fuckin' Boy Scout," was away visiting his uncle in upstate New York. The time had come for

Kurland to get even for Holt's betrayal. Using a passkey, Kurland quickly and quietly entered the basement of the 75th Precinct, through the rear entrance. It was now well after midnight, and Kurland knew that most of the house would be out on patrol. In minutes, he found himself in front of a locker marked HOLT, STEVEN ROBERT, SGT., where he easily slipped the lock and wrapped his handkerchief around Holt's .38 police special, which had been secured in a box at the bottom and to the rear of the locker. Kurland placed the weapon in a small canvas bag and was in his van headed back to Building 1 of Bush Terminal in less than forty-five minutes.

Kurland walked swiftly across the factory floor. He held Holt's gun firmly by the grip, which was still wrapped in the handkerchief to avoid finger or palm prints. He had the weapon at his side and to the rear so it could not be readily seen.

Coles saw what Kurland was doing, and his heart began to beat rapidly as he looked on, helpless to do anything.

Kurland ignored Perone's greeting, "Hey, Boss, that didn't take long, did it?"

Hiram and Ramon were lying facedown in roughly the same position as when the sergeant left the factory. Kurland walked in their direction, never taking his eyes off them.

Coles watched on in horror. When Kurland reached the two brothers, he knelt next to Hiram's head and placed the gun against his temple. The metal click of the trigger produced a sickening popping sound that reverberated across the empty floor.

"What have you done to my broth—" Ramon never finished his sentence, because Kurland kicked him in the back of the head. Quickly Kurland bent over him, placed the gun to his temple, and completed the executions. Kurland then inspected both men, each with a single hole in the left side of his temple; he seemed pleased.

Coles began to gag, then to vomit, doing all he could to suppress the noise, and quite suddenly he passed out.

"Boss, what the fuck did you do that for?" Ruben broke the silence, giving voice to the bewildering shock he and Perone felt.

"Empty out your fuckin' pockets, you piece of shit," commanded Kurland as he drew back the hammer of his gun and pointed it at Ruben. Ruben let spill from his right pants pocket three hundred-dollar bills and four fifty-dollar bills. At the same time, he fell to his knees, sobbing and pleading, "Please, boss, please let me live, I beg you." Turning to Perone, he said, "Gabe, please help me."

Kurland released the hammer, put the gun in his shoulder holster, and said flatly, "We got a job to do. Let's go."

After loading the bodies of Hiram and Ramon Rodriguez into the rear of his van, each wrapped in an oil-stained blanket, Kurland and the other two set out toward Robert Moses State Park in Suffolk County. The raging snowstorm made the driving treacherous, but it didn't matter, because the events of the evening had brought much satisfaction to Sergeant Joseph Kurland. He smiled as he thought, *But the best is yet to come!*

The men drove in silence, mostly because Ruben and Perone had no idea where they were going and were much too afraid to ask, and because Kurland was spending this quiet time reflecting . . . and planning.

On the way back to Brooklyn, at nearly 5:30 in the morning, as the van crossed over the line dividing Queens County and Brooklyn, Kurland ordered Ruben to drive back to Bush Terminal. "Let's check out the factory. I want to make sure that there's nothin' left to cause us a problem."

"Sure, Boss," Ruben responded, certain now that his crisis had passed.

The noise of the door to the fourth floor opening roused Major Coles from his deep sleep. He peered over the side of his loft as the three men walked to the center of the room. The contents of the three bags they carried were soon emptied on the floor, and they began counting and dividing. Coles was astounded by the sheer volume of the stacks of money. When Kurland and Perone had finished counting the money from their respective bags, the sergeant slowly rose from his kneeling position next to his bag of money and walked over to Scott Ruben. In a flash, Kurland took Holt's weapon, with the handle still wrapped in a handkerchief, and placed a bullet neatly behind Ruben's ear. This was followed by an eerie silence, with both Perone and Coles frozen with fear.

Finally Kurland broke the quiet with the sound of his boots, walking over to Ruben's money sack and spilling it out. He began to divide it. Then he said, without looking up, "Gabe, never trust a fuckin' thief."

Ruben's body was wrapped mummylike in sheets and then in plastic, to hold down the stench from the decay. Then it was placed in the rear of the subbasement of Building 1, in an abandoned tool shop long ago forgotten by the management of Bush Terminal.

Ruben's body would be found when Kurland was ready to spring the final phase of his trap.

When Moore had finished, no one spoke. It was too difficult for anyone to absorb the depravity, the quintessential evil created by a New York City police officer.

District Attorney Crowley described how Perone, when faced with a prison term that would have kept him behind bars for life, pled guilty to an added charge of perjury and agreed to testify against Kurland. He would be sentenced according to his original agreement. Afterward, Crowley announced to the group that he would personally try the case against Kurland.

EPILOGUE

It took the jury less than seven hours to convict Kurland of all three charges of murder in the second degree.

Shortly before Thanksgiving Day 1992, Judge Michael McGowan sentenced Joseph Kurland to three consecutive sentences of twenty-five years to life. Kurland was confined to Attica State Prison. Because he was a police officer, he is kept segregated from the other prisoners. His parole eligibility will not occur until he serves seventy-five years, which will keep him in prison for the rest of his life.

Gabe Perone is serving twelve and a half to twenty-five years, also at Attica State Prison. He, too, is segregated from the rest of the prison population.

Police Commissioner Nevins retired early in 1993 to Phoenix, Arizona. His reforms were embraced by successive police commissioners, and systemic corruption has not reappeared. The commissioners have been aided by a new breed of chiefs committed to preventing any return to cyclical corruption.

Brendan and Peggy Moore withdrew to the tranquility of Lookout Point.

Robert and Shannon Mulvey still live in Delhi, New York.

Kenneth J. Rattigan was reelected district attorney of Queens County in the fall of 1993.

Brooklyn District Attorney Buddy Cooper retired in 1993 and resides in Israel with his wife, Boo.

Larry Green still practices law.

In the fall election of 1994, District Attorney Jim Crowley defeated Governor David Laurel and became New York State's first Republican governor in two decades.

In June 1995, Governor Crowley elevated Judge Michael McGowan to the New York State Court of Appeals, the state's highest court.

Wally Goss resigned from the office of the Suffolk County district attorney and was named by Governor Crowley New York State's inspector general, the state's integrity watchdog, with jurisdiction to investigate every agency in New York State.

Bernard Pressler resigned in November of

1993, after Rattigan's reelection and the election of a new mayor. He sent the following letter to District Attorney Rattigan: "Kenny, it's time for me to get off the merry-go-round. I've had a good run, but it's time to go. Please watch your back. Bernie." Pressler lives in Naples, Florida, where he plays endless rounds of golf with former police commissioner Lou Guido and former chief of department Keith "Cookie" Nolan. They never discuss the job.

By the mid-1990s, serious crime had plummeted throughout New York City as Pressler's legacy of reform, Crime Crash, was institutionalized by the NYPD.

With Dominican and Jamaican families arriving in record numbers, their leadership resolved to eliminate drug dealers from their communities. Accordingly, the phrases "Dominican drug dealers" and "Jamaican drug gangs" have disappeared from the headlines. Today, Dominicans in New York City are mostly known for their player contributions to Major League Baseball, and Jamaicans are recognized for their contributing leadership to the annual Caribbean Day Parade on Labor Day in Brooklyn, the largest parade in the United States.

Shortly after the dismissal of all charges against Steven Holt, Police Commissioner

Nevins assigned him to the Emergency Service Unit of the New York City Police Department. "You know, Steven," he said, "if I didn't send you to ESU, your Uncle Robert would never forgive me."

On September 11, 2001, Lieutenant Steven Robert Holt, assigned to Truck 1, ESU, responded with his partner to the scene of the World Trade Center disaster. Both officers entered the lobby of World Trade Center, Tower 2, and headed up the stairwell in search of a large group of civilians trapped by smoke conditions between the fourth and fifth floors. As they reached the fourth floor, they began to shout to the people in the stairwell, "Police, police, head down in this direction."

Steven heard a woman's voice. "Thank God. We're coming, Officer."

Suddenly the police command center broadcast: "Central to all units, this is an emergency. You are to immediately evacuate from World Trade Center, Tower 2, K. I repeat" — the voice was urgent — "immediately withdraw from World Trade Center, Tower 2, K."

"10–4," Holt replied. "This is Truck 1, ESU. We are leading a group of civilians out of Tower 2, K."

That was the last transmission recorded

from Lieutenant Steven Robert Holt. Neither his remains nor those of his partner were ever found. At the time of his death, Steven Holt was thirty-seven years of age. He and his wife, Lee, were the parents of three children.

AUTHOR'S NOTE

While a great deal of what is told in this story is true, particularly the systemic corruption in many parts of the New York Police Department found in the '70s and '80s, it is important that I acknowledge the vast positive changes made by the NYPD to eliminate organized police corruption and to credit those responsible.

First of all, Raymond Kelly, while serving as police commissioner under Mayor David N. Dinkins, responded aggressively to the recommendations of a police corruption investigative panel headed by retired Justice Milton Mollen. Commissioner Kelly changed the name of Internal Affairs from Division to Bureau and raised its status within the NYPD by the appointment of a handpicked three star chief who reported directly to him. Additionally the commissioner encouraged experienced superior officers to serve in IAB and to recruit police officers of all ranks from the field and to indoctrinate and train them to root out police corruption. Commissioner Kelly took the Mollen Commission report recommendations and went far beyond them, creating a broad design that he was confident would institutionalize anti-corruption programs within his department.

With the change of the mayoral administration, Commissioner Kelly was not retained. Fortunately his successors had the good sense to keep his blueprint for ending the cyclical police corruption which had plagued the NYPD, reoccurring roughly every twenty years for more than a century.

Once again police commissioner under Mayor Michael R. Bloomberg, Raymond Kelly continues to hold the integrity of his department as one of his highest priorities. He has been aided in this effort not only by his chiefs and other superior officers but by the police unions, particularly those with the highest number of members, the PBA and the SBA, as well as the smaller unions representing other superior officers.

The story as it relates to two scandal-ridden police units is largely true but the fictionalized portion of the story is meant to suggest how police corruption could lead to tragedy for two police officers and to murder.

ABOUT THE AUTHOR

Charles J. Hynes has been the district attorney of Brooklyn, New York, for seventeen years. A veteran trial lawyer, he earned his spurs as the special prosecutor appointed by Governor Mario Cuomo in the famous 1987 Howard Beach murder case. He also teaches at St. John's, Fordham, and Brooklyn law schools. He lives in Brooklyn, and this is his first novel.

The employees of Thorndike Press hope you have enjoyed this Large Print book. All our Thorndike and Wheeler Large Print titles are designed for easy reading, and all our books are made to last. Other Thorndike Press Large Print books are available at your library, through selected bookstores, or directly from us.

For information about titles, please call:
  (800) 223-1244

or visit our Web site at:
  www.gale.com/thorndike
  www.gale.com/wheeler

To share your comments, please write:
  Publisher
  Thorndike Press
  295 Kennedy Memorial Drive
  Waterville, ME 04901